One with the Father

One with the Father

A Novel of Mysticism, Heresy,
and Rebellion in the Middle Ages

RICHARD EVANOFF

RESOURCE *Publications* · Eugene, Oregon

ONE WITH THE FATHER
A Novel of Mysticism, Heresy, and Rebellion in the Middle Ages

Resource Publications
An Imprint of Wipf and Stock Publishers
199 W. 8th Ave., Suite 3
Eugene, OR 97401
USA

www.wipfandstock.com

PAPERBACK ISBN: 978-1-6667-7110-7
HARDCOVER ISBN: 978-1-6667-7111-4
EBOOK ISBN: 978-1-6667-7112-1

Cover art: Suiboku by Peter Comaroff

Contents

I

The Estate

§1

The wall went around the entire estate and Justin had never once been outside of it.

§2

In the early morning Justin would climb the turret of the manor house and look east to see the blood-red horizon before dawn and watch the ocean give birth to the sun. It was especially nice in spring when the air was fresh and clean. Justin had absolutely no conception that another world might lie on the other side of that horizon. For him, what he perceived was all that could be known and, therefore, all that actually existed.

He would return to the turret just before the noonday meal and look to the south, where in summer the hot sun shone down on strips of land yellow with grain alongside a wide road—a highway actually—leading to a village. Occasionally Justin would observe peasants working in the fields. They were always too far away for him to see their faces but appeared to be in their prime. Beyond the flatlands were the hills, and somewhere in the hills the village, which Justin had never set foot in and knew nothing about. A cross appeared in a fold between two hilltops, although Justin could not see the church it was attached to since it lay hidden in the valley.

In the evening Justin would climb the turret again to watch the sun slowly set behind an ancient tree-covered wold with a shorn top to the west, painting the heavens crimson, darker than the scarlet skies of morning, more similar to the rust-colored leaves that flew from the craggy trees in autumn. But Justin never wondered what lay beyond that wold and had no

1

desire to climb it and find out. He would watch the sun finally expire behind the jagged skyline and then return downstairs for his supper.

At night Justin would make his final visit to the turret to watch stars appear one by one in the northern sky, though they held no wonder for him. Milky moonlight poured down on the treetops of the forest where his father hunted. In winter the boughs were covered with radiant white snow. The dark spaces between the trunks of the pines where the deadwood had fallen were mysterious and haunting, but they cast no spell on Justin. Then Justin would feel the chill of the night and begin his descent back down the turret.

After returning to his room, Justin would tumble into his bed, draw the curtains, slide under the warm blankets, lay his head on the soft feather pillow, and gaze up at the golden silk canopy. He was completely content and knew he was safe, just as his father had always told him. Within the walls of the estate no one could harm him. His security was complete. There was nothing to fear.

§3

The manor house was positioned at the very center of the estate. Although by no means a castle, the estate was larger than most. It had intentionally been built far from the village on a large swath of land that sloped toward the sea. A narrow but deep brook ran along the southern wall, which served as a moat separating the estate from the fields where the peasants worked, with a drawbridge that could be lowered across it, connecting the estate to the highway. A wooden dock had been constructed just upstream from the drawbridge, with a small boat tied to it. Along an outer side road leading to the wolds were the mill, which ground grain into flour for their bread, the brewery for making ale, and the winepress, which crushed grapes into rich red juice, later to be fermented and stored in casks in the cellar of the manor house. Justin had never been to any of these places, however, since they lay beyond the walls of the estate.

The wall itself was made of cut flat stones, set one above the other without mortar. It was neither sturdy nor high, and the spikes that had been set along the top of the wall were spaced too far apart to be of much use preventing intruders from clambering over it. Stretching his hands upward, Justin could just manage to touch the top of the wall with his fingertips. It would have been easy for him to climb the wall and pull himself across but, of course, he did not. Fearing attacks from the peasants, Justin's father, as lord of the manor, had been granted a license from the baron to build the wall, although it fell far short of his expectations in terms of both size and strength.

The grounds inside the walls were expansive. After passing over the drawbridge and through the gatehouse, there was a chapel immediately to the right. In the morning, after finishing his daily ritual of greeting the sunrise, Justin would join his father and mother in the chapel for morning prayers. The village priest would come each Sunday to celebrate the Eucharist and offer the sacrament to Justin's father and mother, and to Justin himself. The three of them would all sit together on a single bench in the otherwise empty chapel. At his father's request, a separate mass was held for the servants, so that Justin and his family would not need to mingle with them.

To the left of the gatehouse, built close to the wall, were the barracks, which housed the men-at-arms, and beyond the barracks, the blacksmith's workshop and the stable where the horses were kept. Given the threats Justin's father faced, he had received further permission from the baron to maintain a small garrison on the estate. Justin had always gotten along well with the soldiers, especially the head guard, Martin, a stalwart but cheerful man. While always treating him with the utmost deference, Martin would play and jostle with Justin when he was still a boy and let him ride horses in the paddock in the corner of the estate on the far side of the stable. Now as a young man Justin met each mid-morning with Martin and other higher-ranking officers, who would teach him how to wield a sword, shoot arrows from a longbow, handle an axe and polearm, and even joust with a lance. The training was turning Justin into a strong, muscular young man, although he was still slight compared to the brawny guards. He also had no experience, of course, with actual combat.

Along the western wall, next to the paddock, were the barns, granary, and storehouses, and beside these the stone house of the bailiff, who supervised the cartloads of food and other goods coming into the estate on a regular basis, and who frequently departed for the village on missions that were never explained to Justin. The bailiff would greet Justin and exchange pleasantries, but never have any genuine conversations with him, leaving Justin unaware of his real function as an employee of his father.

A long dirt driveway led from the gatehouse to the main entrance of the manor house, with grassy lawns on either side. The yard on the right, almost large enough to be called a field, extended all the way around the mansion down to the eastern part of the estate where the orchards were located. Straight ahead, the drive widened as it approached a large open courtyard in front of the house, where there was a portico with steps leading up to the main entrance. To the left a much narrower lane hugged the side of the building until it connected with an alley running from the warehouses past the bailiff's house to the servants' quarters, which were located on the grounds sloping gently upward towards the wolds, just across the alley from the door to the manor's kitchen. Refusing to allow servants to stay inside the house, Justin's father had provided a lodge divided into separate rooms for them to share among themselves.

The servants said even less to Justin than the bailiff, only the bare minimum required to end an exchange as quickly as possible, never smiling at Justin nor to anyone else. They were all immaculately clean and well dressed in simple but sturdy clothes made of linen and wool, with plain designs and dull hues. Any articles of clothing made of velvet or satin were prohibited, for these were reserved exclusively for the nobility. The colors red and purple were forbidden as well.

The servants, as well as the guards, were all young. The youngest were in their late teens, the same as Justin, others in their twenties or thirties, but none were older than forty. Justin noticed that whenever anyone began showing signs of age, that person would simply disappear from the estate and be replaced by someone younger. In fact, the oldest residents on the estate were Justin's own father and mother, although they both maintained a youthful appearance. Justin's father was broad and muscular, having a closely trimmed beard, while his mother was always elegant, her hair finely coiffed and her neck smelling of sweet perfume. There were never any children on the estate. As he was growing up, Justin had no playmates his own age and was always surrounded by adults.

The alley continued from the servants' quarters past a sizable garden where leeks, cabbages, turnips, and peas were grown, along with other seasonal vegetables and herbs. Near the far corner of the manor house, set in the wall a few steps down, was a door that was always locked. Justin had once asked Martin what was behind the door. He replied simply that it led to the "dungeon" and that no one was permitted to enter it. Justin had no idea what a dungeon was nor the purposes it served but sensed that he should not inquire into the matter any further. Justin had never seen anyone go into or out of the door of the dungeon, even though the window of his own room on the second floor was located just above it.

§4

In the northwest corner of the estate was a fishpond, built of stone and supplied with water from a narrow stream, which flowed from the wolds under the western wall into the pond and then exited a small portal, allowing the stream to continue its path through the hunting grounds to the north. The northern wall was punctuated further down by a gate, smaller than the main gate on the opposite side of the estate and less secure. Immediately below the gate was a wooded area that had originally been part of the forest but was now completely swept clean of underbrush.

In the middle of the grove amongst the trees was the residence of Justin's teacher, whom Justin visited each weekday afternoon to be tutored. Justin was only allowed into the front room of the small wooden cottage, where his lessons were conducted. One of the adjoining rooms was the library. Its door was always open, although Justin had never been inside of it. The room was cluttered with codices and manuscripts, randomly cast not only on the shelves, but also on the large wooden table that occupied the center of the room and even on the floor itself.

Justin was not permitted to read any of the books unless his teacher had fetched them for him. Although he often read the classics, including ancient Greek and Roman epics, any works of religion, including even the Bible, were specifically proscribed. The only books of philosophy he was permitted to peruse were those having some connection to his other studies, which included not only grammar, rhetoric, and logic, but also arithmetic, geometry, astronomy, and music. Justin was accomplished at playing the lute and sometimes even composed his own melodies. He practiced writing on a wax tablet with a stylus, carefully erasing whatever he had written after a lesson was finished. He sometimes wrote verses as well but was never given a quill or ink to keep a permanent record of his poetry on expensive imported paper.

The door of another room adjoining Justin's classroom was always closed. Justin had never seen it open until one day when he came sooner than expected for his lessons. Upon entering the cottage, Justin did not find his teacher waiting for him as usual but noticed that the door to the other room was slightly ajar. He peeked inside and saw that it was lined with wooden tables, on which numerous bottles and pots were strewn. On the far side of the room was a fireplace, with a cauldron hanging over the embers. A sulfurous smell wafted through the open door, lingering in Justin's nostrils even after he had moved away and returned to sit down at his desk.

Shortly thereafter the teacher came scurrying out of the room, shutting the door behind him. Surprised to see that Justin had already arrived, he hurriedly assumed his usual position across the desk from him and said, "I have told you to be here punctually, neither early nor late. You must not enter the cottage until the clock has struck two."

The clock the teacher was referring to was a large mechanical clock he himself had constructed in a tower atop the manor house, opposite the turret Justin visited every day. The bell of the clock sounded just as the teacher was speaking.

"My apologies," Justin replied, turning his head back to the door his teacher had just closed. He continued staring at it for several moments, even though he dared not question his teacher about what he had been doing in the room.

The teacher finally broke the awkward silence by saying, "I suppose you are curious about what lies behind that door."

Justin looked back at this teacher but did not answer.

"If I tell you, do you promise not to reveal a word of what I say to your father?"

Justin nodded nervously. The teacher's eyes lit up. He went back to the door and opened it, giving Justin another view of the apparatus inside.

"This is my laboratory," he beamed proudly. "The room in which I prepare my potions!"

Justin summoned the courage to ask, "Potions? What kind of potions?"

"You might say medicines, although their purpose is not to heal people but to prevent them from becoming sick."

"Certainly I have never seen a sick person on the estate," Justin said, his muscles beginning to relax. "And I have never been sick myself. I do not even know what it means to be sick."

"There is a reason for that."

"Then you are not only a teacher, but also a physician!" Justin exclaimed.

"Yes, I am both a scholar and a physician, but more than these I also practice the art of alchemy."

"I am sorry, but I do not understand. I have never heard the word *alchemy* before."

"Shall I teach you about it?"

"Indeed, I would like to learn."

"Alchemy is the ancient wisdom of the universe, the one true theology that comprehends both God and his creation."

The teacher began to finger the gold medallion that always hung from a chain around his neck.

"An alchemist," he continued, "studies the four basic elements—earth, air, water, and fire—and how different arrangements of these fundamental building blocks of nature create everything that exists. A tree, for example, is composed of one particular combination of these elements, and when its wood is burned, the fire inside the tree is released, the water evaporates into air, and the ashes return to dust. By investigating how these components interact with each other and fit together, alchemists seek to understand how one substance may be changed into another."

He took off his medallion and held it out to Justin.

"Do you know what this is made of?"

"I have no idea."

"Hold it in your hand."

Justin took the shiny medallion from his teacher and pressed it gently between his thumb and fingers. The metal was heavy, but soft and malleable.

"It appears to be made of gold," Justin said.

The teacher smiled.

"It not only *appears* to be gold. It *is* gold. And I have made this gold from lead."

"But how is that possible?" Justin asked.

"If we know what things are made of and the processes by which they might be changed, it is possible to transmute any substance into another, even lead into gold."

"Then alchemy is a form of magic!"

The smile faded from the teacher's face.

"Alchemy is not magic," he said emphatically. "It is science. God created the universe in the same way that humans make a clock, just like the clock I assembled in the tower. And once God had set the world in motion, he allowed it to go its own merry way, tick-tock, without any interference and no capriciousness whatsoever."

"So God ensures that everything happens with complete regularity."

"If God did not exist, it would be necessary to invent him. How else to explain the marvelous order we find in nature? It must have been designed by an intelligent being, just like the clock!"

"As I have learned from the books you have assigned me, the ancients believed that each force in nature is personified by the god who rules over it: Zeus rules the sky, Poseidon the sea, and Gaia the earth."

"Yes, but have I not taught you that those are the gods of mythology, merely the fabrications of minds that did not yet truly comprehend the universe? The more enlightened thinkers of the past held that there is one powerful demiurge who moves but is not moved, a single driving force that sets the world in motion. Science has now advanced to the stage where we know that this power is none other than God almighty!"

Justin thought for a moment, then conjectured somewhat timidly: "Perhaps what you have just said is a myth, too, and science will one day discover that the universe requires no external energy to get it going and is perfectly capable of designing itself."

"That's preposterous!" the teacher said with a dismissive hiss. "Only a fool would believe such a thing. If there were no God, all would be chaos, just like in the beginning before the creation."

"I suppose you're right," Justin said.

"The fact that the universe is governed by an immutable set of laws which are the same everywhere proves that God exists."

"Yet the cosmos is vast. How do we come to know that the same rules apply from one place to another?"

"Through observation. We can learn more about God's creation by carefully examining it bit by bit than by reading all the philosophical treatises that have ever been written. There is nothing in the mind that was not first in the senses. God reveals himself through nature. Only science will lead us to true knowledge of what exists in the world and show us how to change things for the better."

"I still think you must be a sorcerer if you are able change one thing into another!" Justin exclaimed.

The teacher's face again became visibly taut.

"No, I am not a sorcerer, but a servant of God," he said firmly. "Jesus himself turned water into wine."

"But mere mortals hardly have the same power," Justin objected.

"We do," the teacher replied. "At every mass, after we partake of the bread and wine, they are transubstantiated into our bodies as flesh and blood."

"I thought that the bread and wine are supposed to turn into the body and blood of Jesus immediately after the priest consecrates them."

"Such incantations have no effect until we have actually consumed the elements. How else would it be possible for us to be fully one with Christ until the bread and wine become our own body and blood, for as the Bible clearly states, the Church *is* the body of Christ, and we are part of that body."

"It is apparently a mystery," Justin said.

"Indeed, for now it is an enigma. But one day we shall find an explanation for how the chemicals of ordinary bread and wine can be transformed into the chemicals that we are ourselves are made of. It is not thaumaturgy, but science. Alchemists do not believe in miracles!"

"Yes, but could not alchemy come from Satan rather than from God?"

"Certainly there are practitioners of the occult arts who seek knowledge from the devil and his demons. But it is only through experiments, not wizardry, that we will learn the secrets of the universe. The aim of alchemy is not wealth or riches, but to purify both the body and the soul, and to make them acceptable to God."

"And how might they be purified?"

"In its natural state the body is weak and frail, subject to disease and death. But the body itself may be rejuvenated and made perfect. The alchemist seeks the philosopher's stone, the primal matter out of which all other elements are made. Powder extracted from this stone can be used to make an elixir, the elixir of life. And whoever consumes this elixir will never become ill but live forever."

"He will become immortal?"

"Indeed. He will always be young and never die. But the soul must also be purified. All evil must be purged from our hearts, just as gold is refined by fire. Only by attaining perfection does a person become acceptable to God, who himself is perfect."

"But surely it is impossible for a mere mortal to become perfect. As the priest tells us regularly at the chapel, we all are sinners."

"Indeed, it is an arduous undertaking. Most people spend thousands of years in purgatory, making great efforts to acquire the perfection demanded by God. But for those who are fortunate enough to have access to the elixir, eternity begins the moment they partake of it."

"And this elixir of life, does it actually exist?"

The teacher's eyes became wide with excitement.

"Yes, it exists! Since time immemorial sages have tried over and over again to concoct the elixir but each time they failed. But now I, and I alone, have discerned how to distill it from the primordial substance out of which all ordinary matter is composed. It has been my life's work!"

"Have you yourself partaken of this elixir?"

"Indeed, I have. The quantities are small, so it is not available to everyone. But I have also given it to your father and mother, as well as to you."

"To me?"

"Yes. Every day my potions are mixed together with your food and drink."

"Does my father know about this?"

"Of course he does. And your mother also."

The teacher suddenly looked away.

"I regret having told you these things," he said, his demeanor now remorseful. "It is your father's responsibility, not mine, to inform you about these matters when he sees fit. He will teach you all you need to know in due course. You have already given me your promise, but I implore you again not to tell your father what we have spoken about today."

"I will not," Justin replied.

The teacher took the medallion back from Justin and pulled the chain over his neck.

§5

In the late afternoon, after his lessons with the teacher but before supper with his family, Justin would stroll through the nearby orchards. On one such occasion, having been dismissed earlier than usual by his teacher, Justin spied a young servant girl picking apples from a tree. He paused on the path and then passed by, thinking not to disturb her, but could not resist turning his head back for a second look. The girl was young and pretty, with golden hair flowing down her neck. Stretching up her arms to pluck apples from the low-hanging branches, she had not noticed Justin. Justin reversed course and approached her.

"Hello!" he called out.

Startled, the girl dropped an apple on the ground, then turned back to see who had spoken to her.

"Good afternoon, sire," she said.

"What are you doing on this fine and glorious day?"

"I am gathering apples, master. For your supper."

Justin picked up the apple she had dropped.

"May I have it?" he asked.

"Why, indeed, whatever you wish. But I fear that the apple is bruised. Let me give you a good one."

She reached into her wicker basket, pulled out the brightest and plumpest of the red apples, and handed it to Justin. He bit into it. The fruit was juicy and sweet.

"Delicious!" he said with a smile.

"I am glad to hear so, sire."

Justin looked carefully at the girl's face. He had noticed her before. She was one of the new servants who worked in the kitchen. She had lustrous eyes, full pink lips, and a dimpled chin.

"May I ask your name?" Justin asked, taking another bite of the apple.

"Constance."

"It suits you," Justin said.

The girl blushed. "How would you know that?"

Justin shrugged. "I don't know, it just suits you."

Justin finished eating the apple and threw the core over his shoulder. The girl picked another apple from the tree.

"How long have you been on the estate?" Justin asked her.

"Just a few weeks, sire."

"Do you like it here?"

"Why, of course," the girl said, but then looked down. "Sir, I apologize sincerely. But I really must finish picking these apples and get back to the house."

"Well, then let me help you."

"No, no," she said demurely. "The duty is mine, not yours."

"Nonsense," Justin replied. He reached up into the tree, picked an apple, and put it into the basket. Justin and the girl continued picking apples in silence until the basket was full.

The bell of the clock at the manor house began to sound in the distance.

"Well, I must take these to the kitchen," the girl said, lifting up the basket and preparing to leave.

"Will I see you again?" Justin asked.

"Oh, sire. Surely you have better things to do than to come to this orchard and help me pick apples."

"At what time are you usually here?"

"About the same time as now. But I've been given strict orders by the steward to return to the house just as soon as the clock strikes five."

"The next time I am able to finish my lessons early, I shall come to see you again."

Constance's eyes met his. There was a look of confusion on her face. Then she turned away and ran back to the manor.

§6

The sun was already beginning to set. Justin walked quickly up the path to the manor house, with a smile on his face. When he reached the front entrance, he rushed past the butler holding the door open for him into the foyer outside the great hall, ascended the curving staircase to the second floor, and took the remaining steps by twos to the top of the turret. He watched the sun as it disappeared behind the wolds, staining the horizon vermillion. The sky seemed more magnificent than he had ever seen it before. Justin thought of Constance but was unable to contrive a plan for how he could escape from his lessons early the following day to meet her again in the orchard.

When the supper horn was blown, Justin descended the staircase, passed through the foyer into a dining room adjacent to the great hall, where his mother and father were waiting for him. The evening meal was a simpler affair than the noon dinner, though still sumptuous, with generous portions of meat, fish, or poultry, fine white bread made from wheat ground at the mill, pottage with vegetables from the garden, new wine from the press or ale from the brewery, and, today, apples from the orchard. The family sat together at a large table adorned with candles, which occupied the center of the room. After saying grace, it was their custom to eat together in silence.

When they had finished eating, Justin's father addressed his wife, "You may retire to your room. I wish to speak to Justin in private."

Justin's mother looked first at her husband and then at Justin. Her eyes were filled with a sorrow Justin could not understand. In the flickering candlelight Justin suddenly realized how much she had changed, from the ageless mother he had known as a young boy into an elderly woman whom he barely recognized now. The changes had been gradual, so Justin hadn't noticed them before. Her hair was still coiffed, but it was graying around the temples. While perfume still wafted from her neck, the skin was creased with wrinkles. She seemed unsteady when got up from her chair, feebly bowed her head, and shuffled out of the room.

"Come, my son," Justin's father said, motioning for him to take a chair closer to his own. Justin walked from his end of the table to his father's and sat down beside him.

"You are reaching the age when it is necessary for me to tell you about matters I have never told you before," his father began. "Someday you will succeed me as the lord of this estate, so you must now acquire an education not to be learned from your teacher or from books, but from the way the world itself is."

Justin looked down at the table and listened obediently. He could not imagine what his father would say next.

"The law of nature," his father began, "is that God created the heavens and the earth. He is, therefore, the master over all that exists. He is present everywhere, knows everything, and has all power in his hands. Nothing happens except by the will of God. Are you with me so far, Justin?"

"Indeed," Justin replied.

His father resumed, "Beneath God are his servants, the angels, who are intermediate between God and humans. Although they are pure spirit, the angels sometimes assume our form to bring us God's messages. And we, as creatures made in the image of God, are only slightly lower than the angels, since we, too, exist forever, either with God in heaven if we have been good or with Satan in hell if we are evil. And below humans are the animals, the plants, and the minerals, which God has given to us and which we have dominion over. In the same way that God rules over us, we humans rule over the world. This, my son, is the law of nature."

Justin's father took a long drink of wine from his brass goblet. Justin waited silently until his father continued.

"The law of society is similar. God has given the king all power on earth to rule over us. The king is subject to no one and his authority over us is granted directly by God. To disobey the king is to disobey God. In the same way that we have first and foremost a devotion to God, who is the supreme Lord of the universe, who gives us his commandments, who protects us when we follow them, and who justly punishes us when we do not, we are compelled to be uncompromisingly devoted to our king, who rules over us, proclaims his laws, guards us from earthly harm, and smites us when we fail him. Disloyalty to the king is treason and will not go unpunished. Do you understand, Justin?"

"Yes, father, I do," Justin replied.

His father leaned back in his chair.

"Then tell me, son, who owns the land that we are living on?"

"Why you, father."

"No, Justin, you are mistaken. This land, indeed all the land in the kingdom, is owned solely by the Crown. The king rewards the highest members of the nobility with vast territories, or fiefs, which they hold directly from the king as tenants-in-chief. These lands may be subdivided into smaller parcels which are granted to under-tenants, such as ourselves, and held as manors, which includes this house, the grounds of this estate, and all the land surrounding it. At each level, vassals must pay homage and swear an oath of fealty to their immediate overlords, in our case to the baron, who rules over not only us but all the neighboring lords as well. The king provides security to the barons in exchange for their military support. We in turn offer military support both to our barons and to the king in exchange for their security. At the lowest level we give security to the peasants, and they give us their labor in return."

Justin did not fully grasp everything his father was explicating to him, but he knew better than to interrupt him by asking any questions.

"As noblemen we pursue excellence—*arête* as I'm sure you have learned from your studies of ancient Greek, from which our English word *aristocracy* is derived. We cultivate our minds through education, our bodies through hardy training, and our souls through devotion to God. We are bound by the code of chivalry, which means first and foremost that we are pious. We safeguard the Church and all it teaches, crusading against and crushing without mercy all infidels and heretics who do not submit themselves to our Lord and King, Jesus Christ, as their supreme master. In turn, God and the Church support us. We must ensure that everyone believes in God. For if the people do not believe in God, they will not obey the Church, and if they do not obey the Church, they will not obey us."

Justin's father leaned forward, picked up his goblet from the table, and took another sip of wine.

"We must have an unfaltering allegiance to our country and king and fight to defend the Crown. We maintain our dignity and uphold our honor by being courageous and strong. We nonetheless show respect and courtesy to others when due, not only to those above us whom we steadfastly serve, but also to the weak, especially women and children. We are generous and benevolent, fulfilling all our duties with magnanimity, not only to the masters who rule us, but also to the peasants whom we rule, instilling in them the virtues of honest toil and service. The peasants are like children, whom we must discipline and nurture, in the same way that a good father brings up his own offspring. We are the champions of all that is right and good, and fight against injustice and evil, but always with humility, for as the Bible teaches us, if we exalt ourselves we shall be humbled, but if we humble ourselves we shall be exalted, even as we have been exalted."

Justin had remained silent throughout this exposition but had tried, the best he could, to appear to be following what his father was saying.

"I have explained to you, my son, the duties we owe to God, to ourselves, and to others. Remember them well because they are the foundation of the social order God has instituted among us. And the glue that holds everything together is loyalty."

He paused.

"You have seen the suit of armor in my room."

It was a statement not a question, but Justin nodded just the same.

"Each dent in that armor was zealously earned defending our baron and our king. In the same way that we must devote ourselves to those above us, those beneath us must devote themselves to us. This is how our society is organized. Each person has their station in life, their own occupations and duties. They know, without needing to be told, where they belong and what they are supposed to do. In days past, all was in order, just as God intended it."

Justin's father then stood up, suddenly animated.

"But recently this order is breaking down. The peasants have always been ignorant, but now they are also becoming lazy. They steal. They cheat. They complain openly about what they rightfully owe us. They are becoming restless. They are no longer faithful, even though they are obliged to serve me, as they have sworn to do, just as I am bound to protect them. This is the sacred bond between us, which they have broken!"

His voice was now trembling with anger.

"What they do not understand is that I myself am not a wealthy man. The baron levies taxes and makes financial demands on me, which I struggle to fulfill. Alas, this manor is all I have and if conditions do not change, I will certainly lose it!"

"Surely that would never happen," Justin said, trying to calm his father.

His father looked at him gravely. "I fear that a great struggle is coming between us and the peasants."

Justin did want to be disrespectful, but could not resist asking, "Pray, tell me father. Why did you not explain all these things to me before? Why did you wait until now?"

His father turned away and was silent for a moment.

"I have my reasons," he said finally. "What is important now is that you should begin to familiarize yourself with the affairs of this estate. I have entrusted the bailiff to give you instructions about how things are managed. He is a trustworthy fellow, but we, as masters of this estate, must know what is going on and always keep an eye on things. Your first assignment will be to learn how to keep records of various transactions that are made and how to be an effective administrator. After that you shall gradually begin to take over the duties which I myself now perform. In time, you yourself will be the lord of this manor. In order to fulfill your responsibilities, you must be properly trained. You shall commence your training tomorrow morning."

With that, Justin's father drained the last swill of wine from his cup, stood up, and quickly left the room, leaving Justin no time to inquire further about how his life was being planned for him.

§7

Early the next day Justin went to the stone house of the bailiff, who led him to the room where the ledgers were kept. The bailiff, though respectful, was businesslike and aloof. Step by step he methodically showed Justin each morning how to keep the books, how rents and fines were collected, how goods were brought into the estate, and how the buildings and grounds were maintained. In a very short time Justin began to understand how not just the estate, but the fief as a whole, was organized. This employment brought Justin no pleasure, but he dutifully accomplished the work set before him, doing exactly as he was told without complaining.

§8

Although Justin no longer trained with Martin and the other soldiers in the mornings, he continued to visit his teacher's cottage for his usual afternoon lessons. He had told Constance that he would meet her again in the orchard, but each day his teacher kept him for the full duration of his study periods, preventing him from leaving before the clock struck five. Over the next few days, he continued to see Constance from time to time as she went about her daily chores but despaired that she might forget about him or, even worse, that he would never be able to meet with her alone again.

Soon, however, the situation changed. Justin walked through the door of the cottage for his usual tutoring and found his teacher collapsed in a chair, staring at the floor and looking distraught. There were no books on the table for Justin to pour over, no wax tablet for Justin to write on.

"Is something the matter?" Justin asked him.

The teacher did not look up, but finally replied, "No, no. It is nothing. We should begin your lesson. Let me fetch some manuscripts from the library for you to read. After that, you may compose a verse, if you like."

The teacher went to the library, retrieved a sheaf of documents from the shelf, returned to the front room, and handed them to Justin.

"And the writing tablet?" Justin asked.

"Ah yes. I forgot."

He went back into the library for the writing tablet and, upon returning, set it down on Justin's desk.

"You may proceed with your lesson," the teacher said.

Justin began reading in silence. An hour passed with the teacher simply sitting in his chair, looking down, saying nothing.

When he had finished perusing the manuscripts, Justin began his composition but could think of nothing to write. His mind was filled with the thought of meeting Constance again. No poetry could express how he felt about her. He saw his lute sitting in the corner of the room and thought that he might play it, hoping the music would inspire him. He knew that tunes are often suggestive of lyrics. But even if Justin could put his longings into words, he would not want his teacher to read or hear them.

Finally, Justin looked up from the blank tablet and said, "May I leave early today?"

The teacher's head snapped up. He took a moment to gather himself.

"I'm sorry," he said. "You startled me. Is there something you need to do this afternoon?"

"I haven't mentioned this to you yet," Justin replied. "But in accordance with my father's wishes I have begun to learn how to manage the estate from the bailiff every morning. Now I have many things to think about."

"Well, I told you, didn't I, that your father would begin your practical education in his own good time."

"Indeed, it is quite different from the education I receive from you."

There was an anxious look on the teacher's face. "You have not spoken to your father about the elixir we discussed previously, have you?"

"No," Justin said. "I will never share what you have told me with him."

The teacher's eyes brightened a bit. "Good. I did not exercise good judgment when I explained my research to you. I simply should have kept my mouth shut. It was only due to my pride . . . ."

The teacher's voice trailed off as he looked up at the ceiling.

"You needn't worry," Justin said. "But recently it seems that my mother is not entirely well."

The teacher was immediately attentive again. "You have noticed? Tell me, what exactly have you observed?"

"Well, she appears rather faint."

The teacher cast down his head, wiping back his hair with his hand.

"Whatever shall I do?" he moaned.

Justin was unsure why his teacher was acting so strangely, but tried to comfort him by saying, "I'm sure it's nothing. Mother will be all right soon."

"No, no, it's all my fault. I was summoned to visit her last night. I examined her. I cannot understand. I have given her a panacea daily but even so she is failing."

Justin did not know what to say. He patted his teacher on the shoulder, picked up his cloak, and hurried out the door, not looking back.

§9

The circumstances, despite being inauspicious, were also fortuitous. Justin congratulated himself for finally being able to quit his lessons early, with plenty of time to meet Constance in the orchard. He raced across the grass towards the apple trees. When he came to the place where he had met Constance previously, however, she was not there. He looked frantically around him, calling out in a loud voice, "Constance, Constance, where are you?"

There was no reply. Surely she would be there if she could. She would not forget him! Perhaps she had been detained by other duties at the manor. Even though it had been one long week since he had last seen her, he knew in his heart that she would come to the orchard every day and wait for him, even if he did not appear. She must want to see him as much as he wanted to see her!

Yet she was not there.

Justin felt her absence like a large hole in his chest. He walked dejectedly through the low-hanging limbs of the trees. Coming to a glade in the orchard, he sat down on the stump of an old tree and buried his head in his hands.

Suddenly from behind him, there was a voice. "Master, is that you?"

He turned and saw Constance approaching him with quickened steps. He stood up and smiled.

"You are here," he said.

"Yes, well, just by coincidence. I often come to pick fruit, but not every day, you know."

"But you came today."

"I heard your voice from the other side of the orchard," she said. "Is there something you need?"

"No," Justin replied. "I was simply looking for you."

"I'm sorry you could not find me. My task today was to gather pears, not apples. Would you like one?"

She held out the same wicker basket she had been carrying before, but this time filled with golden-green pears. Justin took one of them and bit into it.

"Delicious," he said.

"That's exactly what you said about the apple I gave you," Constance smiled, but only briefly, quickly regaining an obsequious demeanor.

Justin nonetheless smiled in return.

"I must apologize for not being able to meet you sooner," he said. "But I'm glad that I could finish my lessons early today. Finally I have a chance to see you again."

"I really must go now, though," Constance said. "The steward has given me strict orders. The clock will strike soon."

"Please, stay with me."

"No, I cannot. It is regretful that I do not have time to talk to you."

"The regret is all mine," Justin said. "I wish to meet and talk with you every day like this."

Constance glanced away, then her eyes returned to Justin's.

"You misunderstand me, sire. I only meant to apologize for not being able to comply with your request."

Justin was flummoxed.

"Do you not wish to see me?" he asked.

"It is not good for us to be together in the orchard like this," Constance answered.

"But why not?"

"It isn't proper."

"I assure you that my intentions are entirely honorable," Justin said.

"That is not what I mean. The point is that you are the son of the lord of this estate and I am but a servant."

"Ha!" Justin laughed. "Does that really matter? Am I not permitted to see whomever I choose?"

"It is dangerous," Constance replied. "Do not force me to choose between the instructions I have been given by the steward and the commands you give me as my master."

"Do not my entreaties carry far greater weight than the dictates of your steward?"

"Well, sir, the choice is yours not mine. I have my duties to perform, so I must come here whenever the steward bids me to. And you, as master of this estate, are of course free to come and go as you please."

"Has the steward told you to come here again tomorrow?"

"He has."

"Good, then I shall come to see you," Justin said. "Let us meet right here, at this old tree stump, so I know where to find you."

The first peal of the bell could be heard from the clock tower.

"As you wish," Constance replied. "But now please let me go. I will be reprimanded severely if I return to the kitchen late."

§10

The next day Justin's teacher was still distressed, and it was easy for Justin to beg to leave early so that he might meet Constance. His rendezvous with her was once again short and inconsequential, but Justin told Constance he would come to see her each and every time the steward assigned her the task of picking fruit in the orchard, which, as it turned out, was not quite every day, but almost.

As the days passed, the teacher appeared more and more distracted when Justin came to the cottage for his lessons. He had lost his enthusiasm for teaching, offering Justin only a bare minimum of comment on his studies and often gazing out the window with a faraway look in his eyes. In time he did not even sit in the front room with Justin but occupied himself behind the closed door of the laboratory. On the one hand, Justin was not at all displeased by these circumstances since they allowed him to leave early to meet Constance at the tree stump whenever she came to the orchard. On the other hand, Justin knew that something was wrong and that whatever it was had something to do with his mother. She was becoming feebler by the day and his teacher was now visiting her on a regular basis.

Constance was initially reluctant to meet with Justin, but over time she seemed to feel more at ease with him. Justin would hurriedly help her gather fruit in the orchard, leaving them time to walk among the trees and chat. Their moments in each other's company were always brief, but soon they were conversing quite freely with each other, at first mostly about the birds and flowers, the squirrels that scampered up the trees, the rabbits that darted through the grasses.

Then one day as they were sitting together on the stump of the old tree, Constance said, "The orchard is so beautiful. It's just like the Garden of Eden."

"The Garden of Eden?" Justin asked. "What is that?"

"You do not know?"

"No."

"But it's from the Bible."

"Oh," Justin said. "I have never read the Bible."

"Neither have I, of course, since I can't read," Constance said. "But the priest often told us this story in his sermons at the village church. Surely you have heard it."

"Not in our church," Justin said, referring to the chapel where he and his family worshipped privately. "I have heard the story about God creating the heavens and the earth, and a few others, but mostly the priest only talks about obedience, the obedience we have to God and king, and the obedience the peasants have to us."

"Well, we certainly hear those sermons, too," Constance said.

"So, tell me about the Garden of Eden."

Constance proceeded to relate the story to him, how God had created the first man, Adam, in his own image, and his wife, Eve, and how they lived together in a wonderful garden, where among the other trees were the tree of life and the tree of the knowledge of good and evil, and they were permitted to eat the fruit of any tree in the garden except from the tree of the knowledge of good and evil, since then they would die, and how Satan appeared to Eve in the form of a serpent and told her that eating the fruit of the forbidden tree would give her wisdom, so she ate of it and tempted Adam to eat the fruit as well, after which they understood the difference between good and evil, and realized that they were naked and corrupted by sin. Then God drove Adam and Eve out of the garden, placing an angel with a flaming sword at the gate to prevent their return, forcing them to live the rest of their days toiling in the fields, among the thorns and thistles, just like the peasants, until they returned to the dust God had made them from.

When Constance had finished the story, Justin asked, "But why would God not permit Adam and Eve to stay in the garden forever, where everything is perfect?"

"Indeed," Constance replied. "Would it not be better to remain in paradise from the time we are born until the time we die, to live in permanent bliss, to know only good and no evil, just as you know only good and no evil in your life on this estate?"

After giving the matter some thought Justin replied, "I am not so sure. I cannot explain why, but recently I have been thinking that it might be better for me to leave this garden. Perhaps I should become an outcast like Adam! It would at least allow me to know more than I know now. I do not wish to remain captive here forever."

"You would disobey your father?"

"I would disobey God, if need be."

"Then you yourself would be like God," Constance said.

Her words were cryptic to Justin, just like the story she had told him, which seemed to have a particular significance for him he could not yet grasp. He wanted to ask Constance more, but the bell began to ring and it was time for her leave, so he did not have an opportunity.

A few days later Justin almost stepped on a snake hiding behind a fallen log near the stump in the orchard. Startled, he picked up a rock and was about to smash it on the head, when Constance stayed his hand.

"Do not kill the snake," she said.

"But you told me that serpents are from the devil!" Justin cried.

"Serpents aren't from the devil. They are from God. God has created the serpents in the same way that he created you and me. They are neither higher nor lower than us. Killing a snake is no different from killing a human!"

Again, Justin was puzzled because he had learned from his father that there is an order to nature and that God had placed humans above the rest of his creation and given them power over it. But Justin kept these thoughts to himself and did not share them with Constance.

"We shall meet again tomorrow," Justin said as they parted.

§11

During their walks the pair also sometimes talked about their daily activities. Constance told Justin about her duties and the various kinds of food she prepared, while Justin told Constance about his studies with his teacher, his sessions with the bailiff, and his ritual of visiting the turret every day at dawn, noon, dusk, and night. Constance was becoming less and less like the other servants, who were cold and unfriendly, and who never spoke unless spoken to. After a while it seemed she had even forgotten that Justin was master of the estate. She would jest with him and talk openly about what she was thinking. It seemed to Justin that Constance knew things he did not know, which made her somewhat mysterious to him. Even though he was the master and she the servant, he felt her to be in some way his superior.

One day, when Constance tripped over a rock, Justin reached out and grabbed her hand. He continued holding on to it even after she had regained her balance.

"Tell me about where you come from, Constance," Justin said.

"I thought you knew, sire. All the servants are peasants from the village, including me."

"I know that, but I have never been to the village, so I have no idea what it is like, nor indeed of anything else that exists outside this estate. You have lived on both sides of the wall, but I have lived only on this side. I want to know what the world is like on the other side."

Constance withdrew her hand from Justin's.

"I cannot speak of these things. You will certainly come to understand them in time. It is not my place to disclose them to you."

"Then at least answer this question: Why did you cross the wall and come to live with us?"

"I am sworn not to tell you, sir."

"No, please tell me," Justin said. "I would like to hear your story."

Constance looked at Justin with imploring eyes.

"I *command* you," Justin said, with mock authority.

Dismayed, Constance immediately replied, "All right. I will tell you, but only if you insist."

"No," Justin said, assuming a gentler tone of voice. "Only if you are willing."

At first Constance said nothing. Then she began to speak, slowly and without confidence.

"I grew up in the village, the village you have never been to and never seen."

Her voice faltered.

"Please go on," Justin said.

Constance regained her composure and began to speak in her own good time, choosing her words carefully. "My father and mother died when I was a young girl. I was brought up by my brother. He tried, he really tried, to take care of me and provided for me the best that he could. But he is a poor man. He gave me everything he had until there was nothing more to give."

"I'm sorry, but I can't understand well. I don't really know what it's like to be poor."

"No, I suppose you don't," Constance said, with a faint smirk on her face. "Poor means wearing rags instead of proper clothes, living in a house with a roof that leaks and lets in the rain, going to bed hungry because you did not have any food to eat all day, shivering at night because you do not have a warm blanket to protect you from the cold."

"But look at the peasants who work for us here on this estate. Surely they are not poor. They wear decent clothes, have ample food, and sleep in comfortable beds. They lack nothing."

"Yes, your father, the lord, certainly provides his servants with everything they need, but it is only to keep up appearances, not out of genuine concern for us."

"I am not sure I understand you."

"Your father does not want you to know poverty, sire, not even the sight of it. That is why you do not really know what it is like to be poor."

"But surely there is enough for everyone. No one can live without food, clothing, and shelter, for these are the essentials of life."

"What you say is true, but those who live in the village have none of these things, at least not in sufficient quantity. We live as frugally as we can, but still there is not enough."

"Then why do they continue living in such conditions? Why don't they make efforts to improve themselves? Surely there is something they could do!"

"The peasants toil in the fields and harvest the crops," Constance said, her voice turning caustic. "They bring you your food. They collect wood from the forest and dig metal from the mines. Everything you have comes from them, and after they have brought it to you, there is next to nothing left for themselves."

"My father has told me that if the peasants were not so lazy and exerted themselves more, they would have nothing to complain about."

Constance glowered at Justin. "You certainly are naive, my lord. The peasants already work every day, from sunrise to sunset, often even on Sundays, though it is prohibited by the Church. They are so tired that by evening there is no time left to do anything more but to go to sleep."

"So, why do they not simply abandon the village and go somewhere else?"

"A few do. They run away to dwell in the forests or become vagabonds traveling from town to town. But they live like hunted animals, for if they are caught, they will surely be punished."

"And those who remain?"

"As you surely must know, master, as serfs they are bound to the land. They are not slaves, but not entirely free either."

"I am not as ignorant as you may think," Justin said, somewhat defensively. "I have been learning about these matters from the bailiff."

"Oh, master, I am truly sorry," Constance said, with barely concealed sarcasm. "It was not my intention to humiliate you. I am sure that your knowledge is much greater than mine, not only with regard to the estate, but about everything else. Still, the kind of knowledge we have is different, for your knowledge comes from records and ledgers. Mine is from what I have seen."

"That is true," Justin replied. "But I do know that while the peasants must give us a percentage of the yield on some of the land they work, they have been given other tracts of land which they are free to cultivate as they please. Indeed, I can see the strips of land from the turret each day. The system is entirely just and fair, I think."

"May I correct you, sire? The land that the villeins use for themselves has not been given to them but only leased. They must still pay rent on it. And surely I do not need to remind you that they are required to work for a certain number of days without payment on the land retained by the lord, your father, leaving them precious little time to tend to their own fields. In addition, they must pay taxes to your father, as well as fees for using your winepress, for grinding their flour at your mill, for feeding their livestock on your pastures, and even for hunting in your forest on the rare occasions the lord permits it. The whole lot belongs to your father, as lord of this manor. He controls everything. The peasants even need his permission to marry! We are not allowed to question his authority or even to petition him for better conditions. Whatever he decides is how things will be and we must never oppose him."

Justin was silent for a moment, trying to reconcile what Constance was saying with what he had been learning from the bailiff about the estate. There seemed to be no connection. Certainly the ledgers he was studying every day showed deficits and amounts due, but they were just numbers. This was the first time for him to hear about how the peasants actually lived.

"Indeed, I am so naive," Justin said finally. "But thank you so much for helping me overcome my ignorance. You have taught me things I would never have learned from my teacher, the bailiff, or even my father. Now I know what life is like on the other side of the wall."

Constance lowered her head as if in a bow, not one of respect but of sadness.

"No, you do not. You only know what I have told you and that is but a fraction of what goes on. To really understand you would need to live among the peasants yourself."

"Certainly there is more to be learned from experience than there is from talking or books," Justin said pensively. "But, Constance, you still have not told me how it is that you came to this estate."

"I shall tell you the next time," she said. "Now I must go."

"Let us meet again tomorrow," Justin said.

§12

And indeed, the very next day Constance told Justin how one day an official from the estate had come to the village to recruit servants. Her brother was offered a small sum of money if he would give permission for Constance to become a scullion at the estate and serve the lord of the manor. He was naturally reluctant to let his sister go but explained to her that it might in fact be best for both of them. She would have clothes to wear, ample food to eat, and a roof over her head that did not let in rain. He, in turn, would be released from the obligation of having to take care of her and, thus, be better able to provide for himself without falling further into poverty.

One week passed and then two. Justin learned many more things from Constance, about her own situation and the peasants' poverty. While always being tender towards her, he did not feel any pity or sorrow. He could sense within her a strength that he himself did not possess, which filled him with admiration. Then one day Justin leaned forward and kissed her, clumsily. And to his surprise, she kissed him back.

"Is this the first time you have done this?" Justin asked her.

"It is."

"For me as well."

Constance blushed, then looked at Justin with shining eyes.

"I shall always remember it," Justin said, adding, as he always did when they separated, "We shall meet again tomorrow."

"Indeed, I have been assigned to gather apples again," Constance replied.

The next day Justin went to his teacher's house but could not find the teacher anywhere. He considered studying on his own, perhaps reading a manuscript or crafting a verse, but then he saw his lute in the corner of the room. Picking it up, he began plucking notes one by one, then two by two in harmony, and as the music filled the air, words began to come to him, which he sang to the tune he had composed:

> O that I could kiss your red ruby lips
> And feel your hair on my own shoulder.
> Your cheeks are like pomegranates,
> Your breath the fragrance of flowers.

Having finished his composition, Justin left the cottage at his usual early hour, although this time without seeing his teacher, and headed straight for the orchard, his lute in hand, eager to see his own eyes reflected in Constance's and to sing the song he had written for her.

But when he reached the old tree stump, Constance was not there. He looked everywhere for her, in both the apple and pear orchards, among all the trees and bushes. He returned to the stump and sat down, filled with anxiety. Then, without thinking, he spontaneously began to sing the same melody he had composed to the accompaniment of his lute, but with new lyrics:

> I sought her whom my soul loves.
> I sought her, but I found her not.
> I called to her, but she gave no reply.
> I will rise now and seek her whom I love.

Justin waited for Constance until after the clock struck five, until the sun went down, but she did not come. When he returned to the manor that evening, the butler, as usual, opened the door for him.

"You are late, master," the butler said. "Your father and mother are already in the dining room, awaiting your presence at supper."

"I shall go immediately," Justin replied. "But first tell me, where is the servant girl who usually gathers fruit in the orchard?"

The butler hesitated and then said, "She has been confined to the kitchen, sire. Her duty now is to help prepare meals for you and your family."

"And why, might I ask, has she been relieved of her former assignments?"

The butler's face was stony. "I think you should know, my master."

It took a moment for Justin to comprehend the butler's words. Then he looked at the butler and said, "You will not tell my father, will you?"

"I swear I shall not," the butler replied somberly. "But I caution you, master. You should not meet this young woman again."

Before going to his mother and father, Justin handed his lute to the butler, asking if he could please return it to the teacher's house.

§13

Justin entered the dining room with a slight tremble that he tried very hard to conceal. As he took his chair, his father said simply, "You are late."

"My apologies, father."

"Where were you?"

"I was in the orchard."

"The orchard? What were you doing in the orchard?"

"Nothing, father. Simply sitting among the trees and thinking about all the things the bailiff has been teaching me."

"Very good," his father said. "There is much for you to learn."

After giving thanks to God for their food, the family commenced eating their supper, in silence as usual.

At the end of the meal, Justin's father rose from the table and said, "The situation is becoming dire. I have business I must attend to. I shall visit the bailiff now and not retire until late this evening."

Justin's father departed, leaving Justin and his mother alone together in the room. Justin looked at his mother. For the past few weeks she had appeared increasingly worn and tired, and this evening she looked even more fatigued than usual.

"Mother," Justin said. "Are you alright?"

"I am fine," she replied.

"But you do not look well."

"Indeed, I have not been my usual self for a long time now."

"Have you been examined?" Justin asked, even though he knew that his teacher was visiting her daily.

"Yes," Justin's mother said. "I suppose you know by now that your teacher is also a physician."

Justin shifted uncomfortably in his seat, but felt compelled to answer, "Yes, he has told me."

"And did he tell you that in addition to being a scholar and physician, he is also a practitioner of alchemy?"

Justin squirmed again in his chair. "Yes, he has told me that as well."

"Alchemy!" his mother sighed with a sardonic smile. "Then I also suppose you have also heard about his potions."

Justin knew he could never divulge to his father what his teacher had told him, but decided that he could confide in his mother, who had always been kind and gentle to him.

"Yes, he has told me about his potions."

"What exactly did he tell you?"

"He claims to have invented an elixir."

"Ah yes, the elixir, the one he makes with red powder from the philosopher's stone, or whatever he calls it. Do you know the purpose of this elixir?"

"Yes," Justin answered. "The teacher has told me that whoever imbibes it will always be young and live forever. Moreover, you, father, and I are being given this elixir every day. It is mixed with our food and drink."

"Do you, too, believe that we shall live forever?"

"Indeed, I hope so," Justin replied.

His mother looked at him wearily.

"You should not be so gullible, Justin. Do you really think that this teacher of yours, this alchemist, has discovered the elixir of life? I tell you, and I tell you earnestly, he has not. Neither the body nor the soul is immortal, for we have no bodies distinct from our souls or souls that can be separated from our bodies. When the body dies, the soul dies with it. This is the way of both God and nature."

"There is no immortality?"

"No one has returned from the dead to tell us, but I am disinclined to think so. We must come to terms with the probability that death is final and there is no afterlife."

Finding his mother's response unacceptable, Justin pounded his fist on the table. "But the priest has told us that if we but believe that Jesus is God's only begotten Son, we shall not perish but have eternal life!"

"The only people who pine for personal immortality are those who are unable to let go of their own shriveled selves and embrace an unlimited God. How can we hope to become one with the infinite if we strive to remain finite beings forever? To be one with the infinite and to be eternal in every moment is true immortality."

Justin could not quite grasp what his mother had just told him, understanding only that she had given up hope for a life in the hereafter.

"Then if we cannot live eternally after we die, why should we not seek to prolong our lives perpetually here on earth, like the alchemist, and avoid death altogether?"

"The only way to avoid death is not to be born," his mother replied.

"But the alchemist's intentions are good!" Justin cried. "He is using science to give us what nature itself does not."

"We should not play God nor tinker with his creation. It is unholy and unnatural to think that we should remain imprisoned in this world forever. To be condemned to live endlessly on this perishable earth, forced to endure the same futilities over and over again, century after century, would not be heaven but hell. To grow old and die is natural, for it is only through death that we can be released from the chains that bind our mortal shells to this world, with all its pain and sorrow."

"But surely, mother, the earth is not filled with pain and sorrow. Look at all the good things we enjoy in this house. Every day our table is laden with food. We drink the fruit of the vine. We wear the finest clothes and sleep in warm beds. We are blessed with every comfort. There could be no greater happiness than that which we have right now. We should not complain about the world God has created but give thanks to him for all that he has provided."

Justin's mother looked at him with an air of resignation.

"You are naive, my son. There are so many things you do not know, so many things to learn."

Upon hearing the word *naive* Justin suddenly wondered how he could have so quickly forgotten everything Constance had been telling him about life beyond the estate. Indeed, for those inside the wall, life was paradise; for those outside, it was perdition. He chided himself for not being able to change his habitual way of thinking.

Justin then said, "Mother, perhaps you are right. I have been naive, but now I am becoming familiar with the ways of the world outside the estate."

"Indeed, I have heard that you are being instructed by the bailiff how to keep the ledgers."

"I know more than what the bailiff is teaching me," Justin said without thinking.

"And who might be imparting this knowledge to you, since I am sure that the bailiff only lets you look at accounts and figures?"

Realizing that he had made an unguarded remark, Justin did not know how to reply. As much as he trusted his mother, he could never tell her about his clandestine meetings with Constance. So he said, "I have been learning these things on my own."

His mother looked at him dubiously. "I rather suspect that you have been speaking with the servants."

"I have not!" Justin declared emphatically, knowing that it was a lie.

"You may not know this, but your father has given strict orders to the servants never to discuss such matters with you and I am quite certain he would not have told you anything himself."

"Indeed, he has only spoken to me in a most general way," Justin said. "And recently I have begun to wonder why."

His mother smiled at him understandingly.

"Your father has compelled me, too, not to reveal anything to you about your situation, but I no longer care what he thinks. This may be the only chance I have to explain it to you, and I think you have a right to know."

She paused for a long moment. Justin was suddenly apprehensive. He could not imagine what his mother would say next.

"Ever since you were a little baby," she began, "your father has sheltered you from all awareness of the world outside this estate. He has forbidden anyone, even me, to speak to you about what life is like beyond these walls."

"But why would he do such a thing?" Justin asked.

"After I gave birth to you, we learned that I would not be able to bear any more children. We loved and cherished you as the only son we would ever have. The village priest came to our chapel to baptize you. After pouring the water on your head and invoking the name of the Father, Son, and Holy Spirit, he prophesied that one day you would become a great spiritual leader."

Justin said nothing but looked at his mother with expectation.

"Your father," she said, "fearing that he would lose the only heir to his estate, vowed on that day never to let you step beyond its walls. He wanted to shield you from any influences which might entice you away from the plans he had already made for you. That is also why he also forbade your teacher to allow you to read any works of philosophy or religion, lest they arouse your interest. In your father's eyes, your entire life has already been decided. You will inherit this estate and become its lord. The plan is fixed and cannot be changed."

It took Justin a moment to digest everything his mother was telling him, but slowly things started to come into focus.

"Your father knew, of course," his mother continued, "that in due time you would learn about affairs outside the estate, but he wanted you to be exposed to these things little by little—just as you are beginning to learn now how the estate is managed from the inside—so that you would not waver from the course he has already set for you."

"You should have told me these things before!" Justin exclaimed.

"Perhaps I should have. But I am telling you now. Look at me, Justin. Do you not see how much I have aged? I have been ill for some time and know that I will die soon. The medicines your teacher prepares for me have no effect. I become sicker by the day."

"If the teacher's potions are useless, why does father not dismiss him?"

"He still believes in him. Your father met your teacher a long time ago during one of his visits to the city. He was impressed with his vast knowledge of alchemy and taken in by his pompous promises of gold and eternal life. So, your father invited him to come to this estate as your tutor, letting him stay in the cottage where he could also set up a laboratory to make his concoctions."

"But surely he is a learned scholar."

"Indeed, your teacher puffs himself up with pretentious wisdom, but he has no real knowledge of life or the world. He is nothing but a quack. Nonetheless, your father has full confidence in the alchemist and the credulity to believe that he has discovered the secret of life."

"Have you not discussed your reservations with father?"

"He cannot be dissuaded, even though he can see me wasting away before his very eyes. Once your father comes to his senses, he will not permit you to see me anymore because he has always endeavored to keep from you any knowledge of old age, sickness, or death, lest it persuade you to make it your mission in life to help others, rather than devote yourself to the continuance of this estate. That is why you have never seen anyone serving us here who is elderly or ailing. They are always dismissed before you have a chance to see them in that condition. And heaven forbid if you should ever be exposed to a dead body."

"Why does father not simply admit the truth?"

"He cannot. He holds on to his convictions unswervingly and refuses to give them up, even when reality contradicts them. Your father thinks he is still young, but he is getting old, too. He wants to continue to enjoy his possessions and riches for as long as he can. He is afraid to die and thinks he can live forever. But once this illusion is shattered, your father will be crushed, and it will be a sorrowful day for your teacher as well."

Justin was perplexed. "But if father truly supposes that he will never die, why does he claim me as his heir? Is that not a contradiction?"

"He is merely hedging his bets. I really do not wish to tell you this, but you should know: even though you are his son, you are expendable. If your father ever became utterly convinced of his own immortality, he would no longer have any need of you."

"And how about you, mother? Do you not wish to live forever?"

"Death is not our enemy but our friend, Justin. Each of us will die someday—me, you, and even your father, whether he realizes it or not. And because we know this, we should be grateful for every single hour we have. We must not fear but embrace the brevity of life, so that we might spend each moment to the fullest, knowing it will never return."

Justin's mother took his hands in hers and squeezed them hard.

"And you, my son, are surely fated to become something other than what your father intends. As long as you remain on this estate under the wing of your father, you will never become a man, but always have the mind of a child. You will obediently do whatever your father tells you to do in-stead of making decisions yourself and taking responsibility for your own life. At some point you must free yourself from the grip your father has on you and leave this estate. Only then will you find your destiny."

"So the priest was right. God has a different plan for my life."

"There are no plans for any of us other than the ones we make for ourselves. But as Jesus has told us, 'Do not lay up for yourselves treasures on earth, but treasures in heaven, for where your treasure is, your heart will be also.' You, too, must follow your heart, Justin."

When she stood up to leave, Justin helped her from her chair to the door. She gave him a long hug at the doorway.

"Farewell," she said.

"Farewell?"

"Good night, then."

"Yes, good night."

That was the last time Justin ever saw his mother. The next day she did not appear at the table for the mid-day dinner.

Justin asked his father, "Where is mother?"

And his father replied, "She will not be joining us for dinner today, nor will she be here at supper."

§14

Less than a week later Justin was awakened in the middle of the night by a great ruckus outside his room. He peered out the window and in the dark below could see the shadow of a guard dragging a man roughly through the alley behind the house. For one brief instant, Justin saw the glint of moonlight on a gold medallion the man was wearing.

Behind the guard was the murky figure of Justin's father, who was shouting above the commotion, "The scoundrel! The charlatan!"

Justin could hear, but not see, the heavy door of the dungeon being unlocked and swung open. A lantern was lit, and Justin heard two sets of footsteps descending the stone staircase. For a moment there was silence. Then one set of footsteps ascended the stairway. A figure emerged from the dungeon and rejoined Justin's father in the alley. In the dim light Justin could now see that it was Martin who was holding the lantern. Martin bowed deeply to his master and then departed down the alley in the direction of the barracks. The lord paused for a long moment outside the dungeon door, then began walking in the opposite direction, stifling the sound of his weeping.

The next morning Justin's father summoned his son to his room, where he was informed matter-of-factly and without emotion that his mother had been called away unexpectedly from the estate during the night and would not return, that Justin would no longer go to the cottage of his teacher for his afternoon lessons, but instead devote himself fully to mastering the affairs and administration of the estate. In addition, he would begin to study the law under the bailiff's supervision.

§15

In the days that followed Justin went each morning to the bailiff's stone house, where he poured over the records of the estate in the morning and studied law in the afternoon, only taking a break for his noonday meal. He no longer visited the turret except at night, when he would look up at the stars and marvel at how vast the heavens are and how small he was in comparison. He began to wonder for the first time what lay on the other side of the ocean to the east, the fields to the south, the wolds to the west, and the forests to the north. In the past the horizons were the borders of a world that did not stretch on forever but only as far as his eyes could see. Now he knew that worlds awaited him beyond those horizons, and he wanted to cross over those boundaries to discover what was there.

He longed to see Constance again but knew there would be no opportunity, at least none to talk with her. Sometimes, though rarely, when looking out the window of the bailiff's stone cottage Justin would catch a brief glimpse of her walking along the alley to one of the storehouses for supplies. On one of her excursions, when the bailiff was out and Justin was alone in the house, he tapped loudly on the shutter, trying to get Constance's attention. He was sure that she had noticed him, but she quickly turned her head and continued on her way to the warehouse. Justin did not see her on her trip back, so he assumed that she had returned to the house by another route, no doubt past the soldier's barracks and up the lane to the main entrance of the manor house.

Justin missed his mother, too. He knew that she had not been called away, as his father had told him. She had died. The alchemist's potions had not been able to save her. He did not know exactly what had become of his teacher, except that he had been put away in the dungeon, a place that Justin could not even imagine. He never saw the door of the dungeon being opened or closed again after that fateful night, so he assumed that no one went to the teacher to bring him food or water. He could not discuss these matters with father, who sat stone-faced and silent throughout mealtimes each day. Justin wondered if his father was grieving for his mother or only for himself, having realized that the alchemist was a fraud and that he himself would not live forever.

Then Justin would think about what his mother had told him. He pondered the difference between fate and destiny and decided that destiny is what you are supposed to do in life and fate is what you end up doing even if it is not what you are supposed to do. While Justin was not sure if life was governed by destiny or fate, one thing was certain: he was thoroughly bored with his new routine at the bailiff's house.

Though his movements were unpredictable, the bailiff left the stone house periodically to do errands around the estate and to supervise incoming shipments of wheat, barley, and oats from the peasants, leaving Justin alone in the room where he labored. At other times, the bailiff would exit the estate in the company of Martin and some soldiers and be gone the entire day. Justin now understood that the purpose of these departures was to collect taxes, rents, and fees from the peasants, which Justin would dutifully record in the ledgers.

One late afternoon when the bailiff returned from a journey to the village, Justin asked him, "Might I be permitted to assist you with your external duties?"

"In good time," the bailiff replied. "You have not yet mastered what needs to be done here on the premises, however. That comes first."

"But I have been making tremendous progress," Justin said. "Surely I also need to know about affairs outside the estate. I would sincerely like to join you on one of your excursions to the village."

"That is entirely your father's decision," the bailiff answered. "I have no control over it."

The real reason, of course, why Justin wanted to accompany the bailiff on a visit to the village was not because he wanted to learn how to manage affairs outside the estate, but because he was becoming increasingly curious about what the world was like on the other side of its walls. He had listened to Constance's stories about life among the peasants in the village, but he wished to see for himself. In short, he wanted to know the difference between good and evil! Despite having access to all the amenities of the estate, life inside its walls was becoming intolerable for him. Their purpose was not to keep out evil, but to keep Justin inside, stultified and in a perpetual state of naivety. With increasing fervency, he yearned to break out of his confinement and leave this prison forever.

One day when the bailiff was out checking an incoming shipment of livestock, Justin spied Constance walking again to the storehouse. Her face was turned away, as always, so rather than tap on the shutter, he ran out of the house and caught up with her, just as she reached the door of the warehouse.

"Constance," he said. "I have been wanting to see you."

Constance looked around her nervously. "No, my lord, we are forbidden to meet."

"Come," Justin said, ushering her inside the warehouse and closing the door behind them.

"I have told you, master. I am not supposed to meet or talk with you. I will surely be cast off the estate if anyone sees me here with you."

"I understand and will not detain you, but there is something I absolutely must confide in you now."

Constance looked at him, not knowing what he would say.

"I want to run away with you. I want to escape from this estate and live a common life among the people. I want to find out what the world outside these walls is really like."

"You have no idea what you're saying," Constance retorted. "Anyone in the village would gladly trade their life for yours. You have every comfort.

There is no reason for you to relinquish your luxury and take up a life of misery. I should not like to do so either."

"Would it not be better for us to be together even if we must share a life of poverty? I have no idea how I'm going to do it, but I have already decided to leave. Either with you or alone. You mustn't tell anyone, of course. But I would like to go together with you. Please. Come with me."

Constance was silent for a moment and then said, "No, I will not go with you. My life here is far from as good as yours, but it is certainly better than the way I lived before in the village. I am sorry, Justin. Right now that is more important to me than you are!"

"Well, at least think about it," Justin said, trying to peck her forehead with his lips.

Constance dodged his advances, picked up what she needed from the storehouse, and hastily departed through the back door.

"I love you," Justin called out after her in as soft a voice as possible. It was the first time he had actually said those words to Constance.

Constance, however, did not turn back to acknowledge them.

§16

Days passed. Justin sat in the cottage every day but could not keep his mind on the ledgers. Even the bailiff noticed Justin's inattention to his duties.

"Is everything all right?" he asked.

"Yes, fine," Justin replied.

"Then you need to get caught up with your work. You're falling behind. You will never learn how to manage the estate at this pace."

But Justin had lost his concentration. All he could think about was leaving the estate. He did not yet have a plan and, worse, could not even imagine one, which pushed him even deeper into despair. He knew that he wanted to run away, but he did not want to leave alone, not without Constance. He knew that he could not fend for himself but would need her to show him how to live in a world that was completely different from his own, the world he had grown up in, the only world he had ever known. But even more, he wanted to be with her. Then Justin considered: if the choice were between leaving without Constance or remaining on the estate to be close to her, even though they could never meet or talk, Justin would stay. Constance was more important to him than anything else in the world. Even if his only contact with her was an occasional furtive glance at her bouncing hair as she passed by his window, it was worth it.

On another day when the bailiff was out and Justin was sitting in the room, looking up at the ceiling, distracted as usual, there was a slight tap on the shutter. Justin peered out and saw Constance, trying unsuccessfully to hide the excitement on her face, forming silent words with her mouth: "Yes! Yes, I will go with you!"

"I will make a plan!" Justin mouthed back. "Just as soon as I can!"

Constance hurried away, not looking back. Justin smiled. Then frowned. He did not have a plan nor could he think of one.

§17

The very next day there was another calamity on the estate. Justin was at the bailiff's house alone, not doing his work as usual, when the bailiff suddenly rushed in through the door.

"Get out," he shouted. "Your father wants you to go to your room inside the manor house immediately."

"But why?" Justin asked.

"There is no time for explanations. Just do as you are told."

Justin left the house, closing the door behind him, but walked as sloooowly as he could, taking the long way back to the house, past the paddock to the stable, where the horses were being readied. At the guardhouse the soldiers already had swords in their scabbards. Some were picking up polearms and axes, others longbows and arrows. Martin was among the soldiers, distributing weapons and shouting commands.

Justin called over to him, "What's going on?"

"It's the peasants," Martin shouted back.

"If it's only the peasants, why do you need your weapons?"

Martin did not reply. One of the soldiers dashed over to Martin and asked, "Should we pull up the drawbridge?"

"No, the lord wants to go out to meet them."

Martin mounted a horse and headed toward the main gate of the estate, the other soldier trotting along behind him. Justin was about to run after them when someone suddenly grabbed him from behind and whirled him around. It was his father.

"What are you doing here?" his father asked sternly. "Did the bailiff not tell you to go to your room?"

"Indeed, he did, father."

"Then that's where you should go."

"Is there going to be a fight?" Justin asked excitedly.

"Not if we can avoid it," his father said.

"But I want to fight!" Justin cried, too thrilled by the idea of picking up a sword and going out to meet the enemy to remember what Constance had told him about the plight of the peasants. "I've been trained, you know!"

"You shall do no such thing."

"Then at least tell me what is happening."

"You do not need to know. Just go to your room and in a short time this will all be over."

He gave Justin a harsh shove in the direction of the manor.

"Now go!" he shouted.

Justin sprinted towards the front entrance. When he looked back over his shoulder, he saw his father already seated in the saddle of a horse. He was wearing a mail shirt, but no helmet or other armor. As with the soldiers, his sword was in its scabbard. But unlike the soldiers, a lance was nestled in his right arm.

Justin did not return to his room, however, but instead ascended the stairway to the turret. From there he looked out over the flatlands to the south and could see a band of peasants, fifty or sixty altogether, walking in uneven ranks up the highway towards the estate. The soldiers had assembled across the brook on the other side of the drawbridge. They were lined up along both sides of the road, some on horses and others on foot. As the peasants approached, Justin's father maneuvered his horse through the gate, followed by Martin. The two crossed over the drawbridge and rode out together to meet the peasants.

"What business have you here?" his father shouted out to the peasants in a voice that was loud enough for even Justin to hear from the turret.

"We have come to speak with you," a muscular young man shouted back. He was clad in breeches brown with mud and a torn, undyed tunic. His black hair and beard were long and wild. Justin noticed that while most of the other men surrounding him were also young, a few were old, with grizzled whiskers, withered skin, and missing teeth. Justin had never seen such people before and none so frail. Ever since his youth he had seen peasants only from a distance, working the fields as he watched from the turret, but he had never gotten a good look at their faces, so did not know their age and assumed they were all young, just like the servants on the estate.

"There is nothing to speak about," Justin's father replied. "You should be doing your work."

"That is what we have come to talk to you about," the young spokesman said. "We will not return to our labors until conditions are improved."

"What conditions do you mean?"

"We have already discussed these matters with your bailiff, who assured us that he would inform you of our concerns. All that we are asking for is relief. We toil all day and give everything to you. Now nothing remains for ourselves."

"Indeed, the bailiff has relayed your message to me. But I cannot see anything wrong with your current situation. Everything is being carried out exactly as we agreed. The amounts are fixed and cannot be changed. I order you now to disband and go back to your duties."

The spokesman looked at the other men around him, then back to Justin's father.

"We will not, sire, until we have come to new terms with you. It is hardly fair to say that we 'agreed' to the conditions you previously imposed on us."

"Nonsense," Justin's father said. "You will disperse immediately, or I will have my soldiers remove you from this place."

There was a moment of silence. Muscles tensed on both sides as the soldiers drew their swords and the peasants stood their ground.

"You can see we have no arms," the spokesman said at last. "We did not come here to fight, but to talk."

Justin's father leaned over and whispered something to Martin. Justin could see his lips moving but, of course, could not hear what he said. Martin nodded his head, looked briefly back at the other soldiers, drew out his sword, pointed it towards the peasants.

He then shouted in a loud voice, "Attack!"

Martin spurred his horse and started off after the peasants, the other men-at-arms close behind him. The peasants immediately turned and scattered across the field, running back in the direction they had come from. The younger ones were swift, and while the lord's horsemen pursued them, they did not cut them down but chased them back towards the village, with Martin leading the charge. The stragglers were a handful of old men, whom the foot soldiers began to slaughter without mercy, stabbing them with their swords, piercing them with polearms, hacking off heads and limbs from their bodies with axes, even after they had fallen to the ground and were already dead. The archers stood at the gate, their longbows ready, but they did not need to draw them.

Justin's father sat on his horse in front of the estate on the other side of the drawbridge viewing the scene impassively. Justin remained in the turret witnessing everything that transpired, unable to comprehend what he was seeing. How could he possibly have told his father that he wanted to fight? These were not simply "peasants," but men having the same flesh and blood that he did and, moreover, the same villagers that Constance herself had once dwelt amongst.

For the first time since his birth Justin had seen suffering and death with his own eyes. His body shook with a feeling he had never experienced before and could not understand. The flawless bubble in which his life had been so delicately contained was now suddenly punctured.

§18

That evening Justin was served supper not in the dining room with his father as usual, but in his own room, to which he had stumbled immediately after seeing the massacre in the fields. That night, while snug and warm in bed, he began to have doubts about his intention to secretly leave the estate with Constance. Before he had looked at it all as if it were a great odyssey, a voyage of discovery, an opportunity to widen his views and learn new things. But now he was consumed with fear. If the world outside was not the adventure he had imagined, but how he had seen it today, Justin was no longer sure he wanted to go there. Perhaps it would be better to stay just where he was and try to crawl back inside the broken bubble so that he might feel secure again.

The next day at dawn Justin climbed to the top of the turret to see the sunrise, something he had not done for a long time. In the morning light he could see no sign whatsoever of the events that had occurred the day before on the southern fields except for streaks of trampled wheat leading off towards the village. Justin spied the small boat still tied to the dock just above the drawbridge, which was now pulled up, and wondered where the boat would take him if he ever climbed into it, cut the cord, and let the frail bark take him down the brook to the ocean and across the ocean to unknown lands he could not yet even envision. But then he put the idea out of his mind. The ocean was too vast, the skiff would sink, and he would drown trying to find realms that had no reality outside his own imagination.

Before leaving for the bailiff's house, Justin's father encountered him in the hallway at the top of the stairway and waved him into his own room. It was more spacious than Justin's, with a grand canopy bed, sitting chairs, a large wooden table, and a full suit of dented armor in one corner.

"Sit down," his father said, motioning to one of the chairs.

Justin dutifully obeyed, while his father strolled over to the room's only window.

"You saw nothing of what took place yesterday?" Justin's father asked him, peering through the glass.

"No, sir, nothing," he replied.

"You were in your room the whole time?"

"Yes, sir, I was," Justin replied, not feeling guilty at all about telling his father a lie.

"Good," his father said. "I must nonetheless explain to you what happened."

He returned from the window and sat in the chair opposite Justin.

"Yesterday our estate was attacked," he began. "With no just cause the peasants descended upon us, hurling invectives and making unreasonable demands. When I refused to make any concessions, they pounced, throwing rocks and stones at our good soldiers, who were forced to defend themselves by any means possible and who drove the peasants back to their homes. This time the peasants had no arms, but it would be easy enough for them to make wooden spears for themselves and to utilize their hayforks and scythes as weapons. If we do not assert our authority and put them in their place, they will surely come to strike us again."

Justin sat in his chair saying nothing. His father was lying, too, of course. Justin had certainly not seen the peasants throwing any rocks or stones.

"So, you see how desperate our situation is becoming. I have already applied to the baron for stronger fortifications and more troops, but so far without reply. It is, as you know, the baron's duty to protect us. But I suppose he is weighed down with burdens of his own at the moment. Ours is not the only manor having troubles. The blight is spreading throughout the land. The only recourse I have is to make an alliance with the lord whose estate lies on the far side of the village where our own villeins live. He has difficulties of his own, but together we shall pool our resources and defeat this defiance on the part of both his serfs and ours. Our mission shall be to chasten the peasants, inculcate them with the virtue of humility, and guide them back to their rightful position, so that order may be restored and the peasants will once again serve God, serve their king, and serve us. Do you understand what I am telling you, Justin?"

Justin nodded his head.

"In a week's time I am planning to hold a great feast in honor of our neighboring lord. I have already communicated with him by couriers riding undetected back and forth during the night between our estate and his, and he has accepted my invitation. The full details of our recent incident with the peasants have been explained to him, so he knows about the bind we are in. We shall discuss these affairs further before the feast. I would like you to also be present for the negotiations. I am sure I do not need to ask for your agreement."

"No, father. Of course, I will be there."

"There is one further matter," Justin's father went on, "which I have proposed to the lord and to which he has already given his consent."

"What might that be, father?"

"That he should bring his daughter, Penelope, with him, and that you and she shall be married in the chapel on our estate on the same day as the feast. So, as you see, the feast will not only be in honor of our esteemed guest but also in honor of your wedding."

His father's proposition was entirely unexpected and Justin did not know what to say.

"Well, son," his father said triumphantly, not even noticing the look of confusion on Justin's face. "Aren't you happy? I have made these arrangements in your own best interests, of course, as well as in my own."

"But, father," Justin stammered. "I am not sure that I wish to marry."

"Of course, you wish to marry," Justin's father said. "You are at exactly the right age and I have found exactly the right woman for you."

"But I have not yet even met her!"

"You needn't worry. She is a few years younger than you and I assure you that she is quite charming."

"Might I have some time to think about it?" Justin asked.

"What is there to consider? The matter has already been confirmed between her father and myself, and that is all that counts."

"But perhaps I shall decide not to marry her."

"The decision is not yours, my son, but mine. Do not be concerned. I am sure that in time you will be just as happily married as your mother and I were . . . I mean, still are."

"Indeed, when is mother coming back to the estate?" Justin asked.

"I'm afraid that she will be delayed for a very long time. Unfortunately she will not be here to attend your wedding, but I am sure that she will send you her blessings and good wishes."

Justin's eyes met his father's. It seemed as if they understood each other perfectly, even if what they understood was completely different.

"Now go," his father said. "You have your duties to attend to at the bailiff's quarters."

§19

Justin spent the next few days at the bailiff's house as ordered, but it was more difficult than ever for him to concentrate on his work. Why, he wondered, was he required to keep the ledgers using expensive imported paper but not permitted to use it to record the poetry, both exuberant and tragic, that filled his soul? Perhaps it was his destiny, as his mother had told him, to become a priest or a religious leader, but his fate, it seemed, was to succeed his father and eventually become lord of the estate. Did he even have a choice, Justin wondered. Is what we do in life determined from the very beginning or are there alternative paths we might follow?

Perhaps it is like a game of cards, Justin thought, the kind he used to play with Martin. The rules are specified in advance and cannot be altered. We cannot choose which cards we are dealt but only how we play them. Once a card has been set down, it cannot be taken back. We cannot decide how others will play their hand, but only how to play the cards we ourselves hold. After each round an entirely new set of conditions is created, which cannot be changed and which circumscribe what we are able to do next. In the same way, we cannot always choose the circumstances life gives us, but we can choose how we respond to them. Once a chain of events has been set in motion, we lose control over the consequences. Each cause has an effect, which then becomes the next cause. Any new situation we create in life constrains us from doing some things but enables us to do others. We reap what we sow.

Still, it increasingly seemed to Justin that he had no choices whatsoever, not even how to play his own cards. Another hand was playing them for him. He could not alter his fate and was bound to do as his father had commanded him. The dream of leaving the estate and running away with Constance had evaporated with his father's announcement of his marriage to the neighboring lord's daughter. Justin considered going through with his original plan to escape but could not think of a way to flee the grounds with Constance without getting caught. Moreover, he was fearful now of what life would actually be like on the other side of the wall. It was a world he did not really know, was scarcely able to fathom, and probably could not navigate, even with Constance's help. Most of all he feared his father, knowing that the consequences would be unbearable if Justin were to go against his wishes. His mother had told him that one day he would need to break free and become his own man, but this did not seem to be the right occasion. He was increasingly unsure that the time would ever come.

Finally Justin decided he could not leave the estate. He would stay. He consoled himself with the thought that at least he would still be close to Constance and able to see her from a distance. Even if during the rest of his life he were only able to meet her for one single moment, he would live for that moment. It did not matter if he were married to another.

Justin was in anguish about not being able to tell Constance what he had been thinking and feeling. No doubt she had already heard the news about Justin's upcoming marriage since her demeanor had changed completely. From his desk at the bailiff's house he would see Constance occasionally pass by the window on an errand to the storehouse, but she always turned her head away, avoiding even a brief look at Justin. The bailiff, moreover, was constantly in the house these days, cursing over the ledgers as he examined them with Justin.

"I tell you," the bailiff said at one point. "The supplies we have on hand will last us a little more than a month, but we'll have none after that. We shall be destitute in a very short time if we do not acquire what we need from the peasants. The matter is urgent. I must inform your father."

With that the bailiff arose from his chair and left the house, leaving Justin alone in the room. By good fortune just a few minutes later the figure of Constance appeared in the corner of the window as she was walking determinedly down the alley. Justin jumped out of his seat, rushed to the door, and silently beckoned her inside. Constance hesitated but then regained her stride and continued straight ahead, impelling Justin to chase after her.

"Hurry," he said in a loud whisper. "There isn't much time."

He grabbed Constance by the arm and pulled her back to the house, then through the doorway, shutting the door behind him.

"I do not wish to talk to you," Constance said, pushing Justin away.

"There is something I must tell you," Justin replied.

"Surely you must know about the confrontation between your father and the peasants last week."

"Indeed, I watched the whole incident from the turret."

"My brother was the leader and four of the villagers were killed by the soldiers," Constance said on the verge of tears.

"I have come to realize just how perilous life can be on the other side of the wall."

Justin's voice did not sound entirely convincing, however, even to himself.

"That is the way things are for us," Constance continued. "And now you know the truth about your father, not just from my words but with your own eyes."

"Certainly I cannot condone his actions."

"Yet soon you will become his heir and end up treating the peasants in exactly the same manner."

Justin reached out to embrace Constance. "I have missed you so much," he said.

"I cannot believe you," Constance responded, avoiding his arms.

"Then you already know?"

"Who does not? All the servants are busying themselves with preparations for your wedding, *sire*."

She pronounced the word with a sneer.

"That is what I want to talk to you about," Justin said.

"There is nothing to discuss."

"I do not wish to marry," Justin continued. "I honestly don't. But father is forcing me to."

"Aren't you man enough to make your own choices in life?"

"As I told you before, what I really want is to run away with you or at least to be with you in any way I can."

"After what has happened, I certainly do not wish to live on this estate any longer either, no matter how good the conditions are compared to those in the village."

"Then why don't you leave?"

"I cannot," Constance replied. "If I fled back to the village, your father would surely have me returned and penalized. If I escaped to the city, how would I be able to make an honest living for myself?"

"So there you are. Neither of us have a choice."

"The choice is yours," Constance said resolutely.

"I do not know what you mean."

"We could still elope, should you choose me instead of her."

Justin was thoughtful for a moment and then said, "I have, of course, considered this. But I can't, Constance. I simply can't. I am afraid. Even with you by my side I am not sure if I could survive life outside this estate."

Constance simply stood there, heaving slightly, eyes to the floor.

"Would it not be better," Justin pleaded, "for both of us to stay here inside these walls? I know I would be married to another woman, but I could still at least behold you on occasion and sometimes be near you. I love you, Constance. I truly do. I must apologize to you sincerely for my lack of fortitude and beg for your forgiveness. If you harbor ill feelings towards me and cannot excuse the dreadful way I am treating you, I fully understand and can accept whatever verdict you reach about me."

Constance raised her chin and looked at Justin intently. "I wish, I wish, I sincerely wish that I could pull myself away from you forever and ever, and never see or think of you again for the rest of my life."

Hearing these words, Justin averted his eyes and let his head fall into his open hand.

"But I could not bear to live in eternal anguish," she then added.

Justin looked up in bewilderment. Constance's face was firm and unwavering.

"My lord, you know that I love you and always will," she continued. "I understand your position and do not reproach you. Certainly I respect your decision. It will not change in any way how I feel about you. If you wish to go ahead with your marriage and to stay on this estate, I shall be happy for you. I have no choice but to remain here as well for as long as your father wishes to keep me. I will also be thankful for any chance there may be to see you, even though we may never truly be with each other."

Justin reached out again for Constance and flung his arms around her. She did not draw back this time but began running her fingers through his hair, then down his neck to his shoulders, holding them tightly in her hands. They kissed, their tongues penetrating each other's mouths, then held each other mournfully, knowing this might be their final embrace but grateful to have this one moment together. Breathing heavily into each other's ears, they did not notice the sound of the bailiff's footsteps as he approached the stone house, did not see him peer through the open window, nor even hear the latch turn and the door open when the bailiff entered the room.

"My lord," the bailiff said forcefully but without anger.

Startled, Justin and Constance disengaged, and looked up sheepishly at the bailiff.

"My lord," the bailiff repeated. "This behavior is unbecoming of you."

"I am sorry," Justin said, awkwardly bowing his head.

"You should not apologize to me, but to your father," the bailiff said.

Justin kicked his foot nervously on the floor. Finally he said, "You know I cannot do that. If my father ever learns of this affair he will certainly disown me."

"It would be much worse for you than that," the bailiff replied. "Perhaps you should not tell him after all, for indeed he would not pardon you."

"You will not tell him, will you?"

"I am not the only one who knows. The butler informed me of your previous encounter with this servant girl. He had seen you walking from your teacher's house to the orchard each afternoon and knew the girl was there at the same time, gathering fruit for the table. He decided to investigate and then told me what he saw."

Justin then remembered what the butler had said to him on the day he could not find Constance and returned late to the manor house. "But the butler swore he would not report the matter to my father."

"He did not. Nor did I. We both know how wrathful your father can be. He has no control over his anger and would do things he later regretted. And now, by continuing your dalliance with this girl, you are endangering not only your position, but ours as well."

The bailiff then turned to Constance and said, "We warned you never to see Justin again. Your willful disregard of our prohibitions cannot be tolerated. It is your fault, not Justin's, that he is in this predicament. The only recourse is for you to leave the estate. You are permitted to go to your room, gather your things, and depart quietly through the main gate. I will give

instructions to the head guard to let you pass and inform the steward of
your departure. I cannot accompany you lest it arouse suspicion. You may
speak to no one and must be discreet. It would not bode well for you if you
disobey my orders."

Justin took Constance by the arm and looked sorrowfully into her
eyes. Constance returned his gaze and said, "Now even I have no choice."

"Come now. Do not tarry," the bailiff said. "You must be off at once."

"Goodbye," Constance said, tearing herself away from Justin's grasp.

"We shall meet again," Justin replied dolefully.

§20

It had rained heavily the night before but on the day of Justin's wedding
the sky was clear and bright. Warm breezes had blown away all the clouds.
The sun was beating down, evaporating the dampness on the ground. As the
morning progressed the air became sultry.

The lord of the neighboring estate arrived early to attend the conference with Justin's father. His regally adorned carriage was followed by a second, less ostentatious one transporting his head guard and administrators.
The occupants were greeted with great pageantry as they passed over the
drawbridge, through the gate, and onto the grounds of the estate. Flags were
waved. Horns were blown. Martin and the soldiers, as well as the bailiff, all
cheered as the coaches wound their way up the drive to the courtyard in
front of the manor house, where Justin and his father were waiting.

The lord stepped grandly out of his carriage, followed by his graceful
daughter. Apparently the lord had no wife or other children since no one
else emerged from the coach. The lord's head guard and administrators got
out of their carriage as well and the entire group joined Justin and his father
just in front of the portico at the main entrance of the mansion.

"Greetings and welcome," Justin's father said, holding out his hand to
the lord without smiling.

The lord took his hand and shook it. His face was equally expressionless.

"Indeed, it is a great pleasure to see you again."

"This is my son, Justin."

"And may I introduce you to my daughter, Penelope."

Penelope curtsied and Justin bowed in return. Penelope was wearing a
blue gossamer veil, which obscured her face. From her eyes alone, however,
Justin could see that she was quite lovely.

The butler held the door for the guests to enter the house. A lady in
waiting escorted Penelope to a parlor next to the dining room, where she
would be served her midday meal, while the men proceeded to the great

hall. The table inside had already been set with a light lunch and ale. The visiting lord and his retinue sat on one side of the table, with Justin's father and his attendants on the other. Justin was seated between the bailiff and his father, with Martin to his father's left.

After exchanging a few more tepid pleasantries and beginning to eat, the two sides got down to business, quickly agreeing that the situation was becoming untenable for both of them. While there had been no confrontation between the neighboring lord and his villeins, conditions were similar to those at Justin's father's estate and the neighboring lord feared the rebellion would spread to his manor as it had to several others.

"Here is the crux of the problem," Justin's father explained. "Since the peasants know they can never win an armed conflict against us, they have begun to withhold grain and other essential goods, which are rightfully ours, and to keep them for themselves. It is nothing more than a backhanded way of laying siege to us. If we do not take action now, we shall be defenseless and obliged to surrender."

After a considerable amount of discussion, a strategy was devised for a brigade from Justin's father's estate to approach the village from the north, while the neighboring lord's troops advanced from the south. After converging on the village the two sides would compel the peasants to make concessions.

"I am sure that our soldiers could do this on their own," Justin's father said to the lord. "But making a joint show of force may in fact be the best way to resolve this matter peacefully. Once the peasants see that you and I have aligned ourselves against them, they will realize that resistance is futile."

"But what if they defy us?" the lord asked.

"Of course we shall dole out severe retribution."

"What do you have in mind?"

"We will burn down the house of their leader."

"That is all?"

"And perhaps kill a few more of the older peasants for good measure. They consume more than they produce anyway and are useless to me."

"It would also set a good example for the rest of them!"

The two men laughed.

Then Justin's father said, "If it pleases my lord, we shall implement our plans exactly one month from today. I shall leave it to my head guard, Martin here, to work out the details with whomever you designate from your side."

"All of your proposals sound fine to me."

"And, of course," Justin's father added, "when the time is right I shall come to your aid and help you deal with the peasants on your manor as well."

"Yes, I agree to these terms," the lord replied.

The two men reached across the table and shook hands.

His father then turned to Justin and said, "And you, my son, shall ride to the village with Martin as his co-leader. You understand more fully now the suffering we endure on this estate and your role in helping to defend it. I am sure that you will be perfectly safe under the care of Martin and am counting on you to devote yourself wholeheartedly to this task. We all hope to live forever, but one day I shall die and you will inherit this manor. You will soon be married and become a man. The time has finally come for you to begin to take charge."

Justin was too shocked by this announcement to make a reply, so he simply nodded his head. To be sure, he wanted to see the world beyond the walls of the estate, but this was not how he wanted to do it, especially not his very first time. He had been trained in the implements of war and until just recently had unthinkingly been willing, even eager, to fight, wanting to test in real battle the military skills he had spent so much time diligently learning. But after he had seen his father's soldiers slay the defenseless peasants on the fields outside the estate, he no longer wanted any part of it, especially since Constance was now back in the village. What he feared most was not being killed—he had decided that the life he was about to live was not worth much anyway—but rather having to kill others. The thought that he himself might be expected to commit what seemed like nothing less than acts of murder appalled him. The pretenses were flimsy and the attack lacked all justification. How could his father possibly believe that those who lived on the estate suffered more than those who lived in the village? Justin nonetheless knew that at some point he would not be able to avoid his responsibilities as successor to the estate, that he would be called upon to perform deeds he did not wish to perform, to engage in actions he would prefer simply to evade. Still, what could he do?

Justin stared at the food in front of him, no longer able to touch it even as everyone else resumed eating and drinking, the two lords and their minions gradually warming up to each other and engaging in friendly banter. When the meal was over, Martin and the bailiff led the neighboring lord's men out of the hall. Justin did not leave with them but lingered at the table with the lord and his father.

"You are dismissed," his father told him curtly. "The lord and I must finalize the matter of your dowry. We shall join you shortly."

"I did not know," Justin replied. "But before I depart may I ask if it is really necessary for me to participate in this mission you are planning?"

His father looked at him tempestuously.

"Of course, you must participate!" Then, pulling Justin's face close to his, he rasped, "Do not embarrass me in front of our guest here by making yourself look like a coward."

"I apologize, father," Justin said sheepishly. "It is not that I am a coward . . . but—"

"You may leave now," his father snapped.

Bowing to his father and the lord, Justin left the room. He passed languidly by the anteroom where Martin and the other lord's head guard were discussing their plans, past the parlor where Penelope was being dressed for the wedding, and then broke into a run just as soon as he was out of the front door of the manor house. He raced across the lawn to the orchard, going straight to the old tree stump where he used to meet Constance. Sitting down, he remembered the times he had spent with her, wondering if he would ever see her again and, if he did, whether it would be under portentous circumstances. Justin would be married soon and after that be chained forever within the walls of the estate. He had never felt so lonely in his life.

§21

Emerging from the orchard, Justin could see that other members of the nobility from the surrounding countryside who had been invited to the ceremony had already arrived. Their carriages were parked in the courtyard in front of the mansion, the horses attended to by servants. The lords and their ladies were all wearing their finest clothes and already walking back down the lane towards the chapel. Justin plodded awkwardly across the open grass, trying to avoid being noticed by them.

He did not join the guests as they gathered in front of the chapel but entered through a side door which led directly to the sacristy, where his wedding clothes were waiting for him. As he was being helped by a servant into his stockings and cotehardie, Justin realized that this would be his last possible opportunity to escape from the estate before being wed. He upbraided himself for not being clever enough to come up with a plan, as well as for not being able to speak up and extricate himself from his father's control, and, most of all, for forsaking Constance and not being true to his own heart. He had made a decision, however, and could not reverse it. Perhaps the choice itself was not a matter of free will in any case, but of fate, with everything already determined.

Before leaving the sacristy, Justin stared at himself in a small looking glass that hung on the wall. His brown hair was cut short, his face shaven, his eyes deep-set and colorless. Here was Justin, heir to his father's estate, about to become wed to Penelope. But who was he really? The person he saw blinking back in the glass was not himself but merely an image. To discover his true self, he reflected, he would need to break the mirror and let his image shatter with it. Then there would be no self at all.

Fully dressed Justin went back outside, shielding his eyes from the noonday sun and breathing a heavy sigh. The stockings were too tight. His cotehardie was uncomfortable in the summer heat. The humidity was making Justin perspire. He pulled at his collar, trying to open some space between it and his skin.

As he was walking over to the party outside the chapel, Justin saw Penelope waiting for him. She was still wearing her veil but was now dressed in a luxurious gown made of gold satin trimmed with blue lace. She did not appear to be sweating. He took his place to the right of Penelope, looking straight ahead at the priest, who was standing on the steps just outside the narthex. The two fathers took up positions beside their respective progeny, with the bridesmaids and groomsmen, all of whom Justin had never met before, just behind and the other attendees to the back of them.

Everyone became quiet. The priest began to ask Justin and Penelope a series of questions—mere formalities—to determine their eligibility for marriage: Were they both of age? Were there any kinship connections between them? Had they had any previous spouses or other relations? "Yes, no, no," Justin and Penelope replied in unison.

Finally the priest asked the question which Justin did want to answer: Did they both freely consent to this union? Justin hesitated for a moment, then replied "Yes," although he knew he did not mean it. Penelope also replied, "Yes," but Justin was not sure if she meant it either.

The priest next turned to the crowd and asked in a loud voice if anyone present knew of any reason why this man and this woman should not be joined together in holy matrimony. He paused judiciously for a response, but since there was none, invited Justin and Penelope closer, pressing their hands together and tying their wrists together with a silver scarf, which felt to Justin like manacles he would never be able to break free from. The priest then asked them to say their wedding vows. Justin's lips were trembling as he repeated the words he had been told to memorize:

"I, Justin, take thee, Penelope, to be my lawfully wedded wife from this day forward, to have and to hold, to honor and to cherish, for better or for worse, for richer or poorer, in sickness and in health, forsaking all others, till death do us part, according to God's holy law, and pledge to you my everlasting fidelity."

After Penelope had said her vows as well, Justin's father handed Justin a gold ring, which he placed on Penelope's thumb, then on her index and middle fingers, saying at each juncture, "In the name of the Father . . . the Son . . . and the Holy Spirit." Finally he slipped the ring onto Penelope's ring finger with the words, "With this ring, I thee wed."

Penelope's father handed a gold ring to his daughter as well, which she presented to Justin in the same fashion. Although it was not customary for the bride to give a ring to the groom, the lord had insisted that Penelope place one on Justin's finger as well to show that this union was not simply between husband and wife, but also between their two families.

The groom was then enjoined to kiss the bride. Lifting the gauzy veil from her head, Justin beheld Penelope's face for the first time. Indeed, she was beautiful, ravishingly beautiful, perhaps the most beautiful woman Justin had ever seen, but she nonetheless disgusted him, for she was not Constance. Penelope had fiery red hair, braided behind her head. Her face was caked with white blaunchet, giving her an artificially pale complexion. Her lips were thickly painted with rouge. Justin did not give her a full kiss, but merely touched his lips to hers, reflexively wiping them afterward with the back of his hand, much to the amusement of the assembled congregation.

The priest then blessed the couple and gave a short homily on the story of how God had created Eve as a companion for Adam, how the sacrament of marriage had been instituted by God from the very beginning, how a man shall leave his father and cleave to his wife and the two become one flesh, how the couple are now bound to each other by unbreakable ties of devotion, even as Christ the bridegroom has taken the Church as his bride. Justin had never heard the priest speak of such matters in any of his previous sermons and was especially astounded when he heard the words, quoted straight from the Bible, that "a man shall leave his father." This was precisely what Justin wished to do.

When the priest had finished, the assembly filed into the chapel for mass. After the departure of Justin's mother, only Justin and his father had attended services together. Now they were no longer alone. The entire sanctuary was filled with people.

§22

The wedding feast was opulent. Additional tables had been brought into the great hall and filled with all manner of food: venison from a deer Justin's father had killed just the day before, along with wild boar, roast pheasant, and other game from the hunting grounds, fish from the fishpond, the finest bread and pies, every vegetable and fruit grown on the estate, all served with honey mead and aged red wine from the manor's cellar.

Justin and Penelope sat together at the front of the room, their fathers on each side, with the groomsmen and bridesmaids seated at an adjoining table. Troubadours entertained the audience, singing songs of courtly love, accompanied by lutes, recorders, and tambourines. The music could hardly be heard above the boisterous laughing and chatter of the guests, although nearly everyone got up to dance at some point. Throughout the evening and well into the night Justin and Penelope sometimes looked at each other, smiling wanly, but hardly spoke. Most of the conversation was carried on across their breasts by their two fathers.

Before the meal was over, Justin's father stood up and asked for the attention of the assembled company. After giving a long-winded and some-what disjointed speech about the auspiciousness of Justin and Penelope's marriage and the new alliance between the two families, he said, "As you all may know, my son is quite gifted at playing the lute. I shall ask him now to sing a song in honor of Penelope, one I am sure that he himself has com-posed for the occasion."

Justin was taken aback by this request, for it was entirely unexpected. Why hadn't his father told him in advance that he would like Justin to per-form an original composition for Penelope at the feast? Had he simply as-sumed that Justin would prepare one for her? But before he could object, his father, beaming broadly, motioned to one of the minstrels to bring a lute to Justin. Justin took the instrument into his hands, looked awkwardly first at his father, then at the guests, though not at Penelope. Standing up and pull-ing the strap over his shoulder, he moved to the front of the table and started to pluck a few notes, singly at first and then in slightly off-key chords. His next move came as a surprise even to himself. He began to sing the song that he had in fact written for Constance, about wanting her kisses and to feel her hair on his shoulder, about her cheeks being like pomegranates and her breath the fragrance of flowers.

The guests listened to Justin's voice and accompaniment with approv-ing smiles on their faces. One of the women wiped a glistening tear from her eye.

Justin paused. Looking away from the audience towards the door of the hall, he then began to sing the second stanza, about seeking the one whom he loves and not being able to find her, about calling to her and re-ceiving no reply, about arising to go to look for her.

Aghast, the guests immediately stopped smiling and began murmuring among themselves. Justin's father shifted nervously in his seat and finally said, "Justin, please, it is enough."

Trying to regain the merriment of the occasion, Justin's father quickly ordered the musicians to resume their revelry. Justin handed his lute back to the bard and turned towards Penelope. She was looking down at the table, her hair covering her face. Penelope's father, sitting beside her, had a disapproving look on his face.

Justin returned to his seat at the table. His father leaned over and said under his breath, "You have shamed me in front of the entire party. You must never dishonor this household again with such flagrancy!"

§23

Meanwhile, the bridal chamber, which in fact was Justin's own room, was being prepared by the servants. Fresh linen sheets were thrown over the bed, with new quilts and feather pillows placed on top.

When the appointed hour arrived, Justin's father announced that the couple would now consummate their marriage. The bridesmaids dutifully came to collect Penelope, leading her out of the room to great fanfare. A short while later the groomsmen ushered Justin to the door of the great hall, where he turned and thanked the guests for coming to join in the celebration of their marriage, then bid them goodnight. After lifting Justin onto their shoulders and tossing him into the air a few times, the groomsmen carried Justin through the foyer and up the staircase to the accompaniment of hearty guffaws.

When they had set Justin down in front of the door to his room, one of the groomsmen shouted gleefully, "Now, go do your duty!"

Pushing them away, as they continued to whoop and laugh, Justin opened the door to his room and slammed it shut behind him. He stood there a long time, waiting until the groomsmen descended back down the staircase, taking their noisy gibberish with them. Penelope was already in the bed waiting for him under the delicate blankets, her head on the soft feather pillow, the curtains drawn, the golden silk canopy above. Somehow it seemed to Justin that the bed did not belong to him anymore. It no longer offered him contentment or security. A viper had slid in between the covers.

"Would you not join me?" Penelope asked at last.

"In a moment," Justin replied, taking a seat in the chair opposite from the bed. "We are still strangers to each other, you know. Do you not think it would be better if we talked first and became acquainted?"

"What is there to talk about?" Penelope answered. "All we need to do now is to consummate our marriage. We can talk later."

"But how is it possible for me to love you if I do not even know you?"

"We shall come to know each other over time. Then we shall fall in love and be forever inseparable."

"How can you be so certain that this will happen?"

"Because that is the way love is."

"Indeed, please tell me what love is," Justin said. "For I have no understanding of it."

"Love is not something you are given, Justin, but something you must earn. You must be valorous and fight for me, protecting me from all harm, to the point that you would be willing to sacrifice yourself for me. You must demonstrate your absolute loyalty and obey my every command. If I wish to be with you, you must stay with me. If I tire of you, you must leave. If tragedy befalls me, you must come to my rescue. If I am sad, you must console me. Even if I do terrible and evil things, you must always stand beside me, no matter what. And you mustn't die before I do or I would be so lonely."

"It all sounds rather formidable," Justin said.

"Well, you asked me what love is and now I am telling you," Penelope replied. "You must love me and only me for all eternity. You must always be virtuous and faithful and show me every courtesy. You must become my vassal and worship me as your empress. You must pay attention solely to me and be jealous of my coquetries, which are certain to occur since men find me irresistible. In short, you must love me unconditionally. That is the meaning of love, Justin. Only a gallant and bold and truly noble man merits the companionship of a desirable woman such as me."

"I must apologize then," Justin said. "For I am hardly worthy of you."

"Whatever do you mean?"

"You seem to have a highly idealized view of love."

"Indeed, Justin. I expect true love, nothing less."

"Well, I am just an ordinary man," Justin said. "Surely unconditional love means loving someone just as they are. I may come to love you unequivocally someday, but after listening to what you just said, I am doubtful if you would ever be able to love me in the same way."

"I can't believe you are so selfish, Justin. You think only of yourself when you should be thinking only of me. Unconditional love is pure love for the other person, with no expectation that your love will ever be requited."

"I completely agree," Justin said. "But it seems that the person you have fallen in love with is not me as I am but your own image of a perfect man who does not exist, except in your own imagination. You would always be more in love with him than with me. I am quite sure I would never be able to live up to your expectations."

"Then you must try, Justin. You must strive to win my love. Am I not worth it?"

Justin made no reply, which seemed to infuriate Penelope.

"It's true, Justin," she said. "I do not love you now, but I want you to love me. That is the only way you can win my heart and deserve my love in return."

"So you desire more to be loved than to love."

"Of course. Are not all women like that? And we desire men with the manhood to give us their unqualified love."

Justin leaned back in his chair and gave no reply.

"Will you not come to me?" Penelope said, turning down a corner of the blanket and exposing her naked breast.

Justin remained seated and did not move.

"Do you love another?" Penelope asked.

Justin did not answer.

"That song you sang tonight, with the verse about seeking someone you could not find, it made me think that perhaps there is someone else whom you would rather be with instead of me. You have not had a slut among the maids, have you?"

At first Justin thought he had not heard Penelope correctly, but when he realized he had, he was pierced to the heart. He almost blurted out an impassioned defense of Constance, but then caught himself, realizing there was no reason why he should associate the word *slut* with her. Instead, he said, "And you? Is there not someone whom you would rather be with as well?"

"No, Justin, I shall want only you to love me."

"Will I be the first man whom you have known?"

Penelope immediately pulled the blanket back over her breast.

"How dare you ask me such a question!" she shrieked. "Of course I have never been with another man my entire life."

"How am I to believe you?"

Penelope glared at Justin.

"I assure you that I am still a virgin," she insisted.

"You would be willing to have our bed sheets examined tomorrow?"

"I will permit no such thing. I am your wife now, Justin. You are supposed to trust me and believe whatever I tell you, but it seems you do not."

Justin slumped down in his chair, putting his face in his hands.

"You are so naive, Justin," Penelope continued, her voice now a low growl. "You are not a man at all. You are nothing but a child. A real man would take me into his arms and make sweet love to me. Indeed, you do not deserve me and I certainly do not deserve you. Tomorrow I shall tell my father that you refused to consummate your love for me and we shall have the marriage annulled."

Penelope turned over with a thump, pulling the blanket over her head. After a few moments, Justin walked over to the lamp still burning on the table beside the bed and blew out the flame.

§24

Justin returned to his chair and sat there in the dark, for how long he did not know, but it was a very long time. Penelope had fallen asleep. All was quiet below. No noise was coming from the great hall. The feast must be over, Justin thought.

He needed to use the privy. Justin opened the door of his room and descended the staircase to the first floor. The butler had already retired it seemed, for he was no longer in the foyer. Peeking into the great hall Justin saw that most of the guests had already departed. Only a few drunken men were still in the room, lying flat on their faces. Empty chalices and plates of half-eaten food were strewn on the tables.

After relieving himself in the latrine, Justin walked back through the foyer to the front door and cracked it open. No one was outside. Stepping onto the portico, Justin noticed that the air was cooler now. He walked on tiptoe down the steps to the courtyard and gazed up at the sky. It was clear and full of stars. It was only then that the idea came to him. He would create his own destiny.

As he proceeded down the drive to the gate, he thought that he might have to scale the wall but was relieved to see that the gate was still open, the drawbridge still down. He was even more relieved to see that Martin, who was supposed to be guarding the gate, was slumped against one of the posts fast asleep. A sword was at his side, which Justin noted with a grin was gleaming in the moonlight but not flaming.

It had all been so surprisingly easy. He had not needed a plan after all. Waving a silent farewell to Martin, the only real playmate and friend he had ever had, Justin stepped across the threshold of the estate.

II

The Village

After crossing the drawbridge, Justin immediately went to the dock where the small boat was jostling about in the brook, untied it from its piling, stepped inside, and set it adrift in the stream. Water from the heavy rains the night before carried the dinghy swiftly away from the estate. Justin did not look back but kept his eyes straight ahead. Further downstream, the brook widened, the water became shallow, the currents faster, with rocks jutting up from the surface. Justin heard the hull splinter as the boat crashed through the rapids. After emerging on the other side into a deeper, calmer, and slower stream, he was relieved to find that there were no cracks in the wood and no water coming in, so he kept the course. Not accustomed to the use of an oar, he simply plucked one from its rowlock and started paddling towards the sea.

The sky was already turning gray by the time Justin reached the estuary where the brook met the ocean. Justin expected that by now Penelope had reported that he was missing. His father would have ordered the servants to start looking for him, and not finding him on the estate, would have then commanded the soldiers to begin the chase outside its walls. Justin hoped that the bailiff or the butler would suggest searching the village, on the assumption that Justin wanted to be reunited with Constance, or, in any case, that no one would notice the missing boat, at least not until later in the day.

Abandoning his little skiff in some reeds on the right-hand side of the stream, Justin sloshed through the marsh to the solid bank and walked from there to a small sandy beach, where he could see the corona of the sun just beginning to brighten the skyline. The scene was not at all unfamiliar to him since he had watched the same event almost every day during his youth. But from this vantage point, it appeared completely different. He was no longer observing the ocean from a distance, but was right there, water meeting sky with no land between him and the horizon.

He knew he could not linger, however. It was possible that someone had already recognized that the boat was gone and a search party had been organized to pursue him down the brook. Justin dreamily imagined going back to the boat and sailing it across the sea to see what lay beyond but, realizing how impractical this would be, decided instead to seek refuge in the woodland which started just above the shoreline. It was a continuation of the forest that wrapped around the eastern wall of the estate and up to his father's hunting grounds, but rather than cross back over the stream and head north, Justin set off in the opposite direction towards the south.

He walked through the ferns and underbrush, careful not to trample anything lest it make his route visible. He stumbled occasionally over fallen tree trunks, but each time picked himself up and pressed on. The ocean was to his left and he could occasionally catch glimpses of it through the trees. He marveled at the darkness of the forest, even though the day was advancing and sunlight was beginning to filter through the canopy of the trees. Here there were no lawns or gardens, no buildings or walls, just wilderness. For the first time in his life Justin felt that he was truly free.

§2

After walking for some time and covering a considerable amount of territory, Justin saw a clearing in the distance and in the clearing a hut, made of wood cut from the trees and covered with grass from the meadows. There was a fire pit in front of the dwelling, surrounded by a circle of stones with logs nearby for sitting. Justin considered making a wide sweep around the place and avoiding it altogether, when a burly man suddenly stepped out the door of the hut.

Immediately noticing Justin, he called out, "Who might you be?"

Justin stopped in his tracks, then approached the man warily.

"I am Justin." He immediately regretted telling the man his name but could not take it back.

"Welcome, Justin!" the man said. He had a broad smile on his face and a jovial manner, which quickly set Justin at ease.

"And where might you be from?" the man asked.

Once again the words slipped out of Justin's mouth before he realized it. "From the estate up the brook to the west of here."

"Well, I can tell by your clothes that you aren't from the village! But it makes no difference. Whether you're a nobleman or a peasant, you're still just a man to me. But what, might I ask, brings a gentleman such as yourself so deep into the forest?"

Justin hesitated. His cotehardie had given away his social standing and he thought it might be better not to reveal anything more about himself. Could the man be trusted? Would he turn Justin in immediately? Nonetheless, Justin needed help since he had no idea where he was or which way to go. It might be better to be truthful.

"I am running away," Justin said.

The man laughed. "Running away, are you? What are you running away from?"

Seeing the man's kind eyes, Justin proceeded to explain his situation, although not in great detail, mentioning only that he could no longer bear life on the manor, that he had fallen in love with one of the servants who was driven off the estate, and that he was now determined to go to the village to find her.

"That's some story," the man said when Justin had finished. "You should be careful, though. Your father's men are sure to come looking for you."

And just then, as if they'd been summoned, there was a noise in the distance, still far away but coming closer and growing louder. Fallen branches were snapping on the forest floor. Low-hanging boughs were breaking from the trees.

"It sounds like horses," Justin said.

"I believe our expected guests have already come to pay us a visit!" the man declared, but with no great sense of urgency. "Come inside my humble abode and I shall give you sanctuary!"

Justin hurriedly followed the man into the hut. To one side, atop the mud floor, was some straw bedding, along with a black pot, a few implements and utensils, and a fishnet. On the other side was a stack of wood, which the man apparently kept under roof to prevent it from getting wet.

"See the woodpile over there?" the man said. "Lie down behind it."

Justin threw himself behind the pile, his back to the wall of the hut. The man began shoveling pieces of wood on top of him until Justin was covered as well as was possible. Finally the man threw the fishnet over the entire heap, crumpling it a bit over the places where Justin was still exposed, and then went back outside.

By this time the horses had arrived. Justin listened as the man shouted out a greeting. The voice that responded could be clearly recognized as Martin's.

"Have you seen a young lad rambling about these parts? He should be easy to spot for he is wearing a cotehardie."

"I have not," the man replied. "Who might you be looking for?"

Martin did not answer. The other men with him did not speak either, though Justin could hear the hoofs of their horses stamping on the ground. Martin dismounted, his feet crunching the dry leaves on the soil as he walked from one end of the camp to the other.

"Let me have a look inside your hovel," Martin said.

"By all means," the man replied. "If you like, please stay and join me for breakfast!"

Justin heard but could not see Martin enter the hut. He felt his heart beat faster as Martin looked about the room. Either Justin was too well covered, which he doubted, or the light was too dim but, in any case, Martin stayed only a moment and then returned outside.

"By whose authorization are you squatting here?" Martin asked the man.

"Why, I need no one's authorization," the man replied. "This area is part of the commons, and this particular patch of woods isn't used by anyone except myself. You're the first other person I've ever seen here my entire life!"

"You still need permission from the lord to live in the forest," Martin said. "I shall have the matter investigated."

"Please do so," the man said cheerfully. "And I am sure that if you inquire thoroughly enough, you will find that I have every right to be here, if not by the laws of men, then by the laws of nature."

"We shall see," Martin said, mounting his horse. "And if you happen to spot the young lad I mentioned, you must journey to the manor house and report it immediately."

"You have my word of honor that I shall," the man replied, touching his heart and smiling with a gracious bow.

Martin motioned for the other horsemen to follow him. Justin listened to the fading sound of the horses tramping back through the forest until he could hear them no more.

The man called to Justin from outside the hut, "It's all right now. You can come out."

Justin scrambled out from under the wood and rejoined the man, who was now at the hearth making a fire.

"Don't worry," the man said jauntily. "They shan't be back, at least not for you."

"But maybe for you? Will you be all right?"

"Ach, don't pay them any mind. I shall be fine no matter what they do."

"Is it true that you need my father's permission to live here?"

"Who owns the land!" the man exclaimed. It was a declaration, not a question.

Justin nonetheless answered, "Why the king, of course."

"The king? I tell you, no one owns the land, not even God. The land is owned by whoever uses it."

The man lit the fire, then sat down on one of the logs and motioned for Justin to sit on the other.

"Now tell me, Justin, is the log I am sitting on mine or yours?"

"Why it's yours, of course."

"And the log you are sitting on?"

"It's mine."

"Then here, let us change seats."

The man and Justin both stood up, each moving to the other's log.

"Now," the man said, sitting down. "Which log is mine and which is yours?"

There was no need for Justin to reply. He simply grinned.

"Something belongs to whoever is using it," the man continued. "This is the law of nature. The laws of men are like the webs spiders spin out of their own bodies, with the purpose of entangling their prey, depriving us of our freedom, and then eating us alive!"

After stoking the fire he said, "Which reminds me. You must be hungry!"

§3

The man went into the hut and returned with a basket of fish, which he began gutting with a small hunting knife.

"I just caught these earlier this morning," the man said. "Before you arrived."

"I noticed on the way here that the ocean is quite near, just beyond the edge of the forest," Justin said.

"Indeed, it's only a short walk from here. I move around from place to place every once in a while, but I never stray far from the ocean. As you can see, I like to fish! I avoid the fens further south, though. The mire makes them uninhabitable, although the hills among them provide a good refuge when needed."

"How did you come to live in a forest by the sea?"

"Well, you see," the man said with a gleam in his eyes. "I'm a runaway like you. Except that I ran away from the village, not a lavish estate!"

Justin and the man continued sitting on their respective logs as the fire burned down, leaving only flaming embers in the pit. After the fish had been cleaned, the man whittled a couple of thin tree branches into skewers.

"Why did you run away?" Justin asked.

"Ha! The short answer is that I was hungry and there wasn't anything to eat!"

The man took two of the fish, impaled them on the sharpened sticks, and handed one to Justin.

"Here. Even you should learn how to cook," he said.

Justin took the skewer and held the fish over the hot coals, watching carefully how the man was grilling his own and following his every move.

"May I ask your name?"

"I'm not sure I have one!" the man chortled. "You don't really need a name if there is no one around to call you by one."

"Then how shall I address you?"

"Well, my mama used to call me just 'Boy,' but since I take fish up to the village every now and then to trade for things I need, the people there call me 'Fisher.' I never took to it, though. I guess I'm just an old hermit so that's what you can call me."

Justin watched the hermit turn his fish over the fire then did the same.

"Is fish the only thing you eat?"

"Some days. But fishing is certainly not my only occupation. There are ample sources of nourishment in the forest as well."

He turned his fish again and so did Justin.

"The earth provides us with a plenitude of food," the hermit said. "There is no reason why anyone should go hungry."

"You have no bread?" Justin asked.

"I do not need bread."

"And no possessions?"

"I don't require much and can carry everything I own in a single bundle!"

The hermit lifted his fish from the fire and examined it.

"Almost ready," he said.

Justin looked at his fish as well. It was becoming silvery brown on all sides.

"Your life must be hard," Justin said.

"Not at all," the hermit replied. "It's easy! I labor only for what I need and after that I enjoy my leisure. It's a simple but fulfilling life."

"If you have so much free time, how do you spend it?"

"Oh, I walk along the beach and watch the waves breaking on the shore. Or I meander through the woods and listen to the songs of the birds. And sometimes I just come here and sit alone by myself. I loaf and invite my soul."

"What do you think about while you're sitting?"

"There is nothing to think about. I just sit!"

The fish was sizzling and ready to eat. The hermit raised the skewer to his lips, took a bite, then pulled a few bones from his mouth and threw them on the ground in front of him.

"You do not say grace?" Justin asked.

"Why should I give thanks to God for these fish when I'm the one who caught them? We should be grateful to the ones who actually provide us with our food."

"Well then, thank you," Justin said with a bow of his head to the hermit.

"Don't thank only me," the hermit said. "Thank the fish, too!"

"Thank you!" Justin then cried to the fish.

"We also should apologize to all the plants and animals whose lives we take in exchange for our own."

Justin looked again at the fish on his stick and called out, "I'm sorry!"

Sinking his teeth into it, he found that the fish was crispy on the outside but moist inside.

"I suppose you never attend church," Justin said to the hermit.

"What ceremonies do I need? I celebrate myself."

"You do not sing hymns?"

"Only of myself."

"You never participate in the sacraments either?"

"What use have I for such rituals? Nature is a sacrament for me and I a sacrament of it. The world is one great enchanted garden. The forest provides me with everything I need."

"What do you eat from the forest?" he asked.

"Alas, I have nothing to offer you just now," the hermit answered. "But come with me tomorrow and I will show you the ways of the woodlands. Once you learn how to take care of yourself, you shall never be without sustenance."

He patted the knife he had used to cut the fish, which was now in the sheath that hung from his side.

"I'll admit that a good knife comes in handy," he said. "But sit me down buck naked in the middle of a forest and I can survive. It's all a matter of seeing ourselves not as apart from our surroundings but as a part of them."

"It would certainly be splendid if you could teach me how to live off the land," Justin said. "But my plan is to go to the village tomorrow. As I told you, there is someone whom I wish to find. Her name is Constance."

"Ah, Constance! I've known her since she was a little girl. But I think it's too dangerous for you to go to the village soon. Your father will surely not give up looking for you so quickly. You are most welcome to hide out here for a while if you like."

"But I cannot endure being separated from Constance," Justin replied. "I really must be reunited with her."

"I understand your longing, even though in my own case I have never desired the companionship of a woman, nor of anyone else for that matter. I am quite content to live alone."

"You never become lonely?"

"Why should I be lonely? I take great delight in my own company."

"But you have no friends?"

"I live with the sun and the moon, the wind and the rain, the animals and the plants. What other friends do I need?"

"So you love no other humans. You only love yourself."

"Well, of course I love myself!" the hermit laughed. "It is only by loving ourselves first that we are able to love others. But you are mistaken if you think that living an isolated life means loathing others. I love all people, every single one of them, even those who hate me."

"Then why do you live here as a recluse among the flora and fauna instead of with your fellow human beings?"

"Listen, before I finally settled here, I traveled round the world, saw everything there is to see. It didn't suit me at all. Life in the forest is so much better. What I hate are not people, but their stupid customs and rules, which simply drag us down into the mud and prevent us from realizing the goodness that is already inside us. You have seen an example of that here today with the soldiers from your own father's estate. The true nobleman is a savage."

"But surely the purpose of culture and breeding is to refine us, to make us better not worse."

"Nay, civilization only corrupts us. Far from helping us improve ourselves, it prevents us from doing better and being all that we might be. Rather than be weighed down by the duties and obligations society imposes on us, let us soar to the sky with our own wings!"

"So you fly solo and need no one?"

"To need or want someone, even if you love them as much as you love Constance, has nothing to do with the other person but is solely about ourselves. We crave their attention to make us feel important or hope to get something from them to satisfy our own selfish desires. But it has nothing to do with love. Love is not taking from others but giving ourselves to them."

The hermit picked up the bones that had piled up at his feet and tossed them over his shoulder. Reaching into his basket, he pulled out another fish.

"Help yourself," he told Justin. "Everything belonging to me as good belongs to you!"

§4

The two men sat around the fire talking most of the day, broiling more fish and eating them until they were satisfied. As evening approached and shadows began to darken the forest, the hermit said, "Tomorrow we shall go fishing in the morning, then tour the forest in the afternoon, where I will show you how to gather more food. Today I provided a meal for you. Tomorrow you shall provide one for me."

"That would be entirely fair!" Justin replied happily.

"Of course, it is! There is no distinction between nobleman and commoner. 'When Adam delved and Eve spanned, who was then a gentleman?' as the doggerel goes. We are all fundamentally equal, not just humans, but everything we find in nature, even the moss and the stones."

"But surely some things are more equal than others," Justin said. "Is it not true that a plant is higher than a mineral, an animal higher than a plant, a human higher than an animal, the angels higher than us, and God the highest of all?"

"Nay, they're all the same to me," the hermit replied.

"So there is no difference between me and a rock?"

"Of course there's a difference! To say we are all equal does not mean we are not different!"

"I still feel superior to a rock," Justin said.

"Ha! You have a very high opinion of yourself. Just look around at everything there is in a forest. It's obvious that each stone, plant, and animal, including us, has a soul. Every single thing is unique, each with its own special features, yet the pieces all fit together like one magnificent mosaic. Break even the smallest pane in a stained-glass window and the whole masterpiece will shatter."

"Yet if everything is equal, why do some trees grow tall while others are short?"

"It depends on lots of things," the hermit replied. "Whether a tree is planted on rocky ground or good soil, how much rain and sunlight it gets, whether thorns and brambles overtake it. Humans are no different. Nature sows within each of us a seed. If we nurture that seed and allow it to grow, we have the potential to become a mighty oak. If we fail to nourish the seed, however, then we remain forever shriveled and frail. That's how nature creates the world."

"I have heard that it is not nature, but God who created the world."

"What's the difference? God is nature and nature is God!"

"But is God not separate from the world he created?"

"There is no God beyond the world we live in," the hermit said. "Ultimately everything is one."

"Yet surely if there is a creation, there must be a creator."

"There are no grounds for holding such a foolish notion."

"Then how was the world created?" Justin asked.

Playfully taking on the air of a learned professor, the hermit stood up and started speaking in grandiloquent cadences, "Well, the way I see it is that in the beginning there was nothing. The earth was without form and void. There was only emptiness moving across the face of the deep."

He pointed his finger upward to the darkening sky.

"Emptiness," he repeated. "The void."

"You're making this all up," Justin said, amused. "The only knowledge we can have is of something. It is impossible for us to know anything about nothing because nothing does not exist."

"It's worse than that, Justin," the hermit replied with a sly grin. "Even if we could know nothing, we wouldn't be able to describe it, and even if we could describe it, no one would understand what we're talking about. The best we can say is that whatever did not exist before everything else has no name. And if you try to give it one, then you don't understand it."

"All right. And then what happened?"

"Then—bang!—there was something."

"Indeed," Justin said with a cynical smile. "Please tell me: why is there something rather than nothing?"

"Don't ask me!" the hermit said defensively. "I'm a scientist, not a philosopher. I can only tell you how it all came about. I can't explain why. All I know is that after God created himself there was something."

"Fair enough. What was the next step?"

Continuing his charade, the hermit said, "Then the one became two. God divided himself into light and darkness, then day and night, dryness and wetness, heat and cold, male and female, and all the rest. There cannot be one without the other. Each is inside ourselves and we must see them as two aspects of the same reality."

"Certainly we can find many such opposites in the world," Justin said. "But most things don't fall so neatly into just two categories."

"Right. That's because after the one became two, the two became three, then the three became the ten thousand myriad entities we see all around us. In other words, things started out simple and gradually became more differented."

"I think you mean *differentiated*," Justin corrected.

"That's what I said. It's all a matter of evolution!"

Then bowing magisterially before sitting back down, the hermit added, "Do you find my exposition convincing?"

"Your views are certainly interesting," Justin replied with a taint of irony in his voice.

"If you don't like my story, you can make up your own!" the hermit sniveled.

"The story our priest at the chapel told us is that God created the world in six days and rested on the seventh."

"That's pure hogwash. The world is still in the birth pangs of creation. God is continually creating the world, even now at this very moment. God never rests."

"Doesn't he take a break now and then on the Sabbath like we do?"

"Well, if he does, then the very next day he's back at it. But I'm doubtful because if nature is God and God is nature, then God is always creating himself as well."

"You're the one who's being foolish if you think that God can create himself."

"If we can create ourselves, why not God?"

"But God is supposed to be unchanging."

The hermit exhaled pompously, resuming a professorial tone. "You fail to see, my dear friend, that everything is in a perpetual state of flux, even God. All things flow. Nothing is permanent. Something is always being brought into existence. Then it is destroyed. After that it is recreated again as something else, just like waves on the ocean and ripples of water on the surface of a river are constantly being formed and reformed. The process goes on forever."

"So, the creation is still unfinished?"

"God and the world make and remake themselves unceasingly!"

"All the way to the end?"

"Indeed, God created the world out of nothing and to nothing it will return. When the world dies, God dies with it."

"So you are an atheist who does not believe in God," Justin said.

"Well, if that is what you want to call me, then so be it. But that's not how I myself think of the matter."

"What do you think?"

Reverting back to his normal demeanor, the hermit said, "Since God incarnates himself in the world, he also incarnates himself in us. He is the seed I told you about, a spark of divine light, inside my own breast. There is no difference between the divine and the human. That is the whole meaning of incarnation. Spirit and flesh are joined together in one body."

"But is not the spirit good and the flesh evil?"

"When God incarnated himself in the world, he saw that it was good. In the same way that we celebrate the goodness of the world we live in, we can celebrate the goodness of our own bodies."

"So you think that you are a god?"

"All things are gods. Not only me, but everything! God's seed is in each of us."

"Even me?"

"Exceptions cannot be ruled out, of course," hermit said, returning to his mirthful mood. "So I am not completely certain in your case. But if a rock is most assuredly a god, then it is entirely possible that you are, too."

"Before I could half-believe your disquisition but now I totally reject it," Justin said. "For I am quite sure that I am not a god."

"Never give up, Justin. There is still hope. Even for you."

"I appreciate your kind words. But the priest at our chapel has told us that God is a being unlike any other, who dwells in the heavens above us. God is King and Jesus is Lord, so we must follow their commandments, even as we follow the commandments of our rulers here on earth."

"Your priest doesn't know what he's talking about!" the hermit said, spitting on the ground.

"But if there is no seed within me, where shall I find God?"

"Don't be so naive, my friend," the hermit said. Somehow his voice sounded just like Constance's when he said the word *naive*. "You yourself must know that you have led a sheltered life and experienced so little. But you will never find God if you think he exists in a realm beyond our own. You do not need to search for God. He is already here, inside our own hearts, in every living thing, in the mountains and the deserts, in each of the stars that hang in the sky at night and each grain of sand that washes onto the beach in the morning."

"How did you come by this knowledge?" Justin asked. "Who is your teacher?"

"We don't need a teacher. Each of us must come to our own understanding of such matters."

"But surely you are now a teacher to me."

"Nah, don't listen to me. I'm just an old hermit. Figure these things out for yourself!"

§5

The forest was almost dark now. Night would soon arrive.

"It is time for us to retire," the hermit said. "We will arise early tomorrow before dawn. You will need better clothes than those decrepit rags you are wearing. I have an extra tunic and pair of breeches in the hut. Let me get them for you. They'll also be more comfortable for you to sleep in."

While the hermit went to get the clothing, Justin disrobed and was standing by the fire in his undergarments when the hermit returned. Justin donned the breeches, tying the drawstring tight. The tunic was made of hemp, which felt scratchy on his skin as he pulled it over his shoulders. He was quite pleased with himself, however. Not only had he changed his clothes, it also seemed as if he had been transformed into a different person.

"They're a bit baggy," the hermit said. "But, of course, they're yours to keep, if you like."

"Oh no," Justin replied. "I could never take a spare set of clothes from you. I'm sure that you will need them."

"A man only needs the clothes he is wearing. Everything else is surplus."

"Then I shall no longer be needing these clothes either," Justin said, pointing to his stockings and cotehardie, which lay in a heap by the fire. "If you wear them, they're yours!"

The hermit laughed. "Why would I want such silly clothes? Please do not burden me with finery! I have no desire to look like a gentleman and would be insulted if someone told me that I did."

"Well, then," Justin said, "I shall burn them!"

"That's the best use they could be put to. They will keep us warm a bit longer!"

Justin picked up his clothes and threw them on the fire.

"I no longer need you," he said with mock solemnity. "I hereby renounce my position and repudiate my entire past. From this day forward I shall devote myself to poverty and live as a man of the people."

He looked gleefully at the hermit, who roared heartily and then said, "I'm not so sure about the poverty bit, though. Look at me. I am not poor. When I go to sleep at night I have a good roof over my head, a warm bed to sleep in, and a full belly. There's nothing wrong with that!"

"Perhaps you're right," Justin said. "I shall satisfy my needs, but no more. In any case, sir, since you did not take my clothes, then at least accept this ring as a gift to show my appreciation for your hospitality."

He took off the wedding ring that Penelope had given him and handed it to the hermit, who accepted it with grace.

"I am always amazed," the hermit said, "at how a worthless little piece of metal such as this can be traded in the market for so many useful things!"

Justin and the hermit stood by the fire until the clothes were reduced to ashes. The hermit doused the remaining embers with water and stirred the fire until it was completely out.

"You shall sleep in my bed tonight," the hermit said, gesturing towards the hut. "And I shall sleep under the trees."

"Please sleep in your own bed," Justin protested. "And allow me to sleep outside."

"The werewolves might get you. Besides, I surely have much more experience sleeping outdoors than you do."

"Are there really werewolves in the forest?" Justin asked.

"The only people who believe in werewolves are those who have never lived in the wild," the hermit said with a laugh. "Though certainly there are wolves—the regular kind—and also wild boars."

"Won't they attack you?"

"Not if you leave them alone. If I don't bother them, they don't bother me! You have never seen a wild boar?"

"I have, but only roasted and on a platter served up for dinner."

"Indeed, they are tasty, but I never kill them myself. It's impossible for me to eat a whole boar before the flesh rots. So I just leave them alone. Now, get a good night's sleep. We shall have a busy day tomorrow!"

§6

The next morning, well before the sun was up, the hermit entered the hut and shook Justin awake.

"Come, it is time," he said.

Justin arose from the straw bed and stepped outside the hut into the brisk air. A few stars could still be seen above the treetops but by the time Justin and the hermit arrived at the shore of the ocean the sky was already turning blue and the skyline was golden with sunlight.

"I should like to know what lies on the other side of the ocean," Justin said to the hermit. "Have you ever been there?"

"You are even more of a fool than me," the hermit responded. "The ocean just goes on and on forever. There is no other side."

"But surely it must end somewhere."

"Nah, it's infinite."

"How do you know that?"

"I don't. What I do know, though, is that if you drink a single drop of water from the sea right in front of you, you will have tasted the whole ocean."

The hermit led Justin to a cove where a small dinghy was moored, not unlike the boat that had carried Justin down the brook from the estate. Inside were some fishnets. The hermit held the boat as Justin got in and then jumped inside himself. The oars were properly settled in their rowlocks and the hermit began navigating the skiff out to sea.

"Let me have a try!" Justin said.

The hermit and Justin exchanged places in the boat. Justin took the oars and began rowing, awkwardly at first, but then with carefully placed dips in the water and strong heaves backward. The boat zigzagged here and there, but the hermit coached Justin until he could steer a fairly straight line with confidence.

When the coast was some distance behind them, the hermit let out the fishnet, twisted it several times, then pulled it back into the boat. There were two fish in the net.

"Here," the hermit said, passing the net to Justin. "Your turn."

Justin took the fishnet, cast it off the side of the boat, unraveled it just as the hermit had done, and pulled it back into the boat. There were three fish in the net.

"I beat you!" Justin exclaimed.

"Beginner's luck," the hermit said.

The two men continued fishing until the basket they had brought with them was half-full, which did not take long, then the hermit said it would suffice, they didn't need any more, and Justin rowed the boat back to shore. After mooring the boat, the hermit showed Justin how to dig clams and mussels on the beach.

When they had collected enough to fill up the remaining half of the basket, the hermit sniffed and said, "You smell worse than I do! Come, let us wash the slime off our bodies."

The hermit stripped off his clothes, ran as far into the water as he could, and then dived beneath the waves. Justin followed him, but entered apprehensively, step by step. The water was cold, not at all like the hot water in the tub he had used for bathing at the manor house, and the stones on the bottom of the sea cut his feet. What he feared most about going deeper, however, was that he did not know how to swim.

"Come on," the hermit howled. "Don't be afraid to put your head under the water!"

"I might drown!" Justin called back. He was now up to his waist in the surf.

"Indeed, you will die and be resurrected!"

The hermit swam over to Justin and pushed his body down under the water, dunking him completely. When Justin's head popped up, he was spurting sprays of mist and gasping for air. The saltwater burned his eyes.

"There. Now you've been properly baptized!" the hermit laughed. "And with more than just a teensy-weensy sprinkle of water atop your crown like they do in church."

Justin laughed back. He began plunging his head down into the water and back up again as if in a frenzy.

"Let me teach you how to swim," the hermit said, showing him some strokes, then holding Justin by the belly so he could practice on his own. A short while later, the hermit let go and Justin glided off through the water, pumping his arms and flapping his feet.

Returning to shore, they slipped back into their clothes, and began walking back to the hut.

"I feel rejuvenated!" Justin said.

"You're a new man," the hermit replied.

After arriving at the hut, Justin built a fire in the hearth and began cooking the seafood for lunch. The two men ate quickly, leaving some leftovers for their evening meal, and then set off for the forest.

The hermit charted a seemingly haphazard course through the woods, showing Justin which plants could be eaten and which could not, how to gather nuts and berries, and even how to set a rabbit snare.

"We'll come back tomorrow and, if we're lucky, we shall have rabbit for our dinner!" the hermit said.

"I have absolutely no idea where we are," Justin replied. "How will you remember where you set the trap?"

"I know precisely where it is."

"You never get lost?"

"The forest is my home. The word *lost* is not in my vocabulary."

"You always know where you are?"

"I am here. Where else could I be?"

"And you always know which way go?"

"If I didn't, my body would ask my shadow to show it to me."

"And if there is no rabbit when we come back?"

"Then it shall be frogs. If you're ever really hungry and have nothing to eat, just go to the marsh and catch some frogs. You can also pick cattails while you're there."

The hermit took in a deep breath of air and with a sweeping gesture of his hand pointed at the trees all around him.

"Who needs a village or a church when we have a forest?" he said with an assured smile. "It is only in nature that we know absolute freedom. In wildness lies the salvation of the world!"

§7

The next day the hermit led Justin back to the exact same spot where they had set the snare and, indeed, there was a rabbit in it, which they took back to hut, skinned, and roasted on the fire. On the following days, they did more fishing and also returned to the forest, where Justin, who was finally beginning to get his bearings, learned how to dig roots, find bird eggs, capture mice, and scrape grubs from under fallen trees. He made a few mistakes, some of which were nearly fatal—such as how to distinguish edible mushrooms from poisonous ones. The hermit promptly corrected him, however, and within a few weeks Justin had learned how to feed himself and survive on his own.

On one occasion the hermit showed Justin some tracks in a clearing.

"Look, I told you," he said. "Those are the burrows of wild boars rooting in the dirt. You can even make out their footprints."

"I should like to see a real boar."

"Well, they're shy creatures actually. It's more likely that you'll hear one rather actually see it."

One day they went to the marsh—to the precise place where Justin had abandoned his boat, although it was no longer there—to catch frogs, just so that Justin could learn the difference between a frog you can eat and a toad that you can't. They also harvested a few cattails to take back with them.

Justin eventually lost track of the time, but approximately one month after his wedding and escape from the estate, as Justin and the hermit were returning in their boat from a morning fishing expedition, they saw huge billows of smoke ascending in the distance from beyond the forest.

"It's the village," the hermit said. "It looks like all the houses are on fire."

Justin began rowing harder. "Then I must go there now."

"I understand."

After they returned to hut, the hermit covered the basket of the fish they had just caught with a piece of cloth and handed it to Justin. "Take this with you. You can share the fish with the villagers but keep the cloth as a bundle. And here is a flask of water as well."

"Thank you," Justin said.

"Be careful!" the hermit shouted out to Justin as he commenced his trek through the forest. "Come and visit me again sometime, if you ever have a chance."

"I certainly will!" Justin shouted back.

§8

As Justin raced through the forest, he recalled the meeting between his father and the neighboring lord just before his wedding, and how they had agreed to exact payment from the peasants in a month's time or let their soldiers loose on the village. He did not think his father would be so cruel as to actually burn the peasants' houses but apparently that was what he had done. It occurred to Justin that the ultimate source of his and everyone else's problems was his father. Even in his own case, the issue was not that Justin was unable to stand up to him, but rather his father's bullying and domineering character. It was he, not Justin, who was to blame! Having reached this conclusion, Justin first felt a tingle of liberation, then a sense of disgust, and finally an uncontrollable rage. He had never before known the taste of pure hatred. If his father were simply out of the picture, there would no longer be any trouble for anyone!

Justin's worries quickly turned to Constance. Knowing that she had returned to the village after being expelled from the estate, his first task would be to find her and see if she was all right.

Emerging from the forest, Justin found a path that led between the fields to the north and the pastures to the south. In the distance he could see that the smoke had already died down in the village. It was no longer rising in great billows but more like wisps of fog evaporating from the ground. When he reached the outskirts of the village, he saw a tall man sitting on a large rock, a staff in his hand, looking down at his feet, shaking his head back and forth.

"What happened here?" Justin asked.

"Can't you see?" the tall man replied. "They've burned our houses and taken all our food."

"Who burned your houses and took your food?"

"The soldiers."

"Which soldiers?"

"The lord's soldiers."

"From the estate?"

"Aye."

"Did any forces approach from the south?"

"Nay, only from the direction of the estate."

Justin then knew that only his father's own soldiers had attacked them. Penelope's father had not sent any forces to join in the attack.

"Was anyone hurt?"

"Two of our men were killed, but everyone else fled to the hills. We just came back a short while ago."

The tall man put down his staff, buried his head in his hands, and began weeping. Justin's first thought was to go directly to the estate and confront his father. He wanted to kill him outright for all the damage he had caused. But instead Justin continued walking straight ahead towards the village.

§9

The path became a road at the edge of the village. Justin paused since he had never actually seen the village before and so had no conception of it. Nestled among the hills, it looked small, but was still larger than he had imagined, extending all the way to the larger foothills of the wolds in the distance. From the turret at the manor house he had only been able to perceive a cross, which seemed to be planted in the hills, but now he saw that it was in fact attached to a spire with a stone church beneath it, set upon a slope on the far side of the village. Beside the church was a cemetery and behind it a compact but well-built house, which he guessed was the rectory where the village priest lived. The barns, which had not been damaged during the raid, were not far from the church, and between them and where Justin was presently standing were the cottages, or what was left of them, since they had been completely gutted. The roofs had been reduced to ashes, the walls had collapsed, posts and boards were smoldering together in heaps. Only the stone hearths remained relatively intact. As Justin began walking down the main road through the village, he saw men sifting through the remnants, while women huddled with their children in the side lanes, crying out with loud voices. No one paid any attention to Justin. It was as if he were invisible.

At the very center of the village was a green, with a path leading from it to the fields beyond. Justin halted there, looking in all directions for Constance, but he could not find her. He continued walking until he had almost reached the other end of the village, where the road met a wider highway perpendicular to it, which, Justin surmised, led north to his father's estate and south to the estate of Penelope's father. The barns were located just on the other side of the highway, with the church and rectory up the slope to the right.

At last Justin spied Constance, standing in a muddy side lane in front of what used to be a house, presumably her own. Justin wanted to wave at her immediately but held his hand. As he came nearer, Constance finally saw him as well. There was a look of stunned disbelief on her face. She raised a leg as if she would run to him, but then checked herself. Justin motioned her back and put a finger to his lips to ensure her silence.

Upon reaching the destroyed house, he saw a muscular young man with long black hair and a beard trying to pull a half-burned beam from the smoking debris. Justin ignored Constance entirely, not even looking at her, and instead addressed the man, "May I help you?"

When the man turned, Justin immediately recognized him as Constance's brother, the leader from the peasant group that had come to the estate to ask concessions from his father and been chased away by the soldiers. Justin did not yet know his name, however, for Constance had never told it to him.

"I don't need any help," the brother said gruffly. "You may be on your way."

Just as soon as he turned back to his task, however, Justin put down his basket, saddled up behind him, and began yanking on the end of the timber. After several mighty heaves the two men managed to dislodge it from the wreckage.

"I would thank you," the brother said, "but I do not wish to incur any debts."

"You owe me absolutely nothing," Justin replied. "I was happy to be of service."

"We have no use for vagabonds around here, so just move on."

"Well, indeed I have been traveling. I saw the smoke from a distance and heard what happened when I arrived at the village. I should like to stay and help."

"Vagabonds are parasites. They live off the labor of others and contribute nothing in return."

"Certainly I am an independent man," Justin said. "But I am not a beggar."

"You may still be a thief."

"I apologize for saying so, but it does not look as if there is anything here for me to steal."

"Well, we are also independent and can manage quite nicely by ourselves," the brother said. "And if you're scrounging for food, we have none to give you."

"I ask for nothing."

Justin retrieved his basket and handed it to the brother. "Here, please take this. You do not need to repay me."

Justin removed the cloth. Upon seeing the fish inside, the brother grabbed the basket by the handle and jerked it away from him.

"Where did you get these?" he asked.

"From the ocean, of course. I was fishing there this morning."

The brother hastily hid the basket in an unburned corner of the house.

"If the others see this fish, they'll expect us to share it with them," he said. "It's not that I'm stingy, but there simply isn't enough for everyone. There would be fighting over it."

"You can have it all," Justin replied.

"Well then, thank you," the brother said.

Constance had remained silent throughout the entire conversation. Justin nodded in her direction and asked the brother, "Is this your wife?"

"No, she is my sister. Her name is Constance."

"And this is my brother, Adrian," Constance said.

Justin was happy to finally learn the name of her brother!

"I am pleased to make your acquaintance, Adrian, Constance," Justin said cordially.

"And what should we call you?" Adrian asked.

"Edward," Justin answered without missing a beat, not wanting to let his real name slip out as he had with the hermit. Constance could barely conceal her surprise at this reply, although she immediately understood Justin's need for a pseudonym.

Justin reached out his hand to shake Adrian's, but Adrian did not offer his in return. Instead he turned and began trying to pull another beam out of the rubble. Justin immediately went over to help him. While they were working, Constance busied herself fetching water from a well located on a small path halfway between the house and the barns, which she used to extinguish the remaining cinders. They worked throughout the afternoon and by the time the sun had begun to set behind the wolds, a section of the site had been cleared, but there was still much to be done.

"The light is fading," Adrian said. "Let's call it a day."

"We should invite Edward to stay with us for supper," Constance said.

"But we hardly have any food," Adrian grumbled. "Only what we could salvage from the house and a wee bit more we might scrape from the floor of the barns."

"With the fish Edward has brought us, we shall have enough."

"Nay, I shall go back to the forest now," Justin said. "I am perfectly able to take care of myself and not in need of anything. In fact, if you have nothing to eat, I can gather food in the forest for you and the others and bring it back with me tomorrow. There is plenty for everyone."

Adrian looked at Justin suspiciously.

"I still do not trust you," he said. "But if you are willing to help us collect food, I shall let you stay. You may sleep tonight in the pigsty."

"With the pigs?" Justin asked uncertainly.

"There are hardly any left. The soldiers took almost all of them, saving only a few for breeding, which we cannot eat, of course. The same with the chickens, sheep, and oxen. We have moved the animals into the barns, where all of the villagers shall sleep tonight as well, huddled together on the hard mud floors. I'm afraid there is no room left for you."

Adrian paused for a moment and then added tersely, "I am sure that the priest would not let you take stay in the church either, unless you are running away from a crime and seeking sanctuary."

"I would prefer to spend the night in the open than in the pigsty," Justin said.

"Suit yourself, Edward."

"I shall return in the morning with food for you. Please enjoy the fish for your dinner tonight."

He bowed slightly to Adrian and caught a glimpse of Constance out of the corner of his eye. She glanced over at him as well, but only slightly, quickly turning her head away.

§10

After returning to the forest, Justin set a rabbit snare before retiring under an oak tree a short distance away. The next morning he gathered greens and roots, just as the hermit had shown him, and stuffed his bundle until it was completely full and he could carry no more. He returned to the snare and was pleased to find a rabbit in it. His intention was to share the food he had collected with the villagers, with the exception of the rabbit, which he concealed inside his tunic and would give to Adrian.

The peasants quickly congregated around Justin when he returned to the village well before noon with his bulging bundle. He distributed the food he had collected as equally as he could among the people, who were grateful for the extra provisions since their own were almost depleted. Having saved a bit for himself, Constance, and Adrian, he walked back to their burned-out home. Upon his arrival, he pulled the rabbit out from under his tunic and handed it to Adrian.

"This is for you," Justin said.

Adrian took the rabbit from Justin. "Where did you get this?"

"From the forest, of course."

"My goodness, man, you should not let anyone know about what you've done. It's poaching. If the lord finds out, he will cut off your hands or dress you in a deerskin and set the dogs after you!"

"But I caught the rabbit in the commons, not on the lord's hunting grounds."

"It makes no difference," Adrian said. "Even the commons are off limits to us, at least for hunting. We have permission only to gather firewood and lumber for our houses, provided we do not cut any of the larger trees. We also have pannage rights in the autumn, when the pigs forage for acorns."

"And for each of these simple privileges we are required to pay a fee to the lord," Constance added pointedly.

Adrian began skinning the rabbit, while Constance went to fetch water from the well. Upon returning, she readied a fire and began washing the roots and nettles Justin had given her and Adrian.

"I should like to help," Justin said, sitting down beside her, risking a pat on her hand as Adrian went to fetch more wood for the fire. Just then a black cat appeared and curled up on Constance's lap.

"You keep a cat?" Justin asked.

"It used to be a stray," Constance explained. "But now it has become my pet."

"It's cute," Justin said. "Does it have a name?"

"I call her Charm, in the hope she will bring me good luck."

"I have heard that black cats are evil omens."

"Don't be so superstitious. I am sure you have heard that a lady who possesses a black cat will be courted by many men."

"And I shall be one of them," Justin said.

"You don't stand a chance," Constance teased.

Just then Adrian returned with some sticks and threw them onto the fire.

"I think we can manage another day or two," he said to Justin. "But I shall organize a party to accompany you to the forest to gather more food tomorrow. The others will remain here to clear the lots. In a few days we shall all go to the forest together to collect wood to rebuild our houses. The first harvest will not be for several more weeks, so we should have time to put up the frames and walls before then, and even thatch the roofs if we're fast enough."

"Your plans seem to be well thought out," Justin said. "Are you the leader of this village?"

"The people here are very simple-minded," Adrian replied. "They are only capable of following their daily routine and if this be broken they have no sense of what to do unless someone tells them. My father used to be head of the village. Not that he had any power. He simply coordinated what needed to be done and assigned everyone their day's work. When he and my mother both died of fever, no one stepped up to take his place, so the responsibility fell to me, even though I was still quite young at the time."

Adrian had finished skinning the rabbit and then held out his knife to Justin.

"Keep this. It's yours," he said. "You shall need a good knife when you go to the forest tomorrow and I see that you do not have one. Fortunately none of our tools were destroyed in the fire, so I shall get another knife from the barn tonight. Oh, and here, please take the sheath as well."

Justin stood up from washing the roots and received the knife and case from Adrian.

"Thank you," he said, taking his seat again next to Constance.

"And I should like if you would not sit so close to my sister," Adrian said.

Justin stood up again and plopped down on the ground next to Adrian.

"My apologies, indeed," he said.

"Stay away from her, Edward," Adrian warned.

Constance had managed to recover a small iron pot, along with a few ceramic bowls and cups from the ruins of the cottage. Everything else had been destroyed. She boiled water in the pot, threw in the roots, and added some of the nettles Justin had collected. Justin meanwhile skinned the rabbit, then shaved the bark off a long thin piece of wood with his knife to make a spit, a skill he had learned from the hermit. He carefully speared the rabbit on the stick, then placed it into two stout Y-shaped branches on either side of the fire. When the rabbit was roasted, he cut half of it into pieces, which were shared among the three of them, saving the remaining half for supper.

While they were eating Adrian related to Justin how the crop had been poor the previous year and there was not enough grain to fill the quota demanded by the lord. The peasants had tried to negotiate new terms based on a percentage of the yield rather than on a fixed amount, but the lord would not relent. Together with a band of soldiers, the bailiff had visited the village numerous times to collect, and the villagers had parceled out any of the stock they could spare, but during the summer months especially they needed to keep some of the food on reserve for themselves until the next harvest. Otherwise they would starve. Finally the villagers decided to go to the manor house itself, with Adrian as their spokesman, to have a word with the lord, but they were driven away by the soldiers, even though they were unarmed, and several of the older men had been brutally killed.

Justin knew about the incident, of course. He had also heard Constance's account of life in the village but was still stupefied at how differently things looked from the other side of the wall.

"You have no recourse to justice?" Justin asked.

"None at all," Adrian answered. "Court would be held at the estate with the lord himself as judge. We could hardly expect him to indict himself and render a verdict favorable to us, now could we!"

"But surely you could appeal to a higher court."

"In principle, but not in reality."

Based on his studies with the bailiff, Justin had always assumed that all people are equal before the law and entitled to a fair hearing. But perhaps some were more equal than others after all.

"And now this," Adrian continued. "The soldiers from the estate descended on us yesterday morning. The bailiff told us that we should settle up and pay what was due or we would suffer the consequences. We pleaded with them to allow us to save some of the food for ourselves, but they threatened to burn down my house if we resisted. The peasants rallied to my defense and there was a standoff. Then the head guard tossed a torch onto the thatched roof of my cottage."

"But why would the soldiers burn down the entire village? Surely it would not be to the lord's advantage to destroy the homes of those whom he depends on to produce his food."

"I don't think that was the guards' original intention. After my house was aflame a scuffle broke out between the peasants and the soldiers, which quickly escalated. We had only our fists, but they had swords and cudgels. The guards killed two of our older men and set a few of the other houses on fire. Then the fire started spreading from house to house. The villagers panicked and scattered. When we returned we found that the entire village had been obliterated and the barns plundered. They took everything we had, except for the animals I mentioned and whatever food in store they could not find, which was not much."

"So what will you do now?"

"What can we do? We need to rebuild our houses and get back to work in the fields. I am quite sure the lord would not allow such a minor mishap as the destruction of our village to lessen his demands on us. He might be able to tide himself over for a while buying food sold in the city, but we have no money to do that."

There was silence after Adrian had finished speaking. Justin had known that the villagers were arrear in their debts from the ledgers he had kept, but he had no knowledge of the methods that were used to collect them nor that his father had the power to wreak such reprisals on the peasants. He had been raised to think that the dealings his father had with peasants were always fair and that any grievances they had against him were unjustified. Now he saw with perfect clarity that the problem was not the peasants' intransigence but his father's. Justin felt complicit in their exploitation, even though there was nothing he could have done. He wanted to apologize not just to Adrian but to all the villagers and beg for their forgiveness, though he knew he could not, lest he give himself away.

§11

After the meal was over Justin accompanied Adrian as he went from household to household giving orders to the villagers about who should go with Justin to the forest to gather food the next day and who should stay back to assist with the recovery. In the afternoon Justin helped Adrian clear the remaining burnt planks from the site of his own cottage, casting them into a pile beside the fire. The pallets had been burned completely, so Constance set about collecting straw to make new bedding, although there were as yet no ticks to put the straw in. She carried the straw to one of the barns, where other women were also making beds.

When she returned to the house, she ignored Justin and asked Adrian instead, "Shall I make a bed for Edward as well?"

Before Adrian could reply, Justin said, "Please do not trouble yourself. I shall sleep again in the forest."

"No," Adrian said. "You shall spend the night here. You need to get up early in the morning to lead the expedition tomorrow. While you are gathering food, I shall remain here with the others to continue clearing the ground."

It seemed to Justin that he had no say in the matter, so he acquiesced. Constance prepared a straw bed with no ticking for him in the pigsty, and after they had finished their supper of leftovers from lunch, he said goodnight to Adrian, Constance, and her cat, Charm, and retired to it. A light rain began to fall. Justin lay down on the bed and felt the cold rainwater begin to seep into the straw beneath him and soak his clothes. He had never felt so uncomfortable, but fell asleep with the thought—no, the wish—that the village might become his new home. With Constance.

§12

The next morning Justin awoke before dawn. He was sopping wet but his clothes quickly dried after the sun was fully up. He met the other villagers who had assembled in the village green and led them into the forest to search for food. The company was made up mainly of women and the older men. Justin was disappointed that Constance was not among them, since he desperately hoped for a chance to talk with her, but she had stayed back in the village with a few others to make simple hemp bedticks while her brother and the remaining men continued clearing any chars that remained on the grounds of their houses.

Justin was impressed at how adept the villagers were at gathering food but was nonetheless able to introduce them to a few edible plants he had learned about from the hermit which they were not familiar with. When he showed them a swarm of grubs lying beneath a rotting log, however, the peasants balked at collecting them, saying they were not fit for human consumption. Well before midday their bundles were full of greens, berries, and nuts. Prior to leaving the forest, the men set some rabbit snares. When they returned the next morning, they found a few rabbits in the traps, which they joyfully added to their bundles. This pattern continued for the next few days. There was plenty of food for everyone, for both their afternoon and evening meals, and even for breakfast, which had never been served on the estate.

"Unlike the nobles, the peasants always have something to eat after they get up," Constance explained to him one morning. "We need the extra fortification for our labors."

Finally the lots had been swept clean and the peasants were ready to begin the reconstruction. The entire village then went together to the forest, half of them with Justin to look for food and the other half with Adrian to cut sturdy trees for rebuilding their cruck houses. To Justin's delight, Constance had been assigned to join the food-gatherers, who quickly dispersed throughout the woodland looking for anything edible they could find.

When they were well out of sight of Adrian and some distance from the others, Justin motioned and called out to Constance, "Look, there are raspberries over yonder."

Constance followed Justin to a raspberry thicket partially hidden by bushes and trees. The two began picking raspberries—slowly—since this was the first time they'd actually had a chance to talk. They kept their eyes straight ahead and avoided looking at each other.

"I am so happy to be able to meet you again," Justin said in a low voice.

"Well, I was certainly astonished when I saw you in the lane that leads to our cottage," Constance replied. "How did you manage to come here?"

Justin told her the story of his wedding to Penelope and his escape, how he had taken the boat down the brook, wandered through the forest and met the hermit, whose hut was in the very same forest but near the sea, and then rushed to the village when he saw the smoke.

"Indeed, we know about the hermit since he used to live here and still visits us from time to time. We have also heard that after you left Penelope, she was completely disgraced and returned with her father to his estate. But why did you leave your new bride? Surely you could have been happy with her."

"I do not think so, Constance. I sincerely regret that I did not confront my father and tell him that I did not wish to marry her, that my thoughts were only of you. I am so ashamed that I simply did not go with you when you were expelled by the bailiff."

"Your father never would have given you permission to leave."

"You are right. He would have done anything to keep me on the estate, even thrown me into the dungeon if he had to."

"Together with your teacher," Constance said. "No one spoke about the matter, but we all knew what happened to him."

"Yes, I suppose the poor fellow died in there. But things have worked out for the best, at least for us. I am here with you now and that is all that matters."

"Indeed. I never expected to see you again."

"I want to stay with you, Constance, not just now but forever."

"Truth be told, I am also happy to see you and would certainly welcome you, but you must keep your identity a secret. If any of the villagers, and especially my brother, find out who you really are, they would exile you from the village or, more likely, lynch you."

"It is fortunate that no one except you knows my face."

"Just after you left the estate the soldiers came to the village looking for you, but they said nothing of the circumstances and did not mention your name, only that you were wearing a cotehardie. When you arrived at the village last week in peasants' clothes, no one suspected that you were the man they were looking for."

"Did any of the soldiers question you specifically?" Justin asked.

"Yes. One of them—I believe his name is Martin—knew who I was. He took me aside and asked me if I'd seen you. I told him I had not, which at the time was perfectly true, of course. In any case, no one from the estate believes you are here now, although they are no doubt still looking for you elsewhere."

"My only concern is the village priest, since he is the same priest who says mass at our chapel on the estate and who performed the wedding ceremony. He would surely recognize me."

"Ha! You needn't worry about him," Constance said. "He never sets foot in the village to minister to us."

Constance hesitated for a moment and then added, "There is one more thing I must tell you, which you surely do not know."

"About what?"

"Your mother."

Justin had not thought about his mother for a very long time.

"Is she still alive?" he asked hopefully.

"No, I'm afraid not. Her grave is in the cemetery beside the church."

Justin took a moment to let what Constance had just said sink in. He finally replied, "Well, I had supposed she was dead and assumed that she must be buried some place, but I knew not where."

"There is a stone cross to mark her resting place, but it is not engraved with her name. Your father does not wish her to be remembered."

"I shall go to see it," Justin said.

There was more that Justin wanted to ask Constance, but he realized that the others might become suspicious if they were away too long.

"We mustn't tarry here," he said. "But let us meet again tomorrow."

Justin pulled his bundle over his shoulder and walked off alone to another part of the forest. Constance remained at the thicket a while longer picking more berries, then finally returned to the others. When the food had been gathered and the trees cut, everyone went back to the village together, some carrying food in their bundles and others wood on their shoulders. In addition to his food, Justin carried a few sturdy poles he had cut, with the intention of building a small shelter in the pigsty to shield him from the rain.

Along the way an older woman hobbled up beside Justin, accompanied by a younger woman at her side.

"I saw you out there in the forest, Edward, going off to pick raspberries so you could have a nice long chat with Constance," the old woman said.

Justin was bemused at how quickly his new name had become known among the villagers.

"Shush, mother," the young woman said. "You are always nosing into other people's business."

Ignoring her daughter, the mother said to Justin, "Well, I just want you to know that you can't pull any wool over my eyes. So you had better mind your p's and q's."

Justin smiled at the old woman but said nothing. She was still quite agile, even though her hair was gray, her forehead creased with wrinkles, her cheeks blotched with liver spots, and her chin sagging with withered skin. So this, Justin thought, is what it means to be old.

The daughter pulled the old woman away, making sure she had no more contact with Justin the rest of the way home.

That evening at supper Adrian said, "I expect that we shall need one more day with everyone in the forest. After that, we can split up again, with some continuing to gather food and timber with Edward, and the others, including Constance and myself, remaining here to plane the wood and begin constructing the frames for our houses."

When dinner was finished, Adrian and Constance headed off to their pallets in the barn, Constance taking Charm with her, while Justin went to the pigsty. He positioned the poles from the forest against the wall and threw a tarp over them to make a small tent. The tarp had been given to him by Constance, along with a hemp tick for his bed, which was a vast improvement over lying directly on the straw. He reminisced about the fine linen sheets of his bed at the manor house and realized, much to his surprise, that he no longer missed them. Justin closed his eyes knowing that the following day there was something very important he needed to do and he must act soon.

§13

Waking earlier than usual Justin made a small fire and prepared breakfast for himself and the others. Constance and Adrian emerged from the barn a little after sunup and joined him at the fireplace.

"Things are moving along well," Adrian said to Justin. "We have food for our bellies and timber for our houses. You must be tiring of all this hard work, Edward, aren't you? Please do not feel obliged to stay. You may leave whenever you want. No doubt you are eager to get going on your merry way again as soon as possible."

Justin had sensed all along that Adrian did not like him but was vexed that he did not seem to appreciate Justin's efforts to help both him and the villagers. Justin did not reply to Adrian's remark, however, fearing that anything he might say would only make him angry.

Soon after breakfast the villagers returned to the forest, separating again into two groups, one to gather food and the other to collect wood. Again, Justin found an opportunity to maneuver Constance and himself away from the others, especially the nosy mother and her daughter, this time to look for mushrooms. They quickly began conversing in the same manner as before.

"This may be the last time I can see you like this," Justin said.

"I think so," Constance replied. "My brother does not want us to be together."

"Why does he hate me so?"

"He does not really hate you. He simply doesn't trust you. He still thinks of you as a vagabond. Even though you have been helping us, he believes you are unreliable, that you have some kind of plot up your sleeve he cannot yet fathom."

"Why would he think that?" Justin asked.

"Because he himself always has some kind of plot up his sleeve and thinks that everyone else is just like him."

"In any case, as you said yesterday, if he knew the truth about me, he would not put up with me for long."

"Perhaps it is better if you left the village."

"Would you go with me?"

"I could not," Constance replied. "Adrian would not permit me to leave."

"We could run away together."

"No, I must stay here with my brother."

Justin was thoughtful for a moment. "First my father, then your brother. It seems that we shall never be together."

"But what else can we possibly do?"

Justin took a long deep breath. "Well, that is what I wanted to ask you."

Constance looked at him searchingly.

"I should like to marry you," Justin said.

Constance could not suppress a laugh. "You must be joking. You cannot marry me. You are already married to Penelope."

"Well, legally I suppose, but, as I told you yesterday, I fled before the marriage was consummated."

"It would still need to be annulled by the Church before you would be free to marry again. Otherwise, you would be a bigamist."

"Who would know except us?"

"It makes no difference. My brother would forbid us from getting married anyway, even if he did not know about your past."

"We do not need your brother's approval," Justin said. "According to the law—and I do know something about the law since I studied it with the bailiff—no permission is necessary. The only requirement is that the man and woman both give their free consent."

"Still," Constance said. "I should not like to marry without Adrian's blessing."

"So you will not accept my proposal?"

Constance thought for a long moment, then said, "I would certainly like to accept your proposal, but it's not that simple. I think we should wait. Give my brother some more time to get to know you. You must prove yourself to him by helping with anything he asks you and showing that you are a trustworthy person. When he said that you are free to leave whenever you want, he was only testing you."

Justin beamed with joy and was about to touch Constance on her arm when there was a rustling in the bushes behind them. Justin turned around quickly and saw Adrian approaching, brandishing an axe in his hand.

"Edward!" he shouted. "I thought I told you to stay away from my sister. If I ever catch you even talking to her again, I shall give you a good thrashing and send you packing."

Justin bowed deeply. "I beg your forgiveness, sir. Indeed, I shall never meet or talk with her again after this."

"Except for necessary matters and in my presence," Adrian said.

"You have my word," Justin replied.

§14

It had been almost a week since Justin had arrived at the village. On his first Sunday there, the villagers prepared to attend mass at the church. Justin, still fearing that the village priest would recognize him, considered making an excuse so that he would not have to go, but then decided it would simply draw more attention to himself as an outsider and potential miscreant. His only recourse would be to keep his head bowed whenever the priest faced the congregants and to cower in repentance when he received the host on his tongue.

After entering the church with Adrian and Constance, Justin was relieved to find that the sanctuary was almost completely dark, even though the shutters of the windows on either wall were open. A gentle breeze wafted in through the frames. Apart from a simple wooden cross atop an altar, an earthen baptismal font, vessels for the Eucharist, and two candlesticks, there were no other furnishings—no stained glass, no iconic paintings, no statues of the Virgin—as there were in the chapel at the estate. There were no benches either, so the parishioners simply flocked together as a group and stood facing the priest at the altar.

Otherwise, the liturgy was indistinguishable from the one Justin had grown up hearing. Even the homily was similar, with its repeated injunctions to obey the Word of God, the Church, and the governing authorities. A key difference was that here the priest placed special emphasis on giving to the lord what was owed him.

"You must pay your taxes, for the authorities are ministers of God," the priest said, quoting scripture. "Pay taxes to whom taxes are due, revenue to whom revenue is due, respect to whom respect due, honor to whom honor is due. The peasants must not resist the authorities whom God has appointed, lest his servants execute his wrath on the wrongdoer. The soil is cursed because of your sin and brings forth thistles and thorns. Nonetheless, it is your lot to toil with the sweat of your brow so that we may partake of what the earth offers us and be given our daily bread from God. You must always remember that despite the hardships and suffering you endure at present, you shall one day receive your just reward in heaven and live with God forever, but only if you first fulfill your obligations to your masters here on earth."

After mass was over, while the villagers were socializing with each other outside the church, Justin walked over to the cemetery. He found the only unmarked stone cross there, which he knew was the grave of his mother. He wanted to kneel before it and pray but was worried that the others might see him. So he just stood there a few seconds, head bowed, remembering the sorrowful eyes of his mother and everything she had told him. The time we have on earth is short. We must be grateful for every moment we are alive and follow our hearts, knowing that one day we will die. How he wished he could hear her voice again and listen to her advice.

The village priest set off in his cart for the estate where, as Justin knew all too well, he would say one mass for his father and another for the servants. The villagers then returned to their homes for their Sunday dinners, which consisted once again of gatherings from the forest, along with any rabbits they may have captured. Justin had found the first brown acorns of the season on the ground the day before, which he threw into his bundle together with some dandelion greens. Adrian scoffed when he saw the acorns, saying they were more suitable for pigs than for humans to eat, but he was hungry enough to accept them gratefully, along with the greens. Constance boiled the acorns in the iron pot, threw out the brown water, and repeated this process several times until the bubbling water was clear. After the acorns were finished, she cooked the dandelion greens in the same pot.

As they ate their meager lunch together, Adrian said to Justin, who was sitting as far away from Constance as possible, "It's all a bunch of nonsense, I tell you. Every week we go to church and hear the same sermon over and over again about how we are supposed to be subject to our masters and hand over what we owe them."

"Why do you go to church, then, if you do not believe what the priest tells you?" Justin asked.

"I do not know myself. We pay a ten-percent tithe to the Church on top of everything we give the lord, plus additional fees for weddings, funerals, even baptisms. We cannot become Christians, get married, or even die without handing money over to the priest."

"I have noticed that he lives well," Justin said.

"Indeed, the rectory is well appointed, much more so than the church, which is our responsibility. That's why it looks so shabby. Recently, though, we have been unable to give the priest anything, so he is tight for supplies as well. I can guarantee you, though, that when he returns from the estate today, his wagon will be loaded with food—food that we produced, that the lord has confiscated from us and given to him!"

Adrian shoveled a spoonful of acorns into his mouth.

"But surely you have faith in God, even if you dislike the priest," Justin said.

"Hardly. Religion is simply a means to keep us in our place. The peasants here will believe anything you tell them. As for me, I think for myself. My sister here, too. She's an independent woman."

"Certainly I do not pay any attention to what the priest says," Constance said, giving a few morsels of food to Charm, who was sitting beside her. "Though perhaps it would be better to say not that I think for myself but that I listen to my heart."

"Heed your brother," Adrian said. "The heart will lead you astray, but the mind will show you the way. And once you know that, it is easy to compel others to follow you. The herd will not move without a herdsman to guide them."

Adrian finished eating the dandelions and handed his empty bowl to Constance for her to clean. She promptly handed it back to him.

"Wash your own bowl," she said. "I am no longer a servant and you are certainly not my master!"

Adrian glared at Constance but proceeded to wash his bowl. He then said to Justin, "Let's get back to work, Edward. There is no rest for us, even on the Sabbath."

§15

For the next few weeks Justin's routine was to gather food in the morning and help Adrian rebuild his house in the afternoon. Vegetables were growing again in the gardens and several new piglets had already been born. With extra food now in storage, fewer were going each day to the forest with Justin. And since almost all the necessary wood had been cut and hauled to the village, the villagers were increasingly preoccupied with constructing their homes.

Adrian's house was making considerable progress. After the frame was up, he and Justin, together with Constance, wove thin branches of wood into wattle, which they placed between the poles and then covered with a mixture of clay, manure, and straw for the daub. Later they raked more straw from the field for the thatch and, after the roof was finished, moved their pallets into the inner room of the house. The final step was to furnish the outer room with a cabinet, table, and chairs made of hewn wood notched and pegged together.

Everyone was happy that they could finally eat dinner and sleep inside the cottage. Adrian was especially pleased. He slapped Justin on his shoulder. "It took you a while to catch on, but after that you did a good job!"

"I have certainly learned a lot," Justin said.

"Well, your delicate hands told me from the very start that you are not a workingman. And I could see from your lack of skills that you aren't the son of a peasant. My guess is that your father was a merchant in town and when his business failed, you set out on your own."

Justin hesitated. Until now Adrian had never asked him anything about his past and he was unsure how to reply. He wished that he had prepared an answer in advance, but he had not.

"Yes, that's right," Justin finally said, and then added, "But I'm glad to have acquired the skills for the life of a peasant now!"

"Well, Edward, I certainly appreciate you lending me a hand. That's why I'm letting you stay inside the house. You helped build it so you've earned the right to sleep in it. Our next task is the harvest, which we shall begin within a few days."

"Indeed, I'm ready to get started."

It seemed to Justin that Adrian was beginning to warm to him! If he worked hard during the harvest, perhaps it would convince Adrian of his good character. Perhaps Justin could even win his approval to marry Constance. He looked over at her and watched her lovingly stroke the tummy of Charm.

After harvesting began, Justin very quickly found out that it is back-breaking labor, much harder than gathering food or building a cottage. The villagers worked first on the wheat, then the barley and oats. The reapers cut the grain with their scythes, while Justin and the others followed after them, raking the stalks and tying them into sheaves, then arranging them into stooks to dry. The air was torrid, his throat parched, but Justin still managed to work up a drenching sweat. His muscles quickly became sore from all the bending and stooping. At night he would be too tired to do anything more than eat dinner with Adrian and Constance, then go to bed aching and wake up the next morning to do it all over again.

In the meantime, women were making ale, the chickens and cattle were being fed, the vegetable gardens tended to. The feast of the first fruits was held. The peasants dutifully presented the priest with loaves of bread, which he blessed. They then set up tables in the village green to enjoy their first taste of the harvest.

The harvest continued in earnest after that, the peasants eager to get it finished. One morning Adrian let Justin try his hand at the scythe, which Justin wielded awkwardly at first but soon got the hang of. By mid-afternoon his muscles were strained to the limit. He wanted to give the scythe back to Adrian but was determined to show no sign of weakness for any task Adrian gave him, so he pressed on.

On the last day of the harvest, as Adrian and Justin were walking back to the village, Adrian was in good cheer.

"You did well!" he said to Justin.

"I gave it my best."

"I can tell. It's hard work but you did your fair share. The harvest is abundant this year. We will be able to pay the lord his due and have enough left over to last ourselves through the winter, perhaps not extravagantly but at least comfortably."

"You must still give the full amount to the lord, even though he took everything from you and burned your houses?"

"It's his prerogative. We are attached to his land and must meet his terms. As you already know, it is impossible to negotiate with him. But finally we will be able to have our fill of bread and ale. We shall have a grand harvest festival this year!"

Adrian beamed broadly. Justin thought that now might be a good time to take advantage of Adrian's high spirits.

"May I ask you a question?"

"Of course. Ask me anything!" Adrian said ebulliently.

It was better, Justin felt, to get straight to the point without hesitating.

"May I have your blessing to marry your sister?" he said.

Adrian stopped dead in his tracks, his smile slowly turning into a frown. He squinted at Justin.

"You want to marry Constance?"

"Indeed I do, but only with your approval."

"She's just a poor peasant girl. Why would you want to marry her?"

"For the only reason that matters: because I love her."

"But she is the only kin I have. You cannot take her away from me."

"I would not. We would live together with you in the village, just as we are living now."

Adrian stood for a moment thinking.

"I cannot answer you now," he said. "But I will consider it."

§16

After the sheaves had dried and the threshing was completed, Justin helped the villagers load the grain into carts to take to the lord, with the remainder being stored in the granary. Justin had often seen carts full of grain coming into the estate when he lived there, but now he knew where the carts came from and all the labor that went into filling them. A tithe was also given to the parish priest, part of which he kept for himself, with the rest being forwarded to the bishop in town. Once the lord and the Church had been given their due, the peasants could keep whatever remained. From his days as a ledger-keeper on the estate, Justin also knew exactly how much it was costing the villagers for the use of his father's mill to grind their bread, his brewery to make their ale, and his blacksmith's shop to repair their broken tools. It had been decided not to use the winepress to make wine this year, but to have cider instead, which could be produced in the village.

As grain continued to be hauled to the estate, preparations were underway for the harvest festival. During this time Justin noticed that Constance was smiling at him more often than usual and was pleasantly surprised when Adrian gave permission for him to talk freely with Constance, although only under his supervision. Justin and Constance confined their conversations to pleasantries and the day's events, but once, when Adrian was called away by a villager to settle a dispute he was having with his neighbor and they were alone in the house together, Justin seized the opportunity to tell Constance that he had asked her brother for her hand in marriage.

"I already know," Constance said.

"Will he give us his blessing?"

"Not yet. But he did ask me if I would be willing to marry you."

"And your reply?"

"Need you wonder?"

"So, it looks as if he will allow us to wed!" Justin said elatedly.

"There are other matters which you have not yet taken into account, however," Constance said in a way that instantly put a damper on Justin's enthusiasm.

"Such as?"

"We still need your father's permission to marry and it hardly seems likely he would give it."

Justin stomped his foot on the mud floor of the house. Charm was startled and ran away to the far corner of the room, where she hid behind the cabinet.

"My father no longer controls me," he said, half-shouting. "Whatever decisions I make are my own, not his."

"But you still need his consent. Not because he is your father, but because he is the lord of this fief. No one in the village may marry without his authorization."

Justin had not thought of this matter before but realized at once the absurdity of asking for his father's approval. Finally he said, "While it may be customary to ask a lord's permission, the law states that no such authorization is needed. We simply keep the whole affair private. My father does not need to know about it."

"Do you honestly think it would be possible to keep such a secret in a small village such as this, where everyone knows everything about everyone else's business?" Constance said. "At some point your father would surely find out. And then he would know where you are. And he would come to get you."

Justin could offer no rejoinder.

"Moreover," Constance continued. "Even if we could persuade the villagers to keep the matter confidential, we would still need to be married by the village priest. You're a fool if you think that the same priest who has just recently performed a wedding ceremony between you and Penelope would turn around and marry us. Since you are still legally married, your marriage to her would need to be annulled first."

Here was another issue Justin had not considered, but which he had a ready answer for. "It is not necessary to have a ceremony. We simply declare our intentions in front of the villagers. In fact, we do not even need to make an announcement, but can simply start living together as a common-law husband and wife. That is sufficient for a marriage to be legally recognized and would be perfectly acceptable to the villagers, even to the Church, assuming it doesn't get wind of my previous ties."

"Perhaps in other places, but not here. We would be ostracized if we did not have a proper wedding blessed by the priest."

"Let us elope, then."

"You are asking me to leave my brother?"

"Well, I have deserted my father. Surely you can abandon your brother. Consider what is important to you."

Constance did not answer.

"There must be a way," Justin said.

"Yet once again you have no plan," Constance replied. She picked up her black cat and turned to leave.

"I shall think of something."

"Will you?" Constance said.

Justin knew that Constance was right. He had given no previous thought to the impediments she had mentioned and had no idea how to overcome them. But then he thought back to his escape from the estate. Even though he had come up with no course of action in advance, it had been easy to simply walk through the gate and leave. Perhaps it would be just as easy for Justin to marry Constance. Things will work themselves out, he told himself, although he was not entirely convinced and had no idea how.

§17

The day of the harvest festival arrived and the villagers turned out in their finest. For the most part these were simply less stained and ragged versions of their ordinary workaday clothes, but a few of the women had made new dresses for the occasion. Tables and chairs were brought out from the houses and placed in the village green, then set with ample quantities of bread, vegetables, beans, fresh cheese, and a roast pig in the center. Casks of ale were brought out, not the weak ale the peasants drank daily, but a stronger variety purposely brewed to maximize its intoxicating effect.

Before the revelry began, Constance whispered excitedly to Justin, "Adrian will announce our betrothal to everyone today, at the end of the festival."

Justin was surprised to hear this news since Adrian had not mentioned anything whatsoever to him about it.

"Are you sure?" Justin asked.

"He told me so!"

"But what of all the objections you raised earlier?"

"Adrian said that after all the trouble the lord has caused us, he no longer felt it necessary for us to ask for his permission to marry. Furthermore, he can see no reason why he should pay a priest to conduct a wedding since we are still so poor. We shall simply announce our intentions to everyone in the green."

"But what will the villagers think?"

"Adrian has already explained the situation to them and won them over. Or, should I say, as the leader of this village he has asserted his authority and forbidden anyone from challenging it. In any case, the villagers dare not oppose him, so there will be no objections to us not having a ceremony at the church. We will simply keep the whole matter to ourselves and make sure that no one informs your father. Nonetheless, the rumor that you have proposed to me has spread throughout the entire village, so the announcement today will be a mere formality. You are probably the only one who has not heard about it yet!"

Justin smiled as he and Constance joined the others at the green and sat down at a table across from Adrian, who was in a jocular mood, eating and joking and sloshing ale from his cup. The nosy mother, who had confronted Justin on their walk back from the forest while gathering food, was sitting just to Justin's left, with her daughter on the other side.

The old mother leaned over to Justin and said in a low voice, "Congratulations on your upcoming marriage, Edward."

"Be quiet, mother," her daughter scolded. "It hasn't been officially announced yet."

"Indeed, it hasn't," the mother said over her shoulder to the young woman. Then turning back to Justin she whispered, "If I were you, I'd do it proper and have it blessed by the priest."

"It shall be done proper," Justin said softly in reply.

"Not without a priest," the mother said, sitting back upright.

Once people had their fill of food and drink, the festivities began. Lacking instruments, the peasants made their own music by singing and clapping their hands. They danced together mainly in circles, which anyone could join, but sometimes in lines where a few of the more accomplished dancers would spin and show off their steps. Other villagers juggled apples in the air or turned somersaults and cartwheels in the grass. The children played leapfrog, hide and seek, and tag. Later in the afternoon two teams were formed, each trying to kick or throw a ball made from an inflated pig's bladder past the other team's markers, which were placed at either end of the road that ran through the village.

By mid-afternoon the villagers began to tire and returned to the tables to eat left-over scraps of food and drink more ale. Suddenly a tall man who had been loitering in the field—the same tall man Justin had met on the outskirts of the village on the first day of his arrival, who had weepingly told him about the razing of the houses—cried out, "They're coming!"

"Who is coming?" Adrian shouted back.

"The soldiers!"

Everyone immediately fell silent.

"Let us go to meet them," Adrian said.

The peasants got up from their tables and followed Adrian up the village road to the highway that led to the lord's estate. Indeed, men on horses were fast approaching. To conceal himself from view, Justin took up a position behind the tall man, who was now standing at the back of the throng. As the company drew nearer, Justin peeked around the man's side to witness what was happening. Finally Justin could see that the company was led by the bailiff, with Martin at his side.

"What business have you here?" Adrian called out to the bailiff.

"We have a matter to discuss with you," the bailiff replied, not getting down from his horse. "We have tallied up the grain you brought us and find that it is short."

"Nay," Adrian replied. "It was the full amount. It was checked by you yourself when we gave it over to you."

"Yes, you presented us with a sufficient quantity for the current harvest, but after checking the accounts, I find that you are still in arrears for the previous year. We will give you one week to hand over what you still owe us."

"Indeed, the harvest this year was good, but we nonetheless have just enough for ourselves to last the winter. We cannot spare any more."

"Your situation is of no concern to me. We simply want our fair due."

"Surely you have enough grain already for the lord and everyone on his estate."

"We do. But it is our intention to sell the surplus in the city. It will fetch a high price. We need to regain the money we lost when we could no longer rely on you to provide for us."

Constance stepped forward and spoke to the bailiff, "You have no right to take our food and sell it to others!"

The bailiff looked carefully at Constance's face.

"I recognize you," he said. "You are the same servant girl who was dismissed from the estate."

"Indeed, and I have done exactly as you commanded. So you may make no claims against me."

"You should be careful about what you say, young woman, or much worse things will befall you."

"I do not care," Constance replied. "You only think about your accounts. You should be more concerned about the people who work for you than how much money you can make for yourselves!"

"It is not the money, but the principle," the bailiff said. "The terms that have been set must be met. I shall not listen to your blather any further."

"Who cares about your principles?" Constance said, ignoring him. "The needs of the people come first."

Martin dismounted from his horse and approached Constance.

"Know your place, woman, and do as you're told," he said.

"And I recognize this man as well," Constance shouted. "He is the same head guard who set fire to our house!"

"Silence!" Martin raged. "Such insolence will not be tolerated."

"I am not afraid of you either!" Constance said defiantly. "We give you everything we have and you still want more. And if we do not give it to you, you kill our men and burn our houses!"

Martin removed the gauntlet from his right hand and grabbed Constance by the arm. Justin ducked his head behind the tall man, then peeped out from behind it again.

"I should like to take you to the fields and give you a good humping," Martin said.

"And I should like to see you castrated!" Constance screamed back.

Martin looked lecherously at Constance, then, replacing his gauntlet, struck her to the ground. As she lay there moaning, Martin kicked her a few times until her sobs finally ceased. She was breathing heavily, but otherwise motionless. Justin was seething with anger but could not step forward to rescue her, nor could anyone else.

As Martin remounted his horse, the bailiff said, "I can see that you have restored your village. It would be a shame to see your houses destroyed again after you have worked so hard to rebuild them."

With that, he reared up his horse, turned it in the direction of the estate, and rode off, with Martin and the other soldiers behind him.

Justin immediately ran over to Constance.

"Are you all right?" he cried.

She made no reply. When he tried to help her to her feet, she pushed him away.

"I can stand up entirely on my own," she said. "No one can knock me down and keep me there."

Justin and Constance, along with Adrian and the other villagers, returned to what was left of their feast and cleared the tables, taking everything back with them to their homes.

§18

The next morning while eating their porridge, Adrian said grimly to Justin, "Something must be done."

"It would seem that you have no options," Justin replied.

"I have already come up with an idea," Adrian said, pointing his spoon at Justin. "I shall assemble the villagers as soon as we finish our breakfast and tell my plan to them."

"And what, may I ask, is your proposal?"

"I shall reveal it to you at the same time I speak with the others," Adrian said. "But I would like you to help me with it."

"I will certainly do what I can," Justin said, although his mind was spinning with doubts.

Adrian looked over at Constance, then back to Justin.

"Edward," he said gravely. "It was my intention to give notice of your engagement to my sister at the festival yesterday, but there was no opportunity. As matters stand, there is one more task I should like you to perform before giving you my final consent. It will prove beyond any doubt that you are one of us."

Justin could not imagine what kind of scheme Adrian had come up with, but he was beginning to feel uneasy. Constance had been silent throughout the entire breakfast, simply sitting there petting Charm. Justin wondered how it all would end.

§19

The villagers gathered in the green, where Adrian had set up a crate, which he stood upon with Justin and Constance on either side of him.

"Friends and comrades," he bellowed to the audience. "You know the situation we are in. We labor every day for the lord and have nothing left for ourselves. When we try to negotiate peaceably with him, he sends his soldiers to kill us. When we are unable to meet his demands, he does not give us an opportunity to make good, but instead burns our houses, making it even harder for us to fulfill the requirements he has set for us. The lord says his terms are just, but we know they are not. And we have no say in them. We must simply follow the dictates of our master."

The villagers began to hiss and boo loudly, all except for the nosy old mother, who, Justin noticed, remained unmoved and silent.

"The situation must change!" Adrian shouted. "And we shall change it!"

A cheer went up from the crowd.

"We must labor not for the lord, but for ourselves!"

The cheering crescendoed.

"I say to you, the land belongs to whoever works it and if the noblemen do not want to work the land, then it is not theirs. It belongs to us!"

The villagers by now had been whipped into a fervor.

After pausing for a moment, Adrian raised his hand in a fist. "So we shall retake the land and make it our own!"

A hush instantly fell over the assembly.

The silence was finally broken by the tall man, the same man Justin had hidden behind the day before. "And how, might I ask, do you intend to make the land our own?"

Adrian looked down on the people intensely. "It is time for us to revolt."

The villagers began to murmur to one another.

"There is no way we could succeed," the tall man said. "We have no weapons and no means to make them. The blacksmith's shop is within the walls of the estate and the lord would scarcely let us use it to forge arms against him."

"The blacksmith is a peasant like us," Justin said. "Perhaps we could enlist his support."

As soon as the words were out of his mouth, Justin remembered that he should not reveal to the villagers how much he knew about the servants who worked for his father. But it seemed that the blacksmith was already well known among the villagers so no one noticed his slip.

"It is too risky," Adrian said. "Winning the blacksmith's confidence would not be a problem, but any covert activity at the workshop would surely arouse suspicions. In any case, we do not need weapons. We have our knives and axes, our sickles and our hayforks. We shall make cudgels with wood from the forest and carve spears with sharp points."

The tall man looked at Adrian skeptically and said, "Those are all excellent armaments no doubt, but no match for the sword and the longbow. We shall be roundly defeated."

"So, tell me, dear sir," Adrian replied. "Which do you prefer: to continue enduring these conditions or to overthrow the present social order and institute a new one that is just and fair for everyone? Those are the only two choices we have."

"'There is no doubt that the present system is less than ideal and cannot be reformed," the tall man said. "But trying to fight against it might only make matters worse. Perhaps a violent revolution is unnecessary. We are, after all, not slaves. We still have some freedoms. Could we not simply refuse to serve the lord any longer and do things our own way?"

"What!" Adrian cried. "If we offer only passive resistance, the lord's men would only come and burn down our houses again."

"Nonetheless, could there not be some kind of peaceful transition? Order must be maintained. We should not try to upend it."

The nosy old woman finally broke her silence. "I agree. As the priest always tells us, to preserve social stability we must be subject to whomever God appoints as our governing authorities."

The mother's daughter, who had been standing beside her the whole time, then said, "Do not listen to my mother here. The lord rules solely by his own power, not because he is ordained by God. I say we should fight."

The tall man was unconvinced.

"An outright struggle would end with losses on both sides," he said. "Perhaps we could have some success against the lord, but his forces would surely be strong enough to come again to our village and burn it to the ground."

"I think not," the daughter said combatively. "The only reason the lord bullies us is because he thinks we will not fight back. We must show him that if he persists in his ways, he, too, will incur losses. Once we have leveled the field, he will have no alternative but to negotiate reasonably with us."

"My intention," Adrian roared, taking back control over the deliberation, "is not to negotiate with the lord but to defeat him. He will not be persuaded with words, but only by deeds. We shall breach the walls of the estate, killing as many as we can and driving off the rest. If every able-bodied man, woman, and child standing here now joins our force, we shall easily outnumber the garrison. The servants at the manor will readily join us, since they are our friends and kin from this very village."

"This is outrageous!" the tall man exclaimed. "Many of us would die. Are you sincerely asking that we lay down our lives for you?"

"Not for me," Adrian said. "But for yourselves!"

"And should we succeed, what then?" the tall man asked.

"We shall pillage the estate and take back what is rightfully ours. After that we shall divide the land equally among us, so that we each will be able to provide for ourselves and our families. What we sow, we shall reap. The fruit of our labor will belong not to the lord but to us, to do with as we please."

There was a palpable stirring among the crowd. Justin felt their enthusiasm begin to seep into his own bosom. He had seen the suffering of the peasants and become convinced of the justice of their cause. It seemed that the only way for the peasants to overcome their subjugation was to vanquish its source. Yet, even though he now hated his father more than ever, he was reluctant to take part in a violent rebellion against him. The lord could not be negotiated with, that was certain. Perhaps more peaceful tactics could be used to overthrow him, but Justin, unable to think of any, berated himself again for his lack of cleverness. Then, there was also the matter of Constance. Justin now understood that this would be his final test to gain Adrian's approval and win her hand. If he failed to support Adrian now, he would have no future, at least no future with Constance, which, for Justin, was a fate worse than dying in a war against the very estate he had grown up in.

"Who is with me?" Adrian cried out to the crowd. A few hands went up, then more, and soon nearly all the villagers had their arms up in the air, even the children. Constance looked at Justin exuberantly and raised her hand. Justin immediately followed suit. The nosy mother and the tall man were the only ones who stood firm without moving.

Adrian looked directly at each of them and called out, "Are you with me?"

The tall man did not answer at first, but then grudgingly lifted his hand and said, "Aye, I am with you, though it be against my better judgment."

"And how about you?" Adrian asked the old woman.

The woman gazed around at the others, all of whom were glaring back at her. "I will only follow whomever God appoints as our leader, but if everyone agrees that Adrian is now our leader, then I will go along with their decision."

She slowly raised her hand.

"Indeed, I shall lead you!" Adrian cried.

The crowd gave out a great hurrah, which Adrian permitted to go on for some time before motioning for silence and saying, "Each of you shall pledge absolute loyalty to me as your commander. And my good friend, Edward here, will be my deputy. You shall obey any orders we give you. The success of our endeavor depends on it!"

There was more cheering and shouting. Adrian then told the villagers they should go to the forest again, to collect hardwood for clubs and cut small trees for spears and sharpen them, while he and Edward began to devise a strategy for storming the estate.

§20

Adrian, Constance, and Justin returned to their cottage. Sitting at the table in their wooden chairs, Adrian, taking charge as usual, laid out his plan of attack. While everyone quickly agreed that the assault should be carried out at night to maximize confusion inside the estate, Constance and Justin both knew that the rest of Adrian's scheme was unfeasible. Adrian wanted to come straight up the highway from the south, batter down the main gate, overtake the garrison, and then proceed to the manor house to capture the lord himself. He had not considered that the night watchman would see them coming well in advance, that the deep brook along the wall would give the villagers no access to the estate once drawbridge was up, that the gate was too strong to be pummeled in any case, and that it would be easy for the archers to simply pick the villagers off one by one from scaffolds behind the wall if they tried to wade across the moat. Justin was cautious about stating his misgivings, partially because he did not want to contradict Adrian, but also because he might unwittingly say something that revealed his familiarity with the estate. Constance, however, was less timid.

"Your plan is impracticable," she said. "Come outside and let me show you something."

Adrian and Justin followed Constance to the lane in front of the house, where she picked up a stick and began to draw the layout of the estate in the dirt.

"I have lived there, you know, so I know the premises well. Here is a better way to carry out our campaign."

Constance then suggested that the villagers cross the brook further downstream from the estate, where they would be unseen.

"Yes!" Justin said unthinkingly, remembering the rapids he had passed through in his little boat on his journey to the sea. "There is a shallow spot where it would be easy for us to get across."

Constance looked sideways at Justin with narrowed eyes and then continued, "We can then walk through the woods to the lord's hunting grounds and pound through the gate on the north wall."

Not noticing Constance's warning and forgetting his own need for discretion, Justin corrected her. "Indeed, the north gate could be battered, but it would take too long and the noise would arouse the soldiers, even from a distance. The wall is not so high, however, and the stones are like footholds, so it would be easier to simply climb over it and enter the estate by stealth."

Adrian looked at Justin warily. "Why do you know so much about the estate?"

Justin stammered for a moment and then said, "On my way here to the village, I tramped through the lord's hunting grounds looking for game, so I have seen the wall with my own eyes. I also crossed the brook at the ford I mentioned."

Constance expeditiously cut in. "I agree with Edward. We should remain undetected for as long as possible. After we are inside the walls of the estate, a small detachment of a dozen or so villagers should go immediately to the alley behind the house. Two or three of them can then enter the manor house through the kitchen door, ascend the stairway to the lord's chamber, and take him unawares. A few others can go to the servants' quarters to arouse the servants and solicit their support, while the remainder secures the house of the bailiff."

As she was talking, Constance pointed with her stick to the sketch she had drawn in the dirt, first to the spot where the kitchen door was located along the alley and then to the positions of the lodge for the servants and the stone house of the bailiff. She shooed away Charm when the cat tried to strut across her map.

"And where do the rest of us go?" Adrian asked.

Constance scratched a few more figures in the dirt and then said, "Everyone else will steal across the lawn between the manor house and the orchards to the barracks, where they can take the garrison by surprise."

"Excellent," Adrian said with genuine admiration. "Do you know the floor plan of the house itself and exactly where the lord will be sleeping?"

"Of course," Constance replied. "I have often been to his room to serve him and can explain the route to whoever goes there to capture the lord."

"We shall not capture the lord, but kill him," Adrian said, "lest he cry out and alert the guards before the others reach the barracks."

Justin bristled when he heard Adrian utter these words and became even more distressed when Adrian next said, "I shall lead the charge to the soldiers' barracks, while you, Edward, shall lead the detachment that goes round to the back of the mansion. I should like you personally to conduct the raid inside the house and to have the honor of slaying the lord. You may use the knife I have given you."

Constance immediately interjected, "I think you should send someone else to take care of the lord. Edward would surely be of more use against the soldiers."

"I applaud your plan," Adrian said. "But you must remember that the final decision about how it shall be implemented is mine. If we split into two groups, it is natural for the main body to be led by me, while the other is led by Edward as second-in-command."

Constance said nothing. Justin was about to make a reply of his own but thought better of it. He hated his father to be sure, but to the point of murdering him? On the one hand, Justin felt a tinge of excitement at the thought of plunging his knife into his father's heart but, on the other, recognized it would be more sensible to simply walk away from the whole sordid affair, which is exactly what he would have done had it not been for Constance. Was it really necessary for Justin to kill his father just to be free from him forever? Was there not another way?

It would be fortuitous if one of the other assailants could be enticed to actually commit the deed so that Justin would not have to do it. Or perhaps luck would present some other alternative which Justin could not yet imagine. In any case, the plan to dispatch his father had been Adrian's, not his own. Justin was not sure if he could carry it out, even though his failure to do so might incur Adrian's acrimony and forfeit his chances of marrying Constance.

"We should also wear scarves over our faces to conceal our identities," Constance said, trying to change the subject.

"Whatever for?" Adrian asked. "You sound as if you are uncertain of our victory. Once we kill everyone on the estate, there will be no one left to identify us."

"As a precaution," Constance responded. "If any of the soldiers escape they shall be able to report us to the authorities."

"All right," Adrian said. "Then we shall all wear masks."

"Do you not think it would also be better if we made alliances with peasants in the adjacent areas?" Constance said. "At some point, word of our rebellion will leak out and be spread far and wide. After that, the baron himself will descend on the fief to crush us and restore order."

"There isn't enough time," Adrian replied. "The bailiff and the soldiers will return within a week for what they say we owe the lord, so our first priority is our own revolt. Upon witnessing our success here, peasants elsewhere will be inspired to foment their own uprisings throughout the entire kingdom."

Adrian then looked at Justin, "Well, what do you think of the plan we have contrived?"

"I am sure it will be successful," Justin replied weakly.

§21

Within a few days the villagers had made spears, cudgels, and other improvised weapons for themselves. Adrian called another meeting at the village green to explain the plan (which he, of course, took full credit for) to everyone and to allocate responsibilities. He divided the villagers into two groups, a larger one which he himself would lead to the soldiers' barracks and a smaller band which Justin would take to the alley between the manor house and the servants' quarters. The two groups would rejoin each other in the courtyard in front of the main entrance once their deeds had been carried out.

The peasants under Adrian's command were to spread themselves out evenly along the lower northern wall and be ready to climb over it when he gave the order, while Justin's detachment was assigned a spot on the far end of the same wall, near the fishpond, since this would provide the shortest route of access to the kitchen door of the manor and the servants' quarters.

Adrian asked if there were any volunteers to accompany Justin for the incursion into the mansion.

A hefty but spry woman immediately shot her hand into the air.

"I will go," she said enthusiastically. "It would be my pleasure to have a hand in taking out the lord."

A stout man with a clean-shaven face standing next to her immediately said, "You shall do no such thing. You might be killed yourself."

"And what if I am? Does it really make any difference to you?" the woman replied.

"Of course. I should be lonely without you."

"You only need someone to cook your dinners and wash your clothes."

"Well, indeed. What would I do if you were no longer here to take care of me?"

"I'm sure you can take care of yourself. Or find yourself another wife!"

Adrian broke off the quarrel by saying, "We still need one more volunteer."

No one raised their hand.

"What about you?" Adrian asked, pointing to the tall man, who had previously been hesitant to support the revolt. "Edward can keep an eye on you."

The tall man kicked at a patch of dirt near his feet.

"All right," he said sullenly. "I will go with Edward."

"It's settled then," Adrian said.

Justin thought that the spry woman was the perfect person to requisition for the unpleasant task he had been asked to perform but was apprehensive about having the tall man along on his mission. The final decision, though, was Adrian's, not his.

Following the description of the manor house Constance had given him, Adrian detailed the route to the lord's room to Justin and his contingent. Justin listened attentively even though he, of course, already knew the way. As the three of them were entering the manor house through the kitchen door, the other members of his detail would awaken the servants and apprehend the bailiff.

After Adrian had finished explaining the remaining plans to everyone, Justin took the tall man and spry woman aside and asked them, "Would either of you be willing to actually kill the lord?"

"Not I," said the tall man. "Should we fail, I would be charged with attempted murder."

"How about you?" Justin asked the spry woman.

"I would be most delighted to murder the lord," she said. "But the honor really belongs to you, Edward, as our leader. Besides, Adrian wishes it."

"All right," Justin said, accepting the inevitable. "Then it shall be my responsibility."

§22

That night after dark the villagers assembled silently on the village green. Justin wanted to reach out and embrace Constance before they parted, but Adrian was close by, so he simply waved at her and said, "We shall meet again."

After taking leave of them, Justin met up with the spry woman and the other members of his detachment. He looked around but could not see the tall man among the group.

"Where is the man who is supposed to accompany us into the house?" he asked the spry woman.

"He has fled," the woman replied. "I saw him running away towards the forest this afternoon. He's a coward, I tell you. That's what he is. No matter, though. He'll make a new life for himself as a refugee and we won't see him around these parts anymore."

"We shall need a replacement," Justin said.

"We'll manage to do the job all right," the spry woman said. "It will be easier just the two of us in any case. Adding a third would only make the task more cumbersome."

She patted the knife at her side. "And should the lord avoid your blow, I will be there to back you up."

The moon was full and offered the villagers sufficient light to make their way down the fields, across the shallow rapids of the brook, and into the forest below the estate. Their route took them round to the lord's hunting grounds on the northern side. When the wall finally came into view, Justin noted the irony of him now wanting to cross over unnoticed into the estate whereas before he had wanted to escape from it.

The villagers positioned themselves along the wall, just as they had been instructed, and tied kerchiefs across their faces. Adrian was stationed at the opposite end from Justin, across from the orchard. Once synchronized, Adrian gave the signal for the company to begin climbing the wall, which was passed all the way up the line until it reached Justin and his group. Justin waved his arm high over his head to indicate he had received the message. The peasants then began scrambling up the wall in unison, avoiding the spikes that ran along its crest.

Scarcely had the attackers reached the top, however, when they were showered with a bevy of arrows. One woman took an arrow in the shoulder. Another penetrated a man's eye. The children began screaming and soon there was mayhem on both sides of the wall.

There were no soldiers near the part of the wall Justin had scaled. He quickly surveyed the situation. The garrison was clustered around the north gate, near the cottage of Justin's former teacher. They had apparently been waiting for the villagers to arrive, so they must have known about the attack in advance. But who had tipped them off?

The villagers had the advantage of being stretched out along the wall and not a few had already managed to scuttle over it. Justin could see Adrian's band emerging from the orchard and moving around behind the soldiers, joined by others who had already crossed over the wall from the other side. With forces still coming over the wall in front of them as well, the garrison was hemmed in on all sides.

Readjusting his scarf, Justin decided to go ahead with the original plan. Motioning for the others to follow him, he jumped down from the top of the wall and began making his way toward the back of the mansion. The group could still split up so that some of them could muster the servants, while he and the spry woman looked for his father, who most assuredly would not be in his room, but nonetheless still hiding somewhere within the house.

What Justin encountered when he entered the alley was not at all what he had expected, however. There, standing just outside the kitchen door, was the bailiff, pointing a sword directly at Justin and his approaching band. Behind him stood the butler and the steward, also holding swords. Even more shocking, behind the butler and steward was a sizable group of servants who had also been armed with weapons from the barracks, with the tall man among them!

Justin's group stopped at a short distance from the bailiff's group.

"You shall go no further," the bailiff said firmly. "Lay down your knives and spears, and we shall not attack you."

"And then what would happen to us?" the spry woman asked.

"We shall put you on trial, of course, and let the lord decide your fate."

"Ha!" the woman cried. "And what do you think the outcome of that trial would be?"

"No doubt you will all be hanged for treason."

"We shall fight you then!" the woman said belligerently.

"You are far outnumbered," the bailiff said calmly. "Look at the servants behind us. They are all from the same village as you, but they have pledged their allegiance to us."

He then pointed to the tall man and added, "Including this fellow here, a true patriot, who was brave enough to forewarn us of your plot."

"It is he and the others who are traitors, not us!" the spry woman retorted.

"To the contrary," the bailiff said in his same unruffled manner. "The servants appreciate the comforts we give them and know full well the consequences they will suffer if they join your insurrection."

The bailiff then turned from the woman to Justin and studied his eyes.

"Your mask does not deceive me, sire. I know exactly who you are."

Now it was the spry woman's turn to be surprised.

"Sire!" she exclaimed. "Just who are you addressing as 'sire'?"

"Why, Justin, the man who is standing right here beside you."

"His name is Edward, not Justin," the woman protested. "And he is no sire, I assure you."

"Of course, he is. He is Justin, son of the lord of this estate."

The spry woman gaped at Justin disbelievingly. Justin averted his eyes, unable to look at her.

The woman stood there dumbfounded for a moment, struggling to digest what the bailiff had just told her. The servants standing behind the bailiff were also visibly dismayed. Then the spry woman glared at Justin with rage-filled eyes and said, "And we thought all along that you were on our side, not theirs. Now I can see that you intentionally laid a trap for us and the others."

Before Justin knew what she was doing, the woman had taken her knife out of its sheath and was lunging at him. The bailiff quickly positioned himself between Justin and the woman, turning his sword toward the woman. Unable to check her momentum, the woman charged into it, with no counterthrust whatsoever from the bailiff. The sword sliced through her flesh, piercing her heart. Desperately clutching her chest as blood gurgled out, the woman fell to the ground.

By this time the other villagers had whipped out their knives and begun throwing themselves at the bailiff's retinue, attacking not only the bailiff and his cohorts, but the servants as well.

In a split second Justin realized that the situation was hopeless. He could either stay and fight with the peasants, facing certain death if he did, or he could flee.

There was no time for reflection. Justin turned and ran back up the alley away from the melee.

§23

As he turned the corner of the manor house, Justin saw that conditions along the wall had changed completely. The lord's guards had taken control and were routing the villagers. A few had taken off through the orchards, with a handful of soldiers in hot pursuit, but most were clambering back up over the wall and running into the forest, the soldiers chasing after them through the gate, which had now been opened. Dead bodies were lying beneath the trees, most of them belonging to peasants. Looking back over his shoulder, Justin saw the steward running after him, but being a rotund man, his steps were slow and cumbersome. The steward stopped suddenly and began calling to the soldiers for assistance.

Without looking back, Justin ran past the fishpond, quickly rescaled the wall, and leaped down the other side. He could hear the shouts of the villagers and soldiers in the darkened woods but saw no one. It seemed that the peasants were running back the way they had come, with the soldiers close behind.

Justin decided not to return to the village and risk being caught by one of the soldiers, so he ran along the small stream that flowed from the fishpond deeper into the hunting grounds. After he had gone some distance he came to a gully which had been carved out by the stream. Jumping behind a large boulder he sat panting heavily through his kerchief, which was still tightly wrapped around his face. The shouting had faded and the forest was now silent, giving Justin time to catch his breath and after that to think.

He wondered, first of all, if he had been a coward to leave the peasants to fight alone against the bailiff and his entourage. On the one hand, he regretted not taking a stance and showing them his solidarity. If a cause is truly just, then it must be worth dying for. On the other hand, it seemed utterly reckless to go arms flailing into a battle one knew he could not win. Justin was quite certain that everyone in the band he had led had been either captured or killed. So who had been brave and who foolish?

Perhaps the entire project had been misconceived from the very start and should never have been undertaken. Would Justin actually have killed his father if he'd had the chance? Was the real reason why he joined the villagers because he genuinely supported their aspirations or simply for his own selfish purpose of hoping to impress Adrian, with Constance as his reward? Certainly it was not that Justin deliberately wanted to lead the peasants into an ambush, as the spry woman had supposed, although he could understand why she might have thought so.

With such misgivings teaming through his brain, Justin sprawled out beside the boulder exhausted. How long he lay there, he did not know, but he must have fallen asleep.

He was suddenly awakened by the sound of twigs cracking under heavy footsteps in the distance. Justin was certain it was not an animal from the forest. Light from the morning dawn was beginning to filter through the treetops. Justin pressed himself against the boulder, not daring to look up over the crevice. As he cowered behind the rock, he hoped that whoever it was would turn and go in a different direction. The stomping was coming closer, however, and almost upon him. Then it stopped.

Before Justin knew what was happening, a man had lunged into the gulch, a knife in his hand. Rolling to one side, Justin avoided being stabbed by the blade. He sprang to his feet, but the man wrestled him back to the ground. In the ensuing struggle Justin's mask was torn from his face. And then the scuffle suddenly ceased. Justin looked up at the man and saw that it was Martin.

"My lord," Martin cried. "I did not know it was you!"

Justin lay there heaving but made no reply.

"You must forgive me," Martin continued. "I thought that you were one of the villagers who had invaded the estate."

"Indeed, I was with them," Justin said without pretense.

"With your clothes and mask, you certainly look like one of them. How did you fall in with the peasants?"

Justin did not have energy to fabricate a story, so he simply told Martin the truth.

"After escaping from the estate, I eventually made my way to the village."

"And you were involved with the rebellion last night?"

"Indeed, I was one of the perpetrators."

Martin took a long moment to ponder this revelation.

"Well," he said finally, "Your father will certainly be surprised to learn this."

"He is all right?"

"We secured him in the dungeon, so I'm quite sure he was not harmed."

"Thank goodness," Justin said.

Martin stood up and helped Justin to his feet.

"Your father was greatly displeased at your sudden disappearance," he said. "He did not know the reason, but you caused him a great deal of trouble, you know. You publicly humiliated not only your father, but also Penelope and the neighboring lord. The treaty between the two families has been completely broken."

"I have no interest in what any of them think," Justin replied.

"It is not my business to interfere with affairs on the estate," Martin said. "But it certainly is my duty to return you to the manor house."

"I shall not go with you."

"I know how you must feel. It is not likely that your father will greet you with open arms. He may even punish you. But he would nonetheless welcome your return. You are still his son after all."

"He does not care that I am his son. He knows now that he will not live forever and only wants me as his heir."

"Why do you say such a thing? Your father has always loved and cared for you."

"Loving someone means helping them become what they want to be, not forcing them to be what you think they should be."

Martin placed his hand on Justin's shoulder and then said gently, "Justin, I have known you since you were a little boy. You and I were friends, remember? I let you ride the ponies in the paddock. I taught you how to wield a sword. Please come with me now. You can start over. This is your only chance."

"I have no desire to go back with you to my father."

Martin removed his hand and took a step back.

"Look at me, Justin," he said sternly. "You may either come with me peacefully of your own free will or, if you resist, I shall be obliged to take you by force."

Justin looked hard at Martin. "If those are the only options you give me, then I will go with you peacefully, though certainly not of my own free will."

"I knew you would see it my way," Martin replied.

The two men climbed out of the ravine and began walking side by side back towards the estate. Indeed, Justin recalled all of the happy times he had spent with Martin but could not erase the memories of how Martin had thrown his teacher into the dungeon, come looking for Justin as he hid in the hermit's hut, accompanied the bailiff to the village to threaten the peasants, and, worst of all, leered at Constance and pushed her to the ground when she had confronted him.

Justin slowly reached down for the knife at his side, withdrew it from its sheath, fumbled it in his hand for a brief moment, then, grasping it firmly, with no thought, no pause for decision, plunged it into Martin's ribs.

Martin fell to the ground groaning. Justin twisted his knife as he removed it from Martin's writhing body. Pulling his head up by the hair, he brought the knife close to Martin's neck.

"Have mercy," Martin gasped. "Spare me, master."

In one clean sweep, Justin drew the knife across Martin's throat, slicing almost halfway through it. Blood spurted onto Justin's hands and tunic. Martin's eyes looked up for one brief instant in horror and then closed. Justin kicked Martin just as Martin had kicked Constance in the village, then left him there and began walking back through the forest.

§24

At the brook, Justin washed the blood from his hands and tried, unsuccessfully, to wipe the blood from his clothes as well. The stains were too deep and could not be removed. The stains on his own heart could not be removed so easily either. He had to admit to himself that it felt good—it had actually felt *good*—when the knife cut through Martin's neck. All the pain that Justin himself had suffered, together with the villagers, had suddenly been released and flushed out of him. Moreover, unlike the ambivalence he had felt about killing his father or helping the villagers in their struggle with the bailiff outside the kitchen door, killing Martin had indubitably been the *right* thing to do. With a single stroke, Justin had both avenged Constance and secured his own freedom.

But now that he had his freedom, what was he to do with it? Certainly he could not return to the estate. But it would be just as difficult for him to go back to the village and risk being exposed or captured. He had been discovered not only by the bailiff but also by the servants. Sooner or later word would get back to the village about what had happened and his true identity would be known. Would the villagers regard him as a champion of their cause, who had forsaken his own privileges to ally himself with them, or as a traitor, who was still his father's son and, therefore, their enemy? Would they know that he had truly taken their side by participating in the revolt, or would they suppose, as the spry woman had, that he had purposefully betrayed them?

At some point Martin's body would be found as well, and while there was no evidence linking Justin directly to the crime, the fact that he had been seen by the steward escaping from the estate and running into the forest would surely implicate him. Even worse, Justin was certain that his father had heard from the bailiff by now of his involvement in the revolt and would perhaps learn of the role Justin had played in planning it, as well as of his intention to assassinate him. If Adrian were caught, it was likely that he would confess everything. And certain that he would be executed. Justin was not sure if his father would demand that he face the same fate.

Now there was nothing for Justin to hope for. He had lost both his home and any prospect of living out the rest of his life with Constance in the village. He had nowhere to turn, no one to talk to, and no one to rely on but himself.

§25

After crossing the brook at the rapids, Justin turned left on the far bank and followed the stream once again towards the ocean. He arrived at the marsh where he had hidden his boat so long ago. Following his former footsteps, he then tramped into the forest to see the hermit.

When he arrived at the place where the hermit's hut had been, however, he saw that it had been knocked down. Pieces of wood were strewn around on the ground, grass from the roof had been trampled into the mud, the stones from the fireplace kicked here and there. Moss was already growing on the stones, so Justin knew that the ransacking had occurred some time ago. And the hermit was nowhere to be found.

This also must have been the work of Martin, Justin thought. As Martin had told the hermit, even though this section of the forest was part of the commons, the hermit still needed the lord's permission to live here. Since the hermit did not have the proper authorization, Martin had returned to permanently remove him, destroying the hermit's hut and no doubt killing the hermit as well.

Justin lifted one of the logs that had been pushed over and set it upright in its original position beside what used to be the fireplace. Sitting down on the log, Justin thought, "Now this log is mine. It is mine because I am sitting on it."

And why, he wondered, could not the whole world be the same way? No one owned the air, no one owned the sea, so why should someone own the land? Why should there be a division between the nobles who protected, the clergy who prayed, and everyone else who worked? Each of these functions could be performed equally well by everyone. If the peasants could pray and protect them themselves, then the noblemen and priests could also work. The land should be owned by everyone—or even better, by no one—just the same as the wind and the ocean.

And whose idea had it been to say that servants must be obedient to their masters? If a man is master of himself, he need never be the slave of another. If, as the hermit had said, God is inside each one of us, then the best way to obey God is to obey one's own heart. The goal, it seemed, was not to eliminate power, which is something each person has within themselves, but all forms of domination which allow one person to have power over another.

When Justin looked within himself, however, he still could not find the seed the hermit had spoken of. Or, if there was one, it was buried so deep in his bowels that it remained hidden. He wanted to start over, to erase what had been his life up until that moment in the same way that he had wiped his wax tablet clean after he had written something on it during lessons with his teacher. After that, he would write a new story for himself, and not just for himself, but for everyone, of a world in which each person has everything they need, where people love and respect each other, without rank.

But then a more disquieting thought entered Justin's mind. If the hermit was right and all people have a spark of God inside themselves, then how could Justin justify having killed Martin? If we truly love God, then must we love not only the God we find within ourselves, but also the God that lives in others? Justin had murdered not only Martin, but also the God that dwelled inside him. And if each person is God, then I alone am not God. It is not up to me to decide whether another person should live or die. If I do not like others claiming authority over me, why should I claim authority over them? The ultimate act of oppression is to kill someone, even if it be for a just cause, for it means permanently depriving them of their freedom.

Before, Justin reflected, he had been thinking only of himself, of his own good, not what was good for others as well. He had acted not out of love, but out of fear—fear that Martin would force him to return to the estate, fear that he would be punished by his father, and, most of all, fear that he would lose Constance. Indeed, Martin had his flaws, but then so did

Justin. They were both compelled by a system neither of them had created to do things they might not do otherwise. Martin, as much as Justin, was trying to figure things out for himself but now Justin had deprived him of that opportunity.

Justin turned these ideas round and round in his mind, trying to refute them and to convince himself that he had simply been meting out justice, ensuring that the actions of both sides were balanced and perfectly equal. But in fact Justin had only succeeded in righting one wrong by committing another. Martin had cried out for mercy, but Justin had not given it to him, and surely mercy is better than justice. Ultimately we must do what is good, not what is right.

The more he thought about it, the more bewildered Justin was that at first he had actually taken pleasure in killing Martin. It was as if a great burden had been lifted from his shoulders. But now there were pangs of guilt and self-loathing deep in his stomach that weighed him down and would not go away. In destroying Martin he had also destroyed himself. And what had all this destruction accomplished? Justin had purged himself of his anger, the slate was now blank, but all this meant was that his soul was now empty, the field was barren. The seed inside him, if there were one, would require both rain and sunshine to grow. Or perhaps it would just die altogether.

§26

Justin considered remaining in the forest and living just as the hermit had, but he knew that he had to make amends with Constance. Or at least try to. There was no hope now that they could marry and he knew he would have to leave her, but he at least wanted to see her one last time to say good-bye. He had become a felon, a wanted man, who would either succeed in evading the guards or be captured by them, returned to the estate, castigated for betraying his father, and then duly tried and executed for his role in the insurrection and the murder of Martin.

He could not take refuge in the village since it would be too easy for the authorities to find him there. Besides, even though he had worked and fought beside the villagers, he was certain they would be contemptuous of his duplicity and hardly willing to give him asylum. Justin was afraid mostly of Adrian, who, if still alive, would hold him accountable for his treachery and perhaps even kill him.

Nonetheless, he wanted to see Constance.

He formulated a plan to return to the village by taking a circuitous route through the forest and approaching it via the pastures on the far south side, so that he would not need to walk through the village itself. Then he could creep up on Adrian and Constance's cottage from the rear. If fortune were with him, he would be able to catch Constance outside the house, get her attention, and then sneak away together if only for a few minutes to talk with her.

He arrived at the edge of the village in the late afternoon and waited behind some bushes on the other side of the well near the house, the same house he had helped Adrian rebuild. After some time he finally spotted Constance emerging from the cottage, carrying an empty water pail, with Charm ambling along behind her. As soon as she reached the well, Justin peaked out from behind the shrubs and called to her in a low voice.

"Constance, come here. It's me."

Constance caught her breath when she saw it was Justin and quickly joined him.

"We must not be discovered here," Constance said, picking up the cat and pulling the bottom of her skirt behind the bushes so as not to be seen. "It's much too dangerous."

"I only need a short time," Justin said. "I am so happy to meet you again."

"And me, you. We thought you had been killed inside the estate."

"No, I made it out. But where is Adrian?"

"We do not know. He did not return and we fear the worst."

"During the attack, I was recognized by the bailiff and the steward as well. Everyone on the estate now knows that I had been living at the village."

"Indeed, the bailiff and some of the soldiers came here this morning looking for you. They suspect that you helped Adrian lead the revolt."

"So, the villagers have learned who I am."

"Indeed, the bailiff told them everything. They know that your real name is Justin, not Edward, and that you are the lord's son. That is why you must not be seen here. A handful of the villagers think of you as a hero for taking up arms against your father, but most are accusing you of being an infiltrator, saying that it was you who provoked the attack on the estate and set them up for defeat."

"But that simply isn't true. The whole idea was Adrian's. You and I only helped with the planning."

"I know that, but no one else does. I have not yet had a chance to tell the villagers the full truth about you, but once I do, I'm sure, or at least hoping, they will change their minds."

"There's one more thing," Justin said. "The reason why the bailiff and the soldiers knew about our attack in advance is because they were tipped off by that tall fellow who was supposed to accompany me into the manor house to kill my father."

"Yes, we knew that he had disappeared."

"He had not run away to the forest, as we had thought, but circled back to the estate and told the lord of our plan, so the soldiers were ready for us."

"There is one thing I must tell you quickly, too," Constance said. "Should you be caught by the guards, you will surely be punished. The bailiff told us that the peasants themselves will suffer no penalty for their revolt, only their leaders, and that includes you."

"I supposed as much about myself and Adrian," Justin replied. "But I'm surprised the lord is letting the peasants off so easily."

"Some say that the reason is because the peasants stood up to the master so he is now willing to come to terms with us, while others say it's because the lord knows he cannot impose any heavy retribution on us lest there no longer be anyone left to work for him. It's probably the latter, of course. Your father realized his mistake the last time when the soldiers inadvertently burned down our village."

Justin took Constance by the hand and said, "Constance, there is not much time. I am here to say farewell. I cannot stay here in the village with you nor can I return to the estate. I have nowhere to go. I must find my own way from now on."

"But at least take me with you," Constance said. "If Adrian is in fact dead and does not return, then I have no reason to stay here either. I am free to go with you. And, moreover, I want to."

"I understand how you feel and have thought of asking you to run away with me," Justin said. "But I do not think it is good for you to accompany me, for I am now a hunted man."

"There is blood on your tunic," Constance said, suddenly noticing.

"It is Martin's. I killed him this morning in the forest."

Constance's face contorted into a frown.

"This is certainly serious," she said.

"So, if I am captured and you are with me, they may treat you as a co-conspirator and perhaps also as my accomplice."

"I am willing to suffer such a fate."

"No, Constance. I myself could not endure it. I must take full responsibility for my own deeds. I cannot involve you, as much as I would like to be with you, now and forever."

A tear streamed down from Constance's eye.

"Be strong," Justin said.

"I shall be all right," Constance replied, straightening up. "I am perfectly capable of taking care of myself."

"I have no idea what will happen, but I will certainly meet you again somehow, somewhere, someday."

Justin reached out to embrace her. They held each other and kissed, the cat between his bosom and hers. Then Constance tore herself away and went running back to her cottage.

Justin looked around and seeing no one, returned to the well to refill his flask with water, which he had emptied during the day. Just as he had put the cap back on, he was startled by the voices of two women who suddenly appeared at the foot of the path leading up to the well. It was the nosy old woman and her feisty young daughter.

"It's him!" the young woman exclaimed.

"The double-crosser!" her mother shrieked.

The two immediately turned and went running back to the village, shouting for everyone to hear, "It's Edward! It's Justin! He's back! By the well!"

Justin had only a moment to consider a course of action. If he ran away in any direction, he would surely be caught by the villagers and mauled to death or worse. His fate would be no different if simply gave himself up to them. He then spied the church just up the hill. The only way out, it seemed, was for Justin to run there for sanctuary.

§27

After Justin was safely inside the church, the priest, hearing the commotion, came out of the rectory and stood in front of the church door, watching the approach of the roaring mob. While their spears and clubs had been confiscated, the peasants were otherwise carrying exactly the same farming implements they had taken with them when they attacked the lord's estate. If any of the villagers still supported Justin, they were not among the protestors.

The priest raised his arms and called out to the crowd as they neared the church.

"Why have you come here? And what is the reason for your discontent?"

"We have come for Justin. He has taken sanctuary inside the church!" a man cried back.

The priest remained calm, but said forcefully, "If he has taken sanctuary, then you may not touch him."

"We assure you he is a rogue. Hand him over to us!"

"No," the priest replied unyieldingly. "We shall follow established procedures. You must remain outside the church until I have had a chance to talk to him."

The crowd shouted back angrily but the priest did not move. He then turned to open the door of the church and stepped inside. There he saw Justin, the same Justin he had baptized, hands clasped together in prayer facing the altar. He went to the windows of the church and opened the shutters to let in air and light.

"What is troubling you, my son?" the priest asked Justin in a compassionate tone Justin had not expected.

"Father, I have sinned."

"Would you like to give me your confession?"

"I will confess only to God, not to you, because only God can forgive me."

"Indeed, only God has the power to forgive, but only a priest has the power to hear your confession and absolve you of your sins."

"I need no intermediary."

"You will not be offered sanctuary by the Church unless you partake in the sacrament of reconciliation. Before that, however, you must also surrender any weapons you may have."

Justin took his knife out of its sheath and placed it on the floor before the priest.

"Now please, let me hear your confession," the priest said.

"If I make a confession, would you tell my father?" Justin asked.

"No, I am bound by the seal of confession not to reveal anything that I hear during confession to anyone."

"But you would nonetheless need to report to my father where I am."

"Yes, I must notify the lord of your presence here in any case, since you are still subject to the law of the land."

"What would happen after I confess?"

"You will need to expiate your sins through acts of penance, which I shall determine," the priest answered.

"But you would still turn me over to my father and I would be summoned to his court."

"You will be given a choice: you may either give yourself up to the civil authorities and stand trial or you may surrender all your possessions and any claim to them, be banished from the realm, and never permitted to return, under penalty of excommunication and execution."

Justin doubted his father would adhere to the law as scrupulously as the priest had just laid it out. Surely he would not allow Justin to simply escape into exile, but would have him followed, hunted down, and either killed or returned to the estate to face whatever fate the lord determined.

"Must I make a decision now?" Justin asked.

"No, you may stay here for a maximum of forty days, during which time you should give the matter prayerful thought."

"Then that is what I shall do."

"You must make a full confession first, however, and sincerely repent of your sins. That is the only way we can keep you here. The Church offers refuge only to those who are penitent, not to recalcitrant sinners."

"All right, then. I shall tell you everything."

And so Justin told his story, from the time he had first met Constance in the orchard until the present. The priest interrupted him occasionally with questions. He was particularly interested to know if Justin had had any sexual relations with Constance. Justin said, truthfully, he had not.

When Justin had finished the priest asked him, "Are you contrite for what you have done?"

Justin replied, "I do not feel contrition for having fallen in love with Constance since this is not a sin at all but something pure and holy. I do not feel remorse for having left my father, since I see now that his only desire was to imprison me on the estate rather than to allow me to make my own way in life. Nor do I feel any guilt over abandoning my legal wife, Penelope. Even though I did not state my true sentiments at the time, which is blameworthy, my consent to marry her was not entirely free but given under duress."

"Vows made before God are not so easily undone," the priest said.

"But the marriage was never consummated," Justin said. "I assure you."

"We cannot simply take your word on that," the priest replied. "There would still need to be a full investigation by the tribunal."

"I am only making a confession," Justin said. "How such problems should be dealt with may be considered later, might they not?"

"Indeed, please continue."

"I repent for having helped to plan the revolt and plotting to kill my father. The only reason I did not exterminate him was not for lack of will but for lack of opportunity, and the intention is just as evil as the deed itself, is it not?"

"You are entirely correct on that point," the priest said.

"I am sincerely contrite for having killed Martin," Justin continued. "This is something I will rue the rest of my days. God has given us his commandment, 'Thou shalt not kill,' and I have broken it."

The priest consoled him, "You must remember, however, that there are exceptions to this commandment. There are cases in which killing is permissible if the cause is just, such as in war or when punishing wrongdoers and heretics. Your sin is not that you killed a man, but that you did not have God's approval, as determined by either the civil authorities or the Church."

"The commandment is straightforward and unambiguous," Justin replied.

"It is up to the Church, not you, to interpret the commandments," the priest reprimanded him. "You must submit yourself to the Church and its teachings. Do you submit?"

Justin had no desire to submit to the priest or to the Church, only to God, but to avoid any further controversy he said simply, "Yes, I submit."

"And do you sincerely repent of your sins?"

"I do," Justin replied, feeling that at least this part of his confession was genuine.

"Then I absolve you," the priest said, making the sign of the cross over Justin and pronouncing the trinitarian formula.

Throughout these proceedings the throng outside the church had become progressively noisier and more unruly. Suddenly there was a loud pounding on the church door. The voice of a man bawled out, "What's going on in there? We shall not wait forever, you know. Release Justin to us now!"

"Excuse me for a moment," the priest said to Justin. "I must quiet the peasants and request that one of them go to the estate to apprise your father of what has transpired here."

The priest stood up and began walking towards the door of the church, but before reaching it he turned to Justin and said, "You disappoint me, young man. I had hoped that one day you would become a great spiritual leader."

As soon as the priest opened the door, the mob outside fell silent. Standing just outside the doorway the priest addressed them in a composed but firm voice. He told them that Justin had made a full confession and asked if anyone would volunteer to go to the estate to inform the lord that Justin was at the church. Several hands immediately went up, the priest acknowledged them, and the messengers hastily departed. The remaining villagers, satisfied with this outcome, began to disperse.

But when the priest went back inside the church, he found that Justin was no longer there and that the knife which Justin had laid on the floor was gone, too.

III

The Monastery

After squeezing through the window Justin scrambled up the hill behind the church. He quickly reached the trees just beyond the cut area that circumferenced the rectory and was well out of sight by the time he heard the priest cry out what had happened. He had a good head start but could hear the shouts of the peasants as they began chasing him up the incline.

Rather than continue his ascent to the top, as the villagers might expect, he cut across the side of the hill, saving both time and energy and also putting more distance between himself and his pursuers. He next went back down into the valley and part way up the next foothill, which he also skirted rather than climbed. Soon Justin could no longer hear the voices of the peasants and found himself alone.

After resting for a moment to catch his breath, he began heading northwest, zigzagging through the hills towards the wolds, where the slopes were less steep but higher and still tree-covered. As evening set in, he camped by a stream flowing gently below one of the wolds, gathered some greens for himself from the forest, which he ate raw for his dinner, and then promptly fell asleep on a soft bed of grass beside the stream.

The next morning he arose early and decided to mount the wold he had been sleeping at the foot of. After bushwhacking his way through the heavy foliage, he finally reached the summit, which was shorn of trees, giving him an unimpaired look in all directions.

From there, to Justin's surprise, he could see his father's estate in the distance, which he recognized both by the general lay of the grounds and by the turret which rose from the manor house, the same turret he had climbed every morning, noon, evening, and night as a youth. So, he deduced, the wold he was standing on now must be the same one he used to watch the sun set behind at dusk. The line of sight was no different, although he saw it now from the exact opposite point of view.

Tiny figures were moving here and there from the manor to the servants' quarters, from the barracks to the stables, from the bailiff's stone house to the granary, but they were too far away for Justin to see their faces. The estate looked so isolated, enclosed on all sides by the wall, no longer standing at the center of the world but at its periphery, small and insignificant.

Justin let his eyes follow the brook beside the estate all the way to the sea, to the estuary where he had left his boat, and beyond to the distant skyline. Indeed, as the hermit had said, the sea went on forever. There was no doubt about that.

The marshy coastline was dotted with small sandy beaches, which extended all the way to the fens, its hills sticking out from the mire and the bogs like islands. Up from the swamps were the woodlands. Justin easily identified the forest where he had met the hermit and gone with the peasants to gather food. Scanning with his eyes almost due south he spotted the village itself, with its distinctive cottages. From this vantage point he could see not only the cross of the church, but the spire and roof as well.

Beyond the village were more fields and, beyond these, another village, which he assumed was the village governed over by Penelope's father. He could not see a manor house, but assumed that there must be one nearby, where Penelope and her father undoubtedly were at this very moment. Far, far in the distance there were larger villages, perhaps towns, but he could not distinguish their features.

Looking north Justin saw that his father's hunting grounds did not go on forever but morphed into a higher, more rugged terrain of boulders and shrubs, a forbidding and uninhabitable frontier bordered by precipitous wave-splashed cliffs that fell into the sea.

Finally, gazing behind him to the west, Justin beheld wolds and valleys undulating towards the horizon, with mountains in the distance. This is the direction he would set off in, vowing to walk until he reached those faraway peaks and, after that, to cross over them. Indeed, the world is much wider than he had thought! If we perpetually walk beyond the vistas of what we have already experienced, will we not discover new terrains, each of which gives us a new partial perspective and at the same time a more expansive view, even though we remain forever myopic and incapable of grasping the whole?

§2

As he tripped down the western side of the wold toward the valley, it occurred to Justin that he was starting a new life for himself. He had no plans, no thoughts about what he would do. He was completely free, having time now to explore a world he had never seen before and could not yet fully imagine. He would be like the wind, blowing where it wishes, not knowing where it comes from or wither it goes. There is no destination, just the journey itself. He had become a vagabond—a real one—who could devote himself solely to finding out what it meant to be alive. The good as well as the bad, he would accept it all, whatever he encountered.

And yet, he felt like a butterfly that had finally broken out of its cocoon and spread its wings, only to find that it could not fly. Now that there was no one to tell him what to do, he did not know what to do. Even though Justin could go anywhere, there was nowhere he wanted to go. No place was home. He was a fugitive, marked with the blood of the man he had killed, condemned to wander aimlessly throughout the earth for all eternity, without ever being able to rest, seeking to fill his vacant soul with something, anything, that would bring him peace.

Justin had formally confessed his sins to the priest at the church, yet even though he had been truly sorrowful, it seemed nothing more than an empty ritual to him and brought him no relief. He was still in anguish over everything that had happened. The Church could provide no salves for the wounds of his heart, no direction about what to do next. Had he stayed he would no doubt be expected to pay in full for his misdeeds. It was not so much the punishment he feared, but the process. Was there not a better way of doing it? Why should he submit to the authorities simply because they are the authorities? Can justice be meted out by those who are themselves unjust? The idea of ducking through the window had occurred to him just as soon as the priest had opened the shutters, but he did not decide to act on it until the priest went to the door of the church to quiet the crowd. Had he made the right decision?

Now, he reflected, there was no God in his heart, only the torment of sin, no seed planted inside him, as the hermit had said, but instead an arid desert in which nothing could grow. If he could not find God within himself, he must look for God elsewhere. But where?

When Justin had first embarked on this journey it appeared to him that the wolds lacked any human inhabitants, but he soon discovered otherwise. He spent the first few days rambling up and down the hills, taking in the scenery, delighting in the trees and meadows, water coursing through the ravines, cascading in small waterfalls over the rocks. The vegetation here was different from that of the forest where he had foraged for plants and berries with the hermit and the villagers, but he was still able to find sufficient food to stave off his hunger and had, of course, unlimited supplies of water from the streams. His only problem was that it was starting to become cold, especially at night. He had his tunic and breeches but longed for a well-knit cloak and hood.

Then one day from high atop a wold, he looked down into a deep valley and saw a narrow river running through it, with a dirt road beside the river. Houses were strung out along the road, surrounded by small plots of cultivated land, with pastures on the slopes. The area could more properly be called a settlement than a village since the houses were spaced far apart rather than clustered close together.

Justin descended from the summit, came to the end of the road, and began walking down it. He saw that the cottages were simple but well kept, about the same size as the houses in the village near his father's estate, but much nicer.

After passing several of the dwellings, he encountered a man wearing a black cloak and hood walking up the road towards him, heading in the opposite direction towards the wolds. Justin said hello to the man, who returned his greeting in a straightforward but not uncordial manner. Justin stopped the man and asked to speak with him.

"It is becoming autumn and I am in need of a cloak," Justin said. "Do you know where I might be able to get one?"

"If you are a beggar, we have nothing to give you," the man said. "You can just keep walking down this road or go back to the hills where you came from."

Despite this curt reply, there was no hostility in the man's voice, as there had been the first time Justin met Adrian.

"I am not a beggar," Justin said. "I work and earn my way."

"So, you are a journeyman?"

"Nay, I have no special skills."

"An itinerant laborer then?"

"Indeed, I am willing to do any odd jobs that might need to be done."

"Well, as you can see, we do not have much farmland and the harvest is already in, so there is nothing for you here."

"Then I shall be moving on," Justin said, beginning to walk away.

"If you need a place to stay," the man called after him without seeming to care if Justin heard him or not, "I would suggest the monastery further down the road, about a mile from here, then up the hill. The monks there help the poor and will also accommodate travelers."

"Thank you kindly," Justin said, turning and giving the man a slight bow.

§3

Justin walked down the road until he saw the monastery, just as the man had said, on the lower slope of a wold, with a small dirt track leading up to it. The abbey was surrounded by a wall, not unlike the wall at Justin's father's estate, although lower and unfortified. The gate, when Justin arrived, was wide open. A monk wearing a black habit was standing just outside the gate handing what appeared to be herbs to a pair of older women. A group of children were playing nearby.

"May the Lord heal both your bodies and your souls," the monk said to the women, blessing them with the sign of a cross.

Justin, having never actually met a monk before, had always imagined them to be highly reclusive and serious, their heads always bowed to avoid meeting the eyes of others, and never talking. But the monk here was warm and affable. He smiled when he said goodbye to the women and waved with a laugh at the children as they joined the women, who were probably their grandmothers, and began walking down the path with them back to the main road.

"Hello, good sir," the monk said with a friendly smile as Justin approached the gate. "I do not recall meeting you before, but is there anything I can help you with?"

"I have been crossing the hills," Justin said. "The air is becoming colder and I am in need of a cloak."

"Then I shall get you one!"

"Oh no. I could not accept any gifts from you. I should like to do some work in exchange for it."

"That is not necessary," the monk said. "As our Lord and Savior, Jesus Christ, has told us, if a man asks for a cloak, give him a tunic as well."

"I already have a tunic."

"Indeed, but it seems that yours is quite smudged and ragged. I shall also bring you a new tunic. Please wait here just a moment."

The monk hurried back into the monastery to fetch the clothes.

Justin had forgotten about the stains of Martin's blood on his tunic, but when he examined them, he saw that they were covered with grime from his journey and no longer red but brown, so did not look like blood at all.

The monk returned and handed a russet cloak and a sturdy tunic made of undyed wool to Justin.

"Why, thank you, indeed," Justin said.

"May God be with you," the monk said. "Might I ask where your travels will take you?"

"I really have no goal nor a route to follow."

"Well, if you just came across the wolds, you probably haven't had a good meal in some time. You would certainly be welcome to have some food with us here before continuing on your way."

"I sincerely appreciate your kind offer, but I should not like to trouble you."

"No trouble at all. Please follow me and I will show you to our guest room."

The monk led Justin through the gate to one side of the abbey, where there was a small room with a table and chair.

"Be so kind as to stay in this room until I return. Please do not wander freely around the grounds, lest you disturb the other monks."

Justin waited in the room as he had been told. The monk soon returned with a plate of food and a mug of ale, which he set on the table in front of Justin.

"I shall come again for the dishes when you are finished," the monk said.

The fare was simple but hearty: beans, bread, and a large quantity of boiled cabbage. Justin was especially grateful for the ale, which was weak, but tasty.

When, after an hour or so, the monk returned to collect the plate and mug, Justin thanked him repeatedly and then said, "I am an able-bodied man. I do not wish to rely on charity. Isn't there something I could do to repay you?"

"No repayment is necessary," the monk replied. "But since you seem to have no definite plans, there are always plenty of odd jobs to be done around here if you would like to stay as a helper to us."

"You mean to actually live and work here?"

"If you are willing!"

Justin deliberated for a moment and then said, "Indeed, I should like to be of service."

"Let me ask the prior first, however. If he agrees, then I'm sure we shall find something for you to do."

The monk departed with the dishes, leaving Justin alone in the room. Justin had never expected this opportunity to be offered to him. He had imagined that he would be constantly roaming from place to place, never settling down, and wondered if, indeed, it would be better for him to stay at the monastery or to move on. Then he considered that it was not as if he were taking vows to become a monk. If things did not pan out, he could leave whenever he wished. So, why not stay for a while and give it a try? The mountains he had vowed to explore someday would wait for him.

A short while later the monk returned to the room with a smile on his face.

"The prior accepts you as an assistant," he said. "Your first assignment will be to wash your own dishes and then to help with any other tasks that need to be done."

"I shall be happy to do whatever the prior asks me," Justin replied.

"We cannot pay you any money, of course, but can give you room and board."

"That is entirely satisfactory to me."

"Fine! You may stay as long as you wish, but throughout your residency here, you must follow the rules for laymen associated with our order. Allow me to review them with you."

"Yes, please," Justin replied.

"First and foremost," the monk said, "chastity is presupposed. I hope that I need not say anything more about this matter to you. The only possessions you may keep are those which you have with you now. You may talk only to me and other lay brothers, and only when outdoors or in these rooms, not in the chapel or any other parts of the abbey. Even so, you may not speak to any of the other monks or the abbot, or even the prior himself, unless you are spoken to first. You must maintain silence when you are working, except for occasions, such as emergencies, when it is absolutely necessary for you to say something. You may go only where you are told to go and only when you are told to go there. You may, of course, quit the abbey permanently any time you choose to do so, but as long as you are employed here you may not leave the grounds without permission from the prior. Regular confession and attendance at mass is obligatory, although you need not join the monks for any of our other prayers. The rule of the abbot is absolute. Although you are not a member of this order and will not take a vow of obedience, you will still be expected to obey his every word. As for your daily duties, you will be informed either by the prior directly or through me, since I am his deputy. Are these regulations agreeable to you?"

"I shall have no difficulty following them," Justin said.

"The rules are strict, but they each have a purpose." The monk added, "As I am not yet ordained, I am unable to hear your confession, but I can still serve as your spiritual advisor, should there be anything you wish to consult with me about."

"Indeed, I shall seek your guidance if necessary."

"Then, we should formally introduce ourselves," the monk said genially. "I am Bartholomew."

"And I am Justin."

"I am pleased to make your acquaintance, Justin. Now, let me show you to the kitchen."

§4

Justin adjusted quickly to his new life inside the monastery. Bartholomew had taken Justin to a room of his own located further down the hallway from the guest room he had first visited, in a wing of the abbey separate from where the monks lived. It was virtually the same as the guest room, although it also included a straw-filled pallet on the floor, a razor for shaving, and a basin, which Justin used for washing himself every morning after rising at dawn with the others. He would then begin his tasks for the day, which included sweeping floors, doing laundry, cooking and cleaning, and caring for the grounds outside the buildings. There were other lay brethren who also worked in the monastery and stayed in the same dormitory, but Justin had little contact with them, even at night when they were permitted to visit each other's rooms. They mostly kept to themselves and were not given to conversation, either with Justin or with each other.

The prior was methodical and exacting, but not unkind. His face was devoid of any emotions, whether happiness, sadness, anger, or fear, his manner even-tempered and purposeful. He knew precisely what he was supposed to do and he did it.

Justin was expected to serve meals in the refectory, where the monks ate in silence while listening to readings of scripture, and to clean up afterward. Once when Justin had failed to notice a spot on the table after the noonday meal, the prior pointed it out to him. Justin promptly wiped the surface clean. When the prior told him that he should be more careful the next time, Justin was annoyed that the prior would be upset over such a trifle. Over time, however, Justin came to see the value of being neat and orderly, and the importance of acquiring self-discipline.

One day outside, after the prior had told Justin to sweep the walkway of the cloister, Justin asked him, "Why must I sweep these stones each day when each day the dust returns?"

The prior replied, "When you sweep the path you are sweeping your own soul."

"But why should we think that dust is bad? Can't we just leave it where it is?"

"It is not the dust itself that is bad, but where the dust is that is good or bad."

"Why are some places good and others bad?"

"They aren't," the prior replied. "Such distinctions are no more than dust in our own minds."

"Then why don't we just sweep them away like we do the dirt on the footpath?"

"If there is no place for the dust to collect, there is no need to sweep it away."

Justin had no idea what the prior was talking about, though he certainly had an interesting way of saying it!

While performing his duties around the monastery, Justin saw the abbot occasionally but since the abbot never spoke to him, Justin never spoke to the abbot either. He had expected the abbot to be stern and foreboding, but in fact he was a gentle old man with graying hair and gleaming eyes, who shuffled rather than walked through the corridors on his way to the chapel or other parts of the abbey. The homilies he gave during mass, always held at mid-morning, were much more varied and uplifting than those Justin had heard from the village priest. The abbot spoke not of God's wrath but of his mercy, not of God's vengeance but of his forgiveness. We may choose, he said, either to live in sin and fall to the depths or to live in grace and be raised up to a higher place. There was much that Justin had never heard before: that God is love and love is God, that we are not Jesus' servants but that he is our friend, and that the Holy Spirit lives in each of us and guides us into all truth. Justin's eyes were opened to a completely different understanding of the Christian faith than he had known as a youth.

The chapel itself was a holy place filled with splendor, overwhelming Justin every time he went there, whether to attend mass or to sweep the floor. The icons and altar and stained glass all made him feel as if he were in the presence of God himself. Yet there were also fixtures that were discomfiting. For example: atop the altar in the chancel was a crucifix, showing the face of the suffering Jesus, yet incongruously gilt with gold leaf. Would Jesus have not been more pleased if the money had been given to the poor instead of wasted on such an expensive decoration? Then Justin considered that since, after all, gold exists in this world, why should it not end up in a church giving glory to God instead of in the hands of a profligate merchant?

In addition to mass, the monks followed the liturgical hours of the breviary, praying eight times a day, including once in the middle of the night, with additional periods for reciting psalms, singing hymns, and reading scripture. The monks would spend the remaining hours perusing sacred works in the library, copying texts in the scriptorium, or engaging in other duties of their own, such as tending the vegetable garden, making wine and ale, and baking bread.

The monastery was not entirely isolated from the surrounding community, however. Each day one of the monks was stationed at the gate to give alms to the poor and medicine to the ill, just as Bartholomew had been doing when Justin first met him. The very sick, the elderly, and those near death were taken to the infirmary, where they were cared for by monks specially trained in the healing arts. A few of the monks served as teachers at a school attached to the abbey for young boys who had been sent there by their parents, some of whom, after receiving a basic education, would go on to become novices and then monks themselves.

Justin had noticed that the monks seemed to have a very different demeanor while they were pursuing their vocation inside the abbey and while they met with ordinary people from the outside. When devoting themselves to rites and prayer, they seemed aloof and withdrawn. They would never speak with each other but instead use hand signals to indicate if they needed something. When engaged with people from the village, however, they greeted everyone cheerfully, were outgoing and sociable, good conversationalists, even loquacious. It was a paradox Justin could not fully understand. Who were these monks and what did they hope to accomplish by retreating to a monastery instead of living like everyone else in the world?

§5

During one of his visits to Justin's room, Bartholomew asked him, "Have you ever considered becoming a monk?"

"No, the idea never occurred to me."

"You may have the makings of one. Of course, you are uneducated and ignorant, but we could teach you."

Despite the rather excellent education Justin had received from his teacher at the estate, Justin did not dispute Bartholomew's characterization of him. Instead he said, "I shall give the matter some thought." Then he asked, "Tell me, Bartholomew, why did you become a monk?"

"Because I wish to make myself pure and holy," Bartholomew replied. "In ancient times hermits went to the wilderness to seek refuge from worldly pursuits and lived in seclusion from others to be solely with God. They spent most of their lives there. One of the desert saints even remained atop a pillar for thirty-seven years."

"Thirty-seven years? How did he get food and water?"

"Children from the village brought it to him in a bucket, which he pulled up with a rope."

"What did he do up there all that time?"

"He would pray, stretching out his arms in the form of a cross or prostrating himself from head to feet. Communion with God was his primary occupation, although people would also come to visit him to ask for spiritual advice. They would climb a ladder part way up the pole and he would speak to them from a distance."

"Did he never descend from the tower and return to normal life?"

"No, he died on top of the pillar, far from the cares of this world but close to heaven."

"Why do monks live in monasteries now?"

"Well, a few continue to live alone as anchorites or hermits with the sanction of the Church. Others are itinerant, preaching the gospel and caring for the indigent, even though they themselves are devoted to poverty. They own nothing and beg for food yet belong to established orders recognized by the Church and are, therefore, highly respected. The worst are the mendicants who wander the countryside either alone or in pairs without supervision. Most of them are heretics who substitute their own views for those of the Church. Having no laws to guide them, they do whatever they like, easily falling prey to temptation and becoming slaves to their own desires. As for the monks here, we avoid exposure to such seductions by secluding ourselves in a cloister set apart from the world, where we can live lives that are blameless."

"Indeed, it seems that life in a monastery is purposely designed to prevent its residents from sinning," Justin said.

"You must not forget the secret sins of the heart," Bartholomew replied. "We are all tempted, even if we manage to avoid committing any overt acts of sin."

"Should we not rather live in the world and actively seek out temptations?"

"Whatever are you saying!" Bartholomew exclaimed.

"What I mean is, instead of trying to shield ourselves from temptations, perhaps we should expose ourselves to them in order to strengthen our ability to overcome them."

"Temptations should be avoided, not confronted."

"But does that not make us weaker?" Justin asked. "Does hiding away in a monastery really solve the problem?"

"Even though sinful deeds cannot be easily committed inside these walls, we are still beset by an ample supply of sinful impulses: not *acts* of murder, theft, or fornication, which we have no opportunity to actually commit, but *thoughts* of anger, envy, and lust, which are constantly popping into our minds. Simply wanting to commit such acts is no less evil than actually committing them."

Justin immediately thought of his plan to kill his father, which according to Bartholomew, was still a sin even though Justin had not actually murdered him, and then of his murder of Martin, something he had not planned on doing but had actually done.

"How should we deal with such sinful desires?" Justin asked.

"We should simply put them out of our minds and pretend they do not exist," Bartholomew replied. "That way they will not bother us and we can remain holy."

"But if we ignore our sinful desires, will they not simply bury themselves more deeply inside of ourselves so that we no longer have any control over them?"

"Surely you are not suggesting that we should allow evil thoughts to have free reign and run rampant in our minds."

"Well, would it not be better for us to dig them up and acknowledge them through confession? It seems that only by uprooting our desires and facing them directly is it possible for them to be purged and eliminated. Instead of trying to maintain the illusion of being a good person, perhaps we should openly admit our faults, which then allows us to change ourselves and make improvements."

"What is even better is to put ourselves in situations where we will not be tempted in the first place. Then, if we are tempted, we should simply repress our desires, which requires enormous willpower. Remaining always on the side of God and fighting the devil is what spiritual warfare is all about. It's a constant struggle!"

"Yet if we truly intend to overcome our spiritual weakness, perhaps it would be better not to disengage ourselves from the world or our own failings but to face them head-on?"

"My dear friend," Bartholomew responded. "We are commanded to be in the world but not of it. The two-fold mission of our order is to pray and to work. We pray for ourselves, for each other, and for all of God's creation. We work both to provide for ourselves and to be of service to others. So we are both inward directed and outward directed at the same time. We are like the ancient Christian communities which held everything in common among themselves and looked after the poor and afflicted."

"Indeed, the people who live in the area surrounding this monastery seem to be much less poor than those in other places I have visited. Is the lord who governs these parts a generous person?"

"The land here is not administered by a lord but by the Church and is looked over by our own abbot."

"The Church controls everything?" Justin asked.

"Absolutely. We administer not only the abbey but all the fields and lands around it."

"So the peasants must cultivate crops for the monastery and pay rent on the land they use for themselves?"

"Yes, they work two days a week for us and also pay a tithe, in addition to the fees they pay for baptisms, weddings, and funerals, of course. But we treat them fairly, which is no doubt why they are better off than those living in most other villages."

"They do not complain?"

"Of course not," Bartholomew said. "They are grateful for the merit they gain by serving God and do it joyfully for their own salvation."

"Do the monks also work in the fields?"

"In the past it was common, but nowadays we devote ourselves to other labors. The lay brethren who stay here also help the peasants, however. Indeed, it will soon be time to plant the winter wheat and rye, and we shall ask for your help as well."

Surely enough, in due time Justin found himself side by side with the peasants plowing the fields, sowing seed, and harrowing the ground. Justin did not mind the labor itself. But he now knew that the situation here, though less onerous, was barely distinguishable from the circumstances on his father's fief.

When the planting was finished, Justin returned to his daily routine at the monastery. His life with the monks was completely different from the life he had had on the estate. There, he was the one who was served; here, he was the one who served. His life was not at all displeasing to him, however, even though the prior was sometimes severe and demanding. Justin never felt as if he were a prisoner, as he had within the walls of his father's estate. It was important to know that he was free to walk through the gate of the abbey and leave it whenever he pleased.

He considered, though, that even if he returned to the world outside, there was nothing there for him to do, or at least nothing that he really wanted to do, except perhaps to see Constance again, whom he thought of often. But he knew this was impossible. The real walls he could not escape from were the ones he had built around himself. Life inside the citadel of his own soul was hollow and devoid of significance.

§6

One day in winter, long after the year's planting and harvesting had been finished, Justin was scrubbing the floor in the library. He saw an open codex on the reading desk and went over to have a better look. The book was written in Greek, which Justin, having learned from his teacher at the estate, had no difficulty comprehending. His eyes fell on a line, which he read aloud: "ἐγὼ καὶ ὁ πατὴρ ἕν ἐσμεν."

Just then Bartholomew appeared in the doorway of the library, with an astonished look on his face. He said nothing but motioned for Justin to resume scrubbing, which Justin promptly did.

That evening Bartholomew visited Justin's room.

"I was very surprised to hear you reading today," he said.

"My apologies for not concentrating on my work," Justin responded meekly.

"Did you understand the meaning of what you were reading?"

"Yes, I did," Justin replied.

"Please translate the passage for me."

"'I and the Father are one.'"

Bartholomew looked at Justin intently.

"I did not know that you are educated," he said. "I had always assumed that you were an illiterate peasant."

Before Justin had been content to let Bartholomew think whatever he wanted about him, but now he felt exposed and did not know how to reply.

"Where did you receive your education?" Bartholomew asked.

Justin dithered for a moment. He did not want to reveal too much and needed to be very careful about how he answered the question. It was better to be as evasive as possible.

"Why, from my teacher, of course."

"And your teacher, who was he?"

"He was a scholar who taught me when I was a youth."

"And where did he teach you?"

This was the question Justin had hoped Bartholomew would not ask him, but now that he had, Justin could think of no other way to answer than to tell the truth.

"On my father's estate," he said.

"So you are in fact a member of the nobility?"

Justin was by now quite nervous. "Yes, I am."

"Then I assume you are not his first son and, therefore, not heir to his estate, so he sent you out to try your fortune elsewhere."

"Yes, that's it," Justin said. It was a lie, of course, but Justin was relieved that he had been tossed a way to squiggle out of his predicament.

"Do you read Latin as well as Greek?" Bartholomew asked.

"I do."

"And what other subjects have you studied?"

"All the usual liberal arts."

"Grammar, rhetoric, and logic?"

Justin nodded his head.

"Arithmetic, geometry, astronomy, and music?"

Justin nodded his head again.

Bartholomew looked at Justin in amazement. "Why, I wonder, would a person with such a thorough education become a wayfarer? You could have gone on to study law, medicine, or even theology. Was your father unwilling to support you?"

"He had fallen on hard times and had nothing to give me," Justin replied quickly.

"Do you know what book you were reading in the library this afternoon?"

"I am sorry, but I have no idea."

"It was the gospel, in the original Greek."

"I have never read the Bible before."

"Was your teacher opposed to religion?"

"Oh no, not at all. But he was not authorized to explain scripture to me. He was more inclined towards science and felt he lacked the qualifications to teach me anything about theology."

Justin knew this was another lie, since the real reason why his teacher had not introduced him to scripture was because his father had forbidden it.

"You have not received any religious education from your priest?"

"No, I only attended mass and listened to his sermons."

"Oh my," Bartholomew said. "This changes everything."

"What do you mean?" Justin asked.

"If you have the propensity and willingness to learn more about the Bible and the Christian faith, then I should be happy to teach you! Remember, I am also your spiritual advisor."

Again Justin did not know how to reply.

"Well, what do you say?" Bartholomew asked.

Justin hesitated for a moment, then said, "If you would be gracious enough to offer lessons to me, I should certainly not refuse them."

"All right then," Bartholomew said jubilantly. "We shall begin tomorrow. You will still need to perform your daily duties, of course, but I shall come here in the evenings to teach you."

§7

Before confession the following day, Justin pondered whether he should disclose to the confessor the lies he had told Bartholomew. Were the lies mortal sins, which would imperil his soul if did not tell the priest, or merely venial sins that he might be able to get away with without confessing? They weren't quite white lies, of course, but it certainly didn't seem as if they would harm anyone, so perhaps they were not so serious after all.

In his previous confessions, Justin had often been at a loss for what to say. He had already confessed his more grievous sins to the priest in the village and did not need to repeat them. The confessions he could and did make to the priest in the monastery were about the spots from the table he had failed to wipe, the dust in the corner he had failed to remove, the leaves he had failed to rake from the ground, and the occasional resentment he felt over the prior's strictness. His confessor would admonish him for his lack of diligence and assign him the penance of washing the bowls twice after dinner even though they were already clean or something similarly trifling.

Yet the shortcomings he confessed seemed petty in comparison with the things that really troubled him. What he really wanted to talk to the confessor about was the vacuity he felt inside himself. Technically, of course, this was not a sin but merely a state of mind which Justin had no control over. Nonetheless, he could not find God either inside or outside his own heart. And, Justin reflected, if one cannot find God in a monastery, then where on earth should one look for him?

The immediate problem, however, was that making a full confession of the lies Justin had told Bartholomew would arouse more suspicion about himself, which he wanted to avoid at all cost. It wouldn't do to simply say in a general sort of way that he had lied. The confessor would want to know what the lies had been about, and there was no way to answer that question without unraveling the whole tale of his past. He wondered again if confession was something that could only be done through a priest or if he could do it himself directly with God, or perhaps even only within his own heart. Weren't there some things that persons should be able to keep to themselves without others knowing about them, especially when the matter in question did not seem to be any of their business? Not everything private needs to be made public.

Justin decided that while it may be all right to deceive others, at least in some situations, and perhaps even to deceive God if he could get away with it, he would never, ever deceive himself, although this, too, might be difficult, he supposed.

He did not tell his confessor about lying to Bartholomew.

§8

That evening Bartholomew came to Justin's room with an extra chair to commence his training.

"Are you ready to begin your lessons?" Bartholomew asked with a smile.

Justin nodded his head expectantly.

"Good!" Bartholomew said. "The very first thing you must know is that fear of the Lord is the beginning of wisdom."

Bartholomew was not one to waste time on pleasantries!

Justin hesitated a moment and then said, "Surely God is to be loved, not feared?" He was careful to raise his voice at the end to make it sound like a question rather than an objection.

"Indeed, we must love God with all our heart, soul, mind, and strength, but fearing him comes first. For God is everything and you are nothing. God created the heavens and the earth, and you are one of God's creatures. While God is all-knowing, all-good, and all-powerful, we, as mere creatures, have absolutely no knowledge, no goodness, no power of our own."

"Indeed, I often feel a complete lack of those things within myself," Justin replied.

Bartholomew, seemingly ignoring Justin's remark, continued, "God is pure and holy but we have been corrupted by the fall of Adam and are stained with original sin. I was born in iniquity and in sin did my mother conceive me. We are by nature the children of wrath and the anger of God abides on us. We are all ugly, rotten sinners who deserve damnation."

"Are not some people good?" Justin asked.

"No, for all have sinned and fallen short of the glory of God. An angry God holds us in his hand over a pit of fire and brimstone. We dangle by a thread, which God may sever at any moment. There is nothing that keeps the wicked out of hell but the mere pleasure of God. He brandishes a sword of divine justice over our heads. It is only God's arbitrary mercy and will that holds him back. The devil is waiting, hell is gaping for our souls, the flames gather and flash all around, ready to swallow us up!"

Throughout this soliloquy, Bartholomew's voice rose steadily until it reached a near-deafening volume.

Terrified, Justin could only cry out, "Please tell me, Bartholomew. What must we do to be saved?"

"There is nothing we can do," Bartholomew replied in a lower, more somber voice. "Our souls are black with sin and can only be made white again through the grace of God. Salvation comes from God alone, not through our own works, lest any man should boast. It is not something we earn through our own actions, but something that God bestows upon us. As humans we are weak and helpless. Only God has the power to save us. We have absolutely no power of our own. Power comes not from within us but from outside ourselves, from an almighty God who has sent his son, Jesus, to rescue us from the depths of hell and to lift us up to dwell with him in heaven. The wages of sin is death, but the gift of God is eternal life through Jesus Christ our Lord!"

Bartholomew's voice had once again become quite agitated.

"If there is nothing we can do," Justin asked, somewhat confused, "then how might we receive this gift?"

"We can only prostrate ourselves before God, our King, submit to his righteousness, and plead for his mercy and forgiveness."

"So there is something we can do!" Justin exclaimed. "We can choose to accept or reject God's salvation!"

"Nay," Bartholomew thundered. "Because we humans are totally depraved, our wills are corrupted to the point that we are not even able to accept God's grace on our own. There is no such thing as 'free will.' The choice is not ours, but God's. God either has mercy on us or he hardens the hearts of those whom he chooses. It is not we who choose God but God who chooses us. God knows everything, so he also knows in advance who will be saved and who will be damned. It is already predestined."

Justin nodded his head but was dismayed by this answer. Having never experienced God's grace, he was apparently not among the chosen. Perhaps he was even among the damned.

"Then I must merely accept my fate," Justin said.

"No," Bartholomew replied, his voice now calm and encouraging. "You must still have faith, for by God's grace alone are we saved through faith."

"But I have no faith," Justin said. "What shall I do?"

Bartholomew looked at Justin sympathetically and said, "If you confess with your mouth that Jesus is Lord and believe in your heart that God has raised him from the dead, then you shall be saved."

"Those are the only conditions?"

"Yes. Whosoever shall call upon the name of the Lord will be saved."

"But how might I call out to a God whom I do not know?"

"Indeed, how are we to believe in him of whom we have not heard? How shall we hear without a preacher? Faith comes by listening to the Word of God. And it is the Church, my friend, which proclaims that Word. How beautiful are the feet of them that preach the gospel of peace and bring glad tidings of good things!"

"So faith can be transferred from one person to another simply by preaching and hearing the Word."

"Not just by *hearing* the Word, but also *believing* it."

Justin was confounded by everything Bartholomew had told him and did not know how to respond.

Finally Bartholomew broke the awkward silence by saying, "Justin, there is no point in me teaching you the doctrines of the Church unless I am sure that you are saved and willing to accept the Church's teachings unconditionally. Will you not pray to God and ask for his salvation?"

"I do not know which words I should use."

"Then just repeat after me: I beg you, God, to forgive my sins. I throw myself entirely on your mercy and agree to fully accept the teachings of your holy Church."

Justin repeated the words but felt nothing. He genuinely tried to believe what he was saying, but the words were not his own. Somehow they seemed insincere and mechanical.

Bartholomew, however, was pleased with Justin's profession. He patted Justin on the shoulder and said joyously, "Now I can welcome you into the fold, for you are truly one of us!"

§9

The very next evening Bartholomew returned to Justin's room and, again with no greeting, began reciting the Ten Commandments to him. When he reached the fifth commandment, "Thou shalt not kill," Justin instantly shuddered.

After finishing the tenth commandment about not coveting thy neighbor's house or slaves or animals or anything that is thy neighbor's, Bartholomew said, "These are the rules God has given us. We must follow them to the letter, exactly as they have been written. They are written by the finger of God himself and set in stone. To violate any one of them is to commit a mortal sin."

"Are there no exceptions?" Justin asked, remembering what the village priest had told him about war and punishing heretics being permissible reasons for killing.

"Of course, there are exceptions. But only if the Church says so. For example, to murder someone violates the fifth commandment, but to execute the murderer is entirely justified."

Justin sat squarely on his chair, trying very hard to make his body motionless.

"Have you broken any of these commandments, Justin?" Bartholomew asked.

"No, I have never broken any of the commandments," Justin said firmly, knowing it was yet another lie.

"Good," Bartholomew said. "If you ever do break one of the commandments, however, you must immediately confess your sin to a priest and receive absolution."

Justin was weary of being constantly being put in a position where it was necessary for him to avoid telling the truth. It did not seem necessary for him to confess his sins once again to Bartholomew since Justin had already received absolution from the village priest. The problem now, of course, was that he had told yet another lie and, thus, apparently broken the eighth commandment about not bearing false witness. Justin immediately decided, however, not to tell his confessor about this lie either.

Trying to shift attention away from his nervousness while appearing interested in what Bartholomew was teaching him, Justin asked, "Do the commandments come from God or from us? Perhaps it is we who conclude killing is wrong, for example, then we say that the commandment comes from God as a way to force everyone to follow it."

"You are confused, Justin," Bartholomew replied, with a touch of irritability in his voice. "This commandment and all the others were given by God to Moses, and they still apply today."

"Well, I suppose it doesn't matter where the commandments come from, they're still good commandments."

"God has not given us his commandments because they are good," Bartholomew said staunchly. "They are good because God has given them to us."

Justin was relieved when Bartholomew moved from the commandments to a recitation of the creed.

"Have you heard this before?" he asked Justin.

"Of course, I have said it many times myself. But I never understood what it means."

"Then let me explain it to you. The creed is divided into three parts, one for the Father, one for the Son, and one for the Holy Spirit, because they are a trinity, one God in three persons. God the Father is the maker of heaven and earth, of all things visible and invisible. What this means is that God and the world he created are different. God lives in heaven and we live on earth."

"But I have heard," Justin said, recalling what the old hermit had told him, "that God is nature and nature is God, and that we, too, each have a spark of the divine within us."

"No, my friend," Bartholomew replied. "This is an abominable heresy. Neither the earth nor we humans can ever be God. God and his creation are two completely separate and distinct things. The natural and the supernatural must be clearly distinguished. God is wholly transcendent to the world, although he acts within it through signs, wonders, and diverse miracles as he wills."

"So there is a gap between us and God."

"Indeed, an unfathomable chasm, which we ourselves cannot bridge on our own. But fortunately God has become one of us in the person of our Lord and Savior Jesus Christ, who is our mediator. This is the second part of the creed. Jesus intercedes between God and us. He and he alone is the connection between us and God."

"We have no direct connection to God ourselves?"

"No, for as the creed states, Jesus is the only begotten Son of God, of one essence with the Father. He is not a created being like the rest of us but instead, for our salvation, came down from heaven and was made flesh and dwelt among us. Whereas we are merely human and have nothing of the divine in us, Jesus Christ was God incarnate, of two natures, both fully God and fully human. He was crucified on a cross and buried, but rose again on the third day, and ascended back into heaven, where he now sits at the right hand of God. He will come again to judge the living and the dead. Those of us who are saved may look forward to the life of the world to come, when we shall be reunited with God and live in his Kingdom forever."

"I have always thought that after the righteous die their souls leave their bodies and go immediately to heaven."

"This is another detestable heresy that was imported serendipitously into the Church from the pagan Greeks and can be found nowhere in either the Bible or the creed. True Christians do not believe in the immortality of the soul but in the resurrection of the dead. After death our souls do not ascend to heaven; instead, at the end of time heaven descends to earth. We shall be given new imperishable bodies and live eternally with God in a new heaven and a new earth!"

"So the Kingdom of God is something that will be established in the future?"

"Yes, but until then the Holy Spirit is with us. As the creed declares, the third person of the Trinity is the Lord and Giver of Life, who proceeds from the Father and the Son, and who together with the Father and the Son is worshipped and glorified. This same Spirit spoke through Moses and the prophets under the old covenant between God and the ancient Hebrews. After Jesus instituted a new covenant with us and ascended into heaven, the Holy Spirit visited the apostles and established his Church, with an unbroken succession of bishops since then, which continues to be the sole source of authority for religious matters. To become a Christian we must be baptized for the remission of our sins and confirm our allegiance to the Church's teachings. Outside the Church there is no salvation. Whoever believes and is baptized shall be saved; those have not accepted Jesus as their personal savior will be cast into hell. We are either with Christ or against him!"

"What of those who have never heard of Jesus? Are they also to be damned?"

"Indeed, there is salvation in no one else, for there is no other name by which we might be saved. As the creed clearly expounds, the Holy Spirit proceeds not from the Father alone to everyone but through the Father *and* the Son, and so is available only to those who have heard of and believe in Jesus."

"Could Jesus not have found a way to spread his message to the entire world instead of to such a small number of people in such a faraway land such a long time ago?"

"That is precisely why he has instructed us to make disciples of all nations, baptizing them in the name of the Father, Son, and Holy Spirit, and teaching them to obey all that God has commanded."

Justin was not entirely satisfied with this answer. Though clouds may occasionally block its light, the sun shines equally on everyone. Why not God? If God is truly one, he thought, is he not the same God for the whole of humanity? Was he merely the tribal God of those whom he had made a covenant with and called his chosen people, or the God of every nation and race? Why would Christ's salvation be offered only to those who were fortunate enough to have had the gospel preached to them? And if the Church is truly catholic, as the creed plainly says, then why does the Holy Spirit not manifest itself at all times and in all places and to all people, regardless of where and when they live? In short, how was it possible for a supposedly universal God, even one in three persons, to be bound to particular geographical areas and particular moments of history? It didn't seem fair!

Justin did not ask these questions openly, but simply listened deferentially as Bartholomew continued his exposition of the creed, detailing a few technical points, which Justin neither fully understood nor was particularly interested in. It seemed quibbling, he thought, to argue over matters such as whether Jesus was the *same* substance as the Father or merely *similar*.

When he had finished Bartholomew asked Justin, "Do you understand the creed now?"

"Indeed, your explanation was very easy to follow," Justin replied. "Was the creed given to us by God like the Ten Commandments?"

"No, it was written several centuries after Jesus lived, by bishops who were called upon by the Roman emperor to distinguish true Christian faith from heresy."

"So it is merely a human creation?" Justin asked.

Bartholomew chastised him, "Do not say such a thing. The creed is not a matter of opinion, but the proclamation of our faith and the foundation for all that we believe!"

"It is, then, a statement of faith, not a statement of fact."

"It is both!" Bartholomew cried. "Not one word of it is false in any way and you must believe it down to the last iota. To avoid heresy, we must follow the teachings of the Church just as they have been handed to us, with no deviation."

"My intention was not to offend you," Justin said. "But as you know I am ignorant about such matters and know not what to believe."

"If you trust that what I am teaching you is true, you shall not be led astray," Bartholomew replied.

"Certainly I am no expert in religion so I will believe whatever you say."

"Just remember that everything I am telling you comes not from me but from the Church. If you disagree with me, you disagree with God."

"I trust you, " Justin said.

Bartholomew stood up, walked across the room, and embraced Justin warmly.

§10

Justin did not entirely trust Bartholomew, however. He understood his own naivety better by now and knew how impressionable and credulous he could be. The flood of new ideas Bartholomew was exposing him to was overwhelming. Rather than drown in them, Justin simply wanted more time to get used to the water and learn how to swim on his own.

For the next few weeks Bartholomew came to Justin's room every evening carrying a book with him written in Latin by one of the Church Fathers, which Bartholomew said was the "catechism." The title, when translated into English, was *Instructing the Unlearned,* which Justin found amusing although not entirely inappropriate for someone in his situation.

Bartholomew's temperament was completely different from the abbot's. Whereas the abbot always spoke in his homilies about the experience of God, for Bartholomew it was all about doctrines and injunctions. Bartholomew was nonetheless a gracious teacher. He did not hesitate to amplify copiously on the texts they were studying and patiently corrected Justin's frequent misunderstandings and misinterpretations of the catechism, reminding him constantly of the danger of trying to understand religious matters in any way that was contrary to the Church's teachings, lest Justin fall into error and become a heretic. Although it seemed that Bartholomew often conflated his personal opinions with God's own truth and could not tell the difference between the two, Justin replied that he would dutifully adhere to all of the precepts Bartholomew was imparting to him.

The basics were clear enough, although Justin sometimes had difficulty making sense of them. Not having studied such matters before, he came to what he was learning with no prior understanding and no preconceptions. He felt free to form his own impressions, even when these differed from what Bartholomew was teaching him. To avoid confrontation, however, Justin never shared his reservations with Bartholomew, although there was much that he found confusing. Some of the Church's teachings seemed contrary to common decency, at times even positively barbaric!

For example: Mary, the mother of Jesus, a virgin betrothed to Joseph, was impregnated by the Holy Spirit. Was this not adultery? If the philandering Zeus could be denounced for his violations of sexual propriety, why not God?

And if Jesus was the bastard son of God and Mary, was he not also an avatar or demigod, just like all the figures in Greek mythology who had one divine and one human parent?

The Church teaches that Jesus died on the cross for our sins. But why would God require the slaughter of his own son in propitiation for iniquity? Was not human sacrifice a bygone pagan practice?

We are told that we must be washed in the blood of the lamb, since without the shedding of blood there is no remission of sins. Did not the ancient heathens practice the gruesome rite of cleansing penitents in the blood of a slain bull?

In baptism we are buried with Christ unto death and then resurrected so that we may walk in the newness of life. But is this not a form of necromancy, in which the initiate is first drowned and then raised from the dead?

In holy communion the bread and wine are transmuted into the body and blood of Christ. Yet is it not cannibalism to feed on a person's flesh and vampirism to drink another's blood, having no life of one's own without it?

In short, Justin wondered, if the Church claims to teach morality, why do so many of its beliefs seem to flout accepted ethical standards? Ordinarily humans are not allowed to break such taboos. Yet religion regards indulging in symbolic acts of transgression as perfectly acceptable. And no one ever questions them.

§11

The main difficulty Justin had, however, was that all he was learning from Bartholomew were dogmas about God and rituals for worshipping him. What he had not learned, and desperately wanted to find out, was how to know God, not simply as an article of faith but as a living reality. There seemed to be an enormous difference between holding certain beliefs about God and participating in religious ceremonies, on the one hand, and actually knowing God and experiencing the divine in one's own life, on the other—in short, how to be genuinely spiritual rather than merely religious. Justin wished that it were the abbot rather than Bartholomew who was instructing him.

When his study of the catechism was finished, Justin decided that it was time for him to begin asking Bartholomew some of the questions he really wanted to find answers for. He thought he'd better start innocuously, though, lest he annoy Bartholomew. So one evening after Bartholomew had come to Justin's room and had seated himself on the floor, Justin asked him point blank, "How might God be known?"

Justin thought it was an easy question but, much to his surprise, Bartholomew was immediately perturbed.

"That's exactly what I have been trying to teach you for the past few weeks!" Bartholomew exclaimed. "Have you not been paying attention?"

"Well, I have certainly listened to every word you said," Justin replied. "But if, as you say, God is completely separate from the world we know, then it would seem that we cannot know him."

"Indeed, we can know nothing about God unless he chooses to reveal himself to us."

"And how does God reveal himself?"

Justin hoped this was the kind of question Bartholomew would like to answer. He was right.

"Through the Bible," Bartholomew said, his manner quickly changing from testiness to enthusiasm. "We can find God's messages to us in the Old Testament, which contains the Law, the Prophets, and Wisdom literature, as well as the New Testament, which tells us about the acts and teachings of Jesus in the gospels and includes other writings by the apostles, mostly their letters to the early Christians."

"In other words, God communicates with us through a book, something like an instruction manual."

"Precisely. All scripture is inspired by God and is profitable for teaching, for reproof, for correction, and for training in righteousness. God speaks to us through the Bible. We in turn speak to God through prayer, addressing him as 'Our Father Who Art in Heaven' because, as I mentioned before, God and humans are completely separate and apart from each other. We're here and he's there. So it's a two-way conversation between two distinct persons, just as you and I are talking with each other right now."

As was often the case, Bartholomew's answers only raised more questions for Justin. While trying to hide his frustration, he plucked up the courage to ask, "If it is truly a two-way conversation, why can't we speak and listen to God directly? Did God only reveal himself to people who lived in the past? Would it not be possible for God to continuously divulge new truths to us in the present and the future as well?"

"With God all things are possible," Bartholomew answered. "But that's not the way it works. The revelation God gave to the ancient writers of scripture is the only one there is."

"The Holy Spirit no longer reveals himself to humans personally?"

"Anyone who claims at this point in time and history to have a special revelation from the Holy Spirit is a false prophet!" Bartholomew said emphatically. "The only true prophets are those who spoke through the scriptures. There can be no new revelations."

"So God only speaks to us through people who lived thousands of years ago?"

"Exactly. And we must believe their testimony. The Bible is the Word of God and God's Word is final. It cannot be changed or challenged. The scriptures are both infallible and inerrant. They contain no errors whatsoever. That is why we must follow them to the letter. It's the only way we can be sure that we are understanding God correctly and doing exactly what he wants us to do."

"Would it not be possible for the Holy Spirit to guide us in ways that are contrary to scripture?"

"Of course not!" Bartholomew said, trying to retain his composure. "For without the Bible how would you know whether the voice you hear is God's or the devil's?"

"Could we not see whether or not the voice leads us to deeds of righteousness and charity, and discern good from evil by looking at the fruits that are produced by our actions?"

"Yet how would you be able to distinguish good from evil conduct apart from a knowledge of scripture?" Bartholomew asked.

"Perhaps wisdom is more important than knowledge. And is wisdom not pure, peaceable, gentle, open to reason, full of mercy, impartial, and without hypocrisy?"

"All that you are saying is well and good, but there can be no wisdom unless we first have knowledge."

"So, we should not follow the Holy Spirit, but the Bible after all," Justin said, not as a question but as a conclusion.

"Assuredly. For the Spirit is beyond our ability to fully comprehend, but the Bible can be understood by anyone, even though there are always

those with itching ears who turn from the truth and follow their own incli-
nations, who base their faith on the shifting sands of myth rather than on
the solid rock of the gospel. That is why we need the Church to interpret the
scriptures for us."

"But how can we believe that the Bible is true if we have never seen or
experienced any of these things for ourselves?"

"God is to be worshipped through faith, hope, and love, as the catechism states!" Bartholomew said, obviously ruffled. "Faith is the evidence
of things not seen. We have hope in that which we have not yet seen. And
we love a God whom we cannot see. We look not at the things which are
seen, but at the things which are unseen, for the things which are seen are
temporal, while the things which are unseen are eternal."

Justin, aware that Bartholomew was becoming increasingly peeved
with his questions, said as politely as he could, "It all seems rather implau-
sible to me. How can we believe in a God whom we are unable to see? And
why do we need to rely on what others tell us instead of trusting our own
experience?"

"Precisely because we ourselves have not been witnesses to God's acts,"
Bartholomew said, making a mighty effort to control his frustration. "We
would not know of Christ's resurrection from the dead, for example, unless
the apostles had seen him afterward and written down what they saw."

"How can we know that Jesus really rose from the grave? It seems so
incredible."

Bartholomew was now openly incensed.

"Because the Bible tells us so!" he cried. "You must have absolutely no
doubt about what you read in the scriptures. As Jesus said, blessed are those
who believe but have not seen."

"But I have not yet read the scriptures," Justin countered. "So I have no
knowledge of such things and, therefore, no knowledge of God."

Bartholomew was instantly contrite.

"Indeed," he said. "I apologize for becoming angry. You are still a baby
in the faith. I should be giving you milk to drink, not solid food which you
are not yet able to digest."

"I apologize to you, as well," Justin said, "for asking so many stupid
questions."

"No, no, it is entirely my fault," Bartholomew replied. "But we shall
remedy the situation! Even though you are not a monk, or even a novice, I
will ask the abbot for a special dispensation so that you may be permitted to
read the Bible, as well as the other books, which are in the library."

"I should like that very much."

"You must still do your regular work, of course, but now that we have finished your catechetical instruction, you will have your evenings free. The monks are usually at prayer during that time, so the room will not be occupied."

As he stood up to leave, Bartholomew added, "I shall accompany you. Laymen must never be left alone in the library, especially when they are reading scripture."

§12

The very next day Justin went with Bartholomew to the library. There was a huge codex on the reading stand. Bartholomew explained that the book was a portion of the Bible that had been made by the monks in the scriptorium, a large room with writing tables and chairs which adjoined the library. Vellum, a parchment made from the skin of a calf, was cut into sheets of the appropriate size and ruled with lines for the text. A quill pen was used to write the text in black ink, with the titles in red or blue. Space would be left for illustrations, which would be colored and then illuminated with gold and silver. The work was tedious, Bartholomew explained, and the monks rarely understood the meaning of the words they were copying.

Before beginning to read the first manuscript, which included the first few books of the Greek Old Testament, Bartholomew reminded Justin, quite solemnly, that it is very easy to misunderstand God's Word, which is why the Bible must always be interpreted in light of Christian tradition, and especially in accordance with the views of the Church Fathers, whom they would also read later.

"You must not rely on your own interpretation of scripture, but solely on the Church's," Bartholomew said. "The greatest evil is for a person to think that they can decide for themselves what is true and false, right and wrong apart from the Church. If at some point in the future a renegade from the true faith were to say that our religion should be based on scripture alone, the result would be a disastrous schism. The Church would no longer be One but split into myriad sects, each believing that its own interpretation of scripture is the only correct one. The Bible must by all means be kept away from the common people, lest they twist its words in ways that undermine the authority of the Church."

Thus, Bartholomew continued, it was his role as Justin's spiritual director to make sure that Justin understood the Bible correctly. After reading a bit, the two of them would talk together to make sure that Justin's comprehension was accurate.

It was a long and arduous process, although in fact longer for Bartholomew than for Justin. Justin would read the passages aloud (it was not a custom to read silently), understanding them immediately and wanting to move on to the passages which followed. Bartholomew, who had a poorer command of Greek, would ask Justin to read more slowly so that he could digest what the words meant. Justin tried to accommodate him but found it challenging since reading fast came naturally to him.

Having time to reflect during these pauses, Justin was bewildered by everything he read. He approached the scriptures the same as he had the catechism, not as someone who had been taught how they should be interpreted beforehand and already knew what they meant, but with fresh eyes, baffled by the contents and struggling to discern their meaning. Bartholomew, on the other hand, once he'd understood the words, seemed to have a firm grasp of the content and confidence that his exegeses were correct. Justin wondered if there was, however, a single correct interpretation of a text? Was it not possible for the exact same words to have different meanings for different readers?

Many candles were burned as Justin and Bartholomew worked their way through the Law and the Chronicles, the Wisdom literature and the Prophets. Reading the New Testament went more quickly, but Bartholomew's explanations became longer. Bartholomew mostly talked. Justin mostly listened.

Much of what Justin read captivated him, because it seemed so much at variance with the religion he had been taught as a youth. He was amazed that the prophets spoke of overcoming oppression, giving food to the hungry, and setting the prisoners free, of justice flowing down like water and righteousness like an ever-flowing stream. He was astounded to hear Jesus say, "Blessed are the poor" and "Woe to the rich" for Justin had always been led to believe that it was the rich who are blessed and the poor who are woeful. Of what use are the secular authorities if, as Jesus plainly said, the Kingdom of God is not of this world but among us? Why should an earthly government be given authority over us and demand that we obey its masters when we have the power to govern ourselves?

On the other hand, when Justin had finished reading the Bible all the way through, from the creation of the world to its apocalyptic end, he found that much of it was simply boring. The tedious genealogies and references to kings and kingdoms and historical events that happened long ago seemed to have no contemporary relevance whatsoever. Why spend so much time reading about the past when it offers us no spiritual insight into the present? Were the encounters our ancestors had with God so much more important than our own? Were their ideas more valid? Should we be bound by the dictums of scripture simply because they are ancient? Rather than closing the canon, should we not continue writing the Bible on the basis of our own experiences and ways of understanding them to this very day? It seemed to Justin that focusing so much attention on bygone eras does not bring one closer to God but, to the contrary, simply makes it easier for us to hold God at a respectable distance.

And then there were the laws, not one jot or tittle of which would pass away until the end of time. What exactly is the purpose of all the endless rules about food, cleanliness, and rituals if we fulfill the Law by loving one another? How could a just God hand down ordinances that condone slavery and the servitude of women; that require animal sacrifice and burnt offerings; that sanction death by stoning to those who serve other gods, who are mediums or possessed by familiar spirits, who curse their parents or blaspheme God, who work on the Sabbath, who commit acts of homosexuality, or who cannot prove their virginity on their wedding night?

There were also parts of the Bible which seemed downright immoral to Justin. God could be loving and merciful at times, but also cruel and heartless, the source of both good and evil, rewarding those who gave him the lavish praise he, like any lord, seemed to enjoy basking in and punishing those who would not follow his dictates. For their disobedience, God ended up hating the humans he had created, destroying all of them with a great flood, save for Noah and his family. He commanded those who venerated him to commit acts of slaughter and genocide. He sanctioned the invasion and conquest of lands occupied by others, the destruction of cities, the slaughter of men and women, young and old, ox and sheep with the edge of the sword, the smiting of nursing infants, children being dashed to pieces, women subjected to rape, those with child being ripped up. He punished even his own people with fire, famine, pestilence, and war. He allowed cannibalism between fathers and sons, daughters and friends. He caused the earth to open up and swallow entire families. He foreordained the hellfire and damnation that awaited anyone who refused to bow down and worship him, as Bartholomew had so vividly explained.

Yet how could one bow down and worship such a God, who seemed to take more delight in retribution and violence than in reconciliation and peace? All of these acts were clearly recorded in the Bible and no amount of exegesis could explain or explain away the atrocities committed in God's name and with his blessing. How can Christians regard such passages as "holy"? Should they not be openly repudiated or even excised from scripture altogether?

Yet Justin found that other parts of the Bible were sheer poetry and quite charming. Many of the stories reminded him of those told by the

classical Hellenic and Roman poets, which he had read under the tutelage
of his teacher on the estate. Did not these ancient authors also say that in
the beginning all was chaos, empty, and void, then from darkness light appeared, distinguishing day from night? Love ordered the cosmos, which
allowed earth and sky to be born, and finally humans were created from
clay, in the form of immortal images from the sky. How was this so different
from the account of God creating the heavens and the earth found in the
Bible? And how did the story of God, in the form of Jesus, being crucified
on the cross and then resurrected from the dead, differ from similar stories
told among the ancient Greeks and Egyptians about gods dying and being
reborn?

Miracles in general were something Justin could only regard with in-
credulity. Even if they happened the way the Bible claimed they did, they
mattered little to Justin since he did not seem to live in a world in which
miracles occur nor had he ever experienced one in his own life. Either the
age of miracles was over or the stories about them were pure inventions
that violate the apparent regularity of the universe. What was the point of
the miracle narratives anyway? To make us awestruck at the persons who
performed them? Even false Christs and false prophets could use signs and
wonders to deceive the righteous. What is important, it seems, is not a person's ability to perform magic tricks, but the spirit of love and compassion
one has, especially for the sick and the poor. When Jesus gave sight to the
blind, was not the real miracle that they overcame ignorance and became
enlightened?

And what of all the other incredible stories from the Bible? Were they
written as records of actual events or as works of fiction with a hidden message? Who would be so foolish as to suppose that God, after the manner of
a husbandman, planted a paradise in Eden or that he walked on two feet
in the garden in the evening? Should such yarns not be taken figuratively
rather than factually? After all, Justin thought, Jesus' parables were stories
that could hardly be interpreted literally either, since to do so would mean
missing their message entirely. Is it really easier for a camel to pass through
the eye of a needle than for a rich man to pass through the gates of the
Kingdom of God? How is it possible for us to enter our mothers' wombs a
second time in order to be born again? Were these not whimsical figures of
speech, which nonetheless expressed profound insights? Why should the
Bible as a whole not be read critically and selectively, just like any other
book, not with the aim of acquiring incontrovertible knowledge about what
happened in the past but for the purpose of gaining wisdom that can be
used in the present?

The dogma that the Bible must be interpreted literally is nothing more than a human postulation not even found in the Bible itself, Justin concluded. Is it not ironic that simpletons who take their interpretations of scripture as literally true end up believing in various fables, while those who see the Bible as a collection of myths are better able to discern its genuine spiritual meaning? The reality a symbol points to may be quite different from what it ostensibly expresses. Should we think of heaven literally as an actual place people go to after they die—a realm that is ultimately unreal? Or should we think of it symbolically as the possibility of a better life in the literal world we live in here and now—something that is very real indeed?

When Justin and Bartholomew began working their way through the Church Fathers, Justin was relieved to discover that scripture could in fact be interpreted on different levels, not only literally but also spiritually. So, Justin thought, we might understand the exodus from Egypt as a literal historical event, but also as a moral lesson about liberating the subjugated. The promised land may be taken allegorically as a reference to a just social order, but also mystically as the experience of the Kingdom of God among us. Justin was not sure if any of these interpretations were entirely accurate, but it didn't really matter. The point was that by moving beyond a literal interpretation of events that purportedly occurred in the past, he could begin to see new possibilities for how we might actually live in the present.

Justin quickly realized, however, that the Fathers of the Church did not always agree among themselves about how scripture should be understood, confirming his suspicion that there is no single "correct" way of construing religious truth, contrary to what Bartholomew was constantly asserting. How can the Church claim ultimate authority over what an individual believes if its teachings are in fact based not on the solid rock of absolute truth but on the shifting sands of hermeneutics? Is the sure foundation of faith the conflicting doctrines of human interpreters or one's own immediate experience of the divine? Of what use are the Church or the scriptures if the Holy Spirit reveals himself to each of us directly, as the Bible itself states? Literally!

The Church Fathers not only disagreed among themselves but also with anyone who opposed their own particular views. As the detailed rants of the Apologists against early heretics clearly showed, ancient Christianity had hardly been a monolithic faith with a single creed agreed upon by everyone but was rather a plethora of competing hypotheses and theories, none of which could claim universal recognition. After all, as Bartholomew had explained to Justin, a significant amount of time had passed before doctrinal disputes began to be resolved by ecumenical councils, the first being convened by the Roman Emperor, Constantine, some three hundred years after the death of Jesus, with the Bible itself not being canonized until decades later. Orthodoxy was a centuries-long process of laborious theological construction, not the One True Faith given to the Church by God from the very beginning. One set of suppositions had prevailed and became the majority position, but had things worked out differently perhaps the views of the heretics would now be esteemed orthodox and those of the Church considered heresy. Why is it so important that everyone adheres to the same beliefs anyway, Justin wondered? Should the Church not be a place where we share our faith with each other, not our intellectual presumptions? Trying to impose unity on everyone only leads to division. Allowing diversity leads to symbiosis. Why should the flowers in a garden all be exactly the same color? Is a garden not more beautiful if it has different kinds of flowers with many different hues?

During their discussions Justin never confronted Bartholomew with any of these apprehensions but confined himself to elementary questions of the sort Bartholomew seemed more comfortable answering. In his heart, however, Justin felt that he would not find what he was looking for by studying books, certainly not the writings of the Fathers or even the Bible itself.

§13

One day after Justin had washed the dishes for the noontime meal and cleaned the kitchen, and the prior had come to inspect his work, Justin gestured to ask if he might speak to him.

The prior looked piqued but motioned back to Justin that he should follow him.

He led Justin into the cloister and then said in a hushed voice, "What is it you want? You know that we should be devoting ourselves to the tasks we've been assigned to and not wasting our time in frivolous conversation."

"I have no one else to turn to," Justin said. "I thought I might ask your advice."

"About what?"

"About my soul."

The prior knit his brows.

"Isn't Bartholomew your spiritual advisor?" he asked. "You should talk to him about whatever it is that's bothering you, not me. I'm not the right person to ask."

"Well, you see, that's the problem. Bartholomew is teaching me many things I cannot understand. I feel he is unable to give me the answers I seek."

"I doubt that I should be able to give you any answers to your questions either."

"But aren't you also a monk in this monastery?"

"Yes, but I am not like Mary in the Bible story, who sat at Jesus' feet and listened to his teachings. I am more like Martha who busied herself in the kitchen preparing meals and serving others."

"Surely one is just as important as the other," Justin said. "May we not do both?"

"Ideally, I suppose. But I do not complain. People tend to be disposed to one activity or the other. In any case it is impossible for one person to do everything."

"How do you find time to study?"

"I do not study," the prior replied. "I can't even read, for Christ's sake!"

"Then how do you know God?"

"I'm not sure I understand what you're asking. I know him because the spirit of truth dwells in me, just like everyone else."

"You do not rely on the scriptures?"

"I do not need to read the Bible to know God."

"Have you never been interested in theology?"

"Theology, ha!" the prior said, not quite letting his lips break into a frown. "No, I could care less about theology. It is much too subtle for my uneducated pea-brain to grasp. No doubt some of the monks go in for that sort of thing with all their expositions and disputations and whatever else it is they do. But it doesn't interest me in the least. We don't need highfalutin theories to know about God or the world. Simple faith is sufficient."

"How do we acquire simple faith?" Justin asked.

"It's not so tough. Jesus said, 'Behold I stand at the door and knock.'"

"So, what must we do?"

"Are you daft?" the prior answered. "You really don't know?"

"I do not."

"You open the door!" he exclaimed.

"And then what happens?"

The prior sighed and then went on in a sing-song manner, "If we hear Jesus' voice and open the door, he will come into us and dine with us, and we with him. Then we will know God and have his power inside us. But if we tell Jesus to go away and refuse to let him in, he remains outside the door. We cannot hear him nor him us and then we are helpless. Does that clarify the matter for you?"

"Not really," Justin replied.

"So what's your problem now?"

"How does this synergy work?"

"*Sinjury?* Speak plain English, man. Stop trying to confuse me with all your big words!"

"What I mean is," Justin resumed, "is salvation something that God does for us or something that we need to do in response to God or perhaps something that has already been accomplished and we just need to realize it?"

"I'm still not sure I follow you," the prior said plaintively.

"Let me try again," Justin said. "It's not only up to God but also up to us? We cooperate with each other."

"I guess," the prior replied, still somewhat befuddled. "We didn't invite Jesus to come to our house. He invited himself. He just shows up at the door. That's something Jesus chooses, not us. But whether we open the door and ask him in is something we choose."

"So once we invite Jesus into our hearts, we are able to discover God and his power within ourselves."

"That's what I just said."

"What is that experience like?"

"Open the door and find out for yourself."

"But can't you tell me at least a little bit about it?"

"It's nothing out of the ordinary," the prior huffed. "It's not like the clouds opening up or angels descending from heaven or voices calling down from the sky or being hit by a thunderbolt or anything like that. We simply do justice, love mercy, and walk humbly with our God. We don't dwell in the past or dream of the future but concentrate our mind on the present moment. We focus on what we are doing right now, whether it be prayer or work."

"Still, is prayer not more important than work?" Justin asked. "This is a monastery after all. The Bible says that the birds of the air neither sow nor reap, nor gather into barns, yet God feeds them. The lilies of the field neither toil nor spin yet they are arrayed in finer clothes than Solomon. Why should we worry about what we eat or drink or how we shall be clothed?"

"I don't care what the Bible says. Somebody has to do the work. We can't leave it all to the peasants!"

"But should we not focus our attention on heavenly matters rather than on the things of this earth?"

The prior was unsure how to answer. Finally he said, "I dunno. Some people look at harvesting grain or spinning cloth as toil, but for me they are just different ways of worshipping God."

"Does God provide for us or must we provide for ourselves?"

"You know," the prior complained. "It really isn't my job to be answering all of your questions."

"I should not ask if I did not value your answers," Justin replied.

"Well, the way I see it," the prior responded matter-of-factly, "is that the Lord blesses us with the land he has given us but we still need to set our hand to it. God makes the plants grow, but it's we who sow the seeds and water them and reap the harvest, which is according to our own labor, not God's. It's common sense, isn't it? Now is there anything you want to know? We really need to be getting back to our own work."

Justin hesitated and then said, "I do have one more question."

"Well, what is it?"

"What is God?"

The prior's face went blank.

"I haven't the slightest inkling what God is," he said testily. "Who can know God? We're all fools and sottish children when it comes to under-standing God."

"You have no idea?"

"Why should I have an idea of God? I don't need an idea of God any more than I need an idea of you."

"But surely you can say something!"

The prior put his finger to his forehead and then said, "How should I answer? God is three pounds of flax, an oak tree in the garden, snow in a silver bowl, a piece of dung."

"Even a lump of shit?"

The prior's face was again expressionless.

"Of course," he said. "Nothing is unclean in itself. Everything is holy."

"But all that you have mentioned are things which we find in ordinary life," Justin said.

"Where else would we find God if not in ordinary life?"

"But are the saints not extraordinary?"

"A saint is simply someone who has succeeded in becoming the ordi-nary person God intends us all to be. The rest of us are still trying to figure that out, so it's we who are extraordinary."

The prior paused, then asked Justin suspiciously, "Why are you asking me so many questions?"

"I simply want to know," Justin replied.

"Sounds to me more like you're just trying to get out of your tasks."

"I'll work overtime if necessary to finish them. But before getting on with my duties, I would like to know how we can measure the level of our spiritual attainment?"

"By how spotless we keep our toilets," the prior responded without blinking an eye. "Now come, for we have toilets of our own to clean."

§14

As he continued his studies with Bartholomew, Justin began listening more carefully to the abbot's sermons. For his Christmas homily, the abbot said:

"Because Jesus is born in us here and now, we make a holiday to celebrate it. Of what use is it that Mary gave birth to the Son of God in history if we do not give birth to the child of God in our own time and place? God became human so that humans might become God. In the same way that God was incarnate in Jesus, he is incarnate in you. God has given birth to us as his begotten children and we, as much as Mary, are also intended to be mothers of God, for God is always needing to be born."

Then on Easter the abbot preached:

"The death and resurrection of Christ was not a singular event in history, but something we may experience for ourselves in the here and now when we die to our old way of life and rise again to a new one. We are buried together in the likeness of Christ's death and raised together in the likeness of his resurrection. Our egoistical self, with all its sins and inadequacies, is crucified and we discover our authentic self, created in the image of God and filled with holiness and truth, not at some distant time or place in the future but at the present moment here in this world."

On Pentecost the abbot explained:

"Humans and God are not separated across a great divide but joined together in one spirit. We are 'partakers of the divine nature,' as the epistle tells us. In the same way that Jesus, as God made flesh, had both a human and a divine nature, we, too, have both a human and a divine nature. Our bodies are not the prison of the soul but the temple of God. The same Holy Spirit that dwelt in Christ dwells in us and it is through his presence that we are deified. The divinity of Christ and our own divinity have the same source. We are one with God, even as Jesus and the Father were one. Jesus is in the Father, the Father is in Jesus, and through the Spirit we are in them and they in us, so that all may be one."

During the long summer months after Pentecost the abbot exhorted:

"When we preach the gospel to those who do not call themselves Christians, we are not attempting to convert them to our own way of thinking. Instead we are sharing the good news which we have received from Jesus, which concerns reconciliation with God and with each other. It matters not if they agree with our opinions about religion, but rather if we are able to trust each other and establish a bond of love between us as brothers and sisters, for we are all children of the same God, who has created every one of us in exactly the same way and filled each of us with his Spirit, regardless of which creeds we subscribe to. Streams with sources in many different lands all mingle their waters in the same vast ocean."

The homilies of the abbot made a great impression on Justin for they seemed to be completely different from what he had been learning from Bartholomew. He wondered how it was possible for Justin and Bartholomew to be listening to exactly the same sermons yet to interpret them so differently. Did Bartholomew not see the discrepancies between what the abbot was preaching and what he himself believed? Bartholomew's mind was already made up. He had his own way of thinking and nothing the abbot said would change it. The heartening words of the abbot did not, in fact, even seem to register with him. Did Bartholomew and the abbot even subscribe to the same religion?

§15

One day Justin worked up the courage to confront Bartholomew with the question that had been bothering him most: "I have been studying God's Word and the Church's teachings for a long time now but still my heart is empty. I must be doing something wrong. What is it?"

Bartholomew seemed vexed.

"I have taught you all that I know," he responded. "Is there something you still do not understand?"

"Indeed, I appreciate the comprehensive tutoring you have given me, but in the end it amounts to nothing if I still do not know God."

"I am sure that there are many things about God that surpass all understanding, but you must have faith."

"But is faith merely a matter of professing the creed and participating in the sacraments? Is it not more than believing in the Bible and what the Church teaches us?"

Bartholomew was becoming exasperated.

"Don't be so slow-witted," he said. "Faith is like leaping from a ledge into the darkness, not knowing where we will land, but trusting the voice of God when he tells us to jump. God commanded Abraham to leave his own country and go to a place that the Lord would show him, not knowing where it would be. That is true faith."

"Yet we do not know where we are going?"

"Jesus said that his disciples should deny themselves and follow him. All of us are blind and cannot find the way on our own. We must simply take his hand and let Jesus take us wherever he leads."

"I'm sorry," Justin said. "But I still do not understand."

"Listen," Bartholomew said abjectly. "Perhaps it would be better if you asked your questions to the abbot. His understanding of these matters far exceeds my own and I am sure that he would be able to explain them to you much better than I can. It seems that I have no talent whatsoever as a teacher."

"But would he be willing to see me?" Justin asked. "I would not wish to trouble him since I am not a monk."

"It makes no difference," Bartholomew said. "Every soul is important. Including yours. I will ask him for an interview."

§16

The next morning Justin awoke before dawn and did something he had not done in a very long time: he went out to see the sunrise. He knew that he was supposed to ask permission from the prior before leaving the monastery, even on a small errand, but reckoned that he could get away with it just once. If he were careful, he would remain undetected, and even if he were found out, the worst that might happen is that the prior would reprimand him and perhaps give him some extra assignments as punishment.

It was worth the risk!

Justin stealthily crept out of his room, left the dormitory, quietly opened the gate, and slipped outside. He walked round to the side of the abbey and ascended a small hill beside it. It was still dark, but the eastern horizon was beginning to turn blood-red behind the distant wolds to the east, the same wolds that he had crossed over from the village and the estate. The scene brought back a flood of memories to him. He could not forget his past, the murder of Martin, or his longing for Constance.

He tried to put these thoughts out of his mind by thinking about something completely different: When we see the sun rising above the horizon, is it the sun that is moving and the earth that is standing still or the earth that is rotating and the sun that is immobile? Would not both appear exactly the same to us? In the same way when we speak of God, is it God who moves around us at the center or we who move around God at the center?

And then the first ray of sunlight appeared from behind the wolds. You do not need to have faith in a sunrise, Justin thought. You just see it. It makes no sense to talk about the "truth" of a sunrise or to have a "belief" about it. You just experience it. Could God not be the same? Faith is about the experience of God, not any ideas we may have of him. The only people who need to say "I believe in God the Father almighty" are those have not yet experienced him. Those who know God do not need to believe in him.

§17

A few days later, Bartholomew told Justin that he had made arrangements for Justin to talk to the abbot. At the appointed time Bartholomew
escorted Justin to the abbot's room, knocked on the door, and waited for
the abbot to answer. The door finally opened and the abbot ushered Justin
inside. Bartholomew stepped into the room behind Justin, but the abbot
said, "Please, Bartholomew. I wish to speak to Justin alone. You may return
to your own room now."

Bartholomew obediently departed, closing the door behind him. Justin had never been in the abbot's room before and had always imagined that
it must be luxurious and ornate. In fact, the chamber was identical to his
own, neither larger nor smaller. The abbot did not sleep on a bed, as Justin
had expected, but on a pallet, the same as Justin's. The only other furniture
in the cell was a table with a basin and a razor on it, just as in Justin's room.
There was, however, no chair.

"I am sorry I do not have a seat to offer you," the abbot said. "But,
please, sit together with me here on the pallet."

Justin sat down, with the abbot positioned diagonally from him.

"Bartholomew told me that you wished to speak with me and I have
wanted to speak with you for some time as well," the abbot said. "The prior
has reported that you are very conscientious and strive for perfection, even
if you do not always achieve it. Of course, none of us are perfect, not even
the prior, although he may sometimes think so."

"I do my best, father," Justin replied.

"Which is all that can be expected. In any case, thank you very much
for your hard work. Bartholomew has also informed me about your studies
and the many questions you ask."

"I sincerely seek the truth, but many times I cannot make sense of
what Bartholomew is teaching me."

"Certainly Bartholomew is ardent in his faith," the abbot replied. "Perhaps a bit overzealous at times, but he is both competent and sincere."

"Indeed, I have found him so on all counts."

The abbot smiled, then sniffled. In the dim light coming in through the
window Justin noticed that the abbot's nose was irritated and red.

"Are you all right?" Justin asked.

"Oh, don't worry about me," the abbot replied. "It must be the dust
inside my room."

"But the floor and walls are immaculate. There is no dust on them."

"I clean them myself every day, yet the dust is still there. We just can't
see it."

The abbot pulled a square piece of ragged cloth from his frock and wiped his nose with it. After concealing the cloth under a fold in his garment, he said, "Now tell me, Justin, what troubles you? It seems that there is something more you are eager to learn in addition to what Bartholomew has been teaching you."

"Yes," Justin replied, somewhat hesitantly. "There is one point which I have not yet been able to understand clearly."

"And what is that, my son?"

"How can I know God?"

The abbot seemed surprised by the question and began coughing. Clearing his throat he said with a slightly embarrassed smile, "Forgive me, but what you are asking for is impossible. God cannot be known. All that we can know is that we know nothing."

"But I have spent the past year or so studying the creed and the catechism, the scriptures and the writings of the Fathers. Surely they can give me knowledge of God."

"Nay, they are only words, Justin. They cannot give you knowledge of God any more than understanding the directions someone gives you to the village is the same as actually going there. Or being told how to shoot a bow and arrow automatically makes you an accomplished archer."

"Yet if God cannot be known, he remains a mystery."

"Indeed. And we cannot construct a fence around the mystery of God with our doctrines and dogmas. It is impossible to draw a circle around God."

"What, then, is the purpose of study?" Justin asked.

"It has no purpose," the abbot answered. "Faith is not something that can be transmitted from one person to another through teaching. You must discover it for yourself."

"And how might I do that?"

"First of all, you must forget everything you have been taught. Only then will you be able to find God's wisdom within you."

Justin felt disheartened. What was the purpose of all the long hours he had spent studying with Bartholomew?

"Is there not something else I can rely on?" he asked.

"Excuse me," the abbot said, pulling out the rag again and blowing his nose into it. When he had finished, he said, "No, you need nothing more. In the end prophecies will fail us. Tongues will cease. Knowledge itself will vanish away."

"Yet is Christianity not founded on a book, the Bible?"

"No, our religion is not based on the Bible, but on faith, hope, and charity."

"Indeed, Bartholomew has told me so."

"And once a person acquires these gifts of the Spirit," the abbot continued, "scripture is no longer needed."

The abbot was wheezing slightly as he spoke.

"But is the Bible not God's Word?"

"No, the Bible is not God's Word. Jesus is. When someone points to the sun, we do not look at the person's finger but at the sun. In the same way, when we read the Bible we do not find truth in the Bible but in what the Bible points to. Any teaching you learn from the Bible is merely a finger which points to the sun. It is not the sun itself."

"May we not at least say that the scriptures are inspired by God?"

"Of course! The Bible is inspired because it has the power to inspire us."

"But does inspiration not mean that God dictated the words of scripture to those who wrote them?"

"There are many who think so, but we humans are not mere horns that God blows his music through. Rather, the authors of the Bible were inspired to chronicle their own experiences and understandings of God in their own language, in the same way one might be inspired to write a song. Yet the song is theirs, not God's. We in turn are inspired by the Holy Spirit to compose our own songs and to share them with each other. It is not that we all must sing together in unison—like some of the chants we do in the chapel, which can be beautiful and peaceful but also at times quite monotonous!—but that we combine each of our unique melodies together to create beautiful harmonies."

"Yet was not the truth that God revealed to the authors of the Bible greater than our own?"

"There is only one truth: the same truth that is revealed equally by God to everyone. We need neither the Bible nor the preaching of the Word to discover it."

"But Bartholomew has told me that the Bible is the only source of truth about God."

"It may lead us to the truth, but it is not the truth itself."

"You are saying, then, that the scriptures are false?"

"Simple-minded people anchor their faith not in the Word of God but in the words of the Bible. If they ever come to doubt that those words are completely true, with no falsehoods or contradictions whatsoever, they easily lose their bearings and are set adrift on a sea of doubt. Mature believers, on the other hand, place their faith in God, not the Bible. You have no need for anyone else to instruct you, neither Bartholomew nor me nor the Fathers nor the Church. Those who merely listen to the word are deluded."

Justin was still unsure how one could have faith in the absence of hearing the words of the Bible, as Bartholomew had told him.

"My understanding, though, is that the only way God speaks to us is through Moses and the prophets, and through our Lord and Savior, Jesus Christ, as recorded in the scriptures."

"Such forms of revelation would be necessary only if God were far away and wholly other, and thus required such a clunky means of communication," the abbot replied.

"So the Bible does not reveal God to us?"

"God reveals himself not through the scriptures but through his presence in our own hearts, minds, and souls. The Bible only records what God has revealed to other people, not what he reveals to each of us personally."

"Then I have nothing to learn by studying the scriptures?"

"You cannot understand God through other people's experiences, but only through your own. Everything you read in the Bible is second-hand knowledge. It might be interesting to see how God has worked in other people's lives, but you do not need to know that to experience God for yourself."

"At least the Bible provides us with guidelines for living, does it not?"

"The scriptures were not written to give us a bunch of rules to live by. Only the spiritually dead think of the Bible as a code of laws written with ink in the pages of a book which must be obeyed to the letter. God's laws are not chiseled on tablets of stone but on the tablets of our hearts. The written code kills, but the Spirit gives us life."

"So we need not follow the Bible?" Justin asked.

"The Bible itself never says that we must follow the Bible. It says that we should follow the Holy Spirit, which dwells inside us and guides us into all truth. God's will is discerned not by reading the scriptures but through prayer and by testing the spirits."

Justin was not quite sure how this was possible but rather than ask, pressed on with his next question.

"What of doctrine? Surely Christian teachings are based on scripture."

"The purpose of the Bible is not to give us dogmas, but to bring us to God. People search the scriptures thinking that in them they will find life, but they miss the point entirely if they do not realize God in their own lives. Theology is not something to be believed but something to be practiced. Faith is not about which creed we adhere to but what we experience."

"Then which words will lead us to God?"

"Truth cannot be stated in words, for they are mere emblems which point to something they themselves are not."

"Can anything be said about God?"

The abbot held back for a moment and then suddenly sneezed. He raised his hand and then sneezed again more ferociously than the first time.

"There," he said. "Now I feel better. I'm sorry I missed what you were asking me before. Could you repeat your question?"

"Can anything be said about God?"

"No," the abbot replied. "Nothing can be said about God. If you try to say something about God, you must use words, but no words ever invented by humans are able to describe God. You might as well sneeze!"

"So God is indescribable."

The abbot sneezed again.

Justin was not sure if the abbot was answering his question or simply unable to control his allergy. So he said, "But if God is real then it should be possible to say something about him."

After wiping his nose once more with the cloth, the abbot replied, "God is not an objective reality to be observed and described, but a real presence within ourselves that is beyond description."

"But the Bible says, 'God is light,'" Justin countered.

"And that is true, but only as a symbol. It would be equally true to say that God is darkness."

"So we may say both that God is light and that God is not light?"

"Indeed."

"But surely that is a contradiction."

"Even more, we may also say that God is neither light nor not-light."

"You are speaking in riddles."

"It is not a riddle but a paradox. God is neither light nor darkness, and yet both."

"I still do not understand," Justin said.

"The point is that anything we try to say about God, or even the world for that matter, can never be absolutely true, for it is only a metaphor. Some people reject religion because it is not science. Others accept religion because they know it is poetry."

"Then God is a delusion."

"Yes. The God we bring into being by thinking of him is not the true God but only an idol of God that we fashion in our own minds."

"You have not yet told me, however, what the word *God* actually refers to."

"It refers to nothing."

Justin was beginning to feel fatigued.

"But surely people must mean something when they use this word," he said.

"Whatever they might 'mean' is their own opinion, for each of us has our own idea of God and all these ideas are different. We might as well discard the word *God* and throw it in the dustbin, since it is simply a term of convenience people use to designate something that cannot be designated. The unsayable cannot be said."

It seemed to Justin that his discussion with the abbot was leading nowhere.

"Then perhaps it is better not to say anything about God at all!" he exclaimed.

"Finally, you are beginning to understand!" the abbot applauded, clapping his hands together. "In the end we must be silent. God is not something to be talked about or known, but something to be experienced, as participants not spectators."

The abbot stood up and walked over to the window of the room, motioning for Justin to follow him. Pointing out the window, the abbot said, "To see scenery through the window is not the same as actually being in the landscape. In the same way, to see God through words is not the same as actually being in God and experiencing him."

Light from outside the room fell on Justin's face.

"I still do not understand what you mean," he said.

"Shall we go outside and see how differently things look from there?" the abbot asked.

§18

Justin followed the abbot out of his room, through the dark corridors of the monastery to the outside door, where the light from the sun dazzled Justin's eyes. At first he was unable to see the path that led round the abbey's walls to the field behind it. The abbot, walking just a few steps ahead, looked like a moving tree, not a man. Gradually, however, Justin's eyes became accustomed to the light and everything became clear. By the time they reached the patch of land they had seen through the abbot's window, Justin felt that he was in a completely different world.

"Smell the air," the abbot said, taking in a deep breath. "It is fresh and invigorating, not at all like the dank, musty fumes in my cell!"

"Indeed, your allergy seems to have cleared up," Justin said.

"I can inhale the wind!"

The abbot then pointed to the sky.

"Now, look at the sun," he said. "Don't look at my finger. Look at the sun!"

Justin raised his eyes, but quickly shielded them with his hand.

"I cannot," he said, "for it is too brilliant."

The abbot beamed. "Indeed! To see the sun you must look at it directly. But if you do, it will only burn your eyes and make you blind. You can only know the sun indirectly, by feeling its heat and walking in its light. In the same way that we never know the sun as it is in itself, we can never know God as he is in himself. We do not know God's essence but only his energies."

"So there is a difference between the two."

"In one sense, yes, I suppose," the abbot replied. "But in another sense, it is difficult to conceive how God could exist apart from his energies or how God's energies could exist apart from him, for the two are inseparable. It is impossible to have one without the other. When we say, 'Lightning flashes,' it is not that there is something called *lightning* which engages in the activity of *flashing*. Lightning *is* the flashing. The 'doer' is nothing more than a fiction written into the deed. In the same way when we say, 'God acts,' it is not that there is something called *God* who acts. God *is* the action. 'God' is nothing more than a fiction we write into the act. The act itself is all there is."

Justin was perplexed. Would it not be even more difficult for him to find God if God is like a sunbeam of energy that cannot be grasped in one's hand?

"I would still like to know where God is and how I might find him," Justin said.

The abbot smiled benevolently at him.

"You do not need to look for God, for he is already with us," he replied. "The same as this sunlight."

"Wherever we are?"

"Whether we be in heaven or hell or any place on earth."

"Indeed, I have learned from the theologians that God is omnipresent," Justin said.

"Well, we must be careful when we try to describe God by using grandiose superlatives such as *omnipresent, omniscient, omnipotent, omnibenevolent,* and the like for these, too, are only metaphors, none of which can be found in the Bible. It may seem that we are giving God a compliment when we use such exalted expressions to describe him, but if we begin to take them literally, it will only lead us into intellectual entanglements from which there is no escape. Religion has nothing to do with any grand ideas we may have about God, but with the immediate awareness of the divine as it is found in ourselves and in the world. It is better to simply say that God is with us, right here, right now."

"But if God is here with us even now, why can we not see him?"

"God is not a being, like the rocks and trees and flowers all around us. He is neither this nor that."

"He is an invisible spirit then."

"No," the abbot said ruminatively. "A spirit is still a being. And God is not a being."

"But if God is not a being, then he does not exist."

"Certainly God does not exist the way most people think he exists."

"Either something exists or it does not exist," Justin said. "There can be no ambiguity."

"Do justice, beauty, or even life itself exist?" the abbot asked.

"Most assuredly," Justin replied.

"God exists in the same manner."

"But none of those things you mentioned are beings!"

"Neither is God," the abbot said. He then looked at Justin with penetrating eyes and asked, "Justin, do you believe in love?"

The question caught Justin completely off guard. Memories of Constance instantly flooded his mind. He did not know how to answer but could not tear himself from the abbot's intense gaze. Finally he said without wavering, "Yes, I do."

The abbot's eyes then softened. "And do you believe in Cupid?"

"Most assuredly not," Justin replied.

"Why do you not believe in Cupid?"

"Because Cupid is a purely fanciful creature made up by storytellers."

"Yet you believe in love?"

"Yes."

"Why do you believe in love?"

"Because love, unlike Cupid, is real."

"And how do you know that love is real?"

Justin looked down so that the abbot could not see him blushing.

"Because it is something I have experienced," he said bashfully.

"Good!" the abbot laughed. "It is wonderful that you have been able to experience love!"

Justin looked up again, relieved by the abbot's unexpected empathy.

The abbot continued, "The God that most people believe in is merely a personification of God, just as Cupid is a personification of love. One is as much a false god as the other. God cannot be personified. Yet he is just as real as love is and can be experienced in exactly the same way."

"This still does not explain how God exists if he is not a being."

"God is beyond being."

"Indeed!" Justin exclaimed, nodding his head up and down. "I have always thought of God as a supreme being who lives beyond the earth in heaven."

"No," the abbot said, shaking his head back and forth. "As I just said, God is not a being, not even a supreme one. If God is something he must have limits and be finite. If God is nothing he has no limits and is infinite."

"Then where is God?"

"He does not live in the distant heavens above, but here with us. To believe in a God who transcends the world is simply a convenient way of getting rid of him, to push him aside so that we might avoid contact with him, to keep him forever separate from us, to desacralize nature and devalue ourselves. Once we start thinking that way, we no longer have any use for God. He simply disappears and conceals his face from us. All that remains is the arrogance of thinking that our paltry good works will lead to human progress."

"So God remains forever hidden."

"Nay, we see God all around us. The physical and the spiritual are not separate from each other. To see the physical as the spiritual and the spiritual as the physical—that is the meaning of the incarnation! Did Jesus not say, 'He who has seen me has seen the Father'? Through the incarnation we are able to see God again in Christ, in ourselves, in each other, and in the world. The veil is removed. We look into a mirror and behold the glory of the Lord, for we are being transformed into his likeness. What we see reflected in the glass is not our own image but God's."

"Yet there is no transcendent God who exists outside the world he created?"

"If so, then we could never know that God exists, for he would be beyond our experience. If God did live solely in an otherworldly realm above the dome of the beautiful blue sky we see above us right now, we could have no contact with him. He would be unknowable and mean nothing to us."

"How, then, is it possible to experience God?"

"The reason why we are able to experience God is exactly because he is not transcendent to the world, but immanent in it. It is God in whom we live, move, and have our being."

"Ah," Justin said, once again nodding his head up and down. "So God is the same as the world after all."

"No," the abbot said, once again shaking his head back and forth. "The world may be a being, but as I keep saying, *God is not a being*. He is neither wholly transcendent to the world nor wholly immanent in it."

"Perhaps then we should think of him as the ground of everything that exists."

"How could God be the ground of all being when he himself is groundless? God is not an empty tray which holds all things, but the empty space in which the tray itself exists."

"Yet surely there must be an underlying first principle for us to stand on even if God himself stands on nothing."

"Nay," the abbot replied. "Being requires no foundation. It is self-contained. The sun does not need a pedestal to stand on or ropes to hold it up. It is perfectly capable of hanging in the sky all by itself. The sky is not carried on the shoulders of a Titan. Nor does the earth rest on the backs of turtles all the way down."

"Is it not a contradiction to speak simultaneously of God's transcendence and his immanence?"

"Not at all, because God is not transcendent on the one hand and immanent on the other. Rather, these are one and the same thing. God transcends all particular beings precisely because he is immanent in all of them. To be beyond all beings means that while God is present in all beings, he cannot be identified with any one particular being. There is a difference between saying that God is transcendent to any particular being, which is true, and that God is transcendent to all beings, which is false."

"So what you are saying is that God lives not beyond nature but within it."

"Indeed, God is not a supernatural being who exists outside the universe, who suspends the laws of nature at his personal whim, who intervenes in the world with miracles, but rather the energy that is diffused throughout nature and flows through it. It is the force that allows the universe to create itself, that causes the flowers to grow, that drives water through rocks, that uproots trees. The exact same energy moves through you and me and everyone and everything."

"So we may distinguish God's essence from his energies after all," Justin said, scratching his chin.

"No more and no less than we can distinguish the dancer from the dance. While they are distinct in our minds, they are one in reality. God is not a noun, but a verb. The word refers not to something that exists but something that happens, not to something that is but something that acts, not to a being but becoming, not to an entity but an event, not to a substance but a process, not to our present reality but a potential that is still to be actualized, within ourselves, within others, and within the world as a whole."

"All of which is another reason why we cannot identify the world as it is now with God."

"Certainly the universe is not the same yesterday and today and forever, and—dare I say—I don't think God is either!"

§19

The sun was beginning to set. A single faint star appeared in the azure sky. Justin thought: I am but one grain of sand in a vast desert, one drop of water in the endless ocean, one star out of the trillions. Who am I that God should find me significant? And yet, despite our finitude are we not also part of the infinite? Do we not participate in the eternal dance of the universe?

"Might I ask you one more question?" Justin said to the abbot.

"Yes, but we must return to the abbey soon. It's getting dark and chilly. Plus, you have chores to attend to and I must prepare for the evening vespers."

Justin turned so that he was facing the abbot directly.

"You have said that the power of God is everywhere," Justin began. "But I am so weak and helpless and have no confidence whatsoever. I feel like I am nothing more than a senseless rock."

"You have a very low opinion of yourself, Justin."

"Yet how might I find the divine energy within myself? Would it not be much easier for me to simply devote myself to God and pray for his assistance, since I have no power of my own?"

The abbot pulled his frock more tightly around him, then replied, "There are two very different approaches to religion, Justin. One is the doty way of devotion, in which we put our faith in a make-believe God created in our own image whom we then mistake for reality, a God whose existence we must always doubt because he is only a figment of our imagination. Piety is the way of those who are spiritually impoverished, who, because they are unable to find the power of God within themselves, think of God as a being that exists outside of and above them, whom they then bow down before and worship, praising the Lord because they can find nothing within themselves worth praising."

"And what is the other approach?"

"The way of actualization in which we are empowered by the God within. We ourselves are icons made in God's image. God engraves himself in us. Any images of God we engrave in our own minds are nothing but counterfeits. We already have the light of God within us and can perceive it directly. This illumination cannot be doubted and requires no faith, for it is self-evident. It is not something we understand intellectually but something we experience. Instead of trying to gain knowledge about God, we should seek to become acquainted with him."

"Religion is not needed?"

"Indeed, Christianity is not a religion, but a way of life. The trappings of religion are totally unnecessary. As the iconoclasts have so graciously reminded us, we should never confuse the symbols we concoct to express our experience of the divine with the divine itself. If we sink into the cesspool of religiosity, it will only make us stink!"

Without looking back, the abbot pointed his thumb over his shoulder to the monastery behind them and said, "The sole purpose of the lofty architecture of our edifices and cathedrals, the beauty of our paintings, sculptures, glasswork, and icons, the haunting music of our liturgy, the poetry of our litanies and prayers, the resplendence of our vestments and engravings, our vessels and utensils, our altars and baptismal fonts, our rituals and ceremonies, is not to draw attention to themselves as aesthetic ornaments, but to edify us. We ourselves are works of art created by the divine."

Justin was impressed, although this did not really answer his question.

"But I cannot find the image of God within myself," he said.

"Well, it may be stained and need a bit of polishing but it's still there," the abbot replied. "It's the same way for everyone."

"So our souls are black with sin."

"No, they are white with light. It is only our own blindness that prevents us from seeing the image in which we have been created. Once the tarnish of ignorance is wiped away, the light of God that has been inside us all along will shine forth. What is opaque will be made transparent."

"Yet we still sin, do we not?"

"Sin is not about breaking the commandments but about preventing ourselves, others, and the earth itself from being all that we can be."

The sun had fully set. The shadows disappeared.

"Yet I cannot find the light within myself," Justin said. "All I see is darkness."

"And you must come to know the darkness that is in you as intimately as you know the light," the abbot replied. "There cannot be one without the other. God dwells in both. We must enter into the divine darkness as much as we dwell in the divine light."

"Why should we not simply avoid the darkness and remain in the light?"

"If all were light how could you distinguish the light that guides you from the light that surrounds it? A pillar of cloud shows us the way by day and a pillar of fire by night."

"And yet if my soul is dark, how can I find my way in the darkness, for the two are also indistinguishable, are they not?"

The abbot swept his arms towards the purple horizon. "Only by walking in darkness can you find your own light, first as a tiny divine spark in your soul and then as a burning bush that will never be consumed, a black light that makes the night white. There will no longer be any images either of you or of God, only I Am Who I Am. The two shall be as one, with no division between them."

"Yet did Jesus not say that he is the light of the world and that whoever follows him will walk not in darkness but in the light of life?"

"Yes, and he also said that *we* are the light of the world. Once we allow the same uncreated light that transfigured Christ to transfigure us, we shall also be illumined. We must not hide our light under a bushel but let it shine forth for all to see."

"Nonetheless, should we not follow the light of Christ rather than our own light?"

"When Jesus said, 'Follow me,' he did not mean that we should blindly tag along after him, letting him lead us by the nose and carefully placing our shoes in his exact same footprints, but that we should walk boldly in the same manner that he walked and find our own way."

"Yet is Christ not our model? Should we not imitate him?"

"Indeed, Jesus is an exemplar of what it means to realize the image of God inside of us. But if we try to mimic Christ, all we end up with is a cheap replica, not the real thing. Rather than striving to be like Jesus, we should simply become what we already are, which is exactly what Jesus did. You must work out your own salvation, Justin. Don't expect others to do it for you, not even Jesus."

"Yet even if I must find my own way, I still need a light to see where I am going."

"Yes, and the same inner light that shone in Jesus also shines in you. We no longer need to walk in the light of Christ for we ourselves have become children of light. Tread neither in the shadows of others nor in their light, but in your own light. Be a lamp unto your own path."

"But the scriptures say that God's Word is a lamp for our feet, a light on our path."

"Indeed, and what is the Word of God but the divine logos that was incarnate in Jesus of Nazareth, the same divine logos that is incarnate in you, which gives you the power to become a child of God? You, as much as Jesus, are the Christ, a son of the living God. God does not live outside the world in a remote heaven, but in it. And the point of intersection between God and the world is us, a fusion of God and humanity, just as it was for Jesus."

"I am God's only begotten son?" Justin's realized that his voice sounded disdainful.

"No, no, not only you, but everyone. We are all begotten by God. Anyone with the hubris to believe that he alone is the Son of God suffers from delusions of grandeur."

"Was not Jesus himself so deluded?"

"Jesus left it to others to call him the Son of God. He usually referred to himself as the Son of Man, who came not be served but to serve. We should think of ourselves in the same way."

"But was he not also called the messiah, the Christ, the anointed one?"

"Certainly. And we too, are anointed by the Holy Spirit, which gives us the right to be called God's children and members of Christ's body. You and I, as much as Jesus, are born of God, just as we in turn give birth to God. God abides in each of us."

"God lives in us?"

"Not just in us but in all things," the abbot said. Then thumping his chest he added, "Christ Immanuel! God with us!"

Justin had never seen the abbot so spirited before.

"But Bartholomew has told me that we have no power of our own, that we must rely solely on the power of God to save us."

"That is correct. It is only possible to be saved through the power of God within you."

The idea was difficult for Justin to grasp.

"You have said that God is here with us," he said, "yet surely this power exists outside of ourselves."

"Nay, Justin. Jesus Christ is in you and he is powerful in you. As one of the Fathers has told us, 'There are many who have sought light and truth but they look for it outside themselves, where it is not.' The power is within you, Justin, where it has always been. It isn't you who do the work but God who does the work in you."

"So are there two powers or only one?"

"These are simply two different ways of describing the same thing. God's power is your power and yours is God's."

"But surely the power that Christ had within him was far greater than the power we have within ourselves!"

"Yet it is exactly the same power, different not in kind but only in degree."

"Even if Jesus was without sin, I am certainly not perfect," Justin admitted.

"In one sense we are already perfect just the way we are, for that is how God accepts us and how we should accept ourselves," the abbot said. "But in another sense, the moment we say we are perfect is the moment we are damned. If God is infinite, then we are also filled with infinite possibilities. We are always climbing higher. Perfection has no end. That is why is some sages say we must be reincarnated countless times before we are sanctified, others that we must spend eons in purgatory to purify our souls, and yet others that even an eternity in heaven would not be long enough to make us fully holy."

"Well, which is it?"

"It doesn't matter. If we live in God, then we shall die in God. And if we die in God, we need not speculate about what happens to us after that. Conversion is only the beginning of a journey in which we let God transform us. To affirm the image of God within us is to acknowledge our capacity for good even if we do not always achieve it. We are all still works in progress!"

"I can come to God just as I am?"

"Indeed, come as you are. And God comes to each of us just as we are, too."

"Does that mean God will save everyone?"

"He already has. God wills all to be saved and destines each of us to salvation through his good pleasure. The grace of God appears to everyone."

"Not just those who have chosen him?"

"It is not we who choose God but God who chooses us. God gives his gift of grace freely to all people. It is not of our own doing!"

"Then why are some people good and others evil?"

"We all wake up to the same sunrise. Some people greet it with their eyes wide open, others with their eyes half-shut. Still others go back to bed and fall asleep again. The question is the extent to which we realize the power of God within ourselves and allow God to act through us. When we allow God to work through us all things may be accomplished."

"How might I find God's power within me?"

"Why search for something you already have? There is no book that can give you all the answers to life's questions, no enlightenment to be found outside yourself. To know yourself is to know God."

"That's a crazy idea," Justin blurted out, giving no thought to his impropriety. "How is it possible to know God by knowing oneself?"

The abbot smiled.

"If God is at the center of all that exists," he said, "then God is also at the center of yourself. And you will find him not by looking without but by looking within."

"How can that be?"

"Whatever is, is God. Soul and mind are emanations from the One and to the One all things return. It is because God is all in all that we are united with him. If God is eternal and without limitation, so is humankind."

"Achieving union with God seems like such an arduous struggle," Justin said forlornly.

"It is not something you strive to achieve, but something you already have. That thou art. At this very moment you are one with God. You simply haven't opened your eyes and noticed it yet."

The abbot then turned and face Justin directly. "Have you ever entertained the idea of becoming a novice?" he asked.

"I have never given the matter much thought," Justin replied.

"You should consider it," the abbot said.

The sky was completely black when Justin and the abbot returned to the monastery. Justin was pleased that the abbot had responded to all of his questions, but disappointed in himself that he could not understand any of the answers, at least not really. Justin castigated himself for not trying harder. Perhaps he should take the tonsure and become a monk after all. Then he could devote the rest of his life to repenting of his sins and trying to find God.

§20

With winter over, Justin was laboring in the fields again, plowing land with the peasants for the spring planting of barley and oats. He had finished his studies of the catechism, the Bible, and the Church Fathers, and it felt good to be doing physical labor again. He had learned much about heavenly things and the spiritual life but was happy to reconnect himself to the earth and practical affairs. He was also glad to be out from under the wing of the prior, who was constantly reproaching him for the smallest of oversights, and even more glad that he no longer had to listen to Bartholomew's long-winded and often dull elucidations of the Christian faith.

As soon as the plowing was finished, however, Bartholomew came to Justin's room to ask if he would accompany him on a visit to an anchorite attached to a church in the nearby town. The purpose of the trip would be to take food to the anchorite but also seek his advice on spiritual matters. Bartholomew already had a specific issue he wished to discuss with the anchorite and encouraged Justin to ask him any questions he might have as well.

Ever since arriving at the monastery, Justin had never ventured far from the grounds, except to work in the fields with the peasants, so while he was not particularly interested in visiting the anchorite, he relished the opportunity to go to a new place. Where he really wanted to go was to the city, which he had never been to before, but he was quite gratified to be able to travel to the nearby local town with Bartholomew.

Bartholomew warned Justin not to be shocked by what he would see. The anchorite was an old man who had been living inside a stone cell for most of his adult life. Unlike the monks at the abbey, who lived communally, anchorites were persons who separated themselves entirely from the world in order to devote themselves to penance and prayer. While subject to the authority of the bishop, they had no spiritual leaders as such and learned directly from God.

Before entering their cells anchorites are consecrated and given a ceremony not unlike a funeral, after which they are regarded as dead to the world. Then they enter their cell, which is cemented in on all sides, leaving only a thin slit, called a hagioscope or squint, looking into the church for them to participate in the Eucharist, and a small window on the outside so that they may receive food and water and communicate with others. There they live out the remainder of their lives contemplating God, but also meeting with anyone who wished to consult with them about the religious life.

"The anchorite we shall visit practices extreme forms of asceticism," Bartholomew told Justin. "No doubt you have witnessed in our own monastery that the monks often engage in long periods of fasting. We wear hair shirts during specific periods to show our repentance and will sometimes even scourge ourselves as an act of penance. Although most anchorites are more moderate, the anchorite we will see eats only the bare minimum to keep himself alive. He is clothed continuously in sackcloth and rarely cleanses himself. Flagellation is a daily practice for him."

"Must we punish our bodies to find God?" Justin asked.

"Penance may involve either suffering as Jesus suffered or doing good to make up for the sins we have committed against others," Bartholomew replied. "Even though our human bodies were created by God, they are still liable to lead us astray, for the desires of the flesh are against the spirit and the desires of the spirit are against the flesh. In such cases we must not beat the air but our own bodies and bring them into bondage, training these decrepit husks to do what they should do, not what they want to do."

Justin quickly agreed to go with Bartholomew and the two men departed a few days later. The town was located further down the valley, at a place where the river widened, with plains on either side. It was small, but much bigger than the village near Justin's father's estate and also more compact. The houses were well built and clustered together along narrow streets, with a mill, brewery, wine press, and a blacksmith's forge all within close distance. Justin and Bartholomew finally came to the parish church, which was large, even imposing, at least compared to any churches Justin had seen before.

Standing in front of it Bartholomew said, "I have already prepared what I wish to speak to the anchorite about. Have you thought of a question yourself?"

"Indeed, I have," Justin replied.

"Good. Before seeing the anchorite, however, we must pray inside the church. Then we shall come back outside and speak to the anchorite separately through the window of his cell."

After they had entered the church and crossed themselves, Bartholomew pointed his finger at a small aperture on the far wall to the right of the altar, which Justin recognized as the squint that allowed the anchorite to witness the mass and receive the host.

Bartholomew knelt down before the altar, bowing his head and clasping his hands in prayer. Justin knelt beside him and prayed that he would be able to find the answer he had been looking for but not yet able to find.

§21

When Bartholomew had finished his prayers, he crossed himself again and bowed, then left the church, with Justin close behind him. Bartholomew said nothing as he led the way around the side of the church to the anchorite's cell. The cell itself was not large, with stone masonry on all sides. There was one small window with a wooden shutter that was closed. Bartholomew motioned for Justin to wait at some distance and then approached the window. He knocked on the shutter gently, which opened slowly, letting light into the cell. From where Justin was standing, he could see no one inside, but watched Bartholomew pass the basket of food he had brought with him through the window and observed him speaking and listening to someone, no doubt the anchorite, although Justin could neither see his face nor hear his voice.

After some time the interview was concluded. Bartholomew returned to Justin and nodded for him to approach the cell. Justin walked slowly toward the window and upon reaching it was finally able to look inside. There he saw a very old man, with long gray hair and emaciated cheeks. He wore a tattered hair shirt over his gaunt body. The man's hands and arms were all bones with no flesh on them. His legs were scarred with the lashings he had given himself. Justin suspected there were many more lacerations on his back although he could not see them. A horrible stench came not only from the cell but from the anchorite himself. When he asked Justin to state his business, Justin noticed that his teeth were broken and his breath was foul.

"I am very pleased to be able to meet and talk with you," Justin said.

The anchorite looked at Justin sternly.

"Can't you see that I am a very busy man?" he said. "I have so many things to do and hardly enough time to do them, especially since I am constantly being interrupted by people who cannot see what is in front of their own noses. So please do not abuse me with formalities. Be brief and to the point."

Justin, taken aback by the anchorite's bluntness, quickly posed the question he had prepared: "Where is God?"

"Ha!" the anchorite exclaimed. "You're no different from that fellow who was here just before you. God is right at the tip of your nose, as I just said. He is closer to you than your jugular vein, nearer to you than you are to yourself!"

"The abbot at our monastery has told me that I would be able to find the light of God within me, but all I see is darkness."

"Good. That means you are making progress."

"I do not understand what you mean."

It was only then that Justin noticed the vermin that were crawling through the threads of the anchorite's hair shirt.

"God may only be found in darkness and a cloud of unknowing," the anchorite said.

"What I seek is not to unknow but to know. I wish to walk in sunlight, not darkness."

"It is impossible to see the dawn if we do not first pass through the dark night of the soul."

"How might we find our way in the dark?" Justin asked.

"We don't," the anchorite replied. "We simply move ahead step by step not knowing where we are going or where we will end up. The voice of God himself will lead us."

"How might I hear the voice of God?"

"Some people think that God speaks to them through earthquakes, wind, or fire, but what you should be listening for is the still small voice within you."

"But I hear no such voice."

"That is because you have not yet spoken."

"I must speak first?"

"God speaks to us with the same voice that we speak to him. They are one and the same voice. If you listen to your own voice, you will hear the voice of God."

"You mean that I must speak to God before God will speak to me?"

The anchorite looked askance.

"When you pray it is not you talking to God, but God talking to himself."

Remembering what Bartholomew had taught him, Justin said, "But I have learned that prayer is a two-way conversation between two distinct persons, just as you and I are having a conversation with each other right now."

"When the God who dwells inside ourselves prays, the same God answers us. There is only one God, not two. Or has no one taught you that yet?"

Justin, though quite aware of his own limited proficiency in such matters, could not understand why the anchorite was being so sarcastic.

"Please tell me, then," he asked, as sincerely as possible. "What words should I use when I pray?"

"You do not need words."

"How then might I speak to God?"

"I, for one, try to avoid talking to myself. It's a sign of asininity. But if you must use words, the Lord's Prayer is a good place to start. Once you have mastered that, you can move on and simply say with all your heart, 'Lord Jesus Christ, Son of God, have mercy on me, a sinner.' Repeat it over and over again until it becomes a part of you. You won't even realize you are saying it. This is what scripture means when it tells us to 'pray without ceasing.'"

"May we not petition God for health or luck or fortune?"

"Why waste your time with such infantile prayers?" the anchorite said. "When we are children we speak as children, understand as children, and think as children, but after we become adults we put away childish things and no longer implore Big Daddy in the sky to 'gimme what I want' or ask him to satisfy all our petty little demands. If we do not know how to pray as we ought to, then it is better to simply allow the Spirit itself to make intercession for us with groanings that cannot be uttered."

Justin sensed that the anchorite was becoming irked by his questions but pressed further.

"May we not also pray to the saints and ask them to intercede for us? Surely our salvation is not a trivial matter."

"Rather than pray to the saints to help you, vow to become a saint yourself and help others."

"But surely if I am in trouble may I not plead for God's help?"

"Such are the prayers of spiritual weaklings," the anchorite said adamantly. "Only those who are unable to realize the power of God within themselves can think of nothing better to do than to get down on their knees and grovel before a graven image they have forged if not in metal then in their own minds, thinking these false gods will work wonders and perform miraculous tricks for them. Do not pray to others for assistance but pray directly to the spirit within you for the strength to deal with any trouble you may encounter in life."

"What if I am not strong enough on my own and the sea of life overwhelms me?"

"You cannot choose the circumstances you are given in life, only how you respond to them."

"But may I not beseech God to change the circumstances of my life?"

"Stop whining," the anchorite remonstrated. "Why do you so persistently think of prayer as some kind of magical incantation? The purpose of prayer is not to change the outward conditions of your life but to change yourself so that you can stand up on your own two feet and face whatever circumstances you meet in the world with the power of God inside you."

"And should I fail?"

"Don't be such a sniveling wimp!" the anchorite cried in exasperation. "The true test of our spirituality isn't how well we respond to success, which is easy, but how well we respond to failure. Both must be accepted and neither allowed to disturb our inner tranquility."

"What if I cannot hear the echo of God's voice when I pray to him?"

"It is because God has nothing to say."

"What then must I listen for?"

"You must hear what God does not say."

"God is silent?"

"Yes," the anchorite said, his voice now a whisper. "And to really know God you must also be silent."

"But silence has no sound."

"It does have a sound."

"Then how might I hear it?"

"God does not need words to speak to you and you do not need words to speak to God. After you get the hang of it, spoken prayer may be dispensed with."

"How do I do that?"

"You just shut up!"

"May I not even think about God?"

"Why would you want to think about God?" the anchorite asked, feigning puzzlement. "If you do, your thought will not be of God himself but only of a picture of God you have painted in your own brain."

"But surely I must think of something!"

"If you must think, then think about your life and all that you have done. Beyond that, think about how you think. You will then see that all of your thoughts are illusions, which you may dispose of. Everything you previously thought about yourself is also an illusion and does not actually exist. You are not the person you think you are. The ego you clench onto so tightly is not the real you."

"Who am I then?"

"To find your true self, the deeper self that we call God, first empty yourself of the 'I' that you think is you," the anchorite explained. "What remains will be the true you, the God within, which, as you will find, is nothing more than a ripple in the ever-flowing stream of life."

"Then I am nothing at all."

"Indeed, that is correct, just as God is no thing at all."

"What is my true self then?"

"It is no longer 'I' but Christ who lives in me."

"So we should meditate upon the Christ within us."

"Yes, but meditation is only an intermediate level of prayer because our thoughts are still focused on the figure of Jesus. An even higher form of prayer is contemplation, in which we give up thinking altogether."

"How is that possible?"

"Sit alone by yourself. Clear your mind of all thoughts. Do not let your mind wander but make it empty. Focus on yourself just as you are. Concentrate on the air you breathe in and the air you exhale, for your breath is the wind of the Holy Spirit blowing into and out of you. It is heard but never seen. No one knows where this power comes from or where it is going."

"What is the purpose of sitting alone and thinking nothing?" Justin asked.

"Once the doors of perception have been cleansed, everything appears just as it is."

"It seems like a waste of time to me."

"Blessed are the pure in heart," the anchorite continued, ignoring Justin's remark. "For only those whose hearts are beyond good and evil, heaven and hell, ecstasy and agony are able to see God."

"But the mind is very restless. What should I do when I stop focusing on my breathing and start thinking about something again?"

"Do not try to make your thought go away or repress it, no matter how evil, but simply acknowledge it, then dismiss it and return to your concentration. Be especially careful that you do not succumb to any phantasms or visions, whether they be malevolent or beatific, for they are but hallucinations that lead us into temptation. The goal is not bliss but equanimity. And there's a difference."

"But what if, after performing all of the exercises you have told me about, I am still unable to hear the voice of God?"

The anchorite frowned.

"Then you will certainly have become one with him!" he shouted. "Now stop bothering me with all these foolish questions and leave me alone!

You don't need my advice. Just go to your room and sit. Commune with your own heart and be silent. Your cell will teach you everything!"

With that the anchorite slammed the shutter of the window shut, leaving Justin standing in front of the crypt mystified.

§22

On their trek home, Bartholomew asked Justin what he had discussed with the anchorite. Justin replied that the matter was private and he did not wish to talk about it.

"I shall not inquire any further," Bartholomew said obligingly.

"And how about you? Would you like to tell me what you discussed with him? Of course, only if you wish."

"It is no secret. You and the others will know soon enough. I have decided to go on a quest."

"A quest? What kind of a quest?"

"You know from your study of the Bible that Jesus went to the desert to pray and remained there forty days and forty nights, just as Moses led the children of Israel in the wilderness for forty years and met God on the mountain."

"Yes, I know the stories," Justin said. "You have also told me about the early saints who went to the desert to find God."

"Well, I should like to do the same—not for the rest of my life, of course, but only for a short time. The anchorite suggested less than a week and absolutely no more than ten days, since it is my first time and I shall fast for the entire period."

"And what is the purpose of this undertaking?" Justin asked.

"We must be tested, as gold is tested by fire," Bartholomew replied. "Testing our faith produces steadfastness, so that we may be perfect and complete, lacking in nothing."

"Is it not a dangerous endeavor?"

"I'm sure I will be all right. I shall take water, though not food, with me."

"What I meant was that when Jesus went to the wilderness he was tempted by the devil."

"Indeed. I have no doubt that I shall meet Satan on this quest. But with God's help, I shall overcome him. This is what I consulted with the anchorite about: how to overcome Satan."

"And what did he say?"

"I'll admit that much of what he said was confusing to me, but the main point was that I should not rely on my own power, which would mean certain defeat, but solely on God's strength, for he is faithful and will protect me from the evil one."

"Does the abbot know of your plan?"

"Yes, I have already asked for his permission. But he told me that before undertaking this mission I should consult with the anchorite, who has much more experience about such matters than the abbot does."

For the remainder of the journey back to the abbey, the two walked together in silence. Justin wondered if perhaps he, too, should consider going to the wilderness to meet God.

§23

Over the next few days, while Bartholomew prepared to mount one of the wolds behind the monastery, Justin continued with his daily chores, repeating over and over again the prayer the anchorite had taught him, "Lord Jesus Christ, Son of God, have mercy on me, a sinner," ceasing only in the evening when he would sit in his room and meditate, not so much on religious matters but mostly on his life and what a mess he had made of it.

He wondered how Constance was spending her time, if she had been able to adjust to life on her own without Adrian, if perhaps she had even met another man and married him. He knew that there was nothing he could do about her now. He had left his former life behind and his decision was final. He simply needed to accept the situation as it was, although he could not so easily quell the yearning he still felt for Constance.

He also thought about Martin. He had been absolved by the priest but could not yet feel absolved by God. The memory of stabbing Martin in the side and then slitting his throat still haunted him. The scene replayed itself over and over again in his mind. He had not yet expiated his sins through acts of penance. Of course, there was nothing he could do that would fully make up for having killed Martin, but perhaps something else that could be done to save the lives of others. He knew not what, but felt he needed to find something.

After his meditations, such as they were, Justin would clear his mind of all thoughts and listen for the voice of God to speak to him. At first it was difficult to simply stop thinking so Justin tried to focus on his breathing, as the anchorite had instructed him, counting each breath and feeling the air flow into and out of him. After a very short while, he would find himself thinking of something again, usually about Constance or Martin, but instead of admonishing himself for his lack of concentration and suppressing the thought, he simply acknowledged it and went back to his breathing.

He would soon begin thinking of something else, however, about his present situation or his future and what he would do with it. Would he end up spending the rest of his days as a helper in a monastery? Should he apply to become a novice and take vows to become a monk as both Bartholomew and the abbot had suggested? To be sure, Justin thought, it would not be unpleasant to fritter away one's life in prayer and study, although he doubted that he was temperamentally suited to a religious vocation. He could not understand at all why the village priest had foretold that he would one day become a great spiritual leader.

Then he would resume his breathing.

Or perhaps he should return to the world outside. He could settle in the town that he and Bartholomew had just visited and work in the fields or take up a trade. He could marry and have children and lead a normal life after all. Or he could become a wanderer with no permanent place to lay his head. He would set out to explore what lies on the other side of the mountains he had seen or even sail away on the ocean towards the horizon to discover where the world really ended.

Then he would return to his breathing.

None of the thoughts Justin entertained gave him as much anxiety as the ache he felt, the utter hopelessness and despair which would not go away, of not having found peace with himself or peace with God. If God and he were truly one, he could not recognize it, and what he could not recognize he could not respond to. His soul was a tree which produced no fruit. The axe would be laid to the root, the tree cut down and cast into the fire.

And then he did not return to his breathing, but gave it up, no longer able to bear the monotony of prayer, the tedium of meditation, the sheer boredom of contemplation. He wondered why he had been so foolish as to think that a vermin-infested monk with broken teeth living locked up in a prison with walls far narrower than his own room could possibly have anything useful to teach him about the world outside.

§24

On the morning that Bartholomew left the monastery to embark on his quest, a special prayer service was held, which Justin had been invited to attend. The monks prayed for Bartholomew's safety on his journey, but most of all for his soul, that he would have the strength to engage in spiritual warfare against the forces of darkness and return to the abbey filled with God's grace. The abbot laid his hands on Bartholomew's shoulders and blessed him. And then Bartholomew departed, alone, from the chapel, through the monastery gate, and began his ascent of the wold. There was no further ceremony. The monks all returned to their daily tasks and so did Justin.

Despite, or perhaps because of, his melancholy, Justin resumed practicing, then not practicing, the prayer techniques the anchorite had taught him, trying to escape from the demons which tortured him while sitting safe and secure in his own room, even though he felt that such nightly devotions were useless. What he could not endure was the insipidity of his own life. It was this that he needed to confront.

The thoughts which interrupted his breathing were increasingly not about himself, however, but about Bartholomew. Through their discussions Justin had found that while he and Bartholomew had completely different dispositions and nearly opposite ways of thinking about almost everything, they had become friends. Indeed, Bartholomew was the only true friend Justin had in the world. Although he could be dogmatic and overbearing at times, Justin still admired and respected him. Bartholomew was sincere. He genuinely believed in the Church and all that it taught and wanted nothing more than to be a good Christian. Even though religion was mostly a matter of rituals and study for him, it was also something that he actually lived. Whereas Justin's life was banal and rudderless, Bartholomew's was full of meaning and significance.

The days passed, then a week. Bartholomew had not returned to the abbey and everyone was starting to become worried about him. Finally after ten days had passed, the abbot called a meeting of all the monks and lay brethren and said that something should be done. He proposed forming a rescue mission and asked if anyone would volunteer. Justin immediately raised his hand. One of the monks promptly followed. The two of them were assigned to climb to the top of the mountain and search for Bartholomew. Should they locate him, alive or dead, they would bring him back to the monastery. The rescuers should take food and water with them to revive Bartholomew and also for themselves.

"What should we do if we do not find him?" Justin asked.

"Do not put yourselves in any danger," the abbot replied. "Look for him as long as you can but when your food and water run out, you must return, even if it is without Bartholomew."

Justin and the monk set out and began climbing the wold behind the abbey. The path was steep, but they hurried as quickly as they could, pausing only briefly to catch their breath. After an hour or so, when they were about halfway up the mountain, they saw a figure coming towards them through the trees. It was Bartholomew. He was still some distance away and had not yet noticed them, but he was stumbling down the path, singing and dancing and throwing his arms into the air like a madman.

"Bartholomew!" Justin shouted.

Bartholomew did not hear him but continued tumbling and reeling from side to side, barely able to stay on the trail. Finally he crashed into Justin, who caught him in his arms.

"Bartholomew," Justin said softly. "It's me, Justin. Are you all right?"

Bartholomew looked up at Justin with a haggard face. One eye was open, the other half-shut, he was drooling from the mouth, his scraggy growth of beard soaked with saliva. Justin looked back into the eye that was open, but then it closed shut. Bartholomew fell out of Justin's arms and collapsed onto the hard mud.

"Is he dead?" the other monk asked.

"He's still breathing," Justin said, reaching down to lift up Bartholomew's head.

The other monk picked up Bartholomew's feet and together the two men carried his thin, almost weightless, body down the mountain. One of the monks had been posted as a lookout and, seeing them coming down the path as it opened onto the grounds behind the abbey, immediately alerted the others. By the time Justin's group reached the gate, the monks were waiting for them, the abbot standing in front.

"Is he still alive?" the abbot asked, as Justin and the monk carried Bartholomew through the gate.

"He is," Justin said.

A few of the monks carefully transferred Bartholomew into their own arms and took him immediately to the infirmary. The monks dispersed and Justin returned to his own room and tried, without success, to pray.

Bartholomew lay in bed for days without waking. Justin visited him every morning, afternoon, and evening between chores, just to sit beside him and hold his hand. The monk in charge continued funneling broth into Bartholomew's mouth, which somehow, miraculously, slithered down Bartholomew's throat into his stomach.

"Will he die?" Justin asked the attendant.

"Whatever happens, he is with God," the monk replied.

Then one day while Justin was sitting with Bartholomew, his eyes suddenly fluttered open. He looked around the room as if he were seeing the world for the very first time. His eyes landed on Justin's face and he said simply, "I am back."

"You never should have put yourself in such danger," Justin cried, throwing his arms around Bartholomew, giving him a tearful hug.

"It was worth it," Bartholomew said.

Justin summoned the attendant, who returned to the room a short while later with a plate of food, which he began giving to Bartholomew in small bites.

§25

Within a week Bartholomew had recovered well enough to return to his own room and a week after that was back to attending prayers and going about his daily routine. The abbot asked Bartholomew if he was ready to share his experience with the other monks. Bartholomew replied in the affirmative, so a convocation was called, which Justin was again invited to attend.

After prayers had been said, Bartholomew stood up before the audience, head bowed, and began to speak.

"First," he said. "I pray to God for humility because he has given me a great gift, which I should like to share with you today. But I must be meek, for this gift comes solely from God, not through my own efforts. I am simply the receptacle of God's divine grace. By myself I am nothing. God is everything."

Bartholomew stood up straight, puffed out his chest, not with pride but with confidence, and then began to tell his tale.

On the first day after beginning his climb to the top of the wold, Bartholomew came to a crossroads in the trail, with two paths leading up the mountain at angles and two leading down. A man wearing a black cloak and hood was standing at the fork between the two paths going up. He was carrying a basket of bread and a gourd of wine. The man asked Bartholomew where he was going.

"To the top of the mountain," Bartholomew replied.

"For what purpose?"

"To pray."

"Then you should go this way," the man said, pointing to the path on the left, which was broad and gentle.

"I think that you deceive me," Bartholomew said. "I shall go the other way."

The man had kept his face shadowed beneath his hood, a sure sign, Bartholomew concluded, that this was his first encounter with Satan.

Turning quickly away Bartholomew began climbing the path on the right. It was narrow and steep, having thorns on either side, which lashed at Bartholomew's arms and neck. Further up he saw a pile of gold coins in the middle of the path. He was tempted, though only briefly, to pick them up and abandon his mission. He might live a decent life in the city with that much money! But then, looking up, Bartholomew noticed that he was almost to the top of the wold. He jumped over the coins as though they were fire and continued on his way.

When he finally reached the top of the wold, he found a small clearing with trees surrounding it. He kneeled down in the very center of the clearing and began to pray. He prayed fervently until the sun had set and the forest was dark, and then continued praying throughout the night until morning sunlight began to filter through the trees. The first day and night had been uneventful. So, were the second, third, and fourth days and nights.

Although he dared not compare himself with Jesus, Bartholomew told the convocation that he was reminded of Jesus praying in Gethsemane before his arrest, trial, and crucifixion, knowing, of course, that whatever ordeals he faced would be far less than those of our Lord and Savior. And he found himself, like Peter and the disciples, unable to keep his vigil, falling asleep at times even while still kneeling. Then he would shake himself awake and resume praying.

He had taken no food with him and was fasting continuously. He drank the water he had brought with him only sparingly. He was becoming dizzy from lack of food and sleep and began losing count of how many days he had stayed on the mountain.

§26

A while later Bartholomew saw through his blurry eyes someone making his way through the trees to the top of the hill, although from the opposite direction in which Bartholomew had come. It was the same man he had met at the crossroads, wearing the same black cloak and hood. Bartholomew still could not see the man's face, but he was carrying the same basket covered with a cloth in one hand and the same sealed gourd in the other. The man sat on the ground next to Bartholomew.

He uncovered the basket, took out a loaf of bread, and tried to hand it to Bartholomew. "Here. You must be hungry."

Bartholomew pushed the bread away.

"Well, if you do not wish to eat, I also have some wine with me," the man said, holding out the gourd to Bartholomew with his other hand. "Please have some to satisfy your thirst."

"I shall not take anything you offer me," Bartholomew said.

"Why are you fasting here in the wilderness, away from the world and all its pleasures?"

"You shall not tempt me, Satan," Bartholomew replied.

"Satan! Whyever do you think I am Satan? I am just an ordinary man."

"Then what is your purpose here?" Bartholomew asked.

"I climbed this mountain simply for my pleasure. As the saint says, people are moved to marvel at the heights of mountains, at the mighty waves of the sea, at the long courses of great rivers, at the vastness of the oceans, at the movements of the stars."

"But they take no interest in themselves."

"I can see that you have read the Church Fathers," the man said. "Yet why should we not take great delight in this world just as it is, which God himself has created and declared 'good'?"

"We should set our minds on things above, not on earthly things."

"So, is that why you have become a monk? I am sure that you are an intelligent man. There are so many good and useful pursuits you could turn your attention to. You could become a merchant and live a comfortable life in the city. Or a trader and travel the world here and afar. Or even an administrator in the court and have control over the affairs of the entire kingdom."

"I have no desire to rule over even all the kingdoms of this world. I wish only to enter the Kingdom of Heaven."

"But are heaven and earth not one and the same?"

"Get thee behind me, Satan!" Bartholomew cried.

"Oh my, I have no idea why you keep confusing me with Satan! As I said, I am just an ordinary person, which is all that you or I can ever be. We should accept the natures God has given us and live in harmony with God's world, not indulge in unnatural pursuits such as starving ourselves to death in the wilderness!"

"Please leave," Bartholomew replied. "I should like to be alone."

"All right," the man said. "The decision is yours. If my presence is not wanted here, then I shall depart."

The man then stood up and began walking down the same path he had come up. Although Bartholomew had successfully rebuffed him this time, he knew this would not be his last encounter with Satan. The devil would wait for an opportune time and then come again to unleash his legions upon him.

§27

And, indeed, the very next night strange things started happening. Vultures began flying overhead. Bartholomew heard sounds coming from the forest, rustling through the underbrush on all sides. Although he could see nothing, he assumed that the noises were coming from wild beasts or perhaps even werewolves. Sometimes the creatures would come quite close to edge of the clearing, but then the crunching on the fallen twigs would cease, as if the beasts were watching him.

A ferocious wind arose and it began raining heavily. Bartholomew was immovable. Or perhaps paralyzed. As he continued kneeling in the mud, fog enveloped him. His stupor increased. He felt as if he were intoxicated or in a daze, unable to think or to move, aware of nothing around him, cognizant only of his own soul. A short time later he lost all awareness, even of his deliriousness. It was no longer Bartholomew experiencing the world since both Bartholomew and the world had ceased to exist. All that remained was the experience itself.

Only then did the fiends of the forest begin to appear to him. One had the body of a horse but the torso of a man. He spoke to Bartholomew in a language Bartholomew could not understand, pointing his finger insistently towards the path that led back down the mountain. Another was a man with goat-like feet and horns, completely naked, with a club in one hand, a serpent in the other, and an enormously erect penis which shot from between his legs like a spear. The lecher whispered into Bartholomew's ear, "Come, let us pray together. For you and I worship the same God." A jester with a bloated stomach was lying on the ground beside a prostitute with her legs wide open.

The wild beasts became demons. Boars with menacing snouts charged at him. Wolves with fanged teeth, growling and snarling, leaped on top of him, ripping his flesh. Birds with splotched wings pecked at him with sharp beaks, some shapeshifting into imps that clawed at him with long talons. Large hairy spiders crawled on his arms, while scaly reptilians with slashing tales and darting tongues slithered around his legs. Fish with venomous spines attacked Bartholomew's feet from the puddles of rain that had formed all around him.

Runnels of water then transported Bartholomew to the far side of the clearing, in the same direction that the man had taken up and down the mountain, the legions still swarming around him. The path disappeared into the trees but soon came to a sudden stop at the edge of a sheer precipice. Bartholomew almost careened over the top but caught himself on a shrub clinging to the rocks.

A voice said, "Bartholomew, behold your suffering. You could end it all right now by leaping down into the pit. If God is truly with you, he will send his angels to bear you up. If God is not with you, then you will die without his mercy. But either way your suffering will cease. Test your faith and see if it is true. Leap!"

Still holding onto the shrub, Bartholomew pulled himself up and looked out over the cliff. The abyss had no bottom.

The earth began to quake, the wind blew the rocks apart, uprooted trees were hurled into the air, lava poured from heaven, the mud boiled. Hailstones of live coals and glowing ashes turned the pitch-black sky incandescent as they pelted down on him.

Bartholomew was in torment and felt an urge—no, a compulsion—to let go of the shrub and jump. But he held steadfast. Then, miraculously, the earth stopped moving, the wind ceased, the rain stopped, and all the fallen angels that had been hounding him evaporated with the fog. He fell back to the ground in convulsions and lay there as if dead.

When he finally opened his eyes, Bartholomew looked up and saw the clouds part. Light streamed down from heaven. The sky was filled with colors he had never seen before. A bliss welled up inside his heart unlike any he had ever experienced. And he prayed to God, "Lord, let me remain in this light with you. I wish this moment could last forever."

Then he heard the voice of God himself say, "No, Bartholomew, you may not remain in the wilderness. You must return to the world, even as Jesus after he was tempted came down from the mountain to preach the gospel. You must report what you have witnessed, warning others of the consequences of sin, but reassuring them that I am merciful and will deliver them from evil."

"But I never want to leave your presence, Lord," Bartholomew said.

"You can never be apart from me," the voice replied. "I am with you always, even to the end of the age."

After Bartholomew had finished recounting his story to the monks in the assembly, he bowed his head deeply and clasped his hands together in thanksgiving.

The chapel was silent for several minutes until the abbot finally said, "Let us pray to God that he will exorcise all unclean spirits from our hearts and minds so that we may perpetually walk in the light of his countenance."

§28

In the days that followed, Justin noticed that Bartholomew had become a transformed person. He had always been good and gentle and kind, but now he was filled with a holy light that radiated outward from his soul to his whole body, to the point that he actually seemed to glow like a lamp he could not hide even if he wanted to, performing his usual duties, but with a sense of dedication and attentiveness that made even the most mundane task seem extraordinary.

Bartholomew had found peace not only with God but also with himself, indeed a peace that surpasses all understanding and a sense of serenity that eluded Justin. Justin sat alone in his room every night, continuing his wordless contemplations, which were constantly interrupted by the question of whether he, too, should undertake a quest to overcome the darkness of his own soul and become enlightened like Bartholomew. He found himself frequently slipping back into discursive prayer, asking God to ignite a fire within himself that could never be extinguished.

He rarely thought of Constance anymore. It was not that he had forgotten her or no longer wanted to be with her, but simply that the situation was hopeless and there was no point in brooding. So he tried to put her out of his mind. On some nights, however, scenes of the times he had spent with her would return unwanted to afflict him, which he could not repress no matter how hard he tried.

In any case, he was bored with life in the monastery. He had already made a firm decision not to ask the abbot to accept him as a novice. There was no future for him here at the abbey as a monk, and while he did not mind the work he was doing at all, it did not bring him any joy or satisfaction either. Justin began to long for something different, but he had no idea what. None of the alternatives he mulled over in his mind really appealed to him. There was no place, really, that he wanted to go, no place that would ever be home for him.

His life was, in fact, about to change dramatically, but he did not yet know it.

Shortly after Justin had been having all these thoughts, Bartholomew came to his room and said, "The abbot has summoned us for an interview. It shall be tomorrow just after morning prayers."

"I can understand why he might want to talk to you, but I can't imagine why he wishes to see me. Do you know?"

"Indeed, I do. I have been conferring with him about this matter for several days now."

"And what exactly is this matter you have been discussing with him?"

"I cannot tell you. The abbot will disclose everything to you in good time."

Then Bartholomew smiled and said, "But it will be a wonderful surprise for you."

Justin looked at Bartholomew quizzically, but he said nothing more and quietly left the room.

§29

The next day Justin appeared outside the abbot's room at the appointed time. Bartholomew was waiting for him. A voice called out from inside the cell for them to enter. They opened the door and stepped inside. The abbot motioned for the two to be seated on the floor, as he sat down opposite them on his pallet. His eyes were gleaming, as they always did, but he spoke in a voice that was, if possible, even softer than Justin had ever heard before.

"Thank you both for coming," the abbot said. And then, addressing Justin, "Before I explain why I asked you to come here, I believe there is something Bartholomew wishes to tell you."

"Indeed, there is," Bartholomew said, smiling to Justin. "I have been remiss in not saying this sooner, but I wish to express my sincere gratitude to you for coming to look for me after my experience on the mountain. I surely would have died if you and the other monk had not come to save me. I feel that we are no longer friends, but brothers."

"I have always thought of you as a friend and brother, too," Justin said. "Although as my spiritual director, you are also my senior."

"Yes," the abbot said, "Bartholomew has told me about your spiritual growth and also about your studies. I was also quite impressed with your earnestness in the discussion we had many months ago. Afterward I had thought to formally ask if you might wish to join us at the monastery as novice, with the intention of becoming a monk in due course. Upon giving the matter much prayer, however, it seems to me that a life of seclusion in an abbey would not suit you."

"I have reached the same conclusion," Justin said straightforwardly.

"Nonetheless, upon further reflection it has occurred to me that you might find a more suitable vocation for yourself if given the opportunity to more fully develop the other talents you have."

"I am not sure what you are referring to, Father Abbot, since I have no particular talents. But I agree that I do not have the proclivity to become a monk."

"Bartholomew has informed me that you are fluent in both Greek and Latin, and that you are an excellent scholar. He has mentioned that he often feels that your wisdom exceeds his own, even though he sometimes finds your questions disconcerting."

"To the contrary," Justin replied. "Bartholomew has always been my guide in both intellectual and spiritual matters. Everything I know I owe to him. And I apologize to him sincerely for my rude inquisitiveness."

"In any case, it has been decided to send Bartholomew to the city to attend university, initially to complete a master's course. After that he might become an ordained priest and perhaps later an abbot such as myself. Or, if he makes good headway with his studies, he may go on to pursue a doctorate in theology and become a teacher or even a theologian. Such decisions require much prayer, of course, but having asked for God's guidance we are determined to send him on his way and to see where his calling will lead him."

Justin said nothing but conveyed his congratulations to Bartholomew with a smile.

"In addition," the abbot continued, "we would like to offer you the opportunity to accompany Bartholomew to the city so that you may also study at the university. You shall follow the standard course of study to become a master and after that decide whether to continue your studies in any specialized field of your choice, such as law or medicine or philosophy."

Justin was instantly excited by the abbot's proposal, but immediately objected, "Your suggestion is very interesting, but as you know, I am a poor man. I would not have the money to pay the fees."

"You needn't worry about costs. An abbey such as ours is not without funds and we will pay the necessary tuition for both you and Bartholomew, as we do for a select few of the brighter boys at our school. We shall also give each of you a small stipend for your living expenses, which Bartholomew will take charge of. As you may know, it is not unheard of for monasteries to offer scholarships to worthy candidates to attend university, regardless of their station in life."

"That would be very charitable of you," Justin said.

"At some point in the future, after you complete your studies and become established in your career, if you have the means to offer us a donation in return, it would be most appreciated, of course. But it would be a donation, not a repayment."

"Indeed, I should certainly want to give you a contribution to thank you for your generosity. But I am still not sure if I am worthy of undertaking such an endeavor."

"You have not told me much about your past," the abbot said. "But I have heard that you were not in line to receive an inheritance and so you left your father's estate to find your own fortune."

This was the same story that Justin had let Bartholomew believe about him, so he replied, falsely, to the abbot, "Yes, that's right."

"Well, then, the only qualification for you to receive our support is that you have lived an upright life and committed no serious crimes. We do not wish any scandal. May we have your guarantee on this point?"

Justin did not want to lie yet again, but not knowing how to respond in a way that was both truthful and would satisfy the abbot, he said simply, "You have my assurance. But perhaps you should give me time to consider more fully the matter of attending university."

"Indeed, there is no rush. You needn't decide now. Please pray about it and give me your answer within a few weeks if you can."

It occurred to Justin that this might also be the perfect time to make a request to the abbot.

"Father," Justin began slowly. "If I may, if you do not object, if I do not seem too forward . . . ."

"Please tell me what you want," the abbot said.

Justin finally released the words from his mouth. "Would you give me permission to go to the mountain to pray, as Bartholomew did?"

The abbot considered for a moment and then said, "Although Bartholomew had a mighty encounter with God in the wilderness, it was still a very dangerous expedition. Therefore, I am inclined to forbid it. I do not wish there to be a similar incident."

"But," Justin said timorously, "if I were to stay for a shorter time and not fast, would I receive your approval? I have experience living in the open."

The abbot pursed his lips and then said, "If you would limit your stay to not more than one week and take sufficient food and water with you, I would give you my consent."

"Indeed, Father. In the meantime, I will pray about this other undertaking you have proposed."

The abbot stood up. Bartholomew and Justin stood up as well.

"May you find the peace of God," the abbot said, blessing them with a smile.

§30

Immediately after his interview with the abbot, Justin returned to his room, fell on his pallet, and began weeping. Why had he told yet another lie, not just one but two, about having left the estate because he was not in line to receive an inheritance and not having committed any serious crimes? Why couldn't he be completely honest and live openly? It was not the first time he wondered why he could not simply erase his past and write a new life for himself on a clean slate.

On the one hand, Justin certainly felt fear about admitting what he had done. He did not want to reveal to anyone who his father was or that he was his father's heir since it would surely end with him being returned to the estate. He especially wanted no one to know about his murder of Martin, which would inevitably result in his trial and execution.

On the other hand, Justin was distressed at having lied not only to Bartholomew, but now as well to the abbot, who had been so kind to him. He wondered why it was so difficult for him to lead a normal life the same as everyone else. He had confessed to killing Martin and been absolved by a priest. Wasn't that enough? If it was the forgiveness of God that mattered, rather than the forgiveness of others, why should he not lie under the circumstances? Was it really necessary for him to carry this burden around with him for the rest of his days? Justin was ready to move on and start over. Why would others not let him?

Justin continued to sit silently night after night, breathing the air in, breathing the air out, in a vain attempt to eliminate such thoughts from his mind.

§31

The day finally arrived when Justin would depart for the mountain. Another prayer service was held, the monks prayed for Justin's safety and for his soul, the abbot laid hands on Justin and blessed him, and Bartholomew said to him with a grin just before he left the gate, "Don't worry I will come to rescue you should you not return within the allotted time!"

Then, carrying the food and water he had been given, Justin commenced his retreat into the wilderness. As he ascended the stony path he reflected that the way up a mountain is the same as the way down. These are simply two opposite ways of describing the exact same reality. The higher we climb the closer we come to the center. And once we have reached the top, the only way to go higher is to come back down.

In what seemed like no time he came to the crossroads that Bartholomew had described and saw that, indeed, the upward path to the left was wide and sloped gradually around the side of the mountain, while the path on the right was narrow and went straight up through a thicket of brambles. There was no man standing there, though, so Justin was left to determine on his own which path to take.

He decided to follow the same route that Bartholomew had taken, and soon found his arms cut and scratched by the thorns. Close to the summit Justin noticed not gold coins, but a cluster of shiny brown chestnuts, which had broken out of their burrs and were strewn over a section of the path. Looking up he saw the branch of a chestnut tree hanging over the path, still full of nuts. He walked around the nuts on the ground and continued up the wold. At the top he found a clearing with trees on all sides, just as Bartholomew had also reported.

Justin positioned himself exactly in the center of the clearing, letting down his basket of food and cask of water as a marker. Standing, not kneeling, in silence for a long time, he cleared his mind of all thoughts and tried, the best he could, to calm his soul. He was surprised how quickly he was able to achieve a state of mindfulness, imperfect though it was. His contemplative exercises must be helping, he thought, even though he hadn't realized it. In one way, he was aware of everything around him, in another he was aware only of himself, and in yet another he was aware of nothing other than his own awareness, conscious only of his own consciousness.

He remained in this state for the whole of the first day. Then he ate some of the food, drank some of the water, and lay down to sleep in the center of the clearing. After awaking the next day Justin began to carry out the plan he had devised beforehand.

In the morning he walked slowly one step at a time towards the east, the direction of dawn and the sun, of birth and infancy, of water and the ocean, of spring and planting. He stayed there for some time experiencing everything but thinking nothing, and then returned to the center.

He repeated the same process by walking at midday to the south, the direction of noontide and earth, of youth and growth, of soil and plains, of summer and blossoming; in the evening to the west, the direction of twilight and the first stars, of maturity and decay, of air and mountains, of autumn and harvesting; and at night to the north, the direction of darkness and the moon, of old age and death, of fire and the desert, of winter and lying fallow, each time remaining for several hours and then returning to the center.

Indeed, Justin concluded, we pass through the stages of innocence, experience, suffering, and redemption. The world is not a trinity, but a quadrinity. And God also seems to require a fourth. God the parent is beyond being and transcendent, the oceanic feeling of being one with the universe. Jesus the offspring is being and immanent, the fusion of the divine and the human, of one's own particularity with something greater than itself. The Holy Spirit is becoming and transformative, creating possibilities for us to be changed into something different from what we currently are. The fourth is Satan, the oft unrecognized impulses lying deep within us which gives us the potential to commit acts of evil.

Nonetheless, beyond these there must be even another—a fifth—something ineffable, a center that is nowhere, a void without form, an absolute nothingness. Yet if the center is wherever we are, then it is also nowhere. Ultimately there is no center. I am here. Where else could I be?

By the end of the day Justin had engraved the sign of the cross in the ground with his feet, each line equidistant from the center. For the next few days he would eat, drink, and sleep again, and wake once more to trace the same pattern.

As he walked he noticed vultures circling overhead waiting to make a meal of him if he were to die. He heard rustling in the underbrush, which he knew to be the sound of wild pigs since he had also seen the burrows they had rooted into the dirt at the edge of the clearing, as well as their telltale footprints. At night Justin heard the howl of a lone wolf, but from a distance, and he knew from having lived with the hermit that he would be safe from any wild animals if he didn't provoke them. There were certainly spiders crawling through the grasses and lizards darting here and there, but he saw no fish, particularly none with spiny fins, nor any centaurs or satyrs or other superhuman figures. The birds were simply birds.

Indeed, the wind on the mountain could be violent at times, kicking up dust and throwing stones into the air, sometimes accompanied by whipping rain that turned the dust to mud and formed rivulets rushing down from the mountaintop on all sides. At other times, however, the fog would lift, the clouds would be swept away, and amber sunlight would pour down from a clear blue sky.

Justin knew from the start that his quest would be different from Bartholomew's. He had no doubt that the experiences Bartholomew had described were in some sense real. Even though when Bartholomew had returned to the monastery there had been no scars on his body from the creatures he claimed had assailed him, he had nonetheless come face to face with the evil inside himself. He had also undoubtedly had a vision of God, although perhaps one which came not from the heavens above, but from within his own soul. And he had been changed by his quest to become a person filled with even more love and humility than he had possessed before. This reality could not be denied and it was something to be valued.

No, Justin had not really expected that his own quest would be the same as Bartholomew's. What he sought were not miraculous experiences but a simple understanding of himself, the world, and God. He did not wish to throw himself into a whirlwind, but merely to calm the storm that seethed inside his own soul. He did not feel that he was making any progress at all, but he did begin to think that maybe he had been searching in all the wrong places and in the wrong way. He had spent five days on the mountain, not the full week he had planned on. But it was time for him to return to the abbey. And from there, to where?

§32

Before going back down the path he had come up, Justin decided to investigate the path on the other end of the clearing, the same trail Bartholomew had mentioned that purportedly stopped abruptly and looked out over a precarious ledge. Indeed, at the end of the path there was a precipice that fell into the valley below and gave one a panoramic view of the landscapes beyond. There was also a bush near the edge, which Justin found was strong enough to hold onto and prevent him from teetering into the abyss.

Moving back from the bush, Justin decided to follow the path that veered sharply to its left. The route wound its way gently down the other side of the mountain and eventually connected to the junction he had encountered on his way up. Near the fork in the path he saw a man wearing a black cloak and hood coming towards him. The man was carrying a basket of bread and a wine gourd.

"Good day," the man greeted him.

"Good day, sir," Justin replied.

The man's face looked familiar, but Justin could not place where he had seen him before. Could this be the same man he had met on the road after his escape through the wolds, who had given him directions to the monastery? Justin could not be sure. The man was neither tall nor short, fat nor thin, young nor old, handsome nor ugly. And he hardly looked like Satan. He was just an ordinary man.

"Are you climbing to the top of the mountain?" Justin asked.

"Indeed, I am. I come here every so often just to enjoy the view. Would you like a bit of my bread and a sip of my wine?"

"It is kind of you to offer, but I am not hungry," Justin said. "I have brought sufficient food for myself. Which path do you usually take to the top?"

"The one on the left, of course. It's a much easier route than the path on the right."

"We each must follow our own path up the mountain, I suppose."

"Moreover, not everyone is climbing the same mountain," man said. "What, may I ask, is the purpose of your visit here?"

"I'm simply enjoying the view, too," Justin replied.

"Wonderful! The air is so fresh and invigorating! A while back I met a monk at this very same spot and later at the top of the mountain. He was fasting and praying. A very excitable chap. I'm not sure why anyone would want to come to a mountain just to fast and pray. Surely we can do that at home!"

"No doubt we can pray and fast anywhere."

"You're right about that," the man said. "Well, it seems you're going down and I'm going up. It's the same path either way. Perhaps we will meet again someday!"

With that the man turned and began climbing the trail on the left. Justin resumed his descent down the mountain, happy he had met the man but doubting if he would ever see him again.

Justin began thinking of what he would say to the other monks after he returned to the abbey. Unlike Bartholomew, he'd had no great visions, even though he had surely learned something. He had come to think that the answer he was looking for could not be found in religion or the Church, that God was not hiding in heaven or even in his soul. Perhaps God is nature and nature is God after all. The two are indistinguishable! And, if so, we no longer need to look for God because we can find him in everything that surrounds us.

Ah, Justin thought, I will be like the old hermit and make nature my home. The forest is my sacred grove, the tree I sit beneath my temple. The limbs are the arches of my cathedral, the branches spires pointing to an unknown beyond. The blue sky is my heaven, the earth my home. The sun is my brother, the moon my sister. The stars are my friends. The wind swirls around me. I inhale the air and it becomes my spirit. The fire warms not just my skin but my heart. I will follow the smoke wherever it leads me. I will run naked through the meadows and bathe in the pools of waterfalls. The mountain springs will slake my thirst and cleanse me. The stones will be my bread, the streams my wine, the rain pouring down from heaven my baptismal waters. Even if a transcendent God no longer exists, the wonder of nature remains!

Or maybe a tree is just a tree, water is just water, stones are just stones. The world is completely disenchanted after all.

Or yet again, perhaps nature embraces not only an immanent God but also an immanent Satan. As the abbot had told him, light cannot be seen if all is light, but only when there is also darkness. The clouds hang over all of us. The rain falls on the just and the unjust. And when the fog lifts, sunlight pours down on both of them as well. Nature is not just the grandeur of mountain peaks, the birds of the air, or the lilies of the field. It is also the sparrow falling, the withering heat and freezing snow, thunderstorms of hail and fire, earthquakes and floods, swarms of locusts and flies, plagues and festering boils, burning cities and rivers flowing with blood. We trust that God is love and his creation good, yet nature is red in tooth and claw.

Perhaps good cannot exist without evil. There is no life without birth, no birth without death. And whether there be any life beyond death, we have only this one brief moment of time to be alive before the worms consume our flesh and shit us out as dust again. There is no purpose in life, neither destiny nor fate, only randomness. Things just happen as they do by chance.

How, then, to affirm life, the joy as well as the sorrow, when it lacks all meaning or direction, to accept the world in all its grandeur and malevolence just as it is? Or perhaps we should protest against it, standing defiant on the ocean until we sink beneath its waves, pointing an accusing finger at God and demanding to know why he had created such a God-awful place?

Justin knew now that he was on his own and must find his own way, with neither the Church nor the Bible to guide him. As the abbot had told him, Justin would need to find his inner light and be a lamp unto his own path. He did not wish to imitate Christ but only to be himself, or better, whatever it was possible for him to become.

These are the things Justin wanted to tell the monks when he arrived back at the monastery, but he knew he could not. He wasn't sure what to believe himself.

§33

When Justin reached the abbey, no one was waiting for him. He walked through the gate and went directly to his room without being noticed. There he lay on his pallet thinking about what he should do. He no longer had any reason to stay at the monastery. A brief image of Constance passed through his mind, but he quickly dismissed it. If another door opened for him, he would pass through it. Water does not flow up the mountain, but down it, always finding the easiest path, not smashing through rocks but going around them.

The next morning Justin appeared as usual for his kitchen duties. The prior was surprised to see him.

"We did not know that you had returned," he said.

"Yes, I came back last night," Justin replied.

"Have you reported yet to the abbot?"

"No, I haven't."

"You should have done so immediately. I will inform him that you are here."

The prior disappeared through the kitchen door and returned in a very short time.

"The abbot wishes to see you immediately," he said.

Justin walked to the abbot's room, paused briefly outside the door, and then knocked. The abbot beckoned him to enter. He was smiling as Justin opened the door and closed it gently behind him.

"You're back early. But I am so glad that you are safe. We were praying for you the entire time. You experienced no difficulties during your trip?"

"None whatsoever."

"Well, you certainly look healthy and robust. Shall we plan a convocation for you soon, so that you may tell us about your experiences?"

"I'm afraid that won't be necessary," Justin replied dejectedly. "My mission was a failure."

"I see," the abbot said, looking at him discerningly. "Could you nonetheless tell me what happened?"

"Nothing happened. My eyes are too attuned to this world to be able to see another world beyond it."

"Well," the abbot said. "Do not be too disappointed. God does not necessarily appear to everyone in majestic visions. We can just as easily see God in a grain of sand and heaven in a wildflower. Everything that lives is holy!"

Justin made no reply.

"Have you prayed about our offer to send you to the university?" the abbot asked.

"I have, Father."

"And what is your decision?"

"As you said, I'm not cut out to become a monk. So I would indeed be grateful for the opportunity to commence my studies."

"Then the matter is settled."

A short time later Justin and Bartholomew passed through the gate of the monastery and began walking towards the city. Justin had been given a new tunic and cloak, Bartholomew a new habit and cowl.

IV

The City

It took Justin and Bartholomew several days traveling on foot to reach the city. A wall had been built around it, not unlike the wall that surrounded Justin's father's estate but vastly higher, more formidable, and encompassing. Passing through the gate Justin was immediately overwhelmed by the throngs of noisy people walking through the narrow streets, as he gingerly stepped over the litter and filth that was everywhere. In addition to the crowds of ordinary townsfolk there were moneylenders and beggars, street musicians and fortunetellers, peddlers of trinkets, vendors of stews and puddings, griddle cakes and pies.

The houses were made of daub and wattle, just like the house in the village he had helped Adrian and Constance build, but they were sturdier and larger, most having three stories. Many of the buildings had shops on the first floor, where merchants displayed expensive cloths, such as satin and silk, and traders sold spices and perfumes. There were workshops for weavers, tanners, and carpenters, and other craftspeople, who hawked their wares beneath signs with pictures showing the kind of goods they had on offer. The guildhall, made of stone not wood, occupied a prominent place in the center of the town, with taverns and inns on either side.

Justin wanted to stop and look at everything he saw, but Bartholomew told him that cities such as these are dens of iniquity, tempting people to indulge not only in luxurious goods and bawdy forms of entertainment but also in drunkenness, prostitution, and gambling, so they should go straight to the cathedral to pray, then to the university, and not be waylaid.

And, indeed, just a short distance further, two women with painted faces and loose-fitting gowns, one pink, one violet, emerged from a doorway and accosted them.

"Would you boys like to spend some time together with us?" the lady in violet asked them.

Bartholomew brushed quickly past them, pulling Justin by the arm.

"See, I told you," he fumed, when they were away from the women.

"I can understand why they might approach me," Justin said, "since I am wearing ordinary clothes. But you are wearing a habit and cowl. Surely they must see that you are a monk."

"It makes no difference. I am ashamed to say, but some of the brothers are prone to commit acts of sexual impurity."

"But monks take vows of chastity."

"And occasionally break them. Not only monks but even priests and bishops."

"Marriage is a sacrament," Justin said. "Why are monks and priests expected to partake in all the other sacraments, but prevented from receiving God's grace through the sacrament of marriage?"

"Ah, but we *are* married," Bartholomew replied. "To Christ and his Church."

The two came to an open market where men were selling meat and bread, along with other essentials, such as salt and coal, while women purveyed poultry, eggs, milk, and vegetables. Once they had passed through the stalls, Justin and Bartholomew found themselves in a large square in front of the cathedral. A stage had been set up in the middle of the plaza and a mystery play was being performed. Despite his eagerness to complete their journey, Bartholomew, to Justin's delight, suggested that they stop to watch it.

The drama was about the last judgment. The lead actor was dressed as a shepherd, others as sheep and goats. The penitents all cried out:

> From the goats my lot divide,
> With thy lambs a place provide,
> On the right and near thy side!

The shepherd then motioned the goats towards a huge burning fire on the left, where devils and demons were gathered, and the sheep to a garden on the right, where saints and angels awaited them.

Bartholomew leaned over and whispered to Justin, "If we succumb to our desires, we shall be on the side of the goats. As the scriptures clearly state, 'Do not be deceived: neither fornicators, nor idolaters, nor adulterers, nor homosexuals, nor thieves, nor the greedy, nor drunkards, nor revilers, nor extortionists shall inherit the Kingdom of God.'"

When the shepherd had duly separated the sheep from the goats and the play had finished, Bartholomew and Justin walked around behind the stage and until they were standing in front of the cathedral itself. It was by far the largest and tallest building in the city, with two soaring spires ascending from either side of the entrance, pointing to God, and gargoyles with menacing faces reminding sinners of all the evil that lay outside its walls. To the left of the cathedral was an infirmary, a squat but long building also made of stone.

Entering the narthex Bartholomew and Justin dipped their right hands in the holy water and made the sign of the cross. Passing into the nave, Justin looked up to see the high pointed arches supported by huge pillars on either side, with frescoes on the vaulted ceilings. There were stained glass windows along each of the walls, depicting various stories from the Bible and the lives of the saints. Justin was entranced by how silent it was inside the cathedral compared to all the hustle and bustle outside. Indeed, here all was holy, if possible even holier than in the chapel at the monastery.

Bartholomew and Justin bowed and approached the stone altar in the chancel, covered with a white cloth and adorned with a cross in the center and white candles in silver candlesticks on either side. Behind and above the altar was a triptych of painted panels depicting the birth, death, and resurrection of Jesus. To the left was a statue of Mary with the baby Jesus in her arms, to the right the tabernacle with a lit red candle in front of it, signifying that the reserved Eucharist, the very body and blood of Jesus Christ, was present. Bartholomew and Justin genuflected before the tabernacle, then prostrated themselves before the altar. After saying their individual prayers, Bartholomew began to say the Lord's Prayer aloud, laying special stress on the words, "Lead us not into temptation."

§2

The university was not unlike the monastery. It was situated directly behind the cathedral and surrounded by a low wall, intended more to demarcate a boundary between itself and the rest of the town than to keep students in or intruders out, with an open gate at the entrance. Inside were the buildings of several colleges, each with their own lecture halls, study rooms, and dormitories for students, in addition to a dining hall, a commons room, and a small chapel. Most of the students were much younger than Bartholomew and Justin, although a few were the same age or older. The headmaster of the college showed Bartholomew and Justin to a room they would share with each other, which had beds rather than pallets, and a desk and chair for each of them.

It had been worked out beforehand that since Bartholomew and Justin had already received a basic education in the liberal arts and were fluent in Greek and Latin, they would forego the usual courses for beginning students and be allowed immediately to take higher-level courses in philosophy, which would be taught by the headmaster himself. Should they pass the examinations for these courses successfully, they would be awarded a master's degree and could then move on to more specialized studies leading to a doctorate if they wished.

The schedule was demanding. Classes would begin at dawn and finish at dusk each weekday, with a break for dinner in between and supper afterwards. Students and professors would eat together in silence, with an occasional short lecture or oration after the evening meal.

Courses were designed around particular works, with time being set aside for students to peruse books in the library. In the morning the master would read a passage from the assigned work aloud to the pupils, with commentaries from other authors and Church documents. The students would then be given time to meditate on what they had heard, both to make sure that they had understood the text and to consider whether there were any topics requiring further discussion. If any potential points of contention were found, both sides of an issue would then be thoroughly debated, with a view towards either proving one of them wrong or showing how two seemingly opposed views might be made compatible. At the end of the disputation the master would present his own conclusions and the matter would be judged resolved.

"There is but one truth," the master told them. "If there is a difference between what we think and what the Church teaches, then it is most certainly we who are wrong. If it appears to us that the Church Fathers contradict one another, then it is only due to our own lack of understanding. The disagreement is only apparent and superficial. Once we are equipped with the tools of dialectical logic and able to dig deeper, we shall see that seemingly antithetical opinions are in fact in perfect harmony with each other. True authority does not oppose right reason nor does right reason oppose true authority."

Justin breezed through the courses. He had never read philosophy, but as with his training at the monastery, he approached what he was learning with a fresh mind and no prior assumptions. The texts were easy enough to understand, although when listening to the master's commentaries he sometimes felt that the master did not really grasp their full significance. What impressed him most was how ignorant the philosophers themselves actually were. They certainly did not agree among themselves and almost always had different ideas about what is true, despite the master's claim that there is only "one truth." Nonetheless, whenever the master asked Justin a question, he always answered it as the master expected him to, not as he really thought. As a result the master was constantly praising Justin for his work, even telling him privately once that he was the best student in the class and would no doubt be able to take his final examination early.

Bartholomew was struggling, however. Theology was obviously much easier for him than philosophy. The Latin and Greek were no problem but, clinging to the idea that there is but one truth, he would often get confused when the philosophers disagreed with each other. With theology one could simply believe what the Church teaches; with philosophy it seemed that any argument used to establish a position could be met by an equally valid counterargument, leaving the matter unresolved. Bartholomew unswervingly believed that the dialectic would eventually resolve all inconsistencies, as the master had suggested, but could not always follow the convoluted chains of reasoning. He would often consult Justin for help, asking him whether this philosopher's idea or another's was the "Truth." Justin tried to explain to him that they were simply different ways of thinking, at which point Bartholomew would throw up his hands and say, "I do not want to know 'different ways of thinking.' I want to know the *Truth!*"

§3

The first term passed with Justin and Bartholomew applying themselves studiously to the assigned readings and the master's lectures. When one text was finished, they began another.

Then on the first day of the second term a new student whom Justin had never seen before appeared in the classroom. He was about the same age as Justin, with long flaming red hair and a wispy beard. It was immediately clear that this recent addition to their class was fond of challenging the master and stirring up controversy. Before his arrival, the lectures had been uneventful and the disputations relatively mild, intended mainly to clear up misunderstandings. The exchanges between the new arrival and the master were quite heated, however. Justin was rather tickled that the usually dull colloquia were now enlivened with some genuine differences of opinion!

"Master," the new student asked on one occasion. "We have learned from our text that a statement must be either true or false and cannot be both true and false at the same time. Could you please tell me, then, is the statement 'I am a liar' true or false?"

"Why, in your case it is definitely true," the master replied with a frown. "I have taught you for a long time now, Roland, but it is evident that you have not absorbed any of my lessons and have no understanding of the truth whatsoever."

So, the new student's name was Roland!

"But if I am a liar," Roland proceeded calmly, "then surely I am lying when I say 'I am a liar,' so the statement must be false."

The master did not answer.

"So perhaps the statement 'I am a liar' is both true and false. Or neither true nor false. Or neither both true and false. Or neither neither true nor false. Or maybe we should just shut up and not say anything at all!"

"You are simply playing with words," the master scoffed.

"Then may I try a different example?" Roland said. "As we all can see, your hair has receded halfway up your head. The statements 'You are bald' and 'You are not bald' are contradictory, so one or the other must be true. But which of these two statements would be true with respect to you?"

There were low snickers among the students, although Bartholomew, who was sitting next to Justin, remained stone-faced.

"I still have hair on my head!" the master shouted. "So I am not bald!"

"Then how many more hairs would you need to lose before we may call you bald?"

The students—all except Bartholomew—erupted into laughter.

"Roland!" the master said sharply, bringing the class back to attention. "You are permitted to leave the lecture hall now."

"But I cannot," Roland replied.

"Of course you can. I command it!"

"You are missing the point, dear master. Would you agree that before I can leave the room I must first walk halfway between where I am now and the door?"

"Of course, that is self-evident."

"And then from my new position I must again walk halfway from there to the door?"

The master was beginning to see the trap that Roland had set for him.

"And from each new position," Roland continued, "I must always go halfway before I can go all the way to the door, which means that I can never leave the lecture hall."

The students were amused but the master now was fuming.

"You are always telling us to think rationally," Roland said tauntingly. "Do you not agree that my logic is impeccable?"

The master stood up from his chair and moved to where Roland was sitting. He raised his hand and was about to slap the unruly student on the face, when Roland wagged his finger and said, "Ah, ah, master. You dare not strike me. And you know why."

The master withdrew his hand and returned to his seat. He then dismissed the class, eliciting a cheer from the students, who were happy to be discharged earlier than usual.

Bartholomew stood up straight away from his chair and quickly left the lecture hall. Justin made his way towards the door, where he happened to bump into Roland.

"I was impressed with your questions," Justin said to him, once they were in the corridor.

"You should ask some yourself," Roland replied with a smile.

"Indeed, I will try to think of one."

"If you need any help, come to my room after supper this evening. We can talk more then."

"I do not know where your room is," Justin said. "And besides, I have heard that it is forbidden for students to visit each other's rooms."

"Meet me at supper, then. After that we can break the rule together!"

With a sweeping motion of his hand, Justin said, "After you."

Roland stepped ahead of Justin, gleefully swinging his hips as he departed.

§4

Justin returned to his room, where he found Bartholomew sitting on his bed infuriated.

"Can you believe his impertinence?" Bartholomew cried.

"You mean the student in class today?"

"Yes, Roland."

"Indeed, he was rather rude to the master."

"The audacity of asking such questions!" Bartholomew exclaimed. "We have come to this university to learn, to be guided by scholars who have spent long years studying these subjects and teaching them. What right does Roland have to interfere with the master's lessons and to deprive us of the opportunity to learn from him?"

"Of course, his manner of speaking cannot be condoned, but it is certainly Roland's right to ask questions to the master."

"Yes, we all have the right to ask questions, but not the foolish sort that he was asking."

"I do not think his questions were foolish at all," Justin said. "They were serious questions and they deserve a serious answer. The fact is, the master was unable to reply."

Bartholomew looked at Justin and scowled, "We must not be puffed up with conceit or have a perverse craving for polemics and disputes about words. The devil delights when we allow our minds to become muddled by such frivolous arguments. We must think clearly and logically. The world God has created is a rational one that can be understood rationally."

"I am surprised to hear you say that," Justin said with a teasing smile, "since you always struck me as being much more of a visionary than a rationalist."

"What has Athens to do with Jerusalem? What concord is there between the Academy and the Church?"

"You mean that there is a difference between philosophy and theology after all?"

"What I mean is that there is no contradiction between faith and reason," Bartholomew said resolutely. "Faith concerns the truths which God has given us through his revelation, while reason deals in the truths we gain through our knowledge of the world and the order we perceive in it."

"But the master has told us that there is only one truth, not two. So certainly the dogmas of the Church must be susceptible to proof."

"To the contrary, the dogmas of the Church must be believed even though they cannot be proven. I believe even though I do not understand and accept by faith what I cannot grasp with my mind."

It was evident that Bartholomew was becoming excited again. Justin, tiring of Bartholomew's incessant certitudes, intentionally started to goad him with questions he knew Bartholomew would find annoying.

"So is God beyond our comprehension?" Justin asked.

"Indeed, God is inscrutable. With our human minds, we see through a glass darkly but after death, when we are joined to God, we shall see him face to face."

"But we cannot see God face to face now in this life?"

"Should any mortal see God in all his glory, he would surely die."

"Therefore, God cannot be known."

"He is known through faith not human wisdom. 'Do not deceive yourself,' the Bible says. 'If you think you are wise, you must become a fool. It is only by becoming a fool that you will be wise.'"

"Then Christianity is foolish!" Justin exclaimed, feeling for the first time that he was getting the better of Bartholomew.

Bartholomew looked warily at Justin.

"Indeed, it is a stumbling block for those who trust in reason. The wisdom of this world is foolishness to God and the foolishness of God is wiser than the wisdom of this world."

"Either way it's foolishness. So, why do you believe in it?"

"I believe *because* it's absurd."

Justin was willing to discontinue the debate as soon as Bartholomew was, but since Bartholomew would not relent, neither would Justin!

"But surely we must know something before we can believe in it," he said.

"I do not know in order to believe; I believe in order to know."

"Then in fact, you know nothing. You just believe."

Bartholomew stood up and faced Justin directly.

"You are twisting my words," he said, his voice rising. "Just as that insipid Roland twisted the words of the master in class today."

"It is not my intention to make you angry," Justin said, knowing this to be only partially true. "I simply want to know."

"If you think you know something, you do not yet know it as you ought to."

"Then how may I know as I ought to?"

"It is not necessary to know. It is only necessary to believe in God."

"Even the devils believe and tremble," Justin said pointedly.

"Faith without works is dead," Bartholomew countered, now visibly upset.

"Yet we must simply believe whatever the Bible or the Church tells us, without question?" Justin asked trenchantly.

"Yes, we must have the simple faith—childlike faith—just as it says in the Bible."

"I am sorry to confront you on this matter, Bartholomew," Justin said. "But your idea of 'childlike faith' sounds to me like nothing more than gullibility. Surely we should agree with something only if we have been persuaded by its truth, not simply because it has been handed down to us by authority."

By this point Bartholomew was raging.

"Indeed, we must never challenge either the Bible, for it is God's Word, or the Church, for it is the body of Christ!" he shouted. "And, let me warn you, Justin: you are treading a treacherous path. If you end up trusting your own reason more than God's revelation and become a freethinker like Roland, you are in danger of becoming a heretic. Submit yourself to God. Resist the devil and he will flee from you!"

With that, Bartholomew stormed out of the room.

"I'm going to the chapel to pray," he said.

§5

When Justin arrived at the dining hall for supper that evening he noticed Bartholomew sitting at the far end of one the tables, sulking. Justin
avoided him, going instead to the opposite end of the table, where he was
soon joined by Roland. The masters entered the room and took their seats
at the high table at the front of the hall. A prayer was said and everyone
began eating, eyes straight ahead with no conversation among them. When
they had finished their meal, one of the masters gave a short exhortation,
telling the students to be diligent in their studies and to never challenge the
authority of their teachers. Then the assembly was dismissed.

Bartholomew abruptly left the room, brushing past Justin without
even a glance. Roland nudged Justin with his elbow, gave him a knowing
look, and led the way out of the hall to his room, which was down the corridor from Justin's.

Once the door had shut behind them, Roland whispered, "Keep your
voice low, of course. We mustn't be heard."

He then reached under his bed and pulled out a flask.

"What's that?" Justin asked.

"Wine," Roland said, uncorking the flask and taking a sip. "Care for
some?"

Roland passed the flask to Justin, who held it to his lips, took a swig,
then passed the flask back to Roland.

"Where did you get this?"

"I bought it, of course," Roland replied. "I always have a supply on
hand."

"You must come from a wealthy family."

"Indeed, my father is a rich man. My mother died a long time ago, but
my sister still lives with him."

"Here in this town?"

"No, he is the lord of a manor. He is also a primary benefactor of this
university."

"Ah," Justin said. "So that explains why you have a room all to yourself.
And perhaps also why the master hesitates to strike you."

"Indeed."

"It seems that you have been a student here for a long time. Why
haven't we seen you before?"

Roland laughed again. "I was suspended! So I have been at home for
the past year."

"Suspended? What did you do?"

"Nothing serious. As you know, the university has lots of stupid rules. It's impossible to follow all of them. But no worry, my father was able to work everything out, at least this time. If I get into trouble again, however, I shall be expelled."

"Doesn't that concern you?" Justin asked.

"Not in the least. If I am expelled, my father would simply start donating money to a different university where I could resume my studies. But I assure you, it will not come to that. The master knows who pays his salary, so he and I remain on what might be called 'good terms' with each other."

Roland took a long draught of wine and handed the flask back to Justin.

"The master is a fool," Roland continued. "He claims to be widely read, but he keeps giving the same old lectures over and over, year after year. He lacks inquisitiveness and never tries to broaden his knowledge by reading something new. Many other works have been written which the master does not even know exist."

"But you have read them all?"

"Of course," Roland replied. "Or at least most of them. I was tutored at home and had access to nearly all the books that have ever been written. Hardly any of them are in our library here."

"How long have you been a student?"

"Since I was sixteen. So about six years altogether. But I'm getting really tired of studying. The lectures are much too easy for me. And boring. The only reason I'm still here is to get a degree. Then I shall obtain a doctorate in law, pursue a career in the court, and later take over my father's estate. How about you? What's your story?"

Justin took another gulp of wine, thinking how he should answer. He did not want to reveal to Roland how similar their backgrounds were, but finally confessed that his father had been the lord of a manor as well.

"I suppose that your older brother will inherit the estate," Roland said, "and that you, as the younger sibling, were sent off to make your own way in the world."

"Indeed," Justin replied, knowing that he was telling a lie. "My father sent me first to a monastery, but I did not have the inclination to become a monk. So he made arrangements for me to come here."

"You were educated at home as well?"

"Yes, by a scholar who was also an alchemist," Justin said, happy to be able to speak the truth at last.

"Ah, a man of science. It sounds exciting."

"I have also studied theology, at least the basics. But this is my first encounter with philosophy."

"Philosophy!" Roland said and then drank some more wine. "It's such a useless discipline. Almost as worthless as theology."

"But is not philosophy the king of sciences and theology the queen?"

"If so, they should get divorced. Theology has no subject matter and philosophy tells us absolutely nothing about the world."

"The master is always saying that the purpose of philosophy is to teach us the correct way of thinking."

"There is no 'correct way of thinking,'" Roland said. "If there were, why do the philosophers and even the Church Fathers disagree among themselves so much? *Sic et non,* Yes and No—that's another book I'm sure the master has never read."

Justin could not recall seeing a book with that title at either the monastery or the university library.

"What is the book about?"

"As I just told you. About how the Church Fathers contradict each other. Some say that faith and reason are in perfect accord with each other, while others say they are completely incompatible. Some say God's foreknowledge determines outcomes and that nothing happens that is contrary to his will, while others say that some events occur by chance and that God may be resisted. Some say that because God is the author of everything, he is the author of evil as well as good, while others say that he is the author of the good alone. That sort of thing."

"Is there no way to settle these disputes?"

"The book is purportedly a set of exercises for students to demonstrate how one idea and its opposite can both be true at the same time by using dialectical reasoning," Roland replied. "But I think the author's real purpose was simply to show how inconsistent the theologians have been. Have a go at it, if you like, but I've never been able to make sense of all those conundrums."

By this time, Roland and Justin were passing the flask rapidly back and forth, quaffing the wine.

"I have thought the same," Justin said, starting to feel a bit woozy. "But my roommate, Bartholomew, says there are no incongruities whatsoever. Ultimately we shall know the truth and the truth will set us free!"

"So, your roommate is Bartholomew, eh? The monk!"

"Yes, the serious student whom the master calls on when he needs someone to reaffirm his remarks. We first met at the monastery and then came here together."

"Well, let me tell you, Justin, there is no truth. Whatever philosophy teaches us is not truth, but simply the various ways in which people have thought about truth. They can't all be right!"

"I agree," Justin said. "But should we not be able to find out which of them is correct? Or if none are correct, then to come up with a new idea that is correct? Surely truth exists."

"No doubt the Church tries to impose its idea of truth on us, but in the end truth is simply whatever we each choose to believe."

Justin's head was beginning to spin from the wine, making it difficult for him to focus his thoughts, but he tried.

"Indeed, I have read the Bible and studied the Church's doctrines," Justin said. "A lot of it seems far-fetched to me. Nonetheless, should we not at least follow the Church's guidance when it comes to ethics?"

Roland took a long guzzle of wine and laughed. "I can see that you have not been in this city long, but you shall find out soon enough."

"Whatever do you mean?"

"The Church is thoroughly corrupt. The priests, and even the bishop, are hypocrites. They are more interested in maintaining their own power than in saving souls. They care only about milking the parishioners for more money. They wear expensive clothes and jewelry. They feast rather than fast. Many of them are drunkards. They take a vow of chastity yet all of them visit houses of prostitution."

"All of them?"

"Well, almost all of them."

Justin had already heard from Bartholomew about monks breaking their vows, but assumed it was a small minority. Still, he could not square what Roland was telling him with what he had experienced in the monastery, where the abbot and the monks lived in simplicity and seemed genuinely committed to leading holy lives.

"How do you know that the clergy visit brothels?"

"Because I have seen them there myself during my own visits."

Roland offered Justin the last bit of wine in the flask, which Justin swallowed in a single gulp.

"There, the flask is empty," Roland said cheerfully.

"It was good," Justin replied.

"Say, the fair will be held the week after next. Shall we go together?"

"Shouldn't we be studying?"

"Life at a university is not all study, my friend! The fair begins on a saint's day, so it's a holiday. We don't have to fret about missing any lectures. As for the final two days, we can just skip classes."

"No, no, I would never skip classes," Justin said.

"Well, then at least come on the first day. I guarantee that you will have a good time!"

"Allow me time to think about it," Justin replied, struggling to stand up. "I must be going but let us meet again when we have a chance."

"Now you know where my room is," Roland said. "You are welcome any time!"

§6

When Justin returned to his room, Bartholomew was sitting at his desk waiting for him.

"Where have you been?" he asked.

Justin went to his own chair, sat down, and tried to steady himself.

"I have been to the chapel to pray," he said, attempting to conceal his lisp.

"You were not at the chapel."

"Yes, I was."

"No, you weren't. For I myself went to the chapel after supper tonight to pray and you were not there."

Justin could not look Bartholomew in the eyes.

"I am sorry," he said. "It was a lie."

Bartholomew was livid. "Now I'm wondering if I can believe anything you've ever told me!"

"I am truly sorry," Justin repeated.

"So, where were you?"

Justin was silent.

"I suppose you were with that no-good fellow, Roland. I saw you sitting beside him in the dining hall."

Again Justin was silent.

"And you smell of wine. Were you drinking together with him?"

Justin looked up at Bartholomew helplessly.

"As I thought. The reason why I went to the chapel to pray was to ask God to forgive me for being angry with you this afternoon. Then I came back here thinking that I would ask you to forgive me as well."

"It is I who must ask forgiveness from you," Justin said. "I should not have lied to you."

"Indeed, you shouldn't have. Every lie must be called a sin. You will never lie to me again." It was an imperative, not an interrogative.

"I will not."

"Then I will forgive you and also ask you to forgive me for my anger."

"I forgive you, too."

"Before mass tomorrow let us visit the priest to confess our sins and receive absolution."

"I shall come with you."

"And you must promise me that you will dissociate yourself from Roland from now on. You may never see him again."

Justin shifted uncomfortably on his bed. He was ashamed for having lied, but still did not like Bartholomew always telling him what to do.

"Shouldn't I at least have the right to choose whom I fraternize with?" he asked.

"Certainly not. Roland will only lead you into temptation. Believe me, Justin, I am only trying to protect you!"

"I am sure that I can resist temptation," Justin said coolly.

"Ha!" Bartholomew exclaimed. "Have you really been tested?"

"In any case, I do not think it is necessary for me to tell you everything about where I have been or what I have done."

"Of course it is necessary. Remember, I am your guardian here. I hold all the money, both yours and mine, and I must report back to the abbot regularly about our activities."

"I understand," Justin conceded to avoid any further argument.

"As you should. I am happy to know that we can remain on good terms with each other."

Bartholomew lay down on his bed to sleep and Justin did the same. The ceiling was spinning above him. He did not know if confessing his lie to the priest the following day would do any good. What was wrong, he thought, was not his lying but the fact that Bartholomew had asked him questions which he had no right to ask in the first place. And even after the truth was out, what right did Bartholomew have to upbraid him? Yet since he had been caught out this time, he knew he would have to go through the formalities of a confession, if not for himself or God, then at least for Bartholomew.

The room spun Justin to sleep.

§7

The next morning Bartholomew and Justin set out for the cathedral. When they entered the square, they saw a man dressed in rags with long unkempt hair gathering a group of people around him. Bartholomew walked over to join the throng and Justin followed. The man stood up on one of the steps in front of the entrance to the cathedral and began to speak.

"I tell you, do not enter this building to confess your sins or attend mass, for the bishop and priests have all sinned. A priest who himself lives in mortal sin is not worthy to hear your confession nor is he able to grant you absolution. You need not confess to a priest, but only to God, who will hear your prayer and absolve you from all sin."

Some of the people in the crowd nodded in agreement. Bartholomew shifted his weight from one leg to the other uneasily.

"Jesus said, 'Blessed are the poor.' But the clergy live lives of wealth and excess. Jesus has told us, 'You cannot serve God and wealth. Go, sell all that you own and give the money to the poor so that you may have treasure in heaven.' But the clergy steal from the poor and accumulate riches for themselves."

More townsfolk joined the assembly, which was warming with enthusiasm to the preacher's words. A few began clapping their hands. Bartholomew, however, was clenching his fists.

"Priests who live in sin do not have the authority to administer the sacraments to you. You do not need the Church nor its sacraments to be saved. You need only to experience the Holy Spirit in your own life. It is not necessary to worship in a magnificent cathedral that has been paid for with our toil and tithes. Do not venerate sacred images, for these are but idols. What agreement has the temple of God with idols? Our bodies are the temple of God. The Holy Spirit lives within each of us!"

The horde by now was cheering.

"Therefore, come out from them and be a separate people, and touch nothing unclean. The Church is no longer of Christ but of the Antichrist. It has ceased to be a house of prayer and become a den of thieves. The temple must be cleansed and the moneychangers driven out. Do not be deceived by false prophets who trick us and lead us astray. The day of the Lord will not come unless there is first rebellion and the lawless one is revealed, the son of perdition destined for destruction."

"Indeed, the day of the Lord is at hand!" one man standing toward the front of the audience cried out. Others began shouting with him.

At this point Bartholomew pushed his way through the sea of people and stood up on the steps opposite the preacher. The crowd, seeing his habit, immediately became silent.

"Please show me your license to preach," Bartholomew demanded.

"I need no license," the man replied.

"You certainly do. Only licensed members of the clergy are authorized to preach in public."

"You mean that only those with a piece of paper signed by the bishop are permitted to spread the good news?"

Bartholomew turned to the crowd and bellowed, "My brothers and sisters, do not listen to this man. For it is he who is a false prophet!"

The preacher put his face into Bartholomew's. "Then please, good monk, point out my errors exactly. For every statement I have just made is either true or a quote from the Bible itself!"

"Even Satan quotes scripture," Bartholomew replied.

"I am only proclaiming the gospel, not as it is given to us by the Church, but as it is given to us by Christ himself. It is the Church which errs, not I!"

"The Church is not in error. Indeed, it is filled with corruption and must be reformed. But reform must come from within, not by breaking away from the Church."

A few people began to slink quietly away.

"Certainly the clergy must be held accountable," Bartholomew addressed the crowd entreatingly. "But we must remember that we all have sinned and fallen short of the glory of God, not only me and you, but the priests and bishops as well. Even the Pope admits that he lives as a sinner among sinners. Yet judge not, lest you be judged! Jesus has instituted his Church and what matters is the authority that he has given to its administrators, not their moral character. Forgiveness comes from God alone. A priest is merely his instrument. God may use even sinners to accomplish his purposes."

"What you are saying sounds to me like nothing more than an excuse for iniquity," the preacher said. "It means that priests who sin will always be granted immunity under the Church. They exercise authority over us but do not exercise authority over themselves!"

More people were walking away and the crowd was beginning to thin.

"I tell you, man," Bartholomew shrieked indignantly. "You are preaching heresy! I shall notify the authorities of your unorthodox views and they will bring their judgment down upon you!"

At this point the preacher, seeing that the townsfolk had for the most part dispersed and were no longer with him, stepped down and began making a hasty retreat. A few others, apparently his companions, ran with him.

Bartholomew shouted after them, "We shall hunt you down and expose you! The greatest threat to the Church are not clerics, but heretics!"

He then turned to the few people still standing with Justin.

"I entreat you to have no truck with deceitful preachers who fashion themselves as apostles of Christ, but to remain true to the Church, which is the only means of salvation."

Then, motioning for Justin to join him, Bartholomew said, "Please accompany my brother and me as we go to confess our sins and participate in the Eucharist."

"We shall follow you," a woman said.

As they were walking up the steps to the cathedral door, Bartholomew asked the woman, "Who is this ravening wolf who comes in sheep's clothing to lead God's sheep away?"

"No one knows his name," the woman answered. "But he stands in front of the cathedral nearly every day giving sermons such as this."

"It shall not continue," Bartholomew said firmly. "We must submit to the Church instead of rebelling against it. Now come, let us be glad to go to the house of the Lord and worship our God almighty!"

Bartholomew turned to enter the cathedral, with Justin and the others close behind.

§8

During his confession, Justin told the priest about the incident with Bartholomew and how he had lied to him. As penance, the priest told Justin that, after a suitable number of prayers and recitations, he should talk with Bartholomew again about the matter and reconcile himself with him. Then the priest said that Justin must resolve not to lie again but to always tell the truth.

Justin asked the priest, "Is it necessary to tell the truth even when a person asks me questions that meddle in my own affairs?"

"If you have committed no sin," the priest responded, "there is no reason for you to hide what you have done. But if you really wish to keep the matter private, then you should simply say nothing. You must always be honest, both to the other person and to yourself."

Justin was satisfied with this reply and felt that it didn't really matter if it came from a priest who was pure and blameless or a fornicator who lived in mortal sin. It was still good advice. He immediately returned to the nave of the cathedral to say his prayers and do penance before mass, as the priest had instructed him. He was later joined by Bartholomew, who knelt down beside Justin and began his own recitations.

When the mass had finished and they were outside the cathedral, Bartholomew said that the priest had told him to reconcile himself with Justin.

"He gave me exactly the same counsel," Justin replied.

The two men asked once again for forgiveness, smiled at each other, and then clasped hands.

"I'm glad that we can be friends again," Justin said.

"We never stopped being friends," Bartholomew replied. "I will always love you with Christian and brotherly love."

Bartholomew reached under his collar and took a chain off from around his neck. At the end of the chain was a silver crucifix.

"Here," he said. "This was given to me by my mother as a present when I left for the monastery. But I should like you to have it as a token of our friendship."

"Oh no, you mustn't give this cross to me. I am not worthy to wear it. And besides, it was a gift from your mother."

"I insist," Bartholomew said gracefully. "Wear it always. The cross will keep you true to the faith and protect you from all harm."

"Well then, thank you," Justin said, pulling the chain over his head and letting the crucifix slip under his tunic and close to his breast. "I will wear it always, even when I'm bathing!"

Bartholomew laughed.

On the walk back to the university, Justin asked Bartholomew about the preacher they had encountered before entering the cathedral.

"Indeed, after confession today I notified the priest about him and he said he would pass my message on to the bishop," Bartholomew said.

"What will happen to the preacher?"

"It is likely that the Inquisition will be summoned to investigate. The inquisitors are very busy these days, however, since heresy is spreading everywhere."

"And what about the preacher's charges of immorality among the priests?" Justin asked.

"These abuses have been festering for some time and are not unknown among those who love the Church," Bartholomew replied.

"Are no actions being taken?"

"Our own abbot has petitioned the bishops to address these matters within their dioceses, but all too often it is the bishops themselves who are part of the problem. The abbot has gone so far as to appeal to the Pope for guidance, but so far without reply."

"What then is to be done?"

"We cannot resolve these issues ourselves but must rely on the Holy Spirit to guide us," Bartholomew said. "No doubt a firm hand is needed, with strict regulations for the clergy. Discipline must be imposed not only on the clerics, however, but also on the people of God. They must not be ensnared by false prophets and heretics, such as the preacher we saw today, who twist the truth to their own purposes and deny the authority of the Church. We, as God's servants, must minister to the masses and preach the gospel to them so that they might be saved and not be misled by recreants who beckon them down the road to perdition."

§9

As it turned out, the inquisitor arrived in the city with his entourage the following week. A convocation was held in the square of the cathedral, which all, or nearly all, of the city's residents attended, including Bartholomew and Justin. The inquisitor was a muscular and not unhandsome man, with a stern emotionless face. His retinue included several guards and assistants, as well as an expert in the law. He was joined on the steps in front of the cathedral by the bishop, who began the proceedings by saying a short prayer. This was followed by the inquisitor delivering a lengthy sermon on the dangers of heresy, which those in attendance listened to with varying degrees of attentiveness. Some were intently focused on what the inquisitor was saying while others seemed to have come to the event only because it had been expected of them. Not showing up could in itself arouse suspicions about one's fidelity to the Church.

When the inquisitor had finished his homily, he then said, "It is my duty today to demand that anyone who is guilty of heresy in any form should present themselves to our tribunal and admit their errors. You should also inform us if you have any friends, acquaintances, or family members who hold beliefs that are contrary to true Christian teachings. We shall certainly treat you leniently if you confess now and help us to locate others who have been disloyal to the Church. Our aim is not to punish you but to lead you back to God. There will be a one-month term of grace in which you may turn yourselves in. If you do not avail yourself of the opportunity to confess your profanation of the faith within this period, then we shall ferret you out and put you on trial in accordance with the procedures of the Inquisition."

After the bishop had blessed the assembly, Bartholomew said in a loud voice for all to hear, "Repent, for the Kingdom of Heaven is at hand. Make straight the way of the Lord!"

The crowd then began to shuffle away, murmuring but with no open complaints.

§10

After returning to the university Bartholomew went to the library to read, leaving Justin alone in his room.

Suddenly there was a light tap on the door. Justin opened it to see Roland standing in the corridor.

"May I come in?" Roland asked.

"No, you shouldn't," Justin said.

"Come on, let me in," Roland insisted, pushing past Justin into the room and closing the door behind him. "It's been more than a week since I last saw you. Why have you been avoiding me?"

"Bartholomew has told me to have nothing more do with you."

"He said that! I can't imagine what he's thinking."

"He claims that you are no good and will have a bad influence on me."

"Since when is Bartholomew ruling your life?"

"I don't have any say in the matter. He controls all the money, you know, and I have none of my own."

"Well, so what? You can't spend the rest of your life taking orders from Bartholomew, can you? Aren't you at least able to choose your own friends?"

"I am not sure," Justin replied.

"Spare me," Roland said dismissively. "You need to stand up to him and be your own man!"

"I suppose you're right, but it's difficult. He's afraid that I might do something wrong."

"Who's to say what is right or wrong? You or Bartholomew? You have to make your own judgments, kid, not let your life be lorded over by others."

At first Justin was offended by Roland's remark, but then realized that Roland had put his finger on the problem exactly, not only with Bartholomew but also his father.

Finally Justin said, "Indeed, whatever I do in life should ultimately be my own decision."

"There you go!" Roland said reassuringly. "Now, the reason I'm here is because the fair will start tomorrow. Will you come with me? You haven't given me an answer yet."

"I know there are no classes, but I need to finish preparing for my final examination. It will be held at the end of this term, you know."

"You still have plenty of time to get ready. Have you ever been to a fair before?"

"No."

"Then this is your chance. Don't miss it! And don't worry about money. I will pay for everything."

Justin considered for a moment and then smiled. "All right. I will go with you!"

"Good! Meet me outside the dormitory just after daybreak. I'll be waiting for you."

"What should I tell Bartholomew if he asks me where I am going?"

"For heaven's sake, man!" Roland cried. "Just tell him the truth!"

§11

The next morning Justin told Bartholomew that he would be going out for the day. When Bartholomew asked him where, Justin replied directly, "To the fair."

"The fair!" Bartholomew exclaimed. "Why on earth would you want to go to the fair? Its only purpose is for merchants to find ways to get people to part with their money. And I shall certainly give you no money to spend needlessly at the fair!"

"I shan't ask you for any money. I just want to see what a fair is like. I have never been to one, you know."

"You really should stay here and prepare for your examination."

"I have already finished reading the texts and only need to review."

"Do not take it lightly," Bartholomew said. "If you fail this exam, you may not be able to go on to study for your doctorate."

Justin was in no mood to have another quarrel with Bartholomew, but he wanted to exercise his newfound sense of honesty.

"I do yet know if I intend to continue my studies after obtaining my master's degree," he said unabashedly.

"What!" Bartholomew screeched. "There will be no other opportunities for you to make a good future for yourself if you do not take advantage of the monastery's offer to pay your tuition all the way through."

"And indeed I am grateful to the abbot," Justin replied. "But I do not think I have the aptitude to be a scholar."

"You certainly have the ability."

"But there is nothing that I would really like to study. To tell the truth, the life of an academic bores me. I can't see the point of anything I'm learning."

Bartholomew was by now obviously disturbed.

"What would you do, then, if you leave the university?" he asked.

"I haven't the slightest idea. I do not wish to study, but there is nothing else I wish to do either."

"You should not waste your talent. You started out far below the other students but now you have moved to the top of the class. That is why the master is allowing you to take your final examination early, before the others."

"I'm sure they will catch up in their own good time."

"You are acquiring a reputation for being precocious," Bartholomew said, changing tactics and trying to flatter Justin.

"I hardly deserve it."

"In any case, you are a much better student than I am. Learning comes easy for you, but not for me."

Bartholomew's mood then turned glum.

"Since today is a saint's day," he said, "I intend to spend the morning in prayer. Then I shall review the master's lessons in the afternoon. There are many points I still cannot grasp."

"Just remember that the master himself is not always clear about what he teaches. But he will eventually catch up, too."

Justin intended his remark to cheer Bartholomew up, but that was not how he took it.

"Do not put yourself above the master," Bartholomew said sternly.

"I was only trying to offer encouragement," Justin said, opening the door. "I must be leaving now."

"Well, stay out of trouble." Bartholomew's voice was now resigned. "I hope you're not going in the company of that deadbeat, Roland."

"Don't worry, I shall be back before dark," Justin replied.

§12

The fair was held in a large field just outside the city walls. Banners surrounded the entire area. Roland and Justin arrived in time to hear the fair open with the ringing of bells. The grounds were soon swarming with people, moving from stall to stall and examining the goods on display. People from out of town exchanged coins with moneychangers. Noblemen and women mingled freely with peasants. The former tended to be more attracted to the merchants selling expensive items, such as gems and jewelry, pewter and woodcarvings, rugs and tapestries, rare fruits and imported wines, while the latter examined more useful handicrafts, such as belt buckles and hats, cups and bowls, pots and candles, cheese and flour.

Roland stopped at one of the stalls selling rings. He picked up several and tried them one by one on his finger.

"Which do you think is more suitable?" he asked Justin. "This gold ring or the silver one?"

"I do not know your taste, Roland. Please choose for yourself."

"I think I shall take the gold one, then."

Roland handed some coins over to the stall keeper, then slipped the ring onto his finger and held up his hand.

"It's rather dandy, isn't it!" he said proudly.

"Indeed, it is," Justin replied, noticing that it looked exactly the same as the wedding ring from Penelope which Justin had given to the hermit. Perhaps he had sold it to this very merchant!

The two spent the rest of the morning walking through the fairground. Around noon, as they were passing by some stalls selling food, Roland said, "I'm hungry. Let's get something to eat. Look, here they have beef ribs and over there they are selling hot sheep's feet. What do you fancy?"

"Whatever you like," Justin answered.

"I would rather prefer a meat pie," Roland said.

They walked around a bit more looking for a shop selling baked goods. After finding one, Roland bought two pasties.

"My treat," he said, handing one of the pastries to Justin. "As I mentioned, I will take care of everything since I know you have no money. Let us go yonder and get some ale, as well."

In the afternoon, they moved to the outer edge of the fairground, where the stalls were larger, with various farming implements for sale, including not just the usual tools, but also plows and carts. Beyond these were corralled areas, where bailiffs in the employ of noblemen bartered over cattle, horses, and sheep, which they would take back to their manors.

Finally they came to a large open space where boys were playing tug-of-war and leapfrog, while girls danced around a maypole. Several games of lawn bowling and quoits had been set up for the adults. Minstrels strolled through the crowd, playing their instruments while the townspeople danced. Bards recited poems and told stories. Among the performers were also jesters and jugglers, acrobats and magicians.

By mid-afternoon various competitions began to be held: races, javelin-throwing, wrestling, and archery matches, all as a prelude to the final tournament: a melee in which two groups of knights on horseback, dressed respectively in red and blue, faced off against each other on either side of the field, then charged towards the center, attempting to knock their opponents off their horses using lances with blunted tips.

When each team reached the other side of the field, those who had not yet fallen turned and charged again to the center, repeating the process over and over. As the bodies fell, most of the men limped off the field on their own power, but a few, obviously injured, needed to be carried off by their squires.

The contest dwindled down to a confrontation between one knight from the red side and two from the blue team. The crowd was yelling its support for the knight in red, who, as the underdog, hardly stood a chance against his two challengers. Yet, with a skillful maneuver, he managed to avoid going between them, running his horse past the knight on the right and felling him with his lance.

The victor in red and the final remaining opponent from the blue team turned again at opposite ends of the field for their final joust. They were both exhausted and breathing heavily.

Roland turned to Justin and said, "If you had any money, I'd bet you that the fellow in red will win."

"Well, as you know, I don't have any money," Justin replied. "And in any case I am not a gambling man."

Just then the knight in blue shouted across to his adversary, "Do you tire?"

"Nay," the knight in red shouted back. "I am ready to strike you down and declare myself the winner."

"We shall see!"

The two knights charged, heading straight towards each other.

The crowd applauded as the knight in red planted his lance squarely on the chest of his rival, who landed on the ground with a thud.

"I told you so," Roland said to Justin.

The victor strode jubilantly back to the cheering crowd, his arms raised in triumph. The fallen knight picked himself and began to walk falteringly towards his teammates, who were standing on the opposite side. Suddenly a rotten apple flew through the air, glancing off the defeated man's shoulder. Children began to make mud balls to fling at the man. Soon the knight, unable to move more quickly, was dodging a barrage of projectiles of various sizes, shapes, and kinds.

Roland picked up a stone and was about to hurl it at the man, but Justin stayed his hand.

"Don't you dare throw anything at that poor fellow," Justin said.

"Why not?" Roland replied. "Losers get what they deserve."

"Should we not have compassion rather than contempt for the harassed and downtrodden?"

"Nay. The weak shall be obliterated both on the battlefield and in life. Only the fittest survive!"

With that, Roland pitched the stone at the knight, hitting him squarely on the back.

"Bullseye!" he laughed gleefully.

Justin spat on the ground. He did not wish to offend Roland, however, and so said nothing more.

§13

As the sun was setting, everyone began to leave the fairground, the peasants and townsfolk to their homes, the knights and nobility to the guildhall, which they had rented for the purpose of holding a large banquet. Justin and Roland were strolling along one of the city streets on their way back to the university when they were approached by two women in flowing dresses, one pink, the other violet. Their heavy make-up made it difficult for Justin to see their faces, especially in the dim light, but he thought that they could be the same two women he and Bartholomew had encountered when they first entered the city so many months ago.

"Do you boys need to go home so soon?" the woman in pink asked.

"Not if you should welcome us to your rooms," Roland replied.

"Indeed, you are welcome," the woman said with a flirtatious smile. "Whom shall you choose?"

"Why you, of course."

"Then you shall come with me and your friend may accompany the other lady here."

Justin looked awkwardly at the woman wearing the violet dress, who had just been designated his companion. She was certainly attractive and he instantly felt an urge to be with her. He was a man after all and it was part of his nature. But he said, "I do not think I should."

"Why not?" Roland said. "I told you before that I would pay for everything. And I meant everything!"

"It's not that. I just can't."

"What's the problem, Justin? Don't tell me that you are still a virgin?"

"As a matter of fact I am."

The lady in violet said, "Don't worry at all. I can teach you everything. Gently."

"No, I will not," Justin said firmly.

"Don't be so obstinate, Justin," Roland said. "It's perfectly all right."

"I am not being obstinate," Justin replied. "I am simply making my own decisions, just as you told me to."

"All right then. Have it your way," Roland said. He then turned to the lady in violet. "My apologies for my friend's rude rejection of you."

The lady jerked her head upward and humphed. Roland and the lady in pink disappeared down an alley, leaving Justin and the other woman alone.

"I suppose there's another girl you fancy," the woman said.

"Indeed, there is." It was, in fact, the first time he had thought about Constance since coming to the city.

"You'd like to marry her?"

"Yes, I would."

"Then I hope you shall marry soon."

"That's impossible. I suppose I will never see her again."

"Did I hear you correctly?" the woman laughed, gesturing with her fingers as if cleaning out her ears. "You may never see her again and yet you are still faithful to her?"

"I am," Justin said.

"Now that's what I would call true love!" she exclaimed. "Oh my, why can't I find a man like you?"

Justin nodded sheepishly, then turned and left. On the way back to the university he could think only of Constance. The memories had returned and along with them the ache of being without her. He realized that he would, in fact, never be able to forget her. Love is not about being with the person you love but about loving them even when you cannot be with them.

When he reached the university, Justin was surprised to see Bartholomew standing outside the dormitory.

"You're late," he said. "I've been waiting for you. You said you'd be back before dark, but the sun set a long time ago."

"I lost track of the time," Justin said. "I hope you didn't worry about me."

"I was more concerned that you would be carousing around with Roland. I'm relieved to see that you are returning alone. Are you sober? Let me smell your breath."

Justin blew into Bartholomew's nose. The scent of ale had dissipated long ago.

"You're fine," Bartholomew said. "Did you enjoy the fair?"

"Immensely," Justin replied.

§14

Roland did not appear in class for the next two days and the discussions after the master's lectures were rather quiet without him. He showed up on the third day—the day after the fair was over—and took his seat rather sulkily. The master glared at him but said nothing.

Afterward in the corridor, when Bartholomew was already on his way to the library, Roland whispered to Justin, "I'm all out of money. But I had a great time spending it!"

"How did you manage to lose all your money in such a short time?" Justin asked.

"Need you ask?" Roland replied.

"So what will you do now?"

"Beg my father for more, of course. I've already written to him."

"And he'll send it to you just like that?"

"Indeed, he will. Just as soon as your examination is finished and the term is over, you and I will enjoy ourselves in the town!"

Over the next few weeks, Justin visited Roland's room often, usually not in the evening when it would arouse Bartholomew's suspicions, but any time they could catch during the day or on weekends. Justin vowed that if Bartholomew ever asked him if he were meeting Roland, he would answer truthfully. It was his right to meet and talk with whomever he wanted. Still, he did not wish to provoke any conflict with Bartholomew, so he kept his meetings with Roland not exactly a secret, but simply to himself.

Roland and Justin talked about everything, not only about Roland's various escapades, which it turned out were considerable, but also about philosophy and life in general. No doubt Roland was a knave. He was vulgar, arrogant, and provocative, even dangerous. The other students avoided him completely and he had no true friends. But then neither did Justin. Of course, he could talk with Bartholomew, but he always needed to be careful about what he said, lest Bartholomew begin reproving him.

With Roland, however, Justin could speak openly about anything. He began to tell him more about his past, about growing up on his father's estate and his stay in the monastery, although he did not mention the circumstances or the specific details. Of course, he would never reveal to anyone his love for Constance or his marriage to Penelope, nor the rebellion or his killing of Martin. But he felt that even if he had told these things to Roland, he would have understood and not been judgmental. One side of Roland was brusque and uncouth, but he had another side as well that was sensitive and understanding, even compassionate.

Roland had, in fact, become Justin's confessor, if not someone who could absolve him from his sins, then at least someone he could talk to about them, with the knowledge that Roland would accept him just as he was without trying to remake him into someone he could not be. Given a choice, Justin would prefer to eat with tax collectors and sinners such as Roland rather than with Pharisees such as Bartholomew.

§15

The day of Justin's examination finally arrived. He was not just prepared but, if anything, over-prepared. He had gone over the texts again and again until he almost had them memorized. He had reviewed all of the arguments to the point that they became a tangled ball of yarn. He needed to unravel them and sweep away all the other useless clutter that had filled his brain. So, during the hour before his exam, he went to the chapel, not to pray, but to simply sit alone in silence, following his breathing, not thinking anything. He had not done any serious contemplation for quite a while but was amazed at how quickly he was able to clear out the cobwebs and achieve a state of mindfulness.

Then he went to the classroom for the examination, taking his place at the front of the room opposite the master's desk. The assembled students became silent as the master addressed them:

"Today we shall examine Justin to determine if he is worthy to be awarded the master's degree. He has chosen to be examined in the area of philosophy, which, as you all know, is an extremely difficult but also highly rewarding subject. This morning I will proceed with a preliminary examination to cover the main points and then test Justin in depth on one specific problem. In the afternoon, we shall open the discussion and students will also be permitted to ask him any questions as they please. Are you ready to begin, Justin?"

Justin nodded his head.

The master then began interrogating Justin, to see how well he understood both the master's lectures and the texts he had been assigned to read. Justin answered the questions effortlessly and in a way that obviously pleased the master.

"I am quite impressed with your exposition thus far," the master said after Justin had responded to all of the general questions. "Allow me now to examine you on one specialized topic, after which we shall break for lunch. The topic is the problem of universals. There are two philosophical positions with respect to this topic. Could you please tell me what they are?"

"One is realism and the other nominalism."

"What is the difference between the two?"

"Realism is the view that both universals and particulars exist, whereas nominalism is the opinion that only particulars exist."

"Please explain to us more precisely what particulars are."

"Particulars are things that are individual and unique. The sea and the sky are both particulars, for instance, since they are distinct things."

"What then is a universal?"

"A universal is a property shared in common by two distinct particulars."

"How might this idea be applied to your example of the sea and sky?"

"If we say that the sea and the sky are both *blue,* then the property they share in common is the color blue, which is a universal."

"And where does this property of blueness exist?"

"Some realists say that universals such as blueness are ideal forms, or ideas, which exist in a transcendental realm beyond the ordinary things of this world. The objects we encounter in daily life participate in these forms, although never perfectly. Nothing that exists in this world is a true shade of blue."

"And what do other realists say?"

"The alternative view is that universals instantiate themselves in particular objects and have no existence apart from them. Blueness is nonetheless real because it is found in objects."

"Is there any way in which these two opposing opinions might be reconciled?"

"It might be said that universals exist as ideal forms in the mind of God but are then instantiated by God in the world he creates."

The master looked at Justin approvingly.

"Excellent!" he said. "You are demonstrating that you not only understand the topic but also how to use the dialectic. Now please explain the contrary position of nominalism."

"Nominalism, as I mentioned previously, is the view that only particulars exist. In its most extreme form it holds that everything is unique, that no two things share any identical properties—that is, universals—in common."

"But surely the words we use to describe things indicate that the same properties may be shared by different objects. If the sea and the sky are both blue, then blueness is a universal which is shared by both of these particulars."

"If you look closely, however, you will see that the color of the sea and the color of the sky are in fact not identical. We speak falsely if we say, 'The sea is blue. The sky is blue. Therefore, the sea and the sky are the same color.' In reality they are different colors."

"So the word *blue* has no meaning?"

"Indeed, words are merely sounds made by our voices or scratches of ink that we apply to paper."

"But words nonetheless refer to real objects and their qualities."

"It is impossible for a word to refer to something. When I say the word *blue* what you hear is a sound not a color. When I write the word *blue* what you see are merely scratches of black ink. You do not see the color blue. Spoken and written words are just as unique as anything else. There is no connection, therefore, between words and the completely different objects they purport to represent."

"If this opinion is true, then it is impossible for us to give a true and accurate description of the world."

"That, indeed, is the theory," Justin replied.

"So, what must we do?"

"We must remain silent."

"We can say nothing?"

Justin said nothing.

The master was perplexed.

"This response can be found neither in the lecture nor in the readings," he said. "What do you mean by it?"

"It means nothing," Justin replied.

"I will assume you are not mocking me. But let us continue. Is there no alternative to this extreme form of nominalism you have just expounded?"

"There is a more moderate version of nominalism known as concep-tualism, which holds that words can be used to refer to qualities that are similar to each other even if they are not exactly the same."

"How is this possible?"

"Rather than begin with an idea, such as the idea *blue,* we look first at the world as it is. We look at the sea. We look at the sky. Although the colors are in fact distinct, the colors appear similar to us so we create a single concept, or word, to designate what are in fact two distinct colors."

"How can a single word be used to represent two entirely different things?"

"All the things we describe as *blue* are similar but also different, even if only slightly. It is impossible for us to give a distinct name to each shade of blue, however, so the concept is a simplification of a much more complex reality."

"How may we determine which shade of blue is 'true blue'?"

"There is no 'true blue,' nor prototype, nor perfect form of any color, but rather a spectrum of hues, which we conceptually divide into separate categories and give names to. That is the central idea of conceptualism. No particular shade of blue can be identified as the 'real' universal blue. A uni-versal is simply an abstraction, which exists neither in the world nor in the mind of God, as realists suppose, but only in the minds of humans."

"Surely the view you have just stated cannot be correct," the master said. "For if humans arbitrarily decide how things should be named, what is to prevent them from falling into error? Words must be grounded in reality and in God's truth, not in the human mind."

Justin replied, "I have merely stated a theory, master."

"To the contrary, you are digressing and taking us quite beyond the ideas you have been assigned to cover."

It was obvious that the master had never heard of conceptualism before.

"May the ideas we have been taught not be improved upon?" Justin asked.

"Your examination is confined to an explanation of the theories," the master said, his voice becoming agitated. "You may not expand on them with your own ill-conceived opinions."

"My apologies, master," Justin said. "In any case, the view I have just stated is not my own."

"And what, may I ask, is your own view?"

"I am afraid you will not like it."

"Nonetheless, please tell me," the master said.

Justin held up his finger and began wagging it back and forth.

Roland sniggered.

The master, however, was furious.

"How dare you insult me and the other students in this room by making meaningless gestures instead of answering my question! Your earlier answers were brilliant, indeed among the best I have ever heard in my long years as a teacher. But now I can see that you should not be allowed to pass this examination and that you are not qualified to proceed to the next level!"

Then the master turned to the students and said, "Today's afternoon session is canceled. There is no point in us continuing with this senseless exhibition of incompetence!"

§16

Back in their room Bartholomew tried to console Justin.

"Except for the end," he said, "you did an excellent job. Whatever did you mean when you wagged your finger?"

"It meant nothing," Justin replied.

"But surely you intended something by it. At first I thought you were flustered—or perhaps imitating Roland."

"Hardly."

"What were you trying to say then?"

Justin was not sure he wanted to get into a conversation with Bartholomew about the topic and doubted that he would understand anyway. He wished he could simply sidestep the question by saying, "I wasn't trying to say anything," or even better, by not saying anything at all.

Instead he replied, "When we look at the trees in a forest, hear the song of a bird, smell a flower, taste an apple, or feel cold wet rain on our skin, the experience itself is enough. We do not need concepts to talk about any of these things since we already know what they are."

"Well, perhaps we do not *need* to talk about them, but we certainly *can* if we want to. That is why we are able to formulate true statements about the world."

"I am skeptical," Justin replied. "Ultimately reality cannot be put into words. There is an enormous difference between the world as we experience it and the world that we describe in language. To really know the world we must give up any ideas we may have about it."

"But surely we should not only experience the world but also think about it."

"To think of a sunrise is different from actually experiencing one," Justin said. "When I watch the sun come up over the horizon in the morning, there is no difference between myself and what I see. No me, no sunrise, just the experience itself. Any ideas I may form about my experience are pure fabrications. And perhaps the same is true of our experience of God. Experience itself is more important than thinking about experience."

Bartholomew stood up and began pacing the room.

"This is something I've been meaning to talk with you about," he said. "I have known you for a long time now. I have taught you about the Christian faith. I have heard your own opinions on various topics. It seems to me that you have a burning desire to find God, yet you reject any teachings that may bring you closer to understanding him."

"I do not think that any teachings can bring us closer to God," Justin said. "Not even the teachings of scripture. It is only the experience of God that matters."

"We must start with a knowledge of God not our own experience, lest we fall into error. Theology is faith seeking understanding."

"Indeed. We should base our understanding on our faith, not our faith on our understanding. Yet theology is not about comprehending the scriptures or the words of the Fathers or the teachings of the Church but making sense of our own experience. Faith is not knowledge or belief but our encounter with the divine. That's where we start. Then we work from there. When compared to our experience, theology is nothing more than straw. Perhaps this is why I understand things differently from the way most people do."

"Not only most people," Bartholomew said, "but also from the Church. I am sincerely worried, Justin, that you are in danger of falling into heresy. Your ideas do not square well with Christian teaching. You are becoming just like the preacher we heard on the steps outside the Church."

"Ah yes, the preacher," Justin said. "Whatever has become of him?"

"The inquisitor has been searching for him, but so far without result. He no longer preaches on the steps of the cathedral but continues to appear at various places in the city. His activities are reported to the authorities, but by the time they arrive he has already disappeared. No one knows where he

THE CITY   237

lives. You yourself should be careful not to spread false doctrines to others, even unintentionally."

"In my case, I never try to preach to or persuade others," Justin said defensively. "I am only seeking to understand my own experience, wherever it leads me. I have learned that the truth cannot be found in philosophy nor, I suppose, in theology."

"You must simply accept what you are taught, Justin. Then you shall be safe."

"I came to this university not to be taught what to think, but how to think. Even though it may be useful to consider the opinions of others, ultimately we each need to find the truth for ourselves."

"Indeed, we should each find the truth. But that's just the point. Any truth we find can never be in disagreement with the Church, for it is the repository of God's truth and safeguards it."

"You speak, rather smugly I think, as if the Church never errs in its understanding of God," Justin said, "which simply means that you have stopped questioning and ceased seeking new and better knowledge. You are no longer interested in the truth, Bartholomew, because you think you have already found it. Should we not regard our ideas about God as fallible and subject to revision?"

"No, for the teachings of the Bible and the Church are infallible. Their truths are final and never changing."

"Yet how do you know that the Bible and the Church are infallible? Where does that idea come from? Is infallibility itself not also a human opinion that the Church has simply adopted as a fixed and unchanging dogma? We should never mistake our own fallible doctrines for absolute truth. Why should all who call themselves Christians be forced to accept a single set of immutable beliefs? If everyone thinks exactly the same, there is absolutely no possibility for a new or better idea to ever arise. Are we not able to move beyond the ideas we have been given and invent entirely new ideas that have never been thought before? If progress in science, the arts, and even philosophy is possible, why not in theology as well? Hasn't the master himself told us that theology is the 'queen of the sciences'? Yet if theology is to be a genuine science, must it not also be rooted in experience? And must not any intellectual formulations we think up to explain those experiences also be regarded as fallible and subject to change?"

"You shall not anger me again with your profane ideas," Bartholomew said obdurately. "I simply say that you should return to the Church. God loves you and so do I. You must consider where you will spend eternity."

Bartholomew stopped pacing the room and looked at Justin, who was lying on his bed staring up at the ceiling as if he were not paying any attention to what Bartholomew was saying.

"Well," Bartholomew said. "Haven't you anything to say?"

Without looking at Bartholomew, Justin finally replied, "I am thinking of quitting the university."

"Why? Simply because you failed your examination?"

"It's not that."

"Perhaps you will be given a second chance. If you study hard during the next year and learn what is expected of you rather than indulging in your own aberrant thoughts, the master might allow you to sit for another examination."

"As I told you before," Justin said. "I simply cannot see the purpose of studying. Learning is vanity. Why should I confine myself to the walls of this university when there is so much of the world I have not yet seen? The knowledge I seek cannot be found in books, but only in experience."

"You are making a pact with the devil, Justin. Do not attempt to go beyond the life you already have but be content with it as it is. I implore you, do not quit the university, at least not yet. What would the abbot say? Give your studies another chance. I'm sure that you will succeed and when you do, you will be able to make a good life for yourself."

Justin looked at Bartholomew drearily.

"The life I make for myself is my own decision," he said.

§17

No classes were held the following week, as there was a recess between terms. Roland's money had arrived from his father and he was eager to spend it. He invited Justin to come along with him on various romps through the city. The first night, after a round of serious drinking at the tavern, Justin came back to the dormitory drunk. Bartholomew, who had been spending the break studying, was naturally upset and asked Justin where he had been.

"To the tavern!" Justin cried lustily. "Eat, drink, and be merry for tomorrow we die!"

"And where did you get money to go to the tavern?"

"From Roland, of course. I went together with him."

"I have told you not to have any association with Roland."

Justin looked up at Bartholomew with bleary eyes and laughed boisterously. "I no longer care what you think. I shall keep company with whomever I please!"

Bartholomew chastised Justin with another lecture about avoiding un-savory characters and leading a good moral life, but Justin wasn't listening. He lay back on his bed in a drunken stupor as the room swirled around him. He was starting to like this feeling!

The following night Roland took Justin back to the street where they had met the two rakes after the fair and then down the alley to a brothel situated at its end.

"I'm not sure I'm ready for this," Justin said.

"If you aren't ready now, when will you be? Surely you're not planning to spend the rest of your life as a virgin, are you?"

"But do you really think we should be going here?"

"My friend, I am beginning to doubt the thoroughness of your studies. Surely you must have read the Church Father who said that if prostitution is removed from human affairs, everything will be unsettled due to lusts."

Roland and Justin were welcomed at the door by a mistress who led them to a parlor, where several men, who appeared to be noblemen or mer-chants, were sitting with women on their laps, fondling and kissing them. Justin nudged Roland when he noticed that one of the men was the bishop from the cathedral, who was attired not in his usual cassock but in clothes every bit as fine as those of the others. Roland gave him a knowing smile in return.

"I shall summon the ladies you requested," the mistress said to Ro-land. She then disappeared into an adjoining room and returned with two women. They were the same women Roland and Justin had met previously in the street, and they were wearing exactly the same dresses.

"Hello," Roland said to the lady in pink. "It is nice to see you again."

"The pleasure is all mine," the woman said with a broad smile.

"You're my favorite, you know."

"And you are my favorite as well. I see that you have brought your friend back with you this time."

"Indeed, I have," Roland replied. Then turning to the lady in violet, he said, "And I am hoping that you will consent to being his companion for this evening."

"Of course," the woman replied. "But only with his consent as well."

Justin nodded to the woman.

"There, the matter is all settled," Roland said. "Let us not waste time in the lounge. Shall we retire to our chambers?"

The women led the men up a stairway to a hall with doors on either side. Roland and the lady in pink entered one of the rooms, Justin and the lady in violet another.

Justin sat down on the bed while the woman stood in front of him.

"So, what has caused your change of heart?" the lady asked, as she began to remove her violet dress.

"It is not my heart that has changed, but my mind."

"In what way?"

"I have been living in a dream," Justin said. "But if one's dream cannot become a reality, then one should face reality."

"Listen," the woman said softly, sitting down beside Justin on the bed. "I am certainly not a dream but a reality."

Justin took off his tunic, then the cross Bartholomew had given him, laying it on the table beside the bed.

§18

On his walk back to the university the next morning, Justin wondered why he had deprived himself so long from doing something that was perfectly normal. He certainly would have preferred to be with Constance, especially for his first time, but that was nothing more than a hopeless dream. He knew that he had betrayed his love for her, but what if he had gone through life without having had this experience at least once? Why should such a marvelous act be regarded as sinful? Our bodies are not evil, as Bartholomew had taught him. They are good!

No, Justin could not feel guilty over what he had done, neither before Constance nor before God. The lady had been so tender, so warm and caring, and even if it were not love, it was something both completely human and completely holy, which should not be denied. He could not condemn the bishop, or any others, for wanting to participate in this sacrament, given if not by God, then by nature.

When he arrived back at his room, Justin was relieved to find that Bartholomew was not there. Apparently he was in the library reading, which was fortunate, since Justin wanted to avoid having a confrontation with him about being out all night. Justin flung himself on his bed and immediately fell asleep, with happy memories in his head.

§19

Later that same afternoon Justin was awakened by a light tapping on his door. Before he could get up from his bed, Roland had already opened the door and entered the room.

"Wake up, man!" he said. "You can't sleep all day. There are still so many things we must do!"

Justin was on his feet by now but his eyes were still blurry. "Surely we need a day of rest, especially after last night."

"We will rest tomorrow. There is one more place I should like to take you to."

"And where is that?"

"You shall see."

Roland handed Justin a pouch with some coins in it.

"Here," he said. "You will need this tonight, along with a bit of luck."

It was dark and beginning to rain as Justin and Roland trekked into a poorer part of the city. Justin pulled his hat down over his face as he followed Roland through a maze of narrow winding streets with high stone walls on either side. Finally they came to an alehouse which did not look like any of the others Justin had seen before. Peering through the open window Justin could see that the tavern consisted of only one small room, cramped with men sitting around tables. They were throwing dice across the tops, with mugs of ale at their sides.

"What kind of place is this?" Justin asked.

"A public house, of course. But it has a reputation."

"A reputation for what?"

"This establishment attracts, shall we say, the lower elements of society."

"You mean peasants?"

"No. Lawbreakers."

"Lawbreakers?"

"Indeed. Poachers, cattle thieves, swindlers, robbers. There is more than one way to acquire money for gambling, you know!"

Justin felt instantly uncomfortable.

"I really think we should leave," Justin said.

"Whatever for?"

"It's dangerous."

"'Tisn't dangerous at all," Roland said. "Playing dice with criminals sounds rather exhilarating, don't you think? I am much more afraid of the townspeople."

"Surely they are upright and decent, are they not?"

"Ah, you still have so much to learn, my friend. Don't you know that they hate us? They wish we would just go away. In their eyes students are ill behaved and arrogant. We get drunk and start fights. All of which is no doubt true, at least on occasion. In any case, there is no peace between town and gown. Murders have been committed on both sides."

"Do not the authorities intervene?" Justin asked.

"Students are legally protected by the Church and exempt from civil law. So if we commit a crime we are tried in an ecclesiastical court and in accordance with canon law. The secular government has no jurisdiction over us. Furthermore, we may not be subjected to any form of physical punishment."

"In other words, we may break the law with impunity?"

"Indeed! Which is great for us, but also why the townsfolk are often tempted to take matters into their own hands. The lynching of students is not unheard of."

Roland winked at Justin and grinned.

"So be careful!" he said.

§20

Roland and Justin shook the rain from their cloaks before passing through the door of the tavern. They were immediately met by the taverner, who had swung round from the bar and blocked Roland and Justin from going any further into the shop.

"You are not welcome here," he said.

"And why not?" Roland asked with a polite smile.

"You're university students, aren't you?"

"Indeed, we are."

"Well, we've had enough of you. You're just a bunch of troublemakers."

"But we have money both to pay and to play," Roland said with mock courtesy.

"And you're haughty, too."

A gruff voice called out from the center of the room, "Let the boys in. We shall be happy to take their money if they care to join us."

Justin turned and saw that the speaker was a man with a pockmarked face. He was sitting at a table with three other ruffians.

"All right," the taverner called back. Then to Roland he snapped, "But no trouble, you hear?"

"Two ales, please," Roland said cheerfully. Then, handing some coins to the man, he added, "And here is the money in advance to assuage your doubts about us."

The taverner accepted the coins with a scowl and then went back to the bar to draw the ale.

While waiting, Roland said to Justin, "Go easy on the drinking tonight. We need to keep our wits about us."

The taverner handed Roland and Justin their mugs. The two walked over and sat down at the table with the pock-faced man and his friends.

"Let's start the pot low," the pock-faced man said, placing a single coin into the center. The others followed suit. The pock-faced man then handed three dice to Roland.

"The first man to land all three dice with the same number wins the pot."

Roland threw the dice, rolling a two, a five, and a six, then handed the dice to Justin, who landed a one, a three, and a four. The dice were passed until each of the players had taken a turn. By the end of the first round none of them had rolled three dice with identical numbers. The second round went much the same. During the third round, however, Roland struck with three fours and took the pot.

"You see," he said to Justin. "Luck is with me!"

They continued playing round after round. Justin did not win any of them, until at last all of his coins were gone.

"I shall stop playing," he said.

"You can still play," the pock-faced man said. "Just bet your tunic or your breeches. If you lose everything, you can leave here stark naked!"

Justin was not sure if the man was serious or joking but, in any case, declined his offer. In the meantime, though, Roland had been winning more than he lost. The pot was growing larger and larger. The others had begun dropping out of the game one by one, until the only players remaining were Roland, who was considerably ahead, and the pock-faced man.

"Here," Roland said, putting all of his money into the center of the table. "I challenge you to one final round."

The pock-faced man glowered at Roland, then pulled some more money out of his pouch and counted it out on the table.

Roland rolled first and came up with two threes and a six.

"Not good enough," the pock-faced man laughed.

Roland handed the dice to the man but was too preoccupied looking at the large sum of money on the table to see him deftly replace the dice they had been using with a different set.

But Justin noticed.

"He's switched the dice," Justin said.

"I have not," the pock-faced man replied.

"You did. I saw you."

"Are you accusing me of cheating?"

"Come on," Roland said to the man. "Hand them over."

"Look," the pock-faced man said, holding the dice out in the palm of his hand. "It's the same set we've been using all evening."

"Fine," Roland said. "But let's roll them a few times to see if they're loaded."

"I shall not have my honor questioned," the man said impetuously.

Roland leaned forward to grab the dice from the pock-faced man but was immediately restrained by one of the man's mates, who leaped from his chair and put a chokehold on him. Wrenching himself free, Roland landed a fist squarely on the thug's jaw. A scuffle broke out. The pock-faced man overthrew the table and charged at Roland, punching him in the stomach while the others held his arms. Men from the other tables rushed over to join in the fray. Justin, who had stepped aside and taken no part in the brawl, decided it was time to take flight. He quickly bolted through the door. The taverner jumped after him, raising the hue and cry just as soon as he was in the street.

As Justin was fleeing down the road, townsmen emerged from the doors of their houses and began chasing after him. It was raining heavily now. Justin slipped and fell in the mud more than once, each time picking himself up and running as fast as he could. His pursuers were closing the gap between them, however. Justin turned a corner and dashed down a ginnel, which he quickly realized had been a mistake. The lane ended abruptly at one of the city's walls, with no outlet on either side. Justin stood there panting from exhaustion. The townsmen were soon upon him.

"It's a student," one of them said.

"Indeed, it is," said another.

"Shall we turn him over to the magistrate?"

"For what purpose? He cannot be tried in court. He'll simply be set free and returned to the university."

"You're right," the first man said. "We should administer justice ourselves right here and now."

"But what has he done?"

"It doesn't matter. The fact that he was making a run for it shows that he's guilty of something. He deserves to be punished."

The men began laying into Justin, kicking and striking him until he was nearly unconscious. Then they picked him up and with a mighty heave threw him into a ditch that ran along the wall. Justin felt blood oozing from his scalp as rain poured into his open mouth. And then all was blank.

§21

When Justin awoke, he found himself lying on a soft pallet in a small dark room. He was wearing dry clothes and covered with a warm blanket. His body had been washed. When he touched his head he felt no blood, only a piece of smooth cloth covering a large aching lump erupting through his hair. Justin had no idea where he was but was too stiff with pain to be able to get up out of the bed and find out.

He lay there for a while, thinking back on what had happened, wondering where Roland was, and chiding himself for having gone with Roland to the gambling den in the first place. His life, as much as the path he had taken to escape the townsmen, was a dead end. It was true that he was despondent over having failed his examination, but was throwing himself into debauchery the best way to deal with it? Bartholomew would find out about the incident sooner or later and not be pleased. Justin would undoubtedly be punished as well, although he did not know how. Yet it was not the punishment he feared as much as the senselessness of it all. Something had to change, but he had no idea what. And, of course, there was no faith for him to fall back on either.

Suddenly the door to the room opened and Justin saw the dim figure of a man in the doorway. The man walked over to the room's only window and pulled back the shutter. Sunlight flooded into the room. The man bent down to examine Justin. It was only then that Justin recognized that he was the preacher.

"It's good that you have finally awakened," the preacher said. "We were all worried about you. You could have died, you know!"

"Where am I?" Justin asked.

"You are a welcome guest in our home," the preacher replied. "We found you several days ago lying half-dead in a gutter near here. It looks like someone gave you a good thrashing."

"Why did you bring me to your house?"

"To take care of you, of course. We shall bring you some food shortly."

"But you could have turned me over to the authorities."

"Ha!" the preacher laughed. "We would hardly do that. You may stay here until you recover, even longer if you like."

The preacher looked at Justin more carefully.

"You look familiar," he said. "Have we met before?"

"Indeed, we have," Justin replied. "Outside the cathedral, when you were preaching."

The preacher was thoughtful for a moment and then said, "Ah yes, you were with that monk who was scolding me about my sermon."

"I would be careful if I were you," Justin said. "That same monk has notified the bishop and the Inquisition is now looking for you."

"I already know. I would hope that you do not turn me over to the authorities either."

"Of course, I would not," Justin replied.

"And what do you think, my friend? Was it right or wrong for me to preach as I did to the multitude?"

"You should be allowed to think and speak as you please," Justin said. "I also find it difficult to accept the authority of the Church and am struggling to make my own judgments about what to believe."

"Well, let us talk more after you are better. And you certainly do not need to explain anything to me about your recent mishap. You were beaten and stripped of your clothes, but we have bandaged and taken care of you."

"I sincerely appreciate your kindness."

"We must love our neighbors as ourselves," the preacher said. "We must also love our enemies and those who persecute us."

Then he added, "Although the latter is admittedly much more difficult."

§22

Over the next few days Justin recovered well enough to be able to move around the house and take dinner with the other occupants. It was a large house, with three stories and many rooms, which were occupied in various combinations by about two dozen men and women altogether, including several children. The house was old and in need of repairs, but well kept. The furnishings were simple, the same as the houses of peasants.

The members of the household each went out during the day to their various occupations, with several of them staying at the house on a rotating basis to look after the children. The preacher, Justin learned, was a cooper who made casks and barrels, and only preached when could find the time. He would wear his hair and dress differently when he was preaching to minimize the chances of being recognized.

In the evening everyone returned to the house to have supper with each other, which they did not call *supper,* however, but a *love feast.* The meal was jointly prepared and then eaten together in a large room that occupied the entire first floor of the house. The fare was simple, but always included bread and wine, consumed not as a sacrament but simply as bread and wine. The mood was merry and boisterous, filled with laughter and conversation, quite unlike dinnertime in the monastery, where the monks were silent and listened to readings of scripture as they ate. The residents saw themselves as forming some kind of religious community, which Justin did not quite understand, but they did not make a show of it. They genuinely seemed to enjoy each other's company and welcomed Justin as if he were one of them.

One day after dinner, when Justin had a moment alone with the preacher, he asked him, "Many people are living here together, yet to whom does the house belong?"

"It belongs to all of us."

"You mean the property is not owned by a single person?"

"No, we have sold our possessions and hold all things in common, breaking bread in our home and partaking of food with gladness and generosity."

"Everyone is regarded as equal?"

"We pool our resources and then distribute them among both ourselves and the poor, each according to his need, with no distinctions. In Christ there is neither priest nor laity, Jew nor Gentile, slave nor free, male nor female, husband nor wife."

"You do not practice marriage?"

"In the realm of God, people neither marry nor are given in marriage."

"So you practice celibacy?"

The preacher laughed.

"Nay," he said. "We are hardly celibate."

"You feel free to be with whomever you want?"

"Not with whomever we want, but with whomever we love and who loves us in return. There's a difference! Nonetheless, we are often accused of sexual immorality by outsiders who have only a superficial knowledge of matters of the heart and think that the only legitimate form of love is between one man and one woman who are married to each other."

"You would permit one person to have many partners?"

"If they love each other."

"Even men with men and women with women."

"If they love each other," the preacher repeated.

"Most people would say that you are simply licentious for having abandoned the custom of marriage."

"Which is preferable: to be married and not to love or to love and not be married?"

Upon hearing the preacher say this, Justin instantly felt the entanglement of his love for Constance, his marriage to Penelope, and his encounter with the prostitute. Somehow he had not gotten it right.

"We are all one family," the preacher continued. "God is our father and we are his sons and daughters."

"But is Jesus himself not God's only son?"

"Jesus was not ashamed to call us his brothers and sisters, for he who sanctifies and those who are sanctified are one. The same Spirit that dwelled in Jesus dwells in us. Jesus is not my King of Kings and Lord of Lords. He is my brother."

"You make yourself equal to Jesus?"

"We have passed from the age of the Father through the age of the Son to the age of the Spirit. All who are freely led by the Spirit are children of God, which is why we call ourselves brothers and sisters of the Free Spirit."

"So you think you are God?"

"Neither more nor less than Jesus."

"Then we should all fall down and worship you!"

"No, no!" the preacher said circumspectly. "You should not worship me but the God that is within yourself, within Jesus, within all of us. Anyone claiming that he alone is God is Satan. If such a man blocks your path, you must slay him!"

"Even if it were Jesus?"

"If he stands in your way, you must kill even him."

"Surely you don't mean that literally!"

"It was not only the Roman soldiers who crucified Christ, but each of us as well."

"For the forgiveness of our sins."

"Indeed. And that is why we must also be crucified with Christ," the preacher said. "Thou shalt worship no other god but the one God and Father of all, who is over all and through all and in all, which includes not just Jesus, but also you and me."

"But does that not mean that God is also our ruler?"

"If God is in each of us, then the Kingdom of God is not a theocracy but a community."

Justin pondered for a moment and then asked the preacher, "Why do you reject the Church?"

"We do not reject the Church. We *are* the Church. The Church is the resurrected body of Christ and we are individual members of it since Jesus is resurrected in each of our bodies as well."

The preacher reached out his arm and said, "Here, touch me!"

"What do you mean?"

"Just touch me!"

Justin reached out his hand and touched the preacher's arm.

"See!" the preacher said. "I am not a ghost. I am real flesh and bones! You have seen me eating as well. Yet Christ has been resurrected in my own body and the same Holy Spirit that dwelled in Jesus dwells in me. Before I was just a corpse, but now I am alive. That is the true meaning of the resurrection of the dead!"

"I'm glad to know that you are still among the living, both physically and spiritually," Justin laughed. "But to rephrase my question, why do you reject the clergy?"

The preacher drew in a deep breath and then said, "Because they have exalted themselves above God and usurped his kingship. We refuse to be ruled over by false priests and bishops. We are a royal priesthood, each one of us, and will not be brought under the power of any other. We strive to maintain the fellowship of the Church. But we reject its authority."

"Yet are you not the leader of the people living here?"

"We have no leaders. Everything is decided by us talking together."

Justin objected, "But if you adhere to no authority, how do you know that your teachings are true?"

"We hold not to the teachings of humans but to the universal gospel," the preacher replied, "which is available to all those who live on earth, regardless of nation, race, gender, kinship, or language. God reveals himself to each of us directly. We do not need the teachings of the Church nor even the scriptures to know God."

"Surely the Bible constrains what you are permitted to believe and do."

"The scriptures are nothing more than pieces of paper with words written on them. We should follow what the Spirit writes in our hearts."

"What if there is a contradiction between what scripture and the Spirit tell us?"

"Then the Bible should be burned!"

Justin recalled what the abbot had told him about following the Holy Spirit rather than the scriptures but was still rattled by this answer.

"In what, then, should we place our faith if not in the Bible?" he asked.

"Solely in the Spirit of God into which we are baptized and which dwells within us," the preacher answered. "To commit ourselves to anything else is idolatry."

"But how does the Holy Spirit communicate with us?"

"There is no dependence upon words and letters but an immediate transmission that is outside the scriptures, a direct pointing into our souls so that we might see into our own nature and realize our Christhood."

"Nonetheless must we still not live by the laws God has given us?"

"The only people who feel obliged to follow the commandments blindly are those who have not been taught by the Spirit and who have no sense of right or wrong in their hearts. Even Jesus' disciples broke the commandments when they gathered grain on the Sabbath. Determining what is right and wrong is not decided by the law but by the gift of discernment, which comes directly from the Holy Spirit."

Justin ruminated on everything that the preacher had been telling him and then said, "Nonetheless, you must obey the civil authorities."

"We swear no oaths, neither by heaven nor earth, neither to the Church nor to the lords. We pay homage and owe fealty to no one."

"Your aim, then, is to undermine the present social system?"

"The Kingdom of Heaven is not a fairyland of the future but something that has already arrived, just as Jesus proclaimed. It is neither here nor there, but among us. It is in this world, but not of it. The way we live now prefigures the life of the world to come, which will only be realized in the fullness of time. Indeed, the day is coming when our present social system will collapse and the ecclesiastical hierarchy with it. A new world order based on love and mutual aid, free from any restraint or external power, will be ushered in. Once all authority has been abolished and there are no more kings, we each may do what is right in our own eyes."

"But until then you are still obliged to follow the law," Justin insisted.

"If there is no property, there can be no law against stealing. If there is no marriage, there can be no law against adultery. If each has what they need, there can be no law against coveting. For us, the only law is love. Those who are led by the Spirit are under no other restrictions. We are not bound by any rule or authority but have passed from the reign of law to the reign of freedom. All things are lawful for us, although not all things are expedient."

"So, you think you are free to do whatever you please!" Justin exclaimed.

"Indeed!" the preacher responded. "For what pleases us are peace, joy, and love; patience, kindness, and goodness; faithfulness, meekness, and self-control. Whoever is born of God does not sin, indeed *cannot* sin, for God's nature lives in us. To the pure of heart all things are pure, but to the corrupt and unbelieving nothing is pure; their very minds and consciences are defiled."

"You would condone theft and murder and rape?"

"It is unfortunate that we are often falsely charged with holding this view, not only by the authorities, but also by others who have appropriated our name and call themselves our brethren. This doctrine is, however, contrary to all that we stand for. We reject any form of domination of one person over another."

"What does it mean to be pure in heart?" Justin asked.

"It means that we have purified our desires. A person born of the Spirit would have no desire to selfishly deprive others of what they need or to kill someone or to have sexual relations with a person who is unwilling. It is only when our hearts have been purified that we are able to see God. And if we are able to see and love the God we find inside our own hearts, souls, minds, and wills, we must also love the God we find in our fellow human beings. We do not seek power over others, but power over ourselves, which we then use to help, rather than to control, others."

"May we see God in this life?"

"This is the only life in which we shall see him!" the preacher declared. "We have already risen from the dead. There is no other resurrection. Those who find God in this world live in paradise. Those who cannot live in hell."

"But how might I find God?"

The preacher did not answer but simply smiled and opened his arms as wide as he could, as if he were trying to embrace not only Justin but the world itself.

§23

The following day Justin informed the preacher of his intention to return to the university.

"Of course, you are free to leave anytime," the preacher said. "But if you would like to stay, you are certainly welcome to join our community here."

"No, I think I should resume my studies, or at least try to. I'm not sure how the headmaster will deal with me, but our new term starts tomorrow."

"Well, please come again and join our love feasts anytime you would like. But I ask you once again not to reveal where I live or this house to anyone, especially the inquisitor, since, as you know, he is looking for me."

"I shall not," Justin said.

He walked through the door of the house into the ginnel, trying to get his bearings. The house was located in the same poor neighborhood as the tavern, along the city wall not far from where Justin had been assaulted by the townsmen. It was a part of town Justin was not familiar with so it took him a considerable amount of time to find his way through the labyrinth of winding passages until he finally came again to the city center.

Justin noticed that a crowd had gathered in front of the guildhall. As he walked closer he saw a young man with fiery red hair and a wispy beard on an elevated platform, standing with his arms and head clasped in a pillory. People were throwing rotten vegetables, dead animals, and excrement at the man, shouting abuse as they did. The filth had so darkened the miscreant's face that Justin was at first not able to recognize him. Then Justin saw a gold ring shining out from under the gunge on the man's finger. It was the same gold ring Roland had bought at the fair and, indeed, the man in the stocks was Roland! He was too busy spitting and cursing as the crowd jeered to notice Justin standing just a short distance away from him.

A man picked up a rock and was about to throw it at Roland, but Justin held his hand.

"Please, don't," Justin said.

"I shall do as I please," the man hissed.

"Should we not have compassion rather than contempt for the weak and helpless?"

"The fellow's a loser. He deserves it."

"Remember the scripture," Justin said. "Let he who is without sin cast the first stone."

"He's the sinner, not me. Why are you defending this scoundrel anyway?"

"He is my friend," Justin replied.

"Ah, I see. So you must be a student, too."

"I am."

"Then get the hell out of here before I throw this stone at you!" the man shouted. "All the students in this town should be banished and sent back to wherever it is they came from!"

The man, still holding the stone in his fist, raised his arm menacingly at Justin, who promptly turned and ran away down the street towards the university.

§24

As soon as Justin opened the door to his dormitory room, Bartholomew leaped up from his desk and confronted him.

"Where on earth have you been?" he cried. "We have been looking everywhere for you!"

"I had a bit of trouble," Justin replied.

"I can see by the bruises on your face and the bump on your head. Come out with it. What happened?"

"I was with Roland."

"Roland! I should have suspected. You've heard what happened to him, I suppose."

"In fact, I was with him on the night of the incident and I saw him again just a short while ago."

"He is still in the pillory?" Bartholomew said, raising his voice at the end to make it a question.

"Indeed he is," Justin replied.

"As soon as they were informed, the masters held a meeting and handed Roland over to the civil authorities."

"I thought that students are protected by the Church in such cases."

"Indeed. But given his past record, Roland was immediately expelled from the university and so is no longer under its jurisdiction. The masters were told that there was another student with him, but Roland refused to give the name of his companion. I had my suspicions, of course—no, not suspicions, I *knew* it was you—but I couldn't confirm that until now. As matters stand, you are also implicated."

Bartholomew sat down on his bed.

"I already know about the fray in the tavern," he said. "But, tell me, what happened to you after that?"

Justin knew he must tell the truth and, in any case, he wanted to.

"I ran away," he started, "but was pursued by men from the town, who caught me and beat me. The next day I awoke in the home of strangers who took care of me and nursed me back to health."

"Who were these strangers?"

Justin's resolve to be completely honest instantly vanished. It was one thing to confess his own exploits to Bartholomew, but quite another to expose the secrets of others.

"I cannot tell you," he said.

"Why not?"

"Do not force me to lie to you again."

"Are they people I know?"

Justin was silent.

"Where do they live?"

"I shall not tell you."

"But you must."

"A priest is prohibited from revealing the details of a confession to others, and I should like to claim the same privilege."

"You are no priest!" Bartholomew exclaimed, standing up straight. "And your manner of speaking leads me to believe that you are shielding a wrongdoer."

"I can assure you he has done no wrong."

"Well, if you will not reveal the truth to me now, it will come out sooner or later," Bartholomew said dourly, flopping back down on his bed. "In any case, you must report to the headmaster immediately and explain everything to him. Even if you are not dismissed by the university and handed over to the civil authorities, you may still be punished, of course."

"But I did nothing wrong. As soon as the fighting broke out, I fled."

"You never should have been in that tavern in the first place."

"What do you think will happen to me?" Justin asked.

"It shall be up to the master to determine your fate. In addition, I shall write a letter to the abbot with a full account of your misbehavior. I had thought I would give you a second chance and not tell him you had failed your examination, but now I think I should inform him about that as well. He had high expectations for you, you know, but you have failed to live up to them."

"Indeed," Justin replied. "You must do what you must do."

§25

An inquiry was held at the university. Justin was brought before the masters, with Bartholomew also in attendance. Justin explained the entire affair to them, just as it had happened. The headmaster censured him for having gone to a gambling den, particularly in the company of Roland, who was known to be a lout. Justin hedged when he was asked about the people who had cared for him, stating simply that they were "strangers." To Justin's relief the master did not press him on this point.

In the end, it was decided that since Justin had not actually participated in the skirmish, but had tried to escape from it, he was not guilty of any serious charges and would not be turned over to the Church authorities for a formal inquest. Instead he would be placed on probation for the entire term and not permitted to leave the university under any circumstances, except to attend mass, and then only with Bartholomew as his chaperone.

After the hearing was over, Justin and Bartholomew returned to their room.

"I am disappointed that you did not reveal who took care of you after you were injured," Bartholomew said.

"I should like to leave the matter alone," Justin replied.

"Even if you will not tell me, I think I know." Bartholomew narrowed his eyes. "I only need to find out where they live."

For the remainder of the term Justin complied with the stipulations of his probation, following the regular routine of attending lectures, which had become hopelessly dull without Roland, reading in the library, having dinner with the other students in the dining hall, and attending mass with Bartholomew. He studied what he was told to study and gave all the correct answers in class, but his heart was not in it. Everyone was pleased except Justin.

Bartholomew had received a reply from the abbot about Justin's misadventures. The abbot, caring as he always was, had told Bartholomew to forgive Justin's misdeeds as the master had, but to keep a watchful eye on Justin and vigilantly monitor the situation. The abbot further instructed Bartholomew to encourage Justin in his studies and to cheer him up when he became dispirited.

Bartholomew shared everything with Justin, telling him, "Don't worry. I shall take care of you!"

In the evenings Justin sometimes went to the chapel, thinking that he should pray, but no words came to him. He tried again to sit quietly and follow his breathing, which brought him some relief. But his mind was invaded by thoughts about what had transpired, not just recently but ever since he had left the estate.

It seemed to him that there was no place he fit in, no place that he really wanted to be. He despised his life at the university and, more than that, despised himself for enduring it and not having the fortitude to leave. Even though there was nothing actually holding him back, it felt exactly the same as when he had been trapped inside the estate.

Yet, where would he go? The ocean and distant mountains no longer held any appeal for him. Even if it were possible for him to return to the village to be with Constance, he no longer wished to do so. That part of his life was over.

He thought that perhaps he should return to the house of the preacher and take up residence with the brothers and sisters there. Their exuberance was so much more refreshing than the solemnity of the monastery. And while the monks at the monastery were thoroughly devoted to their faith and practice, there was no freedom, either to come and go as one pleased or, more importantly, to think on one's own as one wanted.

Even though they were regarded as heretics, the brothers and sisters of the Free Spirit had a sincerity and genuineness about them that Justin could not find in the Church. The beliefs the preacher had shared with him were odd and definitely contrary to the way Christianity was ordinarily understood, or at least to the way Bartholomew had explained it to him, yet somehow they made perfect sense. Justin was still not sure at all about what he himself believed, but he felt there might be something more that he could learn from the preacher. At least he wanted to find out.

§26

The term ended and with it Justin's period of probation. Justin celebrated Christmas with Bartholomew at the cathedral and then told him that he wished to attend a festival that would be held on New Year's Day, if only to escape the confines of the university, which he had been holed up in for so long.

Bartholomew immediately replied that he would not be going and tried to dissuade Justin from attending as well.

"You probably have no knowledge of this festival," Bartholomew said. "Some parishes continue to hold it, but it has been widely condemned by the higher authorities in the Church due to its excesses."

"Excesses?"

"Yes, it started out as a religious feast but has now degenerated into a day of drunken orgies. Anything taboo is permitted, with no need to confess or do penance afterward."

"I have heard that it is called the 'Feast of Fools,' in accordance with scripture, which says that we should be 'fools for Christ.' Surely if the celebration is based on the Bible, it cannot be all bad."

"In fact it is based on an ancient Roman holiday to honor the pagan god Saturn. On this day the social order was inverted: lords waited on their servants, while servants were permitted to abuse their masters. In the Christian version the common people become the clergy, and vice versa, with a young boy being appointed bishop."

Justin laughed. "Surely there should be at least one day out of the year in which the rulers are brought down from their thrones and the humble are exalted. Does the Bible not say, 'The last shall be first, and the first last'?"

"You misunderstand the true meaning of scripture," Bartholomew replied vehemently. "The feast subverts God's holy order. I cannot condone it but I cannot prevent you from attending either. I am sure that the ceremony held in the cathedral will be beyond reproach. The boy bishop will then lead a procession through the town, which should still be within the bounds of propriety. After that, however, the licentiousness will begin in earnest. I should hardly need to warn you not to indulge in any illicit behavior yourself. You must return to the university immediately after the parade is over and avoid any further trouble."

"You needn't worry about me," Justin said.

"You have been on your best behavior recently, so I hope I can trust you," Bartholomew said. He then added ominously, "But just remember that even though your probation is over, you are still being watched."

Bartholomew then left the room, presumably to go to the chapel yet again to pray.

§27

When Justin arrived at the plaza outside the cathedral on the day of the feast, he was surprised to find that no one was there. The entire city was eerily silent.

But when he opened the doors of the cathedral his ears were immediately met with the noise of the rabble inside. The scene was far from being "beyond reproach," as Bartholomew had told him, and even more decadent than Justin could have imagined.

Priests were in the choir singing bawdy hymns, while parishioners shouted words of blasphemy. Men were dressed as women and women as men. A few had stripped off their clothes and were running and leaping nude through the nave. Girls were dancing lewdly in the aisles as boys played dice in the transepts. Young children parodied the clergy, swinging censers with burning dung, which filled the air with a heavy foul-smelling smoke. Black pudding was eaten from the altar. Mugs of ale were sloshed around.

Above the ruckus, on the central panel of the triptych behind the altar, a suffering Jesus looked down from his cross, while the statue of Mary stood serenely to the left holding an innocent baby in her arms. The red candle atop the tabernacle had been snuffed out.

As Justin stood in the cathedral witnessing all of these things, a monk in a black habit quietly entered from the rear and took up a position in the far corner opposite Justin. Justin noticed that he was the only person not joining in the mayhem. The monk stood silent and motionless, sometimes peeking one eye around the corner of the black cowl he had pulled over his face. He seemed to be less interested in the spectacle itself than in observing those participating in it.

Suddenly a horn was blown and a hush fell over the audience as they parted to make way for a donkey with a young boy on it, which had just passed through the doors of the narthex. The boy, wearing a white alb, rode the donkey directly through the center of the nave towards the sanctuary. The congregation began placing holly branches before the feet of the ass and singing,

> He hath put down the mighty from their seat
> and hath exalted the humble and the meek!

The boy dismounted the donkey and ascended the steps of the chancel, where he was greeted by the bishop of the cathedral, who took off his gold chasuble and placed it around the boy's shoulders. With mock gravity, the bishop then took off his miter, also colored gold, and said with a loud voice as he placed it on the boy's head, "I now pronounce you 'Lord of Misrule.'"

The crowd applauded and cheered. The bishop handed his crozier to the boy, who then blessed the congregation with exaggerated waves of his arms. The response was a clamorous "Heehaw!" A buffoon from the assembly then went to where the bishop was standing, bonked him on the head with an inflated pig's bladder, and proclaimed solemnly, "Now let us go naked into the tavern and drink without end!" The parishioners responded with an equally clamorous "Amen!"

The boy bishop remounted the donkey, which was then led out of the cathedral back into the square, with the parishioners following. Once everyone was outside, they all donned masks, caricaturing kings and queens, noblemen and noblewomen, doctors and city officials, panderers and harlots. People sang and danced, some of them acting out burlesque scenes with obscene gestures.

Justin was swept along with the crowd, elbowed and bumped from one side to the other, even though he himself did not take part in their whooping and gyrations. He certainly did not wish to dampen the festive mood, but simply could not see the point of their merriment. Amidst the noise his mind drifted back to the times he had stood alone atop the tower on the estate looking out over vast open vistas, without a single sound in the sky. But he was quickly jolted back into reality when a burly man accidentally swung his arm around and knocked Justin to the ground, without so much as an apology. Picking himself up, Justin noticed out of the corner of his eye the same monk with a black habit and cowl, whom he had seen in the cathedral, now tagging along listlessly at the end of the pageant.

Justin rejoined the twistings and turnings of the crowd, but when they came to the side street that turned off in the direction of where the preacher lived, he wiggled himself free and set off to find the narrow ginnel that led to the preacher's house. Looking briefly back over his shoulder, he saw the crowd continuing its way down the main boulevard. The monk in black was no longer following them.

§28

Justin knocked on the door of the preacher's house, and when it opened the preacher himself was there to greet him with a hearty hug.

"Welcome," he said. "We haven't seen you in a very long time. It is so good that you could come back to visit us!"

He ushered Justin into the room and motioned for him to have a seat at the table, where the communalists were gathered for their usual love feast.

"We have just begun to eat," the preacher said. "Please join us."

Everyone exchanged greetings and Justin sat down on a chair beside the preacher's. He was handed a slice of bread and a cup of wine, while more food was heaped onto his plate. As the brothers and sisters were chatting among themselves, the preacher asked Justin, "What is the occasion for you coming to see us today?"

"I attended the feast at the cathedral and the parade afterward," Justin replied, "When I saw the street leading to your house, I decided to drop by. I hope you do not mind my intrusion."

"No, not at all. We ourselves never attend the feast. It's much too rowdy and, in any case, brings no benefit."

"Indeed, it was much more raucous than I had expected. Why do the Church and the authorities permit such travesties?"

"To let people blow off steam," the preacher said. "If you wish to sub-jugate people, you must also give them the opportunity to taste what they think is freedom and equality, even if it is just for one day out of the year. Bend a sapling too far in one direction and it will snap back at you just as soon as you let it go. A mature oak, however, has equanimity. It is not so easily bent one way or the other."

"I have heard to the contrary that a strong old oak will break more easily in a storm than a young green reed that bends with the wind. The hard and stiff will be broken, while the soft and supple will prevail."

"Well, no doubt both sayings are true, each in their own way."

"But should we not try to resolve the inconsistencies?" Justin asked.

"Nay!" the preacher laughed. "Paradox is essential! How else can we get at the truth? No statement is ever true in itself. It must always be taken together with its opposite."

Indeed, Justin thought, that is the true meaning of dialectics! He then said, "Surely, though, the festival serves a useful purpose. Peasants are al-lowed to become noblemen, merchants may become kings, a child may become a bishop. The high is made low and the low made high, just like it says in the Bible."

"But the high and low still remain. You have simply turned them up-side down."

The preacher moved his hands vertically so that the right hand was on top of the left, then the left on top of the right.

"What is your own view then?" Justin asked.

"There is neither high nor low, no up or down," the preacher said. "Ev-ery valley shall be raised up, every mountain and hill made low. The uneven ground will be made level and the rough places a plain."

The preacher was now moving his left and right hands horizontally back and forth, side by side with each other.

"As matters stand, however, the Church and the government still have ultimate power over us, do they not? What shall we do?" Justin asked.

"As the Bible says, 'Resist not evil.' If they slap us on one cheek, then we shall turn to them the other. We do not fight back, for we hold that it is wrong to do unto others what we do not want them to do unto us. Our goals cannot be achieved through violence. Peaceful ends can only be pursued through peaceful means."

"Do you not fear the Inquisition?"

"The wicked Church at present persecutes all who refuse to condone its sins and actions," the preacher replied. "It does not flee from city to city, as we do, but rules over all the nations. Seated in the grandeur and pomp of this world, it is feared by kings and emperors. Rather than tending the sheep, it kills them. But the sheep bear all in patience, making no defense against the wolf."

"But is not your attempt to overthrow the bishops and clergy just as power hungry? Do you not wish to set yourselves up as the true Church of Christ?"

"There is no 'true Church.' We are perfectly content to let the institutional ecclesia go its merry way as long as we are also allowed to go ours. We do not try to overthrow the Church but simply to persuade people to withdraw their support from it."

"Nonetheless, you are a heretic," Justin said.

"Was Jesus not also a heretic? He criticized the religious establishment of his day and tried to point us in a new and better direction. That is all we are attempting to do as well."

"And Jesus was crucified for challenging the authorities."

"Indeed, and we may be crucified as well. Literally!" the preacher said. "Or stoned or burned or thrown to the lions as the early Christian martyrs were. In times past Christians were oppressed. Now they have become the oppressors. We may defend our faith by dying for it, but never by killing others."

"Yet should you die, your beliefs would die with you, never to return."

"Perhaps. Yet it is also possible that they would be born again in a far distant future and find new life among people who never knew us, in times and places we cannot even imagine."

When the meal and conversation were finished, the preacher accompanied Justin to the entrance of the house.

"Your door has no lock," Justin observed.

"That's because everyone is given hospitality here," the preacher replied.

"What if a thief should break in to rob you of your belongings?"

"He can have anything he wants. It wouldn't be stealing. We would simply give it to him or, if no one were here, he could just help himself."

Once outside and standing in the ginnel, the preacher gave Justin another warm hug. Justin felt as if his soul had been cleansed or at least that he had learned something new and precious.

"The door is always open for you, too," the preacher said. "Please come to visit us again anytime you like. You needn't even knock."

"I shall return before this holiday season is over," Justin replied. "For our classes will resume after that. Perhaps at some point I shall choose to stay here with you permanently!"

"You would be most welcome!" the preacher said.

As Justin walked away and the preacher went back inside, neither of them noticed a dark figure wearing a black habit and cowl emerge from a gap between two of the houses.

§29

When Justin returned to the dormitory at the university Bartholomew was not in their room, which was unusual because it was already night and Bartholomew was not the sort to stay out late, even if he only went to the library or to the chapel to pray.

Justin lay back on his bed and thought about everything the preacher had told him. He reflected back to his time on the estate and his life in the village with Constance. Was not the social order his father had so vigorously defended based solely on raw power, with those who have it ruling over those who do not? The claim is that power is given to the authorities so that they may maintain order and insure that their subjects lead tranquil and peaceful lives in godliness and dignity. But is it not obvious that the real purpose of the system is to allow those with power to compel others to be their servants and do their bidding?

And surely, as the preacher had said, the solution is not simply to flip the present order over so that those on the bottom are now on the top, but to make everything flat. The end result would not be that everyone becomes perfectly "equal" or the "same," but rather that no one person would ever be able to illegitimately exercise power over another, even if they wanted to.

It was also becoming increasingly obvious to Justin that religion is used, or misused, to keep everyone in their place by making them drunk on the idea that the Kingdom of Heaven is not something that is already here among us, as Christ himself declared, but a glorious land above the sky that we go to after we die. What better way to keep the minds of the people off their present injustices, to keep them from trying to change things and to make a better world here and now, than by focusing their attention on their future life in heaven?

Anyone, such as the preacher, who challenged the authority of the Church or the nobility would either be wooed like a sheep back to the pen or, if that failed, expelled from the flock and left to the wolves. The task, then, was not to overthrow our present leaders and install new ones who would purportedly act in our interest, but rather to abolish the entire hierarchical system itself. Otherwise, any challengers who succeeded in fomenting a revolution and overturning the social order would simply become the new tyrants who would lord it over the others and attempt to impose their rule on everyone else, just the same as before.

Justin had almost fallen asleep thinking these thoughts when suddenly the door to the room burst open and he saw in the doorway a dark figure wearing a black habit and cowl, which he instantly recognized.

"It was you," Justin said.

"You know?" Bartholomew replied, taking off his cowl. "I told you this morning that you would be watched and that's exactly what I've been doing."

"You've been following me all day?"

"Of course. You went first to the cathedral, where I stood in the back of the nave and was forced to watch all those despicable antics. I cannot believe that the bishop would permit such acts of desecration in the House of God."

"I saw you there," Justin said. "But I did not think it was you."

"Believe me, I shall report everything I saw back to the abbot, who will issue his strongest condemnation of this so-called feast and the clergy who participated in it."

"But I thought you said that the offices of the Church must be respected, even if those who fill them are impious."

"That is still true," Bartholomew said. "But corruption in the Church must nonetheless be plucked up by the roots. It is no wonder that the masses no longer have faith in the Church when they see priests and bishops engage in such sacrilege."

Bartholomew folded his habit and placed it under his bed.

"I kept my distance when you joined the procession," he continued. "But there was no place for me to hide. When you stumbled and looked up I thought you had recognized me."

"I saw only a figure wearing a black habit and cowl."

"My intention all along was simply to make sure you did not get into trouble. I never anticipated that after shadowing you through the back-streets you would end up at the house of the preacher."

"How did you know it was the preacher I visited?"

"At first I did not, but then I saw you and the preacher embracing in the alley when you departed."

In a flash Justin realized the gravity of the situation.

"Surely you have not reported the preacher to the authorities!" Justin cried.

"Indeed, I have. There is no doubt that the inquisitor and his assistants have already gone to the preacher's house to detain him and round up his followers."

Justin reached under his bed for his own cloak.

"I must go to them immediately," he said.

"Not so fast," Bartholomew said, positioning himself between Justin and the door of the room. "The trouble you are in now is far more serious than your episode at the tavern. If the inquisitor learns that you were in the house with the heretic, then you, too, shall be thought of as one of them or at least as one of their supporters."

"So, you did not tell the inquisitor I was there?"

"No," Bartholomew replied. "I am sure that I should have. But I said nothing."

"Was that not a lie?"

"It is not a lie to conceal information one is not asked to give, but I may still be accused of shielding heretics."

"Why were you willing to protect me?"

"Because you are my friend, Justin, and I care about you. Tell me that you have not fallen victim to the preacher's heresies."

"It is true that I visited the preacher's house. But I never joined his association."

"I have long suspected that you were falling into heresy, so I am relieved to hear you say so," Bartholomew said. "You must forsake the preacher and all his teachings now and forever. I will say nothing to the inquisitor this time, but should you ever embrace any heretical views of any kind, I shall be obliged to inform him."

"I am quite sure that you would," Justin said, barely able to conceal his loathing of Bartholomew.

"I cannot tell you how concerned I am that you may be straying from Christian teachings, but please be assured that I shall give you every opportunity to return to God and the true Church," Bartholomew said in a gentle voice. "Let us take some time to pray together and seek God's guidance."

Justin was enraged at Bartholomew for having told the authorities about the preacher, but could think of nothing to do, so he bowed his head while Bartholomew said a prayer asking God to forgive and help Justin. Justin did not wish to be forgiven or helped, however.

§30

A public inquiry was held the very next day, which Justin and Bartholomew both attended. Once again, nearly all the townspeople were there, flooding the square in front of the cathedral.

The inquisitor and his retinue were standing on the steps, accompanied by the bishop, who had his miter back on his own head and now stood solemnly before the assembly. Guards then brought the preacher out of the cathedral, setting him up on a stand for all to see.

The inquisitor then explained that the man standing before them, commonly known as "the preacher," had been accused of heresy by a person whose name would be withheld. The preacher and his fellow heretics, including the children, had been taken into custody and questioned. The latter would be dealt with separately since it had been determined that they had not actively expounded their false doctrines to others. The inquisitor further explained that the preacher had denied being a heretic, but upon further questioning was found to be holding opinions contrary to the teachings of the Church, which he publicly avowed and obstinately defended.

The inquisitor mentioned that several witnesses who had observed the preacher spreading heresy at various places in the city had already come forward and then asked if there were any others who would be willing to testify against him.

"You may inform us later in private," the inquisitor said. "The identity of any and all witnesses will be held in the strictest confidence and not revealed to the accused."

Just as soon as the inquisitor had finished speaking, however, a woman called out, "Indeed, I have seen this man preaching heresy right here on the very steps of this cathedral, just where you are standing, and I am not ashamed to say it openly in public!"

Justin recognized her as the woman who had joined Bartholomew and him for confession the first time they had heard the preacher speak.

"And I!" shouted out another man, and then another and another. Bartholomew himself enthusiastically joined in the chorus. The throng soon became unruly, with everyone crying out accusations. Or almost everyone, since a few of the townspeople stood by impassively, not saying anything, including a woman standing immediately next to Justin.

"Burn him!" the crowd began to chant.

It was only then Justin realized that these were exactly the same people who had been participating in the festival the day before, who had so wantonly danced around the golden calf while the tablets of the law shattered all around them.

The inquisitor raised his hands and demanded silence.

"I see that we shall have no difficulty finding witnesses," he said.

His assistants meanwhile had already gone into the swarm, taking the names of people who would volunteer to make statements.

Bartholomew looked at Justin, scrutinizing his reaction. Justin was distraught but made no movement. The woman on the other side of Justin, however, wriggled. Justin thought he heard her say in an almost inaudible whisper, "We are far too many for you to find all of us."

The inquisitor then dismissed the assembly, telling the crowd that a just trial would be held, a verdict rendered, and punishment administered, all in due course.

§31

The crowd dispersed and Bartholomew and Justin began walking back to the dormitory. Along the way, Bartholomew said to Justin, "It is essential now that the preacher be found guilty."

"Surely you can't be hoping for such an outcome," Justin replied, with a hint of disgust in his voice that went undetected by Bartholomew.

"Indeed, I am. For I was the first to formally accuse him. If the preacher is found innocent, then I will be charged with making a false accusation and defaming him. I myself would face legal penalties, possibly even imprisonment for life."

"That would hardly be just, now would it?" Justin said.

"Certainly not," Bartholomew said gravely, failing to note Justin's sarcasm. "But I am confident that the inquisitor will find him guilty. The preacher is obviously teaching false doctrines and there are witnesses against him. The evidence is very clear."

"Can we be assured that the Church will treat the preacher fairly?"

"Of course, they will. The Inquisition is a vast improvement over the older forms of justice. In days of old vigilantes would have simply taken matters into their own hands and done with him as they pleased. Heretics were also condemned capriciously by the nobility, who realized, as they do even now, that their authority is derived from the Church and that any attack on the Church poses a threat to their own rule. Heresy is not only a violation of God's commandments and canon law, but also treason against the state, which is why we now have civil laws against heresy as well."

"So, why not just let the secular powers deal with heresy?"

"Because they have no authority in doctrinal matters and are unable to determine on their own whether a teaching is genuinely heretical or not."

"Which is why a tribunal is established by the Church."

"Indeed. The Inquisition is essentially an inquest, a method of inquiry, an investigation. Compared to the dark ages of the past, heretics are now protected by the Church and given a rigorous trail based on testimony and proof. They are not convicted arbitrarily."

"What happens if a person is found to be guilty of heresy?" Justin asked.

"In instances in which people fall unwittingly into error simply because they are too ignorant to know the truth, the Church will offer them instruction and correct their views."

"There is no penalty?"

"A mild penance may be imposed, such as reciting prayers, fasting, or going on a pilgrimage."

"And if the heresy is willful?"

"If they recant, it is possible that they will still be whipped, but more likely they would simply be stigmatized," Bartholomew replied. "In the case of the preacher's associates, if they renounce the preacher and his teachings, I would expect them to have a yellow cross sewn into their clothes as a sign of humiliation. They may be given a lighter sentence, though, if they are willing to testify against others who share their beliefs."

"And if they do not abjure the preacher's doctrines?"

"Since they are only guilty of believing heresy but not of preaching it, they would most likely be exiled from the city, but marked on their foreheads with a red-hot iron first so that no other municipality would accept them. In any case, their house will certainly be confiscated. It is a source of income for the Church."

Justin and Bartholomew reached the entrance to the university, but instead of going directly to their rooms, Bartholomew suggested that they continue their conversation in the commons room, which students could use freely. Inside the room was a table with benches to sit on and a fire going in the fireplace, which while not quite heating the entire room took off some of the chill.

After they had seated themselves, Justin asked, "And what will happen to the preacher?"

Bartholomew swung himself around so that he could face Justin directly.

"The best outcome would be for him to make a full confession and recant," he said. "That is certainly what the Church wishes. After all, the purpose of the Inquisition is not to condemn heretics but to save them."

"And if he were to remain silent?"

"Then he would probably be cast into prison."

"For how long?"

"For as long as necessary," Bartholomew replied. "The Church authorities would visit him periodically and ask for a recantation. He would be released just as soon as he adjures, even if it takes years, and then be given an appropriate penance."

"Do you think that he will confess?"

"If he refuses to do so freely, he might also be tortured."

"Tortured?" Justin asked, dismayed. "What kind of torture would the preacher be subjected to?"

"I suppose he would be stretched on a rack or have his hands tied behind his back and then be hung from the wrists on a strappado, with weights being added to the feet if necessary, although this increases the chance of the arms and shoulders being dislocated. But there are other methods. I am sure the authorities would use every available means to insure the salvation of his soul."

"Are there no restrictions?"

"The Church takes every precaution, of course. Torture must have the approval of the bishop. It may not be unnecessarily brutal or result in permanent injuries, nor result in bloodshed, mutilation, or death. A member of the medical profession is always present to stop the procedure if it goes too far."

"Do the inquisitors themselves actually conduct the torture?"

"No, it is conducted by his assistants, who are not members of the clergy. If an inquisitor is present while torture is actually being administered, he must seek absolution."

"If torture is a sin then do not the torturers also require absolution?"

Bartholomew was uncertain how to answer this question, so Justin asked another.

"What, then, is the role of the inquisitor?"

"He merely tries to elicit the truth."

"But is it likely that a confession obtained under torture will be valid?"

This question was obviously an easier one for Bartholomew to answer.

"Not in itself," he said. "A person who makes a confession while being tortured will be asked to confirm his confession again later when he is no longer being tortured. If he then denies what he originally confessed, his initial testimony will be regarded as insincere and he may be tortured again. In any case, the heretic's final confession must be completely genuine. Throughout the process, of course, heretics are constantly reminded of the many benefits they will receive if they do confess sincerely."

"Including no further torture?"

"Well, torture may also be used to compel heretics to testify against their fellow travelers. Witnesses as well may be tortured if their testimony seems unreliable."

Bartholomew's stolid way of talking about such nefarious deeds was beginning to grate on Justin, so he started to make his questions more pointed.

"But does torture not go against the principles of Christian charity?" he asked.

"To the contrary," Bartholomew replied. "Torture is a form of Christian charity. Many heretics would not confess without the beneficence of torture, which is why we must pray that the torture is effective. It is far better for the body to suffer than the soul to perish. I myself should prefer having momentary pain inflicted on me in this life to being condemned to spend eternity in hell."

"Surely it is only through persuasion, not violence, that people are won to the faith!" Justin exclaimed.

"What is important is not the means but the end," Bartholomew said. "What we hope for is that the heretic will confess his errors and then recant."

Justin wondered, as he often did, why it was so difficult to get Bartholomew to see any point of view which differed from his own.

"Do you think the preacher will retract his teachings?" Justin asked.

"I doubt it. I rather suspect that he will hold to his opinions and attempt to defend them to the end."

"Why would he do that?"

"Because he is under the delusion that his teachings are correct," Bartholomew said. "That is why he maintains his innocence. He knows full well that what he preaches is contrary to Christian dogma but has the audacity to believe that he will be able to convert the Church to his own way of thinking."

"On the other hand, if what the Church teaches is true, it should be able to persuade the preacher to change his mind without the need for any coercion."

"People of his sort are never open to the truth if it conflicts with their own entrenched notions. Their minds are already made up and will never change. The only persuasion they understand is the fear of pain or death."

Justin suspected that the inability to change one's views in light of evidence and argumentation applied more to Bartholomew than to the preacher.

"What should happen if even after all measures have been taken the preacher refuses to recant?" he asked.

"Then the Church must reluctantly admit that it has failed and excommunicate him," Bartholomew answered. "After that, he would be handed over to the civil powers for execution. As the Bible clearly states, the punishment for prophets and dreamers who rebel against the Lord God shall be death."

"The Church would not execute him themselves?"

"No, it does not have the authority. The Church would not want to participate in such acts in any case since its mission is to save not to condemn. Although the bishop must give his consent to an execution, clerics are forbidden to kill. Remember the commandment against killing."

Justin was appalled at Bartholomew's specious reasoning.

"So, the Church simply passes the responsibility on to the state," he said cuttingly. "If clerics are forbidden to kill, shouldn't the state be forbidden to kill as well?"

Only then did Bartholomew notice that Justin was not simply asking questions but challenging him.

"It seems to me," he grumbled, "that you are not interested in understanding the true meaning of the Inquisition and its efforts to root out heresy. Your intent is only to question the authority of the Church."

"No," Justin replied. "It is an honest question and it deserves an honest answer."

"You must understand, my friend," Bartholomew said with great deliberation, "that the purpose of the Inquisition is not condemnation but salvation. We love and pray for our enemies. Our desire is not to put heretics to death, even though that is what they deserve, but to correct them so that they may be rescued from eternal damnation. The Church is concerned not only about the soul of the heretic but also about the debilitating influence that heresy has on civilization. If heretics are allowed to preach their doctrines unimpeded, they will subvert the Church and its true teachings, upend the nobility and their just rule, and confuse the masses, who abhor heresy and will fiercely resist it. It is in everyone's best interest not to disrupt the present social order but to passionately defend and preserve it. The Inquisition tries—sincerely tries—to bring heretics back into the fold so that they will respect the clergy, the civil authorities, and the will of the people. It is because we love even those who are contemptible that we offer them every possible means to return to the truth. But if these sick souls reject our generous offers of therapy and refuse to be made healthy, then the only recourse is to annihilate them. The choice is theirs: either join us at the wedding feast and come properly attired or be cast into the outer darkness."

When Bartholomew had finished this soliloquy Justin could not suppress the feeling that it was the Church rather the preacher who was guilty of heresy. At the same time, however, he could not overcome his own feelings of guilt at having unintentionally revealed the preacher's whereabouts by going to his house after the parade during the Feast of Fools.

In the meantime, the fire had gone out in the fireplace. The commons room was now cold and damp. Justin and Bartholomew returned to their own room and huddled under their blankets.

§32

The inquest into the preacher's activities did not take long and a burning was scheduled just a few days later. The atmosphere in the plaza in front of the cathedral was festive, not unlike the atmosphere at the Feast of Fools a short time before. People were laughing and joking, shouting "Burn him!" and making crude mimes of what it looks like when a person is set aflame at the stake. Justin stood silently among the crowd, together with Bartholomew, who was also silent.

"There is still hope that he may recant," Bartholomew said. "Right up until the moment the fire is lit, even after."

Faggots had been arranged into a pyre around the stake. The bishop and inquisitor appeared on the steps in front of the cathedral, followed by the preacher, wearing a white robe and escorted by two guards. The preacher had evidently been tortured, for his right arm, disjointed from the shoulder, hung limply at his side. His face was haggard, although it still had a look of fierce determination in it.

A priest strode in front of the man, the palms of his hands joined together, pleading with the preacher in a low voice, "Please repent. You may still repent. God will forgive you if you repent."

The magistrate ascended the steps and joined the retinue, at which point the crowd began chanting in a steady rhythm, "Burn him, burn him, burn him!"

The inquisitor silenced the crowd and shouted with a loud voice, "We do not wish to see this man burnt nor should you! We have prayed that he would repent and return to the true Church. This he has chosen not to do, however. Instead, he has held tenaciously to his own false beliefs, despite our best efforts to show him the errors of his ways and persuade him to forswear them. Throughout the course of this trial he has freely explained his views to us and has steadfastly maintained his innocence, even though he readily admits that his teachings are contrary to those of the Church. I shall now read the charges on which this man has been convicted."

He turned for a moment to look at the preacher, who was standing slightly behind him, while the priest continued to intone his pleas for a recantation. The inquisitor then unrolled a long scroll of vellum and began reading.

"The charges against the accused are as follows:

"First, he believes that there is no distinction between God and his creation, and, therefore, that he is also one with God the Father almighty, maker of heaven and earth.

"Second, he believes himself to be a son of God in the same way that our Lord and Savior Jesus Christ is the only begotten Son of God.

"Third, he believes himself to be in direct communion with the Holy Spirit, whose guidance he follows exclusively, even when it contradicts Christian teachings and the Bible.

"Fourth, he believes that he is free from all obedience to the Church, which he regards as evil, and that he does not need the Church to intercede for his salvation.

"Fifth, he believes that laws are made only for those who do not know the Spirit, and that those who know the Spirit are not bound by any law, either divine or human.

"Sixth, he believes that he is not subject to the governing authorities and disavows any oath of fealty to those whom God has appointed as our just rulers.

"Seventh, he believes that he is beyond sin and does not require the sacrament of penance, nor any other sacraments, to receive the grace of God.

"Eighth, he believes that prayer should not be directed to God above but to one's own divinity through silent contemplation.

"Ninth, he believes that the Kingdom of God may be joyfully entered into in this life, so that one need not seek the Kingdom of Heaven in the afterlife.

"Tenth, he has promoted these teachings among the unwitting masses and has gathered about him a community which does not hold to the sacrament of marriage, and, therefore, indulges in all manner of iniquity, including fornication, sodomy, and other obscenities."

When the inquisitor had finished reading, he rolled up the scroll, turned again to face the preacher, and said, "Will you not renounce these teachings, which we, God's holy tribunal, have found you guilty of holding?"

The preacher looked the inquisitor straight in the eyes and replied, "Will not you renounce the false teachings of the Church and proclaim instead the most excellent creed of ours, which you have just articulated so eloquently?"

The inquisitor turned back to the crowd and raged, "There, as you can see, we need not condemn this man, for he has condemned himself!"

"You are the Antichrist!" the preacher roared.

"It is you who are the son of perdition!" the inquisitor shouted back.

The crowd erupted into another round of jeers, demanding in unison that the preacher be burned.

The inquisitor then turned to the magistrate and said, "We have found this man guilty of perverting our nation, of refusing to bow down before the government, and of saying that he himself is Christ the King. I, therefore, hand him over to you, as representative of the civil authorities, so that you may administer whatever punishment you see fit."

The magistrate took a step forward and replied in a loud voice for all to hear, "The state sincerely appreciates everything that the Inquisition has done to try this man and bring him to justice. I am an impartial and fair ruler, and firmly hold that in all things the state must follow both the Church and the will of the people. So I pronounce that this heretic before us now shall be sentenced to death by being burned at the stake in the presence of those assembled here."

A deafening cheer arose from the crowd. The magistrate nodded his head towards the guards holding the preacher. They brought him down the steps to the pyre and tied his hands behind the stake. The priest was with the preacher the entire time, ever more loudly and insistently begging him to recant.

Bartholomew, who had stood motionless beside Justin throughout the proceedings and refused to join in with the crowd, began praying, "Lord God almighty, please intervene and give this man the conviction to repent. Do not consign his soul to eternal hellfire and damnation."

The faggots were lit. The fire first caught the lower parts of the preacher's robe, then slowly rose up his body. Through the smoke Justin caught his eyes. The preacher smiled at him. After that he neither flinched nor screamed. Just as the flames enveloped him, however, he cried out defiantly for everyone to hear, "Strive to bring back the God in you to the divine in all!"

A cold winter wind blew through the air. Members of the crowd approached the fire to warm their hands.

§33

Justin scarcely spoke to Bartholomew in the days that followed, even though they still shared the same room. Lectures had resumed at the university, which Bartholomew attended with his usual assiduity. Increasingly worried that he lacked the ability to pass his examinations, he was also spending considerably more time in the library. Justin no longer had any interest in the classes, however, and was almost always absent. He would wander through the city from morning till night, marveling at how quickly everything had returned to normal after the preacher's burning. Throngs filled the streets, the shops were open, people were buying and selling, eating and drinking, and carrying on as they always had.

One day while attempting to avoid the noisy crowds, Justin found himself, unexpectedly and not knowing why, standing in front of the house of the preacher. He was about to try the door when he noticed it had a new lock. Justin put his ear to the wooden panel but could hear no voices coming from inside.

Bartholomew no longer rebuked Justin for his lack of diligence and staying out late, greeting him sullenly whenever he returned to the room. He had written again to the abbot about both the abominations committed during the Feast of Fools and the incident with the preacher. He did not mention that Justin had been discovered visiting the preacher's house but did express in the strongest possible terms his increasing misgivings about him.

A reply eventually arrived, which Bartholomew did not show to Justin, but which Justin found tucked under the corner of Bartholomew's mattress one evening when Bartholomew was at the library. The abbot began his letter by saying that the preacher should not have been burnt but rather persuaded to recant.

"There is no occasion for violence and injury, for religion cannot be imposed by force," the abbot wrote. "The matter must be carried on by words rather than by blows. Torture and piety are widely different. It is not possible for truth to be united with violence nor justice with cruelty. Religion is to be defended, not by putting to death, but by dying; not by cruelty, but by patient endurance; not by guilt, but by good faith. If you wish to defend religion by bloodshed, torture, and guilt, it will no longer be defended, but will be polluted and profaned. For nothing is so much a matter of free will as religion."

The abbot then said that the Feast of Fools was an anathema and that he would report Bartholomew's account of the recent event to the higher ecclesiastical authorities, but he also advised both Bartholomew and Justin to continue to attend mass at the cathedral and participate in the sacraments.

As for Bartholomew's fears that Justin was straying from the faith, the abbot wrote that Bartholomew should engage Justin, if he could, and try to gently bring him back to a state of grace. If his efforts failed, then Bartholomew should simply give Justin time to reflect on these matters for himself, with the confidence that God would eventually reveal himself to Justin in his own heart. Justin's salvation was, after all, in God's hands, not Bartholomew's. As Justin read the letter he thought that perhaps the reason why Bartholomew rarely spoke to him these days was not because he had given up on Justin but simply because he was following the abbot's instructions. Either way Justin was relieved that he was no longer being regaled with Bartholomew's self-righteous sermons.

Justin had just finished reading the abbot's message when the door to the room suddenly opened and Bartholomew appeared in the doorway. Seeing Justin seated on his own bed, Bartholomew rushed over to him and snatched the letter from his hand.

"What are you doing with this?" he cried. "You have no right to touch any of my personal belongings!"

Justin made an embarrassed apology to Bartholomew, then left the room, exited the university, and began walking aimlessly through the darkness.

§34

Justin spent the whole night tramping through the city, not knowing, not caring where his footsteps took him. In the morning, when sunlight began to filter its way into the narrow alleys between the houses, Justin saw a dead rat curled up against one of the walls. Since the streets were routinely swimming with filth, it did not particularly attract his attention. A bit further down the alley, however, he saw another black rat, then another, and after that one after another all the way to the alley's end. On his way back to the university Justin continued to see dead rats here and there, not knowing what to make of them.

In the following days Justin made it a routine to spend his nights in his room with an untalkative Bartholomew and his days roaming the city. The number of dead rats on the streets increased exponentially with each cycle, until finally measures began to be taken to collect the rats, pile them onto carts, and take them to a barren field outside the city walls, where they were burned. Shortly thereafter people began to die. At first it was thought that the deaths were isolated incidents, so there was no outcry in the city. Rumors were beginning to spread, however, that the plague had already struck several nearby cities and villages. Although some people became anxious that they too might catch the disease, others scoffed that the disease was a hoax and the deaths were natural. In any case, there was nothing to be concerned about, they said. God would protect them.

For a while everything looked much the same as it had before. People carried on with their daily business, ignoring what was transpiring all around them. Soon, however, things began to change. Justin noticed that fewer and fewer people were out and about, until finally the streets were empty, except for occasional furtive figures darting here and there.

On one of his excursions Justin heard a cry come from inside a house as he was passing by. A woman rushed out the door, almost knocking him down. She grabbed Justin by his tunic and implored, "Help me! Please! It's my husband. He's ill."

Justin followed the woman back into her house. She led him to a room where a man was lying on a bed, stripped bare. Large lumps rose from his thighs, reaching all the way up to his groin. Open sores appeared on his neck and armpits. The rest of his skin was dark with contusions. He was groaning and coughing. The woman kneeled beside him and began whimpering.

Justin bent down and caressed the man's forehead, which was covered with beads of sweat. He could feel the man's fever and was startled back upright when the man began heaving and vomiting blood.

"I shall summon a doctor," Justin said softly to the woman.

He ran back into the street and went straight to the infirmary adjacent to the cathedral. He tried the door, but it was locked. Justin began knocking loudly while impatiently tugging at the handle. When the door finally opened, a rotund matron immediately stepped between the doorjambs, barring his way.

"You must not come in here," she warned, "unless you yourself are ill and require medical attention."

"It is not me," Justin replied breathlessly, "but a man who lives just a short distance from here. He desperately needs a physician."

"I am sorry," the matron replied. "But there are no physicians available. As you can see, all of our physicians are completely occupied caring for the patients we already have here."

She gestured with her head for Justin to look behind her. The building had the appearance of a large corridor, long but narrow, with beds lining the walls on either side, each of them occupied, some holding two or more patients, all of whom were moaning and wailing. Pallets had been placed on the floor between the beds, filled with more writhing bodies. A handful of physicians were attending to the infirm, assisted by nuns. In the light that filtered through the tall windows, Justin could see the telltale lumps and streaks of red, which indicated that the people being treated had been afflicted with exactly the same disease as the man he had just left.

"I know not what to do," Justin said, on the verge of tears.

"Bring the man here," the matron said. "I am not sure that we can do anything either, but we shall look after him the best we can."

Justin thanked the matron and returned as quickly as he could back to the house of the sick man. Just as he arrived the man's wife was coming out the door. Her face was blank and expressionless.

"Is he dead?" Justin asked.

The woman did not answer. Justin brushed past her and went back to the room where the man's body was lying. The groanings and heavings had stopped, but the boils and lesions remained. The woman reappeared in the doorway to the room.

"He was a good man," she sobbed. "I cannot understand why God would have taken him . . . and in such a horrible way."

Justin put his hand on the woman's shoulder, attempting to console her. He could think of nothing to say to alleviate her grief.

Finally he said, "I will help you to bury him."

Justin lifted the man onto his shoulders and carried him out of the house. He walked with his heavy burden through the narrow alley back to the main street, where he saw a cart being pulled by a young man, filled with dead bodies, all bearing marks of the same disease.

"Just throw him up there with the others," the man said. "I can give you a hand."

Together the carter and Justin lifted the dead man's body and hoisted him to the top of the heap.

"I could also use some help pulling the cart if you have time to spare," the man said. "It is rather heavy."

And so Justin helped the man pull the cart to the city gate and from there down a long winding road to a site not far from the fairgrounds where a mass grave was being dug. Parts of it were already full, the bodies tossed one on top of the other, arms and legs akimbo. Other carts were lined up in front of the grave, the carters patiently waiting their turn to dump their cargo into the pit. A group of men was already digging the hole wider.

As Justin and the man he was helping maneuvered their cart to the end of the queue, Justin asked him, "Do the dead not get a grave of their own?"

"The cemetery is reserved for the wealthy," the carter said. "Only the poor are interred here."

"Are there no priests to administer last rites to them?"

"That's only for the rich, too. The families of these pitiable folk can't afford the fees the priests charge for a burial service."

When Justin and the carter's turn came, they tilted their cart and watched the bodies tumble into the grave. The carter made the sign of the cross, while Justin bowed respectfully.

The two men worked all day, going back and forth between the city and the grave, filling cartload after cartload with dead bodies. When the late afternoon sun fell behind the distant horizon, the carter said, "This is our last load for today, but there will be more tomorrow."

"I should be happy to help you again," Justin replied.

"Meet me at daybreak in front of the cathedral."

The two men pulled their empty cart back to the city. More bodies had already been brought out into the streets, but the carter said nothing and departed in silence. Justin began his weary walk back to the university.

§35

After arriving at the dormitory, Justin found Bartholomew lying on his bed in their room. Justin began telling him about everything he had seen and done, but Bartholomew was unresponsive, pulling his blanket over his head as if he did not wish to hear. Justin continued his story anyway, until Bartholomew finally peeped out from under the covers and said, "It's the infidels' fault."

"The infidels?"

"The plague originated among those unbelievers in the east, whom God is no doubt punishing for their failure to embrace the true faith."

"Why, then, has the disease spread to Christian territory as well?" Justin asked. "Surely God would not wish to punish Christians."

"Of course, he wouldn't," Bartholomew replied. "But he may nonetheless punish those who have fallen away. You have seen for yourself how our town has become infested with heretics. God will see to it that they are either brought back into the Church or exterminated. Those among the faithful who have been lax in their duty to root out heresy will also be punished. Only the truly righteous will be spared."

"So you do not worry?"

"Why should I? I am a righteous person. I cling to the Church. There is no reason for me or others like me to fear. God is on our side!"

Bartholomew started to become fraught as Justin pressed him with more questions.

"So that is how you can continue to go about your daily routine, as if nothing were happening?"

"I am not going about my daily routine," Bartholomew said. "You have not noticed since you are always out, but I have been staying in my room every day."

"You are not attending classes?"

"They have been canceled. The master has given us strict orders not to leave the university."

"Yet you did not tell me?"

"If you were here, you could have heard it for yourself."

Bartholomew was now sitting upright on his bed. Justin looked away.

"I can tell you this, however," Bartholomew said. "It is likely that the city will soon be sealed off. The gates will be locked and no one will be allowed in or out."

"So you are content to burrow in your room while the pestilence goes on all around you?"

"God is a hiding place for me, who protects me from trouble and delivers me from harm. Yea, though I walk through the valley of the shadow of death, I will fear no evil, for God is with me."

"But what of those who are suffering and dying? Should we not help them?"

"The best way we can help is to pray for them, which is what I do not just every single day but every single hour. Otherwise, we should not interfere with God's judgment!"

"I do not believe your prayers will have any effect," Justin said.

Bartholomew got up from his bed, walked over to Justin, placed a hand on Justin's jaw and cheeks, and jerked his face around until their eyes met.

"That is because you have also become an unbeliever," he seethed. "If I were you, I would be very careful going out among sinners. The same judgment that is befalling them may befall you as well!"

With this act, Justin's dislike for Bartholomew finally turned into actual hatred, the same kind of hatred he had felt toward his father and toward Martin. He wanted to kill Bartholomew. He really did! But instead of giving in to his impulse, he turned and collapsed on his bed. Justin could not sleep but lay there thinking about what he would do. The answer in fact was starting to become clear to him.

§36

The next morning Justin went to the square in front of the cathedral at dawn and met the man with the cart.

"Thank you for showing up," the carter said. "There are few people who are willing to do this kind of work."

"I can see that the streets are deserted."

"The only people out and about these days, except for carters such as us, are the thieves. They loot the merchants' shops and accost anyone stupid enough to be walking around looking like they might be carrying money with them."

Justin and the carter began pulling the cart into the street.

"Most everyone stays shut up inside their houses," the carter continued. "No one ventures out. People simply leave the bodies outside for us to pick up, just like they leave their garbage. They refuse to greet us or even say goodbye to their loved ones."

As Justin and the carter traversed the city, they saw more and more rotting bodies, which they collected and threw onto the cart. Some were beginning to putrefy. Others were already necrotic. Gangrene had set in on the victims' fingers and toes, lips and noses. When Justin lifted one of the bodies into the cart, its arm came off in his hand.

Each time the cart was full, Justin and the carter pulled it to the mass grave outside the city, where they dumped the bodies and then returned to the city to gather more.

As they were drawing the cart through the city Justin asked the carter, "What actually causes the disease?"

"I don't know," the carter said. "Some people say it's in the air. Others claim you can get it just by looking at someone who already has it."

"Do you think that only evil people catch it?"

"Not at all," the carter replied. "You can see for yourself. It's affecting everyone—priests and laity, the nobility and commoners, good people, bad people—without distinction."

The two passed by a house where they saw a woman sitting in the doorway, with a baby in her arms. She was rocking the baby gently and singing a lullaby to it.

The man walked over to the woman, examined the baby, and then said, "She is dead, my lady. Would you allow me to take her away?"

"No," the woman smiled. "She is not dead but just asleep. I shall take her back to her crib, where she will be safe."

The woman arose and went back inside her house, still holding the baby and slamming the door behind her.

Justin and the carter continued to cart bodies to the mass grave for the next several days. The hole had been expanded, but there were fewer diggers than before and also fewer carters. Each day they would make several trips to the grave, the cart always loaded high with fetid flesh and protruding bones. Each night as they reentered the city, they could see more and more bodies piling up in the streets, some neatly stacked, others sprawled out as if they had died on the very spot where they lay. Lamentations were pouring out of nearly every house that Justin passed. The noise was, if anything, more unbearable than the silent sights and smells. The dead had already suffered and were now at peace. The living continued to suffer, knowing that only death would bring them relief.

"We shan't be able to keep it up," the carter said one evening. "There are simply too many bodies and not enough carters."

"I shall meet you again tomorrow," Justin said.

"I don't think so. I am already too weak to go on."

The carter pulled up his tunic and lifted his arm.

"Look," he said.

There was a small cyst and a short red groove in his armpit.

"You have caught the disease!" Justin exclaimed.

"Indeed, I shall be next," the carter replied without emotion. "Here, let me give you the cart. I won't be able to meet you tomorrow, but if you are willing, you could continue on your own."

Justin took hold of the cart from the carter.

"But be careful," the carter said. "You could catch the disease yourself."

"Do not worry," Justin said, pulling out the cross Bartholomew had given him and showing it to the carter. "I have this to protect me."

The carter reached into his own tunic and pulled out his own cross.

"Indeed, I have one, too," he said with a faint smile.

The carter returned to his home, Justin knew not where, while Justin made his way back through the streets of the city, pulling the empty cart behind him. Perhaps he would see the carter again after all, under different circumstances.

§37

As Justin passed the guildhall on his way back to the university he noticed that a sign had been posted saying that a quarantine would be imposed the very next day. The gates of the city would be closed and no one would be permitted to enter or leave. Justin and all the townsfolk would remain captive inside the municipal walls until the affliction had passed.

Approaching the cathedral Justin saw that a small crowd had gathered in the plaza. The bishop was on the steps, crying out with a loud voice, "This is God's retribution on us for having departed from his ways. Repent and call upon the mercy of God to save us!"

People were on their knees, hands folded, looking up to the sky, offering loud and earnest prayers of petition to God to rescue them from this tribulation. One woman, obviously devout but unable to pray, was laughing and screaming hysterically. Justin then recognized that she was the same woman who had accompanied Justin and Bartholomew into the cathedral for confession on the day they had first met the preacher, the same woman who had also publicly accused him of heresy before the inquisitor.

A group of flagellants wearing white robes with rent cloth exposing their hind skin and pointed white caps marked with red crosses was making its way through the crowd. In one hand they carried a crucifix, in the other a scourge having three leather tails, each tipped with a sharp barb, which they flung over their shoulders to beat themselves on their bare backs. Their flesh was streaked with red stripes, but they emitted no cries, only a steady litany of invocations and responses proclaiming their sins and begging God for forgiveness. At intervals they would prostrate themselves on the ground, extending their arms in the form of a cross, and then leapfrog over one another, administering a stroke of their whip to the person beneath them.

"Crucify me," one of the flagellants said to Justin as he passed by.

§38

Justin parked his cart beside the entrance to the university and returned to his room, where he found Bartholomew kneeling beside his bed in prayer. Although Justin had entered quietly and said nothing, Bartholomew spoke harshly to him, "Do not disturb me. For I am now at peace with my-self and with God."

Justin lay down on his bed and tried to sleep. Tossing and turning, visions of what he had seen the past few days danced in his brain, refusing him the oblivion he so intensely desired.

Turning over, Justin saw that Bartholomew had finished his prayers and was sitting on his bed, his eyes wet with tears.

"Is something wrong?" Justin asked.

"I have just received word that the abbot has died," Bartholomew replied.

Justin bolted up, instantly alert.

"From the plague?"

"Yes, from the plague."

Justin shook his head vigorously, unable to believe what he had just heard. Then he said to Bartholomew, "But I thought you said that God would only strike evil people dead, not the righteous. And if there ever was a good and decent man, it was the abbot."

"Yes. And to all appearances no doubt you are right. But the abbot could have been a wretched sinner in ways we cannot fathom. Only God knows everything. It is God's right to judge, not ours."

Justin slumped back down on his bed, twisting his body so that he would not be facing Bartholomew.

"People were eating and drinking, marrying and being given in mar-riage, up to the day Noah entered the ark," Bartholomew continued. "Then the flood came and destroyed them all. But just as Noah and his family were saved, God shall leave us a remnant and give us a secure hold within his holy place."

Justin turned round and propped his head upon his hand. "And you, no doubt, shall be part of that remnant."

Bartholomew wiped his eyes and said, "God will send his angels with the great sound of a trumpet, and they will gather together his elect from the four winds, from one end of heaven to the other. In the twinkling of an eye the dead will be raised incorruptible. We shall all be changed and given new bodies. Then the righteous will be caught up together in the clouds to meet the Lord, whom we will be with always."

"And you shall be among the elect."

"Indeed, my salvation is certain. For I am one of the righteous."

"Aren't you being a bit sanctimonious?"

"Not at all," Bartholomew said, his face no longer showing any grief. "I am simply telling you, with all humility, that those who call upon the name of the Lord shall be saved. Those who do not will be damned."

Justin sat up in his bed, wrapping his arms around his knees.

"And what of infants who have committed no sin? The other day I saw a baby dead in its mother's arms. Is that baby one of the elect or is she one of the damned?"

Bartholomew immediately replied without hesitation, "If she had not been baptized, then she will not enter the Kingdom of Heaven, for she is stained with original sin."

"But you, who have committed actual sin, will be saved."

"I have been baptized. I have repented. My sins have been forgiven."

"Why does God ask us to forgive those who trespass against us if he himself is unwilling to forgive those who trespass against him, whether they have repented or not?"

"Certainly God is willing to forgive everyone, but only if they bow down in sincere contrition and confess their wretchedness to him."

Justin looked away in repulsion and then said, "Tell me this, Bartholomew. If, as the Church teaches and you sincerely believe, God is both omnipotent and omnibenevolent, then why does evil exist?"

"Evil is merely the absence of good."

"So, you mean that evil does not exist?" Justin said. "It seems to me that the plague is not simply the absence of good, but a genuine evil. The suffering people are experiencing is real, not an illusion. If God is all-powerful, why doesn't he do something about it?"

"Indeed, as even heathens acknowledge, almighty God has supreme power over all things, being himself supremely good. He would never permit the existence of anything evil among his works. It is precisely because he is omnipotent and omnibenevolent that he can bring good even out of evil. The fact that there is evil as well as good in the world is itself good. In other words, it is *good* that evil exists. If this were not so, then the existence of evil would not be permitted by our all-powerful God. Without a doubt God can just as easily refuse to permit what he does not wish as he can bring about what he does wish."

"That still does not explain why God would not wish to put an end to our suffering."

"We live in a fallen world, Justin. If we suffer, it is not God's fault, but our own. God created the world perfect. It is we humans who have corrupted it with our sin."

"We have no control whatsoever over tempests and plagues, earthquakes and other natural disasters. How can we possibly be held responsible for the havoc they wreak? It seems that God has no control over them either!"

"No, Justin. God is in control and he uses whatever measures he chooses to bring us to repentance."

"The bishop claims that God is using this pestilence to punish us for our sins. So it is still God who is causing us to suffer and God who is evil."

"God may justly punish us for our sins, not because God is evil but precisely because he is righteous. God cannot endure evil."

Justin was not satisfied with this answer at all.

"But if God is indeed good and has genuine love for his creation and God is also almighty and has the power to prevent human suffering, why would he allow an innocent baby to suffer and die, as the precious little baby I told you about? This is the God that you expect me to trust? To fall down before and worship?"

"God moves in mysterious ways," Bartholomew said. "We must never question his deeds but always have faith that all things work together for good for those who love the Lord."

"Then I cannot love such a God," Justin said. "Nor can I believe that such a God loves me."

"Watch what you are saying, Justin, for you are falling ever deeper into heresy. Even if we are upright and God takes everything away from us, we should praise rather than curse him. The God we worship is a compassionate and gracious God, abounding in love and mercy."

"To the contrary, Bartholomew, the God you worship is Satan."

Bartholomew looked venomously at Justin.

"You blaspheme!" he shouted. "God is the supreme being over all creation."

"If I were an inquisitor I would put God on trial and find him guilty for all the evil he permits yet is unwilling to stop, even though he has the power. After that I would give him the death penalty, just like the preacher—or Jesus for that matter."

"You heretic!" Bartholomew screamed contemptuously. "You have it completely backward, just like the devil himself. We do not stand in judgment of God. God stands in judgment of us. No mere mortal can ever be higher than God."

"Perhaps I am not higher," Justin said. "But I am almost certainly better. Although I do not always do good, it seems that I have more compassion than God does for those who suffer. And although I do not have absolute power as God supposedly has, at least I try to use what little power I have to relieve the suffering of others, those whom God almighty will not help."

"I shall not listen to your heresies any further!" Bartholomew cried, holding his hands over his ears. "I am reporting you to the inquisitor!"

With that, Bartholomew fled from the room, not suspecting that before he returned Justin would simply walk out the door, into the street, through the city, and beyond the city gates into the cold winter night.

V

The Return

§1

The devastation was everywhere. Justin passed through hamlets and villages, seeing the calamity of death all around him. His only companions on the roads in between were the flagellants, who traveled from place to place preaching their gospel of penitence, marching in a somber line, flailing themselves and each other on their backs with their whips, repeating their invocations to God, asking for his forgiveness and mercy. But God, it seemed, was in no mood to be forgiving and merciful.

In each of the settlements Justin entered, he was never far from the sound of wailing, as wives cried over their dead husbands, husbands cried over their wives, fathers cried over their daughters, and sons cried over their mothers. In some houses, however, there was no crying, only silence.

Bodies were piled high on every street. There were virtually no carters left to carry them away, but Justin would always stop to help any he came across to fill their carts and carry the bodies to the graves that had invariably been dug just beyond the outskirts of each and every town he visited.

More than once Justin saw children weeping on the steps outside their houses, with no one to take care of them. The carters would ignore them, excusing themselves by saying that they already had too much to do and could not be expected to do any more.

"Better to let him die," one of the carters told Justin when they saw a young peasant boy sobbing alone in front of his house, his neck streaked and his arms covered with lumps. The boy had no cloak and was shivering with cold. He held out his hand, begging for food and water.

"Whatever we do for the least of these, we do for ourselves, do we not?" Justin said. "Perhaps we should let the dead bury the dead and take care of the living instead."

"His suffering will end soon," the carter replied. "Then he will surely know the solace of heaven."

"If God can make everything perfect in heaven, why not here on earth, which he has created and declared 'good'?"

"Ha!" the carter said, pulling away his cart. "This earth is hardly 'good.' It is nothing but a vale of tears. Our home is not here but in the world beyond."

Ignoring the carter, Justin gathered the boy in his arms and gave him a sip of water from his flask. Then he began rapping on the doors of each successive house looking for someone to take him in. Most people would not even open the door. They simply shouted to Justin that he should go away. A few peered out their windows but, as soon as they saw the diseased boy, slammed the shutters shut.

Justin carried the boy out of the city and into the fields, where he scrounged for leftover grain from the harvest to feed the boy and then himself. That night Justin slept with the boy at his side, listening to him moan and wheeze.

The next morning Justin propped up the boy's head in the crook of his arm and tried to pour water into his mouth, but it only gurgled from his lips and would not go down.

The boy nonetheless looked up at Justin and said, "Thank you."

Justin had never seen such vacant eyes before, devoid of all hope. Then the eyes closed.

Justin shoveled out a shallow grave with his hands, laid the boy inside, and covered the body with dirt. He reached for the crucifix beneath his tunic and held it tightly between his fingers. Justin wanted to say a prayer, but he could not.

§2

Justin spent the rest of the winter in these labors, his only compensation the morsels of food he would be given on rare occasions by some of the peasants or townsfolk in exchange for his services as an itinerant undertaker. In time he became immune to the suffering, indifferent to the stench of rotting bodies, no longer caring if the sick people he cared for lived or died. He had become just like the carters, knowing that he could not save everyone. The task was too great. There was no point in even trying. His heart became calloused, his soul a vacuum. Justin could not understand why he himself had not caught the disease. It certainly was not because he was among the truly righteous. He checked his body daily for the telltale lesions and buboes, but never found any. If he had, he would have accepted them gladly.

Justin began to walk erratically, following whatever road he happened to be on, having no destination, just as when he had fled the village, no longer caring where he went or where he ended up, wishing now only that the journey were already over. His life was as empty as the eyes of the boy he had watched die, staring out at a world he could not comprehend. Why, Justin wondered, do I keep putting one foot in front of the other when I am not only going nowhere but there is nowhere to go?

Spring was coming. The peasants who could were returning to their fields for the next round of plowing. Wishing to avoid both them and the hard work they would surely ask him to help with, Justin retreated to the forests where he scavenged for food and slept beneath the stars. When he awoke one morning he found that the ground he had been lying on was not flat but sloping. He was at the foot of a wold. He decided to climb it, which took him a good part of the morning. After he finally reached the peak he found that there was nothing but more wolds on the other side, stretching to the horizon as far as his eyes could see.

This, he thought, would be his new objective: to go deeper and deeper into the wolds until he was lost and could never find his way back out. Then he would lie down on the ground and go to sleep and never wake up. Consciousness would be extinguished. His body would deteriorate. Justin had no desire to go to heaven, only to pass into nonexistence, to become after he died what he had been before he was born.

Justin spent the next few days climbing one wold after another, never looking back. One day, as he was in a valley filling his flask from a brook, he saw the reflection of his face in the water and noticed how much he had changed. His hair and beard were long, his face wrinkled not with age but with despair. The hollow eyes in the stream gazed back into his own. He looked up at the wold in front of him and knew this was the last he would climb.

"Enough," he said to himself. He had succeeded in having absolutely no idea where he was and felt that this qualified as being lost. He knew only that he was "here." After ascending to the top of this final wold, he would lie down in the dirt and stay there until his flesh rotted away and his body returned to dust.

Finally—finally!—he had discovered a purpose in life, to die alone and unknown at a place where he would never be found. Justin started to climb the wold with great expectations, putting one foot in front of the other determinedly, sweating despite the cold, panting with exhaustion, eager to reach his goal. When the summit came into view, he could see the crystal-clear blue sky above and the sun shining down benevolently.

Justin hauled himself up over the last rock and stood in the clearing atop the wold, which somehow seemed familiar to him. He expected to see only more wolds extending into the distance, but instead, much to his surprise, he caught sight of the estate nestled in the valley just in front of him, looking just as he had seen it at the very beginning of his journey after he had fled from the village. His pilgrimage had not been to a distant site, but a circle leading him back to the very place he had started. Was it fate that had brought him here or some underlying yearning he did not understand?

But something had changed. There were no tiny figures moving about from one building to another. All seemed eerily silent. Most noticeable was a huge gap in the northern wall of the estate, starting near the cottage of his former teacher, the alchemist, and extending halfway up to the fishpond. The gate itself was gone and the stones were lying in piles of rubble.

Justin's first inclination was to go at once to investigate, but then he caught himself. Why would he want to go back? There was no reason to. His aim now was different. Still, he thought, would it not be nice to return, to be once again within the walls of the estate, where all was safe and secure? Why could things not be the way they used to be, when his world had been a garden in which there was no knowledge of good and evil?

Justin let his eyes wander from the manor house, where his father and mother had raised him, to the orchards, where he had first met Constance, and beyond the orchards to the sea sparkling with diamonds of sunlight. He saw again the estuary where he had left his boat and the forest where he had met the hermit and foraged for food with the peasants, then, looking further south, the village where Constance must still be and the spire of the church he had escaped from.

"I will certainly meet you again," Justin had told Constance just before their final embrace at the well. Yet now it was no longer even a hope for him, despite being so close to her once more.

Turning his face to the north Justin looked beyond his father's hunting grounds and the forest where he had killed Martin to the desolate wasteland beyond, with its boulders and shrubs, the ground still white with snow even though it was spring. It would take the rest of the day for Justin to reach it, but it seemed a better place to die than the wold he was standing on now. He consoled himself that for one afternoon at least he could take in the panorama of his life, recalling everything that had happened, and dream that night of everything that could have been.

§3

The wasteland was even bleaker up close than it had been from a distance, a sandy snow-covered heath, with almost no vegetation among the boulders, except for the shrubs, and no food to forage. The wee bit of water in Justin's flask was all that he had.

Justin traversed the windswept landscape until he came to a bald patch with no snow between two boulders, where he took off the cross he had worn ever since Bartholomew had given it to him. Without ceremony he scooped out a bit of sand, buried the cross inside the hole, and tamped the grave down hard with his foot.

"I shall have no more use for this," he said aloud, as if to make it official, or perhaps just because he wanted to hear the sound of his own voice.

The wind was blowing hard. The air was frozen. Justin pulled his cloak tightly around him, as he continued his walk across the sterile terrain towards the sea. There was no beach as there had been on the shore near the hermit's hut, only cliffs dropping straight into foaming waves that crashed onto the jagged rocks beneath. Justin looked out over the shimmering water and for one brief moment considered tossing himself off the ledge into the ocean. But this, he felt, was the wrong way to go about it. He did not want to force the situation, but to die naturally, to act without acting, to achieve his goal not through what he did but through what he did not. He would not jump. He would stick with his original plan and starve himself to death instead.

There was a bush with overhanging branches near the side of the cliff, tall enough to be called a tree, and a single white flower peeping up through the snow just beside it, mysteriously, since the wasteland was still as cold as winter. Justin plopped himself down beneath the tree and sat there looking out towards the eastern horizon, vowing not to move from the spot until his life-blood dried up and his skin, nerves, and bones had wasted away. This would be his final resting place!

Yet Justin felt no peace. His mind was in torment. The image of the young boy who had died in his arms returned to haunt him. What kind of life had the boy led before contracting the disease? It was probably not at all like Justin's childhood. When Justin had been the same age as the boy, everything was perfect, there was no suffering, no grief, no sorrow. Justin saw himself playing on the grounds of the estate, jostling with Martin, and riding horses around the paddock.

Yet even if the boy's short life had been hard, had he not enjoyed it? Did he not also have his happy moments, laughing with his friends, going to festivals, having dinner with his parents, being loved by his mother? Why could such joyful times not last forever? Why were they punctuated by times of travail? Why, when he breathed his last, had the boy's eyes, which once had undoubtedly gleamed with hope and anticipation, been so emotionless? Why had God abandoned him?

Justin began to follow his breathing, just as he had learned long ago from the anchorite, trying to calm his mind. He inhaled the air. His abdomen expanded. His head would rise. He exhaled the air. His abdomen contracted. His head would bow. In and out, he observed the heavings his body, the violent surgings of his soul.

He would see the boy's face, acknowledge it, and then go back to focusing on his respirations. For a few moments he would think nothing, then the image of the boy would reappear, he would acknowledge it again, and resume tracing his sighs. But the storm would not be abated. The waves continued to rise and fall. The sea of his soul could not be stilled. But so what? It made no difference. Justin knew that he would perish eventually, sooner rather than later.

The hours passed. As the sky blackened, no stars could be seen. Night became day. Day became night. Night became day again. Justin did not move. He did not lie down. He did not sleep. He'd had nothing to eat and was hungry, ravenously hungry. But he refused to get up and go back to the woods to look for food. He sipped at the water in his flask from time to time until it was gone. He was becoming delirious, slipping in and out of consciousness. The earth groaned in travail. The sea and sky before him congealed into a single mass of blue, one color not two. The howling wind and the roar of the tide joined in unison with Justin's cries, clotting into a single scream.

§4

Then in the light the flower beside him metamorphosed into a figure, white and formless. It had no face, but when the apparition spoke he recognized the voice as his mother's.

"Justin," she called to him. "Your cries have awoken me. Why are you in such anguish?"

"Mother!" Justin called back. "You have returned to me from heaven!"

"Nay, Justin. There is no heaven."

"But is not heaven the place people go to after they die? Surely that is where you must be and where I will be going soon, if not to the other place."

"The only people who believe in heaven are those who have not yet found it within themselves," his mother said. "God is not the God of the dead but of the living."

Justin squinted to see if he could get a better look at the figure. He could not.

"Surely we can hope to one day leave this valley of weeping and dwell in an idyllic realm in the skies," Justin said, "where all tears have been wiped away and death is no more. My only desire is to flee from this earth and to live forever in heaven."

The voice of his mother replied, "We should no more wish to be imprisoned in heaven than to be imprisoned in hell. Why would you want to rise beyond the clouds to a place where there is no sorrow or crying or pain, instead of doing as Jesus did when he became flesh and dwelt on earth? The Kingdom of Heaven is here among us, at this very place, this very moment."

"The place where I am now is assuredly not heaven, but hell," Justin said dejectedly.

"Nay, Justin, there is no hell either. Heaven and hell are places that dwell inside us, not we inside them."

"So they are mere fictions of the imagination?"

"No, they are very real places, but they exist here on earth not in some great beyond."

"Even if that be true, heaven is still preferable to hell."

The voice said, "There can be no hell apart from heaven nor heaven apart from hell, for they are married to each other. In this world there are both joy and sorrow, a time to laugh and a time to weep, a time to dance and a time to mourn."

"Why can we not be always happy and never sad?"

"Certainly we need not feel guilty about enjoying whatever smidgen of happiness we might find in a world that is also so heartbreaking, but if we wish to be only happy, it will only make us more unhappy."

Justin tried to sit erect to see the phantom face to face, but he did not have the strength.

"You must eat of the tree of knowledge," his mother's voice continued, "and know that there is evil as well as good in the world. Both must be embraced even as they embrace each other."

"Surely we should embrace what is good and spurn what is evil," Justin replied.

"The universe is neither good nor evil but indifferent to us, yet we are not indifferent to it. When we find something good in the world, we say it comes from God. When we find something evil, we say it comes from Satan. But the world itself is beyond good and evil. There is but one reality, Justin, the one that you inhabit right now. The rest is what you make of it."

"Then I should like to escape from this reality and sail across the ocean and find another world, where all is perfect, where I can eat only the fruit of the tree of life and never perish, where there are neither thorns nor thistles, where my security is complete and there is nothing to be afraid of, where I can live in peace and happiness forever."

"And after you have entered this land of milk and honey, could you be truly happy there?" the voice asked. "Would you become smug and complacent in your rapture? Would you pat yourself on the back and congratulate yourself for having attained your own personal salvation? Or would you look back and think of those who remain here on the opposite shore, those who continue to suffer? Would you not wish to return to help them? Would you not want to turn and sail your boat back across the ocean to rescue them, vowing not to enter the promised land yourself until everyone could go there with you? Why do you think only of yourself and have no concern for others?"

"But what about Jesus? Did he not fly away to heaven, where he now sits at the right hand of God, far from the horrors of this earth, enjoying eternal delight? Why does he not return to help us?"

"God does not dwell in heaven, Justin, and Jesus never left you. He is with you always and lives in you here and now. When you suffer, he suffers with you. What happens next is not up to God, but up to you."

"It is not my duty to save humanity," Justin said scornfully. "It is God's. And he's doing a pretty miserable job of it. Why has he forsaken us? Why does he not listen to our prayers when we cry to him in our times of trouble? If God has the power to do good, why is the world so evil?"

"God struggles through us to overcome evil in the world. So if we give up the struggle, what is God to do?"

"Well, he should certainly do something. How long must we wait before God acts?"

"Perhaps God is waiting for us to act."

"But how are we, as mere mortals, supposed to overcome evil?"

"Not by running away from it, but by facing it head on. It's time to grow up, Justin, and start acting like an adult, not a whimpering child. Expecting your Father in heaven to do everything for you is simply a way to avoid taking responsibility yourself. Stop being so adolescent."

"Surely we do not have the power. Only God can rescue us!"

"God is not some kind of conjurer in the sky, who waves a magic wand to make everything right. Or a puppeteer, who pulls the strings of the universe to make it move in accordance with his will. Nor does he contravene the laws of nature for our own personal benefit. That is the God of superstition and fairy tales. And you are no miracle-worker either! If a boulder is about to fall down on you, do you pray to God or say 'abracadabra' in the hope that it will remain suspended in mid-air and not hit you? No. You simply step out of the way. God does not interact with the world through miracles. It is through the power within yourself that God acts."

"Am I then equal to God?"

"Each and every one of us must abdicate any claims to power and glory, emptying ourselves and taking the form of a suffering servant, as Jesus did. We should humble ourselves and become obedient unto death, even if it be an unjust death we do not deserve. We must carry the death of Jesus in our bodies. Only then may the life of Jesus be manifested in our mortal flesh."

"Why did God not rescue Jesus from the cross? Or, if he were truly God incarnate, why did Jesus not use his power to come down from the cross on his own? He saved others but he could not save himself."

"When Jesus died, God died, too."

"So, God is dead."

"There is no God beyond the world we inhabit, only the living God that exists inside our own hearts. Should we let that God die, God would cease to exist altogether."

"Surely Jesus will save us!" Justin cried.

"Rather than pray to Jesus for salvation, take up your cross and become a savior yourself. Instead of exalting Jesus as our Prince and Protector, as Lord of Lords and King of Kings, we should stand together with him as allies. There is no power outside of ourselves to redeem us, only the power of God working through us, with Jesus at our side. Jesus does not take away our suffering, but shares in it, even as we share in the suffering of others."

"The power to transform suffering into joy is God's, not mine."

"The same energy that moves through the world moves through you, Justin, constantly destroying what has been created to make all things new. The ground must be cleared before new seeds can be planted. The old must die for the new to be born. This present heaven and earth will pass away. And a new heaven and earth will be built by God working through us."

"What if, in the end, the universe simply peters out and becomes motionless? I cannot see the point."

"Certainly whatever is not constantly being born is constantly dying. Yet in the interval God is continually creating and recreating the world and we are part of that process. If the world is to become a better place, it will be because you yourself have made it so. The goal is to transform the world, Justin, not to try to escape from it."

"Nay, mother, the world can never be made good for it is intrinsically evil. Just look at the misery that exists all around us. This world was created not by God but by Satan."

"No doubt suffering is an unavoidable part of life," the voice of his mother replied. "There is suffering in birth, in aging, in illness, in death. The only way to overcome suffering is to free oneself from this cycle."

"I wish that you had not given birth to me."

"Indeed, if you had never been born, you would never need to suffer!"

"Then I should like to end my existence this very minute. The world is so absurd."

"You are right. The only serious question in life is why we do not kill ourselves."

"Well, I have decided that life is not worth living. I need not go to hell for I am already there. Surely I am one of the damned."

"I quite agree," his mother said. "You have become a revenant, one of the living dead. Unlike me, who is physically dead but spiritually alive, you are physically alive but spiritually dead, still awaiting the true resurrection."

"There is no resurrection of the dead."

"A seed must be dead and buried before it can grow and produce fruit. God must also be dead and buried before he can be resurrected in you."

"Mother, everything you say is very excellent, but your words have no meaning for me. I have tried, I have sincerely tried, ever since I left the estate, to find the seed of God inside my heart, but it is not there. Why has God forgotten me and hidden his face so that I may never see it? The only thing he ever shows me is his backside!"

"Indeed, all is absence. And the only reason why you cannot see God is because you have not yet emptied yourself of everything, including the expectation that you will find God in your own heart. You must ask God to rid you of God. You must descend into hell before you can ascend into heaven, pass through the dark night before the dawn breaks, die before you are reborn, suffer as Jesus did on the cross before you may be resurrected. Only then will you see that God is not something you find but something you create, just as you do not find but create your own meaning and purpose in life."

"Yet how might I empty myself?"

"Make yourself nothing. Have no faith, no hope, no love. Drain your soul, annihilate your ego, so there is room for God to fill your heart with his power. There can be no union with God without spiritual negation. Once you have discovered that your true self is in fact no self, you will also know that the true God is no God at all but the God you already are."

"But how might I drain my soul?" Justin asked.

"Purge yourself of every desire, even the desire for God, your desire for heaven. Desire is the root of suffering. The reason you are in anguish is because you wish that everything would be other than it actually is. So you must let go."

"I must no longer care and become apathetic?"

The voice replied, "Apathy may mean either that we just don't care and are totally indifferent to what happens, or that we really do care but know that we must simply accept things as they are before seeing what it is possible for us to change."

"But if there is absolutely nothing in my heart, I would no longer be able to care," Justin said.

"No, because it is only after you have emptied your heart that it may be filled again with faith, hope, and love. Instead of selfishly wanting and needing to be loved by God, we should let God's love flow out of us. To truly be the God of love that is inside your heart, mind, and soul, you must love yourself just as you are, others just as they are, and the world just as it is. I am glad that I gave birth to you, Justin. I hope that you will be glad, too, even though you are now in agony."

Justin sat for a moment in reflection and then said, "It is so fortunate that I have been able to see you again, mother, even if you are only a ghost."

"I am not a ghost, Justin, but simply a memory of yours, a figment of your own imagination."

"But still, it is nice to hear your voice and to listen to your comforting words."

"Well, the voice may be mine," the figure replied, beginning to melt back into a white flower. "But the words are yours and yours alone."

Suddenly Justin's eyes were opened and he knew, like God, the difference between good and evil. The tree of life is the same as the tree of knowledge. And he understood, like God, that he would also die, just as God had died in Jesus on that same tree. We all must die before we can be resurrected.

§5

When Justin looked up, he saw nothing. Absolutely nothing. No God in the Holy of Holies, no Jesus in the sepulcher, no Holy Spirit in the tabernacle of his soul, not even a soul for the divine spark to occupy. All had been forsaken.

Then Justin shouted in a loud voice, "I give up my spirit!"

The curtain was torn in two. The veil had been removed, the shackles broken. The stone of his heart had been rolled back. Demons vomited from Justin's mouth. The legions cried. Thunder rolled. The earth shook. The rocks were split. The graves opened. The sun's light failed. Darkness covered the land.

The vision was from neither God nor himself, neither sensuous nor imaginary, neither a mirage nor a reality. Its source did not matter for it had none.

When Justin arose, the heavens did not part. His face did not shine like the sun. His clothes were not a radiant white. Rain did not fall down from a crystal clear sky. Blossoms did not spring up all around him. A dove did not descend from heaven and alight on him. A voice did not say, "You, too, are a beloved child of God, with whom I am well pleased."

No, all was silence. The tomb of his soul was now empty, his heart a fathomless abyss.

There was no ecstasy in the moment, but the exact opposite: a wordless feeling of serenity, knowing that everything was now all right. There was no longer anything to fear. Justin was content, completely safe and secure, not because he had retreated back into a mighty fortress, a bulwark never failing, but because he could now live outside its walls with the courage to face whatever he encountered.

The wilderness was the same as it had always been, empty and desolate, no voices, no visions. It was not the world that had changed, but Justin.

§6

Justin collapsed beneath the tree and fell into a deep sleep, a sleep with no dreams, a sleep in which he no longer existed. When he awoke he struggled to get up but could not. His body was ravaged from fasting. He was hungry but not strong enough to traipse all the way back to the forest to gather food. He was thirsty but his flask was empty and the nearest stream a good hour away.

"So, I shall die here after all!" he said to himself, fully aware of the irony.

But why not? I can see now that life is a gift we did not ask to receive, he thought. Yet even if the end comes today, I am ready for it. Is dying not a part of life and death a part of nature? We should not despise death but welcome it. Rather than long for eternal life, can we not just as easily accept the absolute nothingness of death?

Justin ran his fingers through the dust beside his head. I should be grateful, he thought! All the world is dust and I am a bit of that dust which has had life breathed into it, so that I might stand up and have a look around. The evening shadows fall. The grass withers. The flower fades. Yet a blossom is no less brilliant if it drops away just after blooming. Even if I were to die here and now, at least I have had this one moment. The birds sing and sing, not knowing that tomorrow they will be no more.

Not only I, but all things must pass. In the beginning God created the heavens and the earth, yet both shall perish. The heavens will vanish like smoke, the earth will wear out like a garment, and those who dwell in it will die like gnats. Then God himself will cease to exist and all will be silence again.

Justin lay there, alternating between consciousness and unconsciousness. He could accept death. He could accept life. He could accept whatever the world offered him.

Suddenly Justin saw a snake slithering towards him. He was too weak to flee or even reach for his knife. He lay there paralyzed as the snake glided closer and closer. This could be yet another way to die, he thought!

Then he saw that the snake was in fact a shadow cast by a man who was now standing next to him, beside the white flower. The man was wearing a black cloak and hood.

"It is you," Justin said, his voice scratchy from thirst. "The man whom I met at the juncture on the wold."

"Indeed, it is I," the man replied, pulling off his hood. "I thought that we might meet again sometime, although I hardly recognized you at first. Are you all right?"

"Of course I am!" Justin cried. He then began laughing ebulliently.

"I wouldn't expect a person in your condition to be laughing. What's the reason?" the man asked.

"At first I thought you were a serpent."

"A serpent?"

"I had no means to kill it, so my plan was to wait until it slid inside my mouth."

"Then you would pull it out?"

"No, for it would only sink its fangs in me."

"But what else could you do?"

"Bite off its head and spew it out!"

Justin let out another long peel of laughter.

"It looks like you could use a bit of water," the man said, pulling out a flask from his side and pouring the cool liquid into Justin's open mouth.

"More," Justin said.

"Don't worry, I have plenty," the man replied. "And food as well. I'm guessing from the way you're talking that you haven't eaten in quite some time."

Justin quaffed the water until he was satisfied. The man helped him to sit up beneath the tree and continued to nurse him, giving him a few bits of bread from his basket, then larger chunks, and finally a few sips of wine from his gourd until Justin could eat and drink on his own.

"You seem to have a fancy for visiting isolated places," Justin said to the man, feeling restored by the bread and wine.

"And you as well," the man replied. "I guess we are both wanderers."

"Are you an angel?" Justin asked.

The man chuckled. "An angel! Perhaps I am, but if so, then one made entirely of flesh and bones."

"You are not a supernatural being?"

"Hardly. I am neither a celestial messenger nor a demon, neither God nor devil. I am just an ordinary man. What are you doing here anyway?"

"I've been running away," Justin said.

"Running away from what?"

"From myself."

"Why did you come here of all places?"

"To find my self."

"And have you found it?"

"No. But what I've discovered is that I have no self. There is nothing for me to find, only the flux of the universe, the flow of life which my no-self is part of. If I were obliged to live this exact same life over and over again an infinite number of times, I would embrace it just as I have lived it, every pain I have endured, every pleasure I have enjoyed, each good thing I have done, and each mistake. I no longer wish to escape from but to affirm the endless cycle of life no matter how magnificent or miserable, to face and accept reality in all its absurdity, and to love it just as it is with all my heart, mind, and soul, until existence itself is no more."

"Indeed, the two greatest commandments are to affirm life and to love unconditionally," the man smiled.

"Or better: to accept the world as it is while at the same time changing it."

"There you go."

"But isn't what I just said a contradiction?"

"Only if you think so," the man said. "And what shall you do now?"

"I shall return."

"Return?"

"To the place where it all started."

"You have been on a long journey?"

"Indeed, I have," Justin said. "Would you like to hear about it? It shall be my confession."

"Well, as I told you, I am just an ordinary man, not a priest. I am certainly willing to listen to your story and to hear your confession, if that's how you envisage it, but I cannot absolve you of your sins."

"It is not necessary for a priest to absolve us of our sins. We need only forgive ourselves and ask for forgiveness from others."

"As we forgive those who sin against us," the man added.

Justin proceeded to tell the man his story, the whole story, from his time growing up on the estate, about his father and mother, the alchemist and the bailiff, his marriage to Penelope and flight to the village, about his love for Constance, his participation in the revolt, his plan to kill his own father and the murder of Martin, about his escape to the monastery, his meeting Bartholomew and the abbot, his constant lying and deception, his encounter with the anchorite and his search for God, his quest up the mountain and his failure to find God, about his life as a student, the temptations of the city and his betrayal of Constance, his flirtations with heresy and the burning of the preacher, the coming of the plague and his confrontation with death.

When Justin had finished his story, he heaved a great sigh and felt cleansed.

"That's some story," the man said. "And now by returning, you are hoping to set things right?"

"I have no idea how it will turn out," Justin replied. "I have wasted my life away and am no longer worthy to be called my father's son. I have sinned against heaven and can expect no forgiveness."

"Well, you never know. Perhaps your father will welcome you back with open arms, and give you his best robe, a ring for your hand, and shoes for your feet, and then kill a fatted calf and hold a great feast for you. Before you were dead, but now you are alive. Once you were lost but now you are found!"

"I am still fearful of meeting my father and also the villagers. They have every right to be wrathful and to retaliate against me."

"So why not just run away and go someplace else? You could avoid all the messiness of dealing with others if you simply withdraw from the world and retreat to the mountains. You could live out your days as a hermit or a desert monk. No one would even know you existed."

"Indeed, that is my last temptation," Justin said.

"Then why not give in to it?"

"Rather than be condemned to spend eternity in bliss, I prefer to return the world I came from and to give myself to others."

The man looked at Justin compassionately.

"Certainly I understand," he said.

"And how about you?" Justin asked. "What is your story?"

"It's similar to yours in some ways, but different in others."

"I should like to hear it, although you needn't confess everything, of course."

"Indeed, my confession would be much longer than yours, so I shall not go into the details. But I do not mind sharing the gist of what I have discovered with you."

"Please," Justin said, leaning his head back against the tree.

§7

The man began to speak:

"God has never left us, so why go looking for him? It is only because we have turned our back on our own true natures that we are unable to find him. We are lost only because our illusions prevent us from seeing our true selves.

"When I set out on my journey, the first thing I discovered is that the world is a labyrinth of crisscrossing roads. I did not know which way to turn and traveled further and further from my home. I was greedy, constantly wanting more and fearful of losing what I already had, obsessed with discerning right from wrong. I tried to sail away across the distant horizon, but the sea has no end. There is no other shore. So I returned. I wandered alone through the wilderness, pushing away the brambles, searching and searching for something I could not find. I hiked up and down distant mountains. I followed wide-flowing nameless rivers. The paths were unending. My strength failed. My vitality was exhausted. But I still could not find what I was looking for. I did not even know what it was. At night I heard only the sound of crickets chirping in the trees.

"I read the scriptures but they did not have the answer. They were nothing more than a long bony finger pointing to a gate I could not yet see. I was unable to discriminate good from evil, truth from falsity. Then I began to see traces of God along the riverbank and under the trees. The grass was trampled. There were footprints in the mud. The fragrance of God filled the valleys. I could smell him on the mountaintops. But I could not yet see him. Yet, just as different golden vessels may be made of the same substance, everything I saw was a manifestation of him and a reflection of myself.

"And then I caught a glimpse of him, although only a glimpse. He quickly ran away into the forest and I chased after him. I found him in a glade. I had passed through the gateless gate. The sun was warm, the wind mild. The branches of the trees undulated in the soothing breeze. Perched on one of them, a nightingale warbled cheerfully. The God I sought could not hide. Yet what artist could paint him? What words could possibly describe him? He cannot be perceived by the senses. The sound of his voice is our own. The source of all things is like dye in cloth, salt in water. They are neither two, nor even one.

"God, however, is not easy to catch. He is accustomed to cavorting wild through the fields. He charges into the highlands and stampedes through misty, impenetrable ravines. He is at home in such surroundings, yet longs for sweeter grasses. His great will and power are inexhaustible. He cannot be confined to a cage, although this is exactly what most people who worship him try to do. The God without is untamable and cannot be broken in. It is the God within whom you must wrestle with throughout the dark night of your soul. You must use your whip to subject him and force him to submit to you, lest he break your joints. But if you persevere, in the end you will prevail and he will bless you. You will see God face to face, yet your life will be preserved.

"So then I tried to bridle the God within me. I whipped him constantly and tethered him with ropes, so that he would not stray away on muddy roads. Holding him tightly by the nose, I would permit no indulgences. But he could not be disciplined. One thought would arise, leading to another and another, an unending train of thoughts. I regarded my thoughts as true, as corresponding to how things are in reality. I believed I was enlightened. But then I realized that while these thoughts indeed spring from my own true nature, they are nothing more than fantasies of a self-deceiving mind. My own chains had become oppressive, so I unbound the God within myself and found that he would stay with me willingly, without coercion.

"My struggle was over. Gain and loss no longer affected me. I had conquered by letting go. It was time for me to go home. Though God is a wild horse that can never be domesticated, I mounted him and buoyantly rode away through the evening mists, free as the air, wearing a straw hat and cape. Notes from my flute serenely dissipated into the clouds. I played the simple tunes of children. When the pipe vanished, I sang the rustic songs of woodsmen. The pulsating rhythm of my beating hands measured the harmonies of my soul. One who already knows does not need to be told. I did not look back. If someone called out to me, I would not turn my head. Nothing could upset me. I would not be disturbed. The horse as well required not even a blade of grass.

"When I finally arrived home, to the garden and my thatched-roof dwelling, I forgot about God completely. I no longer needed him. He himself had been nothing more than a thought, a delusion to me. The whip and rope were abandoned. The red sun hung over the morning sky. We slept together in tranquil repose, yet each of us alone. I knew not where he was. We were no longer two, but one. Or no longer one but neither. Once the rabbit has been snared you no longer need a trap. Once a fish has been caught you no longer need a net. Once a raft has transported you across a river, you may abandon it. Once a ladder has been climbed, you may throw it away. Words are nonsensical. If there is nothing to speak about, we must remain silent. Gold is separated from dross. The moon emerges from the clouds. Light is sundered from darkness. A single ray shines forever out of the void before creation.

"I killed God. I sacrificed him on the altar of my soul for the remission of my sins, so that he could be resurrected in me. And then there was nothing. Whip and rope, God and self, merged into nonexistence. The azure sky is vast and infinite. It cannot be measured. Ideas cannot comprehend it. A snowflake falling on a blazing fire quickly disappears. We behold the spirit of the patriarchs. There is no longer a mind to be confused. All is serenity. I do not seek enlightenment nor does it seek me. I am the Christ. I am not the Christ. A thousand eyes cannot see me. I am now invisible. There is no room for pride or the stink of holiness. If the birds strew hundreds of flowers at my feet, their praise would have no meaning to me.

"And yet, after I had retraced my steps back to the origin and returned to the source, I found that my entire journey had been in vain. I should have stayed home and been content to see and hear nothing from the very start. What is there to strive for? The truth had been there all along. Sitting in silence I observed the waxing and waning of life, birth and decay, integration and disintegration, creation and destruction. The sea is blue. The mountains are green. The flowers are red. That is all. I was detached from the world, detached from myself. There is neither outside nor inside. I determined that I should remain in my true abode, unconcerned that the rivers outside continue to flow and are always changing.

"But who can remain so content and placid? The beauty of my garden could not be perceived. My soul could not be seen. The wisest know me not. I closed the door of my cottage and returned to the world in my ragged, dirty clothes. I had no maps to guide me for I had burned them and put all their images out of my mind. I went my own way, making no attempt to follow in the footsteps of those who had gone before me. I needed no staff to support me, no rucksack, no food, no money, not even a change of clothes. I entered the marketplace with open hands, taking only bread and a wine gourd with me. I avoided the priests and bishops, the monks and holy saints, and ate with tax collectors and sinners. I drank with fishmongers and butchers. In the faces of the hungry and the thirsty, the naked and the poor, the strangers I met and the prisoners I visited, I saw my own face. This is now my home. And no one knows who I am."

When the man had finished, Justin said, "I would like to embark on such a journey myself. But I would not know the way."

"There is no way," the man said. "Except the one that you yourself make."

"How will I know if the path I am on will lead me home?"

"If wherever you are is home, how can you ever be lost?"

"But the journey seems so long."

"Nay, your journey is almost over."

"Perhaps I should run away, as you suggested, and let this cup pass from me."

"No, as you yourself have said, you must return, even though you will sweat great drops of blood. It is no longer your will, but the will of something greater than yourself."

"At least before I depart, I wish to understand everything that you have just told me."

"There is nothing to understand."

The man reached down, plucked the mysterious white flower at Justin's side, and handed it to Justin.

Justin smiled.

"You, too, are now an ordinary man," the man said, wagging his finger at him.

§8

"I hope to see you again," Justin said to the man when the two parted.

"You're on your own now," the man replied with a grin, pulling up his hood. He set off northward, deeper into the wasteland.

Justin started in the opposite direction, towards the estate, sliding between the boulders and slipping around the shrubs like water finding the easiest way down the mountain. At last he arrived at the edge of his father's hunting grounds. He tramped through the forest until he came to the ravine where he had hidden from Martin on the night of the revolt and then to the very spot where Justin had plunged his knife into Martin's heart.

The bread and wine the man in the black coat had given him had revived Justin a bit, but he had still not recovered completely from his delirium. He heard the blood of Martin calling to him from out of the ground.

"Why did you kill me?" the voice asked. "Did God not make me as much as you in his own image? Am I not also a son of God whom you have crucified? The martyrs cry out with a loud voice, 'How long, dear Lord, holy and true, before you will judge and avenge our blood on them that dwell on the earth?'"

"I cannot even ask for your forgiveness," Justin said, looking down at what appeared to be a huge pool of blood at his feet. "For what I have done can never be undone."

"Whoever smites a man so that he dies shall surely be put to death. Wound for wound, stripe for stripe, and life for life."

"Indeed, that is justice."

Then the voice of Martin softened. "But God desires not justice but mercy. So, I will pray to God that he have mercy on you."

"I do not deserve it."

"None of us do."

"You do not wish to see me avenged?"

"Vengeance is not mine but the Lord's. We must love not only our neighbors but also our enemies, just as we love ourselves."

Justin kneeled on the ground and felt Martin's blood soak through his breeches, oozing its way up until it covered his entire body.

"May I ask, then, for your forgiveness?" Justin asked.

"I should ask for yours first," Martin's voice replied.

"But surely it is I who have committed the greater sin."

"We are all sinners who have fallen short and failed to achieve the glory God intended for us. That is why we must forgive each other, even as God has forgiven us."

"Well, I certainly forgive you."

"And I forgive you, too. You did not know then what you know now."

"That's what makes it all the worse," Justin replied. "It is something I will never forget."

"Perhaps not. But God will. He blots out our transgressions and re-members our sins no more. Though our sins are like scarlet, they shall be white as snow; though they are red as crimson, they shall be like wool."

Justin stood up. The blood had vanished. The red stains had disappeared. His breeches were now as white as wool. Justin placed the white flower he had been carrying in the dust where Martin had died.

§9

Justin continued through the undergrowth of the forest until he came to the wall of the estate, the same wall that he had climbed over with Adrian and the others during the revolt. But now the wall had been breached, just as he had observed from the top of the wold. Moss was collecting on the stones. The wooded area on the other side was unkempt and full of brush, the trees untrimmed.

Crossing the threshold into the estate, Justin walked over to the cottage of his teacher, the alchemist, and tried the door. It was locked. He opened the shutter and peered inside. There was the desk Justin had studied at, the chair the master had sat in, both covered with dust. In the corner was Justin's lute, the strings all broken. Cobwebs hung from the ceiling and the corners of the room.

The door of the library was open. The books were rotting and covered with mold, their words no longer having any meaning. The door of the laboratory was closed. Apparently no one was interested anymore in finding the elixir of life. Science had been forgotten. The last time Justin had seen the alchemist was from the window of his own room on the night the discredited man had been taken to the dungeon, his gold medallion gleaming in the moonlight.

Proceeding the long way round to the main entrance of the house, Justin passed by the orchards. The trees were withered and bore no fruit. He was tempted to go beneath the branches and look for the old tree stump where he used to meet Constance, but pulled himself away, realizing that despite trying to forget her, he was still waiting for her, yet not knowing if she had been waiting for him.

Justin curved upward past the chapel where he had listened to so many dull sermons about being subservient to both God and the nobility, the same chapel where he had sweated through his wedding with Penelope. He saw the main gate he had taken flight through, what seemed like a lifetime ago, still intact, though the drawbridge now was down. The barracks along the southern wall were empty. There were no horses in the stable.

The lane from the gatehouse to the manor was rutted with wheel marks and in disrepair. The grass on either side was knee-high. The portico and door to the house were the same as before. Justin hesitated before opening it, filled with trepidation. Nothing seemed right, yet he fully expected to soon be standing face-to-face with his father. What would his father say when he first saw him? How would he react? Justin knew that his father would not welcome him back with open arms nor plan a great feast in his honor. No, he would reprimand Justin severely. The only question was what happened after that. Justin doubted that his father would shield him from any charges. It was far more likely that he would abandon him and turn him over to the higher authorities for punishment.

The front door creaked loudly as Justin opened it and stepped inside the foyer. The floor was covered with grime. Shards of broken glass were everywhere. All of the chairs had been overturned. No one was in sight. The doors of the great hall were closed, but loud boisterous voices were coming from inside.

Justin yanked the doors open.

Before him was a group of men seated around the table, with plates of half-eaten food and half-empty glasses of wine strewn across its top. The men were simultaneously laughing and quarreling, exchanging obscenities, then slapping each other on the back with convulsions of glee.

His father was not among them.

Suddenly above the din a man's voice cried out, "Look, my friends, who has just appeared in our doorway. Dare I say it is Justin, the man whom we used to know as Edward, who took such a hasty departure from us a long time ago!"

Another man stood up and scrutinized Justin's face.

"He needs a haircut and a shave but indeed it's him," he said.

A third man, sitting at the head of the table, then arose and called out, "Justin, come join us in our banquet."

At the sound of the man's voice the assembly fell silent. Justin instantly recognized him as Adrian, his black hair and beard even longer and wilder than before.

Giving a swift kick to the man who was sitting beside him, Adrian offered Justin the man's chair. Justin approached the head of the table and sat down.

"We never expected to see you again," Adrian said, pouring wine into a glass and handing it to Justin.

"And I as well never expected to see you here seated at my father's table."

"Where have you been?"

"On a long journey," Justin replied.

"Well, welcome back," Adrian said, piling food on a plate and setting it before Justin. "We are delighted to have you once again in our company."

"I did not think you would greet me so warmly."

A stout man with a long scar down his clean-shaven face, sitting on the other side of Justin, pushed himself away from the table and said, "I'll have to admit, after we learned your true identity, we were all ready to kill you. But you fled into the wolds and we could not find you. It was only later, after Constance had explained the whole situation to us, that we finally understood."

"Indeed, we thought at first that it was you who had betrayed us by alerting the estate that we would attack," Adrian said.

"It was not I," Justin said, "but that tall fellow who was supposed to accompany me on the raid into the house. He deserted us and absconded to the estate."

"So we have heard," Adrian replied. "Now we know that we should express gratitude to you for taking our side. You forsook your nobility to become one of us."

The scar-faced man then said, "But I shall not forgive you for abandoning the group you led to kill your father. The woman who was run through by the bailiff's sword was my wife, leaving no one to cook and clean for me! We heard the story from the bailiff himself when he came looking for you."

Justin then recognized that the scar-faced man was indeed the husband of the spry woman who had accompanied him on the mission to assassinate his father on that fateful night.

"Certainly I am sorry," Justin said. "But to set the record straight, your wife tried to attack me. The bailiff merely intervened in my defense."

"I don't care," the scar-faced man said. "You shouldn't have run away, but stayed and fought, like my wife. She was not the only one who was killed. All the others were as well. And look at me. I myself got this scar in the incursion. I am no deserter."

"Your wife and the others were all fools," Adrian said. "They could have fled like Justin. Or like me. It is certainly worth killing for a good cause, but hardly worth dying for one. You were a hero, Justin."

"To the contrary, I was a coward, just as the man here insinuates," Justin said.

"He who fights and runs away, lives to fight another day," Adrian replied.

"But she who is in battle slain, can never rise and fight again," the scar-faced man rebutted.

"You are right," Justin said to the scar-faced man. "I should not have abandoned my comrades."

"It's unforgivable," the scar-faced man snorted. "But if that's an apology, I accept it."

"We heard that a guard chased after you," Adrian said, screwing up his eyes. "His dead body was found in the hunting grounds to the north. You don't happen to know anything about it?"

Justin looked down at the table.

"I am ashamed to admit it," he said. "But it was I who slew him. His name was Martin."

Adrian smiled. "That is nothing to be ashamed of, my good man! It's one less soldier defending the whole corrupt system."

Justin hesitated and then said, "Perhaps it is the system itself that should be destroyed, not the people who defend it."

"I can't tell the difference," Adrian replied. "In any case, you'd better keep low. You are wanted for helping me lead the first revolt. The bailiff has also accused you of murdering Martin. After witnessing your flight, he saw the steward calling out for a soldier to chase you. The steward didn't see who the soldier was, but apparently it was Martin who responded. So that makes you the chief suspect. I was never near the place, so this is one deed they cannot pin on me. You needn't worry, though, since neither the bailiff nor the steward is here any longer and they are not likely to return."

Upon hearing this news, Justin was immediately tense.

"Surely you would not turn me over to the authorities?" he asked.

Adrian was amused. "Do you really think we would do that? Of course not! No one here would ever say a single word against you, even though we know now that it was you who did it. Your confession shall remain forever our secret!"

The other men beat their fists on the table and grunted their agreement.

Adrian gestured to the plate in front of Justin. "You haven't touched your food. It looks like you have not had a good meal in some time!"

"Indeed, I haven't," Justin replied, beginning to shovel meat, vegetables, and bread all at once into his gullet. He had forgotten how hungry he still was and had not had such sumptuous food in a very long time.

"But you, Adrian, what happened to you after the revolt?" Justin asked, after washing down his food with a long draught of wine. "You did not return to the village and it was feared you had been killed."

"Nay, I escaped through the forest and down to the sea. Then I ran south along the shore to the fens, where I met Fisher, who took care of me."

"Fisher?" Justin said. "You mean the old hermit who used to live in the forest?"

"You know him?"

"Yes, we met once a long time ago. I am relieved to hear that he is still alive."

"Well, I knew I had to hide out for a while until things cooled down. I returned to the village only later and tried to stay out of sight of the authorities."

"The village has not been affected by the plague?" Justin asked.

"Not at all," Adrian replied. "We have heard about it, of course, but it seems to be confined mainly to the other side of the wolds. Not a single person in our own village has been infected and the situation is much the same in the surrounding area. As you know, the pocket of land we live in is fairly isolated."

"So, what did you do after returning to the village?" Justin asked.

"We planned a second revolt but were better prepared this time. We were no longer just a band of peasants but a militia."

"A militia!" Justin exclaimed. "Where did you get the weapons?"

"We stealthily acquired longbows and arrows, swords and polearms, from unscrupulous merchants in the town. We also made alliances with peasants from the surrounding estates and enlisted their support. By joining together we were successful in overthrowing the lord and taking over the estate. The same peasants who aided us are planning uprisings of their own this very moment, which I am helping to coordinate. When the time comes, we shall offer them our solidarity in return."

Adrian leaned forward. "I tell you, Justin, the revolution is spreading. People everywhere are tired of being peons and are ready to take up arms against oppression. In time the nobility shall fall. We will topple even the king. Then the entire realm will be ours and we shall be its rulers."

"Indeed, we are all standing behind Adrian," the scar-faced man said.

Justin hesitated for a moment and then said, "And my father. What has happened to him?"

Adrian took a long sip of wine.

"Justin," he said slowly. "I know that you had no love for your father. You were even prepared to kill him during the revolt. So I shall tell you bluntly: I smote him with my sword and cut off his head. When I held it up by the hair for all to see, the head was still alive. He grimaced. His eyes fluttered. He tried to scream but no sounds came out of his mouth. This went on for several seconds until he finally succumbed. Then we threw him head and body into the dungeon."

Justin winced.

"You showed him no mercy," he said.

"Mercy!" Adrian exclaimed. "He did not deserve mercy. He deserved justice! After all the suffering he put us through, we working day and night for him, while he took everything we had. If we hadn't killed him, he eventually would have reasserted his authority and continued lording it over us. He had to be killed, Justin. It was the only way."

Justin put down his fork and stopped eating.

"And what happened to the others on the estate?" he asked.

"They all were either slain or fled, even those whom we expected would rally behind us. The servants—our own fellow peasants from the village—had enjoyed the master's comforts for so long that in the end they took his side. Before we could persuade them to join us, those who had not been killed ran away and sought refuge with the lord of the neighboring manor, together with the bailiff and other retainers. That tall chap was among them."

"But how did you manage to break down the wall?"

"We amassed along the northern side of the estate as we had before, but this time we had a mighty assembly, equipped with trees we had felled for battering rams. We did not even try to make it a surprise attack, but instead blew trumpets to draw out the soldiers. When they climbed over the wall from the other side, we drew our bows and shot them with arrows just as soon as they reached the top. Then with a great shout we smashed the wall with our rams. The stones crumbled and the wall fell down flat. The wall was much weaker than we had expected. We fought the remaining soldiers on the grounds of the estate, slaying most of them, although a few got away through the main gate on the opposite side. The bailiff had already prepared the horses for them. Then we made straight for the manor, where we found your father cowering in his room. He refused to relinquish control and would not flee with the others. What happened after that I have already told you."

"So now you have taken over the estate."

"Yes, it is ours! We are now the lords over all. There is no one to oppress us anymore. We live like kings. The cellar is full of wine. The women bring us food regularly. And we sit back and enjoy all the luxuries that we had been deprived of for so long. Isn't it wonderful?"

"Indeed, it is," Justin said, rising from the table.

"Are you leaving?" Adrian asked. "Do you not wish to stay here with us and feast until your belly is bloated and drink until you have lost your mind?"

"Nay, I have had enough," Justin said. "I aim now to go to the village."

"Ah, I see. You are eager to see Constance."

"Is she still living in the village?"

"She is."

"Then I should like to meet with her again."

"I fully understand. But let me tell you, I withdraw my permission for you to marry her."

"Is she already married?"

"No, but you are!" Adrian laughed, getting up and slapping Justin on the back. "The story of how you left your wife on the night of your wedding has spread far and wide. The woman claims that the marriage was never consummated, but no one believes her. What we all want to know, Justin, is whether you did or did not do it after you lay on the bed with her. You're not afraid of women, are you?"

Justin looked Adrian cold in the eyes but did not reply.

Adrian leaned back in his chair and said, "I do not know what has happened to you, Justin, but I can see now that you are different. It seems that you are no longer one of us after all."

Justin turned towards the door. When he had passed through it, the revelry resumed, the rowdy clamor and offensive jokes, which sounded to Justin like the cackles of imps.

§10

Passing over the drawbridge Justin saw the boat tethered to the dock, the same boat he had navigated down the brook to the sea, which had been retrieved from the marsh and brought back to its mooring. He was no longer tempted to get into that vessel and sail it across the oceans, for he knew now that the sea has no end and, even if it did, he would not be content to live on a distant shore, no matter how splendid, but would yearn to return home, no matter how wretched. He had no thoughts of remaining on the estate itself, but still wanted to live in the land that surrounded it. This was home for him now.

Walking on the highway to the village, Justin thought of all that Adrian had told him. His father had certainly received the "justice" he deserved. Justin could not say that he missed his father, at least not in the same way that he missed his mother, but somehow he wished that before his father had died, there had been a chance to talk to him, to tell him everything he had thought and done, openly and without fear. He doubted that his father would have listened to him or, even less, condoned his actions. It was Justin's fault that he was never able to stand up to his father. Yet he had blamed his father, not himself, for his own inadequacies, and that was why he had wanted to kill him. He longed to meet him in a vision, as he had his mother and Martin, but there was none. Perhaps there could not be. Perhaps there would be no reconciliation. Perhaps this was something Justin would simply have to live with for the rest of his days.

Then Justin's thoughts turned towards Constance. Despite his best efforts, he had never been able to forget her. Each time he would put her out of his mind, she would pop back in. The best way to remember something is to keep telling yourself over and over that you should forget it. But perhaps Constance had tried to forget about Justin as much as he had tried to forget about her? It was not as if they would rush into each other's arms at first sight and pick up exactly where they had left off. That would not be right in any case, for Justin had betrayed his love for Constance the night he slept with the prostitute. He could not ask Constance for her forgiveness. He would not even try. Justin would be content simply to see Constance again, even if it were for only one short time. It did not matter if she accepted or rejected him.

As he approached the village he saw women in the fields, tilling the ground in pairs, one guiding a plow and another goading the oxen. There were no men. Justin tromped over clumps of earth to two of the women, whose struggles to keep the furrows straight had been unsuccessful. Without saying a word, Justin took the handles of the plow from the guide and began plowing.

"Why, Justin, it's you! Welcome back!" the woman exclaimed, tagging along beside him.

"You recognize me?"

"Of course. Under all that hair, your eyes are still the same. And everyone knows your real name now and exactly who you are. *Edward.* How tedious. Couldn't you have chosen a more daring alias that suits you better?"

Justin smiled at the woman and then realized that she was the feisty young woman he had known when he lived in the village. When the older woman in front stopped prodding the oxen for a moment and looked back over her shoulder, he saw that she was the feisty young woman's mother.

"Indeed, it is Justin," the mother said. "You have come home! Before we thought of you as a traitor, but Constance has told us the truth about you!"

Justin continued plowing while the young daughter ran to tell the others that Justin had returned. When Justin reached the end of the field, he rotated the plow and began another furrow going back in the direction of the village. In the distance he could see a young woman with blonde hair standing in the dirt apart from the others looking at him. She was too far away for Justin to be able to see her face, but he knew it was Constance. Justin looked down at the soil beneath him and kept plowing.

§11

When the day's work in the fields was finished, Justin trudged back with the women to the village. Constance joined them from where she had been working. Justin and Constance walked together side by side, though he did not look at her, nor she at him. They said nothing to each other but did not really need to.

Tables had been set up in the village green, in the same spot where the harvest festival had been held, but seemingly permanently, for the wood was fading and stained with rain marks. The women prepared a communal meal, with Justin helping. Then they all sat down at the tables to eat. Constance took a seat next to Justin, although they had still not spoken a word to each other. The feisty young woman and her mother were sitting just across the table from them.

"Tell us what has happened to you since we saw you last," the young woman said as they were eating.

"Ah, it's a long story," Justin replied. "I shall relate it to you another time. But what of your situation now in the village? I met Adrian at the estate just before coming here and he told me about your second revolt."

"Indeed, we succeeded this time. We are no longer slaves to that filthy lord who used to be your father."

"Speak respectfully," the woman's mother said. "You should not insult Justin's father like that, especially in front of Justin."

"Mind your own affairs, mother," the daughter replied. "If Justin is to be one of us, he must think as we do, whether that repugnant man was his father or not."

"Well, I understand how you feel," Justin said. "But now that Adrian is in charge, is everything going well?"

"Ha!" the young woman said. "I would hardly say 'going well' is the right expression. Adrian is just as much of a bastard as your father was. Before we scraped and bowed before your father. Now we scrape and bow before our Great Leader, Adrian. He thinks he is God. Things have hardly changed at all, at least not for us. The men stay at the estate day and night, eating and drinking. Every few days the women take food to them, all the way from here to the manor house and back again. The only time the men come to the village is when they want to fuck their wives."

"Watch your language," the mother upbraided her.

"Well, it's true. Fucking. That's all they care about. They give no thought to the fact that it is we women who are doing all the work while they play at being noblemen. Look at the plowing we did today. Where were the men while we were out in the fields?"

"But that is the way of the world," the mother said. "Men rule and women serve. Wives submit yourselves to your husbands. It's in the Bible, as the priest so often tells us."

"Well, I do not have a husband and do not want one. But even if I were married to a kindly gentleman I certainly would not subject myself to him. I do not wish to be tyrannized over by anyone."

"You still must submit to the governing authorities and Adrian is our ruler now. As servants we must obey our masters with fear and trembling, in the same way that we submit to God our Father."

"On the contrary, we must obey God rather than men," the daughter said sharply. She then added, "And why do we always refer to God as 'our Father' instead of 'our Mother' anyway? Perhaps God is a woman!"

"Or both," Justin put in.

"Or neither," Constance said. It was the first time for Justin to hear her voice again.

"Whatever," the daughter replied. "If God really exists, we should abolish him. We do not need rulers. It makes no difference to me if our master is a nobleman or Adrian, a husband or a wife, a man or a woman, or both or neither. I wish to be a slave no longer, but a master, not of others but of myself. If we each have control over ourselves, we no longer need to be controlled by others. I cannot be free until all human beings are free. It is only when we see that we are neither completely independent from, nor completely dependent on, each other that there will no longer be a distinction between lordship and bondage. Once we learn to love wisdom, rulers and ruled will be one and the same."

"Ah," the mother said derisively. "So if we all just become philosophers there will no longer be any kings."

"It is probably true," Justin interjected, "that most people prefer to be told what to do than to think for themselves."

"Aye, and that is precisely the problem!" the daughter cried. "That is why we continue to wander around in a daze, like sheep without a shepherd."

"And also why do we need a good shepherd to lead us," the mother said.

"But if we are no longer sheep, we no longer need a shepherd," Constance said.

"We are still obliged to acknowledge Jesus as Lord and to obey him," the mother responded.

"Jesus does not call us servants but friends and we should return the compliment," the daughter said. "Jesus is not my Lord, but my buddy."

"Indeed, why think of him as our master and we as his disciples?" Constance added. "We walk neither in front of, nor behind, but beside him. Jesus is our companion just as we are companions with each other."

"I quite agree," the daughter said. "The Church stole Jesus from us and it's time for us to steal him back!"

"Nay, Jesus must be worshipped as our Lord and King," the mother countered.

"I refuse to bow down and praise Jesus as our Great Leader either."

"Yet we still need rulers," the mother continued. "We need those who can establish and maintain order. Otherwise all would be chaos."

"I want no one to rule over me, not even Jesus. I am perfectly capable of ruling myself."

"You are, are you?" the mother snapped back. "God has given all authority to Jesus, not to you. If there were no God, everything would be permitted. No immortality, no morality."

"Even though everything is permitted, that doesn't necessarily mean we'd want to do everything that is permitted," the daughter said.

"Indeed, and that is exactly why God has ordained those who have power over us to tell us what we should and should not do."

The daughter looked at her mother with exasperation.

"We all know exactly what should be done," she said. "We do not need anyone else to tell us, neither the lords nor even God. We must work together, men and women alike, each of us plowing the fields and harvesting the crops, maintaining our houses and mending our clothes, cooking our food and eating together. Both the toil and the fruits of our labor must be shared, each contributing to the best of their ability and distributing to each as they have need."

"You're dreaming, young lady. We must have rules and a ruler to enforce them."

"There are no rules," the daughter said. "That is why we are always making them up."

"Without rules no one would work and we would be even poorer than we are now."

"To the contrary, the more regulations there are, the poorer we all become."

"Don't you know that people are basically selfish?" the mother said. "What would keep us from breaking the commandment, 'Thou shalt not steal'?"

"If everything is shared and each has enough, we have no need for laws to protect our property. Increasing the number of laws simply increases the number of thieves."

"Without rulers it would be each person for themselves, a mere war of all against all. We need the lords and knights to protect us."

"The more weapons men have, the more distress they cause throughout the land. We should beat our swords into plowshares, our spears into pruning hooks, and not learn war anymore. The lion will lie down with the lamb and a little child shall lead us!"

"La-di-da," the mother said. "What a quixotic vision! I suppose the next thing you'll be telling us is that we should all become vegetarians!"

"I wish to build castles neither in the air nor here on earth. What I am saying is that the best government is one which governs least."

"Nay," Constance broke in. "The best government is one which governs not at all."

During the conversation Constance's black cat, Charm, a bit older and fatter than before, had wandered over to the village green and was now sitting in her lap.

"Whatever do you mean, Constance?" the mother asked.

"In days of old, laws were not needed because people trusted each other and knew what was right in their hearts. Nothing was forbidden and there were neither legislators nor judges. It is only if our natural dispositions have been corrupted that we become evil and need government. But if we are virtuous we can get along very well without it."

"You are quite mistaken, my child," the old woman said. "You seem to think that without a strong leader to tell us what to do, the people will reform all by themselves and suddenly become honest. Then we shall all be rich and at peace!"

"Look at us here," the young woman said, addressing her mother. "Are we robbers and murderers, or knights and warriors? Do we not have good will towards each other? Can we not talk with each other sensibly and make decisions on our own instead of letting some else make them for us? We should establish our own commonwealth and have nothing further to do with the king, the lords, or the government. Do not be conformed to this world but come out and be a separate people! The land belongs to everyone and should be held and worked by all. True freedom lies where people receive their nourishment and preservation, and that is in the use of the earth. Property is theft and should be abolished. Whatever we produce can be mutually exchanged with each other. We do not need money!"

"You are so unrealistic," the mother replied.

"Certainly we do not live in the best of all possible worlds," Constance said. "But we are each able to cultivate our own fields and make the world better."

"I agree," the young woman said. "Let us have no desires for wealth and power, but return to a good, simple life. If we no longer need to work for the nobility, we can produce just what we need for ourselves and no more. With the time leftover, we shall each be able to enjoy our lives to the fullest."

When the meal was over, the entire group cleared the table and washed the dishes together, Justin as well as the women. Before everyone left to return to their houses, the young woman said, "Well, at least tomorrow is Sunday. We do not have to plow."

"No, we shall all go to church," the mother said.

"The priest is still here?" Justin asked.

"Indeed," Constance replied. "He is obliged to remain in his parish and could not flee with the others. But he stays locked up in his rectory every day and emerges only on Sunday morning to say mass at the church."

"And how about you, Justin," the young woman asked. "Where will you spend the night?"

"I shall sleep in the barn," Justin replied.

"No, you will not," Constance said. "You shall stay with me."

The ladies all giggled, except for the mother, who said sternly, "But no hanky-panky."

Her daughter laughed. "What she means is 'no fucking'!"

§12

Just as soon as Justin and Constance had entered the cottage and the door was shut behind them, Constance set down the cat and flung herself at Justin. Justin stepped back, however, avoiding her advances.

"Justin," she said, looking confused. "I am so happy to see you. I thought that you would be happy to see me, too."

"Indeed, I am happy to see you," Justin said. "It is so wonderful that we are now together again in the same room with each other."

"Then, please take me into your arms."

"No, I may not embrace you," Justin said, turning away.

"Is something the matter? Surely you can tell me," Constance pleaded.

Justin looked back at her.

"Yes, I shall tell you."

Then after a long pause he said, "Constance, you know that I loved you once and I love you still. But during the time I was away, I thought I would never see you again. At first, I thought of you every day, but little by little it became more difficult. In fact, I tried very hard not to think of you at all, to put you completely out of my mind."

"But I thought of you every day the entire time you were gone. I did not know if you would come back or not, but I never gave up on you, Justin. I knew that I would love only you and no one else for the rest of my life."

"I wish I had been as faithful as you," Justin said. "But I have betrayed your love."

Constance looked at him uncomprehendingly.

"I committed my virginity to a prostitute," Justin said forthrightly, with no beating about the bush.

She stared at him with composed eyes, then broke away and stood in the corner of the room.

"Don't you see?" Justin continued. "It is impossible for me to ask for your forgiveness because I cannot even forgive myself."

"But at least you have returned."

"Perhaps I should leave," Justin said.

"No, you may stay," Constance replied. "But I shall sleep in the other room."

§13

The next morning after he woke up, Justin saw that Constance had already prepared a simple breakfast for them, which they ate together in silence. As they were cleaning their plates Constance said, "You must not go to church today."

"Indeed, I do not wish to face the priest. Even more than before, I must avoid being recognized by him."

"It is understandable. You are still wanted for having helped plan the first revolt. And the priest knows that you are the one who killed Martin."

"Of course. I made a full confession to him," Justin said. "Do you think he would hand me over to the authorities?"

"I am sure he would," Constance replied.

"But priests are not supposed to reveal what they hear in confessions."

"He would still be obliged to turn you in and he may find a way to let them know what you did, even if only indirectly."

"It no longer matters. I deserve to be executed. I deserve justice."

"You do not deserve justice, Justin. You deserve mercy."

"It is kind of you to say so, but that is not the law of the land. As you know, I have studied the law and am quite familiar with it."

"You are not subject to the law of the land, Justin, only to the law in your own heart. There is a difference between breaking the law because you want to do evil and breaking the law because it prevents you from doing good. Even if you did something wrong and need forgiveness, you must never submit to the law—not out of fear of what the governing powers might do to you but simply because they are not entitled to control you."

"No doubt that is true."

"Do two wrongs make a right?" Constance continued. "If killing is wrong, would it not be just as wrong for the authorities to execute you for your crimes as it was for you to kill Martin? 'Thou shalt not kill.' Which part of this commandment is difficult to understand? Of course, our self-proclaimed masters are willing to make all kinds of exceptions to the law when it suits them. As far as they are concerned, your sin is not that you killed a man, but that you did so while fighting on the side of the peasants. They intentionally interpret their decrees in ways that allow them to justify their own acts of murder while condemning those exact same acts when committed by any who oppose them."

"What you say is undeniably the case," Justin said. "That is the way the law works. Rulers do not draft laws because they are 'right' but simply because they have the power to make and break them as favors their interests. Nonetheless, I feel genuinely sorry for what I did and feel that I should confess my crimes to the authorities."

"You have already confessed to the priest and to God. You do not need to make any further confessions except to the persons you have wronged."

"I have asked Martin for forgiveness, at least in my own heart," Justin said, thinking back to the vision he had had in the forest. "I know that I have committed a grievous sin, but what should I do?"

"Indeed, to acknowledge your wrongdoing and repent, that is the first step," Constance said. "What you did was wicked not because you broke the law, but because you deprived another man of his life. That is something that can never be changed."

"Then how can I make things right?"

"Atonement is not about punishment but reconciliation. You must be reconciled to yourself, as well as to those whom you have offended. Asking others for forgiveness is of no use if you do not first forgive yourself."

"Well, I suppose that I am now reconciled with myself," Justin said. "And with Martin, to the extent that is possible."

"And your father?"

"I have tried, the best I can," Justin said. "But he, like Martin, is already dead, so there can be no restitution. I must still expiate my sins, do penance, and pay my debt to society."

"Indeed. And your penance should be much greater than anything a priest would ever assign you. It is not a matter of simply performing a few trivial good works as recompense but trying from now on to live every day of your life the very best that you can. And the way to be reconciled to society is not to be cut off from it, but to return. You must rejoin our community, Justin, and we must welcome you, so that you might become part of us again, work together with us, help and be helped when there is need, share in both our joys and our sorrows, come what may."

Justin looked up and smiled at Constance. She smiled back at him. Charm came over and nuzzled against Justin's leg. Justin picked the cat up and held it in his arms.

"There is one more reason why we shall not go to church this morning," Constance said briskly.

"Why is that?"

"I shall cut your hair and shave your beard. But before that you must go to the well, draw some water, and wash up. You stink!"

Justin did as he was told and when he returned to the cottage, he saw that Constance had laid out a fresh set of clothes for him, borrowed from Adrian. After donning them, he sat down in the chair, while Constance fetched the shears. She pulled out his hair in her hands and began cutting.

The air was cool on Justin's neck. When the hair was finished, she started on the beard, trimming it first with the scissors, then shaving him with a razor, undoubtedly also Adrian's. When his face was like satin, Constance ran her hand down it, then turned Justin's head to hers and kissed him.

"I do not need permission from the lord, the law, the Church, or even God to express my love for you," she said. "I only need permission from you."

"I wish to be reconciled with you as well, Constance. Will you forgive me?"

"You do not need to ask," Constance replied, pulling Justin around and holding him tightly in her arms. "There is nothing to forgive."

Nor anything more to be said.

§14

How Justin and Constance spent the morning while the others were at church cannot be told. They did not join the other women for the noonday meal either, but instead stayed together side by side on the pallet all afternoon talking. Justin related to Constance everything that had happened to him since he had seen her last, about both his experiences and his spiritual struggles.

"Finally," he said. "I feel that I have found peace."

Constance curled up beside him, with Charm just at the top of her head.

"You know," Justin said, holding Constance tighter. "I should still like to marry you."

"That isn't necessary," Constance replied. "We shall always be together."

"I am absolutely certain of that. But don't you think it would be better if we made it official?"

"I have already said that we need neither the Church's permission nor the law's to be with each other. Moreover, nothing has changed. You are still legally married to Penelope. You cannot be legally wed to both her and me at the same time. That would be bigamy."

"Yes, and as I told you before and tell you again now, the marriage was never consummated. I shall have it annulled."

"Don't be so stupid," Constance said. "You would only expose yourself to the authorities. Besides, an annulment is out of the question now."

"Why is that?"

"Did Adrian not tell you?"

"He only mentioned that Penelope claimed the marriage had not been consummated, then asked me about what happened between us that night. Of course, I told him nothing."

"Everyone knows about Penelope's situation now. She has become a laughingstock throughout the realm!"

"I have not yet heard the details."

"After you fled the village, Penelope's father tried to arrange a marriage between her and the son of another lord he wished to make an alliance with, but the tribunal refused to give him permission. At first, the lord claimed that Penelope was free to marry because you were presumed dead and Penelope was, therefore, a widow. Having no evidence of your death, however, the tribunal rejected this plea. The lord then declared that Penelope's marriage with you should be annulled on the ground that it had never been consummated, a point which Penelope herself testified to."

"An annulment should not have been a problem," Justin said. "Penelope was telling the truth about what happened—or should I say, did not happen—on our wedding night."

"Indeed, if you were not in so much trouble and had been here to verify that fact, the case might have been settled rather smoothly. But in your absence, the tribunal insisted that Penelope be examined by a midwife to determine whether or not she was still a virgin."

"I have already told you that nothing happened between us on the night of our wedding, Constance. I swear to it!"

"Of course, I believe you," Constance said.

"So it should not have been a problem for Penelope to be tested either."

"Except that her father refused to allow her to be submitted to an examination."

"For whatever reason?" Justin asked.

"Can't you guess?"

"I suppose he would claim that it was an affront to his honor and an indignity to Penelope."

"Why are you always such a dimwit?" Constance laughed wryly. "Of course, that is exactly what Penelope's father said, but no doubt the *real* reason was because Penelope would have failed the test!"

"You still do not believe me."

"No, no, not because of you, but because she had been with someone else. Apparently her father knows all about it as well. He himself might have molested her for all we know."

"You should not spread such rumors," Justin said.

"Certainly I would not. But how else would you explain the lord not permitting her to be examined? Penelope herself has protested that she never had another lover, but she is unable or unwilling to offer any proof."

"Perhaps she had a mishap. Even if she didn't, she or her father certainly could have used that as an excuse had there been an examination."

"Who would believe them?"

Justin could make no reply.

"In any case, both the Church and the civil authorities have upheld your marriage with Penelope," Constance continued. "The baron's court also decided that your father could keep the dowry, which further aggravated the situation."

"So what you're saying is that it is still to the lord's advantage to avoid handing Penelope over to a midwife for a test. If he did, the marriage could not be annulled. Penelope would then lose all hope of remarrying and the lord would forfeit his right to reclaim the dowry, whatever has happened to it by now."

"Indeed. But all of this is to your advantage as well. If it ever comes out that Penelope is not a virgin, you yourself would be in an even more dangerous situation."

"I cannot see why. There is no possible reason."

Constance looked at Justin with bemusement.

"Sometimes your lack of common sense amazes me," she said.

"I still cannot understand."

"Because then everyone would think that your marriage with Penelope had indeed been consummated, even if you both claim otherwise."

Justin pondered for a moment and then said, "Even so, what is wrong with that? Surely neither Penelope nor her father would expect me to return and live together with her as man and wife."

"Well, at least you've got that right," Constance applauded. "But if your marriage is upheld, it would be unbearably awkward for you and Penelope to live either together or apart. That leaves only one other option."

"What would that be?"

Constance exhaled with exasperation. "Shall I spell it out for you?"

"Please," Justin replied.

"Right now Penelope is living her days as a spinster at her father's estate. Despite her beauty no man even dares to look at her under the circumstances. Her father desperately wants to marry her off to someone else, but as long as she is legally married to you and the marriage cannot be annulled, it would need to be dissolved in some other way."

The situation was slowly beginning to sink into Justin's head.

"So the only way Penelope would be able to marry again is if I were dead," Justin said.

"Finally you're catching on!" Constance exclaimed. "The sacrament of marriage is like the sacrament of baptism. Once it has been performed, it cannot be unperformed. Divorce is not an option. 'Till death do us part,' as you vowed to Penelope at your wedding. No doubt everything would be much easier for the lord if you were no longer alive."

Everything was clear to Justin now.

"If the lord ever found me, it should not be too difficult for him to have me executed, either for treason against my father or for the murder of Martin."

"Or both," Constance said. "But don't worry, he will never find you here."

"Even if I should be safe, the law is still in force."

"As we have already discussed, the purpose of the law is to protect the interests of the nobility, not ours. It has no legitimacy for us. We hardly need to obey the law if we can get away with it."

"But if I am still legally married to Penelope, would it not be adultery for you and I to simply live together?"

"There is no such thing," Constance said. "There is only love and we should be free to share our love with each other."

"The Church would also disapprove."

"I have absolutely no respect for the Church in such matters."

"What would the villagers think?"

"That we are living together in a common-law marriage, the same as most of them are."

"Yet if a common-law marriage also has legal status, would I still not be committing bigamy?"

"In the law's eyes perhaps, but not in mine," Constance answered. "What I am trying to tell you, Justin, is that love and marriage are two completely separate things. Sometimes they overlap with each other, but sometimes they don't."

"We still must consider the opinions of others."

"Who cares what the authorities, the Church, or anyone else thinks? This is between you and me, Justin. It concerns no one else and they have no right to interfere."

"That nosy old woman would certainly disagree with you."

"I am sure that even she will respect our privacy once she sees how committed we are to each other."

"And what about Adrian?" Justin asked. "He explicitly told me that I could not marry you."

"I keep telling you, Justin," Constance said, her voice becoming frustrated. "We are not getting married in any sense of the term. Even if Adrian refuses to give our relationship his blessing, I no longer care what he thinks."

"What, then, should we do?"

"There is nothing we need to do. You and I are together now and that is all that matters."

"Then I shall take care of you," Justin said gently, his eyes twinkling.

Much to Justin's surprise, Constance immediately sat up on the pallet.

"Whatever do you mean?" she asked testily.

Taken aback, Justin replied, "Just what I said. I shall take care of you forever."

"I do not wish to be taken care of, Justin."

"You do not need me?"

"No, I do not need you. If anything should ever happen to you, I am perfectly capable of taking care of myself."

"So you do not want to be with me?"

"Of course, I want to be with you," Constance said. "Though not because I need you to support me or because I depend on you, but simply because I love you. We must each stand on our own two feet, Justin, even if we stand close to one another. The only way I could endure being without you after you left the village is because I have never relied on you and can do things on my own. If I had leaned on you, I would have fallen down when you went away. We must never cling to each other, Justin, neither me to you nor you to me. Although we are together, we are also each alone."

"That sounds so distant and cold," Justin said.

"Nay, it is the purest form of love there is: to be with someone but never to fetter them. If a butterfly flutters into your open palm, you will only crush it if you try to hold on to it by closing your hand."

"But if I keep my palm open, the butterfly might fly away."

"Indeed, it might. But love cannot be bound."

"Constance, you are everything to me," Justin said, as tenderly as he could. "I cannot live without you."

"Do not put blinders on your own eyes or place such a heavy burden on me."

"I only want you to love me."

Constance feigned a slap on Justin's face.

"How selfish!" she cried. "You should not want to be loved, Justin, but to love. If you need to be loved, then you have no love to give. Your cup is empty and can only be filled by draining another person's cup into your own, which leaves that other person with nothing. It is only if the cups of two people are full to begin with that they can drink from each other's cups."

Justin lay back on the pallet and looked up at the ceiling.

"I have been so ignorant about love," he said. "And never understood it until now."

Constance's eyes began to soften.

"You have always been so naive," she scolded him gently.

"Indeed, I still am."

Constance's face broke into a smile. She tousled his newly cut hair. Then Justin touched her on the forehead and said, "My cup is overflowing."

"And so is mine," Constance replied.

The cat snuggled in between them and began purring.

§15

That evening as Justin and Constance were walking along the road from the cottage to the tables for the communal supper, they met the young woman and her mother they had talked with the night before.

"We did not see you in church this morning," the young woman said, with a knowing smile. "Nor for the noonday meal."

"Indeed, we did not come. We had other things to do."

"I hope you were not—you know—doing anything sinful," the woman's mother said. "You should be ashamed of yourselves if you were."

"Mother, leave them alone," the young woman said. "What they do is their own business. Someone should put a scold's bridle round your head and push the clamp down hard on your tongue."

Then turning to Justin she said, "Did Constance give you a haircut?"

"Yes, and a shave, too."

"Your skin must be soooo smooth," the young woman said. "Anyway, you look the same as the man I remember from before, but there is something different about you. I can't quite put my finger on what it is."

After joining the others, they all sat down at the tables, Justin and Constance once again across from the young woman and her mother. As those gathered were preparing to say grace, the young woman said to everyone, "I do not think that we should give thanks to God, but rather to each other! For it is nature that has given us every seed and the fruit of every plant, and we ourselves who have put this food on our table with our own labor!"

"Amen!" said the others, all except for the young woman's mother.

"You blaspheme," she said to her daughter. "Of course, it is God alone who gives us what we eat and all the other blessings we have."

Justin wanted to interrupt and give his own views on the subject but thought it best to keep his mouth shut.

To his surprise Constance intervened and said, "Indeed, mother, it is God alone who provides our food by working through nature and through us."

The young woman then said, "Well put, Constance. In any case I'm tired of going to church every Sunday and listening to the same homily over and over again about how we should subject ourselves to God and the authorities. 'Submit' and 'submit' are the priest's two favorite words. He is trying as hard as he can to get us all back into line. But I shall no longer be subject to anyone. No gods, no masters!"

The women, who had been giving the conversation their full attention, all cheered.

The mother then turned to her daughter and said, "Adrian is an exception, of course. Tomorrow we must take food and supplies to him and the others."

"I refuse. If Adrian wants anything, he can come and get it himself. I will no longer take any provisions to either him or his henchmen."

"I shall certainly take food and supplies to Adrian tomorrow," the mother said. "You seem to be forgetting what a great man he is. Without Adrian we would still be suffering under the master. We are no longer subject to the lord, yet it is also unmistakable that God has designated Adrian to take his place, so we should do his bidding. Surely you would not defy Adrian as your God-appointed ruler."

Constance corrected her. "Do you not mean *self*-appointed?"

"God-appointed or self-appointed, Adrian is not my ruler and neither are you," the young woman said to her mother. "There is barely any food left to take to him anyway. It has been a hard winter, you know."

"Yes, we must make do as long as we can," Constance said. "We haven't even finished planting the new crop yet."

"And the men are not helping us with the plowing!"

"Indeed," Constance continued. "We should not give them any more food until they return here to work the same as we do."

"Nor welcome them to our beds!" one of the other women hollered.

A loud hurrah went up from everyone.

"So, what will you do tomorrow?" Justin asked the young woman.

"I shall do nothing, except go to the fields to plow," she replied. "I shall not take food to Adrian either now or in the future."

"You do not fear him?"

"Of course, I fear him. He is a violent man with a violent temper."

"But if we all stick together, neither he nor the other men can harm us," Constance said. "And we shall have our way."

"Oh my," the mother said. "You would stand up against your own brother?"

"It makes no difference if he is my brother or not. I will stand up against anyone who tries to oppress us."

The young woman then called out to the others, "How about the rest of you? Will any of you go with my mother to take food to Adrian and his men tomorrow?"

"We shall not!" the women all cried, almost in unison.

"I will go alone then," the mother said, fuming but determined.

"You would not be able to manage on your own," her daughter said.

"I shall nonetheless try. A worthy woman is like a merchant ship bringing bread from afar."

"How about you, Justin? What will you do?" the daughter asked.

"I shall stand beside Constance," Justin replied.

"Just don't stand too close," the young woman chided, imitating the voice of her mother.

§16

The next day everyone woke early and went to the fields to plow, all except for the mother, who filled her basket with as much food as she could, although it was still a scant amount, and began shambling up the highway to the estate. Justin guided the plow from one end of the field to the other as Constance goaded the oxen. He watched the mother out of the corner of his eye until she disappeared around a bend in the highway, wondering how Adrian would react when she arrived at the mansion and told him about the new situation.

The plowing was hard as usual and the sun hot enough to help Justin work up a good sweat. In the mid-afternoon he saw the mother, her basket empty, returning down the highway, together with Adrian and his cadre of men. The women all dropped their plows and gathered around Justin and Constance, waiting for Adrian's group to cross the field to where they were standing.

"You did not bring us our food today," Adrian said when he had reached Justin and the others. The man with a scar on his face was standing beside him.

"Nay, but my mother took something to you," the young woman said. "You should be grateful."

"But that's not the arrangement. You must not neglect your duties."

"Nor should you neglect yours."

"What other duties do I have except to humbly serve as your leader? It is you who must be grateful to me."

"You should be out here helping us with the plowing," Constance said.

"That is not my role," Adrian replied, "My role is to lead, yours is to work."

"We require no leaders."

The scar-faced man then said, "But do you not appreciate all that Adrian has done for you—for all of us? We owe it to Adrian for overthrowing the lord."

"Indeed, we are thankful to Adrian for what he has done," Constance replied. "But now we no longer need either him or you, at least not as our leaders. We are perfectly capable of making our own decisions. You are welcome to join us, if you like, but we will no longer bring you food nor take any orders from you."

"Without me, you would still be slaving under the master," Adrian said.

"It makes no difference whether we slave under the master or we slave under you," Constance said. "We are still slaves."

"But on your own you are powerless. You need a leader to organize you, just like our own father did in days past."

"Certainly I respect our father and I respect you. But we are completely able to coordinate our activities without your help."

"You would not know what to do."

"We shall learn and educate ourselves."

Adrian was becoming exasperated.

"We shall take a vote then," he said finally. "Let us all decide together who our leader will be. I have every confidence that I will win the majority's support."

"What good is a vote?" Constance countered. "Even if the majority agrees on someone, we would continue to have a leader. There would still be those who give orders and those who take them. No. We shall decide things among ourselves, not by taking votes, but by talking with each other and reaching a reasonable agreement."

"That would simply be another form of oppression," Adrian replied. "If the group decides everything, we would lose our freedom as individuals."

"To the contrary, we shall each enjoy as much individual freedom as we like when our actions do not affect another person. But when we need to take actions that involve others, then all those who may be affected by a proposal should be allowed to participate in the discussion about what will be done."

"You think that we can resolve all our problems just by talking about them?"

"If we have good will towards each other, we are perfectly capable of working together," Constance said. "We all face the same problems, we all want to deal with them, and we all have ideas about how to remedy them. So, why not pool our resources and see what happens?"

"Everything would just fall into disarray!" Adrian protested. "You would be disagreeing with each other all the time and never be able to get anything done!"

"Well, so what? No system is perfect, but it would certainly be better than the one we have now."

Justin broke into the conversation at this point.

"Adrian, do you not remember what you yourself told us long ago, when you were whipping up support for the first revolt? You said, 'The land belongs to whoever works it and if someone does not work the land, it does not belong to them.'"

"What I meant is that the land belongs to us—the peasants, not the lords. And it is up to the peasants to decide how the land is managed."

"Is that not exactly what Constance is suggesting?"

"She has it wrong, though," Adrian said. "The peasants have a right to self-determination. The nobility may not interfere. Freedom means that we may choose whatever form of governance we please."

"Does freedom mean simply substituting one form of authority for another or abolishing authority altogether? Concentrating power in the hands of a single leader or spreading it out among the people themselves?"

"Power in the hands of a leader is perfectly legitimate if it is the will of the people and he governs with their consent."

"Well, you hardly have everyone's consent, Adrian. The only people who support you are your loyal cronies. Before you worked the land for my father. Now the women are working the land for you. We should all like to adopt the principle that you yourself have advocated: Whoever does not work shall not eat. Are you not willing to share in the labor with us?"

"I will do nothing of the sort," Adrian replied.

"We shall not force you," Justin said. "But neither will we give you food or anything else that we have produced with our own labor unless you help us produce it."

"You are being unreasonable, Justin."

"We would never deny you the freedom to do as you choose. But we also have the freedom to decide how the fruit of our labor will be distributed."

"It is not me but you who are setting yourself up as a leader and trying to dictate your own rules to others," Adrian said stonily.

"Certainly there is no reason for anyone to simply accept what I say, for I am no leader," Justin replied. "Let us hear what the others think. We have nothing to fear by listening to them."

For a moment everyone was silent. Then the young woman said, "Well, you already know my opinion. I agree with Justin."

"As do I," Constance said. "What about the rest of you?"

Again there was a moment of silence. The scar-faced man then said, not to Adrian but to everyone, "We should consider what the women and Justin have been saying. After all, we began this revolt because we thought the master was treating us unfairly. Simply replacing one master with another does not solve the problem one bit. We need to change the whole system and find a new way of doing things. We can no longer organize ourselves from top to bottom but must stand together side by side."

"What do you others say?" Justin asked.

Some of the men began to murmur their approval, then more, until it seemed that all the men had been won over. All, that is, except Adrian.

"I care not what the rest of you think," he said. "I have fought, and fought hard, to conquer that manor house. If the rest of you don't want it, that's fine. Then I shall make it my own. I hereby proclaim myself its sole owner!"

Yet again there was silence. Then the scar-faced man said, "Aye, Adrian, you may have it. 'Tis yours and yours alone. We no longer have any use for the estate."

"And what shall *you* do?" Adrian asked.

"I shall pick up this plow and commence plowing," the scar-faced man replied, which is exactly what he did.

Others started to join him, some spreading out across the fields and some returning to the village to get more implements.

"You are all committing treachery against both me and the movement," Adrian shouted out after them before turning around and beginning to walk back in the direction of the estate.

Justin caught up with a group of peasants returning to the village in time to hear the young woman ask her mother, "And what is your opinion?"

"I do not approve of what has transpired here, not one bit," the older woman replied. "But you hardly expect me to return to the estate and live with Adrian, now do you?"

§17

Afterward when they were alone again in the cottage, Constance said to Justin, "I cannot quite understand why the men changed their minds so quickly."

"They were convinced by my cogent arguments!" Justin said somewhat boastfully.

"Indeed, you were very persuasive," Constance said. "But it was something else. Somehow the men were inspired by you."

"I cannot imagine why."

"It was not what you said but . . . I don't know. It's like salt that seasons the food or yeast that raises the bread but cannot be tasted. There is something special about you, Justin. Something you have now which you did not have before."

"There is nothing special about me," Justin said looking down. "I am just an ordinary person."

§18

And so the men and women worked together plowing the fields, then sowing the seeds and harrowing the soil. Gardens were planted with cabbage, garlic, and leeks, as well as flax and hemp for sale in the town. The cows were taken out to pasture, the milk used to make cheese and butter. The sheep were sheared and the wool used to make fresh sets of clothes. When the haymaking was finished, the weeding began, a loathsome task that was detested by all, but with everyone pitching in, they made short work of it.

In the evenings Justin and Constance would lie on their pallet, together yet apart, making love then separating. They were like the strings of Justin's lute, the notes distinct yet in harmony with each other, or two trees growing side by side, neither standing in the other's shadow. The wind passed through the spaces between them. The ocean pulsed between the shores of their hearts. They were joyous in each other's company, yet each was still alone.

One midsummer morning, just before the harvest of the first fruits, when stocks of food were at their lowest, a decision was made for some of the villagers, with Justin in their company, to go to the forest to forage for wild plants. Shortly after they had filled their bundles, Justin saw a man with a huge basket and a bundle slung round his back making his way through the trees. As the man drew near, Justin recognized him as the old hermit.

Justin hailed him, "What a surprise! I thought I should never see you again!"

"You never know who will show up, now do you," the hermit grinned. "What have you been doing?"

"Gathering food."

The hermit looked inside Justin's bundle. "Well, I can see that the lessons I gave you so long ago were not in vain."

He then pointed to his own bundle and said, "And look here. I have brought plenty of food with me as well!"

The villagers swarmed around the hermit, greeting and hugging him. They knew the man well, of course—"Fisher" as they called him—since he used to live among them and occasionally came back to the village to trade. He had not been seen in quite some time, however. As the group was walking back to the village, the peasants recounted to him all that had taken place since his last visit.

"Aye," the hermit said. "I have seen Adrian and heard about your troubles. But now you have succeeded. Wonderful! You have won your freedom!"

Justin told the hermit about going to the site where his hut had been and finding everything destroyed. It was just after the first revolt, so Justin had worried that the hermit might have been killed.

"No cause for alarm," the hermit said. "You should know me better than that. When the soldiers came after me, I made a clean escape. I know the forest much better than they do! I made my way down to the fens, which are even more of a maze than the forest. It was easy to lose them. I just waded through the mire until I came to a knoll and then set up camp. Somehow Adrian found his way there after his own brush with the law."

"And where are you living now?"

"Back at the same place where you first met me. I like being near the sea. Rebuilding the hut was easy. It's even nicer than before. I laid down some planks for a floor, to keep my shoes out of the mud. The fens convinced me that I do not like muck on my feet."

"Well, no one shall bother you anymore."

When they reached the village, the other villagers, joined by Constance, set aside what they were doing and all sat down together at the communal tables. Justin offered the hermit a chair, saying, "Here, this seat is yours now."

"Indeed, it is!" the hermit laughed.

He set his basket on the table and removed the cloth cover.

"Have a look," he said to the villagers. "Fresh fish. I caught them just this morning. And I shall trade all of them with you for a new tunic—and breeches if you have any. As you can see, mine are getting rather tattered."

"We have just been making new clothes," Constance said. "I shall fetch some for you."

"And I'll throw in these rabbits for free," the hermit said, reaching into his bundle and pulling out two, already skinned. He then took out a smaller sack and said, "These grubs, though, are mighty precious. I shall only let you have them for a chicken in return."

Constance opened the sack and looked inside. The grubs were still moving.

"We thank you most assuredly for your generous offer," she said, shrinking back. "But I think we shall decline."

"Makes no difference," the hermit chortled. "I can eat them myself. Grubs are just as good as roast chicken if a man is hungry enough."

Constance went back to the cottage to get new clothes for the hermit. When she returned she had a tunic and breeches in one hand and a cackling chicken in the other.

"We shall throw in the chicken for free as well," she said. "As you can see, it's still alive, just like the grubs."

The hermit bowed graciously. "Well, thank you kindly. It always amazes me that the rich are so stingy despite their wealth and the poor are so generous despite their poverty."

"You have it wrong," Constance replied. "It's the rich, not us, who live in poverty."

"I stand corrected! Just set the chicken down and let it run around so that it can enjoy the last day of its life."

Some of the villagers went to cook the fish, while others prepared the greens they had gathered from the forest. The tables were set and they all sat down to eat.

"I'm sorry we have no bread to give you," Justin said. "But we shall be harvesting soon and after that we shall bake bread aplenty. The feast of the first fruits will be held in another week and the harvest festival after that. You should come and join us."

"Nay, I am not one for feasting," the hermit said. "It just makes me fatter than I already am."

"I thought that since we are now free from the lord you might, in fact, wish to move back to the village and live with us."

"Ha!" the hermit said with a hearty laugh. "You shall not know real freedom until you come to live in the forest like me."

"No doubt we each must find our own way."

"But you are certainly welcome to come visit me anytime down at my hut. We shall go hunting werewolves together."

"I would love to," Justin smiled.

The meal over, the hermit stood up to leave, putting the clothes into his bundle and the still squawking chicken into his basket.

Justin walked with him back to the road.

"You're a changed man," the hermit said with a knowing smile. "I can tell."

"Indeed, I have had many experiences since the last time I saw you."

"Well, you needn't tell me about them. The details don't matter. But I can see that you finally found what you were looking for."

"I suppose I have," Justin replied.

"It's just like my nose," the hermit said. "It's been there my whole life, but I didn't even realize I had one until one day I crossed my eyes and there it was, smack dab in the middle of my own face."

The hermit waved goodbye with a loud hoot and started off down the road back towards the forest.

§19

Following the first harvest, a small group of villagers paid a visit to the rectory to invite the priest to join them for the feast of the first fruits, although they did not bring bread for the priest to bless. At the same time they informed the priest that they would not pay a tithe to the Church this year. The priest protested that the peasants were still obliged to give him his due, even if they would not be giving a percentage of the produce or paying any taxes to a lord.

The villagers politely replied that the priest would no longer receive any provisions of any kind from them, but that he was welcome to join them in the fields and help with the rest of the harvest, in which case they would treat him as one of their own and give him his fair share. Otherwise, he could continue to live in the rectory for as long as he wished, but he would be on his own and obliged to provide for his own needs.

The priest demurred. The terms they were offering were unacceptable, he said, and against the will of God. The duty of the clergy is to pray; the duty of the peasants is to work. Before the priest had closed the door of the rectory in their faces, one of the peasants said, "We are able to pray by ourselves and you are able to work like us."

A different group of villagers returned the next day to repeat the offer, taking with them a basket of food to tide the priest over until he could manage on his own. But when they knocked on the door of the rectory, there was no answer. Apparently the priest had departed quietly during the night. After that both the rectory and the church were empty and left to collect dust. The villagers had long ceased attending mass in any case.

The harvesting continued, men and women both working together, until the day of the grand harvest festival arrived a month later. The tables were set, as usual, with all manner of food from the season's offerings, along with a roast pig and enormous quantities of strong ale.

Justin and Constance were sitting, as they usually did, across from the young woman and her mother. They had hardly begun eating, however, when they heard the steady drumming of hoof beats coming from the end of the village. The villagers all stood up and went to have a look.

There, coming down the road, was a large battalion on horseback, led by none other than the lord of the neighboring manor, the father of Penelope. To his left was Penelope herself, in a flowing purple gown and, to his right, much to Justin's disbelief, his old cohort from the university, Roland, who was dressed now in the proper clothes of a nobleman, though still wearing the gold ring he had bought when he and Justin had gone to the fair. Just behind them was the village priest, the same priest who had baptized Justin and prophesied that he would become a great religious leader, the same priest Justin had confessed his murder of Martin to, the same priest who had so recently left the village because the villagers would not give a tithe to him. And beside the priest was the bailiff, the same bailiff Justin had learned from when he still lived with his father, the same bailiff who had ordered Constance to leave the estate, the same bailiff who had accused him of murdering Martin. Bringing up the rear was a fully armed regiment of knights wearing mail and metal breastplates.

The lord called the company to a halt just in front of the dumbstruck villagers. He then announced in a loud voice, "We have come to reestablish order on this fief. Everything has fallen into disarray. The baron will not stand for any anarchy on his holdings nor will the Crown tolerate any insubordination among the peasants."

Although Justin could see both of their faces clearly, neither Penelope nor Roland had yet noticed Justin standing among the peasants.

"After long negotiations, the baron has granted me authority over this manor," the lord continued. "I am naming my son here, Roland, as your new master, with my daughter, Penelope, as his adjunct."

So, Justin thought, Roland was not only the son of a nobleman but also the brother of Penelope! How had they not stumbled across this fact during their many conversations together at the university? The only hint was that the color of the hair on both of them was the same burning shade of red.

The lord continued, "From here we shall march to reclaim the manor house, but first we must round up the leaders of your rebellion. I assure you they will be given a fair trial, but once proven guilty, they shall be executed."

Constance stepped forward and shouted out, "If you wish to round up our leaders, then you must take all of us. We have no leaders. We have all been in this together."

"Well, you have a leader now," the lord replied. "Not only the land but also the peasants who live here belong to me from this day forth. With Roland as your new overseer, we shall need you to continue working for us, just as you did for your previous lord. We have heard that the main instigator of your revolts is a man named Adrian, and that he was assisted by Justin, the heir to this fief. Are either of these men among you now?"

A few of the knights dismounted from their horses and began approaching the crowd. The young woman could not restrain her mother from breaking away and running up to the lord.

"You will find Adrian sitting in the great hall of the manor house," she whispered to him.

"Thank you, my dear woman," the lord said. "We shall go there forthwith to apprehend him."

The woman did not return to her daughter, who was beside herself with fury, but moved to a different part of the crowd. The lord then addressed the assembly again.

"Are there any others here who have been party to plotting these revolts? If so, you should step forward now. We shall find you sooner or later in any case and it is to your advantage to cooperate with us. You have my promise that we will treat you charitably and not torture you."

The knights were standing immediately in front of the villagers now, none of whom moved. Justin remained unseen. His mind was racing. He considered stepping forward but was reminded of what Constance had told him. He did not wish to cooperate with the authorities simply because they had the law on their side. He was then tempted to flee but he knew that if he did, he would instantly be chased down and slaughtered by the knights. If he tried to hide his face, it would only attract attention to himself. Once again he had no plan!

After a few tense moments, the bailiff finally pointed directly to Justin and cried out, "Look who is here! The other leader of the revolt!"

Penelope gasped. Roland seemed just as astonished to see Justin as Justin had been to see him.

Two knights came over, grabbed Justin by the arms, and dragged him before the lord.

"Justin," the lord said with mock courtesy. "It has certainly been a long time since I last saw you."

Justin did not reply.

The lord shouted out to the villagers, "Justin shall accompany us to the estate. The rest of you will remain here. I shall leave a contingent to watch over you lest you try to flee."

Justin's hands were tied together with a rope by a knight, who then mounted his horse, leaving Justin to stumble along behind him. Justin looked back over his shoulder and saw Constance standing tight-lipped in the crowd.

"We shall meet again," he mouthed to her.

§20

As they were going along the highway to the estate, Roland pulled his horse up beside Justin.

"My sister just told me that you are the man who deserted her," he said.

"I did not know that Penelope was your sister," Justin replied. "You were not at the wedding."

"Of course not. I had already left for university by then. It was only after the master suspended me the first time and I returned home that I heard about what happened. When I resumed classes last year, I never suspected that the same 'Justin' who had married my sister and treated her so badly was you. How could you even think of acting in such a manner? And you didn't do yourself any favors either. You should have just stayed with her and accepted your station in life instead of trying to fight it."

Justin did not look up at him.

"You are so naive, Justin," Roland continued. "Don't you know that the best way to get along in this world is to outwardly conform to what people expect of you, then to privately do whatever you want? The only thing you must avoid is getting caught, in which case you will suffer public humiliation."

"Indeed, the last time I saw you, you were locked in a pillory," Justin said.

"I am sorry that I was too preoccupied at the time to see you in return!" Roland laughed. "In any case, it's good you got away. But had you been apprehended, you could have done what I did, which is to simply apologize, no matter how insincerely, so that people will trust you again. After that you may regain your position in society and no one will think the worse of you. If a prince avoids those things which admittedly make him odious or contemptible, he will have played his part well and meet no danger or inconveniences should he indulge in any other vices. In fact, some of those acts that appear to be virtues bring certain destruction, while others that are seemingly bad may procure peace and security."

"You have no intention of resuming your studies at the university?" Justin asked.

"Certainly not. I was permanently expelled and no other university would accept me, despite my father's offers to make a generous donation. But it makes no difference. Those who know the ways of the world do not need a formal education and certainly not a degree. And, as you now know, my father has new plans for me and those are the plans I intend to pursue. You should have simply followed the plans your father had set for you as well."

Justin continued to stagger along behind the knight's horse and said nothing.

"You have no reply?" Roland asked.

"No," Justin said. "By all means, please carry on with your monologue."

"Well, I am finished. But I can say this, Justin. You are not the same person I knew at university. I can tell just by looking at you. You have completely disgraced yourself and are no longer a man of honor. I doubt that you can understand anything I've been saying to you anyway. You're a loser."

After a short pause, Roland added balefully, "Oh, indeed, there is one more thing I must tell you: Your problems go far beyond the wrath of my father. There are others who are itching to make claims against you as well."

Justin could not discern exactly what Roland meant but supposed he was referring to Penelope. Before he could say anything further, however, Roland had already pulled his horse away and rejoined his sister.

§21

Once the company had reached the estate Justin saw that the grounds were thick not only with grass, but also weeds, growing ever taller. The lord halted just in front of the main entrance to the manor house, dismounted, and motioned to the knight in charge of Justin to bring him forward.

"I shall need you to identify Adrian," the lord said.

The bailiff and the priest dismounted as well and joined the master as he entered the house with Justin and a few other knights, leaving the others outside. The floor of the foyer was covered with slippery mold and beginning to crumble.

The entourage passed through the doors of the great hall and found Adrian sitting at the head of the grand table all by himself. His hair and beard were gnarled, his arms spindly, his body scraggly. In front of him was a plate of gnawed bones and some half-rotten vegetables. Beside the plate was a large flask of wine and beside the flask a nearly empty glass. Stains covered the table. On the floor next to Adrian was a huge pool of vomit. Justin was dismayed to see Adrian living in such squalor.

"I assume this is Adrian, the man who led the revolt," the lord said to Justin.

Refusing to cooperate, Justin did not answer. Adrian, however, having overheard the lord, called out, "Indeed, I am Adrian. Greetings and welcome to my estate. You are a most honored guest!"

His speech was slurred. He was obviously inebriated.

"This estate is no longer yours," the lord said flatly. "Now it is mine."

"Surely you jest," Adrian garbled back. "Who are you anyway?"

"The lord to whom the baron has given this house and the entire fief as well. I have come here to take possession of it in accordance with the law."

"The law!" Adrian yowled. "I am the law here now. I came, I saw, I conquered. The estate belongs to me. I have gained my freedom and no one shall take it away from me!"

"If you have no respect for the law, then I shall have no qualms about taking the estate by force," the lord said. "It seems that the only thing you understand is power."

"Indeed, power is the law and the law is power!"

Adrian was slobbering all over himself at this point.

"He is mad," the bailiff scoffed.

Justin tried to take a step forward to help Adrian but was held back by his guard.

"And who is this with you?" Adrian asked, rolling his head in a stupor. "Surely you did not need to bring Judas along to betray me with a kiss. I am the one you seek and freely admit it!"

"That is all we need to know," the lord said, motioning to two of the knights to take Adrian into their custody. Adrian laughed drunkenly as he rose from the table, slipped in his own puke, and fell down to the floor. The knights pulled Adrian to his feet and led him out of the room, followed by the others.

"Take him to the dungeon," the lord said. "That should sober him up. And take Justin with him. We shall indict them tomorrow, then commence with their trial."

Penelope was standing just outside the entrance of the mansion when the knights emerged with Justin and Adrian. She scurried up to Justin and walked alongside him for a short distance as the group went up the narrow drive toward the alley behind the house.

"I have been completely shamed because of you," she hissed at Justin. "I shall never marry again."

"Indeed, I must apologize very sincerely for what I did to you," Justin replied.

"I will never forgive you," Penelope said. "And that wench you left me for. I don't know who she is or what she looks like, but rest assured, I shall find her and make sure that she never marries either."

Before Justin could say anything more, Penelope had veered away and returned to the others.

Approaching the alley, Justin saw the bailiff's house and the warehouses, then, turning the corner, the servants' quarters. The garden had a few scrawny vegetables in it, which Adrian had apparently tried to grow. The knights led Justin and Adrian to the dungeon, lit a lantern, and unlatched the door. Stench from below wafted up into the open air.

The knights yanked the two men down the stairway. Once inside the room, the knight with the lantern held it high, lighting up the entire chamber. Justin was startled by the sight of a severed head and detached body lying on the floor. The torso, once apparently broad and muscular, was putrid and swarming with worms. The hair and beard on the head were matted but still intact. The features of the face, though contorted, were still distinguishable.

"Do you recognize this man?" the knight asked Justin, holding the lantern closer.

"Yes," Justin replied. "It is my father."

"How about that one over there? There's no face left, but do you know who it might be?"

In the far corner was a skeleton, the skull covered with dry black skin, the teeth clenched and clearly visible. A chain hung round the bones of the neck, with a corroded brown disk resting on the rib cage. It was the alchemist's medallion. Justin walked over and touched it. Flakes of rust crumbled into the palm of his hand.

"No doubt this is my former teacher," Justin said.

"We shall inform the lord," the knight said.

The other knight threw Adrian into the corner near the door, where he lay groaning, too drunk to care, not even knowing where he was. Justin sat down across from his father and leaned his back against the cold stone wall. The knights ascended the stairway, taking the lantern with them, leaving Justin and Adrian alone in the darkness.

Justin could not cry, but only reflect. So this was the immortality his father and the alchemist had finally ended up with.

Justin must have fallen asleep. He was awakened by the voice of Adrian calling out through what seemed to be his dreams.

"Is someone there? I can hear you snoring," the voice said.

Startled, Justin opened his eyes to the pitch-black chamber and called back, "It is I, Justin."

"Justin!" the voice of Adrian said. "Where in heaven's name are we?"

"Don't you know? We are in the dungeon."

"The last thing I remember is being dragged from the hall by two knights. After that it's all a blank."

"You were very drunk at the time," Justin's voice said.

"But I also remember seeing a nobleman there. He was making some kind claim about the estate now belonging to him."

"Indeed, that was the lord of the neighboring fief. As he told you, though you may not remember, the baron has given this house and the surrounding lands to him."

"He cannot do that," Adrian's voice cried back through the darkness. "We have won the estate and it belongs to me now."

"I am sorry, Adrian, but you have failed."

It seemed to take Adrian some time for the notion to sink in.

Finally Justin heard Adrian's voice say, "You have failed, too."

"Indeed, we all have failed."

"If you had only listened to me, we could have prevailed. It was imperative that we stick together. But no, you and the others insisted on abandoning me and going your own way."

"No one wanted to follow you, Adrian."

"Well, even if they did not want to follow me personally, they still need someone to guide them."

"The villagers are perfectly capable of guiding themselves as long as there is no outside interference."

"You are truly a dreamer, Justin. You think that if everyone simply isolates themselves from the rest of the world and creates their own little utopia, all will be fine. You have no awareness whatsoever of the forces that surround you on sides, just waiting for their chance to take back control and reassert their authority over us. We must be able to defend ourselves and meet their power with our own power. Look at what has happened to us now. The nobility has come to oppress us once again because we were not prepared."

"Surely it would be more effective to just eliminate hierarchy altogether and spread power equally among everyone, would it not? So that no one person may ever oppress another."

"No doubt you are right. In the end that is the way it should be. Freedom will only be achieved when the peasants no longer bow down before tyrants but become a dictatorship themselves. But how do we get there? Why is it that right now a very tiny minority—the nobility and the Church—are able to lord it over the rest of us, even though we are by far the vast majority? It is only because we are complicit in our own oppression. If we unite and rise up together, and exert our power and defeat them, then we ourselves shall be in control and can work together to create a new and glorious future."

"Please explain to me, Adrian," the voice of Justin said. "How do we form such alliances?"

"As I told you, we were already beginning to make connections with peasants throughout the kingdom, until you interrupted things. One revolt by one group of peasants on one estate means absolutely nothing and is easily quashed, as has just now happened to us. But a revolution of all the peasants throughout the land against the nobility could not be stopped. If we all act together, we could crush both the Crown and the Church in one fell swoop."

"Certainly I can see the value of having the peasants form one big union to fight against their masters. But instead of fomenting a bloody revolution, could the peasants not simply withdraw their support from the nobility, in the same way they withdrew their support from the priest or, for that matter, even from you? No violence is necessary. The state does not need to be abolished. We simply allow it to wither away on its own."

"And how would you do that?"

"By not giving anything to the lords or the Church and letting them provide for themselves. Or, if they prefer, by accepting our invitation to join us, so that we all work together and share what we produce equally."

"Do you really think the authorities would ever go along with such an idea? They know that the only way they can maintain their high position in society is by standing on our backs. They would prefer to exterminate us completely before they would allow us to govern ourselves or to share power jointly with them. And that is why we must exterminate them completely first, with us leading the masses."

"Indeed, we need organization and coordination, but what usually happens is that the leaders then take over and try themselves to control the people, telling them what to think and do, just like you did."

"The reason why people need to be told what to think and do is because they don't think and do for themselves. They are all gullible and will follow whatever foolish populist despot comes along and tells them what to do. That is why it is important for them to have an enlightened commander who takes them in the right direction."

"Once the peasants understand their situation, they can make their own decisions about which direction to go in."

"Ha!" the voice of Adrian said. "On their own the peasants are ignorant and stupid. They only care about what they are going to do today— what they will eat, what they will drink, what clothes they will wear. They have been duped into believing that if they work harder in support of their masters, their own lives will be improved. They do not have the big picture about how the established order works and what they can do to change it."

"And how do we give them 'the big picture'?"

"We educate them! We show them how they have been hoodwinked by the nobility, how the Church holds out the promise of heaven to them if they will but submit to their lords here on earth. We must eradicate this false way of thinking, Justin, this entire ideology and religion, and inculcate the peasants with new doctrines which show them how to overcome their oppression. Indeed, we shall be the new lords and new priests who teach the masses, for it is we who understand such matters, not them. We are the vanguard that leads the troops into battle, for it is only we who know the way forward."

"Would it not be preferable to simply give people time to think things through for themselves and reach their own conclusions?"

"Nay, Justin, the people must not be allowed to think for themselves, for they would simply revert to their old ways. Their thoughts must be strictly controlled. Any opinions which are contrary to what we teach them must be completely suppressed."

"So we simply replace the dictates of the nobility and the Church with dogmas of our own."

"Indeed. We must expose the deceptions of the ruling classes and propagate the truth!"

After a short pause Justin's voice said, "It seems to me that the people are more intelligent than you think, Adrian. Or, if not, then they are capable of becoming intelligent. Rather than follow the views of just one person, such as yourself, or one group of people who all think alike, would it not be better for the peasants to meet together and discuss among themselves how to manage affairs in the village, to share their ideas with each other and rationally arrive at solutions that everyone can support, and then to confederate with other like-minded villages and towns for the purpose of mutual cooperation? Even if we are never able achieve all of our ideals, at least they give us goals to move towards. Are we not capable of making perpetual improvements?"

"Ah, Justin. You are naive. You are so naive. It would take not just centuries but millennia before people could acquire such wisdom on their own and achieve the paradise on earth we all dream of. But you and I are living right at this moment, so it is we who must take action and the time to act is now."

The voice of Justin fell silent. He no longer knew how to reply to Adrian's arguments. Indeed, perhaps it was naive of him to believe that the world would change on its own spontaneously if only people began to think and act differently.

"There is one more thing," Adrian said. "If something should happen to me but you are set free, I plead with you to carry on the campaign."

"I will," Justin said with as much determination as he could muster.

"Is that a promise?"

"I shall do my best to find a way."

Justin knew it could not be Adrian's way, but, as usual, he could think of no other plan, at least not just then. He wasn't sure if anyone else had a good plan either.

§23

It was not long after this conversation, that Justin heard the turn of the bolt and the door of the dungeon creaking open. Sunlight cascaded down the stairway, bringing with it a breath of fresh air. Two guards appeared and commanded Justin and Adrian to ascend the stairs. Once outside, they were met by two additional guards, who promptly shackled the men's wrists with iron chains. With guards in front and behind, Justin and Adrian were led away from the dungeon and down the alley.

When the company turned the corner of the manor house, they were immediately confronted by a large throng of people gathered in the courtyard, spilling down the drive and onto the overgrown lawn. They were all from the village and were speaking in hushed tones to each other. As soon as the villagers saw Justin and Adrian, they fell silent and stared at them grimly. In the middle of the crowd was Constance, standing on tiptoe and waving furtively at Justin. When she finally managed to catch his eye, Justin noticed that her face was flushed with anguish.

Justin and Adrian were led through the main door of the house into the foyer and from there to the great hall. All the floors had been swept and everything wiped clean. The table had been turned sideways to give the hall the appearance of a courtroom. Seated in the middle was the lord, with

Roland to his right and Penelope to his left. The priest, the bailiff, and a few other deputies were standing to one side. Justin noticed that the tall man, who had deserted the villagers just before their first revolt and joined his father's servants, was also there, standing next to the steward.

The guards deposited Justin and Adrian in the center of the room and took up positions behind them.

The lord then stood up and addressed the two men. "You are both accused of sedition against the former lord of this estate, which is the main purpose of our investigation today. We must also inquire into the lord's demise, as well as the death of his faithful guard, Martin. To be entirely fair, however, before proceeding, I should like to give each of you the opportunity to reply to these allegations."

"I admit to everything," Adrian said immediately.

"You would like, then, to enter a formal plea of guilty?"

"Yes. I plead guilty. It was I and I alone who planned both revolts, I who led the peasants, I who killed the guard, and I who beheaded the former lord of this estate."

Justin was mystified by the strange mix of fact and fiction in Adrian's declaration.

"You feel no remorse for your actions?" the lord asked.

"None whatsoever," Adrian replied. "Everything I have done I would do all over again if given the opportunity."

"I see," the lord said, sitting back down and pressing the palms of his hands together. "And you, Justin, is there anything that you would like to say?"

But before Justin could reply, Adrian spoke again, "Justin is innocent. He had nothing to do with plotting the first revolt. The plan was entirely mine. As for the second revolt, Justin wasn't even here, so he couldn't possibly have taken part in it."

"You are thereby taking credit as the sole leader of both insurgencies?"

"Indeed. You must set Justin free and allow him to return to the others. If you are willing to retain the other villagers as your serfs, then you must keep Justin as well, for he is now one of them."

"I wish I could believe you," the lord said. "But I presume that Justin's real motive for participating in the rebellion was because he became impatient about inheriting his father's estate. To hurry things along, he schemed to overthrow the lord and proclaim himself the fief's new master. Indeed, even now—and for as long as he lives—it would be possible for Justin to lay claim to this manor. Despite the arrangements that have been recently made for me to take over the estate, the baron might still regard him as its rightful heir."

Adrian replied, "I am sure that it would be advantageous for you to find Justin guilty, so that you can get him out of the way, not only so that he would not be able to challenge your claim to the manor but also so that your daughter could remarry! I assure you, however, that Justin is blameless."

The lord was unsettled by Adrian's remarks. Finally he said, "And may I assure you as well that my intention is not to get Justin 'out of the way' but simply to learn the truth about this incident so that justice may be served. I should like to hear from Justin himself."

After some hesitation, Justin replied, "Certainly I would not make any claim to this estate. For I no longer consider myself to be my father's heir. As Adrian has said, I have thrown my lot in with the peasants."

"But how might we be sure?"

"You have my word," Justin answered.

"And that can be trusted?" the lord said snidely. "In spite of your denial of any wrongdoing, I have no doubt that you still have designs upon this estate. But we are digressing from the issue at hand. I have not yet heard your own reply to the charges."

"I have no reply to make," Justin said. "I only ask that you remove the remains of my father and my former teacher from the dungeon and give them a proper burial."

"Indeed, I have been informed of the unfortunate situation," the lord said. "It is being taken care of right at this moment. We are very aggrieved over the death of your father and especially the vicious manner in which he was killed. Undoubtedly this event occurred while you were away, so we shall lay the blame on Adrian since he has already confessed to doing it. Regarding your teacher, I know nothing about the cause of his death, since he has been there much longer than your father. In any case, we give you our deepest condolences."

The lord bowed graciously to Justin. He then continued, "What I am concerned with at the moment, however, are not these matters but rather with your role as a leader in the first revolt. We know that you participated in it, for there are eyewitnesses. What we are asking, however, is whether or not you helped to plan it."

"I have already told you he is innocent," Adrian again cut in. "How could you possibly expect a halfwit such as Justin to know how to concoct such a scheme?"

"I am sure that Justin is much cleverer than he appears," the lord said to Adrian. "And although you have confessed your guilt and assumed full responsibility for these crimes, Justin himself must still be interrogated."

At this point the bailiff stepped forward and said, "May I address your lordship?"

"Of course," the lord said.

"I, for one, have no doubt that Justin helped plan the revolt. It was too well coordinated. Everyone who participated was fully familiar with the layout of the estate. That knowledge could only have come from Justin himself, although that former servant girl, the sister of Adrian, may have been involved as well."

Justin braced himself for the bailiff to now reveal how, a long time ago, he had caught Justin kissing Constance in his own house and then expelled Constance from the estate. But he did not. Instead the bailiff said, "And I also suspect that it was Justin who murdered the guard, Martin."

"Could you please tell us the basis for this accusation?" the lord asked.

"To start from the beginning: On the night of the first revolt I myself witnessed Justin here, together with a band of villagers, attempt to enter the manor house through the kitchen door, undoubtedly with the intention of assassinating Justin's father."

The lord looked at Justin as if expecting a reply, but Justin did not offer one. Turning back to the bailiff, the lord said, "Please relate to us what happened next."

"There was an altercation, after which Justin fled. While I was occupied with the marauding villagers, the steward chased after him, but unable to keep up, he called out for help. One of the soldiers responded and set out in pursuit, though the steward could not see who it was. Martin's mutilated body was later found in the hunting grounds, however, so it must have been Martin who pursued Justin and Justin who killed Martin."

The lord looked at the steward. "Will you confirm the bailiff's story?"

"Indeed, it happened just as he has said," the steward replied, flapping his double chin vigorously up and down.

"Are there any others who can substantiate this claim?" the lord asked.

"Yes, this man here," the bailiff replied, pointing to the tall man.

"Is the bailiff's report true?" the lord asked the man.

"Indeed, it is," the tall man said. "It was I who found Martin's body after the bailiff ordered me to go looking for him."

"What do you say to this charge?" the lord then asked Justin.

Before Justin could answer, Adrian intervened yet again, "As I have already told you, I am the one who killed the guard. You may lay the blame entirely on me."

"Impossible!" the bailiff replied. "On the night of the revolt you were chased through the orchards by some of the soldiers and were clearly seen vaulting over the eastern wall. The soldiers chased you to the brook, which you waded across and then made off towards the sea. After that the guards lost track of you but, in any case, you were nowhere near the spot where Martin's body was found."

"How could anyone possibly have recognized me in the black of night?" Adrian cried. "Once again, I am telling you that Justin is completely innocent of any of the charges you have made against him! If there is anyone who must assume all guilt and be sacrificed for these sins, let it be me. If your intention is merely to use Justin as a scapegoat, then you should set him free to wander in exile if you do not wish to allow him to return to the village."

"I should hardly believe the testimony of this dishonorable man," the bailiff said to the lord. "He is nothing but a rogue, no doubt with reasons of his own for wanting to shield Justin."

The lord then looked at Justin and said, "The good bailiff here has made three charges against you: that you in fact helped Adrian plot the first revolt, that you intended to assassinate your own father, and that you yourself killed the guard, Martin. How do you plead?"

Justin thought for a moment, trying to recall what he had learned about the law from the bailiff. Finally he said, "I wish to enter a plea of innocent. Your evidence is simply a matter of my word against those of my accusers."

"Would it not be easier for you to simply admit to everything you have done?"

"I admit to having participated in the revolt," Justin said. "But as for the other charges, there is no corroborating evidence, so they carry no weight. Mere hearsay may not be accepted as truth."

"What is truth?" the lord replied. "We all know you are guilty. No evidence is necessary."

"You might have been able to get away with that argument in the past, when lords had absolute authority. But the legal system is rapidly changing, as you know, and you must also follow the law, the same as those whom you govern."

"Why do you know so much about the law?" the lord asked.

"Because I have studied it," Justin replied. "I am only informing you of what the statutes declare. If you distrust me, please ask the bailiff, for it is he who taught me the law."

The lord looked at the bailiff for a reply. The bailiff seemed confounded.

"Justin is quite right about the law on each of the points he has made," the bailiff said. "As it turns out, we are unable to establish with complete certainty that Justin was party to planning the revolt. We have no way of knowing what was going on in his mind the night he approached the manor house and can only assume that his intention was to murder his father. And there are no eyewitnesses who can verify that the soldier who chased after Justin was Martin or that it was Justin who killed him. Indeed, the evidence is entirely circumstantial."

"So, we are back where we started from," the lord said, barely able to conceal his consternation. "Without concrete proof, how are we to reach a conclusion that would withstand legal scrutiny?"

Before the bailiff could answer, however, the lord turned to the priest and asked, "Has Justin revealed anything about these affairs to you in his confessions?"

The priest looked not at the lord, but at Justin, with penetrating eyes, forcing Justin to lower his head.

"I am not permitted to divulge what a penitent discloses to me in confession," the priest said, "though I would certainly encourage anyone who has committed a crime to openly admit it in a court of law when called upon to do so."

"But did Justin not seek sanctuary in the church after the first revolt and the murder of the guard?" the lord asked, his voice more urgent. "And are you not duty-bound to hear his confession if he is to be given refuge?"

"Indeed," the priest answered, not looking away from Justin. "But I may not break the seal of confession, which I am sworn to uphold."

The lord was chagrined.

"You must tell me what Justin confessed," he demanded. "If you do not, I will have you thrown in the river and drowned!"

The priest then turned and bored his eyes into the lord's.

"Then you shall make me a martyr," he said unshaken.

"I should be happy to!" the lord came back.

"After which you will be excommunicated from the Church," the priest added, "which would hardly put you in good stead with the baron either."

Justin looked up to see the lord look down, crestfallen. The priest was intrepid, showing no emotion on his face and giving no indication whatsoever that he knew more than he was telling.

The bailiff stepped forward again and said, "May I make a suggestion?"

"Yes," the lord said wearily.

"It is not necessary for the priest to reveal what Justin confessed. We can still establish the truth beyond any reasonable doubt and convict Justin in a manner that is legally sound."

"And how might we do that?"

After a pause the bailiff said, "Submit Justin to an ordeal."

"An ordeal?" The lord raised his eyebrows.

"In the absence of compelling evidence, my proposal is that we let God determine Justin's innocence or guilt."

"But I do not have the authority to conduct an ordeal. Any procedures which involve the judgment of God can only be administered by the Church."

"The Church no longer condones ordeals," the priest said resolutely, "and members of the clergy are forbidden to participate in them."

"You would not have the approval of the king either," Justin said. "Edicts have been issued proscribing the ordeal in criminal cases."

"But your lordship does not need permission from either the Church or the Crown to conduct an ordeal," the bailiff said. "You are the law here, my lord, so the decision is entirely up to you."

"Ordeals are antiquated," Justin said. "There have been no trials by ordeal for more than a hundred years."

"On that point you are wrong," the bailiff replied. "Ordeals may have been banned but they continue to be carried out by local lords in remote areas. The only reason they appear to be rare is that they are never recorded."

Then turning to the lord, the bailiff said, "Under these extraordinary circumstances, an ordeal may be expedient. It would put you above reproach, if not entirely in the eyes of the law then at least in the eyes of the people."

The lord sat silently for quite some time. No one knew what he was thinking, but no one dared to interrupt his ruminations. Then suddenly his eyes brightened, his face lit up, as if he had had an epiphany.

"The old ways are often the best ways!" he said at last. "I accept the bailiff's suggestion. We shall have an ordeal for Justin."

The lord looked at the priest for confirmation. The priest glared back at him scathingly and said, "You shall not test the Lord your God!"

"We shall nonetheless proceed," the lord said, "even if we do not have your blessing."

The lord then stood up from the table and prepared to leave.

"While Justin's case remains pending," he said. "Adrian's guilt has been clearly established, has it not? Let us go outside and tell the people our verdict."

§24

The entire group exited the mansion and stood on the portico outside the entrance, facing the crowd in the courtyard, the lord in front, with Roland and Penelope on either side and the others just behind. Justin and Adrian still had chains on their wrists and guards were holding their arms.

"Why did you defend me in there?" Justin whispered to Adrian.

"So that you may live to fight another day," Adrian whispered back. "I already know there is no hope for me. If I must be sacrificed for the cause, then so be it. But in return for my favor, I am counting on you to take over from me and lead the people in my stead. Do not forget that while we were in the dungeon you promised to carry on the campaign if something should happen to me. You may have betrayed me, Justin, but I shall never betray you. Please, in turn, do not betray the people."

Amidst the noise from the villagers, the guards did not overhear these remarks. The villagers quickly hushed, however, when the lord began to address them.

"After much deliberation," he bellowed, "we have reached a decision about how to handle the cases of the two men before you here, Adrian and Justin. Adrian has made a full confession and we find him guilty of treason against the former lord of this estate and for mercilessly beheading the lord himself."

The crowd became visibly tense, although no one moved.

"Given the seriousness of his offenses," the lord went on, "Adrian shall be duly punished by being dragged back to village, where he shall first be quartered. Each of his limbs shall be tied to horses pulling in opposite directions until they are detached from his body. His torso shall then be flayed and burned until he is dead, after which his arms and legs will be dipped in tar and placed on poles raised at the north, south, east, and west corners of the village as a reminder to all of you of the consequences of revolt, which shall not be tolerated on this manor nor anywhere else in the entire kingdom."

There was a shudder when the villagers heard the lord's words. Justin looked out and saw Constance standing at the same spot she had been before. She was looking at him intently, her face otherwise devoid of emotion.

"I assure you that this punishment is not harsh but just. Those who are violent will meet a violent end. If any man shall kill with the sword, by the sword he must be killed. This is the command of holy scripture."

The villagers looked at one another but said nothing.

"As for Justin," the lord continued, "the results of our investigation are thus far inconclusive. We are unable to determine whether he should be convicted for conspiracy against the former lord of this estate and the murder of the guard, Martin. We have, therefore, decided to submit him to an ordeal, which shall be conducted by myself, with the assistance of the bailiff and the guards."

Murmurs arose among the villagers at this announcement, which the lord quickly quelled by raising his hand. Justin detected a trace of relief on Constance's face. Perhaps Justin would be able to pass the ordeal?

"The priest shall be invited as an observer," the lord added, "but will play no role in the ordeal itself."

The priest seemed surprised by this announcement and quickly addressed the crowd, "I have informed the lord that the Church does not approve of ordeals, but it seems that he has already made up his mind about this over my stringent objections."

The lord, fearful that the priest would undermine his authority before the peasants, immediately rejoined, "While we fully respect the opinion of the priest, Justin has been accused of committing crimes against the realm, over which the Church has no jurisdiction."

The lord then beckoned to the priest, who reluctantly stepped forward. Grabbing him by the arm and pulling him closer, the lord said, "We must allow no divisions among us, but always strive for unity. There can be no enmity between the Church and the state, between God and the world, between those who rule and those who are ruled, for we are not enemies but friends!"

The priest stood by, steaming but unable to say anything further.

"There is one further item of business which must be attended to," the lord continued. "As you all know, the servants who previously worked at this manor house fled to me for protection during the second revolt and subsequently swore allegiance to me. I have taken good care of them in the interim and will reinstate all of them as servants on this estate effective immediately."

The lord nodded in the direction of a group of servants who had assembled to one side of the lawn, apart from the crowd. Their heads were all bowed.

The lord then addressed the villagers directly, "The reason why I have called the rest of you here today is not only for you to hear the results of our trial, but also to ask you to formally swear an oath of fealty to me as your new lord, as well as to my son, Roland, who has been appointed as the new executor of this estate. He shall be assisted by my daughter, Penelope, at least until such time that she is able to find more suitable accommodation. In return for your loyalty, we shall pardon your treachery and grant a general amnesty, with the proviso that if any of you should ever rise up against the nobility again, either here or elsewhere, you shall be punished just as you will witness Adrian being punished today."

The lord then stepped forward and opened his arms to the crowd in a conciliatory gesture.

"With this holy man and God himself as our witnesses," he said, "I ask all of you now to bend down on your knees before me and to swear that you will never again undertake a rebellion against our just rule and that you will serve both me and your new lord, Roland, with all diligence until the end of your days, as both the law and the Lord of heaven requires you."

The villagers began falling down one by one, extending their hands and touching their foreheads to the ground, pledging their devotion in loud voices, until at last the entire assembly was prostrate before the lord.

All, that is, except Constance, who still stood where she had been standing, her head jutting up from her erect body in a proud gesture of defiance.

The lord was perplexed for a moment, but then called out to her, "Do you refuse to obey me?"

The villagers, still kneeling, turned their heads to see whom the lord was speaking to.

"You may have the power to subject me, but I am not your subject," Constance cried back belligerently.

The lord motioned to a guard and said, "Take her into custody."

As the guard was going to retrieve Constance, a woman near the front of the crowd said in a hoarse whisper to Penelope, "That's her. She's the one Justin left you for!"

Justin immediately recognized her as the mother of the feisty young woman from the village. Her daughter, crouched beside her, was desperately tugging at her sleeve, trying to shush her up.

The lord, overhearing her remark, motioned to another guard and said, "Detain this old woman. I wish to speak with her as well."

Justin noticed a look of triumph on Penelope's face as the guards brought Constance and the old woman to a place near the steps of the portico.

The lord then shouted with a loud voice to the gathering, "By participating in this ceremony and paying homage to me and my children, we, in our magnanimity, hereby absolve you of your past transgressions and accept you as our loyal serfs. You are now dismissed and enjoined to return to the village to behold Adrian's execution. Exactly one week from today you shall return to the river to witness Justin's ordeal."

The villagers rose to their feet. Adrian was led down the steps to the courtyard, where a horse was waiting for him. After stripping off all of his clothes except for his undergarments, a guard tied one end of a rope around the chains on Adrian's wrists and the other to the horse, then mounted the horse and began to drag Adrian down the drive towards the highway that led to the village, followed by a retinue of knights also on horseback, the priest accompanying them apparently to administer Adrian his last rites.

Adrian turned his head the best he could back to the lord and began shouting obscenities. The peasants in turn began to hiss and scream at
Adrian, heaping scorn and ridicule on him.

"Take these two women back into the great hall for questioning," the
lord said to the bailiff, indicating Constance and the old woman. "And see
that Justin is returned to the dungeon."

§25

One of the guards led Justin back into his chamber and removed the
chains on his wrists. In the light from the lantern Justin noticed that the bodies of his father and the alchemist had been taken away. The guard handed
Justin a single scrap of bread and a flask of water, and then departed, taking
the light with him and leaving Justin alone in the inky darkness. Justin ate
from the bread piece by piece, washing each one down with a swig of water.

His first thoughts were of Constance. Her action had surprised him,
not because, indubitably true to her heart, she had defied the lord, but because she had done it so visibly. He would have expected her rather to be
more surreptitious, to make an outward show of conformity and then to go
her own way, without provoking an open confrontation that would put her
in jeopardy. Perhaps she had done it because she could no longer endure
being controlled by others or perhaps to show her solidarity with Justin. He
did not know.

Justin was also astonished at how quickly the old mother had abandoned Adrian and embraced the lord as her new master. Had she not only
a short time ago declared that Adrian had been appointed by God to take
his father's place as her leader? But just as soon as the neighboring lord had
asserted his sovereignty over the manor, she had switched allegiances again.
Her loyalty, of course, was not to any of the leaders, but only to God!

Now the old woman had also revealed the identity of Constance to
the lord and would no doubt tell him everything she had seen, including
the fact that Justin and Constance had begun living together, even though
everyone knew by now that Justin had been legally married to Penelope. It
seemed there was no way out of the quagmire Justin was in.

No doubt both Penelope and her father would prefer to simply sweep
the entire affair under the rug and the most convenient way to do that was,
indeed, to simply eliminate Justin, as both Constance and Adrian had said.
If Justin were dead, he could no longer lay claim to the estate and Penelope
would be free to remarry.

Subjecting Justin to an ordeal would neatly solve this problem. The os-
tensible justification would be that if Justin were innocent of the accusations

that had been made against him, God would intervene and preserve him from harm. If he failed the test, however, it would be taken as proof of his guilt. But since ordeals were, or at least seemed to be, purposely designed to set defendants up for failure, Justin knew that his own chances of passing the test and being acquitted were virtually nil. No doubt this was the "epiphany" the lord had experienced at the end of Adrian and Justin's trial.

The only question remaining was what kind of ordeal Justin would be subjected to. The easiest to pass was the corsned, more commonly known as the morsel of execration. Justin would be forced to eat a piece of barley bread together with some cheese. If he choked, he was guilty. If he could swallow all the dry crumbs without gagging, he was innocent. Contrary to the other forms of ordeal, this method was based on a presumption of innocence and, therefore, not too difficult to pass. Predictably a trial by ingestion was usually reserved only for members of the clergy and Justin doubted that he would be submitted to it.

A more grueling type was the ordeal by hot water, in which Justin would be asked to retrieve an object, such as a coin or stone, from a cauldron of boiling water. If he were guilty, his arm would be scalded and not heal. If he were innocent, he would either suffer no injury or be miraculously cured within three days. Similarly excruciating was the ordeal by fire, which would oblige Justin to walk a certain number of paces carrying a rod of red-hot iron in his hand. His innocence would be established if the iron did not leave him with festering sores. Another was the ordeal of being thrown into a pool of cold water. If guilty, Justin would float. If innocent, he would sink. Even though a rope would be tied around his waist to pull him up should he remain underwater too long, it was not uncommon for the victim to simply drown.

None of these options seemed to offer Justin any hope of being proven innocent. This time, it seemed, there would be no escape.

§26

A week later a guard came to retrieve Justin.

"It is time for your ordeal," he said.

"Indeed, let us get on with it," Justin immediately replied.

Justin was led up the steps of the dungeon into the alley outside and taken to the front of the manor house, where the lord, Roland and Penelope, the bailiff and the priest, and additional guards were waiting for him. The company then made their way down the long drive to the drawbridge.

As they crossed over it, Justin saw the boat still moored at the dock by the side of the brook. He recalled how the boat had carried him away the night he had fled the estate and thought about how different everything would be if only he had stayed. He would still be together with his father, preparing to take over the fief, married to Penelope, perhaps even starting a family, and just as innocent and naive as he had ever been. Yet if he had it to do all over again, he would not change a thing. He had no regrets for having thrust himself into the world outside the walls of the estate to find out what was there. Would that it were possible to climb into that boat again and sail away, taking Constance with him!

Justin acknowledged the thought then quickly put it out of his mind.

The villagers had already gathered on the bank of the brook just below the drawbridge to watch the spectacle. Understanding now that he would be subjected to the ordeal of being thrown into the stream to see if he would sink or float, Justin began to prepare himself. Since the hermit had taught him how to swim he was not afraid of the water. He would simply allow himself to plummet to the bottom of the creek, which would prove his innocence, and then hope that he would be rescued and pulled back to the bank before he drowned.

With Justin now standing before the assembly for all to see, the lord addressed them:

"Since our previous interrogation of the accused was inconclusive, we find ourselves in a situation where we have no other choice for determining whether Justin is guilty or innocent of the charges that have been brought against him than by carrying out an ordeal, in which we shall ask God himself to render judgment."

Before the lord could continue, the priest stood up and addressed the crowd in a loud voice, "May I remind everyone that the Church does not sanction ordeals and that I am here today solely as a witness to ensure that the correct protocol is not violated."

"I assure you that there will be no trickery," the lord said. "Let us begin the ordeal without further delay."

He then motioned to the guards, who removed Justin's tunic and breeches, revealing the loincloth he was wearing underneath. A rope was tied around Justin's waist. Two guards then picked Justin up and carried him to edge of the brook, while another held the rope.

Before giving the order to cast Justin in, the lord said, "Let us pray."

Everyone bowed their heads except for Justin, who continued looking straight ahead into the water.

"We beseech you, O merciful God," the lord said, raising his arms to heaven, "to reveal the truth to us about the charges that have been leveled against Justin. We shall throw him into the brook here, at its deepest part. If Justin is innocent, please show us a miracle and allow him to sink to the bottom of the brook without drowning. If he floats back up to the surface, however, we shall know that he is guilty."

As soon as the lord had finished praying, he let his arms fall.

The guards threw Justin into the currents. Justin took in a large gulp of air before hitting the water. He allowed himself to sink deeper and deeper until he finally touched bottom, where he folded his knees into a sitting position and flapped his arms gently to hold himself down.

Then he waited. He did not know how long the lord would keep him underwater but felt that he could hold his breath as long as was necessary. He waited some more. There was no tug of the rope, no attempt to rescue him. He was hanging on the best he could, pacing himself by allowing short puffs of air to escape from his mouth. He sensed that the lord was intentionally hindering the guard from pulling him up so that Justin would drown and be done with for good. Justin tried to ignore his urge to dart up to the surface. Just a bit longer, a bit longer.

But then he could wait no more. He was unable to resist his own will to live, his instinct for survival. Involuntarily Justin pushed himself with his legs towards the rippling light above him. His head splashed up through the water. Gasping for air, he remembered the strokes the hermit had taught him and swam back to the bank, where he was hauled ashore by the guards.

Standing there, panting, with body bent, Justin heard the lord say, "Only the devil could have taught him to swim like that!"

"He could have learned on his own," the priest retorted instantly.

"Nay, the result is unambiguous. Justin is clearly guilty!"

"The ordeal proves nothing," the priest replied, "for it was not properly executed. You failed to give the order to pull Justin back up out of the water after it had already been established that he had sunk to the bottom. Had Justin not been able to swim, he surely would have drowned!"

"God has given us his judgment," the lord shot back angrily, "which is always righteous and true."

"Perhaps in your eyes, but not in mine and not in God's."

"Not only in my eyes and God's but also in the eyes of my loyal subjects, who will surely confirm that the ordeal was conducted flawlessly."

Looking out over the peasants, the lord then called out in a loud voice, "Does anyone here question my adjudication?"

The villagers stood by silently, making no reply.

"See," the lord said to the priest. "I have their full confidence and support! There is nothing further for us to discuss. I have not yet decided how Justin shall be punished but will announce his sentence tomorrow."

Justin was helped back into his breeches and his tunic thrown over his shoulders. The guards began leading him and the others back towards the drawbridge, as the crowd quietly dispersed.

§27

Justin was taken back to the dungeon, where he spent a sleepless night, nibbling from the bread he had been given by one of the guards and rationing his water. He could not imagine what his sentence would be. No doubt it would be as severe as Adrian's. Certainly it could not be any worse. And what had happened to Constance? Justin knew that she would not reveal any details that might further incriminate him, but he was still worried about what the lord might do with her.

There was no way for Justin to estimate how long he had been in the chamber. All light was blocked by door and it was impossible for him to hear the clock's bell from inside its thick walls. It seemed like a considerable amount time, however. The lord had said that Justin would be sentenced on the very next day after his ordeal, yet nothing had happened.

Finally the door to the dungeon opened. Apparently it was night again for the only light Justin saw was from the lamp of the guard who came down the steps and handed him another scrap of bread and a new flask of water. The guard then ascended the steps without saying a word.

On what must have been the following night, the guard reappeared with more food and water.

"Why have I not been summoned for my sentencing?" Justin asked him.

The guard made no reply.

A few more days passed, or perhaps weeks or months, Justin could not be sure, punctuated only by the same routine of the guard periodically bringing him bread and water, always at night, saying nothing, then leaving him alone in darkness. Justin languished in his cell, not understanding the long delay.

Finally, tiring of his own despair, Justin sat up straight and cleared his mind, emptying it of all thoughts, all worries, all confusion. He had become an anchorite, confined within the walls of his cell, unable to get out, yet no longer wanting to. It hardly mattered where he was or how long he had been there. He had ceased to exist in space and time. He cared not what he was, what he had done, or what he would do, only *that* he was, just as he is, right here in this place, right now at this moment, something neither he nor anyone else could change. If God is I Am Who I Am, then I, too, am what I am.

§28

Then one day as Justin had been sleeping, he was awakened by the sound of the dungeon bolt being thrust out of its slot. He opened his eyes to see the door being opened. Bright light flooded into the chamber. Two guards came down to get him. When Justin tried to stand up, he found that his knees were wobbly from a lack of movement. As he ascended the stairs the light grew ever more intense, blinding his eyes, which had grown accustomed to being in total darkness.

When he stepped out into the alley, he saw a figure standing before him. The sun was directly behind his head, giving him the appearance of an angel.

"Justin, it's me," the figure said.

Although Justin could still not make out the figure's face, he recognized the voice. It was Bartholomew's!

"I am glad to see you," Bartholomew said, "although I am not at all pleased with the circumstances that brought me here."

"Bartholomew, is that really you?" Justin asked, his voice cracking.

"Indeed, it is I."

"I never expected we would meet again."

"I have heard all the details about your situation and am here to help you," Bartholomew said.

"I do not think there is anything you can do for me at this point," Justin replied.

"It is indeed doubtful that I will be able to offer much assistance with your legal problems. The purpose of my visit is entirely different."

Justin could still not see Bartholomew's face, but the voice was kind and gentle.

"Pray tell me, then, what is the reason for your visit?" Justin asked.

"I have come to save your soul," Bartholomew answered.

"Save my soul?"

"Indeed. I am here with the Inquisition."

"The Inquisition?"

"Yes, I was unable to finish my studies at the university. I simply do not have the aptitude for scholarship. So I gave up my ambitions to become a priest and was called by God to renounce my monastic vows and join the holy Inquisition as a lay assistant. Heresy is spreading like wildfire throughout the realm and there are simply not enough guardians of the faith to keep up with it. There can be no greater vocation than to rescue souls from eternal damnation. It is, I assure you, a most noble and honorable profession."

"So I am to be put on trial for heresy?"

"You have deviated from the sound doctrines of the Church and must be given the opportunity to recant."

Justin's eyes had adjusted well enough that the alley and its surroundings were beginning to come into focus.

"It is clear to me now, Justin, that you have been a liar the entire time I have known you," Bartholomew continued, in a tone that was more sorrowful than accusatory. "Worst of all was the lie you told the abbot. You said that you had not committed any serious crimes just so that he would give you a scholarship for your education but now I find that you have been accused of both revolt and murder!"

Justin hung his head and said, "I must beg forgiveness from both you and the abbot for not having been completely honest about my background and situation."

"Of course, I would forgive you, seventy times seven times if necessary, but the abbot has already passed on to a better world, or at least we hope, so any apologies to him would be futile. In any case, my main concern now is not how you betrayed the abbot and me, but how you have betrayed the Church. In addition to making amends for your past misdeeds, you must also retract your views. That is the purpose of our inquiry today. The inquisitor is waiting for you now in the great hall, which the lord has kindly given us permission to use for your interrogation."

"And what is your role in all of this?"

"I am the inquisitor's deputy. I have no authority over spiritual matters but discharge any duties which the clergy are prohibited from performing."

"I once thought that you were my friend," Justin said.

"I still am!" Bartholomew exclaimed. "Right now I am the best friend you will ever have, Justin."

"Yet you will participate in trying me for heresy."

"Certainly I do not wish to do so, but considering the views you hold, which I have heard with my own ears, there is no choice."

"How did you know where to find me?" Justin asked.

"After you fled our dormitory room that night long ago, I searched everywhere for you. I even wrote a letter to Roland, asking if he knew of your whereabouts. I thought you might try to contact him again, since the two of you were such good chums at the university."

"So it was Roland who informed you that I was being held here." It was now clear to Justin that the other person Roland had alluded to who was itching to make claims against him was not Penelope but Bartholomew.

"Indeed. Immediately after he had seen you, he sent word to me. It was not a mere coincidence but God's will that the two of you crossed paths again. Just as soon as I heard what had happened to you, I relayed the information to the inquisitor, who straightaway dispatched a courier on horseback to the lord demanding that he take no action in your case until we had a chance to speak with you. Fortunately his message arrived just in time!"

"I thought my case has already been decided. All that remains is for me to be sentenced."

"No," Bartholomew said. "The priest has told us about your ordeal. He suspects that subterfuge was involved. It seems that the lord's intention was to simply do away with you by letting you drown."

"So a final decision has not yet been made?"

"The Church is insisting that your case be reviewed before the lord is allowed to proceed any further. While the outcome is uncertain, the charges against you are nonetheless formidable and we fear for your soul. Should you be found guilty and executed before making a full confession of your heretical views and repenting, it would be too late."

Justin could finally see Bartholomew's face clearly. It had become harder and even more determined since he had last seen him, although there was still an unmistakable glint of charity in his eyes.

"You look different," Bartholomew said to him. "I cannot quite say why, but somehow you are different from when I knew you before."

§29

Bartholomew was no longer wearing the black habit Justin had always seen him in, but a plain crimson robe with a pointed hood. The insignia on the guards' uniforms indicated that they belonged not to the lord but to the Inquisition. Bartholomew motioned to the guards to take Justin to the front of the manor, two in front and two behind, with Bartholomew bringing up the rear. Justin noted that his wrists had not been chained this time, as they had been during his trial with Adrian.

Once inside the great hall, the group was met by the inquisitor, the same muscular, handsome inquisitor who had presided over the burning of the preacher. He was seated at the table, with the village priest to his right and a vacant chair to his left. No others were present. Bartholomew promptly occupied the empty seat, leaving Justin standing alone in the center of the room with the four guards behind him.

The inquisitor opened the session with a prayer and then addressed Justin.

"We have heard about the civil charges that have been made against you. As Bartholomew may have told you, we are in the process of appealing the lord's decision to the baron, whom we are asking to convene a new trial for your case. The lord is by no means pleased by this turn of events, but he has graciously acceded to our request to conduct an investigation into the charges of heresy that have also been made against you and to allow you to respond to them. Have you anything to say before we begin these proceedings?"

Justin made no reply.

"I see," the inquisitor said. "Since you refuse to speak, please allow me to read out the charges against you, as conveyed to me by your former associate and my present aide, Bartholomew."

The inquisitor unrolled a scroll which lay on the table before him and began his recitation. The document opened with a brief summary of Bartholomew's struggles to indoctrinate Justin into the Christian faith shortly after he had arrived at the monastery and the precocious manner in which Justin scrutinized everything he was being taught rather than simply assenting to it. Although his questions had at first been seemingly sincere, they were later accompanied by challenging remarks, which gave Bartholomew the distinct impression that Justin never truly accepted the instruction he was being given.

The report then related the story of Justin's examination at the university and his exposition of the theory that words are ultimately meaningless. When asked by the master to state his own views, Justin made a mockery of him by simply wagging his finger. Later Justin had told Bartholomew that all ideas, including our ideas about God himself, are merely human creations, and that one's experience of God takes precedence over the teachings of the Church and holy scripture itself. Christian dogma, in Justin's view, is not eternally valid but subject to revision in light of one's own experience.

Mention was next made of Justin's association with the preacher. Although Justin had never actually joined the Free Spirit group, Bartholomew suspected that he had absorbed many of the preacher's heretical teachings, specifically the beliefs that God exists solely within the created world and not apart from it, that one should put faith in oneself as an incarnation of God, and, therefore, that a person is obliged to follow neither God's commandments nor the secular authorities but solely the spirit within oneself.

The inquisitor concluded with Bartholomew's account of how, on the last night he had seen him, Justin had profaned God by denying his omnibenevolence and omnipotence, claiming that if God is truly good and almighty he would never permit humans to suffer unnecessarily but would be compelled to save them from all misfortunes, whether caused by others, by nature, or even by God himself when exercising his righteous wrath, and concluding, therefore, that God is in fact Satan and should be sentenced to death for his injustices. This last charge, the inquisitor added, was the most serious.

When he had finished reading from the document, the inquisitor then re-rolled the scroll and set it down on the table before him.

"Well, Justin," he said. "How do you reply to these charges?"

Again Justin gave no answer.

"My dear friend," the inquisitor said as beneficently as he could. "Please understand that it is not our wish to see you condemned, but rather to reconcile you both with the Church and with God. It is to your benefit to repent of your sins and heresies, in which case our faithful priest here would grant you absolution and you would be given an appropriate penance. If necessary, however, we may be obliged to employ stronger methods to extract a confession from you."

Justin remained taciturn.

"In the absence of any reply to these charges, you leave us no choice," the inquisitor said finally. "It is indeed unfortunate that this inquiry could not be held in the city, where we would have at our disposal all the necessary implements of torture, which we would apply most mercifully to you. We were unable to carry the rack or wheel with us, however, nor could we find a lawyer able to accompany us for legal counsel. Unfortunately, the doctors are all too busy as well, caring for victims of the plague. So I shall now turn you over to Bartholomew, who shall duly perform his duty within the limits of both the law and medical guidelines, all with the aim, of course, of welcoming you back into the Church's loving arms."

Bartholomew looked at Justin gloomily, then stood up and walked out of the room. The inquisitor's guards took Justin by the arms and dragged him to the door. Justin could see that one of the guards was carrying a whip. On its handle were inscribed in Latin the words *Soli Deo Gloria*— "Glory be only to God."

§30

Bartholomew walked alone, ahead of the group at some distance, heading towards the orchard. Justin noticed that the lawn had been mowed and the trees trimmed. The estate was beginning to return to how it had been before.

Along the way, the guards began to shove Justin about and mock him.

"Why do you heretics always go around claiming to be the Son of God?" one of them asked, striking Justin with his hand.

"Hail to our great spiritual leader!" exclaimed another, spitting in Justin's face. "Let us pay homage to our King!"

"I think we should array him in a purple robe and put a plaited crown of thorns on his head, just like Jesus," said a third.

"And do not forget to give him a reed as his scepter!" said the fourth.

Bartholomew was too far in front to hear what the guards were saying or perhaps simply not paying attention. He walked, eyes straight ahead, without looking back. When he reached the trees at the edge of the orchard, he stopped for a moment to give the group time to catch up and then led them to a clearing, where there was an old tree stump. Justin recognized it as the same stump where he used to sit together with Constance a long time ago. He had returned to the Garden of Eden.

Bartholomew told the guards he wanted some time alone with Justin. After they had stood aside at some distance, Bartholomew looked at Justin imploringly.

"I still consider you my friend," he said. "Please do not force me to torture you."

Justin looked down and did not answer.

Bartholomew placed his hand on Justin's shoulder and smiled gently. "If you would simply make a full confession, everything would be so much easier. Since you expressed your heretical views to me in private and I alone have knowledge of them, there are no other witnesses to corroborate the allegations I have brought against you. I myself am in jeopardy of being charged with making false accusations if you do not fully confess what you know to be true."

"I have nothing to confess," Justin said.

"It would not only be to my advantage, but to yours as well, if you confess, for then you could be reconciled with the Church."

"I have no desire to be reconciled to the Church."

"It may be the only way to save your life, Justin, and certainly the only way to save your soul!"

"I have no soul to save."

"Yet you claim to be a god?" Bartholomew asked.

"So it is said."

"Well, I for one have never claimed that you are a god."

"I am sorry, I did not mean you personally, but the Bible. Are you not familiar with scripture? When Jesus was accused of blasphemy he did not say that he himself was God but instead quoted the Psalm: 'You are gods, all of you, sons of the most high.'"

Bartholomew looked puzzled.

"You do not believe in the Bible?" Justin asked.

"Of course I do," Bartholomew replied. "But if you do not claim to be a god, then how do you think of yourself?"

"I am just an ordinary person."

After a thoughtful pause Bartholomew said, "It makes no difference. The ideas you expound are contrary to Christian teachings and must not be taught to others."

"Whatever beliefs I hold are my own private affair," Justin said. "I have never tried to teach them to others as you have tried to teach your beliefs to me."

"But how can you trust your personal convictions? They may be in error."

"Perhaps they are," Justin replied. "And, if so, then I will simply change them. I am not like the Church, which is unable to admit that it might err because it thinks that the truth it promulgates is absolute and unchanging, the same for all people at all times in all places."

"Indeed, we must have certainty, which is what the Church provides us with. How else could we be sure of our salvation? We cannot be left to our own subjective whims."

Justin looked at Bartholomew earnestly.

"Certainty is the greatest enemy of the truth," he said. "For if we feel certain about something, we are incapable of changing our views, even when we find something better. We must never try to impose what we take as 'certain' on others. They may in fact understand matters much better than we do!"

"You are nothing but a skeptic," Bartholomew said.

"Indeed, I am a skeptic. Yet you know, do you not, that the Greek word *skeptikos* means 'inquirer'? And since inquiry never ceases, skeptics go on searching. Truth is endless and no one can claim to have grasped the whole of it. Should we not test everything and hold fast to what is good? Seek and you shall find. And what we find is that there is always something more to seek. It is only by doubting what we currently believe that we are able to grow and learn new things. Otherwise we end up stuck in the rut of our own minds and can never get out. Do not block the way of inquiry, Bartholomew. Quench not the spirit!"

"Without the authority of the Church, people would be free to believe anything they want!"

"We are constrained only by spiritual discernment and persuasive arguments," Justin said. "Is it not possible for the Church to be a community of inquirers who, together with the rest of humankind, openly share their insights with each other, mutually trying to improve their understanding of the world and their place in it by getting rid of archaic ideas and replacing them with better ones? But instead the Church has become a fossilized institution that simply attempts to force its own inflexible views on everyone, which is precisely why it remains so backward and quaint. Yes, we are part of an ongoing tradition, yet our duty is not to slavishly follow what people believed thousands of years ago, but to be continually renewing and developing that tradition. For that to happen, the Church must allow a plurality of opinions and stop insisting that its own opinions are the only correct ones."

Bartholomew replied, "Justin, the Church can never permit people to substitute their own human opinions for God's own truth. And that also applies to you. How can you possibly presume that you are the only person in the world who comprehends the sense of our religion? Do you really think that you understand Christian principles better than the learned scholars who have spent their lives interpreting the scriptures? Is your spirituality greater than that of the saints? On whose authority do you challenge the one true holy faith, given to us by the perfect lawgiver Christ himself and passed down to us by our ancestors? Do you put your own views above those of the apostles who have spread the gospel to all parts of the earth, the martyrs who have shed their blood for it, and the ecumenical councils that have confirmed the orthodoxy of our creeds? Please do not equivocate but answer candidly."

Justin faced Bartholomew squarely, planting his feet firmly in the ground.

"I place my trust neither in the scriptures nor in the dogmas of the Church, for they are full of contradictions," he said. "Whatever convictions I have are based on my own experience, which cannot be doubted. I will not be convinced by anything if it is contrary to the truths I have learned not through books or teachings, but in life."

"Your so-called 'truths' must still be consistent with plain reason," Bartholomew said.

"Not when common sense is used merely to uphold conventional wisdom or the general consensus."

"We must not be like sheep gone astray, each turning to their own way."

"How can you possibly ask a person to go against their own conscience and deny them the freedom to hold whatever beliefs they choose, if these be in accordance with what they have seen with their own eyes, heard with their own ears, and perceived in their own hearts? I stand here before you. What else can I possibly do? If the Church insists that there are certain things I must believe before it will accept me, then it is the Church that is in error, not me."

"Your convoluted rationalizations are unacceptable, Justin. I ask you once more for a simple answer to a simple question: Do you affirm or do you deny the teachings of the Church?"

"I neither affirm them nor deny them," Justin said.

"I cannot understand. You must do one or the other, but not both."

"There is nothing to understand. It is not necessary to have beliefs about what we experience, any more than we must 'believe' in what we can clearly see with our own eyes."

"Experience alone is insufficient," Bartholomew said. "You must also have faith."

"But I do have faith," Justin replied.

"*Simple* faith, like I told you before."

"You only think your faith is 'simple' because you have lived with it so long and become accustomed to it," Justin said. "My faith is in fact far simpler than yours!"

"Please explain your 'simple faith' to me."

"Simple faith does not mean unquestioningly acceding to all the excessively complicated ideas about God which you have tried to teach me, but rather experiencing the divine within ourselves. The dogmas of the Church are simply irrelevant and make no sense to me."

"But have I not elucidated them to you?" Bartholomew asked.

"Indeed, you have," Justin replied. "And I have learned a great deal from you. I have come to understand that I, like all people, am not a perfect person, that I am capable of doing better than I have actually done, that I must acknowledge my shortcomings and wrongful deeds, since it is only by admitting our faults that we are able to see how we might improve ourselves, that I must confess my sins if not to a priest then to God, the God I find within myself, that I am capable of dying to my old way of life and being resurrected to a new one, of being born again and having my sins washed away, of loving myself as I am and others as they are, of being reconciled both to myself and to those whom I have wronged, of seeking forgiveness and sharing in the sufferings of others, of being transformed through the renewal of my mind and allowing the spirit within me to transform the world, not through any good works of my own but through faith by allowing God to work through me, of praying that God's Kingdom may come among us here and now, that his will be done on earth as it is in heaven, and that we may live together in a new social order of peace and goodwill with the whole of humankind. Surely these are the essentials. What else is required?"

"Everything you have said is so true and perfectly compatible with what the Church and scripture teaches," Bartholomew countered. "But more is demanded of you. You must also believe."

"I have no need for beliefs, for surely they are of little consequence. If something is true, it is true whether we believe it or not. Simply believing something fervently does not make it true and disbelieving it does not make it false."

"Yet I believe and you do not. When I have doubts, I cry out to God, 'I believe. Help thou my unbelief!'"

"Even if there are differences in our ways of thinking, are they not insignificant? We may be divided in our beliefs, but are we not united in the results? I am sure that you are much more fastidious than I am about saying prayers and attending services, but we are both trying to experience what we take to be God, are we not? All the rest is mere theology, which can be endlessly debated, but has it has no bearing whatsoever on what we experience."

"You are so naive, Justin," Bartholomew said. "To avoid heresy, you must also subscribe to true Christian precepts. You must affirm the creed. You must believe that God is our majestic Lord and King, who created the heavens and the earth, and yet dwells not in the things he has made but beyond them, for he is distinct from his creation. You must acknowledge that Jesus is our sure foundation and that Peter is the rock on which Christ has built his Church, which the gates of hell shall never prevail against, and that Peter's successors, who rule over our Church, hold the keys to the Kingdom of Heaven, and that whosoever they bind on earth shall be bound in heaven and whosoever they loose on earth shall be loosed in heaven. And now, since I have been invested with the Church's authority, I have the power to either bind or loose you. I beg you, Justin, to repent and allow me to set you free."

Justin looked at Bartholomew with expressionless eyes.

"This is your last chance, Justin!" Bartholomew cried. "Tell me, what exactly do you believe?"

Justin held up his finger and began wagging it.

Tears began to form in Bartholomew's eyes.

"I cannot believe your impudence," he stammered.

Bartholomew then motioned for the guards to rejoin him.

"Strip him," he said.

The guards removed Justin's tunic. As soon as Bartholomew saw his bare neck, he said, "You are no longer wearing the cross which I gave you."

"Indeed, I buried it."

"You buried it?"

"I no longer had any use for it."

"This is clearly a sign that you have repudiated your Christian beliefs!" Bartholomew exclaimed.

"How could I repudiate my beliefs when I had no beliefs to repudiate?"

Bartholomew turned away in revulsion. He motioned to the guard who had been carrying the whip to hand it to him. The other guards then bent Justin over the stump of the tree and positioned his hands so he was clutching the thick roots growing deep into the soil.

Bartholomew raised his eyes to heaven and said, "Not my will but God's be done. Even if You were to tell me to sacrifice my own son on a pyre, I have an absolute duty to obey You. I must do whatever You command, no matter how wrong it may seem. I give thanks to You, O Lord, that I have a clear conscience, secure in the knowledge that I am simply carrying out Your bidding."

He then pulled back the scourge and struck it on Justin's back. A red stripe immediately appeared. Justin flinched but did not cry out.

"Confess," Bartholomew pleaded, hitting Justin again. "It is not enough for you to simply tell me what you do or do not believe. You must also confess that you are wrong. Admit your errors and withdraw them."

There was no response from Justin. Bartholomew cracked the whip again and again, repeating the word *confess* over and over. Soon Bartholomew was openly weeping, but he did not stop flogging Justin. The lashes became harder and harder, Bartholomew's shrieks louder and louder. The streaks on Justin's back flowed together into a solid film of blood.

Finally one of the guards said, "Sir, do you not think that your blows are excessive?"

"The regulations state that the maximum number is forty," another guard said.

"Do not stop him," a third guard said. "The damnable heretic deserves it."

"No, the purpose of torture is not punishment but repentance," the fourth guard said.

Bartholomew paid no attention to any of the guards, but continued thrashing Justin, until finally, exhausted, he set down the whip, fell to the ground, and began sobbing.

"Why, Justin, why?" he wailed. "Why did you make me do this to you?"

§31

Justin was taken back to the dungeon, where one of the guards, who seemed to be in no mood to treat him gently, threw him down the steps into the cell. Justin landed in a heap on the floor, his back stinging with a pain greater than he had ever felt before. How long he lay there, he did not know. He was neither asleep nor awake. He could not turn over and did not even notice when he was later brought food and water.

Days passed or so it seemed. Then Justin's eyes suddenly fluttered open, only to confront once again the pitch black and total silence of the cell. Near his hand he could feel a half-eaten piece of bread and beside it a water flask, which, when he shook it, he found was half-empty. He could not remember having consumed the bread or drunk the water.

Justin struggled to sit up and, succeeding, ran a finger along his back. It was covered with raised welts, but there was no blood and the pain was no longer sharp but dull. He greedily ate the remaining bread and gulped down the water.

Justin sat alone in silence. Though his body be chained, tortured, and imprisoned, his soul would always be free, he thought, for it was no longer his alone but one with the soul over all. In persecuting Justin, his tormentors had also persecuted themselves. The walls of his cell could no longer contain him. So why try to escape?

Sometime later, Justin heard the bolt turn again in its cylinder. The door opened and light poured into the chamber. A guard came down the steps, shining his lantern first on Justin's back then on Justin's face.

"Your wounds are healing," he said. "The lord wishes to speak with you again."

Pulling Justin to his feet, the guard began helping him up the steps.

"I do not require your assistance," Justin said, breaking loose from the guard's grip. "I can climb the steps perfectly well on my own."

As he stumbled through the door into the alley, Justin's eyes were once again dazzled by the light. He could just barely make out the face of a servant waiting for him, his arms stretched out with an open robe to cover Justin's upper body. The servant caught his breath when he saw the welts on Justin's back protruding from the skin in long ridges. He threw the robe over Justin's shoulders and quickly departed. A detail of guards then appeared in Justin's clouded vision. Justin began to regain his sight and balance as he walked along with them to the entrance of the manor house.

§32

When the group entered the great hall Justin found the lord and the others seated in their usual positions, now joined by the inquisitor and Bartholomew. After Justin had been deposited in the center of the room, the lord gestured dourly to the inquisitor, who had apparently been given permission to speak first.

"In addition to the criminal charges that have been brought against Justin," the inquisitor began with great solemnity, "he has also been accused of holding to doctrines which are contrary to Church dogma. After careful examination, however, we have found that Justin is not guilty of heresy, as originally alleged, but of apostasy, for it seems that he has abandoned his faith and no longer holds to any beliefs whatsoever. Having refused to reaffirm his faith, he has, in effect, renounced it. Nonetheless, Bartholomew has made entreaties on Justin's behalf and in accordance with the great mercy the Church bestows upon all sinners, we still have hope for Justin and are not yet ready to hand him over to the civil authorities for punitive measures to be taken against him."

The lord sat in his chair impassively as the inquisitor continued.

"We are also questioning the results of Justin's ordeal, which the priest claims was not carried out fairly. Rather than reach a verdict on the basis of evidence and testimony as the Inquisition does, the lord has relied on entirely outmoded and arbitrary practices, and apparently tried to bend them to his own will. Surely the methods of the Inquisition are a great advance over earlier forms of justice based on mob rule or the whims of the civil authorities. We have, as you know, appealed to the baron to have the lord's verdict invalidated and are asking that Justin be granted a new trial conducted by unbiased judges and based on sound legal procedures."

The lord interrupted, "It is ironic, is it not, that by insisting on evidence and testimony, the Church is now substituting the judgment of men for the judgment of God, while we, the civil authorities, are prepared to base our final verdict solely upon divine providence in the form of an ordeal."

"You must not confuse your own personal judgment with God's," the inquisitor said. "If one's own opinion is correct it will conform both to the judgment of God and to the judgment of men."

"I assure you that I have not entirely neglected the judgment of men," the lord contested, "but have sought, in accordance with ancient law, to conduct a compurgation, which would allow Justin to profess his innocence under oath. If twelve honorable men could be found who would stake their reputations by swearing that Justin is telling the truth, I would certainly release him."

"A compurgation only establishes the credibility of the accused, not his guilt or innocence," the inquisitor said.

"The point is moot," the lord replied. "For we have not been able to find a single man among the nobility willing to testify on Justin's behalf. We have not consulted any of the serfs, of course, since their word is not to be trusted."

"Indeed, your efforts have been wasted, for compurgation is also a discredited form of judgment that may still be appealed to with respect to debts, but is no longer recognized in the case of felonies, which must be judged solely on the basis of their merits."

"Nonetheless, I shall not let the results of the ordeal be challenged," the lord said, "for it was conducted in a fair and transparent manner, as everyone who was present will certify, including the peasants. It is my intention to see that Justin's sentence is fully commensurate with the crimes he has committed."

"Not before the baron has weighed in on the matter," the inquisitor countered. "I have no doubt that since the evidence against Justin is purely circumstantial and without substantial proof, he will be acquitted of all charges. In any case, the Church should not like Justin to be wrongly executed nor to face the last judgment unrepentant. Our recommendation, therefore, is that you turn Justin over to us, so that he might be confined in the bishop's prison under our supervision for as long as necessary in the hope that after reflecting upon his situation he would eventually repent. We should be most happy to assure him of his eternal salvation if he would simply reconvert to the true Christian faith. Justin may still be turned over to the baron for an impartial trial after that."

"And just how 'impartial' was the torture the Inquisition recently subjected Justin to?" the lord asked. "Do you really think you can extract an honest confession from a man by beating him half to death? It is you, not me, who hands down arbitrary judgments on the basis of your own actions rather than God's."

As the lord was delivering these remarks, Justin glanced over and saw Bartholomew sitting at the table with a cold and stern face. He quickly turned away when he saw Justin looking at him.

The inquisitor then said, "You should know, of course, that the judgments of the Church take precedence over the judgments of the civil authorities, for God is above all. We, therefore, must insist that you place Justin in our custody."

"You are mistaken," the lord replied. "As you should also know, my dear friend, the secular powers are not beholden to the authority of the Church."

"It seems that we have reached an impasse," the inquisitor said, "which can only be resolved by appeal to the Pope, who as the vicar of Christ is God's representative here on earth."

"There is no impasse," the lord cried. "If an appeal is necessary, it should be made not to the Pope but to the king, who has a divine right to govern civil affairs apart from the Church, for he has been ordained directly by God to rule over every person, not only the peasants, but also the clergy and the Inquisition itself. I am fully prepared stand by my original judgment and to proceed with Justin's sentencing."

The inquisitor looked at the lord piercingly.

"Should you do so we shall see that the Church excommunicates you and petition not just the baron but the king to strip you of your privileges!" he said.

The lord remained firm.

"I shall not permit you to intimidate me!" he raged. Then, composing himself again, he added, "There is, however, one further matter which must be settled before we can proceed."

"What is that?" the inquisitor asked.

The lord cleared his throat and spoke in a halting manner which suggested that his words had been carefully chosen and memorized in advance. "You are already familiar with the fact that Justin and my daughter, Penelope, who is sitting here beside me, were married in a formal ceremony in the chapel of this estate by the priest who is also with us today. And you know how on the night of their wedding, Justin so irresponsibly abandoned his new bride."

"Yes, I have heard about this," the inquisitor answered. "And I have also heard that both you and Penelope have claimed that the marriage was never consummated, but that your request to have the marriage annulled was denied by the tribunal unless Penelope were willing to submit herself to an examination to prove her virginity, which you refused to allow."

"Indeed, that was the case. I must now inform you, however, that we are prepared to have Penelope examined and will ask the tribunal to reconsider the case."

"So finally you are willing to have your claim backed up by hard evidence," the inquisitor said.

"Yes!" the lord exclaimed. "And our intention is to prove that the marriage between Justin and Penelope was in fact consummated!"

A gasp went up in the room. No one was more surprised to hear the lord say this than Justin, who quickly cried out, "I assure you that Penelope and I never had any carnal relations with each other!"

"You will speak only when given permission," the lord chastised him.

"Why are you changing your story now?" the inquisitor asked the lord. "You should have told the tribunal the truth from the very start."

"That is easy to explain," the lord replied. "Penelope was so humiliated at the time that she was unable to reveal to anyone what actually happened, not even to me. Just last night, however, she finally told me everything, which is why I, as a man of God, now have a duty to speak the truth and make things right."

"Nonetheless, for Penelope to have originally made a false claim before the tribunal is a mortal sin," the inquisitor said.

Penelope shifted uncomfortably in her seat, looking at her father as if for reassurance. Roland was fidgeting as well, his eyes darting back and forth nervously. Had it been Roland who deflowered Penelope, Justin wondered.

"Indeed," the lord said. "Penelope has committed a lamentable iniquity, even though her actions are completely understandable. She will most certainly confess her sins, beg absolution for them, and perform appropriate acts of penance, as the priest sees fit."

Turning to the priest the lord bowed deeply. "Might I suggest that she be obliged to make a pilgrimage to the city, prostrate herself before the altar of the cathedral, and offer a generous donation to the bishop?"

The priest nodded his approval. "Indeed, pilgrimages, prostrations, and alms-giving are all acceptable ways to demonstrate penitence."

The inquisitor then said, "But if what the lord is saying is true, then Justin should also be returned to Penelope as her lawfully wedded husband."

"Impossible!" the lord replied triumphantly, as if the tide were finally turning in his favor. "For there is one additional charge that must be made against Justin, which I should very much like you to hear."

The lord made a motion with his hand to the guards. They immediately went to the doors of the hall and opened them.

And there, standing in the doorway, was Constance.

§33

Two escorts brought Constance into the room and deposited her in the center of the hall next to Justin. When Justin turned to look, he saw that her face was filled with anxiety. Justin attempted a smile, but the muscles of his mouth would not move.

"The woman before us now is Constance," the lord began, "a peasant girl who was previously employed on this estate but who was expelled by the good bailiff here after it was discovered that she had been carrying on an illicit affair with Justin prior to his marriage to Penelope. We now know that the reason why Justin abandoned my lovely daughter on the night of their wedding was because he wished to be reunited with Constance. We have learned from an old peasant woman that after Justin arrived in the village, he took up residence with Constance in her home, together with her brother, the usurper Adrian, and made a proposal of marriage to her, despite the fact that he had just been legally married to Penelope."

"But no wedding was performed between Constance and I!" Justin protested.

"I have already admonished you not to speak without permission," the lord fulminated. Then turning to the inquisitor he continued, "What Justin has just said is correct. There was no wedding. Nonetheless, Adrian was prepared to announce their betrothal at the harvest festival until events intervened. In the aftermath of the revolt against the previous lord of this estate, Justin left the village and fled to a monastery, where he sought to conceal himself and avoid prosecution. From there, you know the story of how Justin met Bartholomew and the two headed off to university together."

"Indeed," the inquisitor said.

"The old woman also told us that upon his recent return to the village, Justin began living together with Constance and to commit habitual acts of adultery with her, in violation of his vows to Penelope, his lawful wife."

"How could the woman possibly know what happened between Constance and me?" Justin asked.

"Justin, I am warning you for the last time," the lord said coldly. "You may only speak when you are spoken to. I shall not remind you again."

"Are you saying that the old woman actually spied on them and witnessed their deeds?" the inquisitor asked.

"I assure you that she was not being prurient," the lord said. "But, indeed, she peered in on them through their window and saw everything that Justin and this shameless hussy did together with each other."

Justin and Constance looked at each other, unable to conceal their dismay.

"If so, then Justin's actions go far beyond adultery," the inquisitor said. "For by cohabitating with Constance, he in fact entered into a common-law marriage with her. Even in the absence of a formal ceremony, Justin is guilty of bigamy."

"That is my point exactly," the lord said. "Justin has not only violated the sacrament of marriage but also committed a public crime, punishable to the same extent as the other charges made against him."

It was obvious now that this was a backup plan the lord had carefully prearranged in the event that Justin could not be convicted of treason or heresy.

Turning next to Justin the lord asked, "In addition to the other heinous crimes you have been accused of, what do say to this new charge? Now you may speak."

"I cannot be guilty of bigamy," Justin said. "For, as I have already told you, my marriage with Penelope was never consummated."

"But we shall soon have proof that it was," the lord said.

"If she has lost her virginity, it must have been to another man!" Justin objected, looking directly at Roland, who was nervously taking the gold ring off his finger and putting it back on again.

"How dare you insult my daughter in such a way!" the lord cried, banging his hand on the table.

"I would swear an oath before any court of law that nothing happened between Penelope and myself on the night of our wedding!" Justin exclaimed.

At this point Bartholomew stood up from the table and said, "No one would believe you, Justin, for I myself would be willing to testify before the tribunal that you are a habitual liar. No doubt you would say anything to try to wriggle out of the numerous charges that have been made against you."

After Bartholomew had sat back down in his seat, the lord said, "If Justin had merely engaged in sexual acts with Constance with no intention of taking her as his wife, his deeds might be excused as a mere moral infraction better handled by the Church than the civil authorities. There is, after all, ample precedent for members of the nobility who are unable to resist temptation to take peasant girls at their will, even to ravish them with impunity, it being well-known that they are incapable of love and unable to appreciate any refinement in such matters."

Constance glared at the lord upon hearing these words. The inquisitor was about to say something, but the lord cut him off.

"That Justin took on a second wife when he was already lawfully wedded to Penelope is inexcusable, however. For having abandoned my daughter, who has suffered so greatly and unjustly, the penalty I impose on Justin shall not be lenient."

The lord then looked directly at Constance.

"As for you, you horrible creature," he said, "your intention to steal Justin away from my daughter is a grievous offense not only against Penelope but also against God and the realm. This despicable wickedness shall not go unpunished, nor shall your impertinent refusal to swear an oath of loyalty to me as your lord and Roland as your new master be overlooked."

Justin glanced over at Constance. Her head was unbowed. The lord then stood up and leaned over the table.

"I shall, therefore, give you a choice," he said. "If you are willing to repent of your sinful deeds and publicly affirm your allegiance to us, we shall drop our charges against you. Roland shall take you into his own household and you will become a maidservant of Penelope's, whom you shall serve to the end of your days. If you refuse this offer, however, then we shall bring the full force of the law against you and see that you are rightfully punished in a manner similar to Justin's."

Constance looked down and was thoughtful for a moment, but only a moment.

She then raised her head and said softly, "I choose to accept your offer, my lord. I shall confess my sins to the priest and profess my everlasting faithfulness to you, to Roland, and to Penelope."

The lord smiled exultantly. Justin was not sure what to make of Constance's announcement, although it had seemed entirely sincere.

Then Constance added, "But only on one condition."

"And what might that be?" the lord asked.

"That I may keep my cat."

"Your cat? Indeed. I had thought not to mention this, but I have also heard from the old woman that you consort with a black cat and frequently visit the forest at night to perform satanic rituals."

Justin, unable to contain himself, immediately began raving, "Those are pure fabrications! Constance is hardly a witch!"

"It certainly seems that she has cast a spell on you!" the lord roared back. "And, as we all know, the punishment for witchcraft is strangulation."

"Your abuse of the law is reprehensible," the inquisitor excoriated the lord. "You cannot base your judgment on the idle babble of an old gossip whose testimony lacks all credibility."

"I shall not press the matter, even though I think it should be in the Church's interest to prosecute cases of witchcraft."

"Indeed, we would, but only if first presented with sufficient evidence, which you obviously lack."

"I assure you that black cats are not from the devil," Constance said. "They have been created by God just the same as you and me."

"All right then, you may keep your cat!" the lord snapped. Then turning to Justin he said, "See how easily Constance has betrayed you. She has no loyalty whatsoever to you. What else might be expected from a whore? But do not worry. We shall reform her and make her into a lady whom everyone would be able to admire. Have you anything to say?"

"Indeed, I would also admire you if you are able to tame her," Justin said.

"It shall be my pleasure to try. I rather take a fancy to her."

The lord then looked at Constance in the same lascivious way that Martin had looked at her at the harvest festival when he threatened to rape her. Justin felt the blood begin to boil inside him. He rushed towards the table where the lord was sitting, his hands outstretched, ready to grab him by the throat, but he was quickly restrained by the guards.

Tussling in their grip he blurted out to the lord, "And I should like to kill you in the same way I killed Martin!"

There was a moment of stunned silence. Then everyone began talking back and forth all at once. This went on for some time until the lord finally raised his hand and said, "So, you finally admit to having slain the guard."

"Yes, I did," Justin said. "And I helped Adrian plan the first revolt and had every intention of murdering my own father if I'd had the opportunity to do so!"

The priest immediately rose from his chair and approached Justin.

"I am glad that you have finally told everyone the truth," he said.

"Indeed, I have already confessed all these sins to this priest," Justin said, looking not at the priest but at the lord. "There is nothing further I need to do."

"There is still the matter of your apostasy," the priest said. "Would you repent now and be restored to the Church?"

"I have nothing to repent of."

"Even though it would not overturn your conviction, you still have the power to put yourself right with God and receive your just reward in heaven."

"I have no power whatsoever, not even God's," Justin said, still looking at the lord. "The Church and the authorities have arrogated all power for themselves. Do with me as you wish."

The priest bent down and kneeled before Justin.

"I humbly implore you to confess your sins, Justin," he said. "I have known you since you were a baby. When I was a young priest, only slightly older than you are now, I baptized you at the chapel. At that time I truly believed I had received a prophecy from God that you would become a great spiritual leader."

"I am no great spiritual leader," Justin said. "I am just an ordinary person."

"I am not sure how I erred," the priest went on. "But I must seriously examine my soul to see why I was so woefully wrong and ask God for his forgiveness. And you should do the same, Justin. To betray your own religion is a grave matter. You must submit to the Church and pray for God's mercy."

Justin then looked straight into the eyes of the priest but said nothing. The priest stood up, faced the inquisitor, and shook his head sadly.

"Justin, your intransigence defies belief," the inquisitor said. "Not only have you admitted your guilt before the law, but you also refuse to accept the most generous offer of grace which the priest has extended to you. I hereby wash my hands of you and turn you over to the lord for him to mete out whatever punishment he thinks is appropriate. The Church withdraws its previous pleas for leniency in your case."

At this point, Justin saw Bartholomew press his hands together in prayer, tears falling from his eyes.

The lord then said, "You are perfectly correct on one point, Justin. I hold absolute power over you as your lord and master. But you must still be reconciled with the Church. It would be better for you to confess to the priest now before you are sentenced. You will not be given a second chance."

Justin was unmoved. He continued looking straight ahead brazenly. Receiving no reply, the lord finally said, "Justin, you are so naive."

Then looking about the room, the lord addressed all present, "Since it has now been established beyond any shadow of a doubt that Justin is guilty of all the crimes he has been accused of, against both the state and the Church, I hereby sentence him to death."

Justin felt Constance's hand reaching for his, but he brushed it aside.

"In anticipation of this outcome to Justin's trial, I have given a significant amount of thought about the method by which Justin should be executed," the lord resumed. "Were it my choice I would prefer that he be sawn in half through the groin. I would be equally delighted to see his belly slit open and stuffed with rats to feast on his intestines or to have him eviscerated so that he could watch his entrails being burned before him. Even to have him executed in the same manner as Adrian would be quite satisfactory. It has been reported that Adrian was still cursing and screaming obscenities when his skinned torso, stripped of its limbs, was thrown onto the fire."

Standing up, the lord began pacing the room, calm and assured, knowing now that he was fully in control and that no one would challenge him.

"It is my intention, however, to keep Justin's body intact," he said, "partly out of deference to the Church's dictum against the shedding of blood and partly so that he may be put on full display as a reminder to the people of the dangers of both apostasy and insurrection against the established authorities. There is one exception, however. Following the suggestion, which I find most exquisite, of my wronged daughter, Penelope, Justin shall first be castrated in retribution for having abandoned his disconsolate wife, who has suffered so greatly and unjustly as a result of his callous disregard of her. Those who distain the sanctity of marriage should not be permitted to enter eternity with the ability to commit such offenses still intact."

A large smirk appeared on Penelope's face. Roland had stopped fidgeting and was snickering as well.

The lord continued, "After his emasculation, Justin will be brought before the people, whom we shall invite to witness the execution. In the same way that Judas betrayed his lord and master and then hanged himself, Justin shall be hung by the neck with a rope until dead for having betrayed both his temporal lords and celestial masters. His body will then be placed in a gibbet and suspended from the turret of this manor house as carrion for the crows and vultures. After three days the corpse shall be taken down and transported to the village, where it shall remain in the square for all to see until Justin's flesh has melted away and his bones have turned to dust."

The lord paused for a moment and then concluded, "That is my decision. This court is now adjourned."

Justin turned to look at Constance, but she was already being hustled out of the room by two guards. She tried to turn her head to see him, but the guards quickly jerked her away.

§34

Justin was then taken not to the dungeon, but to the blacksmith's workshop to be fitted for his gibbet.

"The lord has told us that he wants the gibbet to be tight enough to keep the body upright," the guard in charge told the blacksmith. "But the spaces between the bands should be wide enough for the birds to eat his flesh and the upper face left open so they may pluck out his eyes."

"I know what I am doing," the blacksmith replied irritably.

Justin was next returned to his chamber, where he sat again in darkness. He did not regret having defended Constance or making a full confession before the lord. He still refused to acknowledge that either the lord or the Church had any authority over him but could no longer bear the incessant legal wrangling and machinations. Why is it that the law so often prevents people not from doing what is wrong but from doing what is right? Most of all Justin was tired of living a lie. Which is better: to pretend to be someone you aren't just for the sake of others or to be true to yourself even if they crucify you? Social stability, it seems, cannot be maintained in the absence of lies and whoever tries to live authentically will be crushed. Whosoever would save his life shall lose it; whosoever shall lose his life will save it.

It was not punishment that Justin feared, but rather his own inability to control himself. He rebuked himself for having lost his temper, for still having had the desire of wanting, really wanting, to kill another person. Would he have actually strangled the lord? Yes, if he'd had the opportunity!

Even when we are redeemed, he thought, we still continue to sin. In a loud voice that echoed against the walls of his cell, Justin repented and asked both himself and the lord for forgiveness, despite no one being there to hear him. By acknowledging his temptation, it no longer had any control over him. The impulse was still there, to be sure, but the desire to act on it had been vanquished.

What would happen next? Justin was once again in a tight situation and had no plan for dealing with it. This time, however, it seemed that there was no way out. He could hardly expect any friends to visit him in prison and help him flee into exile. Or the peasants to revolt again, overthrow the lord, and liberate him. Or a yeoman outlaw and his merry band to suddenly appear and rescue him. Or Constance to come and magically spirit him away to a place beyond the horizon where they could live happily ever after. Or even God to descend on a machine from heaven and suddenly make everything right. Indeed, life was governed by fate, not destiny. Things must be accepted just as they are, not as we want them to be.

Then there was nothing more to think, nothing more to do. He began to follow his breathing again but realized he no longer needed to. His mind was already empty.

After what must have been a few days, the door of the dungeon opened and the guard informed Justin that the time of his execution had arrived.

It is finished, Justin thought. Today is a good day to die.

§35

Justin's gibbet, assembled now and gleaming in the sun, had been set next to the wagon that would serve as the scaffold for the hanging. The gallows consisted of a single upright post with a horizontal beam jutting out from the top, supported by a diagonal brace. A noose dangled over the floorboards of the wagon, a hook having been drilled into the bar to keep the rope in place.

Unable to walk to the wagon, which had been situated on the lawn between the house and the orchards, Justin had to be carried there by two guards. Despite the bandages, blood was trickling down Justin's thighs and dripping onto the ground. The guards lifted Justin up a short flight of wooden steps to the bed of the wagon, holding him firmly in a standing position beside the noose so he would not fall down. Justin's back was to the horses that would pull the wagon out from under him when the lord gave the word. A stableman in waiting was holding the reins.

The executioner who followed the guards up the steps was a tall man wearing an iron mask that completely covered his head, with only two slits for his eyes. As he was tying Justin's hands behind his back, he said to him in a low voice, "I do not wish to do this to you, but I have been ordered to. I am just an ordinary man, you know. I do as I'm told."

Justin did not reply but looked out at the faces of those who had assembled in the yard to witness the execution. Standing in the very front row were the lord, Roland and Penelope, the inquisitor and Bartholomew, the bailiff and the priest, in the same order as at his trial. Just behind Penelope was Constance, held tightly by a guard. Beside Constance was the feisty young woman. Her mother was nowhere to be seen. The servants still in the employ of the lord stood to one side, while the remaining villagers were scattered across the lawn.

In the distance, leaning against an apple tree in the orchard apart from the others was the old hermit, Fisher, his face shielded from the sun and cast in dark shadows. He was wearing the new tunic and breeches which Constance had given him. Justin thought he could also see the silhouette of another figure standing in the umbra of the forest not far from the old tree stump where he used to meet Constance. He was clothed in a black cloak with a black hood pulled down over his eyes.

Justin looked at Constance. With a mighty effort, he succeeded in giving her a wan but sincere smile. She smiled back at him, holding up her black cat. Constance then tapped the lord on his shoulder.

"Might I have one last word with him?" she asked.

"For heaven's sake no!" the lord replied angrily.

"Allow her," Penelope said softly to her father. "For she has truly loved Justin in a way that I would never have been able to."

The lord looked at Penelope, then nodded his consent to Constance. The guard released Constance. She walked to the foot of the steps but did not climb them.

"I have brought Charm with me for good luck," she said in a voice that was just barely audible.

"There is no such thing as luck," Justin replied feebly, hoping that Constance could hear him. "But I am sure that you will have many suitors."

"Yet it will always be you whom I love."

No, Justin thought, Constance had not abandoned him, nor would he abandon her, even after he had breathed his last. Their lives had each been a candle, glowing brightly. Put the two flames together and the light grows even stronger. But now it was time for the candles to be separated. The flame on one of the candles would be snuffed out, but the other would keep on burning. Yet the flame was not only hers, but his as well.

"I shall not see you again." Justin said.

"I know," Constance replied, her voice breaking. "Yet you shall be with me always and I with you."

Constance turned and went back to her position in the crowd. The guard did not grab onto her, however, but let her stand freely next to her friend, the young woman.

The priest then ascended the steps. Kneeling directly in front of Justin, he said, "Repent, my son, and pray for forgiveness."

"It is I who should forgive you," Justin responded. "And I pray that God will forgive you as well."

"You have it backwards, Justin. We need forgiveness neither from you nor from God, for we stand on the side of righteousness. It is you who must repent. This is your very last chance to save your soul from eternal hellfire."

"I should prefer to commit my spirit into the hands of the Father himself than to the powers of this world," Justin said.

"Indeed, you must submit to God, but also to the Church and those whom God has appointed as our rulers."

The tall executioner placed a coarse black blindfold over Justin's eyes and tied it behind his head.

"Submit," the priest said. "Submit."

The hangman then put the noose over Justin's head.

"Submit," the priest said again.

The young woman turned to Constance and murmured, "This priest is so ignorant."

"He doesn't know what he's doing," Constance said, not taking her eyes off Justin.

"If God is willing to forgive Justin's sins, then why not everyone else?" the woman asked. "Even if he is guilty, Justin deserves mercy, not justice."

The knot was tightened around Justin's neck, forcing him to gag slightly. He could still hear the voice of the priest asking him over and over again to submit, then joined by the sound of Bartholomew weeping uncontrollably as the clock struck five.

The lord motioned to the stableman. The two guards who had been propping Justin up let go and quickly descended the steps, with the hangman and the priest just behind them. The stableman prodded the horses and the cart slowly pulled away from the gallows.

The rope stretched taut. Justin began to choke as the cord slowly strangled him. He struggled instinctively but vainly to raise his tied hands and loosen the ligature around his neck. His body twitched and lurched from side to side. He continued convulsing a while longer until his very last breath was cut off. Then his body went limp, swinging back and forth in the wind, the rope creaking in its hook.

"Behold the man!" the lord proclaimed loudly. "Justice has been served!"

In a barely audible voice the young woman said, "Surely this man was innocent."

"We shall not forget you, Justin," Constance whispered tearfully. "You will be resurrected in our hearts and live there now and evermore. The same spirit that guided you shall guide us as well, now and forever."

"And we shall carry on with the mission we started together with you," the woman added. "Perhaps someday, if not in our lifetimes then before the close of the age, our vision shall be realized and we shall all live together in love and peace and freedom."

Justin's body was taken down from the gallows and placed into the gibbet, which was then fastened shut and carried back into the manor house, where it was carried up to the turret. Constance and the others could see the guards attach the gibbet to a chain hanging from a pole which protruded out from the tower. The body was perfectly perpendicular to the tower's circular wall. The familiar wold was in the distance. The setting sun cast a golden nimbus round Justin's head.

The next morning, although no one was there to witness it, the sun rose again out of the sea, illuminating Justin's face with scarlet light. On the third day the gibbet with Justin's body, torn by the birds but still in one piece, was taken to the village and hung in the square, just as the lord had ordered.

§36

After that everything returned to how it had been before. The peasants went back to their fields, the priest to his rectory, the bailiff to his stone house, the guards to their barracks, the servants to their quarters. Roland's first act after taking charge of the manor was to have the wall rebuilt and fortified, permission having been obtained from the baron. After returning from her excursion to the city to do penance, Penelope was duly ensconced as second-in-command, with Constance as her maid. While she allowed Constance to continue caring for the cat, Penelope claimed Charm as her own and in time had many suitors.

Then one morning Constance and her cat were nowhere to be found on the estate. The boat that had been moored at the dock near the drawbridge was also missing.

Annotations

A theological novel written in reply to Dostoyevsky's *The Brothers Karamazov* and Tolstoy's *The Kingdom of God Is Within You, One With the Father* stands at the intersection between mysticism and anarchism in the Christian heritage, while simultaneously interweaving insights and archetypes from a variety of other spiritual traditions—Eastern, Western, and indigenous—into what is hopefully a fast-paced, engaging narrative. With its controversial, even subversive, religious and political themes, this novel will certainly not be for everyone, though some may find that the wisdom articulated by the sages of old speak as much to the enigmas of the present as to those of the past. The advantage of including philosophical passages and dialogues (in the tradition of Plato and Berkeley) in a work of fiction is that various positions may simply be presented, rather than advocated or seen as expressions of the author's own personal views, so that readers may make of the arguments what they will. My hope is that those who reach the end of the book will feel not that they have been given an answer but rather that they have been asked a question, possibly more than one.

Parts of the novel are intended to reveal the tremendous amount of theological diversity within Christian thought, as well as similarities between Christianity and other spiritual traditions, all of which are part of our common human heritage. Cultural appropriation is not at all inappropriate if done appropriately. Fritz G. Wallner in "Intercultural Philosophy: The Viennese Program" in *Intercultural Philosophy: New Aspects and Methods,* ed. Fritz G. Wallner, Florian Schmidsberger, and Franz Martin Wimmer (Frankfurt am Main: Peter Lang GmbH, 2010), p. 16, uses the term *strangification* to refer to a process of transferring ". . . a proposition system from its original context to a different context"; for a practical application, see Vincent Shen, "Appropriating the Other and Transforming Consciousness into Wisdom: Some Philosophical Reflections on Chinese Buddhism" in *The Dialogue of Cultural Traditions: A Global Perspective,* pp. 283–305, ed.

William Sweet, George F. McLean, Tomonobu Imamichi, Safak Ural, and O. Faruk Akyol (Washington, DC: The Council for Research in Values and Philosophy, 2008).

A related concept is *integration,* which involves combining ideas from different cultural systems into a relatively coherent higher-order conceptual framework or "third culture" (*cf.* hybridity, pastiche, eclecticism, syncretism, bricolage); see Richard Evanoff, "Integration" in *Key and Contested Concepts in Intercultural Discourse,* ed. Monika Kirloskar-Steinbach, Gita Dharampal-Frick, and Minou Friele (München: Verlag Karl Alber, 2012), pp. 139–145. An excellent example of an attempt to integrate insights from Buddhist and other traditions into a Christian framework is Benjamin Riggs, *Finding God in the Body: A Spiritual Path for the Modern West* (Shreveport [Louisiana, USA]: Benjamin Riggs, 2017).

The plot and situations in the novel are entirely original and the characters purely fictional. Any resemblance to real persons either living or dead is purely coincidental. Like folksongs and the Bible itself, the novel includes numerous allusions, often in the form of quotes and misquotes, paraphrases and misparaphrases, from a variety of sources, in some cases intentionally taken out of context or presented tongue in cheek. Whereas plagiarism involves copying someone's work with the hope it will remain undetected, allusions assume readers will know that a given phrase or passage is taken from other sources. Since the allusions in this novel are derived from a wide variety of works, some of which may be obscure and not widely known, all the original source materials have been meticulously documented in these annotations for any who may be interested. How these sources should be interpreted in the context of the novel is an entirely different matter, of course. The novel has been written in a way, however, which requires no prior knowledge or other background information on the part of general readers.

While no quotation marks or citations are given in the text itself (to avoid clutter), the references provided below can be easily matched to the appropriate passages in the respective sections of the text. Direct and near-direct quotes are taken only from works and translations not currently under copyright. No copyright violations have been committed. Unless otherwise noted, scriptural references are adapted from the American Standard Version of *The Holy Bible* (New York: Thomas Nelson and Sons, 1901), which is in the public domain, although often with changes in wording and other modifications. With all sources, my general approach is not exegetical (trying to determine the intended meaning of an author), but eisegetical (reading one's own meanings into a text). Scripture itself has been more or less interpreted in this way for the past two thousand years anyway, whether consciously acknowledged or not. The novel playfully draws on the insight of recent literary criticism that the same text can be interpreted in highly different, even contradictory, ways, depending on the intentions of the interpreter.

While there is no pretense that *One with the Father* is entirely "realistic" or completely accurate in its portrayal of how people in the Middle Ages thought, spoke, and lived, the details are nonetheless, for the most part, historically authentic. In some ways the book qualifies as metafiction, loosely defined as "a novel which imitates a novel rather than the real world"; see John Barth, "The Literature of Exhaustion" in *Metafiction,* pp. 161–171, ed. Mark Currie (London: Routledge, 1995 [1967]), p. 161. At times the novel intentionally conflates different geographical areas, historical periods, and religious traditions within the framework of the story, and includes occasional inaccuracies, as well as cultural, literary, philosophical, and theological anachronisms, all of which are duly noted below. I prefer to acknowledge these myself to the extent possible rather than have them pointed out by others. If any errors remain, I will be happy to correct or note them in any future editions of this book.

GENERAL

The following works were consulted for general information about medieval life and history: John Guy, *Medieval Life* (Oxford: Bodleian Library, 1995); *The Plantagenet Encyclopedia,* ed. Elizabeth Hallam (New York: Crescent, 1996); May McKisack, *The Fourteenth Century: 1307–1399* (Oxford: Oxford University Press, 1959); David Nicolle, *The Medieval World: Civilization from 1000 to 1500 A.D.* (New York: Barnes and Noble, 1997); Norman Cohn, *The Pursuit of the Millennium: Revolutionary Millenarians and Mystical Anarchists of the Middle Ages,* 2nd ed. (New York: Oxford University Press, 1970); and Ian Forrest, *The Detection of Heresy in Late Medieval England* (Oxford: Oxford University Press, 2005).

I. THE ESTATE

§2. The novel is set in the mid-fourteenth century in an unspecified area with a topography similar to that of Lincolnshire, England, the "ocean" being the North Sea (obviously there is no point in Europe from which it is possible to watch the sun rise over the Atlantic Ocean). Justin's view from the turret is based on a mandala in the form of a cross, with five points: a center (the turret); east (dawn, birth, water, spring); south (noon, youth, earth, summer); west (dusk, maturity, air, autumn); and north (night, death, fire, winter). The mandala has affinities with the one described in Joseph Epes Brown, *The Spiritual Legacy of the American Indian* (Wallingford: Pendle Hill, 1964), pp. 13–16; see also *Black Elk Speaks,* as told to John G. Neihardt (New York: Pocket, 1959), Chap. 3. The mandala reappears in Part III, §31 of the novel.

§3. Descriptions of medieval weaponry and the life of knights in general can be found in Andrea Hopkins, *Knights* (New York: Shooting Star, 1990). The term *bailiff* is used in this novel to designate a medieval *Advocatus* or *Vogt,* who manages affairs on a fief, not a modern legal official.

§4. Medieval education consisted of the seven traditional liberal arts: the *trivium* (grammar, rhetoric, and logic) and the *quadrivium* (arithmetic, geometry, astronomy, and music). Alchemy was practiced in the ancient cultures of both the East and the West; for an introduction to medieval European alchemy, see Lawrence M. Principe, *The Secrets of Alchemy* (Chicago: University of Chicago Press, 2013), Chap. 3. On the relation between alchemy and both psychology and religion, see Carl Jung, *Psychology and Alchemy,* 2nd ed., trans. R. F. C. Hull, Vol. 12 of the *Collected Works of C. G. Jung,* ed. Herbert Read, Michael Fordham, Gerhard Adler, and William McGuire (Princeton: Princeton University Press, 1968 [1952]). Archetypal sorcerers include Simon Magnus and Merlin; see Robert De Boron, *Merlin* [late 12th–early 13th century] in *Merlin and the Grail,* pp. 45–114, trans. Nigel Bryant (Cambridge: D. S. Brewer, 2001). "God created the universe in the same way that humans make a clock" is derived from the analogy between a watch and a watchmaker found in William Paley's *Natural Theology: Or, Evidences of the Existence and Attributes of the Deity, Collected from the Appearances of Nature,* 2nd ed. (London: R. Faulder, 1802). The pseudo-scientific concept of "intelligent design" associated with creation science is forcefully criticized by the evolutionary biologist, Richard Dawkins, in his book, *The Blind Watchmaker: Why the Evidence of Evolution Reveals a Universe without Design* (New York: Norton, 1996). The notion that God created the world and then had no further involvement with it is a central tenet of deism. The quote "If God did not exist, it would be necessary to invent him" is translated from Voltaire's *Épître à l'Auteur du Livre des Trois Imposteurs* [1770] and appears in James Parton's *Life of Voltaire* (Boston: Houghton, Mifflin, 1882), Vol. 2, p. 554. The notion that external forces are necessary for the world to be made can be traced back to surviving Paleolithic artifacts, which suggest that creation was seen either as birth or as analogous to human craftsmanship; the invention of pottery in Neolithic times likely gave rise to several prehistoric myths in which ". . . the creator-god is imagined as a divine potter who fashions men out of clay";

quoted from the *Encyclopedia of World Mythology,* produced by Phoebus and Octopus (New York: Galahad, 1975), p. 13. In Hesiod's *Theogony,* Earth (Gaia) bears Heaven (Uranus) and Sea (Pontus), as well as Mountains (Ourea); see Hesiod, *Theogony and Works and Days,* pp. 1–33, trans. M. L. West (Oxford: Oxford University Press, 1988 [c. 700 BCE]), pp. 6–7. Plato's [c. 428–347 BCE] writings on the demiurge can be found in the *Timaeus* in *The Dialogues of Plato,* pp. 442–477, trans. Benjamin Jowett, Vol. 7 of *Great Books of the Western World,* ed. Robert Maynard Hutchins (Chicago: William Benton, 1952), §28, p. 447. Aristotle's [385–322 BCE] writings on the unmoved mover can be found in the *Physics* in Vol. 1 of *The Works of Aristotle,* pp. 259–355, trans. R. P. Hardie and R. K. Gaye, Vol. 8 of *Great Books of the Western World,* ed. Robert Maynard Hutchins (Chicago: William Benton, 1952), VIII, §5, 256a–258b, pp. 340–344. Following Aristotle, Thomas Aquinas in *The Summa Theologica,* trans. Fathers of the English Dominican Province, revised by Daniel J. Sullivan, Vol. 19 of *Great Books of the Western World,* ed. Robert Maynard Hutchins (Chicago: William Benton, 1952 [c. 1265–1273]), Vol. 1, First Part, Question 3, Article 3, p. 13, wrote that because it is impossible for something to move itself, it must be moved by something else, but since the chain of movers cannot be infinite, there must be ". . . a first mover which is moved by no other, [which] everyone understands to be God." The principle of self-organization is implicit in Darwin's theory of natural selection in *The Origin of Species* (Harmondsworth: Penguin, 1968 [1859]) and can be applied to the evolution of the universe as a whole at the physical, chemical, biological, psychological, and sociological levels; see Erich Jantsch, *The Self-Organizing Universe: Scientific Implications of the Emerging Paradigm of Evolution* (Oxford: Pergamon, 1980). Chaos and complexity theory further investigate how order breaks down; see Mitchell M. Waldrop, *Complexity: The Emerging Science at the Edge of Order and Chaos* (New York: Touchstone, 1992). "There is nothing in the mind that was not first in the senses" is a near direct quote from Thomas Aquinas, *Truth [Quaestiones disputatae de veritate],* trans. Robert W. Mulligan (Chicago: Henry Regnery, 1952 [1256–1259]), Vol. 1, Question 2, Article III, Argument 19, p. 69. Scriptural sources: Gen 1:1–2; John 2:1–11; Acts 8:9–24; 1 Cor 12:27.

§5. Scriptural sources: Gen 3:6.

§6. This section provides a summary of the medieval cosmology known as the "Great Chain of Being"; see Arthur O. Lovejoy, *The Great Chain of Being: A Study of the History of an Idea* (Cambridge: Harvard University Press, 1964 [1933]). The word *fief* refers to a unit of land of any size that is granted by an overlord to a vassal, regardless of rank. The words *manor* and *estate* may be used interchangeably to refer to the smallest unit

390 O N E   W I T H   T H E   F A T H E R

of land controlled by a single lord, usually of the lowest rank. In this novel, however, depending on the context, the word *manor* is sometimes used as short for the *manor house,* where a lord lives, while *estate* is generally used to refer to the grounds within the walls surrounding and including the manor house. Manor houses are described in Philip Warner, *The Medieval Castle* (New York: Barnes and Noble, 1993 [1971]), pp. 233–234. General details about life inside large estates are taken from Fiona MacDonald and Mark Bergin, *A Medieval Castle* (London: Simon and Schuster, 1990) and R. J. Unstead, *See Inside a Castle* (New York: Barnes and Noble, 1986). A classic work on chivalry is Baldassare Castiglione, *The Book of the Courtier,* trans. by Charles S. Singleton (Garden City: Doubleday, 1959 [1528]). Scriptural sources: Gen 1:1, 26; Ps 8:5–8; Jer 23:24; Luke 14:11; Rom 13:1; Heb 1:14; 2:7; 1 John 3:20.

§8. An oblique allusion is made to Stéphane Mallarmé's "blankness of the white paper," cited in Jacques Derrida, *Dissemination,* trans. Barbara Johnson (London: Athlone, 1981 [1972]), p. 230; *cf.* Stéphane Mallarmé's poem "A Throw of the Dice Will Never Abolish Chance" ["Un Coup de des Jamais N'Abolira le Hasard"], trans. Daisy Aldan (New York: Tiber Press, 1956 [1897]).

§10. Justin's privileged and sheltered surroundings as a youth resemble those of Siddhartha Gautama [the Buddha, 5th–4th century BCE] and Francis of Assisi [c. 1181–1226]; see the annotations for Part I, §13 and II, §5. Other archetypal examples might be the characters Freder in the movie, *Metropolis,* directed by Fritz Lane (Babelsberg: UFA, 1927) and Truman Burbank in *The Truman Show*, directed by Peter Weir (Los Angeles: Paramount Pictures, 1998). Scriptural sources: Gen 1:1; 2:7–3:24.

§12. The first poem was inspired by the Song of Solomon. Lines 1, 2, and 4 of the second poem are adapted from Song of Solomon 3:1–2; line 3 is adapted from a phrase which does not appear in the American Standard Version but does appear in 3:1 of the Revised Standard Version of *The Holy Bible* (Cleveland and New York: World, 1962).

§13. The section includes a paraphrase from William Blake, *The Marriage of Heaven and Hell* in *William Blake,* pp. 93–109, ed. J. Bronowski (Harmondsworth: Penguin, 1958 [1793]), p. 94: "Man has no Body distinct from his Soul" and a quote adapted from Friedrich Schleiermacher, *On Religion: Speeches to Its Cultured Despisers,* 3rd ed., trans. John Oman (London: K. Paul, Trench, Trubner, 1893 [1821]), p. 83: "In the midst of finitude to be one with the Infinite and in every moment to be eternal is the immortality of religion." In the film, *Nosferatu the Vampyre,* directed by Werner Herzog (Munich: Werner Herzog Filmproduktion, 1979), the vampire (an undead creature who cannot die) says, "Time is an abyss, profound as a thousand nights. Centuries come and go. To be unable to grow old is terrible. Death is not the worst. There are things more horrible than death. Can you imagine enduring centuries, experiencing each day the same futile things?" Tradition holds that shortly after his birth it was prophesied that Siddhartha Gautama would become either a great king or a spiritual leader; to avoid the latter, his father intentionally tried to prevent him from being exposed in his youth to any sight of old age, disease, and death; see John B. Noss, *Man's Religions*, 5th ed. (New York: Macmillan, 1974), pp. 119–121. "Death is not our enemy but our friend" is adapted from the Jewish rabbi, Joshua L. Liebman's *Peace of Mind* (New York: Bantam, 1961), p. 106. Scriptural sources: Pss 32:8; 37:23; Prov 16:9; Matt 6:19–21; John 3:16; 1 Cor 15:42.

§19. There is no mention of playing cards in England until the 15th century; see Compton Reeves, *Pleasures and Pastimes in Medieval England* (Oxford: Oxford University Press, 1995), p. 79. Viewing life as a game of cards has some affinities with the doctrine of *karma,* found in Hinduism, Buddhism, Jainism, and other Indian traditions. The terms *enables* and *constrains* are derived from the structuration theory of Anthony Giddens as developed in *The Constitution of Society* (Cambridge: Polity, 1984), but have implications that extend far beyond sociology. Scriptural sources: Gal 6:7.

§21. The phrase "break the mirror" appears in the poem "Break the Mirror" in Nanao Sakaki, *Break the Mirror: The Poems of Nanao Sakaki* (San Francisco: North Point, 1987), p. 108. The wedding vows are adapted with revisions from "The Form of Solemnization of Matrimony" in *The Book of Common Prayer* (New York: The Protestant Episcopal Church in the United States of America, 1892), pp. 277–280. Scriptural sources: Gen 2:18–24; Rev 19:7.

§23. Penelope's view of love is not "I want you, I need you, I love you," but more similar to the chorus of Cheap Trick's song "I Want You to Want Me" from the studio album *In Color* (New York: Epic, 1977).

§24. Scriptural sources: Gen 3:24.

II. THE VILLAGE

§2. In a letter to James Madison dated September 6, 1789, Thomas Jefferson wrote, "the earth belongs in usufruct to the living"; see *The Papers of Thomas Jefferson*, Vol. 15, ed. Julian P. Boyd (Princeton: Princeton University Press, 1958), p. 392.

§3. The opening stanza of Walt Whitman's poem "Song of Myself" [1892] in *Complete Poetry and Selected Prose by Walt Whitman*, ed. James E. Miller, Jr. (Boston: Houghton Mifflin, 1959), p. 25, includes the lines "I

392   ONE WITH THE FATHER

celebrate myself, and sing myself"; "For every atom belonging to me as good belongs to you"; and "I loafe and invite my soul." "There is nothing to think about. I just sit!" is a short description of Buddhist *zazen*, which literally means "sitting-meditation"; see the annotation for Part III, §21. The practice of apologizing to "plants and animals whose lives we take in exchange for our own" can be found in Native American spiritual traditions; see Lois J. Einhorn, *The Native American Oral Tradition: Voices of the Spirit and Soul* (Westport: Praeger, 2000), p. 95: "Before killing animals or cutting trees, Native People express their appreciation to the particular animals and trees for giving of their lives." The use of the phrase "great enchanted garden" to describe a sacralized world comes from Max Weber, *The Sociology of Religion,* trans. Ephraim Fischoff (Boston: Beacon Press, 1963 [1922]), p. 270. "I live with the sun and the moon, the wind and the rain, the animals and the plants" alludes to Francis of Assisi's "The Canticle of Brother Sun" [c. 1224] in *Francis and Clare: The Complete Works,* trans. Regis J. Armstrong and Ignatius C. Brady (New York: Paulist Press, 1982), pp. 37–39. Although Jean-Jacques Rousseau never used the term *noble savage,* the basic idea can be found in his book, *Discourse on the Origin of Inequality,* trans. Franklin Philip (Oxford: Oxford University Press, 1994 [1755]). Scriptural sources: Mark 12:31; Luke 6:27.

§4. The phrase "When Adam delved and Eve spanned, who was then the gentleman?" was used in a sermon delivered by the English priest, John Ball, during the Peasants' Revolt of 1381; see the entry for "Ball, John" in Vol. 3 of the *Encyclopaedia Britannica,* 11th ed., ed. Hugh Chisholm (Cambridge: Cambridge University Press, 1910–11), p. 263 and the annotation for Part V, §22. The illogic of "some things are more equal than others" is taken from George Orwell, *Animal Farm* (Harmondsworth: Penguin, 1987 [1945]), p. 114: "All animals are equal but some animals are more equal than others." The Great Chain of Being is introduced in the annotation for Part I, §6. The metaphor of a seed's potential to actualize itself can be found in Aristotle's *Metaphysics,* trans. W. D. Ross, in Vol. 1 of *The Works of Aristotle,* pp. 499–626 (*op. cit.*), IX, §7, 1049a–1049b, pp. 574–575. The Stoic expression "seminal divine word" [*lógos spermatikós,* λόγος σπερματικός] denoting the divine presence in each person can be found in Justin Martyr [100–165 CE], *The Second Apology,* trans. Thomas B. Falls, in Vol. 6 of *The Fathers of the Church,* ed. Hermigild Dressler, et al. (Washington, DC: Catholic University of America Press, 1948), Chap. 13, p. 133. Animistic religions see everything that exists as possessing a soul; Shinto, for example, holds that *kami* (神), variously translated as *gods, spirits,* or *powers,* are present in all natural phenomena; see William K. Bunce, *Religions in Japan: Buddhism, Shinto, Christianity* (Tokyo: Charles E. Tuttle, 1955 [1948]), pp. 99–102. Panpsychism, the view that mind pervades everything that exists, is a perennial concept in Western philosophy, beginning with the claim made by Thales [c. 626–c. 548 BCE], often regarded as the first philosopher in the Western tradition, as reported in Aristotle's *On the Soul* [*De Anima*], trans. J. A. Smith in Vol. 1 of *The Works of Aristotle* (*op. cit.*), pp. 631-668, I, 5, 411a, p. 641, that "all things are full of gods." For a survey of both historical and contemporary treatments of panpsychism, see William Seager, *The Routledge Handbook of Panpsychism* (New York: Routledge, 2019). The pantheistic view that "God is nature and nature is God" can be traced to Stoic philosophy, particularly Chrysippus [279–206 BCE]; see Dirk Baltzly, "Stoic Pantheism," *Sophia* 42(2):3–34. A Christian version of pantheism can be found in John Scotus Eriugena, *Periphyseon [The Division of Nature]*, trans. John O'Meara (Washington, DC: Cumbarton Oaks, 1987 [c. 867 CE]), Book IV, 759A–759B, pp. 401–402. Pantheism was also advocated by Almaric of Bene [c. late 12th century–early 13th century CE] and David of Dinant [c. 1160–c. 1217 CE]; see the respective entries in Chas S. Clifton, *Encyclopedia of Heresies and Heretics* (New York: Barnes and Noble, 1992), pp. 12–13 ("Almaric of Bene"); p. 35 ("David of Dinant"). Benedict de [Baruch] Spinoza championed the view that nature and God are coterminous in *The Ethics* [1677], trans. R. H. M. Elwes, in *On the Improvement of the Understanding, The Ethics, Correspondence* (New York: Dover, 1955), preface to Part IV, p. 188. The ancient Greek Sophist, Gorgias [483–375 BCE], is reported by Sextus Empiricus [160–210 CE] in *Against the Logicians,* Vol. 2 of *Sextus Empiricus,* trans. R. G. Bury (Cambridge: Harvard University Press [Loeb Classical Library], 1935), Book I, §65, p. 35, as having written a book entitled *Concerning the Non-existent* or *Concerning Nature* in which he established three main points: "firstly, that nothing exists; secondly, that even if anything exists it is inapprehensible by man; thirdly, that even if anything is apprehensible, yet of a surety it is inexpressible and incommunicable to one's neighbour." In his lecture "What is Metaphysics?" [1929], trans. David Farrell Krell in *Martin Heidegger: Basic Writings,* 2nd ed., pp. 89–110, ed. David Farrell Krell (New York: HarperCollins, 1993), p. 110, Heidegger asks, "Why are there beings at all, and why not rather nothing?" Lao-Tze [aka Lao Tsu, Lao Tzu, Laozi; 6th century BCE?] in the *Tao-Teh-King* [aka *Tao Teh Ching, Dao De Jing*], trans. Paul Carus (Chicago: Open Court, 1898) holds that the Tao cannot be named: "The name that can be named is not the eternal name" (Chap. 1, p. 97). The division of one into two parallels the *ying–yang* symbol of Taoism: "Reason [the Tao] begets unity; unity begets duality; duality begets trinity; and trinity begets the ten thousand things. The ten thousand things are sustained by *Yin* [the negative principle]; they are encompassed by *Yang* [the positive principle], and the immaterial. *Ch'i* [the breath of life] renders them harmonious" (*Ibid.*, Chap. 42, p. 119). *Three* is also an important number in Christian theology (the trinity of Father, Son, and Holy Spirit) and Neoplatonism (Mind and Soul are emanations of the One; see the annotation for Part III, §19). "All things flow" is a translation of the Greek phrase *pánta rheî* (πάντα ῥεῖ) ascribed to Heraclitus [c. 535–c. 475 BCE] in Plato's *Cratylus* in *The Dialogues of Plato*, pp. 85–114 (*op. cit.*), 401, p. 94. "Nothing is permanent" is a statement of the Buddhist idea of *anitya* ("impermanence"); see Junjirō Takakusu, *The Essentials of Buddhist Philosophy*, ed. Wing-tsit Chan and Charles A. Moore (Delhi: Motilal Banarsidass, 1947), p. 17. The clause "just like ripples of water on the surface of a river" echoes the Heraclitan fragment, "One cannot step twice into the same river, nor can one grasp any mortal substance in a stable condition, but it scatters and again gathers; it forms and dissolves, and approaches and departs" in Charles H. Kahn, *The Art and Thought of Heraclitus: An Edition of the Fragments with Translation and Commentary* (Cambridge: Cambridge University Press, 1979), LI, p. 53. There are parallels as well between Heraclitan process thinking and the scientific concept of dissipative structures developed by Ilya Prigogine in *From Being to Becoming: Time and Complexity in the Physical Sciences* (New York: W. H. Freeman, 1980), pp. 83–84. Scriptural sources: Gen 1:1–24, 31; 2:2; Ps 47:7; Matt 13:3–8.

§5. After renouncing his father and his inheritance, Francis of Assisi is reported to have stripped himself of all his clothes in a courtyard and was then covered by a bishop; see Giotto's painting, *Renunciation of Worldly Goods*, aka *St. Francis Renouncing His Father* (Florence: Basilica di Santa Croce [Bardi Chapel], c. turn of the 14th century). Following his "Great Renunciation" of worldly wealth and leaving his father's house, Siddhartha Gautama similarly exchanged his rich clothes for the coarse yellow robe of a monk; see Noss, *Man's Religions* (*op. cit.*), p. 121.

§6. The phrase "if you drink a single drop of water from the sea right in front of you, you will have tasted the whole ocean" echoes the line "the great ocean has one taste" from *The Udāna* [date uncertain but considered by some to be one of the earliest Buddhist texts] in *The Udāna and the Itivuttaka: Two Classics from the Pali Canon*, pp. 1–110, trans. John D. Ireland (Kandy: Buddhist Publication Society, 1997), p. 70. The clause "my body would ask my shadow to show it to me" alludes to a line from Han Shan [c. 9th century CE], *Cold Mountain* in *Cold Mountain Poems*, pp. 21–72, trans. J. P. Seaton (Boston: Shambhala, 2009), Poem II, p. 23. Taoist sages often retreated to nature to escape the social strictures of Confucianism; see the painting *Walking on Path in Spring* by Ma Yuan [c. 1160–1225 CE] (Taipei: National Palace Museum, late 12th–early 13th century). In "Walking" [1862] in *Walden and Other Writings*, pp. 597–632, ed. Brooks Atkinson

(New York: The Modern Library, 1950), Henry David Thoreau writes on p. 597: "I wish to speak for Nature, for absolute freedom and wildness, as contrasted with a freedom and culture merely civil,—to regard man as an inhabitant, or a part of and parcel of Nature, rather than a member of society" and on p. 613: "In Wildness is the preservation of the World."

§14. An allusion is made to Friedrich Nietzsche's concept of "herd morality," found in *Beyond Good and Evil* [1886] in *Basic Writings of Nietzsche*, pp. 191–435, ed. and trans. Walter Kaufmann (New York: The Modern Library, 1968), §202, p. 305. Scriptural sources: Gen 3:17–19; Ps 78:52; Matt 6:11; Luke 11:3; Rom 13:1–7.

§15. Scriptural sources: Lev 23:10.

§17. "No one can knock me down and keep me there" alludes to the chorus of Chumbawamba's song "Tubthumping" on the studio album *Tubthumper* (London: EMI, 1997).

§19. "Propaganda of the deed" has been a popular slogan among insurrectionary anarchists; see Michael [Mikhail] Bakunin, "Letters to a Frenchman on the Present Crisis" in *Bakunin on Anarchism*, pp. 183–217, ed. and trans. Sam Dolgoff (Montréal: Black Rose, 1980 [1870]), pp. 195–196: "All of us must now embark on stormy revolutionary seas, and from this very moment we must spread our principles, not with words *but with deeds, for this is the most popular, the most potent, and the most irresistible form of propaganda*" [italics in the original].

§25. The phrase "wipe his wax tablet clean" is virtually synonymous with the idiom "wipe the slate clean." There are overtones with the idea of a "blank slate" (*tabula rasa*) in Aristotle's *On the Soul* [*De Anima*] (*op. cit.*), III, 4, 429b–430a, p. 662. A similar expression "white paper" was used by John Locke in Vol. 1 of *An Essay Concerning Human Understanding* (New York: Dover, 1959 [1690]), Book II, Chap. 1.2, p. 121 to refer to the condition of the mind prior to experience. Scriptural sources: Gen 9:6; Eph 6:5; Col 3:22.

§27. Scriptural sources: Exod 20:13; Matt 5:21–22.

III. THE MONASTERY

§2. Lame Deer in John (Fire) Lame Deer and Richard Erdoes, *Lame Deer, Seeker of Visions* (New York: Pocket, 1994 [1972]), p. 31, says, "I was a wanderer, a hippie Indian. I knew nothing then. Right or wrong were just words. My life was a find-out. If somebody said, 'That's bad,' I still wanted to experience it. Maybe it would turn out to be good." The phrase "condemned to wander aimlessly throughout the earth for all eternity, without ever being able to rest" references the literary archetype of the eternal wanderer found in the stories of Cain, the Ancient Mariner, the Flying Dutchman, and the Wandering Jew (dissociated from any anti-Semitic implications). Scriptural sources: Gen 4:14–15; Mark 4:5–6; John 3:8; Hos 9:17.

§3. Scriptural sources: Matt 5:40.

§4. Roshi Soen Nakagawa [1907–1984] is quoted by Robert Aitken in *Original Dwelling Place: Zen Buddhist Essays* (Washington, DC: Counterpoint, 1996), p. 18, as saying: "When you sweep the garden, you are sweeping your own mind." Mary Douglas in *Purity and Danger: An Analysis of Concepts of Pollution and Taboo,* Vol. II of *Mary Douglas: Collected Works* (London: Routledge, 1996 [1966]), p. 36, mentions "the old definition of dirt as matter out of place." Daisetz Teitaro Suzuki in *An Introduction to Zen Buddhism* (New York: Grove Press, 1964), p. 48, quotes Hui-neng [683–713 CE], the Sixth Patriarch of Zen in China, as saying, "As there is nothing from the first, / Where does the dust itself collect?" Scriptural sources: Ps 103:8; Matt 26:9; John 12:5; 15:15; 16:13; 1 Cor 6:19; 1 John 4:8.

§5. Simeon Stylites the Elder [c. 390–459 CE] lived atop a pillar located near Aleppo, Syria for thirty-seven years; a biography of Simeon was written by an anonymous author shortly after his death; see *The Life of Saint Simeon Stylites: A Translation of the Syriac Text in Bedjan's Acta Martyrum et Sanctorum,* Vol. IV, trans. Frederick Lent (Merchantville: Evolution, 2009 [c. 459 CE]); originally published in the *Journal of the American Oriental Society* 35:103–198 [1915]). Chap. 1 of *St. Benedict's Rule for Monasteries,* trans. Leonard J. Doyle (Collegeville: Liturgical Press, 1948 [516 CE]), p. 1, distinguishes between four different kinds of monks: (1) Cenobites who live in cloisters under the rule of an abbot; (2) Anchorites or Hermits who live alone although still under the guidance of the Church; (3) Sarabaites who live singly, or in twos or threes, with no supervision from the Church; and (4) Gyrovagues who travel from place to place on their own. In the medieval period established monastic orders included the Benedictines and Cistercians; sanctioned mendicant orders included the Franciscans and Dominicans; lay houses included those for Beghards (men) and Beguines (women); heretical groups of itinerant lay preachers included the Cathars and Waldenses, among others. "Prayer and Work" (*ora et labora*) is a motto of Benedictine monasticism; see Anselm Grün, *Benedict of Nursia: His Message for Today,* trans. Linda M. Maloney (Collegeville: Liturgical Press, 2006), pp. 30 *ff.* Scriptural sources: Matt 5:21–22, 27–28; John 17:15–18; Acts 2:44–45; 4:34–35.

§6. Scriptural sources: John 10:30. The original Greek is from *The New Testament in the Original Greek,* ed. F. H. A. Scrivener (Cambridge: Cambridge University Press, 1894), p. 267.

§7. Scriptural sources: 1 John 5:17.

§8. The section incorporates reworked language and quotes from Jonathan Edwards' sermon "Sinners in the Hands of an Angry God" (Boston: J. Kneeland, 1772 [1741]) and Augustine, *The Enchiridion of Augustine, Addressed to Laurentius; Being a Treatise on Faith, Hope, and Love* [423 CE], trans. J. F. Shaw, in *The Works of Aurelius Augustine, Bishop of Hippo*, Vol. IX, pp. 175–260, ed. Marcus Dods (Edinburgh: T. and T. Clark, 1877), Chap. XXXIII, p. 200. The latter includes a statement on original sin, further articulated by Augustine in *A Treatise on the Grace of Christ, and on Original Sin* [418 CE] in *St. Augustin: Anti-Pelagian Writings*, pp. 213–255, trans. Peter Holmes, Robert Ernest Wallis, and Benjamin B. Warfield in *Nicene and Post-Nicene Fathers*, Vol. 5, ed. Philip Schaff (New York: Christian Literature Company, 1887). For Augustine's views on predestination, see *The Enchiridion of Augustine* (*op. cit.*), Chap. XCVIII, pp. 242–244 and *On the Predestination of the Saints* [c. 428–429 CE] in *St. Augustin: Anti-Pelagian Writings* (*op. cit.*), pp. 493–519. For John Calvin's views on predestination, which were heavily influenced by Augustine, see *Institutes of the Christian Religion*, trans. John Allen, 3 vols. (Philadelphia: Philip H. Nicklin, 1816 [1559]), especially Vol. 2, Book Three, Chaps. XXI–XXIV, pp. 414–484. Predestination presupposes that humans have no free will and that salvation is effected through God's power alone (one power = monergy); in their debate on the topic Desiderius Erasmus [1466–1536] attacked predestination and defended free will, while Martin Luther [1483–1546] did the opposite; see *Discourse on Free Will: Desiderius Erasmus and Martin Luther,* ed. and trans. Ernst F. Winter (London: Bloomsbury, 2013 [1961]), which includes excerpts from Erasmus's *The Free Will* [1524] and Luther's *The Bondage of the Will* [1525]. Several of the views expressed by Bartholomew in this section have affinities with those of the Jansenist sect within Roman Catholicism, some of whose propositions were condemned as heretical in papal bulls issued by Innocent X in 1653 and Clement XI in 1713; see the entry for "Jansenism" by J. M. Gres-Gayer in *The New Catholic Encyclopedia*, 2nd ed., ed. Berard L. Marthaler et al. (Farmington Hills: Gale, 2003), Vol. 7, pp. 715–720. The anonymously written tract "Heaven or Hell: Which One Will You Choose?" (Lebanon, Ohio: Fellowship Tract League, no date) was also consulted when writing this section. Scriptural sources: Gen 1:1; Deut 6:5; Job 42:2; Pss 51:5; 62:1; 145:17; 147:5; Prov 9:10; Hab 1:13; Matt 22:37; Mark 12:30; John 3:36; 15:16; Acts 2:21; Rom 3:23; 5:12; 6:23; 8:29–30; 9:18; 10:3, 9, 13–17; 1 Cor 15:22; Eph 1:5; 2:3, 8–9; Rev 4:8.

§9. In Plato's *Euthyphro* in *The Dialogues of Plato*, pp. 191–199 (*op. cit.*), 9–10, p. 195, Socrates asks ". . . whether the pious or holy is beloved by the gods because it is holy, or holy because it is beloved of the gods."

Leibniz, in his essay, "Reflections on the Common Concept of Justice" [c. 1702] in *Gottfried Wilhelm Leibniz: Philosophical Papers and Letters,* 2nd ed., pp. 561–573, trans. Leroy E. Loemker (Dordrecht: Kluwer Academic, 1989), p. 561, similarly writes, "It is generally agreed that whatever God wills is good and just. But there remains the question whether it is good and just because God wills it or whether God wills it because it is good and just." Quotes are taken from the Nicene Creed, originally formulated at the First Council of Nicaea in 325 CE and amended at the First Council of Constantinople in 381 CE; the texts of both the Apostles' Creed and Nicene Creed in English can be found in Philip Schaff, *The Creeds of Christendom,* 4th ed. (New York: Harper and Brothers, 1877), Vol. 1, pp. 27–29. For an interesting liberal, yet mystical, interpretation of the Apostles' Creed, see W. F. Cobb [William Frederick Geikie-Cobb], *Mysticism and the Creed* (London: Macmillan, 1914). On the view "that God is nature and nature is God, and that we, too, each have a spark of the divine within us" see the annotations for Part II, §4 and Part III, §19. A key point of contention during the First Ecumenical Council of Nicaea in 325 CE was whether Christ should be described as being of the *same* essence (*homooúsia,* ὁμοούσια) or a *similar* essence (*homoioúsia,* ὁμοιούσια) with the Father; in Greek the only difference between the two words is whether an iota (*i,* ι) appears or does not appear between *homo* and *oúsia*; hence, the English expression "quibbling over an iota." A later point of contention was that whereas the original formulation of the Nicene Creed, which continues to be used in the Eastern Orthodox Church, states that the Holy Spirit proceeds solely "from the Father," the Western Roman Church later added the words "and [from] the Son," a phrase known as the *Filioque.* Despite the seemingly small change in wording, one theological concern, among others, is whether the Holy Spirit operates apart from the work of Jesus of Nazareth [c. 4 BCE–c. 30 CE] (i.e., is universal and available to the whole of humankind throughout history, even those who have never heard of Jesus) or only through Jesus (i.e., is particular and available only to those who respond to the gospel as revealed by Jesus at a specific time and place, in Palestine two thousand years ago). For an overview and history of the phrase "Outside the Church there is no salvation" (Latin: *extra ecclesiam nulla salus*), see Sandra Mazzolini, *"Extra Ecclesiam Nulla Salus?*: What Has the Catholic Church Learned about Interfaith Dialogue since Vatican II?" in *Pathways for Interreligious Dialogue in the Twenty-First Century,* ed. Vladimir Latinovic, Gerard Mannion, and Peter C. Phan (Basingstoke: Palgrave Macmillan, 2016), pp. 41–52. Despite its popularity among fundamentalists and evangelicals, the notion that one must accept Jesus as their "personal savior" is nowhere to be found in the Bible. In the title song of the rock opera, *Jesus Christ Superstar,* by Andrew

Lloyd Webber and Tim Rice (London: Decca, 1970), Judas similarly asks Jesus why he chose to bring his message to such a limited audience in such a remote country at such a distant time. Scriptural sources: Gen 17:1–8; Exod 20:2–17; 31:18; Deut 5:6–21; Isa 26:19; Jer 31:31–33; Matt 6:9; 12:30; 22:31–32; 28:19–20; Mark 16:16; Luke 11:23; 22:20; John 1:14; 3:13; 15:26; Acts 1:9; 2:1–4; 4:12; 24:15; Rom 8:34; 1 Cor 15:42–53; Phil 3:21; 1 Tim 2:5; Heb 2:4; Rev 21:1–4.

§10. The catechism referred to is Augustine's *On the Catechising of the Uninstructed* [*De catechizandis rudibus*, which may also be translated as *Instructing the Unlearned*, c. 400 CE], trans. S. D. Salmond, in *The Works of Aurelius Augustine, Bishop of Hippo* (*op. cit.*), Vol. IX, pp. 265–335. On Zeus's philandering, see Edith Hamilton, *Mythology* (Boston: Little, Brown, 1969 [1940]), p. 27. On baptism with the blood of a slain bull in the pagan mystery religion, Mithraism, see the entry for "Baptism" in Udo Becker, *The Continuum Encyclopedia of Symbols*, trans. Lance W. Garmer (New York: Continuum, 2000), p. 33. A hymn from the Mithraic cult includes the line, "Thou hast redeemed us too by shedding the eternal blood"; quoted in Andreas Sofroniou, *Mythology: Legends from Around the Globe* (Morrisville: Lulu Press, 2017), p. 517. Charges of infanticide and cannibalism were frequently made by the ancient Romans against the early Christians; see the brief summary in Stamenka E. Antonova, "Barbarians and the Empire-Wide Spread of Christianity" in *The Spread of Christianity in the First Four Centuries: Essays in Explanation*, pp. 69–86, ed. W. V. Harris (Leiden: Brill, 2005), p. 77, and the defense of Christianity by Tertullian [c. 155–c. 220 CE] in *The Apology*, trans. S. Thelwall, in *The Ante-Nicene Fathers*, Vol. III, pp. 17–55, ed. Alexander Roberts and James Donaldson (Buffalo: Christian Literature, 1887). George Bataille in *Eroticism: Death and Sensuality*, trans. Mary Dalwood (San Francisco: City Lights, 1986 [1957]), p. 36, sees religion as involving a "duplicity" concerned with "reconciling what seems impossible to reconcile, respect for the law and violation of the law, the taboo and its transgression." Scriptural sources: Matt 1:18; 26:26–28; John 6:53–57; Rom 3:25; 6:4; 1 Cor 15:3–4; Heb 9:22.

§11. The notion that God continues to reveal himself directly to people through the Holy Spirit was a key tenet of Montanism, a sect founded by Montanus in the 2nd century CE, ultimately denounced as heretical for placing personal prophecies above those of the Bible; see the entry "Montanism" in Clifton, *Encyclopedia of Heresies and Heretics* (*op. cit.*), pp. 98–99. During the Protestant Reformation, various radical reformers, particularly forerunners of the Anabaptists, including Nicolaus [Nikolaus] Storch, Thomas Müntzer, and the Zwickau Prophets (all active during the first half of the 16th century), claimed direct inspiration from the Holy Spirit; see

William R. Estep, *The Anabaptist Story: An Introduction to Sixteenth-Centu-ry Anabaptism,* 3rd. ed. (Grand Rapids: William B. Eerdmans, 1996), p. 22. Continuous revelation is rejected by the Catholic and Orthodox Churches, as well as most contemporary Protestant denominations; exceptions include Friends and Quakers who associate the Holy Spirit with an "inner light," which supports an idea of continuous revelation; see the annotation for Part III, §19. The *Catechism of the Catholic Church* [English translation], 2nd ed. (Washington, DC: United States Conference of Catholic Bishops, 2019), p. 23, states, "There will be no further Revelation." Doctrines of the inerrancy and infallibility of scripture were not asserted until the post-Reformation period; see Ronald Hendel, "The Dream of a Perfect Text: Textual Criticism and Biblical Inerrancy in Early Modern Europe" in *Sibyls, Scriptures, and Scrolls: John Collins at Seventy,* pp. 517–541, ed. J. J. Collins (Leiden: Brill, 2017), especially p. 529. For a contemporary fundamentalist perspective on Biblical inerrancy, see Norman L. Geisler and William C. Roach, *Defending Inerrancy: Affirming the Accuracy of Scripture for a New Generation* (Grand Rapids: Baker, 2011). In the Bible, wisdom (personified as Ἁγία Σοφία, *Hagía Sophía,* "Divine Wisdom") is one of the gifts of the Holy Spirit (1 Cor 12:8). The Biblical method for determining whether a voice is "God's or the devil's" is not on the basis of scripture but through spiritual discern-ment (διακρίσεις πνευμάτων in Greek, *discretio spirituum* in Latin; 1 Cor 12:10) and manifestations ("by their fruits ye shall know them"; Matt 7:20); see Ernest E. Larkin, *Silent Presence: Discernment as Process and Problem,* 2nd ed. (Denville: Dimension, 1998) and Nancy Caciola, *Discerning Spirits: Divine and Demonic Possession in the Middle Ages* (Ithaca: Cornell Uni-versity Press, 2003). In *The Book of Margery Kempe,* trans. B. A. Windeatt (Harmondsworth: Penguin, 1985), p. 78, Julian of Norwich [1343–c. 1416] advises Margery Kempe [c. 1373–c. 1438] that acts against charity are "not the influence of a good spirit, but rather of an evil spirit." "God is to be worshipped through faith, hope, and love" is a direct quote from Augus-tine, *The Enchiridion* (*op. cit.*), Chap. III, p. 176; this book was also used for catechetical instruction; see also the annotation for Part III, §17. Scriptural sources: Matt 6:9; 7:20, 24–27; 19:26; John 20:29–31; Rom 8:24–25; 1 Cor 2:10–14; 3:2; 12:8, 10; 2 Cor 4:18; 2 Tim 3:16; 4:3–4; Heb 1:1–2; 11:1; Jas 3:17; 1 John 4:20.

§12. While Roman Catholicism, Eastern Orthodoxy, and Anglican-ism interpret scripture in light of tradition, many Protestant denominations have adopted the principle, originally formulated by Martin Luther, of *sola scriptura,* i.e., the view that scripture is the sole authority for doctrine and practice; see the quote from Luther in the annotation for Part V, §30 and also Keith A. Mathison, *The Shape of Sola Scriptura* (Moscow [Idaho, USA]:

Canon Press, 2001), p. 95. Books were in fact not read by candlelight in medieval libraries for fear of fire. For an overview of Greek and Roman mythology, see Hamilton, *Mythology* (*op. cit.*). Hesiod's account of creation can be found in his *Theogony* (*op. cit.*), pp. 6–7. Ovid's account of creation can be found in *The Metamporphoses,* trans. Horace Gregory (New York: Viking, 1958 [8 CE]), pp. 31–33. For examples in ancient mythology of gods dying and being reborn, see J. G. Frazer, *The Golden Bough: A Study in Comparative Religion* (London: MacMillan, 1890), Vol. 1, Chap. 3, pp. 301–320 (Osiris); 320–329 (Dionysius); and 330–362 (Proserpine [Persephone]). Allegorical interpretations of the Hebrew Bible [referred to by Christians as the "Old Testament"] were pioneered by the Hellenistic Jewish philosopher, Philo of Alexandria [c. 20 BCE–c. 50 CE]; see, for example, his *Allegorical Interpretation of Gen, II., III. [Legum Allegoria]* in Vol. 1 of *Philo,* pp. 146–473, trans. F. H. Colson and G. H Whitaker. (Cambridge: Harvard University Press [Loeb Classical Library], 1981), Book I.II, pp. 147–149: "It is quite foolish to think that the world was created in six days or in a space of time at all. Why? Because every period of time is a series of days and nights, and these can only be made such by the movement of the sun as it goes over and under the earth: but the sun is part of heaven, so that time is confessedly more recent than the world. It would therefore be correct to say that the world was not made in time, but that time was formed by means of the world, for it was heaven's movement that was the index of the nature of time." The ancient Christian theologian, Origen [c. 184–c. 253 CE], also of Alexandria, writes in *De Principiis [First Principles],* trans. Frederick Crombie, in *The Ante-Nicene Fathers,* Vol. IV, pp. 239–382, ed. Alexander Roberts and James Donaldson (Buffalo: Christian Literature, 1885), Book IV, Chap. 1, §16, p. 365: "And who is so foolish as to suppose that God, after the manner of a husbandman, planted a paradise in Eden, towards the east, and placed in it a tree of life, visible and palpable, so that one tasting of the fruit by the bodily teeth obtained life? and again, that one was a partaker of good and evil by masticating what was taken from the tree? And if God is said to walk in the paradise in the evening, and Adam to hide himself under a tree, I do not suppose that anyone doubts that these things figuratively indicate certain mysteries, the history having taken place in appearance, and not literally" [Greek text]. In IV.1.9, p. 357 of the same work, Origen says that the reason why some people are led into erroneous views, false opinions, impious statements, and ignorant assertions about God is because ". . . holy Scripture is not understood by them according to its spiritual, but according to its literal meaning" [Latin text]; see also IV.1.7, p. 355: "Many, not understanding the Scriptures in a spiritual sense, but incorrectly, have fallen into heresies" [Latin text]. Origin's three-fold method of interpretation distinguishes the following levels of interpretation: (1) "flesh" [literal, historical]; (2) "soul" [moral], and (3) "spirit" [mystical]; see IV.1.11, p. 359 [Greek text]: "For as man consists of body, and soul, and spirit, so in the same way does Scripture . . . ." Thomas Aquinas lists four ways of interpreting the Bible in *The Summa Theologica* (*op. cit.*), Vol. 1, First Part, Question 1, Article 10, pp. 9–10: (1) historical or literal; (2) allegorical; (3) tropological or moral; and (4) anagogical. Allegorical interpretations of scripture were largely rejected at the beginning of the Protestant Reformation by both Luther and Calvin in favor of literal, historical interpretations; see David R. Law, *The Historical-Critical Method: A Guide for the Perplexed* (London: T&T Clark, 2012), p. 37. For Luther's treatment of *Genesis,* which includes his deprecation of allegory, see *The Creation: A Commentary on the First Five Chapters of the Book of Genesis,* trans. Henry Cole (Edinburgh: T & T Clark, 1858 [1544]). Modern Biblical criticism begins with David Friedrich Strauss, whose *Life of Jesus: Critically Examined,* 4th ed., trans. George Eliot (London: Swan Sonnenschein, 1902 [1835]) rejected both literal (supernatural) and rationalistic (naturalistic) explanations of the New Testament in favor of a mythic perspective, which sees the gospel narratives as expressing spiritual rather than historical truths, a view which continues to inform contemporary Biblical criticism. Scriptural sources: Gen 6–8; Exod 31:15; Lev 10:2; 11:1–15:33; 20:6, 9, 13, 27; 23:1–44; 24:16; 25:44–46; Num 6:10–14; 11:1; 16:32–33; Deut 7:1–2; 13:6–16; 17:2–5; 21:10–14; 22:20–21; Josh 6:20–21; 1 Sam 15:3; Pss 145:8–9; 146:7; Isa 13:16; Jer 19:9; Ezek 5:10–17; Hos 13:16; Amos 5:24; Matt 5:18; 7:24–27; 9:27–31; 19:24; 24:24; Mark 8:22–26; Luke 6:20, 24; 17:21; 18:35–43; John 3:3–7; 4:48; 9:1–7, 25; 14:26; 16:13; 18:36; Rom 13:8; Rev 21:8.

§13. As opposed to *monergism,* the idea advocated by Augustine, Luther, and Calvin, which holds that God is the sole energy at work in salvation and which, therefore, denies free will in favor of predestination (see the annotations for Part III, §8), Roman Catholic, Eastern Orthodox, and Arminian theology supports *synergism,* the view that God's grace and the free will of humanity cooperate in effecting salvation. For an Eastern Orthodox perspective on the synergy between God's grace and the free will of humanity, see Timothy Ware, *The Orthodox Church* (Harmondsworth: Penguin, 1983 [1964]), pp. 226–227. The Church Father, John Cassian [c. 360–c. 435], an advocate of synergism, writes in *The Conferences of John Cassian,* trans. Edgar C. S. Gibson in *A Select Library of Nicene and Post-Nicene Fathers of the Christian Church,* Second Series, Vol. XI, pp. 291–545, ed. Philip Schaff and Henry Wace (New York: The Christian Literature Company, 1894), Conference 13, Chap. 13, p. 430: ". . . the grace of God always co-operates with our will for its advantage . . . ."; see also Chap. 12, p.

429: "It cannot then be doubted that there are by nature some seeds of good-ness in every soul implanted by the kindness of the Creator: but unless these are quickened by the assistance of God, they will not be able to attain to an increase of perfection, for, as the blessed Apostle says: 'Neither is he that planteth anything nor he that watereth, but God that giveth the increase'" (1 Cor 3:7). "Do not dwell in the past, do not dream of the future, concentrate the mind on the present moment" is a phrase attributed to Gautama Buddha [Siddhartha Gautama]; quoted in Bukkyō Dendō Kyōkai, *The Teachings of Buddha* (New Delhi: Sterling, 2004), p. 123. In two collections of kōan, the *Hekiganroku* (*Blue Cliff Record*, compiled in the 12th century CE) and *Mumonkan* (*The Gateless Gate*, compiled in the 13th century CE), the following answers are given by Zen masters in reply to students' questions about what the Buddha-nature is: "three pounds of flax" (*Mumonkan* #18, pp. 71–72); "a *kanshiketsu*" (= "dried shit-stick," used instead of toilet paper; *Mumonkan* #21, pp. 77–78); "the oak tree in the garden" (*Mumonkan* #37, pp. 110–112); "snow in the silver bowl" (*Hekiganroku* #13, pp. 182–184); see the respec-tive pages in *Two Zen Classics: Mumonkan and Kekiganroku*, trans. Katsuki Sekida (New York: Weatherhill, 1977). Scriptural sources: Deut 28:8; Jer 4: 22; Mic 6:8; Matt 6:25–34; Luke 10:38–42; John 14:17; 15:16; Rom 14:14; 1 Cor 3:6–8; Col 3:2; Rev 3:20.

§14. The abbot's Christmas sermon includes a composite of reworked passages adapted from Meister Eckhart's [c. 1260–1328 CE] Sermon #1, "This is Meister Eckhart from whom God hid nothing" in *Meister Eckhart: A Modern Translation,* trans. Raymond Bernard Blakney (New York: Harp-er and Row, 1941), p. 95; Sermon #2, "This is another sermon" (*ibid.*), p. 103; and Sermon #2, "Creation: A flowing out but remaining within," trans. Thomas O'Meara, in *Breakthrough: Meister Eckhart's Creation Spirituality in New Translation,* ed. Matthew Fox (New York: Doubleday, 1991), p. 66. The last sentence of the second paragraph is adapted from a saying of Eckhart's quoted in Megan McKenna, *Keepers of the Story: Oral Traditions in Religion* (New York: Seabury, 2004), p. 86. Constantine N. Tsirpanlis in *Introduction to Eastern Patristic Thought and Orthodox Theology* (Collegeville: Liturgical Press, 1991), p. 66, quotes the following from Athanasius [4th century CE]: "He (the Son of God) became man, that we might become God." While the doctrine of deification, also referred to as *divinization* or *theosis,* can found in the patristic writings accepted by the Roman Catholic and other Western traditions, it is most fully articulated in Eastern Orthodox theology; for a concise introduction see Ware, *The Orthodox Church* (*op. cit.*), pp. 236–242. In his opening speech delivered on September 11, 1893 at the World's Par-liament of Religions held in Chicago, Swami Vivekananda quoted from a Hindu hymn, "As the different streams having their sources in different places all mingle their water in the sea, so, O Lord, the different paths which men take through different tendencies, various though they appear, crooked or straight, all lead to thee"; from *The World's Parliament of Religions,* ed. John Henry Barrows (Chicago: Parliament, 1893), Vol. 1, p. 102. Scriptural sources: John 17:21–23; Rom 6:3–11; 8:9; 1 Cor 3:16; 6:17; Gal 2:20; Eph 4:22–24; 2 Pet 1:4.

§15. The expression "leap of faith" can be found in Søren Kierkegaard's *Concluding Unscientific Postscript,* trans. David F. Swenson and Walter Lowrie (Princeton: Princeton University Press, 1941 [1846]), p. 15. Scriptural sources: Gen 12:1; Matt 16:24; Phil 4:7.

§16. The following anecdote is related by Tom Stoppard on p. 66 of his play, *Jumpers,* 2nd ed. (London: Faber and Faber, 1986 [1972]): "Meeting a friend in a corridor, Wittgenstein said: 'Tell me, why do people always say it was *natural* for men to assume that the sun went around the earth rather than that the earth was rotating?' His friend, 'Well, obviously, because is just *looks* as if the sun is going round the earth.' To which the philosopher replied, 'Well, what would it have looked like if it had looked as if the earth was rotating?'" When asked in an interview if he believed in God, the psychologist Carl Jung replied, "I don't need to believe; I know"; an excerpt of the interview is included in Don Cupitt's documentary *Sea of Faith,* Episode 2: "The Human Animal," broadcast by the BBC in 1984.

§17. Diogenes Laërtius in *The Lives and Opinions of Eminent Philosophers,* trans. C. D. Yonge (London: Henry G. Bohn, 1853 [date unknown but probably between the 2nd and 4th centuries CE]), p. 69, attributes to Socrates the view that "he knew nothing, except the fact of his ignorance"; see also Socrates' remark in Plato's *Apology* in *The Dialogues of Plato,* pp. 200–212 (*op. cit.*), 21, p. 202: "I neither know nor think that I know." The sentence "And we cannot construct a fence around the mystery of God with our doctrines and dogmas" is a response to the contention of Timothy Ware in *The Orthodox Church* (*op. cit.*), p. 28 that the purpose of the first six ecumenical conferences held from 325–681 CE was not to explain the mystery of God, but to ". . . exclude certain false ways of speaking and thinking about it. To prevent men from deviating into error and heresy, they drew a fence around the mystery; that was all." The anonymous author of *The Cloud of Unknowing* [late 14th century CE] in *The Cloud of Unknowing and Other Works,* trans. Clifton Wolters (Harmondsworth: Penguin, 1978), p. 66, writes that before God can be known we must enter a "cloud of forgetting"; the title of the chapter this phrase appears in is "The Cloud of Forgetting must obliterate all things" (p. 53). In *On Christian Doctrine* [*De doctrina Christiana,* 397 CE], trans. J. F. Shaw, in *The Works of Aurelius Augustine, Bishop of Hippo,* Vol. IX, pp. 1–171 (*op. cit.*), Book I, Chap. XXXVII, p. 32, Augustine writes,

"... these are the three things to which all knowledge and all prophecy are subservient: faith, hope, love"; the title of Book I, Chap. XXXIX, p. 32 is "He who is mature in faith, hope, and love, needs Scripture no longer"; see also the annotation for Part III, §11. Thomas Müntzer [1489–1525] in Hans-Jürgen Goertz, *Thomas Müntzer: Apocalyptic, Mystic, and Revolutionary,* trans. Jocelyn Jaquiery, ed. Peter Matheson (London: T and T Clark, 1993), p. 143, similarly writes, "If someone had never had sight or sound of the Bible at any time in his life, he could still hold the one true Christian faith because of the true teaching of the spirit, just like all those who composed the holy Scripture without any books at all"; for a Buddhist parallel see the annotation for Part IV, §22. "Do not mistake the finger pointing at the moon for the moon itself" is a Zen Buddhist saying; see Julius Evola, *The Doctrine of Awakening: Self-Mastery According to the Earliest Buddhist Texts,* trans. H. E. Musson (Rochester: Inner Traditions, 1996), p. 224. Gregorian chants are composed of a single melody sung in unison. The "sea of doubt" is the opposite of Matthew Arnold's "Sea of Faith" in his poem, "Dover Beach," in *New Poems* (London: Macmillan, 1867), pp. 112–114. The notion that God is "wholly other" and known only through revelation is propounded by Karl Barth in his commentary, *The Epistle to the Romans,* trans. Edwyn C. Hoskyns (London: Oxford University Press, 1933 [1922]). On discernment, see the annotation for Part III, §11. "God is light. God is not light. God is both light and not light. God is neither light nor no-light" is a tetralemma; the *catuṣkoṭi* is a similar four-valued system of logic advanced by Nagarjuna [c. 150–c. 250 CE] of the Mādhyamika school of Buddhism, which asserts (1) p; (2) not-p; (3) p and not-p; and (4) neither p nor not-p; each of the above may also be negated to form four additional truth values; a ninth category is the negation of all eight preceding values, i.e., "none of the above" or silence (*śūnyatā*); see Jan Westerhoff, "Nagarjuna's catuṣkoṭi," *Journal of Indian Philosophy* 34(4):367–395 (2006). Jainism posits a similar seven-valued system of logic in which each predication is prefaced by the word *possibly*; see Pragati Jain, "*Saptabhaṅgī*: The Jaina Theory of Sevenfold Predication: A Logical Analysis," *Philosophy East & West* 50(3):385–399 (July 2000). Christian apophatic theology (aka the *via negativa*) claims that any statement made about God can never be absolutely true; cataphatic theology (aka the *via positiva*) claims that any statement made about God is at best a metaphor; on the difference between the two, see Vladimir Lossky, *Orthodox Theology: An Introduction,* trans. Ian and Ihita Kesarcodi-Watson (Crestwood: St. Vladimir's Seminary Press, 1989), Chap. One, Section ii, "The Negative and the Positive Way," pp. 31–35. Negative theology was also advocated by the Jewish scholar and philosopher, Moses Maimonides [1138–1204], in *The Guide for the Perplexed,* trans. Michael Friedländer

(New York: Cosimo, 2007). Similar ideas can be found in ancient Greek, neo-Platonic, Hindu, Buddhist, Islamic, Baháʼí, and atheistic thought. The notions that religion is untrue because it conflicts with science and that God is, therefore, a delusion can be found in Richard Dawkins, *The God Delusion* (London: Black Swan, 2007). In his article on Fritz Mauthner [1849–1923] in Vol. 5, pp. 221–224 of *The Encyclopedia of Philosophy,* ed. Paul Edwards (New York: Macmillan and the Free Press, 1967), p. 223, Gershon Weiler writes that for Mauthner, "The highest degree of critical attitude is silence. The critique of language merely leads up to it, for the critique tries to 'say the unsayable'. . . . All that philosophers have endeavored and failed to say can become present in mystical silence. Mauthner declared himself an adherent of a 'godless mysticism' (*gottlose Mystik*)—godless because, from the point of view of the critique of language, 'God' is but another unwarranted substantive"; see also Fritz Mauthner, "Der Friede in gottloser Mystik" ["Peace in Godless Mysticism"] in *Der Atheismus und seine Geschichte im Abendlande* [*Atheism and Its History in the West*] (Heppenheim: m-presse, 2010 [1921–1923]), Vol. 4, pp. 282–354. On the "unsayable," see William Franke, *A Philosophy of the Unsayable* (Notre Dame: University of Notre Dame Press, 2014). The phrase "as participants not spectators" alludes to John Dewey's criticisms of the "spectator theory of knowledge" in *The Quest for Certainty: A Study of the Relation of Knowledge and Action* (New York: Minton, Balch, 1929), p. 196: "If we see that knowing is not the act of an outside spectator but of a participator inside the natural and social scene, then the true object of knowledge resides in the consequences of directed action." In Buddhism knowledge of the scriptures is compared to seeing scenery through a window, while religious experience is compared to actually being in that scenery; see Evola, *The Doctrine of Awakening* (*op. cit.*), p. 224. Scriptural sources: Matt 22:37; John 1:1; 5:39–40; 14:17; 16:13; Rom 10:17; 12:2; 1 Cor 13:8, 13; 2 Cor 3:2–6; Gal 1:12; 2 Tim 3:16; Heb 1:1–2; 8:10; Jas 1:22; 1 John 1:5; 2:27; 4:1.

§18. In the myth of the cave, Plato writes of a prisoner who breaks free from his chains and ascends to the outer world, "When he approaches the light his eyes will be dazzled, and he will not be able to see anything at all of what are now called realities"; see *The Republic* in *The Dialogues of Plato,* pp. 295–441 (*op. cit.*), Book VII, 516, p. 388. The metaphor of humans not being able to grasp the sun directly but being able to experience its light and heat is used by the medieval Byzantine theologian, Gregory of Palamas [c. 1296– c. 1359], to express a distinction between God's essence and his energies; see George C. Papademetriou, *Introduction to St. Gregory Palamas* (Brookline: Holy Cross Orthodox Press, 2004), especially pp. 42–43. Friedrich Nietzsche writes in *On the Genealogy of Morals* [1887] in *Basic Writings of Nietzsche,* pp. 449–599, ed. and trans. Walter Kaufmann (New York: The Modern Library, 1968), First Essay, §13, p. 481: ". . . the popular mind separates the lightning from its flash and takes the latter for an *action,* for the operation of a subject called lightning . . . . But there is no such substratum; there is no 'being' behind doing, effecting, becoming: 'the doer' is merely a fiction added to the deed—the deed is everything." Benjamin Lee Whorf similarly writes in *Language, Thought, and Reality,* ed. John B. Carroll (Cambridge: MIT Press, 1956), p. 243: "We are constantly reading into nature fictional acting entities, simply because our verbs must have substantives in front of them. We have to say 'It flashed' or 'A light flashed,' setting up an actor, 'it' or 'light,' to perform what we call an action, 'to flash.' Yet the flashing and the light are one and the same! The Hopi language reports the flash with a simple verb, *rehpi:* 'flash (occurred).' There is no division into subject and predicate . . . ." "Religion has nothing to do with any grand ideas we may have about God, but with the immediate awareness of the divine as it is found in ourselves and in the world" is adapted from Schleiermacher, *On Religion,* (*op. cit.*), pp. 82–83: "The usual conception of God as one single being outside of the world and behind the world is not the beginning and the end of religion . . . . [T]he true nature of religion is neither this idea nor any other, but immediate consciousness of the Deity as He is found in ourselves and in the world." "He [God] is neither this nor that" is a restatement of the Hindu concept *neti-neti,* usually translated into English as "not-this, not-that," but as "no, no" by F. Max Müller in the *Brihadaranyaka-Upanishad,* Vol. XV of *The Sacred Books of the East,* ed. F. Max Müller (Oxford: Clarendon Press, 1884 [c. 700 BCE]), II.3.6, p. 108. In *The Mystical Theology* in *The Divine Names and Mystical Theology,* pp. 209–222, trans. John D. Jones (Milwaukee: Marquette University Press, 1980), Chap. 1, §1, p. 211, Pseudo-Dionysius Areopagite [5th–6th century CE] speaks of God as "beyond being." The connection between a belief in God's transcendence and his ultimate disappearance as a way to free human activity from God's interference is explored in both Richard Elliott Friedman's *The Disappearance of God: A Divine Mystery* (Boston: Little, Brown, 1995) and Eric Fromm's *You Shall Be as Gods* (Greenwich: Fawcett, 1966); Fromm describes his orientation as both "radical humanism" (p. 12) and "nontheistic mysticism" (p. 18), the latter the equivalent of Mauthner's *gottlose Mystik;* see the annotation in Part III, §17. An inevitable consequence of removing the divine from earth (as in ancient animistic and pagan cults) to heaven (as in the great monotheistic religions of the West) is a desacralization of the world; according to Peter L. Berger, *The Sacred Canopy: Elements of a Sociological Theory of Religion* (Garden City: Anchor, 1967), p. 113: ". . . the 'disenchantment of the world' begins in the Old Testament." In the allegorical film *Circle of Iron (The Silent Flute),*

directed by Richard Moore (Los Angeles: Embassy Pictures, 1978), the main
character, Cord, goes through numerous trials to be able to read a book
which will show him the meaning of life; when he is finally able to open it,
he finds that each of the book's pages is a mirror; the original story, written
by Bruce Lee, James Coburn, and Stirling Silliphant, was intended, according to the opening credits, to "... capture not only the spirit of martial arts
but a part of the Zen philosophy he [Bruce Lee] lived by"; see also the annotations for Part III, §19 and Part V, §6. Part I of Herbert Spencer's *First
Principles*, 4th ed. (New York: D. Appleton, 1898 [1864]), pp. 2–126, is entitled "The Unknowable." The notion that the world as a whole may be con-
ceived of as a being is similar to the Gaia Hypothesis, which sees the earth
not as a collection of organisms but as an organism itself; see James Lovelock,
Gaia: A New Look at Life on Earth, 2nd ed. (Oxford: Oxford University
Press, 1995). Paul Tillich writes in his *Systematic Theology: Three Volumes in
One* (Chicago: University of Chicago Press, 1967 (1951–1963) Vol. 1, p. 156:
"The religious word for what is called the ground of being is God"; in Vol. 2,
p. 12, Tillich posits "... not the God of traditional theism but the 'God above
God,' the power of being, which works through those who have no name for
it, not even the name God." The Titan referred to in this section is Atlas. The
expression "turtles all the way down" (an infinite regress) is derived from
the mytheme found in Indian, Chinese, and native American mythology
that the world rests on the back of a turtle. The relation between the immanence and transcendence of the divine is eloquently expressed by Black Elk:
"We should know that he [the Great Spirit] is within all things; the trees, the
grasses, the rivers, the mountains and all the four-legged animals, and the
winged peoples; and even more important, we should understand that He is
also above all these things and peoples"; quoted in Brown, *The Spiritual
Legacy of the American Indian* (*op. cit.*), p. 18; see also the annotation for
Part I, §2. Note, however, that the abbot attacks rather than defends panen-
theism, the view that "God is both immanent in and transcendent to the
world," as well as pantheism, the view "God is the same as the world," in favor of seeing immanence and transcendence as two sides of the same coin.
"This-worldly" transcendence and religious naturalism (as opposed to su-
pernaturalism) are expounded by the Unitarian Universalist theologian,
Jerome A. Stone, in *The Minimalist Vision of Transcendence: A Naturalistic
Philosophy of Religion* (1992) and *Religious Naturalism Today: The Rebirth of
a Forgotten Alternative* (2008), both published by the State University of
New York Press in Albany. Images of a force that "... that causes the flower
to grow, that drives water through rocks, that uproots trees" are from Dylan
Thomas's poem "The Force That Through the Green Fuse Drives the Flower"
[1934] in *The Norton Anthology of Modern Poetry*, ed. Richard Ellmann and

Robert O'Clair (New York: W. W. Norton, 1973), pp. 903–904. Near equivalents may be the dualistic idea of an élan vital as a force distinct from matter, as developed by Henri Bergson in *Creative Evolution,* trans. Arthur Mitchell (Mineola: Dover, 2012 [1907]) and Asian concepts of energy (*qi* or *chi,* 氣 in traditional Chinese; *ki,* 気 in Japanese). A nondualistic conception of mass-energy sees the two as equivalent and convertible: $E = mc^2$. Thomas Hobbes in *Elements of Philosophy,* Vol. 1 of *The English Works of Thomas Hobbes,* trans. William Molesworth (London: John Bohn, 1839 [1655]) similarly holds to the materialist view that all that exists is matter in motion, i.e., in a nonduality with each other. On nondualism as a philosophical concept, particularly in Buddhist thought, see David Loy, *Nonduality: A Study in Comparative Philosophy* (New Haven: Yale University Press, 1988). It may be hypothesized that the concept of nonduality has the potential to overcome a number of dichotomies in Christian theology, including those between God and creation, the three persons of the Trinity, the divine and human natures of Christ, the deification or *theosis* of humans, the presence of Christ in the sacrament of holy communion, monergy–synergy (predestination vs. free will), God as a force acting within rather than from outside the world, etc. The nondualistic notion that we are unable to distinguish "the dancer from the dance" (similar to our inability to distinguish "lightning from its flash") is derived from William Butler Yeats' poem "Among School Children" [1928] in *The Norton Anthology of Modern Poetry* (*op. cit.*), pp. 140–142. In *No More Secondhand God and Other Writings* (Carbondale: Southern Illinois University Press, 1963), p. 28, R. Buckminster Fuller, a Unitarian, writes, "God, to me, it seems, is a verb not a noun"; on April 20, 2015 the Episcopalian bishop, John Shelby Spong, posted on Twitter @JohnShelbySpong: "God is not a noun, that demands to be defined, God is a verb that invites us to live, to love and to be." Scriptural sources: Ps 139:7–8; Isa 59:2; Mark 8:24; John 14:9; Acts 17:28; 2 Cor 3:18; Heb 13:8.

§19. The distinction between the "doty way of devotion" and the "way of actualization" has parallels with the distinction made in Buddhism between "other-power" (*tariki,* 他力), characteristic of some schools of Buddhism, such as Pure Land Buddhism, which see people as incapable of saving themselves and so invoke the power of a celestial Buddha, Amitābha, to attain nirvana, and "self-power" (*jiriki,* 自力), characteristic of Zen, in which salvation is achieved through one's own efforts. From a genuinely nondualistic perspective the two approaches are simply two aspects of the same phenomenon: if the "I" does not exist as a distinct entity separate from everything else, then when "I" acts, it is indistinguishable from the universe (God, the One, the name that cannot be named, absolute nothingness, whatever) acting through "me"; see Steve Bein, "Self Power, Other Power, and Non-dualism in Japanese Buddhism," *Proceedings of the XXII World Congress of Philosophy* 6:7–13 (2008). "The way of actualization" has parallels to the concept of *self-actualization* in humanistic and transpersonal psychology, as developed by Abraham Maslow in books such as *Motivation and Personality* (New York: Harper, 1954), *Toward a Psychology of Being* (Princeton: Van Nostrand, 1962), and *The Farther Reaches of Human Nature* (New York: Viking Press, 1971). The Greek word for *image* is *icon* (εἰκών). The notion that religion is more a matter of experience than of knowledge and that we might directly perceive the light of God within us was emphasized particularly by Symeon the New Theologian in *The Discourses*, trans. C. J. deCatanzaro (Mahwah: Paulist Press, 1980 [late 10th century CE]). Distinctions between mediate vs. immediate knowledge, knowledge-about vs. knowledge of acquaintance, knowledge by description vs. knowledge by acquaintance, intellect vs. intuition have been made respectively by Kitaro Nishida in *An Inquiry into the Good,* trans. Masao Abe and Christopher Ives (New Haven: Yale University Press, 1990 [1911]), p. 4; William James, *The Principles of Psychology* (New York: Dover, 1950 [1890]), Vol. 1 pp. 221–223; Bertrand Russell, "Knowledge by Acquaintance and Knowledge by Description," *Proceedings of the Aristotelian Society* 11:108–128 (1910–1911), pp. 108 *ff.*; and Henri Bergson, *An Introduction to Metaphysics,* trans. T. E. Hulme (Indianapolis: Bobbs-Merrill, 1955 [1903]), pp. 21 *ff.* The distinction is similar to that made in the German language between *wissen* (to have knowledge about something) and *kennen* (to be familiar with something), which is difficult to make in English since these two distinct ways of knowing are both rendered by the word *know.* The phrase "Christianity is not a religion" echoes the idea of "religionless Christianity" found in Dietrich Bonhoeffer, *Prisoner for God: Letters and Papers from Prison,* trans. Reginald H. Fuller, ed. Eberhard Bethge (New York: Macmillan, 1959 [1943–1945]), p. 123: "If religion is no more than the garment of Christianity—and even that garment has had very different aspects at different periods—then what is a religionless Christianity?" Iconoclasm, the view that outward forms of religion are an impediment to spiritual experience and should, therefore, be destroyed, is a recurring tendency in the Judeo-Christian (and other) religious traditions, starting with the Biblical prohibition against making graven images in the Ten Commandments, followed by the Iconoclast controversies in the Byzantine Church during the early medieval period, the iconoclasm of Reformed Protestantism during the Reformation, and continuing all the way up to the modern period with proscriptions against art and some forms of music in some Christian denominations; see Alain Besançon, *Forbidden Image: An Intellectual History of Iconoclasm,* trans. Jane Marie Todd (Chicago: University of Chicago Press, 2000). The phrase "enter into the divine darkness" is taken from Pseudo-Dionysius, *The Mystical Theology* (*op. cit.*), Chap. 1, §3, p. 213. The expression "inner light" is used by Friends and Quakers to refer to the light of God within oneself; see George Fox, *Journal* (London: Friends' Tract Association, 1891 [1694]), Vol. 1, p. 36: "I was glad that I was commanded to turn people to that inward light, Spirit, and grace, by which all might know their salvation, and their way to God; even that Divine Spirit which would lead them into all truth, and which I infallibly knew would never deceive any." Rufus M. Jones, in *Social Law in the Spiritual World: Studies in Human and Divine Inter-Relationship* (New York: Swathmore Press, 1904), p. 149, further writes, "The Inner Light is the doctrine that there is something Divine, 'something of God' in the human soul." In the Quaker tradition the inner light is equated with the guidance of the Holy Spirit within oneself in support of the idea of continuous revelation; see the annotation for Part III, §11. The concept of a "divine spark" is central to Gnosticism, a heretical sect which flourished at beginning of the Christian Era; see Dan Merkur, *Gnosis: An Esoteric Tradition of Mystical Visions and Unions* (Albany: State University of New York Press, 1993), p. 111. The term *uncreated light*, also referred to as the *Light of Tabor* (after Mt. Tabor, the purported location of Christ's transfiguration) in the Eastern Orthodox tradition, was associated by Gregory Palamas with the divine light experienced by those who attain union with God; see Papademetriou, *Introduction to St. Gregory Palamas* (*op. cit.*), p. 33. A classic work on imitating Christ is Thomas à Kempis, *The Imitation of Christ*, trans. Richard Whitford, ed. Harold C. Gardiner (Garden City: Image, 1955 [c. early 15th century CE]). "Be ye lamps unto yourselves" is a saying ascribed to the Buddha in the *Mahāparinibbāṇa Sutta* [4th century BCE?], trans. T. W. Rhys-David, quoted in *The Teachings of the Buddha*, 2nd ed., ed. Jack Kornfield (Boston: Shambhala, 1996), p. 124. In Christianity the statement "You are the Christ" is traditionally reserved only for Jesus of Nazareth, despite numerous passages in the New Testament which speak of believers as also being the sons/daughters/children of God. In Buddhism, however, "You are the Buddha" may be applied to everyone; see Ed Russo, *You Are Buddha: Translation of the Vajrayana* (Pittsburgh: Illuminated Publications, 2014), especially p. 84. Religious statements such as "You are the Christ" and "You are the Buddha" may be taken as performative rather than descriptive uses of language: e.g., when parents give a name to a baby, the speech act is performative because it brings the name into being; later when someone uses the name to refer to the baby, the speech act is descriptive because the name has already been created; see J. L. Austin, *How to Do Things with Words*, 2nd ed., ed. J. O. Urmson and Marina Sbisà (Oxford: Clarendon Press, 1975). On the meaning of the expression "the Son of Man" (ὁ υἱὸς τοῦ ἀνθρώπου, also translated "Son of Adam") and Jesus' use of it to refer to himself, see Robert W. Funk, Roy W. Hoover, and the Jesus Seminar, *The Five Gospels: What Did Jesus Really Say?* (New York: HarperCollins, 1993), pp. 76–77. The Hebrew word *messiah* means "anointed one" and is translated into Greek as *Christ*. In the Eastern Orthodox sacrament of chrismation a baptized person is anointed with oil as a seal of the gift of the Holy Spirit, reflecting the bestowing of the spirit on the apostles on the day of Pentecost, which marks the beginning of the Christian Church (Christ's body). "There are many who have sought light and truth but they look for it outside themselves, where it is not" is a quote from Augustine in Meister Eckhart's Sermon #2, "This is another sermon" in Blakney, *Meister Eckhart* (*op. cit.*), p. 105. "Come as You Are" is the title of a contemporary Christian song by [David] Crowder, appearing on his studio album *Neon Steeple* (Brentwood: Sparrow Records, 2014). "Just As I Am" [1835] is the title of a hymn written by Charlotte Elliott, included in the Lutheran *Service Book and Hymnal* (Minneapolis: Augsburg, 1958), Hymn #370; it was the signature invitation hymn at Billy Graham's crusades. The phrase "Know thyself" was inscribed at the Temple of Apollo in Delphi and frequently referred to and quoted by Greek philosophers, including Socrates, who in Plato's *Phaedrus* in *The Dialogues of Plato*, pp. 115–141 (*op. cit.*), 229, p. 116, says, "I must first know myself, as the Delphian inscription says." The idea that self-knowledge leads to knowledge of God can be found in *The Gospel of Thomas*, trans. Thomas O. Lambdin, in the *Nag Hammadi Library*, 3rd ed., pp. 124–138, ed. James M. Robinson (New York: HarperCollins, 1988 [c. 1st–2nd century BCE]), Saying 3, p. 126: ". . . the kingdom is inside of you and outside of you. When you come to know yourselves, then you will become known, and you will realize that it is you who are sons of the living Father." The phrase "all the answers to all life's questions" is taken from the film *Circle of Iron* (*op. cit.*), which also includes the line: "There is no book . . . no enlightenment outside yourself"; see the annotations for Part III, §18 and Part V, §6. Christian Neoplatonism draws on Plotinus's [c. 204–279 CE] theory of emanations; see the following passages from the *Enneads*, 7 vols., trans. A. H. Armstrong (Cambridge: Harvard University Press [Loeb Classical Library], 1984): "For there is a kind of centre [the One or God], and around this is a circle shining out from it [mind, *noûs*, νοῦς], and beyond these another, light from light [soul, *psyché*, ψυχή]: but outside these there is no longer another circle of light but this next circle [matter, *húle*, ὕλη] through lack of its own light needs illumination from another source" (IV.3.17, p. 89); ". . . there is the One [the center] beyond being . . . and next in order there is Being and Intellect [*noûs*], and the nature of Soul [*psyché*] in the third place. And just as in nature there are these three of which we have spoken, so we ought to think that they are present also in ourselves . . . . Our soul then also is a divine thing . . . ." (V.1.10, pp. 45–47); "'But it [*noûs*] contemplates God,' we might say. But if anyone is going to admit that it knows God, he will be compelled to agree that it also knows itself" (V.3.7, p. 93). The goal of Neoplatonic contemplation is to realize unity with the One (*hénosis*, ἕνωσις). In the documentary, *Mysteries of the Jesus Prayer,* directed by Norris J. Chumley (New York: Magnetic Arts, 2010), Father Neilos of St. Catherine's Monastery, Mount Sinai, Egypt, says, "Knowledge of God is also a knowledge of oneself and if God is eternal and without limitation, so is mankind." "That thou art" is a translation of the Hindu phrase *tát tvam ási* found in the *Khândogya Upanishad* [early 1st millennium BCE], trans. F. Max Müller in *The Upanishads,* Part 1, Vol. 1 of *The Sacred Books of the East,* ed. F. Max Müller (Oxford: Clarendon Press, 1879), VI.8.7, p. 101: "Now that which is that subtile essence (the root of all), in it all that exists has its self. It is the True. It is the Self, and thou, O Svetaketu, art it." Scriptural sources: Gen 1:26: 2:24; Exod 3:2, 14; 13:21; 20:4; 1 Kgs 8:12; Pss 8:3–4; 18:11; 97:2; 119:105; Isa 7:14; Matt 1:16, 23; 5:14–16; 16:16; 17:1–8; 19:26; 26:63–64; Mark 9:2–3; 10:45; Luke 4:18; 9:23; John 1:1–14, 41; 3:16; 8:12; 12:35–36; 15:16; Acts 2:1–4; 1 Cor 11:1; 15:28; 2 Cor 13:3–5; Eph 1:4–6; 5:8; Phil 2:12–13; 1 Thess 5:5; 1 Tim 2:4; Titus 2:11; Heb 4:15; 1 Pet 2:22; 1 John 2:6, 20, 27.

§20. Scriptural sources: 1 Cor 9:26–27; Gal 5:17.

§21. "He is closer to you than your jugular vein" is adapted from *The Qur'ân,* trans. E. H. Palmer, Vol. IX of *The Sacred Books of the East,* ed. F. Max Müller (Oxford: Clarendon Press, 1880), Part II, L:16, p. 243. The phrase ". . . nearer to you than you are to yourself" is derived from Meister Eckhart's Sermon #6, "The Kingdom of God is at hand" in Blakney, *Meister Eckhart* (*op. cit.*), p. 129. The anonymous author of *The Cloud of Unknowing* (*op. cit.*), p. 61, writes, "When you first begin, you find only darkness, and as it were a cloud of unknowing"; see also the reference to the "cloud of forgetting" in the annotation for Part III, §17. The "dark night of the soul" is the theme of the poem, "The Dark Night," by St. John of the Cross [1542–1591] in *The Poems of St. John of the Cross,* pp. 19–21, trans. John Frederick Nims (Chicago: University of Chicago Press, 1979). "God speaks to us with the same voice that we speak to him. They are one and the same voice" is a play on Meister Eckhart's Sermon #23, "Distinctions are lost in God" in Blakney, *Meister Eckhart* (*op. cit.*), 206: "The eye by which I see God is the same as the eye by which God sees me. My eye and God's eye are one and the same— one in seeing, one in knowing, and one in loving." The distinction drawn on in this section between verbal, meditative, and contemplative (silent) prayer overlaps imprecisely with the three levels prayer distinguished by

Hesychasm in Eastern Orthodoxy spirituality: (1) catharsis/purgation/purification; (2) theoria/contemplation/illumination; (3) theosis/deification/union with God; a principle text is *The Philokalia*, a collection of spiritual writings composed from the 4th–15th centuries CE and initially compiled in 18th century; the first four volumes have been translated by G. E. H. Palmer, Philip Sherrard, and Kallistos Ware (London: Faber and Faber, 1979–1999); see especially St. Symeon the New Theologian [949–1022 CE], *The Three Methods of Prayer* in Vol. 4, pp. 67–75. "Lord Jesus Christ, Son of God, have mercy on me, a sinner," known as the *Jesus Prayer*, is widely practiced in the Eastern Orthodox tradition. In some Buddhist sects, the Buddha and bodhisattvas (saints) are seen as powerful figures whom powerless people pray to for help; in other sects adherents vow to *become* a bodhisattva and help others; see "The Four Vows" in Isshu Miura and Ruth Fuller Sasaki, *The Zen Koan* (New York: Harvest, 1965), pp. 35–36. Within Christianity there is a parallel difference between the conventional view that Jesus is someone whom powerless people pray to for help and the mystical view that it is possible to realize the power of Christ within oneself; a similar distinction might be made between those who pray to the saints for help and those who become saints to help others; *cf.* the distinction between "other-power" and "self-power" in the annotation for Part III, §19. James Dillet Freeman, a minister of the Unity Church and poet whose poems were taken twice by astronauts (Buzz Aldrin and James B. Irwin) to the moon, states, "Prayer is valuable not because it alters the circumstances and conditions of your life, but because it alters you"; quoted by Rev. Dr. Raymont L. Anderson in *Moving Mountains: The Journey of Transformation* (Bloomington: AuthorHouse, 2012), p. 140. "God has nothing to say" and "God is silent" echo the following lines from John Cage's "Lecture on Nothing": "I have nothing to say and I am saying it . . . . We need not fear these silences" in *Silence: Lectures and Writings by John Cage* (Middletown: Wesleyan University Press, 1961), p. 109. "[Silence] does have a sound" was inspired by the title of the Simon and Garfunkel song "The Sound of Silence" on the studio album *Wednesday Morning, 3 A.M.* (New York: Columbia, 1964). To "think about how you think" is *metacognition*, a skill that may be applied to spirituality as much as to other forms of thinking. The phrase "a ripple in the flow of life" applies the concept of dissipative structures to the Heraclitan flux (see the annotation for Part II, §4) and may also be associated with the stream of consciousness discussed by William James in *Principles of Psychology*, Vol. 1 (New York: Henry Holt, 1890), pp. 348 *ff*. On the use of breathing techniques in both Zen meditation (*zazen*) and Christian contemplation, see William Johnston, *Christian Zen*, 3rd ed. (New York: Fordham University Press, 1997), pp. 78–80. The Greek word *pneûma* (πνεῦμα) may be variously translated as *breath, air, wind,* and *spirit.* In *The Marriage of Heaven and Hell* (*op. cit.*), p. 101, William Blake writes, "If the doors of perception were cleansed every thing would appear to man as it is, infinite." *Beyond Good and Evil* is the title of a book by Friedrich Nietzsche; see the annotation for Part II, §14. In *The Way of a Pilgrim,* trans. R. M. French (New York: HarperCollins, 1965 [1884]), which tells the story of an anonymous nineteenth-century Russian mendicant, the following instructions for saying the Jesus Prayer are given on p. 90: "... [A]s you draw your breath in, say, or imagine yourself saying, 'Lord Jesus Christ,' and as you breathe again, 'have mercy on me.' Do this as often and as much as you can . . . . [W]hatever you do, be on your guard against imagination and any sort of visions . . . . [I]nward prayer should be kept free from visions, lest one fall into temptation." Practitioners of *zazen* are similarly instructed to count their breaths and to dismiss *makyo* ("devils in the objective world") taking the form of "visions, hallucinations, fantasies, revelations, illusionary sensations" when meditating; see the lecture by Zen master Hakuun Yasutani [1885–1973] in Philip Kapleau, *The Three Pillars of Zen,* 2nd ed. (Garden City: Anchor, 1980), p. 41. When the desert saint, Abba Moses [330–405 CE], was asked for advice, he replied, "Go, sit in your cell, and your cell will teach you everything"; from *The Sayings of the Desert Fathers,* trans. Benedicta Ward (Kalamazoo: Cistercian Publications, 1975), p. 139. The Bodhidharma [5th–6th century CE], a legendary monk who is traditionally regarded as having brought Chan (Zen) Buddhism from India to China, reportedly spent nine years meditating in front of a wall, a practice known as *pi-kuan,* or "wall-gazing"; see D. T. Suzuki, *Essays in Zen Buddhism: First Series* (London: Rider, 1953), pp. 184–186. Scriptural sources: Exod 20:4–5; 1 Kgs 19:11–12; Matt 5:8; 6:9–13; Luke 18:13; John 3:8; Rom 8:15–17, 26; 1 Cor 13:11; Gal 2:20; 1 Thess 5:17.

§22. The practice of going on a quest to seek God or find spiritual enlightenment can be found in many religious traditions and is also regarded as a mythic and literary archetype; see Joseph Campbell, *The Hero with a Thousand Faces,* 3rd ed. (Novato: New World Library, 2008 [1949]), Part I. Examples include the *Epic of Gilgamesh* [c. 2100 BCE], Homer's *Odyssey* [c. 8th century BCE], and *The Quest of the Holy Grail* [early 13th century CE]. In *The Sacred Pipe: Black Elk's Account of the Seven Rites of the Oglala Sioux,* ed. Joseph Epes Brown (Norman: University of Oklahoma Press, 1953), pp. 44–66, Black Elk describes a Hanblecheyapi, or "crying for a vision" [vision quest] ritual; see the annotation for Part III, §31. In the Judeo-Christian tradition, the theme of "going to the wilderness to meet God" can be found in the stories of Moses receiving the Ten Commandments from God at Mt. Sinai, Jesus being taken to a high mountain during his temptation in the wilderness, Jesus being transfigured on a mountain (traditionally identified with Mt. Tabor), Jesus praying in the Garden of Gethsemane at the foot of the Mount of Olives, and Jesus being crucified at Golgotha (traditionally regarded as a hill or mountain). On the desert saints, see John Chryssavgis, *In the Heart of the Desert: The Spirituality of the Desert Fathers and Mothers,* 2nd ed. (Bloomington: World Wisdom, 2008). Scriptural sources: Exod 19:20; Num 32:13; Matt 4:1–11; 17:1–2; 26:30; Mark 1:12–13; 14:26; Luke 4:1–13; 22:39; John 19:17; 2 Thess 3:3; Jas 1:2–4; 1 Pet 1:7.

§23. Scriptural sources: Matt 3:10; 8:20; Luke 3:9; 9:58.

§25. In Western and African folklore, crossroads are regarded as places of liminality, where it is possible to meet and make deals with the devil; Robert Johnson's songs "Cross Road Blues," "Me and the Devil Blues," and "Hellhound on My Trail" on the album *Robert Johnson: King of the Delta Blues Singers* (New York: Columbia, 1961 [1936–1937]) are sometimes cited in support of the legend that Johnson sold his soul to the devil to improve his guitar-playing ability. Athanasius writes in *The Life of Saint Antony,* trans. Robert T. Meyer (New York: Newman Press, 1978 [c. 4th century CE]), §11–12, pp. 29–30, that on his way to the wilderness the desert saint Anthony the Great [251–356 CE] found a large disk of silver and later gold along the road, put there by the devil to tempt him. Scriptural sources: Matt 7:13–14; Mark 14:32–41.

§26. On April 26, 1336, the Italian poet Petrarch [Francesco Petrarca, 1304–1374 CE] climbed Mt. Ventoux for no other purpose than to see the view. In a letter to his spiritual advisor, reproduced as "Ascent of Mont Ventoux" in Henry Reeve, *Petrarch* (Edinburgh and London: William Blackwood and Sons, 1878), Chap. VIII, pp. 83–89, Petrarch includes the following quote from Augustine on p. 88: "There are men who go to admire the high places of mountains, the great waves of the sea, the wide currents of rivers, the circuit of the ocean, and the orbits of the stars—and who neglect themselves." See *The Confessions of St. Augustine,* trans. F. J. Sheed (New York: Sheed and Ward, 1942 [397–400]), Book Ten, XIII, p. 180. Scriptural sources: Gen 1:31; Matt 4:1–11; Mark 1:12–13; Luke 4:1–13; Col 3:2.

§27. Images in this section are drawn from St. Athanasius, *The Life of Saint Antony* (*op. cit.*) and from the following paintings: Michelangelo, *The Torment of St. Anthony* (Ft. Worth: Kimbell Art Museum, 1487–1488); Matthias Grünwald, *The Temptation of St. Anthony* (Colmar: Unterlinden Museum, 1512–1516); and Joos van Craesbeeck, *The Temptation of St. Anthony* (Karlsruhe: Staatliche Kunsthalle, c. 1650); medieval surrealism is replicated in twentieth-century versions, such as Max Ernst, *The Temptation of Saint Anthony* (Duisburg: Lehmbruck Museum, 1945) and Salvador Dalí, *The Temptation of St. Anthony* (Brussels: Royal Museum of Fine Arts, 1946). Prior to his enlightenment Siddhartha Gautama was similarly besieged by demons summoned by Mara, the god of Desire and Death, who "assailed him with wind and rain and hurled at him such deadly missiles as uprooted trees, boiling mud, fiery rocks, live coals, and glowing ashes that turned the pitch-black darkness incandescent"; quoted from Noss, *Man's Religions (op. cit.)*, p. 124. "I wish this moment could last forever" alludes to Faust's bargain with Mephistopheles in Johann Wolfgang von Goethe, *Faust*, trans. Ann Swanwick (New York: Frederick A. Stokes, 1887 [1832]), p. 76: "When to the moment I shall say, / 'Linger a while, so fair thou art!' / Then mayst thou fetter me straightway, / Then to the abyss will I depart." Scriptural sources: Gen 19:24; 1 Kgs 19:11–12; Ps 89:15; Matt 28:20; Luke 4:9–11; Rev 9:1–2.

§28. Scriptural sources: Phil 4:7.

§31. "The way up a mountain is the same as the way down" references Heraclitus's fragment, "The way up and down is one and the same" in Kahn, *The Art and Thought of Heraclitus (op. cit.)*, CIII, p. 75. Koan #46 in the *Mumonkan (op. cit.)*, p. 75, includes the question: "How can you proceed on further from the top of a hundred-foot pole?" "The higher we climb the closer we come to the center" corresponds horizontally if not vertically to the following line from Plotinus's *Enneads (op. cit.)*, V.1.11, pp. 49–51: "He [the One or God] is not divided, but abides, and as he does not abide in place he is contemplated in many beings, in each and every one of those capable of receiving him as another self, just as the center of a circle exists by itself, but every one of the radii in the circle has its point in the center and the lines bring their individuality to it." The Hanblecheyapi, or vision quest ritual, described by Black Elk in *The Sacred Pipe (op. cit.)*, involves placing five poles on the top of a mountain, one in the center and four equidistant from the center in the four directions; the "lamenter" [seeker of a vision] walks to each of the outer poles, which represent the four great powers of the universe, offers a prayer, and then returns to the center, which symbolizes the dwelling place of *Wakan-Tanka* [the Great Spirit]; see the annotations for Part I, §1 and Part III, §22. The pattern described by Black Elk is the same as a Greek cross, an archetypal figure which was used as a religious symbol in pre-Christian times as well. The cross also forms a mandala based on the number *four*, which has parallels in numerous religious and cultural traditions, variously representing the directions (east, south, west, north), the times of day (morning, afternoon, evening, night), the spheres (sun, earth, stars, moon), the life cycle (birth, growth, decay, death), the phases of life (infancy, youth, maturity, old age), the elements (water, earth air, fire), topography (oceans, plains, mountains, deserts), the seasons (spring, summer, autumn, winter), agriculture (planting, blossoming, harvesting, lying fallow), and spiritual stages (innocence, experience, suffering, redemption), the latter derived from William Blake's *Songs of Innocence* and *Songs of*

Experience in *William Blake* (*op. cit.*), pp. 26–59. On the concept of a qua-ternity encompassing the traditional Christian Trinity plus Satan, see Carl Jung, *A Psychological Approach to the Dogma of the Trinity,* trans. R. F. C. Hull, in *Psychology and Religion: West and East,* 2nd. ed., pp. 107–200, Vol. 11 of the *Collected Works of C. G. Jung* (*op. cit.,* 1969 [1948]), especially pp. 164–192: "The Problem of the Fourth"; see also *Concerning Mandala Sym-bolism,* trans. R. F. C. Hull, in *The Archetypes and the Collective Unconscious,* 2nd ed., Vol. 9, Part I of *The Collected Works of C. G. Jung* (*op. cit.,* 1969 [1950]), pp. 355–384. The center of a Greek cross represents a fifth, so the mandala is in fact a quintinity, the same as that described by Black Elk. The concept of an *oceanic feeling* was derived by Roman Rolland from his studies of the 19th-century Hindu mystic, Sri Ramakrishna Paramhansa, published in *The Life of Ramakrishna* (Calcutta: Advaita Ashrama, 1970 [1929]) and conveyed in a letter dated December 5, 1927 to Sigmund Freud, who wrote about it (rather dismissively and with less profundity) in *Civilization and Its Discontents,* trans. Joan Riviere (Mineola: Dover, 1994 [1930]), Chap. 1, pp. 1–8; see J. Moussaieff Masson, *The Oceanic Feeling: The Origins of Religious Sentiment in Ancient India* (Dordrecht: D. Reidel, 1980), Chap. II, "The Oceanic Feeling: Origin of the Term," pp. 33–50. The phrase "absolute nothingness" (*zettai mu,* ぜったい無) is from Kitaro Nishida, *Intelligibility and the Philosophy of Nothingness,* trans. Robert Schinzinger (Tokyo: Maru-zen, 1958), p. 130. The idea of there being "no center" is discussed in Masao Abe's essay, "Kenotic God and Dynamic Sunyata" in *The Emptying God: A Buddhist–Jewish–Christian Conversation,* pp. 3–65, ed. John B. Cobb, Jr. and Christopher Ives (Maryknoll: Orbis, 1990) and is also consistent with Jacques Derrida's concept of *decentering,* as presented in "Structure, Sign, and Play in the Discourse of the Human Sciences" in *Writing and Difference,* pp. 278–294, trans. Alan Bass (London: Routledge, 1980 [1967]).

§32. On "God is nature and nature is God," see the annotation for Part II, §4. In *My First Summer in the Sierra* (New York: Houghton Mifflin, 1998 [1911]), p. 250, John Muir writes, "In our best times everything turns into religion, all the world seems a church and the mountains altars." "The sun is my brother, the moon my sister" alludes to Francis of Assisi's "The Canticle of Brother Sun" (*op. cit.*); see also the annotation for Part II, §3. Other images from this same paragraph are drawn from the poem, "The Secret Place" by Richard Evanoff, published in the January 1994 issue of *Japan Environment Monitor* 60:2. On the "disenchantment of the world," see the annotation for Part III, §18. Alfred Lord Tennyson's poem "In Memoriam A. H. H." (Lon-don: Macmillan, 1890 [1850]), Canto 56, p. 84, includes the following lines: "Man . . . trusted that God is love indeed / And love Creation's final law / Tho' Nature, red in tooth and claw / With ravine, shriek'd against his creed."

The ability to affirm life despite suffering is a key tenet of Nietzsche's philosophy; see Friedrich Nietzsche, *The Will to Power,* trans. Walter Kaufmann and R. J. Hollingdale (New York: Vintage, 1967 [1906]), Book Four, §1032, p. 532: "If we affirm one single moment, we thus affirm not only ourselves but all existence"; see also the annotation for Part V, §6. The phrase "standing defiant on the ocean until we sink beneath its waves" alludes to a line in Bob Dylan's song, "A Hard Rain's a-Gonna Fall" from the studio album *The Freewheelin' Bob Dylan* (New York: Columbia, 1963). References for allusions in the penultimate paragraph are given in the annotation for Part III, §19. Scriptural sources: Gen 6:17; Exod 7:20; 8:24; 9:10, 14–15, 23–24; 10:13–14; Job 21:26; Isa 1:7; Matt 5:45; 6:26–28; 10:29; Luke 21:11.

§33. An allusion is made Lao-Tze, *Tao-Teh-King* (*op. cit.*), Chap. 8, p. 100: "Superior goodness resembleth water. Water in goodness benefiteth the ten thousand things, yet it quarreleth not. Because it dwells in places which the multitude of men shun, therefore it is near unto the eternal Reason [Tao]." The first two lines of William Blake's poem "Auguries of Innocence" in *William Blake* (*op. cit.*), p. 67, are "To see a World in a Grain of Sand and a Heaven in a Wild Flower." "Everything that lives is holy" is a near-direct quote from Blake's "A Song of Liberty" in *The Marriage of Heaven and Hell* (*op. cit.*), p. 109.

IV. THE CITY

§1. The city is fictional but inspired by Oxford, England, which, in addition to being a cathedral town, was the only city in England other than Cambridge to have a university in the 14th century. For descriptions of medieval towns and cities, see *Fourteenth-Century Towns,* ed. John D. Clare (San Diego: Harcourt Brace Jovanovich, 1993). The poem beginning with the line "From the goats my lot divide" is excerpted directly from *Dies Irae* [c. 13th century], rendered into English by Edward Slosson (New York: Anson D. F. Randolph, 1866), Stanza XV, p. 13. Scriptural sources: Matt 6:9–13; 25:31–46; 1 Cor 6:9–10.

§2. For a general introduction to medieval universities see Robert S. Rait, *Life in the Medieval University* (Cambridge: Cambridge University Press, 1918). For a survey of medieval scholasticism, see Maurice de Wulf, *An Introduction to Scholastic Philosophy: Medieval and Modern,* trans. Peter Coffey (New York: Dover, 1956 [1907]). For an introduction to dialectical logic, including its use in the Middle Ages, see Nicholas Rescher, *Dialectics: A Controversy-Oriented Approach to the Theory of Knowledge* (Albany: State University of New York Press, 1977).

§3. The maxims that "a statement must be either true or false and it cannot be both true and false at the same time" are two laws of bivalent logic stated in Aristotle's *Metaphysics* (*op. cit.*): (1) the law of the excluded middle: ". . . there cannot be an intermediate between contradictories, but of one subject we must either affirm or deny any one predicate" (VI, §7, 1011b, p. 531); and (2) the law of non-contradiction: ". . . contradictory statements are not at the same time true" (IV, §6, 1011b, p. 531). The *liar's paradox* and *paradox of the heap,* also known as the *sorites paradox,* were articulated by the ancient Greek philosopher, Eubulides of Melitus [4th century BCE]; see Glenn W. Erickson and John A. Fossa, *Dictionary of Paradox* (Lanham: University Press of America, 1998), pp. 63–64 and 196–199 respectively. A paradox of Zeno of Elea [5th century BCE], mentioned in Aristotle's *Physics* (*op. cit.*), VI, 9, 239b, p. 323, is paraphrased with interpolations by Charles M. Bakewell in *Source Book in Ancient Philosophy,* 2nd ed. (New York: Charles Scribner's Sons, 1939), p. 24, as follows: "You cannot traverse an infinite number of points in a finite time. You must traverse the half of any given distance before you traverse the whole, and the half of that again before you can traverse it. This goes on *ad infinitum,* so that . . . there are an infinite number in any given space, and it cannot be traversed in a finite time." Reference is made again in this section to the system of logic known as the *catuṣkoṭi,* or tetralemma; see the annotation for Part III, §17.

§4. Tertullian in *The Prescription Against Heretics,* trans. Peter Holmes, in *The Ante-Nicene Fathers,* Vol. III, pp. 243–265 (*op. cit.*), Chap. VII, p. 246, wrote, "What indeed has Athens to do with Jerusalem? What concord is there between the Academy and the Church?" Thomas Aquinas [1225-1274 CE] subscribed to a two-fold theory of truth: the truth of faith and the truth of reason do not contradict each other; see *Contra Gentiles,* trans. Anton C. Pegis (Notre Dame: University of Notre Dame Press, 1955 [1259-1265 CE]), Book I, Chap. 7, Sec. 1, p. 74. "I believe even though I do not understand and accept by faith what I cannot grasp with my mind" is a modified quote from Bernard of Clairvaux's [c. 1090-1153 CE] *Sermons on the Song of Songs* in *Life and Works of Saint Bernard,* trans. Samuel J. Eales, ed. Dom John Mabillon (London: John Hodges, 1896), Sermon LXXVI, §6, p. 471: "I say with confidence that the blessed and eternal Trinity, which I do not understand, I believe in, and thus hold by faith that which I do not grasp with the understanding." "I believe because it's absurd" is a translation of the Latin phrase *credo quia absurdum,* an imprecise rendering of a line frequently attributed to Tertullian; see Tertullian, *On the Flesh of Christ,* trans. Peter Holmes, in *The Ante-Nicene Fathers,* Vol. III, pp. 521–542 (*op. cit.*), ed. Chap. 5, p. 525, where the actual quote is given: "it is by all means to be believed, because it is absurd." "I do not know in order to believe; I believe in order to know" is adapted from Anselm, *Proslogian*, trans. Thomas Williams (Indianapolis: Hackett, 2007 [1077-1078]), Chap. 1, p. 81: "For I do not seek to understand in order to believe; I believe in order to understand." Scriptural sources: Exod 33:20; Job 36:26; Matt 18:3; Mark 10:15; Luke 18:17; Rom 11:33; 1 Cor 1:23–25; 2:5, 14; 3:18–19; 8:1–2; 13:12; Col 2:2–3; 1 Tim 6:4; 2 Tim 2:23; Jas 2:17, 19; 4:7.

§5. Peter Abailard [Abelard] in *Sic et Non* [*Yes and No*]: *A Critical Edition*, ed. Blanche B. Boyer and Richard McKeon (Chicago: University of Chicago Press, 1977 [1120]) juxtaposes quotes from the Church Fathers to show how they seemingly contradict one another, challenging students to use dialectical reasoning to resolve the discrepancies. Scriptural sources: John 8:32.

§6. "Every lie must be called a sin" is a direct quote from Augustine, *The Enchiridion* (*op. cit.*), Chap. XXII, p. 192.

§7. The Donatist heresy, prevalent in the 4th and 5th centuries CE and revived during the Middle Ages, held that sacraments performed by sinful priests are invalid. A number of heretical movements active in the late medieval period, including the Fraticelli (Spiritual Franciscans), the Brethren of the Free Spirit, the Petrobrusians, and the Waldensians, railed against the wealth of the clergy, the necessity of the sacraments, and/or the use of images in the church; see the respective entries in Clifton, *Encyclopedia of Heresies and Heretics* (*op. cit.*), p. 47 ("Fraticelli"), pp. 47–48 ("Free Spirit"); pp. 111–112 ("Petrobrusians"); pp. 131–133 ("Waldensians"). While heresy was widespread in continental Europe, it was virtually unknown in England until the appearance of John Wycliffe and the Lollards in the latter half of the 14th century; see Malcolm Lambert, *Medieval Heresy: Popular Movements from Gregorian Reform to the Reformation* (New York: Barnes and Noble, 1992). In *Luther's Table Talk*, trans. Henry Bell, extracts selected by James Macaulay (New York: John B. Alden, 1885 [1566]), p. 43, Luther is recorded as saying, " . . . the Pope exalted himself over and above God. Therefore he is properly called the Antichrist . . . ." "The devil can cite Scripture for his purpose" is a line spoken by Antonio in William Shakespeare's *The Merchant of Venice* [1605] in Vol. 1 of *The Plays and Sonnets of William Shakespeare*, pp. 406–433, Vol. 26 of *Great Books of the Western World*, ed. Robert Maynard Hutchins (Chicago: William Benton, 1952), Act I, Scene 3, p. 410. Clement VI, Pope of the Roman Catholic Church from 1342–1352, is quoted in Antony Stockwell, *The Unholy Popes and the Debasement of Western Civilisation*, Vol. 1 of *A Corrupt Tree: An Encyclopaedia of Crimes Committed by the Church of Rome against Humanity and the Human Spirit* (Bloomington: Xlibris, 2013), p. 182, as having said that he "lived as a sinner among sinners." Scriptural sources: Ps 122:1; Joel 1:15; Matt 6:24; 7:1, 15;

19:21; 21:12–13; 24:24; Mark 2:7; Luke 6:20; Rom 3:23; 1 Cor 6:19; 2 Cor 6:16–17; 11:13; 2 Thess 2:3; 1 John 2:22.

§8. A distinction is made in ancient Greek between four different kinds of love: charity or unconditional love (*agápe*, ἀγάπη), brotherly love or friendship (*philía*, φιλία), natural affection (*storgé*, στοργή), and romantic love (*érōs*, ἔρως); see C. S. Lewis, *The Four Loves* (London: Geoffrey Bles, 1960). The Inquisition began in France in the 12th century and was continued in various forms in continental Europe until the Spanish Inquisition was officially abolished in 1834. With the exception of actions taken against the Knights Templar during the early part of the 14th century, the Inquisition was not active in England until the 15th and 16th centuries, initially against Lollardy and later during the reign of Mary I ("Bloody Mary"). General works on the inquisition in the Middle Ages include Edward Burman, *The Inquisition: Hammer of Heresy* (New York: Dorset, 1984); Bernard Hamilton, *The Medieval Inquisition* (New York: Holmes and Meier, 1981); and Henry Charles Lea, *The Inquisition of the Middle Ages* (New York: Barnes and Noble, 1993 [1887]). Scriptural sources: 2 Pet 2:1; 3:16.

§9. Scriptural sources: Isa 40:3; Matt 4:17; John 1:23.

§12. The phrase "survival of the fittest" was coined not by Darwin, but by Herbert Spencer in *The Principles of Biology*, Vol. 1 (London: Williams and Norgate, 1864), pp. 444–445: "This survival of the fittest, which I have here sought to express in mechanical terms, is that which Mr. Darwin has called 'natural selection, or the preservation of favoured races in the struggle for life.'" The concept was later used in defense of the now-discredited view known as *Social Darwinism*. Scriptural sources: Matt 9:36.

§14. Scriptural sources: Mark 2:16.

§15. The word *mindfulness* is a rough equivalent of the concept of *samādhi* found in the Hindu, Jain, Buddhist, and Sikh traditions; see Suzuki, *Essays in Zen Buddhism: First Series* (*op. cit.*), pp. 82–83. *Samādhi* is usually translated into English as *concentration*, which has the connotation of being intellectually focused, but might be better translated as *immediate awareness*; see the annotation for Part IV, §16. The contrast between intellectual and spiritual forms of concentration can be instantly distinguished by comparing Auguste Rodin's sculpture *The Thinker* (Paris: Rodin Museum, 1904) with virtually any statue of the Buddha, e.g., *The Great Buddha* at Kōtoku-in in Kamakura, Japan. For a general introduction to the problem of universals in medieval thought, see W. T. Jones in *The Medieval Mind*, Vol. 2 of *A History of Western Philosophy*, 2nd ed. (New York: Harcourt, Brace, and World, 1969), pp. 185–196. The main views presented are those of Plato [c. 428–347 BCE], Aristotle [385–322 BCE], Augustine [354–430 CE], Boethius [c. 477–524], Roscelin of Compiègne [c. 1050–1125], Peter

Abelard [1079–1142], Thomas Aquinas [1225–1274], Duns Scotus [1226–1308], and William of Ockham [1285–1347]. The syllogism "The sea is blue. The sky is blue. Therefore, the sea and the sky are the same color" is not original, but from memory, though I can no longer remember or locate the source. The notion that objects and their qualities cannot be communicated through language is attributed to Gorgias by Sextus Empiricus in *Against the Logicians* (*op. cit.*), Book I, §83–87, pp. 43–45; see the annotation for Part II, §4. An allusion is made to the finger wagging of Cratylus [5th century BCE] in Aristotle, *Metaphysics* (*op. cit.*), IV.5, 1010a, p. 529; a parallel can be found in the third koan, "Gutei Raises a Finger," of the *Mumonkan* (*op. cit.*), pp. 34–36; see also the annotation for Part V, §7.

§16. The approach to "pure experience" described in this section was inspired by the writings of William James in *Essays in Radical Empiricism* (Cambridge: Harvard University Press, 1976 [1912]) and Kitaro Nishida in *An Inquiry into the Good* (*op. cit.*); cf. the concept of *immediate awareness* in the annotation for Part IV, §15. The sentence "When we look at the trees in a forest, hear the song of a bird . . ." is adapted from Richard Evanoff, "Pure Experience and Constructivism: Western and Asian Perspectives," *The Aoyama Journal of International Politics, Economics, and Communication* 95:41–59 (November 2015), p. 42. "Faith seeking understanding" (*fides quaerens intellectum*) is the subtitle of Anselm's *Proslogian* (*op. cit.*); see also the annotation for Part IV, §4. The infallibility of the Roman Catholic Pope was not formally declared until the First Vatican Council of 1869–1870; the doctrine of the infallibility of the Bible did not appear in Protestant circles until the rise of fundamentalism as a reaction to modernism and liberal Christianity in the late 19th and early 20th centuries; see also the annotation for Part III, §11. On theology as a science, see Thomas Aquinas, *The Summa Theologica* (*op. cit.*), Vol. 1, First Part, Question 1, Articles 1–5, pp. 3–6. At the end of his life Aquinas is reported to have said, "Everything I have written seems like straw by comparison with what I have seen and what has been revealed to me"; quoted in *Albert and Thomas: Selected Writings*, trans. and ed. Simon Tugwell (New York: Paulist Press, 1988), p. 266. The relation between science and fallibilism is discussed in Charles Sanders Peirce [1839–1914], "The Scientific Attitude and Fallibilism" [written at the end of the 19th century and first published in 1940] in *Philosophical Writings of Peirce*, pp. 42–59, ed. Justus Buchler (New York: Dover, 1955). An allusion is made to Goethe's Faust, who longs to give up his pursuit of knowledge in order to encounter life outside his study; see the annotation for Part III, §27.

§17. The line ". . . if prostitution is removed from human affairs, everything will be unsettled due to lusts" is derived from St. Augustine, *On Order* [*De Ordine*], trans. Silvano Borruso (South Bend: St. Augustine's Press, 2007 [late 4th century CE]), Book II.4.12, p. 65: "Remove prostitutes from the social order . . . and lust will destroy it." Scriptural sources: Eccl 8:15; Isa 22:13; Luke 12:19; 1 Cor 15:32.

§19. An overview of lawlessness in the Middle Ages and how it was dealt with by the authorities is provided in Andrew McCall, *The Medieval Underworld* (New York: Barnes and Noble, 1979). On the relation between "town and gown" (conflict between townspeople and students) in medieval times see Rait, *Life in the Medieval University* (*op. cit.*), Chap. VII.

§20. Raising the "hue and cry" was a method used in medieval times to summon common people to help in the apprehension of a criminal; see Samantha Sagui, "The Hue and Cry in Medieval English Towns," *Historical Research* 87(236):179–193 (May 2014).

§21. Scriptural sources: Matt 5:44; Mark 12:31; Luke 10:30–37.

§22. Communal houses for lay persons who wished to devote themselves to the religious life without taking monastic vows were established in the Low Countries, Germany, and France starting in the 12th century, generally with separate houses for women (known as Beguines) and men (known as Beghards); see the annotation for Part III, §5. Some but not all of these groups adopted tenets promoted by the heretical movement known as the Free Spirit, which was influenced in part by the teachings of Joachim of Floris [c. 1135–1202 CE], who associated the age of the Father with the Old Testament and the Law, the age of the Son with the New Testament and the Church, and the age of the Spirit with a new age based on love and freedom that would begin around the middle of the 13th century; see the respective entries in Clifton, *Encyclopedia of Heresies and Heretics* (*op. cit.*), pp. 20–23 ("Beghards"/"Beguines"); pp. 47–48 ("Free Spirit"); pp. 71–72 ("Joachim of Floris"). Compare ". . . if a man blocks your path, you must slay him!" with "If you meet a Buddha on the road, kill him," attributed to the Chan (Zen) master, Linji Yixuan [9th century CE]; see Peter Manseau and Jeff Sharlet, *Killing the Buddha: A Heretic's Bible* (New York: Free Press, 2004), pp. 1–2. The final words of the Nicene Creed are "we look for the resurrection of the dead, and the life of the world to come"; see Philip Schaff, *The Creeds of Christendom* (*op. cit.*), Vol. 1, p. 29. The Protestant Reformer, Martin Luther, advocated the "priesthood of all believers"; see the following line from *The Babylonian Captivity of the Church,* quoted in *A Compend of Luther's Theology,* ed. Hugh T. Kerr (Philadelphia: Westminster, 1966), p. 137: ". . . we are all priests, as many of us as are Christians." "The scriptures are nothing more than old scraps of paper with words written on them" alludes to the line "The scriptures are nothing more than useless paper"; quoted from the Zen master, Rinzai (Linji Yixuan, who flourished in China in the 9th century CE), in Julius Evola, *The Doctrine of Awakening* (*op. cit.*), p. 224.

The following lines are attributed to Bodhidharma: "A special transmission outside the scriptures; No dependence upon words and letters; Direct pointing at the soul of man; Seeing into one's nature and the attainment of Buddhahood"; quoted in Suzuki, *Essays in Zen Buddhism: First Series* (*op. cit.*), p. 176; see also the annotation for Part III, §21. On the difference between apocalyptic and realized eschatology, see John F. Walvoord, "Realized Eschatology," *Bibliotheca Sacra* 127(508):313–323 (1970); the distinction is similar to that made between apocalyptic and sapiential eschatology noted in the annotation for Part V, §4. The term "prefigurative politics" was coined by Carl Boggs in "Marxism, prefigurative communism, and the problem of workers' control," *Radical America* 11(6):99–122 (1977). The phrase "new world order" is taken from H. G. Wells' book *The New World Order* (London: Secker and Warburg, 1940), which advocates the creation of a world government to achieve international peace (an idea diametrically opposed to anarchism); the expression has also been used by various politicians, including Woodrow Wilson, Mikhail Gorbachev, and George H. W. Bush. *Mutual aid* is a key anarchist concept; see Peter Kropotkin, *Mutual Aid: A Factor in Evolution* (Montréal: Black Rose, 1989 [1902]). The slogan "No law but love" is widely adopted by the Restoration Movement (which includes the Disciples of Christ, Christian Churches, and Churches of Christ); see Douglas A. Foster, Paul M. Blowers, Anthony L. Dunnavant, and D. Newell Williams, eds., *The Encyclopedia of the Stone–Campbell Movement* (Grand Rapids: William B. Eerdmans, 2004), p. 688. Purity of heart may be linked to the Buddhist concept of overcoming desire, as explicated by Gautama Buddha in his "Sermon at Benares," compiled in Lewis Browne, *The World's Great Scriptures* (New York: Macmillan, 1946), pp. 145–149; see the annotation for Part V, §4. Scriptural sources: Exod 20:14–15, 17; 34:14; Judg 17:6; Matt 4:9; 5:8, 33–37; 22:30–32; Mark 2:23–28; 12:30–31; Luke 3:16; 6:1–5; 17:21; 24:39–43; John 3:16; 15:19; 17:14–16; 18:36; 20:27; Acts 2:44–46; 4:32–35; Rom 2:14–15; 8:2, 11, 14–16; 13:1; 1 Cor 2:10–16; 3:16; 6:12; 12:27; 2 Cor 6:18; Gal 2:20; 3:28; 5:1, 18–22; Eph 1:10; 2:4–5; 4:6; Phil 3:10–1; Titus 1:15; Heb 2:11; Jas 5:12; 1 Pet 2:9; 1 John 3:9; Jude 1:12; Rev 1:18; 14:6; 19:16.

§23. Scriptural sources: Matt 9:36; John 8:7.

§26. The Feast of Fools is described in David S. Schaff, *The Middle Ages: A.D. 1049–1294*, Vol. 5 of Philip Schaff's *History of the Christian Church* (Grand Rapids: William B. Eerdmans, 1979 [1907]), pp. 463–464 and Max Harris, *Sacred Folly: A New History of the Feast of Fools* (Ithaca: Cornell University Press, 2011). A description of the Saturnalia festival can be found in William Warde Fowler, *The Roman Festivals of the Period of the Republic: An Introduction to the Study of the Religion of the Romans* (London: Macmillan, 1899), pp. 268–273. Contemporary expressions of what has been termed the *carnivalesque* can be found in the writings of the Marxist literary critic, Mikhail Bakhtin, members of the Situationist International (Guy Debord and Raoul Vaneigem), and the anarchist, Hakim Bey (Peter Lamborn Wilson); see Gavin Grindon, "Carnival Against Capital: A Comparison of Bakhtin, Vaneigem, and Bey," *Anarchist Studies* 12(2):147–161 (2004). Scriptural sources: Matt 20:16; Luke 1:52; 1 Cor 4:10.

§27. The depiction of the Feast of Fools presented in this section is no doubt an exaggeration, although many of the details are historically authentic. The couplet is a direct quote from the "Magnificat" in "The Order for Daily Evening Prayer" in *The Book of Common Prayer* (*op. cit.*), pp. 22. The following lines, sung during the Feast of Fools, are quoted in Rosemarie Taylor-Perry, *The God Who Comes: Dionysian Mysteries Revisited* (New York: Algora, 2003), p. 23: "Let us drink: take from us, we beseech thee, Bacchus, all our clothes, that we may be worthy, with naked bodies, to enter into the tavern. Unto us all, drink without end." Scriptural sources: Luke 1:52; John 12:13–15.

§28. The section includes a paraphrase of a quote attributed to Confucius [551–479 BCE] in Dr. Purushothaman, *What Confucius Said* (Kollam: Centre for Human Perfection, 2014), p. 177: "The green reed which bends in the wind is stronger than the mighty oak which breaks in a storm." A paraphrase is also included from Lao-Tze, *Tao-Teh-King* (*op. cit.*), Chap. 76, p. 135: "Thus the hard and strong are the companions of death. The tender and the delicate are the companions of life"; *cf.* "The Oak and the Reed" in Rev. T. James, *Aesop's Fables: Complete* (Philadelphia: Claxton, Remsen, and Haffelfinger, 1876 [c. 6th century BCE]), Fable CLXVIII, p. 168. The Golden Rule, in either its positive or negative forms, is found in nearly every major religious tradition, ancient and modern. The maxim "We must pursue peaceful ends through peaceful means" appears in Martin Luther King, Jr., *Where Do We Go From Here: Chaos or Community?* (Boston: Beacon Press, 1986 [1968]), p. 194. Nonviolence has a long history in the Christian, Hindu, Jain, and Buddhist traditions. This section includes adaptations of the following lines quoted in Clifton, *Encyclopedia of Heresies and Heretics* (*op. cit.*), p. 6, from a document entitled "The Vindication of the Church of God," written around 1250 CE in defense of the Albigensian (Cathar) heresy: "The words of Christ contradict the wicked Roman Church. For it [the Catholic Church] is not persecuted for the goodness or justice which is in it, but on the contrary it persecutes and kills all who refuse to condone its sins and its actions. It flees not from city to city, but rules over cities and towns and provinces and is seated in grandeur in the pomp of its world; it is feared by kings and emperors and other men . . . . And above all does it persecute and kill the Holy Church of Christ [i.e., the Albigensians], which bears all in patience like the sheep, making no defense against the world." Cathars and Albigensians were also strict pacifists. Scriptural sources: Deut 13:10; Isa 40:4; Dan 3:20–21; 6:16; Matt 5:39; 7:12; Luke 3:5; 6:31.

§29. Eliminating all forms of domination is a key theme in anarchist thought; see, for example, Julia Tanenbaum, "To Destroy Domination in All Its Forms: Anarcha-Feminist Theory, Organization, and Action 1970–1978," *Perspectives on Anarchist Theory* 29:13–34 (2016). The notion that religion is used "to keep everyone in their place by making them drunk" echoes Marx's idea that "religion is the opium of the people"; see Karl Marx, "Contribution to the Critique of Hegel's Philosophy of Law" in *Marx and Engels: Collected Works*, Vol. 3, pp. 175–187 (New York: International, 1975 [1844]), p. 175. The phrase "glorious land above the sky" is from a song by Joe Hill, "The Preacher and the Slave" [aka "Pie in the Sky"] in *Songs of the Workers* [aka *Little Red Songbook*], 35th ed. (Chicago: Industrial Workers of the World, 1984 [1911]), pp. 12–13. Scriptural sources: Matt 3:10; Luke 15:3–7; John 10:1–18; 1 Tim 2:2.

§30. Scriptural sources: Exod 32:1–19.

§31. Works providing background information on the Inquisition are cited in the annotation for Part IV, §8. For a general introduction to the history and techniques of torture, see George Riley Scott, *A History of Torture* (London: Senate, 1995). Although the use of torture to extract confessions was first authorized by Pope Innocent IV in 1252, it should be noted that the modern Roman Catholic Church is opposed to both torture and capital punishment. The following Latin phrase can be found in Sancti Bernardi [Bernard of Clairvaux], *Sermones super Cantica canticorum* (Rome: Editiones Cistercienses, 1958), Sermo LXVI, §12, p. 187: "*fides suadenda, non imponenda*" (English translation: "faith through persuasion, not imposition"). Augustine in a letter to Donatus [408 CE] writes, "We love our enemies and pray for them. Hence, we desire that, by making use of judges and laws that cause fear, they [heretics] be corrected, not killed, so that they do not fall into the punishment of eternal condemnation. We do not want discipline to be neglected in their regard or the punishment they deserve to be applied"; from *The Works of Saint Augustine: A Translation for the 21st Century*, ed. Boniface Ramsey, Part II—Letters, Vol. 2: *Letters 100–155 (Epistulae)*, trans. Roland Teske (Hyde Park: New City Press, 2003), Letter 100.1, p. 15. The terms *therapy* and *annihilation* are derived from the theory of Peter Berger and Thomas Luckmann in *The Social Construction of Reality: A Treatise in the Sociology of Knowledge* (Garden City: Anchor, 1966), pp. 112–116, that those who fail to conform to socially accepted norms are typically subjected either to *therapy* (an attempt to reintegrate them back into society) or *nihilation* (an attempt to marginalize or even eliminate them from society). Scriptural sources: Exod 20:13; Deut 13:5; Matt 5:44; 22:9–14; Mark 8:36.

§32. The ten charges against the preacher expand on the core beliefs held by the Brethren of the Free Spirit condemned by Pope Clement V in his bull of 1311; see the entry for "Free Spirit" in Clifton, *Encyclopedia of Heresies and Heretics* (*op. cit.*), pp. 47–48; see also the annotation for Part IV, §22. In "On the Life of Plotinus and the Order of His Books" in Plotinus, *Enneads* (*op. cit.*), Vol. 1, §2, p. 7, Porphyry [c. 234–c. 305] reports that the last words of Plotinus were "Try to bring back the god in us to the divine in the All!"; *cf.* Schleiermacher, *On Religion* (*op. cit.*), p. 81: "Would they but strive to annihilate their personality and to live in the One and in the All!" Scriptural sources: Matt 27:22–23; Mark 15:13; 16:13–14; Luke 23:31.

§33. The abbot's letter includes slightly revised direct quotes from Lactantius, *Divine Institutes* [c. 303–311 CE], trans. William Fletcher in *The Ante-Nicene Fathers*, Vol. VII, pp. 9–223, ed. Alexander Roberts and James Donaldson (Buffalo: The Christian Literature Company, 1886), Book V, Chap. XX, pp. 156–157; the book was written towards the end of the major persecutions of Christians in the Roman Empire when thousands were martyred.

§34. For a vivid first-hand description of the Black Death, see the introduction to the first day of Giovanni Boccaccio's *The Decameron*, trans. Guido Waldman, ed. Jonathan Usher (Oxford: Oxford University Press, 1998 [1353]), pp. 6–14. For a modern scholarly treatment, see Philip Ziegler, *The Black Death* (Phoenix Mill: Alan Sutton, 1991 [1969]). This and the following sections touch on themes also found in Albert Camus, *The Plague*, trans. Stuart Gilbert (New York: The Modern Library, 1948 [1947]).

§35. Scriptural sources: Pss 23:4; 32:7.

§37. For a gripping account of flagellation in medieval Europe, see Norman Cohn, *The Pursuit of the Millennium* (*op. cit.*), Chap. 7.

§38. On "original sin" see the annotation for Part III, §8. The problem of evil is a trilemma, which David Hume in *Dialogues Concerning Natural Religion*, ed. Henry D. Aiken (New York: Hafner, 1966 [1779]), Part X, p. 66, attributes to the ancient Greek philosopher, Epicurus [341–270 BCE]: "Is he [God] willing to prevent evil, but not able? then is he impotent. Is he able, but not willing? then is he malevolent. Is he both able and willing? whence then is evil?" Theodicy attempts to solve the problem by showing how an omnipotent and omnibenevolent God can permit evil; see, for example, Gottfried Leibniz, *Theodicy: Essays on the Goodness of God, the Freedom of Man, and the Origin of Evil*, ed. Austin Farrer, trans. E. M. Huggard (London: Routledge and Kegan Paul, 1952 [1710]). One of the greatest literary treatments of the problem of evil can be found in Fyodor Dostoyevsky's *The*

Brothers Karamazov, trans. Constance Garnett (New York: New American Library, 1957 [1880]), Book V, Chap. 4 (entitled "Rebellion"), pp. 218–227. For a more or less orthodox response to the problem of theodicy, see C. S. Lewis, *The Problem of Pain* (London: Centenary, 1940). The paragraph beginning with "Indeed, as even heathens acknowledge . . ." consists of direct quotes, near-direct quotes, and paraphrases, from Augustine, *The Enchiridion* (*op. cit.*), Chap. XI, p. 181 and Chap. XCVI, p. 241. "God Is in Control" is the title of a contemporary Christian song by Twila Paris, appearing on her studio album *Beyond a Dream* (Houston: Star Song Records, 1993). "God moves in mysterious ways" is adapted from the title of the hymn "God Moves in a Mysterious Way" [1773] by William Cowper in the Lutheran *Service Book and Hymnal* (*op. cit.*), Hymn #484. The heretical Albigensians, Bogomils, and Cathars identified the God who created and rules the world with Satan; see the respective entries in Clifton, *Encyclopedia of Heresies and Heretics* (*op. cit.*), pp. 6–12 ("Albigenses"); pp. 24–26 ("Bogomil"); pp. 29–31 ("Cathari"), and the annotation for Part V, §4. Elie Wiesel's play *The Trial of God,* trans. Marion Wiesel (New York: Schocken, 1979) was inspired by an actual incident at Auschwitz during the Second World War in which three rabbis put God on trial and found him guilty for permitting the Holocaust. Scriptural sources: Ezra 9:8; Job: 1:21–22; Pss 75:7; 86:15; Ezek 18:25–29; Joel 2:32; Hab 1:13; Matt 6:14; 7:1; 24:31; Luke 17:27; Acts 2:21; Rom 2:1–2; 8:28; 10:13; 1 Cor 15:52; 1 Thess 4:16–17; Heb 10:30; 1 John 2:19; 3:20.

V. THE RETURN

§1. The expression "vale of tears" can be found in the writings of various Christian authors, including Boniface [c. 675–754 CE]; see *The Letters of St. Boniface,* trans. Ephraim Emerton (New York: Columbia University Press, 1940), p. 35; the phrase is derived from Ps 84:6, translated in the American Standard Version as "valley of weeping"; this latter phrase also appears in Part V, §4. Scriptural sources: Gen 1:31; Ps 84:6; Matt 8:22; 25:37–40; Luke 9:60.

§2. One of the few pilgrimages in the world in which the ending point is the same as the starting point is the Shikoku Pilgrimage associated with Kukai (Kobo Daishi), who established the esoteric Buddhist school, Shingon-shu, in Japan. The same motif can be found in lines from the song "Sitting" by Cat Stevens [aka Yusuf Islam] on the studio album *Catch Bull at Four* (London: Island, 1972) and in Hermann Hesse's first novel, *Peter Camenzind,* trans. Michael Roloff (New York: Bantam, 1969 [1904]). Scriptural sources: Gen 2:8–9.

§3. Reference is made to the Taoist concept of "acting without acting" (*wei wu wei,* 為無為); see Raymond Blakney's explanation of this phrase in his translation of Lao Tzu's *The Way of Life* [*Tao Teh Ching*] (New York: New American Library, 1955), pp. 39–40. This section also utilizes the description of Gautama Buddha vowing to sit beneath a Bodhi tree, or tree of knowledge, until he attained Enlightenment, found in Noss, *Man's Religions* (*op. cit.*), pp. 123–124, and specifically the following quote attributed to the Buddha in Kenneth J. Saunders, *Gotama Buddha: A Biography Based on the Canonical Books of the Theravadin* (New York: Association Press, 1920), p. 21: "Though skin, nerves, and bone shall waste away, and life-blood itself be dried up, here sit I till I attain Enlightenment." On the problem of evil, see the annotations for Part IV, §38. The scream was inspired, in part, by Edvard Munch's painting, *The Scream* (Oslo: National Gallery, 1893). Scriptural sources: Mark 4:35–41; Rom 8:22.

§4. An allusion is made to the title of Blake's *The Marriage of Heaven and Hell* (*op. cit.*). Reference is made again to the title of Nietzsche's *Beyond Good and Evil*; see the annotations for Part II, §14 and Part III, §21. The boat story illustrates the vow of a bodhisattva in Mahayana Buddhism not to enter Nirvana (heaven) until all other beings precede him; see the annotation for Part III, §21. The phrase "eternal delight" comes from Blake, *The Marriage of Heaven and Hell* (*op. cit.*), p. 94: "Energy is Eternal Delight." On the problem of theodicy, see the annotation for Part IV, §38. The phrase "times of trouble" is from Ps 9:9 and also quoted in the first line of The Beatles' song "Let It Be" from the studio album *Let It Be* (London: Apple, 1970). John Dominic Crossan in *Who Killed Jesus?: Exposing the Roots of Anti-Semitism in the Gospel Story of the Death of Jesus* (San Francisco: HarperSanFrancisco, 1995), p. 47, makes the following distinction between apocalyptic and sapiential eschatology: "In apocalyptic eschatology, we are waiting for God to act. In sapiential eschatology, God is waiting for us to act"; sapiential eschatology is similar to realized eschatology; see the annotation for Part IV, §22. The Patripassian heresy, which arose in the 2nd century CE, held that since God the Father was fully incarnate in Christ, God himself was crucified on the cross; see the entry for "Patripassianism" in Clifton, *Encyclopedia of Heresies and Heretics* (*op. cit.*), p. 110. The phrase "God is dead" can be found in Friedrich Nietzsche's *The Gay Science* [2nd ed. 1887], trans. Walter Kaufmann (New York: Vintage, 1974), Book Three, §125, p. 181 and *Thus Spoke Zarathustra* [1892] in *The Portable Nietzsche*, pp. 103–439, ed. and trans. Walter Kaufmann (Harmondsworth: Penguin, 1968), "Zarathustra's Prologue," §2, p. 124. References are also made in this section to the death of God theology of Thomas J. J. Altizer in *The Gospel of Christian Atheism* (Philadelphia: Westminster, 1966) and the process theology of John Cobb and David Ray Griffin in *Process Theology: An Introductory Exposition* (Philadelphia: Westminster Press, 1976). "Certainly whatever is not constantly being born is constantly dying" is a less poetic rendering of a line from Bob Dylan's "It's Alright Ma (I'm Only Bleeding)" on the studio album *Bringing It All Back Home* (New York: Columbia, 1965). The dualistic views that the spirit is "good" while the body is "evil" and that Satan or a lesser demiurge rather than God created the world are recurring themes in many Christian heresies, including Bogomilism, Catharism, Gnosticism, and Manichaeism; see the respective entries in Clifton, *Encyclopedia of Heresies and Heretics* (*op. cit.*), pp. 24–26 ("Bogomil"); pp. 29–31 ("Cathari"); pp. 49–54 ("Gnosticism"); pp. 87–90 ("Manichaeism"), and the annotation for Part IV, §38. The Four Noble Truths of Buddhism proclaimed in Gautama Buddha's "Sermon at Benares" in Browne, *The World's Great Scriptures* (*op. cit.*), pp. 145–149, are that (1) everyone suffers; (2) the cause of suffering is desire; (3) suffering is destroyed when desire is overcome; (4) the way to overcome sorrow caused by suffering is to follow the Buddhist path. Birth, decay, disease, and death are specifically mentioned as sources of suffering in the first of these truths. The aim of freeing oneself from the cycle of life, death, and rebirth (*saṃsāra*) is found in the Indian religions of Hinduism, Jainism, Buddhism, and Sikhism; see also the annotations for Part I, §13 and Part IV, §22. Antinatalism is the view that because life is suffering, it is better not to be born; see, for example, David Benatar, *Better Never to Have Been: The Harm of Coming into Existence* (Oxford: Oxford University Press, 2008); antitnatalism has affinities with the teachings of some Gnostics, including Marcion [85–160 CE], that marriage and procreation should be proscribed because they contribute to ". . . the imprisonment of more souls in the material world"; see the entry for "Marcion" in Clifton, *Encyclopedia of Heresies and Heretics* (*op. cit.*), pp. 90–91. Absurdity was a central concern of Albert Camus's philosophy; the first two sentences of his *The Myth of Sisyphus*, trans. Justin O'Brien (Harmondsworth: Penguin, 1975 [1942]), p. 11, are: "There is but one truly serious philosophical problem and that is suicide. Judging whether life is or is not worth living amounts to answering the fundamental question of philosophy." Revenants are depicted in medieval folklore as reanimated corpses (undead creatures similar to vampires) and have affinities with zombies in voodoo and African traditions; see David Keyworth, *Troublesome Corpses: Vampires and Revenants from Antiquity to the Present* (Southend-On-Sea: Desert Island, 2007); Nancy Mandeville Caciola, *Afterlives: The Return of the Dead in the Middle Ages* (Ithaca: Cornell University Press, 2016); and Mambo Chita Tann, *Haitian Vodou: An Introduction to Haiti's Indigenous Spiritual Tradition* (Woodbury: Llewellyn, 2012), Chap. 3; a zombie is the polar opposite of a spiritually

aware person; the primary fear is that one will become rather than be attacked by a zombie. Nietzsche quotes Meister Eckhart's "I ask God that he
rid me of God" in *The Gay Science* (*op. cit.*), Book Four, §292, p. 235; see
Blakney, *Meister Eckhart*, (*op. cit.*), p. 231. The image of the "dark night of
the soul" from *The Poems of St. John of the Cross* (*op. cit.*), pp. 19–21 is re-
prised here; see the annotation for Part III, §21; the phrase "union with God
by the way of spiritual negation" appears in the same poem. The term *kenōsis*
(from κένωσις in Greek) may be used to refer either to Christ "emptying"
himself to become human in the incarnation or to the spiritual experience
of "emptying" oneself of ego and desire so that God might dwell in one's
soul; for a comparison of the concept of *kenōsis* in Altizer's death-of-God
theology and the concept of *śūnyatā* ("emptiness") as understood by philosophers in the Kyoto School, including Kitaro Nishida, Keiji Nishitani,
and Masao Abe, see Steve Odin, "*Kenōsis* as a Foundation for Buddhist–
Christian Dialogue: The Kenotic Buddhology of Nishida and Nishitani of
the Kyoto School in relation to the Kenotic Christology of Thomas J. J. Altizer," *The Eastern Buddhist* 20(1):34–61 (1987). For Nishitani's treatment of
ekkénōsis (ἐκένωσεν in Phil 2:7), meaning to "self-empty" or "make oneself
nothing," see *Religion and Nothingness,* trans. Jan Van Bragt (Berkeley: University of California Press, 1982), pp. 58–59; see also Abe's "Kenotic God
and Dynamic Sunyata" in *The Emptying God* (*op. cit.*), pp. 3–65 and Altizer's
response, "Buddhist Emptiness and the Crucifixion of God," in the same
volume, pp. 69–78. For the ancient Greek Stoics apathy (ἀπάθεια) was not
indifference but the ability to accept things as they are; Epicetus in *The
Enchiridion* in *The Works of Epictetus,* 4th ed., Vol. 2, trans. Elizabeth Carter
(London: F. C. and J. Rivington, 1807), p. 297, held that in any situation we
should determine "Whether it concerns the Things which are in our own
power, or those which are not; and, if it concerns any Thing not in our
Power, be prepared to say, that it is nothing to *you*"; *cf.* what has come to be
known as the "Serenity Prayer" written by Reinhold Niebuhr: "O God, give
us serenity to accept what cannot be changed, courage to change what
should be changed, and wisdom to distinguish the one from the other,"
quoted in John Bartlett, *Familiar Quotations,* 14th ed., ed. Emily Morison
Beck (Boston: Little, Brown and Company, 1968 [1934]), p. 1024. To accept
things as they are is similar to the Zen Buddhist concept of *kono mama*
(このまま, "just like that," or more colloquially "let it be"); see D. T. Suzuki,
Mysticism Christian and Buddhist (London: Unwin, 1979 [1957]), Chap. 7.
Scriptural sources: Gen 2:9, 15–17; 3:5, 18; Exod 33:20–23; Deut 34:4; Josh
5:6; Pss 9:9; 10:11; 16:11; 22:1–2; 84:6; Eccl 3:4; Isa 43:11; 53:1–12; Jer 11:14;
Matt 10:38; 22:32; 24:35; 27:40–43, 46; 28:20; Mark 12:30–31; 15:34; Luke
9:23; 17:21; 21:33; John 12:24; Acts 1:9; 5:30, 31; 1 Cor 13:11, 13; 2 Cor

4:7–11; 13:15; Eph 3:17–20; 4:9-10; Phil 2:4–8; Heb 12:2; Rev 2:7; 17:14; 21:1–5; 22:2.

§5. Nishida's concept of "absolute nothingness" from *Intelligibility and the Philosophy of Nothingness* (*op. cit.*), p. 130, reappears here; see the annotation for Part III, §31. The empty Holy of Holies, sepulcher, and tabernacle form a trinity (Father, Son, and Spirit). In his *Histories*, Gaius Cornelius Tacitus [c. 56–c. 120 CE] wrote that when the Roman commander, Pompey, conquered Jerusalem [in 63 BCE] and entered the temple he found that "...the place stood empty with no similitude of Gods within, and that the shrine had nothing to reveal"; quoted from Tacitus, *The History of Tacitus*, trans. Alfred John Church and William Jackson Brodribb (Cambridge and London: Macmillan, 1864 [100–110 CE]), Book V, §9, p. 270. Practices related to purgation, exorcism, and/or purification can be found in most of the world's religions, including Hinduism, Buddhism, Taoism, Shinto, Judaism, Christianity, Islam, and Native American traditions. Richard H. Robinson in *The Buddhist Religion: A Historical Introduction* (Belmont: Dickenson, 1970), p. 18, says that when Siddhartha Gautama attained enlightenment while sitting under a bodhi tree facing east, "The earth swayed, thunder rolled and rain fell from a cloudless sky, blossoms fell from the heavens ...." The distinction in ancient Greek between εὐφορία (*euphoria* or intense pleasure) and εὐδαιμονία (*eudaimonia* or well-being) can also be applied to spiritual experiences; compare Gian Lorenzo Bernini's sculpture, *St. Teresa in Ecstasy* (Rome: Santa Maria della Vittoria, 1647–1652), with its obviously erotic imagery, and virtually any statue of the Buddha. The ultimate goal of mystical experience is not ἔκστασις (*ecstasy* or bliss) but acceptance and reconciliation; "heaven" as well should perhaps be interpreted as reconciliation rather than as bliss. The English translation of the opening lines of Martin Luther's hymn, "Ein feste Burg ist unser Gott" [c. 1527–1529], trans. Frederick H. Hedge, in the *Service Book and Hymnal* (*op. cit.*), Hymn #150, is "A mighty fortress is our God, A bulwark never failing." Scriptural sources: Ps 46; Matt 3:16–17; 17:2, 5; 27:51–52; Mark 1:11; 5:2-13; 9:7; Luke 3:22; 8:27-33; 9:29, 35; 23:44–46; 24:2–6; 2 Cor 3:16; 2 Pet 1:17.

§6. See the *Meditations* of the Roman Stoic philosopher, Marcus Aurelius [121–180 CE], in *Marcus Aurelius*, trans. C. R. Haines (Cambridge: Harvard University Press [Loeb Classical Library], 1916), Book IX.3, p. 235: "Despise not death, but welcome it, for Nature wills it like all else." Allusions are made to a line from Kurt Vonnegut's novel, *Cat's Cradle* (New York: Delacorte, 1963), p. 181 ("And I was some of the mud that got to sit up and look around"); Matsuo Basho's [1644–1694 CE] haiku やがて死ぬけしきは見えず蝉の声 (*yagate shinu keshiki wa miezu semi no koe*), translated by R. H. Blyth in *Haiku, Vol. 3: Summer–Autumn* (Tokyo: Hokuseido Press,

1982), p. 820, as "Nothing intimates, / In the voice of the cicada, / How soon it will die"—the poem is also quoted by J. D. Salinger in "Teddy," *Nine Stories* (New York: The Modern Library, 1959 [1953]), p. 282; and the title of George Harrison's studio album *All Things Must Pass* (London: Apple, 1970). In Friedrich Nietzsche's *Thus Spoke Zarathustra* (*op. cit.*), Third Part, pp. 271–272, after a shepherd bit off the head of a snake that crawled into his mouth while he was sleeping, he spit it out and began laughing. The phrase "affirm the endless cycle of life" alludes to Nietzsche's concept of the eternal recurrence, which indicates a willingness to affirm the life one has lived even if obliged to live it over again in exactly the same way an infinite number of times; see *The Joyful Wisdom* [aka *The Gay Science*], trans. Thomas Common, in Vol. 10 of *The Complete Works of Friedrich Nietzsche*, ed. Oscar Levy (New York: Macmillan 1924), §341, pp. 270-271. Rather than hope for the annihilation of the soul in Nirvana or eternal life in heaven, the wheel of life (*saṃsāra* in Indian traditions) may be embraced; see Takakusu, *The Essentials of Buddhist Philosophy* (*op. cit.*), pp. 18; 24–31. Since expressing the doctrine of the eternal recurrence in the indicative mode is both scientifically dubious (it violates the law of entropy) and morally problematic (it seemingly hopes that historical atrocities will actually be repeated), the idea is probably better stated hypothetically as a thought experiment: "*If* the same pattern of events were to repeat itself endlessly over infinite periods of time, I would affirm it." A similar conception of affirmation can be found in a saying attributed by Paul E. Szarmach in *An Introduction to the Medieval Mystics of Europe*, ed. Paul E. Szarmach (Albany: State University of New York Press, 1984), p. 6, to the medieval mystic, Smargadus [c. 760–840 CE], in relation to the concept of compunction: "We must face the fact of our miserable human condition head on, accept it, and even come to love it in a certain way." "Affirm life" is a two-word summary of Nietzsche's philosophy; "love unconditionally" is a two-word summary of Christian philosophy; the dictums are not incompatible, conceivably even two different ways of saying the same thing; see also the annotation for Part III, §32. Similarly the injunctions to both affirm and negate the world are not contradictory but complementary; see John Dominic Crossan, *The Birth of Christianity* (San Francisco: HarperSanFrancisco, 1998), p. 259: "It [apocalyptic eschatology] is a basic and unusual world-negation or rejection as opposed to an equally basic but more usual world-affirmation or acceptance." To isolate oneself from society in order to attain wisdom and then return is an archetype that can be found in many hero stories; see Joseph Campbell, *The Hero with a Thousand Faces* (*op. cit.*), Part I, Chap. 3. After sitting beneath a bodhi tree and attaining enlightenment, the Buddha returned to preach the Sermon at Benares, despite being tempted to enter directly into Nirvana (heaven); see the annotation for Part IV, §22 and Part V, §4. After being tempted by Satan in the wilderness, Jesus returned to preach the Sermon on the Mount. Timothy Ware in *The Orthodox Church* (*op. cit.*), p. 48, characterizes the pattern of St. Anthony and his successors as a *"withdrawal in order to return"*: "A monk must first withdraw, and in silence must learn the truth about himself and God. Then, after this long and rigorous preparation in solitude, having gained the gifts of discernment which are required of an elder, he can open the door of his cell and admit the world from which formerly he fled." As flight attendants tell passengers on an airplane: "Put your own oxygen mask on first before trying to help others put on theirs"; the pattern of a Buddhist bodhisattva is similar; see the annotations for Part III, §21 and Part V, §4. In the film *Circle of Iron* (*op. cit.*), after Cord reaches an island representing (perhaps) nirvana, the keeper, Zetan, pleads with Cord to take his place, so that Zetan might be freed from spending eternity in paradise; Cord chooses, however, to return to the world, leaving Zetan imprisoned in heaven, much to his chagrin; see the annotations for Part III, §18 and §19. Scriptural sources: Gen 1:1; 2:7; Ps 102:11, 25–26; Isa 40:7; 51:6; Matt 6:14–15; 22:36–40; Luke 15:11–32.

   §7. This bulk of this section is a Christian reworking of the Ten Oxherding Pictures and loosely based on the accompanying verses attributed to the Chinese Zen Master Kou-an Shih-yuan [Kakuan, c. 12th century CE]; the following English translations have been consulted: Suzuki, *Essays in Zen Buddhism: First Series* (*op. cit.*), pp. 149–151; 371–376; Kapleau, *The Three Pillars of Zen* (*op. cit.*), pp. 314–323; and Paul Reps, *Zen Flesh, Zen Bones* (New York: Doubleday, 1989), pp. 136–155. Allusions are made to the titles of the song "I Still Haven't Found What I'm Looking For" by U2 on the studio album *The Joshua Tree* (Dublin: Island, 1987) and the Bob Dylan film *Don't Look Back,* directed by D. A. Pennebaker (New York: Leacock-Pennebaker, 1967), as well as the title of the *Mumonkan* (*op. cit.*), which may be translated as "gateless gate." The phrase "dark night of the soul" from St. John of the Cross, "The Dark Night" (*op. cit.*), is once again alluded to; see the annotations for Part III, §21 and V, §4. The Buddhist raft parable is from the *Majjhima Nikāya* [3rd–2nd century BCE], §22, as retold in Suzuki's *Essays in Zen Buddhism: First Series* (*op. cit.*), pp. 150–151. The following sections from Ludwig Wittgenstein's *Tractatus Logico-Philosophicus*, trans. D. F. Pears and B. F. McGuinness (Atlantic Highlands: Humanities Press, 1961 [1921]), p. 74, are referenced: "My propositions serve as elucidations in the following way: anyone who understands me eventually recognizes them as nonsensical, when he has used them—as steps—to climb up beyond them. (He must, so to speak, throw away the ladder after he has climbed up it.) He must transcend these propositions, and then he will see the world aright"

(§6.54) and "What we cannot speak about we must pass over in silence" (§7). An allusion is made to the Buddhist "Flower Sermon" as found in the sixth koan, "Buddha Holds Out a Flower," of the *Mumonkan* (*op. cit.*), pp. 41–42. Alluded to again are the finger wagging of Cratylus and the koan "Gutei Raises a Finger"; see the annotation for Part IV, §15. Scriptural sources: Gen 1:1–4; 32:24–30; Matt 25:35–40; Mark 2:15; Luke 9:3; 22:42–44.

§8. An allusion is made again to Lao-Tze's comparison of superior goodness and water in *Tao-Teh-King* (*op. cit.*), Chap. 8, p. 100; see the annotation for Part III, §33. Scriptural sources: Gen 4:10; 9:6; Exod 21:12, 23–25; Lev 19:18; Isa 1:18; 43:25; Hos 6:6; Matt 5:43–44; 22:39; Luke 23:34; Rom 3:23; 12:19; Col 3:13; 1 John 1:9; Rev 6:10; 7:14.

§9. The proverb, "He who fights and runs away . . ." and its rejoinder are attributed to various writers and adapted here from Oliver Goldsmith's *The Art of Poetry on a New Plan* (London: J. Newbery, 1762), Vol. 2, p. 147. Agnes Strickland in *Lives of the Queens of England* (Philadelphia: Lea and Blanchard, 1847), Vol. IV, pp. 211–212, gives the following account of the beheading of Anne Boleyn: ". . . [Her] eyes and lips were observed to move when her head was held up by the executioner. It is also said, that before those beautiful eyes sunk in the dimness of death, they seemed for an instant mournfully to regard her bleeding body as it fell on the scaffold"; the report that she was still alive after her beheading is probably apocryphal and medically improbable. Scriptural sources: Josh 6:20.

§11. This and subsequent sections draw on anarchist thought in general, especially the ideas of Pierre-Joseph Proudhon anthologized in *Property Is Theft: A Pierre-Joseph Proudhon Anthology*, ed. Iain McKay (Edinburgh: AK Press, 2011) and Peter Kropotkin's *The Conquest of Bread* (Montréal: Black Rose, 1990 [1892]), and Christian anarchist thought in particular, including Leo Tolstoy's *The Kingdom of God Is within You*, trans. Constance Garnett (Lincoln: University of Nebraska Press, 1984 [1894]), Dorothy Day's *Loaves and Fishes: The Inspiring Story of the Catholic Worker Movement* (Maryknoll: Orbis, 1997 [1963]), and Jacques Ellul's *Anarchy and Christianity*, trans. Geoffrey W. Bromiley (Grand Rapids: William B. Eerdmans, 1991 [1988]). For a more specific introduction to anarchist tendencies in the Middle Ages, see Ian Forrest, "Medieval History and Anarchist Studies," *Anarchist Studies* 28(1):33–59 (2020). There are also affinities between anarchism and the concepts of *subsidiarity* and *distributism* in Catholic social thought; see the following quote from Pope Pius XI's encyclical, *Quadragesimo Anno* [1931] in Dualta Roughneen, *Subsidiarity: A New Principle?* (Newcastle upon Tyne: Cambridge Scholars, 2017), p. 14: "Just as it is gravely wrong to take from individuals what they can accomplish by their own initiative and industry and give it to the community, so also it is an injustice and at the same time a grave evil and disturbance of right order to assign to a greater and higher association what lesser and subordinate organizations can do." "Great Leader" was the title that Kim Il-sung, the founder of North Korea, gave himself; authoritarian tendencies can be found in fascist, communist, and even liberal regimes. The English anchorite and mystic, Julian of Norwich, wrote of visions she experienced in the year 1373 in which she ". . . saw that God was rejoicing to be our Father; rejoicing too to be our Mother"; see Julian of Norwich, *Revelations of Divine Love*, trans. Clifton Wolters (Harmondsworth: Penguin, 1966 [1670]), p. 151. In contrast to Voltaire's "If God did not exist, it would be necessary to invent him" (see the annotation for Part I, §4 above), Michail [Mikhail] Bakunin in *God and the State*, trans. Benjamin R. Tucker (New York: Mother Earth, 1916 [1882]), p. 14, wrote, "[I]f God really existed, it would be necessary to abolish him." In "Man, Society, and Freedom," an unfinished note on *God and the State*, in *Bakunin on Anarchism*, pp. 234–242 (*op. cit.*), p. 237, Bakunin writes, "I am truly free only when all human beings, men and women, are equally free." The master–slave dialectic can be found in G. W. F. Hegel's *The Phenomenology of Mind*, trans. J. B. Baillie (New York: Harper and Row, 1967 [1807]), in the section entitled "Independence and Dependence of Self-consciousness: Lordship and Bondage," pp. 228–240; see especially p. 234: "The one is independent, and its essential nature is to be for itself; the other is dependent, and its essence is life or existence for another. The former is the Master, or Lord, the latter the Bondsman." Plato's view that in the perfect state philosophers must become kings or kings become philosophers can be found in *The Republic* (*op. cit.*), Book V, 473, p. 369. The anonymous lines, "Do not walk in front of me, I may not follow / Do not walk behind me, I may not lead / Just walk beside me and be my friend," are frequently misattributed to Albert Camus. "The Church stole Jesus from us and it is time for us to steal him back!" echoes Bono's introduction to U2's performance of "Helter Skelter" live at the McNichols Sports Arena in Denver, Colorado on November 8, 1987, included on the album *Rattle and Hum* (New York: Island, 1988): "This song Charles Manson stole from The Beatles, we're stealing it back." The phrase "If there were no God, everything would be permitted" is derived from the question Alyosha asks Dimitri in Fyodor Dostoyevsky's novel, *The Brothers Karamazov* (*op. cit.*), p. 534: "'But what will become of men then,' I asked him, 'without God and immortal life? All things are lawful then, they can do what they like?'"; *cf.* Nietzsche, *Thus Spoke Zarathustra* (*op. cit.*), Fourth Part, p. 386: "Nothing is true, all is permitted." The phrase "From each according to his ability, to each according to his needs" can be found both in Karl Marx, *Critique of the Gotha Program* in *Karl Marx and Frederick Engels: Selected Works* (Moscow:

Progress, 1977 [1875]), p. 19 and in James Guillaume, "On Building the
New Social Order" in *Bakunin on Anarchism*, pp. 356–379 (*op. cit.*), p. 361;
the second half of this idea is also expressed in Acts 4:35: ". . . distribution
was made unto each, according as any one had need." Paraphrased quotations have been taken from Lao-Tze, *Tao-Teh-King* (*op. cit.*), Chap. 57, p.
126: "The more restrictions and prohibitions are in the empire, the poorer
grow the people. The more weapons the people have, the more troubled is
the state . . . . The more mandates and laws are enacted, the more there will
be thieves and robbers," as well as from Chuang Tzu [c. 369–c. 286 BCE],
Zhuang Zi, trans. Herbert A. Giles (London: Bernard Quaritch, 1889),
Chap. 7, p. 94: "The goodness of a wise ruler . . . covers the whole empire, yet
he himself seems to know it not. It influences all creation, yet none is conscious thereof" and Chap. 11, p. 119: "But if their [the people's] natural
dispositions be not perverted nor their virtue laid aside, what room is there
left for government?" The direct quote "a mere war of all against all" is from
Thomas Hobbes' preface to *The Citizen* [*De Cive*] in *Man and Citizen*, ed.
Bernard Gert (Indianapolis: Hackett, 1991 [1642]), p. 101. In "Civil Disobedience" [1849] in *Walden and Other Writings*, pp. 635–659 (*op. cit.*), p. 635,
Henry David Thoreau states, "That government is best which governs least,"
followed by "That government is best which governs not at all." Ovid writes
in *The Metamorphoses* (*op. cit.*), p. 33: "The first millennium was the age of
gold: / Then living creatures trusted one another; / People did well without
the thought of ill: / Nothing forbidden in a book of laws, / No fears, no
prohibition read in bronze, / Or in the sculptured face of judge and master."
During the Protestant Reformation, some radical reformers, broadly associated with the Anabaptists, advocated principles consistent with Christian
anarchism, including a separation of believers from the established ecclesiastical authorities, a refusal to participate in civil governments, an advocacy
of nonviolence and pacifism, a prohibition against taking oaths, nonconfor-
mity to the ways of the world, and in some cases communal living; a key text
is the *Schleitheim Confession*, attributed to Michael Sattler [1490–1527] and
adopted by Swiss Anabaptists in 1527, trans. John Howard Yoder (Harri-
sonburg: Herald Press, 1977). Since the radicals advocated a strong separation between the Kingdom of God and the kingdom of the world, and
refused to seek protection from any secular authorities, they were often
subjected to severe persecution by both Roman Catholics and so-called
"Magisterial" Protestants, such as Lutherans and Calvinists, who aligned
themselves with temporal powers; successor groups to the Anabaptists include the Brethren, Hutterites, Mennonites, and Amish; see William R. Estep, *The Anabaptist Story* (*op. cit.*). Gerrard Winstanley in *The Law of
Freedom in a Platform* [1652] in *The Works of Gerrard Winstanley*, pp.

500–600, ed. George H. Sabine (New York: Russell and Russell, 1965), p. 519, wrote, "True freedom lies where a man receives his nourishment and preservation, and that is in the use of the earth"; Winstanley was a key spokesperson for the True Levellers, or Diggers, a radical Protestant group that appropriated common land in England in the mid-17th century to grow their own food and advocated the abolishment of both property and money. The slogan "Property is theft" [*La propriété, c'est le vol*] was coined by Pierre-Joseph Proudhon and translated as "Property is robbery" in Pierre-Joseph Proudhon, *What Is Property?: An Inquiry into the Principle of Right and of Government*, trans. Benjamin R. Tucker (Princeton, Massachusetts, 1876 [1840]), p. 11. Remarks by Constance in this section have been adapted from the following lines in Voltaire's *Candide,* trans. Robert M. Adams (New York: W. W. Norton, 1966 [1759]), p. 77: "All events are linked together in the best of possible worlds" and ". . . we must cultivate our garden." The desire to "return to a good, simple life" based on producing for consumption rather than wealth is a key tenet of voluntary simplicity; see Duane Elgin, *Voluntary Simplicity: An Ecological Lifestyle that Promotes Personal and Social Renewal* (New York: Bantam, 1982). Scriptural sources: Gen 3:16; Exod 20:15; Eccl 5:18; Isa 2:4; 11:6; Mic 4:3; Matt 28:18; Mark 6:34; John 10:11–14; 15:15; Acts 2:36; 4:35; 5:29; Rom 12:2; 13:1–4; 1 Cor 10:23; 2 Cor 6:17; Eph 5:22; 6:5.

§13. In Plato's *Republic* (*op. cit.*), Book I, 338, p. 301, Thrasymachus states, ". . . justice is nothing else than the interest of the stronger." Scriptural sources: Exod 20:13.

§14. Scriptural sources: Ps 23:5.

§15. A scold's bridle, or branks, was not used in England until the 16th century at the earliest; see Scott, *A History of Torture* (*op. cit.*), pp. 240–242. The anarchist slogan "No gods, no masters" was derived from the title of a journal first published in 1880 by Auguste Blanqui: *Ni Dieu ni Maître* [*Neither God nor Master*]; the original French expression is also quoted by Nietzsche in *Beyond Good and Evil* (*op. cit.*), §22, p. 220; §202, p. 306. Women withholding sex from their husbands as a way to change their errant behavior is described in Aristophanes' play, *Lysistrata* [411 BCE], trans. Jack Lindsay, in *The Complete Plays of Aristophanes,* ed. Moses Hadas (New York: Bantam, 1962); the same tactic has been employed in other cultures, ancient and modern. Scriptural sources: Gen 1:29; Prov 31:14; Rom 13:1.

§16. This section critiques both authoritarian forms of Marxism and representative democracy in favor of what has variously been called *participatory democracy, discursive democracy,* or simply *anarchism,* and alludes to the discourse ethics of Jürgen Habermas, as articulated in *Moral Consciousness and Communicative Action,* trans. Christian Lenhardt and Shierry

Weber (Cambridge: Polity, 1990) and *Justification and Application: Remarks on Discourse Ethics*, trans. Ciaran Cronin (Cambridge: MIT Press, 1993). Scriptural sources: 2 Thess 3:10.

§17. Scriptural sources: Matt 5:13; 13:33.

§18. The second paragraph of this section alludes to images found in the chapter "On Marriage" in Kahlil Gibran's *The Prophet* (London: William Heinemann, 1980 [1926]), pp. 16–19. Scriptural sources: Mark 12:41–44.

§20. Some of Roland's remarks are near direct quotes from Nicolò Machiavelli, *The Prince*, 3rd ed., trans. Henry Morely (London: George Routledge and Sons, 1889 [1532]), Chap. XV, p. 99: ". . . for if we consider things impartially we shall find some things in appearance are virtuous, and yet, if pursued, would bring certain destruction; and others, on the contrary, that are seemingly bad, which, if followed by a prince, procure his peace and security" and Chap. XIX, pp. 113–114: "That a prince make it his business . . . to avoid such things as may make him odious or contemptible, and as often as he does that he plays his part very well, and shall meet no danger or inconveniences by the rest of his vices."

§21. "I came, I saw, I conquered" is a translation of the Latin phrase attributed to Julius Caesar [100–44 BCE]: "*Veni, vidi, vici*"; see Plutarch [c. 46–c. 119 CE], *The Life of Julius Caesar* in *Lives*, Vol. VII, pp. 441–609, trans. Bernadotte Perrin (Cambridge: Harvard University Press [Loeb Classical Library], 1919), Chap. 50, p. 563. Scriptural sources: Mark 14:45; John 18:4–8.

§22. This section draws on ideas found in William Godwin, *An Enquiry Concerning Political Justice*, ed. Mark Philp (London: William Pickering, 1993 [1793]); Mikhail Bakunin, *Bakunin on Anarchism* (*op. cit.*); Karl Marx and Friedrich Engels, *Manifesto of the Communist Party*, trans. Samuel Moore (Moscow: Progress, 1975 [1848]); Frederick Engels, *Anti-Dühring*, trans. Emile Burns (Moscow: Progress, 1978 [1878]), especially pp. 339–341; Frederick Engels, *Socialism: Utopian and Scientific* in Vol. 3 of *Karl Marx and Frederick Engels: Selected Works*, pp. 95–151 (Moscow: Progress, 1977 [1892]); V. I. Lenin, *What Is to Be Done?*, trans. Joe Fineberg, George Hanna, and Robert Service (London: Penguin, 1988 [1902]); and Leon Trotsky, *The Permanent Revolution*, trans. John G. Wright and Brian Pearce (Seattle: Red Letter Press, 2010 [1930]). Local peasant revolts occurred periodically throughout late medieval Europe; two major revolts were the English Peasants' Revolt of 1381 led by Wat Tyler and the German Peasants' Revolt of 1524–1525 instigated in part by Thomas Müntzer. "One big union" is a slogan adopted by the Industrial Workers of World (IWW); see Thomas J. Hagerty and William E. Trautmann, *One Big Union* (Chicago: Charles H. Kerr, 1911). For an anarchist perspective on confederations, see

Murray Bookchin, "The Meaning of Confederalism," *Green Perspectives* 20:1-7 (1990). Scriptural sources: Matt 6:31; Rev 20:2-7.

§23. The priest, John of Nepomuc [c. 1350-1393], was drowned in the Moldau [Vltava] River for allegedly refusing to violate the seal of confession to King Wenceslas IV of Bohemia; see the entry for "John of Nepomuc, St." by B. B. Szczesniak in *The New Catholic Encyclopedia* (*op. cit.*), Vol. 7, pp. 977-978. Trials by ordeal were increasingly opposed by the Church during the Middle Ages. The Fourth Lateran Council of the Catholic Church, held under Pope Innocent III in 1215, forbid members of the clergy from blessing or consecrating ordeals, although it did not proscribe secular authorities from conducting them; see the subentry "The Medieval Order" by L. E. Boyle under the main entry "Ordeal" in *The New Catholic Encyclopedia* (*op. cit.*), Vol. 10, pp. 626-628. Ordeals were banned in England by King Henry III in 1219 and replaced by evidentiary jury trials, first stated in Clause 39 of the Magna Carta of 1215 under King John; nonetheless, ordeals continued to be conducted in Europe well into the 14th and 15th centuries, albeit with declining frequency and virtually no recorded cases in England; they were revived in the 16th and 17th centuries in both Europe and North America in connection with witch-hunts; see Robert Bartlett, *Trial by Fire and Water: The Medieval Judicial Ordeal* (Oxford: Clarendon Press, 1986). Scriptural sources: Lev 16:7-10; Deut 6:16; John 18:38.

§24. For the reference to "So that you may live to fight another day," see the annotation for Part V, §9. The description of Adrian's method of execution has similarities with that of Robert-François Damiens [1715-1757], as described by Michel Foucault in *Discipline and Punish: The Birth of the Prison,* trans. Alan Sheridan (New York: Vintage, 1977 [1975]), pp. 3-6. "Those who are violent will meet a violent end" alludes to Lao-Tze, *Tao-Teh-King* (*op. cit.*), Chap. 42, p. 119: "The strong and aggressive do not die a natural death"; *cf.* Matt 26:52b: "for all they that take the sword shall perish with the sword." The phrase "You may have the power to subject me, but I am not your subject" echoes the response given by William of Wallace to King Edward I upon being accused of treason: "I cannot be a traitor, for I owe him no allegiance; he is not my sovereign; he never received my homage"; quoted in Patrick Fraser Tytler, *Lives of Scottish Worthies,* Vol. 1 (London: John Murray, 1831), p. 279. Scriptural sources: Matt 26:52; Jas 4:4; Rev 13:10.

§25. Descriptions of various types of ordeals are given in Riley, *A History of Torture* (*op. cit.*), Chap. XXIII, pp. 227-233.

§26. The description of Justin's ordeal in this section is highly simplified since the accused would normally undergo considerable spiritual preparations beforehand and also be bound by the arms and legs prior to being thrown in the water; see Scott, *A History of Torture* (*op. cit.*), pp. 227–233.

§27. The distinction between "what" a person is and "that" a person is can be found in the anonymously written *The Epistle of Privy Counsel* in *The Cloud of Unknowing and Other Works* (*op. cit.*), p. 164. An allusion is made to the Zen concept of *kono mama*, identified with the name of God, "I Am That I Am," in Exod 3:14 and defined as the "is-ness of a thing" in Suzuki, *Mysticism Christian and Buddhist* (*op. cit.*), p. 102; see the annotation for Part V, §4. Scriptural sources: Exod 3:14; John 8:58; 1 Cor 15:10.

§28. Scriptural sources: Matt 18:21–22; 2 Cor 11:14.

§29. A list of general books related to the Inquisition can be found in the annotation for Part IV, §8. On instruments of torture being inscribed with the phrase "*Soli Deo Gloria*," see Rosemary Ellen Guiley, *The Encyclopedia of Witches, Witchcraft, and Wicca,* 3rd ed. (New York: Facts on File, 2008), p. 347. Scriptural sources: Matt 27:14.

§30. One definition of the word *catholic* is "that which has been believed everywhere, always, by all"; see Vincent of Lérins, *A Commonitory: For the Antiquity and Universality of the Catholic Faith Against the Profane Novelties of All Heresies* [c. 434 CE], Chap. II, trans. C. A. Heurtley in *A Select Library of Nicene and Post-Nicene Fathers of the Christian Church,* Second Series, Vol. XI, pp. 131–156 (*op. cit.*), p. 132. The English word *skeptic* is derived from the Greek term *skeptikós* (σκεπτικός), which means "inquirer" or "investigator"; the ancient Greek Skeptics characteristically neither affirmed nor denied the truth of any proposition. "Skeptics go on searching" is quoted from Sextus Empiricus, *Outlines of Pyrrhonism,* Vol. 1 of *Sextus Empiricus,* trans. R. G. Bury (Cambridge: Harvard University Press [Loeb Classical Library], 1955), Book I.1, p. 3. On the virtues of doubt, both secular and religious, see Peter L. Berger and Anton C. Zijderveld, *In Praise of Doubt: How to Have Convictions Without Becoming a Fanatic* (New York: HarperOne, 2009) and Brian D. McLaren, *Faith After Doubt: Why Your Beliefs Stopped Working and What to Do About It* (New York: St. Martin's Essentials, 2021). "Do not block the way of inquiry" is quoted from Peirce's "The Scientific Attitude and Fallibilism" (*op. cit.*), p. 54; see the annotation for Part IV, §16. The concept of a "community of inquirers" is derived from Peirce's essay "The Fixation of Belief" [1877] in *Philosophical Writings of Peirce* (*op. cit.*), pp. 5–22, and may be plausibly applied to both scientific and religious communities. Johann Eck, while interrogating Martin Luther at the Diet of Worms in 1521, asked him, "Martin, how can you assume that you are the only one to understand the sense of Scripture? Would you put your judgment above that of so many famous men and claim that you know more than they all? You have no right to call into question the most holy orthodox faith, instituted by Christ the perfect lawgiver, proclaimed throughout the world by the apostles, sealed by the red blood of the martyrs, confirmed by the sacred councils, defined by the Church in which all our fathers believed until death and gave to us as an inheritance, and which now we are forbidden by the pope and the emperor to discuss lest there be no end of debate. I ask you, Martin—answer candidly and without horns—do you or do you not repudiate your books and the errors which they contain?" Luther replied, "Unless I am convinced by Scripture and plain reason—I do not accept the authority of pope and councils, for they have contradicted each other—my conscience is captive to the Word of God. I cannot and I will not recant anything, for to go against conscience is neither right nor safe. God help me. Amen." Luther then reportedly added, "Here is stand, I cannot do otherwise." All quotes are from Roland H. Bainton, *Here I Stand: A Life of Martin Luther* (Nashville: Abingdon, 1978 [1950]), pp. 181–182; see also the annotation for Part III, §12. The expression "peace on earth, good-will to men" is from Henry Wadsworth Longfellow's anti-war poem, "Christmas Bells," in *Longfellow's Poetical Words*, Vol. 11 (London: George Routledge and Sons, 1878 [1866]), pp. 21–22; the poem was set to music in 1872 by James Baptiste Calkin as the Christmas carol, "I Heard the Bells on Christmas Day," which appears in *A Collection of Christmas Carols*, 6th ed., ed. Benjamin Bloomfield (Scotts Valley: CreateSpace, 2019), p. 89. An allusion is made again to the finger wagging of Cratylus; see the annotation for Part IV, §15. In his interpretation of the story of Abraham and Isaac, obeying God involves what Søren Kierkegaard refers to as a "teleological suspension of the ethical"; see *Fear and Trembling*, trans. Walter Lowrie (Princeton: Princeton University Press, 1954). Scriptural sources: Gen 1:1; 22:1–13; Deut 25:2–3; Ps 82:6; Isa 53:6; Matt 5:23-24; 6:10; 16:18–19; 27:26–31; Mark 9:24; 12:31; 15:15–20; Luke 2:14; 11:9–10; 17:21; 22:42; 23:3; John 3:3; 10:33–36; 19:1–7; Acts 22:16; Rom 12: 2; 3:23; 6:5–6; 1 Cor 3:11; Eph 4:32; Phil 3:10–11; 1 Thess 5:19–21; 1 John 1:9.

§31. The following quote from Mahatma Gandhi [1869–1948] appears in the *Dictionary of Proverbs*, compiled by Grenville Kleiser (New Delhi: A. P. H., 2005), p. 208: "You can chain me, you can torture me, you can even destroy this body, but you will never imprison my mind." To be "one with the soul over all" references the concept of an Oversoul, similar to the concepts of soul (*psyché*, ψυχή) in Plotinus and *Paramātman* (absolute *ātman* or universal self) in Hindu, Jain, and Buddhist thought; see also Ralph Waldo Emerson's essay "The Over-Soul" [1841] in *The Portable Emerson*, pp. 209–227, ed. Carl Bode and Malcolm Cowley (Harmondsworth: Penguin, 1981).

§32. On the development of the concept of the "divine right of kings" in medieval Europe in relation to conflicts between Church and State, see John Neville Figgis, *The Divine Right of Kings,* 2nd ed. (Cambridge: Cambridge University Press, 1914).

§33. Vern L. Bullough in "Prostitution in the Later Middle Ages" in *Sexual Practices and the Medieval Church,* pp. 176–86, ed. Vern L. Bullough and James Brundage (Buffalo: Prometheus, 1982), p. 185, summarizes the medieval attitude towards fornication between the nobility and the peasantry as follows: "If a nobleman desired a peasantwoman so strongly that he could not resist the temptation, he was free to rape her on the spot since a courteous approach would only be wasted on a woman who could not possibly feel love." On bigamy in the Middle Ages, see Sara McDougall, *Bigamy and Christian Identity in Late Medieval Champagne* (Philadelphia: University of Pennsylvania Press, 2012). For medieval methods of capital punishment, see Stephen Currie, *Medieval Punishment and Torture* (San Diego: ReferencePoint Press, 2014), chap. 5. Following the Latin maxim "*Ecclesia non novit sanguinem*" ("The Church does not know blood"), the Inquisition was opposed to forms of execution that involved the shedding of blood, which is why other methods were used against heretics, especially burning at the stake; see Isaac Disraeli, *Curiosities of Literature* (London: Frederick Warne, 1866), Vol. 1, p. 168. Scriptural sources: Matt 27:5, 24.

§34. The contribution lying makes to maintaining social harmony is a theme of the feature film, *Liar Liar,* directed by Tom Shadyac (Universal City: Universal Pictures, 1997). For an overview of revisionist perspectives on lying, see Brian Martin, "Telling Lies for a Better World," *Social Anarchism* 35:27–39 (2003–2004). Allusions are made to Socrates being offered the means to live in exile rather than drink the hemlock in Plato's *Crito* in *The Dialogues of Plato,* pp. 213–219 (*op. cit.*) and to the legend of Robin Hood. The notion of God descending from heaven to make everything right is related to the *deus ex machina* device used by ancient Greek dramatists, such as Euripides [c. 480–c. 406 BCE], in which actors playing the parts of gods would descend from a crane to resolve a seemingly insoluble conflict in way that enabled the play to have a happy ending; later Christian ideas of divine intervention are not dissimilar. On "Things must be accepted just as they are," see the annotation for Part V, §4. The phrase "This is a good day to die" appears at several points in *Black Elk Speaks* (*op. cit.*), p. 10; p. 84; p. 101; and p. 227, and may be interpreted as expressing the courage and equanimity that allows one to face death instead of futilely trying to run away from it. Scriptural sources: Matt 16:25; Mark 8:35; Luke 9:24; John 19:30.

§35. In fact, executioners rarely wore masks or hoods in the Middle Ages. When Jesus appeared before him, Pilate said "Behold, the man!"; the original Latin expression, *ecce homo,* was used by Friedrich Nietzsche as the main title of his last book, written in 1888 and published in 1908: *Ecce Homo: How One Becomes What One Is* in *Basic Writings of Nietzsche* (*op. cit.*), pp. 671–791. Scriptural sources: Zech 12:10; Matt 28:20; Luke 6:36; 23:34, 46, 47; John 19:5; Acts 1:18; Gal 2:20; Titus 3:1; Jas 2:13; 4:7; 1 Pet 2:13–14.